D1068100

DESOLATION MOUNTAIN

Also by William Kent Krueger

Sulfur Springs
Manitou Canyon
Windigo Island
Tamarack County
Ordinary Grace
Trickster's Point
Northwest Angle
Vermilion Drift
Heaven's Keep
Red Knife
Thunder Bay
Copper River
Mercy Falls
Blood Hollow
The Devil's Bed
Purgatory Ridge
Boundary Waters
Iron Lake

DESOLATION MOUNTAIN

A Novel

William Kent Krueger

ATRIA BOOKS

New York London Toronto Sydney New Delhi

An Imprint of Simon & Schuster, Inc.
1230 Avenue of the Americas
New York, NY 10020

This book is a work of fiction. Any references to historical events, real people, or real places are used fictitiously. Other names, characters, places, and events are products of the author's imagination, and any resemblance to actual events or places or persons, living or dead, is entirely coincidental.

First Atria Books hardcover special edition August 2018

ATRIA BOOKS and colophon are trademarks of Simon & Schuster, Inc.

For information about special discounts for bulk purchases, please contact Simon & Schuster Special Sales at 1-866-506-1949 or business@simonandschuster.com.

The Simon & Schuster Speakers Bureau can bring authors to your live event. For more information or to book an event contact the Simon & Schuster Speakers Bureau at 1-866-248-3049 or visit our website at www.simonspeakers.com.

Manufactured in the United States of America

10 9 8 7 6 5 4 3 2 1

Library of Congress Cataloging-in-Publication Data is available.

ISBN 978-1-9821-0774-1
ISBN 978-1-5011-4748-7 (ebook)

For Randalyn Nickelsen Clark,
whose beautiful spirit is with us always

DESOLATION MOUNTAIN

AUTHOR'S NOTE

Many years ago, in a stand-alone thriller titled *The Devil's Bed,* I first introduced readers to the character of Bo Thorson, who plays a significant role in the following story. Over the fifteen years since that book's publication, I've received a consistent flow of requests from readers to bring Bo back. It wasn't until I conceived of the plot for this current novel that I saw a way to resurrect him. I always thought that Bo Thorson and Cork O'Connor were the kind of men who would appreciate each other and might look forward to cracking open a couple of brews and trading tales. I hope you enjoy his presence, and if he intrigues you, I encourage you to pick up *The Devil's Bed,* in which his full history is made clear.

CHAPTER 1

He watches the boy on the steep rise above him. He is that boy and he is not. The boy is intent on the sky, a witch's brew of swirling gray clouds. He is anxious, waiting. The boy. And him. For what, neither of them knows. The air smells not of the evergreen all around but of something foul. Diesel. Fire. A breeze blows across his face carrying a different smell, even more foul. Burning flesh. The boy holds a compound bow, complicated, powerful. An arrow is notched. The boy's stomach is taut. His body knows something his mind does not, something terrible. The boy watches the sky, and he watches the boy.

The bird appears out of the dark boil of clouds. Wings spread broad, catching the wind. Curling in a wide arc above the hill. The bird—clearly an eagle now—lets out a screech. High-pitched. Then another.

The boy raises his bow.

The eagle circles, near enough that the boy can see details. Golden irises, saffron beak, long, dangerous talons. The eagle cries again.

The boy draws back the bowstring. Calculates trajectory, wind speed. Leads the bird. Takes a breath. Eases it out. Lets the arrow fly.

The great bird twists in an explosion of feathers. Tries to right itself. Begins to plummet.

The boy lowers the bow. Watches an egg drop from the eagle. Watches the eagle in its fall, lost among the evergreens. The boy stands still as death. He feels uncertain, as if there is still more to be done, but what that is he doesn't know. He turns and stares down the hillside. At the young man who stares back. Him. And not him.

Neither of them understands.

Then the boy on the rise above him sees something, which he senses now at his own back. From the look on the boy's face, from the way his eyes grow huge, he understands that what is behind him is enormous and terrifying and threatens them both. He feels its breath break against him, hot and hungry. He should turn, face this beast whatever it is, but he's paralyzed with fear. The boy on the hill opens his mouth to cry out. At the same moment, he opens his.

The sound of their one scream wakes him.

The old man sat on the other side of the fire, listening. Old? He was ancient, with more years behind him than any living thing in the dark of that great forest—turtle, owl, deer, wolf, bear, all were children in comparison. The years, kind to no one, had done their best to weather his flesh, weaken his muscle, erode his bone. His body displayed none of the power and comeliness that had so marked it when the twentieth century was young. Time had etched lines long and deep into his face. His white hair hung over his shoulders in spidery wisps. The weight of ten decades of living had bent his spine, but only slightly. In the firelight, he appeared to be the ghost of a thing, not the thing itself.

And yet the young man who stared at him across the fire perceived only wisdom, only possibility.

"Many times you have seen this vision?" the old man asked.

"Many times," the young man answered.

"That is all of it?"

The young man nodded. "All of it."

"The eagle is sacred. Killing an eagle, that is a terrible thing."

The fire popped. An ember leapt from the flames, landed on the jeans the old man was wearing. The old man gazed up at the stars and didn't seem to notice.

"Your leg, Henry," the young man said.

But the ember had burned itself out.

"And so," the old man finally said, as if speaking to the stars. "Why now?"

The young man didn't understand the question. "Why now what?"

The old man's eyes came back to earth. "You tell me."

The young man knew better than to press this elder, his mentor. He considered his reply.

"Now, because it worries me. It's a portent, Henry. Something terrible is going to happen. My visions are always about terrible things. I've never had one that's hopeful."

"They have proven helpful," the old man pointed out. Then he asked again, as if it were a new question, "Why now?"

"If you mean why have I come to you only now, it's because I thought I could figure this out on my own. But I don't have a clue. I need help, before it's too late."

The old man closed his eyes, looked as if he were about to sleep. Then, "Too late for what?"

"If I understood the vision, I would understand that."

"Maybe so. Maybe not. Visions are tricky. They can be the thing itself, or the shadow of the thing."

"If it's only a shadow, why does it scare me so much?"

The old man took a stick from the fire, the end still licked by tongues of flame. He moved it toward the young man's face. The flames came nearer and nearer, until the young man could feel the heat on his cheek, the fire only inches from his flesh. But he didn't flinch.

"You are not afraid?" the old man asked.

"I believe you won't burn me. Or if you do, there's purpose in it."

"A vision is like that." The old man returned the stick to the fire. He stared deeply into the young man's face, his eyes dark, hard, gleaming in the flickering light. "Who is the boy?"

"I'm the boy," the young man answered. "And I'm not."

"What is this beast that frightens you?"

"I don't know. It's behind me. I never see it."

"And who is it you are afraid for, Stephen O'Connor?"

"For the boy," Stephen answered. "And for me." He leaned toward the old man. "And I don't know why, Henry, but for you, too."

CHAPTER 2

Anyone who knew Tamarack County, Minnesota, and the town of Aurora, in particular, knew Sam's Place. The old Quonset hut turned burger joint sat on the shoreline of Iron Lake. Behind it was blue water, a vast expanse. South rose a copse of poplar trees at whose center lay the ruins of an old ironworks. Aurora itself was a stone's throw west, just beyond the raised bed of the BNSF railroad tracks. A short, unpaved road crossed the tracks, connecting Sam's Place with civilization.

Corcoran Liam O'Connor stood in the parking lot, appraising the sign he had just affixed with sheet metal screws to the side of the Quonset hut. The sign read: TRY OUR NEW WAABOO BURGER! Cork had made the sign himself, at the workbench in his garage, with the help of his five-year-old grandson, Waaboo—legally, Aaron Smalldog O'Connor. The family nickname for the little guy was Waaboozoons, which, in the language of the Ojibwe, meant "little rabbit." It had been shortened to simply Waaboo. The exclamation point was entirely little Waaboo's handiwork.

It was late afternoon, late September. The leaves of the poplar trees were like gold doubloons. The air was cool, the sun a lazy yellow. There were no customers lined up at the serving windows. They would arrive eventually, Cork knew, closer to suppertime. He appreciated this quiet period, between the hustle of the lunch crowd and what would come.

A green Forester turned up the road, bounced over the tracks and into the lot. The driver parked and got out. She was tall, pretty, with hair the color of corn silk. She opened the back door and helped a child from his seat. They stood with Cork, looking at the sign.

"Me," little Waaboo said with great pride, pointing toward his name.

"A hundred people are going to eat you up tonight." Cork opened his mouth wide as if to take a bite out of his grandson. Waaboo danced back, happily.

"Any sign of Stephen yet?" Jenny asked. She was Cork's daughter, Waaboo's mother.

Cork shook his head. "He's with Henry. So who knows?"

"Has he said anything to you yet?" Concern shaded her words.

"Whatever it is, I'm sure he's sharing it with Henry." Cork stepped to the sign, brushed at a spot of what looked like dripped black paint but turned out to be a spider. "When he's ready, he'll tell us."

"He's a darkpoople," Waaboo said.

"Darkpoople?"

"We've been reading *The BFG,*" Jenny explained. "Roald Dahl. Waaboo's creating his own dictionary of words."

Cork laughed. "Darkpoople. You nailed him, little guy."

"Waaboo and I can stick around until he shows," Jenny offered. "Rainy's going to cover, if necessary."

"I want to stay," Waaboo said. "I want to help Baa-baa." His name for Cork. Not one of his new, made-up Roald Dahlish words. It was what he had always called his grandfather.

"For a while, then," she agreed.

Inside, the place smelled of deep-fry oil and of the meats that had sizzled on the griddle, decades of aromas soaked into the walls. The Quonset hut was divided into two parts. The front was Sam's Place, with all the food prep equipment, big freezer, storage shelves, stainless-steel sink. The back was an office Cork used for both the business of Sam's Place and his own work as a private investigator. There was a round table and four chairs, all of sturdy maple, old and worn. A little kitchenette with a small refrigerator, a microwave, a coffeemaker, counter space, sink. A couple of tall, gray file cabinets stood against the wall, one for documents pertaining to Sam's Place, the other for the files related to Cork's investigations. He didn't advertise that side of his business doings anymore. He had a reputation. Those who needed him found their way.

"Can I have an ice cream cone?" Waaboo asked, addressing his grandfather, not his mother.

"Whoa," Jenny said. "I thought you just wanted to help."

"Yes. But I'm hungry."

"Just a cone, Jenny," Cork said. "Won't spoil his dinner."

"A small one."

Waaboo sat on a chair at the serving window, licking his cone, a chocolate and vanilla twist. Cork scraped the griddle. Jenny sliced tomatoes.

"Are you going to the town meeting tomorrow night?" Jenny asked.

"I'm working here, remember? You put together this week's schedule."

"I'll get one of the kids to cover."

Cork had always hired high school students to staff Sam's Place in season. For many, it was their introduction to the working world. He tried to be firm in what he asked of them but patient in his oversight.

"That's okay. There'll be plenty of people attending. Senator McCarthy will get an earful without me."

Jenny said, "It's a chance to see the senator up close."

"I've seen Olympia McCarthy up close. She's a fine woman, but still just a woman."

"A lot of people are pinning a lot of hope on her. Daniel's agreed to put Waaboo to bed. Rainy's going with me."

"Then you two make plenty of noise for the rest of us."

An old Jeep rattled over the railroad tracks.

"The prodigal son," Cork said. "You and Waaboo are free."

A few minutes later, Cork heard the Quonset hut door open and Stephen appeared. He smelled of woodsmoke and evergreen sap. He shed his gray hoodie, hung his backpack on a hook. The backpack looked heavy, and Cork knew it was full of college textbooks.

"Sorry I'm late. Hey, Waaboo!" He tousled the boy's hair. In appearance, Stephen more resembled his nephew than his father or sister. His Anishinaabe genes dominated—dark hair, almond eyes, broad, bold facial bones. He was twenty years old and walked with a limp that was becoming less and less noticeable with time.

"How's Henry?" Cork asked.

"Old." Stephen bent toward Waaboo. "You gonna eat that whole thing?"

"Yes."

"I haven't eaten all day. I could sure use a lick."

"Uh-uh."

"Come on." Stephen lunged toward the cone.

Waaboo swung away, protecting the treat with his free hand. "No-o-o-o."

"Grinch."

"Darkpoople."

"Darkpoople?"

"Grab . . ." Waaboo hesitated. "Grabgrubber."

"Don't know what you're saying, but it doesn't sound good."

"How about a Waaboo Burger?" Cork suggested.

"Waaboo Burger? I saw the sign. What is it?"

"Patty made of ground bison instead of hamburger."

"Named after me," Cork's grandson said proudly.

"When did we start offering that?"

"Today. Jenny and I have been talking about it for a while. Being a college man now, you've just had other things on your mind. What do you say? You can't sell customers on it until you're sold on it yourself."

"Sure."

Cork dropped a patty on the griddle, buttered two bun halves.

"We're out of here," Jenny said. "Come on, kiddo. You can finish that cone on the way home. I've got to get dinner going. Joining us, Dad?"

"No, I'll stay here and close tonight."

"I think I'm supposed to close," Stephen said.

"I'll take it."

Stephen didn't argue.

When the others had gone, Stephen stood at an empty serving window, staring toward the copse of poplars to the south. Stephen had been doing a lot of staring lately. Something had set a hook in him, snagged his senses. College, perhaps. Stephen was in his first semester at Aurora Community College, taking classes to fulfill his general requirements in preparation for an eventual degree in criminal justice studies. The same route Cork had taken long ago when he started on the road to becoming a cop. But he hadn't seen any real enthusiasm for the coursework, and in truth, he wasn't at all certain his son was cut out to wear a badge. So was it a girl, maybe? For a couple of years, Stephen had been in an on-again, off-again relationship with a young woman on the rez, Marlee

Daychild. During the past month or so, it had been in the off mode. Cork didn't know if this was Stephen's doing or Marlee's. His son had always been private, hesitant to reveal a lot about himself, and that had been especially true lately. What Cork had sensed, what all the O'Connors had sensed, was a growing restlessness in Stephen, which Cork told himself was natural in a young man. One of the thoughts he'd had was that maybe it was time for Stephen to leave Aurora. Maybe if he was away from all that was familiar, at least for a while, it might be easier for him to see the path he needed to travel. It was possible this was what Stephen had been discussing with Meloux, seeking the old man's advice.

But there was another possibility. Stephen saw things others did not. He had visions. And so Cork understood that what was weighing on his son, what held Stephen's attention while he stared at what appeared to be nothing, might well be something his eye couldn't see.

CHAPTER 3

"All the buzz on the rez is about the town meeting tomorrow night," Rainy said as she undressed. "Everyone at the clinic, everyone who comes in, Senator McCarthy is all they're talking about."

Rainy Bisonette, Cork's wife, worked at the tribal clinic in the town of Allouette on the Iron Lake Reservation. Trained as a public health nurse, she was also a member of the Grand Medicine Society, a Mide, a healer in the traditional way. They'd been married only since the previous April, not even six months. Still on honeymoon, Cork often thought, especially whenever he watched her shed her clothing.

"She's a safe raft in a stormy sea," Cork said. He was already in bed, his back against the headboard.

Rainy stepped out of her jeans and unbuttoned her blue work shirt. She was full-bodied, but not heavy, having spent the last several years before her marriage seeing to the needs of her great-uncle, Henry Meloux, living in a cabin without running water or electricity, with only a wood-burning stove for heat, fed with wood she'd chopped herself. She knew hard work. When she drifted her hands across Cork's body, he could still feel the calluses.

"She'll listen," Rainy said. "Everyone believes we'll be heard."

"And that she'll carry that message forward. Good thing to believe."

She'd slipped off her bra and had reached for her nightshirt, but she paused and studied him in the light of the lamp on the nightstand. "You don't?"

"I believe she'll listen. I'm not sure I believe it'll do any good."

"She's a U.S. senator. She has influence."

"The other side has more. And they hit harder and they don't play fair."

She slipped the long nightshirt over her head and down her body, then joined him in bed, where she leaned against him. "You sound like you believe the battle is already lost."

"Not lost. But I've been in battles like these before. There are always casualties." He changed the subject abruptly. "Talked to Stephen lately?"

"I've tried. He's burrowed deep inside himself."

"He's like a sleepwalker. I tell him something, and, poof, it's gone from his head."

Rainy flipped her long black braid so that it hung at an angle between her breasts. Her fingers slowly traced the strands of the plaiting, in a way that made Cork think of rosary beads. "I'm wondering if he's seen something."

"I've wondered that, too. But it could be just that he's getting used to college. Or maybe it's Marlee. There's nothing like a woman to addle a guy's brain."

"I'm going to ignore that remark," Rainy said. "He hasn't gone out with Marlee Daychild in weeks. And he just seems so unsettled. More and more I'm thinking he's had another vision, Cork. And I think this one scares him."

They both knew Stephen had a right to be afraid. Before the bullet that caused his limp was fired, Stephen saw the man who would shoot him in a vision. He saw his mother's death years before it happened. He saw the threat from a monster, a murderer of young women who'd called himself Windigo and who'd tried to kill Cork and Jenny. It hadn't escaped their notice that Stephen's visions had always foreshadowed terrible things.

Cork said, "I wish he'd share what he's seen."

"It would be an unburdening," Rainy said.

"Practically speaking, it might help us get ready for whatever's coming."

"Something to do with the proposed pit mine, you think?"

For years, a large corporation had been at work to secure the permits necessary to begin a huge open-pit mining operation that would extract copper, nickel, and a number of heavy metals from an area adjacent to both the Iron Lake Reservation and the Boundary Waters Canoe Area Wilderness. In Tamarack County, a region once wealthy because of the iron ore that underlay everything, the issue had been divisive. With the iron mines having closed or closing and good-paying jobs evaporated, there was a considerable element applauding the possibility of the return of industry. On the other side were the Iron Lake Ojibwe and many other groups who feared that the mine would ruin the pristine wilderness and the clean water. Their fears weren't unfounded. While iron mining had brought wealth, at least for a time, it had made much of the North Country resemble the barren surface of the moon.

"I'm thinking something more personal." Cork put his hand over hers as she worked her braid, stilled it. "He talks to Henry. Could you talk to Henry?"

"I can try. But what's between Uncle Henry and Stephen will probably stay between them, unless Stephen indicates otherwise."

"Maybe a sweat?"

"Until Stephen is ready to share, he'll be as hard to crack as a walnut."

"A sweat couldn't hurt."

"I'll suggest it. You smell good, by the way. Like French fries. How'd the new Waaboo Burger do?"

"A winner. Everybody loved the bison patty, and everyone who knows our grandson loved the name."

"Doesn't surprise me a bit. The world loves Waaboo."

Rainy picked up a book from the nightstand and prepared to read. It was a novel titled *Downwind of the Devil*. The author was Jennifer O'Connor. When she wasn't helping run Sam's Place or involved in all she did as mother and wife, Jenny wrote stories. *Downwind of the Devil* was her first published novel, a fictionalized account of the hunt for a missing Ojibwe girl, in which she and her father and the monster who called himself Windigo were deeply involved. It had done well enough that Jenny was under contract for a second novel. She wouldn't tell her family what it was about, but they all suspected it would be another telling of a story in which some of them played a part.

Cork picked up the book he'd been reading every night for a week, *To Kill a Mockingbird*, one of the many American classics he'd never read, but one that both Jenny and Rainy had insisted he should. Within ten minutes, his eyes fluttered closed. He felt Rainy slip the book from his hands, turn out the light, and he was wrapped in a blanket of sleep.

CHAPTER 4

Next morning, well before sunrise, Cork heard Stephen leave the house. He slid from bed and stood at the window, watching Stephen walk away in the blue, early light, and his heart twisted. His son was struggling and Cork didn't know how to help. Rainy had advised patience. Which was the same advice her great-uncle Henry Meloux might have offered. Good advice, Cork knew, but it didn't mean he wouldn't suffer along with his son. He dressed quietly, hit the bathroom, went downstairs to make coffee. A few minutes later, he stood on the front porch, sipping from the steaming mug in his hand and breathing in the cool air of approaching dawn. Gooseberry Lane was quiet, the neighbors still abed.

With the exception of a few years as a cop in Chicago, he'd lived in Aurora, Minnesota, his whole life. His roots on his mother's side went back to a time long before white men muscled their way into the North Country and began the destruction of the natural order, a ravaging that had never really ended. His Anishinaabe heritage might not show on his face, but it shaped his conscience. As he stood in the cool, evergreen-scented air, in the fresh feel of that fall morning, he understood the calm probably wouldn't last.

He was more and more certain that Stephen had had a vision, seen something, and the things that Stephen saw had always been monstrous.

He picked up the morning paper from where it had been thrown under the porch swing and headed back inside. Rainy was awake and up, pouring coffee from the pot he'd made. He heard footsteps coming downstairs, heavy, probably Daniel English, his son-in-law, ready for work. Daniel was an officer with the Iron Lake Ojibwe Department of Conservation Enforcement. When explaining, he generally referred to himself as a game warden. Like Jenny, he was a writer, a poet. Like his aunt Rainy, he was full-blood Ojibwe, an enrolled member of the Lac Courte Oreilles Band of Lake Superior Chippewa.

"That coffee smells good," he said as he entered the kitchen. He wore his willow-green uniform. Rainy poured him a cup of the brew.

"You're up early," Cork noted.

"A lot on the agenda today. We've had reports of a couple of poachers on the rez. We've tried tracking them, but they keep slipping away."

"Jenny tells me you won't be going to the town meeting tonight," Cork said.

"I'm on Waaboo duty. Putting our little guy down for the night." Daniel sipped his coffee and looked satisfied. "You're not going either, I understand."

"Somebody's got to sell the new Waaboo Burger."

Daniel dropped a couple of slices of bread in the toaster. "How'd it go yesterday?"

"Sold like hotcakes."

"Waaboo was excited last night. He kept saying, 'People are eating me.'"

Rainy laughed. "Everybody could use a little Waaboo in them."

After Daniel had gone, Cork put on his jacket and kissed Rainy.

"You haven't had breakfast yet," she said. "Where are you off to?"

"To talk to Henry."

"About Stephen? I'm not sure he'll tell you much."

"Can't hurt to ask."

"I told you I'd talk to Uncle Henry myself."

"When will you see him next? Between your clinic work and the town meeting with the senator, your schedule's packed." He kissed her again. "Meet you in bed tonight."

He drove north out of Aurora, along a graveled county road that followed the shoreline of Iron Lake. The woods were a mix of broadleaf and needle in which autumn had created great islands of gold and red among the evergreens. The cabins along the lake, mostly resorts and summer homes, looked deserted now, but on weekends they were still alive with activity and would continue that way until the leaves had been stripped from the trees and the color was gone. Come winter, the population of Tamarack County would shrink significantly.

He parked at a double-trunk birch several miles north of town, locked his Expedition, and began the long walk through the forest, following a path familiar to him since childhood. The sun was just about to rise, and the strip of clear sky above the path was a pale red, the color of water mixed with blood. On either side of him, the birds, those who had not yet wisely headed south, cried to one another with harsh, territorial challenges. Squirrels chattered at his intrusion. He startled a doe and her two fawns, who bounded away and disappeared among the trees. Everything about the morning and the walk along this familiar path, which normally would have calmed him, felt unsettling. The blood-colored sky, the contentious birds, the angry squirrels, the startled deer, all seemed to signal threat. He thought maybe this was a glimpse of what Stephen must feel when he'd had one of his ominous visions.

A mile in, he crossed onto rez land. A mile farther, he broke from the trees onto Crow Point. He stood at the beginning of a broad meadow filled with tall grass and with wildflowers still blooming—marigolds and oxeyes and asters and Canadian horseweed. On the far side rose two simple cabins, between them an outhouse. The nearer cabin had been Rainy's for many years. Now its sole occupant was Rainy's aunt by marriage, a septuagenarian named Leah Duling. The far cabin had been on Crow Point for more than eight decades and during all that time occupied by Henry Meloux, who was Rainy's maternal great-uncle and more than a hundred years old.

Smoke came from the stovepipes on both cabins, but Cork headed toward Meloux's place. Before he arrived, the door opened.

"I've got oatmeal with walnuts and dried blueberries ready," Leah said from the threshold. "Henry told me you won't have eaten."

Without any forewarning, Meloux was expecting him, one of the many mysteries of the ancient Mide. Cork found the old man at his small table, a book opened before him. When he was young and a renowned hunter, Meloux's eyes were like those of an eagle. His vision, though no longer eagle-sharp, was still good enough that he didn't require glasses. Cork saw that the book was *Downwind of the Devil.*

"She tells a good tale, your Jennifer," Meloux said, looking up. He was a part of the events at the heart of the story. "But she has simplified much."

"Most readers aren't as astute as you, Henry." Cork removed his jacket and sat with the old man. "I want to talk to you about Stephen. I think he's had a vision, and I think he's shared it with you."

"First, we have some breakfast," Meloux said.

Leah dished up oatmeal for them all and joined them at the

table. Meloux gave a blessing in Ojibwemowin, most of which Cork didn't understand.

"Maple syrup?" Leah offered.

Cork knew she'd tapped the trees and boiled down the sap herself. She was well into her seventies, but seemed younger, the effect, Cork suspected, of life on Crow Point in the company of Meloux.

They ate in silence. The hot oatmeal sat well on Cork's empty stomach. When the meal was finished, Meloux said, "Let us build a fire, Corcoran O'Connor. We will smoke and talk."

Leah wasn't invited to join them, and she made no comment as Meloux gathered his tobacco pouch and pipe, eased on his old plaid mackinaw, and walked out the door.

"*Migwech,* Leah," Cork said in thanks.

She glanced where Meloux had gone. "He probably won't say anything to you, but he's worried."

"About what?"

Leah shrugged. "He doesn't say anything to me either."

Cork followed Meloux across the meadow along a path that ran between two rock outcrops. On the far side, Iron Lake stretched away, mirroring the morning sky, and near the shoreline was a stone fire ring. Sawed sections of hardwood had been spaced around the ring for sitting, and cut firewood was laid up against one of the outcrops. Cork had helped Meloux build more fires here than he could remember. He gathered wood and kindling, used his pocketknife to curl off dry tinder, built a small tepee at the charred center of the fire ring. Meloux handed him a wooden match, and Cork struck a flame.

While Cork fed the growing fire, the old man took pinches of the mixture—tobacco and red willow—from his beaded pouch. He offered these to the four directions of the earth, and to the center, then put a bit into the pipe bowl. Cork sat with him. Meloux lit the tobacco mixture and they smoked together, while the fire crackled before them.

"Something's coming, Henry," Cork finally said.

The old man replied, "You have visions now?"

"I feel it."

"What do you feel?"

"Unsettled. Watchful."

"Afraid?"

"That, too. Stephen has had a vision."

"He told you this?"

"No, but he's clearly troubled, and he won't talk about it. Except to you. He's shared the vision with you, hasn't he?"

"You ask a question I cannot answer."

Which Cork took as an answer. He leaned toward the old man. "It must be a frightening vision, because it worries you, too."

Meloux's eyes were soft brown and unreadable. "You see into my heart now?"

"Leah told me. What is it that you know?"

"Not the answer you are looking for. But I will tell you this. These woods are alive, and all that is living speaks. To a human who listens, knowledge is given. Stephen listens. Maybe the spirit of what is alive here has spoken to him. Maybe if any man quiets himself enough, he also can hear what is being said."

"You've listened, Henry. What have you heard?"

"I was talking about you, Corcoran O'Connor. I believe if you quiet yourself, what it is that you are looking for will become known to you."

"I've never had a vision." Cork heard the brusqueness in his voice and tried to calm himself, tamp down his frustration. "I doubt I ever will."

"A vision is not everything." Meloux's face took on a soft cast. "You have a keen mind, Corcoran O'Connor, and a warrior's heart.

You also have a warrior's impatience. Quiet yourself. Use your head and your experience and the quiet, and perhaps you will not need a vision."

"You listen, Henry, better than Stephen, better than anyone. Can't you just tell me what you know?"

Meloux took a good while to answer. The wind shifted. The smoke from the fire drifted across Iron Lake, casting a dark, gray shadow over the blue surface.

"There is a beast in these woods that does not belong here," Meloux finally said. "What exactly, I do not know. But it is huge and it is evil. And that is all I can say."

CHAPTER 5

At a quarter to three that afternoon, Stephen turned his steps toward Sam's Place. He was scheduled to work until closing with his father and with a high school senior named Naomi Burns. The day was warm but overcast, thin clouds muddling the sky. He walked along the streets of Aurora with his hands in his pockets, his shoulders slumped. Fallen leaves as colorful as pieces torn from a Mediterranean tapestry littered the sidewalks. Over the course of his twenty years, he'd been down these streets a thousand times, knew them like he knew the lines that crossed his palms. They were part of who he was and also part of what he struggled against. It was comfortable, this small, familiar town, this isolated county. Every day he slid into life there like a finger into a glove. More and more, he'd begun to think that to understand the man he was at heart, he would have to separate himself from all that was familiar.

His father had abandoned Aurora when he was a young man and spent nearly a decade in Chicago before returning. His sisters, too, had left. College took Jenny away for a long time before she returned and settled down to family life in Aurora. Annie had been gone forever—in Iowa and New Mexico and California and now in South America, for a second time. Stephen had seen only a little of the world, and he'd begun to hunger for more. He'd also started to wonder, if he were far away, would the terrible things he sometimes saw not be able to find him?

His father was inside Sam's Place, preparing for the dinner crowd, which would begin arriving in an hour or so. Naomi was there, small and quiet, with streaks of color like cotton candy in her hair. She stood at the prep table, tossing coleslaw in a big stainless-steel bowl. His father looked up from the burger patties he'd been preparing next to the grill.

"Where've you been?"

"Around," Stephen replied.

"I tried to call."

"I didn't feel like talking."

Cork wiped his hands on some paper toweling. "How about we talk now?" He led the way into the back of the Quonset hut, poured himself some coffee from the pot he'd made earlier, held the mug out in offering to Stephen, who shook his head.

"I went to see Henry," his father told him. "I figure you've had a vision, and since you won't talk about it to anyone except maybe him, I went to find out what he knows."

Stephen's first thought was that this was a trespass, that his father had stepped across a line. Then he realized that, in its way, it might be an unshackling. He couldn't share the vision himself because it felt too personal, too close, and was still too indecipherable. What good would it do to bring others in if it accomplished nothing except to make them as afraid as he was? Now that what he'd seen was in the open, he thought differently. He had no illusions that his father, who could sometimes be a stump when it came to sharing his own emotions, could help him understand the meaning and purpose of the vision. Even Henry had been unable to do that. But he felt as if a weight had been lifted from him, and now his father might help to shoulder some of the burden.

"So he told you?" Stephen said.

Cork shook his head. "But he admitted that he believes something bad is out there in the woods, and he doesn't know what it is. Look, Stephen, I don't want to intrude on a thing so personal to you as a vision. But if there's something out there, something really bad, don't you think it would be best to figure out what it is? Maybe together we can do that."

"Henry couldn't help me," Stephen said.

"I'm not Henry. I see the world in a different way. Maybe my perspective can be of some use."

Stephen considered this, considered also how good it felt, even for a moment, to have the burden of the vision off his shoulders. He made his decision, and he shared with his father what he'd seen: the boy on the steep rise who was him and not him; the eagle appearing from the sky; the boy with the bow in his hands; the arrow flying; the eagle falling; the dropped egg; staring at the boy, him and not him, and the boy staring back, both of them ignorant of the meaning in all this; and at the end, the sense of something monstrous looming at his back.

In the serving area, Naomi plopped a burger patty onto the grill, and the sizzle seemed inordinately loud.

"The boy is you and not you," Cork said. "I have dreams like that."

"This isn't a dream, Dad." Stephen heard the note of impatience in his voice and tried to soften. "It's so different."

"I understand. I'm just trying to get the lay of the land here. The hill, is it a place you recognize?"

"In that way, it's like a dream. It seems familiar, but not like a real place."

"The boy. Can you describe him?"

"Fourteen or fifteen, maybe. Dark hair. Dark eyes. A little shorter than me."

"You a few years ago."

"But not me, Dad."

"Native?"

"Maybe."

"The eagle. Is it like a real eagle?"

"Yes," Stephen said, thinking that this wasn't getting them anywhere. Then he realized something. "Not exactly like a real eagle."

"What's different?"

"The tail feathers should be completely white, but other colors are mixed in."

"What colors?"

Before Stephen could answer, Naomi called to them, "We've got incoming."

Through the doorway into Sam's Place, Stephen could see a couple of cars pulling into the parking lot. Behind them came two more.

"We'll talk later," his father said, and they turned to the business of a burger joint.

The town meeting with Senator McCarthy was scheduled for that evening. It was expected to draw a good audience, a huge number of Tamarack County residents with strong feelings on both sides of the mining issue. The dinner crowd came early and heavy. Cork had called in another of the kids on his roster, and he and Stephen and the high schoolers worked to move the lines at the windows. The Waaboo Burger continued to be a big hit, and the spicy fries, another recent addition to the menu, went fast.

Near six, while Cork was bent over the grill, the whistle atop the Aurora firehouse began a prolonged blast. Almost immediately, the phone on the wall in the Quonset hut rang. Cork handed the spatula to Stephen and took the call. The whistle, Stephen knew, was the signal for the volunteer firemen to assemble. His father wasn't a volunteer, but he was a part of the Tamarack County Search and Rescue team, and sometimes the whistle blast and the need for the team went hand in hand.

When Cork returned, he had removed his apron, and he threw it in the wicker basket where all the dirty aprons went.

"What is it, Dad?"

"A plane's gone down on the rez. Out on Desolation Mountain."

A brief image flashed through Stephen's mind. An eagle shot from the sky. "You're going? I want to go, too."

Cork opened his mouth, and Stephen fully expected to have to argue his right to be there. But his father simply nodded and said to the kids at the serving windows, "We're shutting down for the night."

CHAPTER 6

Tamarack County Sheriff Marsha Dross walked quickly up the old logging road where nearly a dozen vehicles had parked—deputies' cruisers, a couple of hook and ladders, an ambulance, and several civilian cars and trucks. Cork waited with Stephen beside the Expedition.

They were in the far east section of the Iron Lake Reservation, spitting distance from the Boundary Waters Canoe Area Wilderness. Before them rose Desolation Mountain, a great uplift of gray gneiss and greenstone, scoured clean by glaciers ten thousand years ago. The mountain stood several hundred feet above the crowns of the evergreens that grew around its base. Higher up, a grove of aspens ringed the formation. The very top was bare rock where only the most basic and tenacious plant life grew, patches of gold lichen that resembled ulcers on the outcrops. The dark mountaintop pressed itself against the darkening overcast of a clouded sky. A storm was coming.

Dross was in her mid-forties and had been sheriff for a number of years. Cork had hired her as a deputy when he wore the sheriff's badge, making her the first woman to don a law enforcement uniform in Tamarack County. She was experienced, tough. But Saturday nights she still put on cowboy boots, tight jeans, a snap-button western shirt, and the white Stetson her father once gave her as a birthday present, and kicked up her heels at the American Legion hall, line dancing. The lower pant legs of the khakis and the Wolverines she wore now were coated in mud.

Without prelude, she said, "It came down in a bog out there." She pointed toward the trees west of the logging road.

"Survivors?" Cork asked.

"So far nothing, but we just started looking and the debris is still burning."

"Know who was in it?"

As if a hand had pressed itself into her face, her eyes closed a moment, and all her features went flat. "We think it's Senator McCarthy. She was scheduled to land at Olson Field this afternoon. Her family was with her."

Olson Field was the small regional airport just outside Aurora.

"But you're not sure?"

"We're double-checking."

"Who called it in?"

"Monkey Love."

His real name was Jameson Love, but no one called him that. Monkey Love was a mixed-blood Shinnob who lived with his uncle Ned Love in an isolated cabin in the shadow of Desolation Mountain. Cork used to haul him in regularly, D and D—drunk and disorderly—at first, then for other offenses that had earned him significant jail time. But Monkey Love got clean and for the past few years had lived quietly, surviving thanks to careful spending of the allotment he received from the profits of the Chippewa Grand Casino and from the cutting and selling of firewood with his uncle.

"Monkey and Ned don't have a telephone at their place," Cork said.

"He hightailed it into Allouette, used one at the tribal office. Some guys from the rez came back out with him. They're up there now with my people. Daniel's one of them."

From out of the west came a crack like an enormous branch splintering, followed by a long rumble of thunder.

Dross's look went as dark as the sky. "Just what we need."

"Okay if we head on in to give a hand?"

"Foster's posted up the road a bit. He'll point the way. Check in with Azevedo. He's coordinating at the crash site."

Sirens screamed in the distance, although there was little need for a siren on the ill-traveled back roads of the rez.

Dross said, "State Patrol," and moved past Cork and Stephen to await these new arrivals.

They walked the logging road as it skirted the base of Desolation Mountain. Cork knew that in Alaska or Colorado or even Vermont they would laugh at the thought of calling this hump of gneiss a mountain. But it was the highest elevation in the county, a landmark that could be seen for miles. Although it was on the Iron Lake Reservation, it was a popular destination for photographers in the North Country, especially in the fall, when the view from the top was a stunning 360-degree panorama of color. Several small lakes were visible from the mountaintop. With binoculars, and if you knew where to look, you could see Ned and Monkey Love's cabin, hunkered among the pines on a lake called Little Bass.

Deputy David Foster waved at them from the side of the road. Cork could see where the undergrowth had been trampled and broken by the passage of many feet. The recently made trail led into mixed-growth forest of pine and poplar.

"How far in, Dave?" Cork asked.

"Couple hundred yards. Gets real mushy halfway there. After that, watch your step."

The trail wove a crooked course among the trees and between

great humps of rounded granite, miniature reflections of the bald mountaintop. A hundred yards in, just as Foster said, the soil turned wet underfoot and their boots began to make sucking sounds. The trees thinned out, and as the ground became softer and mushier, the pines and poplars gave way to tamaracks and tall ferns. Up ahead, from somewhere still out of sight, came the shouts of men. Also from that direction came another long roll of thunder.

They reached the scene, a boggy area, roughly circular and a hundred yards in diameter, full of reeds and cattails. The men already there were spread out across the marsh and around the edges. Those that had ventured into the reeds stood in brackish water up to their thighs. Close to the far side of the marsh, a group of the volunteer firemen had surrounded a large section of fuselage that was sending up a thick column of black smoke. Cork could see wreckage everywhere, but that one piece of fuselage appeared to be the only debris still burning. The firefighters wore yellow packs and were laying down a spray of suppressant foam where the smoke billowed.

Deputy Azevedo stood with a group of men Cork recognized from the Iron Lake Reservation, Daniel English among them. Cork headed their way, Stephen on his heels.

"Lots of debris in the woods," Daniel was saying as he pointed southwest of the marsh. "Looks like the plane clipped the treetops and began to break apart there."

"All right," Azevedo said. "Take your guys and see what you can find. But don't touch anything. Yell if you find someone alive."

When he saw Cork and Stephen, Daniel lifted his chin to acknowledge them, then turned toward the woods, the four Shinnobs from the rez trailing him. Cork knew them all. Ned and Monkey Love, Phil Hukari, who, like Daniel, was a tribal game warden, and Tom Blessing, who worked with Native youth.

Azevedo turned to Cork. "As soon as the fire's out, we'll check the fuselage. Cockpit's over there, sunk in the mud." He nodded toward a section of debris shaped like a white bullet and almost hidden by reeds. "We broke the windows out. Two bodies inside. I don't figure what's in that burning fuselage is going to be any more hopeful."

"Any idea how many passengers?"

"We think the two pilots, Senator McCarthy, her husband and son, and McCarthy's personal assistant. If this was McCarthy's plane. We've radioed in the registration number but haven't received confirmation yet."

"What do you need us to do?"

"The plane broke up pretty good. Hit the trees back there, like English said, then plowed into the marsh. If you're willing, follow the line it took coming down through those trees and across the marsh." He eyed Stephen and hesitated before going on.

"Looking for bodies," Cork said.

"Yeah," Azevedo acknowledged. "I've already got some guys on it, but I could use more."

Someone already in the marsh called to the deputy, and Azevedo waded in.

When he wore a badge, Cork had been on the scenes of dozens of brutal accidents—car wrecks, lumbering mishaps, explosions, fires. He'd seen life wrenched from the human body with nightmarish violence and in unimaginable ways. But that was far outside Stephen's experience, and the father in Cork hoped that they wouldn't find what might remain of the passengers from the destroyed plane. Yet Stephen was ahead of him, already wading into the reeds and the black water and the suck of the mud beneath it all.

Chapter 7

Moments after they entered the bog, brilliant tendrils of lightning crossed the sky to the west, and only a second passed before the air seemed to shatter. Roy Berg, the fire chief, hollered to everyone to clear the water. Although the broken section of fuselage still smoldered, Berg and his men abandoned their work and made quickly for the shoreline. Cork called to Stephen but got no response. Cork thought he understood. Stephen wanted to press forward, take the risk, find what there was to find, answer the questions. This fallen plane was part of his son's vision, and he had to know why.

"Stephen," Cork called sharply.

Another bolt of lightning, then thunder like the end of the world. Reluctantly, Stephen followed his father to safety.

A driving rain descended. Cork and Stephen hunkered beneath the trees a good, safe distance from the marsh water. After a while Daniel English joined them, along with the other men from the reservation.

"Anything?" Cork asked.

"Tail section and wings. Sheared off as the plane clipped the treetops," Daniel replied. "Everything's pretty torn up."

"You called it in, Monkey? What did you see?" Cork asked.

Monkey Love looked like the Devil had walked all over him, the result of years of addiction to booze and drugs. He was emaciated. His face bore scars from drunken fights in bars and alleyways, and his damaged right eyelid was beset with a persistent droop. He had unusually long arms and fingers—he'd been called Monkey all his life—and more often than not, he could be found puffing on a cigarette hand-rolled from American Spirit tobacco. When he spoke, it was like a rasp over metal.

"Was sitting on the crapper with the door open." Monkey and Ned Love had no running water at their cabin. They used an outhouse for taking care of business. "Got a good view of the mountain from there. Saw the plane come over it. They all do when they're headin' toward the airport. But this one was strange, kinda cockeyed and real low. Going way too slow, seemed. I lost it, then heard a lot of popping, like gunshots or somethin'. Then whump. I swear I could feel it hit. Got out of that crapper, and there was Uncle Ned, lookin' at the trees west of the cabin."

"Did you locate it right away?"

"Wasn't hard," Ned Love said, taking up the story. "Could see where the smoke was coming from. Got there pretty quick."

Ned Love had always been a quiet man, a lifelong bachelor and hermit, content to live in basic isolation. He was tall and thin, like Monkey, but with a vibrancy that Cork had always attributed to Ned Love's connection with the land he called home and his decision, long ago, to draw his life from it. A good deal of the man's sustenance came from trapping and hunting and fishing. Aside from Henry Meloux, Cork couldn't think of another human who knew more about harvesting food from what grew in the Northwoods.

"See anybody alive?"

"Just pieces of that plane and the fire. Figured Monkey and me couldn't do nuthin' but we oughta let somebody know, so I told him to hustle his butt to Allouette."

"And you guys came back with him?" Cork addressed this to the others from the rez.

"It was like Ned says," Phil Hukari replied. He didn't look Native. Young, blond, balding, he was mixed-blood from Oregon, his Native heritage Nez Perce. Much like Daniel, he'd come to Minnesota because of a woman. His wife, Sue, taught early childhood education on the rez, and everyone loved her. "The fuselage piece was in flames when we got here. Nothing we could do about that. Did a quick perimeter search just in case somebody got thrown clear. Then the first responders showed up, started hitting the fire with foam. Then you and Stephen." He looked at the sky. "Then this damn storm."

Finally it happened, exactly the reason Berg had cleared the marsh. A searing electric bolt hit the water. As if a bomb had gone off, the flash was blinding, the sound deafening. Even where he stood among the pines and tamaracks, many yards from the edge of the bog, Cork felt the jolt of the current rip through the ground under his feet.

"That's all she wrote," Tom Blessing said in a stone voice. "If anyone was still alive somewhere in that bog, they're dead now."

Blessing was full-blood Iron Lake Ojibwe. Like a lot of Native youths, he'd gotten into trouble young. He'd belonged to a gang on the rez called the Red Boyz and still bore the brand that was part of the initiation ritual. A set of bloody circumstances had tied him and Cork together in a way that changed them both, and after that, Blessing had abandoned the Red Boyz and now counseled troubled Ojibwe teens.

Moments after the flash, Cork got his first glimpse of the men in olive-green ponchos, a half dozen of them, spread out around the marsh along the shoreline, moving slowly. They held boxes in their hands, electronics of some kind. Cold rain cascaded down his face, and he had to wipe his eyes to see the men clearly. They were like wraiths, dark, silent figures, ignoring the dangers of the storm.

"Who're they?" Daniel asked.

Cork squinted but could see nothing that would be helpful in answering Daniel's question.

Deputy Azevedo intercepted one of the figures. They talked. The deputy stepped back. The men in the ponchos continued on their way. After they'd completely circumnavigated the marsh, they sifted among the trees and were gone.

Although the storm was violent, it was also brief and passed quickly. When the lightning was far to the east, well beyond Desolation Mountain, the fire chief gave the all clear and the search resumed, along with the dousing of what flames sent up smoke from inside the broken fuselage.

Cork realized that Stephen was no longer with him. He did a scan of the dark woods at his back and saw Stephen standing by himself, arms hanging at his sides, staring down at something. Cork jumped brambles and quickly made his way to where his son had become a statue with a bowed head.

There it was. A plane seat. Torn from its moorings. Bolt holes empty. Padding exploded from the ripped upholstery. Cork wondered if the passenger still strapped in the seat, a young teenager judging from his size, was the kid from Stephen's vision. It would have been hard to tell. The face resembled raw meat loaf.

Stephen turned to his father and asked a question Cork couldn't even begin to answer.

"Why?"

Rainy and Jenny had dinner waiting, macaroni and cheese and peas. It was one of Waaboo's favorites, and also Stephen's. The men stripped off their muddied clothing, cleaned themselves, and took their chairs at the table in the dining room. Stephen sat next to Waaboo, who loved his uncle and made grunting noises at him, like a pig. Stephen returned the grunts, but his heart wasn't in this play.

When they'd finished the meal and Waaboo had been read to and taken upstairs to bed, Stephen removed himself from the others and sat in the porch swing, rocking and processing. The night air felt clean after the storm. The sky had cleared, a waxing moon had risen, and the front yard under the elm was a complex tapestry of moon shadow and silver light.

Rainy joined him on the swing. Like Meloux, she had been nurturing Stephen in his own desire to become Mide, though nothing formal had begun. It was all preparation.

"You're struggling to understand," she said.

"Why do the visions come if there's nothing I can do about them, if they don't help prevent the horrible things that happen?"

"I've never had a vision, so I can't answer that."

"I don't want this. I don't want to see these things."

"I understand. But do you have a choice?"

He stared at the complex pattern of light and shadow on the lawn. "I tried to stop it from coming. I tried to close my mind."

"Even if you don't understand, maybe you should open yourself to acceptance, believe there's purpose, although what that might be isn't clear, at least at the moment." She looked up at the sky. "The Great Mystery."

This was one of the more poetic interpretations of Kitchimanidoo, which was also translated as the Great Spirit or sometimes the Creator. Stephen, in his efforts at spiritual understanding, had come to believe that whatever you called this spirit—God, Allah, Kitchimanidoo—it was an integrated consciousness on a cosmic scale, the interconnectedness of all creation. When he was grounded, centered, he understood and, exactly as Rainy was counseling, worked at acceptance. But at that moment, all he felt was frustrated, cut off, full of anger and rejection.

"If I'd understood, maybe all those people would still be alive."

"Or maybe not. Who can say? It seems a lot to take on your shoulders, responsibility for this."

"If I'd only understood in time."

"Stephen," she began.

"I'm going for a walk." He shoved himself out of the swing and rushed headlong across the yard and down Gooseberry Lane.

Cork stepped onto the porch. "Where's he going?"

"To be with himself."

"Maybe I should go after him."

"I don't think he's ready to talk." She watched the figure growing small and dark. "He feels responsible."

"For the plane crash?"

"For not keeping it from happening. He believes he failed because he didn't understand his vision."

Jenny and Daniel joined them.

Cork asked, "Waaboo's down?"

"Sound asleep." Daniel leaned against the porch railing. "I was just listening to the radio. It's all over the news."

"Do they know how many were on the plane with Senator McCarthy?" Jenny asked.

"Her husband, her son, an aide, and the two pilots. That's the working count. NTSB is on the scene now. I suppose we'll know more tomorrow."

"Do they have any idea what caused it?"

"They're still looking for the black box."

Cork shook his head. "I wish to God they hadn't hustled us out of there. I can't help feeling there was more we could have done."

At the same time Stephen had discovered the boy's body still strapped in its seat, another influx of searchers had arrived. Among them were FBI personnel, agents from Minnesota's Bureau of Criminal Apprehension, and first responders from other communities in Tamarack County. Control of the scene moved into the hands of the FBI, and all the others were asked to stand down and clear the marsh. Floodlights were brought in. Cork, Stephen, Daniel, and the others made their way back to the logging road, the lights behind them glaring and unnatural. And within Cork, maybe within them all, a disturbing sense of something important left undone.

"Could you have saved anyone?" Rainy asked.

"I don't think so. But maybe some questions could have been answered."

"Like what?"

"Monkey says there was something odd about the plane, how it was flying, low and slow and canted. No one talked to him about that. Not Dross's people, not the FBI. He and Ned were first on the scene. But no one bothered to question them." He looked at Daniel and added, "Or you and the others who weren't far behind, for that matter."

"We spoke with Azevedo, but just briefly," Daniel replied. "He was the one doing all the talking with the FBI, but I don't know if he said anything about us."

"The sheriff?" Rainy asked. "Where was she?"

"Marsha stayed on the logging road, coordinating the flow of the other responders," Cork said. "I didn't see her at the scene until the FBI was telling the rest of us to stand down."

Jenny looked puzzled. "That seems unusual. Shouldn't she have been in charge?"

"Azevedo's been her go-to incident commander for a long time now," Cork explained. "Marsha trusts him with a scene. I'm guessing she was in communication with all the other agencies, making quick decisions, trying to keep a handle on things. Situation like this, it can be chaos, explode in your face."

"Mom!"

"Thought Waaboo was down," Cork said.

Jenny rose. "Probably picking up all our unsettled vibes." She and Daniel headed inside.

On the porch, alone with Rainy, Cork stared at the sky, where the glow of moonlight outshone the stars. "I don't know how to help him."

"He'll find his way."

"I understand where he's coming from. What good is a vision if it saves no one? Just makes you feel useless."

"You're both wishing you could have done something more."

"Moot point. What's done is done. I'm going inside. Coming?"

"I think I'll wait out here a bit longer," Rainy said.

Cork studied the empty street. "He may not be home for a good long while."

Rainy continued to rock in the porch swing, and Cork called it a night.

The house wasn't completely dark when Stephen finally returned. A light had been left on in the hallway. He shed his jacket and climbed the stairs to his bedroom, where he lay fully clothed on top of the covers. He'd found no answers on his long, solitary sojourn. Moonlight slanted through his window. Shadows invaded his room. He stared at the ceiling, seeing a body full of shattered bones strapped in a plane seat, a face no longer human. He was certain he wouldn't get any rest. But sleep stole over him with surprising suddenness.

And in the night, the vision came to him again.

CHAPTER 8

"Pilot error."

Cork was reading the *Duluth News Tribune.* It had been nearly a week since Senator Olympia McCarthy's plane plowed into a bog near the base of Desolation Mountain, killing everyone on board.

"That's what they're calling it. Not officially yet. Not until they've sifted through everything, which'll take weeks. But at this point they don't have a better explanation."

Rainy was at the kitchen counter, pouring her first cup of coffee that morning. "They still haven't talked to you or to Daniel. Have they talked to anybody who was out there?"

"According to the article, the investigation is ongoing. God only knows what that means."

In the first days following the crash, the world had become glaringly aware of Aurora, Minnesota. The hotels, normally filled with leaf peepers at this time of year, had filled instead with journalists and television reporters. Every day, the main street carried traffic equal to that of a busy summer weekend. The road to Desolation Mountain was a constant stream of coming and going, although the authorities had blocked access to the crash site itself.

That area was still cordoned off while the NTSB continued documenting the scene and collecting debris. But Cork knew that news was only news if it was fresh, and it was fresh only for a heartbeat. After a few days, if nothing sensational came to light, people's interest moved on. Aurora would soon be back to normal. Out of the limelight. He hoped.

"The funeral is tomorrow in the Twin Cities. A private affair," Cork said, relaying what he'd learned from the newspaper story. "Then a public memorial at the cathedral next week. They're expecting thousands."

Rainy joined him, propped her elbows on the table, sipped her coffee. "Minnesota lost a senator. The little guy in America lost a champion."

"Speculation is that our governor is going to arrange to have himself appointed to fill her seat." Cork folded the newspaper. "So for the next four years, the little guy in America will still be lacking a champion. And the question becomes, what do you do now?"

"What do *I* do now?"

"About the mine."

"Cork, you talk about that mine as if you have nothing at stake. It could ruin a lot of the water on the rez, to say nothing of the Boundary Waters."

"I'm well aware of the potential."

"Then why aren't you angry, like the rest of us?"

"Rest of us? There are a lot of folks in Tamarack County who'd be overjoyed to see that mine begin operation. Jobs coming back. It's been a long time for some of the men who worked the iron mines."

"But it's so shortsighted. In the long run, all I see is devastation."

Jenny entered the kitchen, Waaboo trailing behind her, still looking sleepy. Jenny wasn't looking so bright-eyed herself.

"Raised voices this early in the morning? Honeymoon's over, I guess."

"I had a bad dream, Baa-baa." Waaboo sat on his grandfather's lap and laid his head against Cork's chest. "It was scary."

"What was it?"

"A monster. He was chasing me."

"Did he catch you?"

"I hided."

"You hid," Jenny said, pouring herself a mug of coffee.

"It had lots of heads, Baa-baa. Monster heads."

Cork hugged his grandson. "Only a nightmare, buddy."

"Did you see Daniel?" Jenny asked.

"Already gone when I got up this morning," Cork told her. "Why so early?"

"He's still trying to track down those poachers. He keeps getting reports, but he can't nail the guys. I thought I heard Stephen leave early, too."

"Gone at first light."

"Did you talk to him?" she asked.

"Nope."

"Know where he was going?"

"No idea. Tight-lipped as ever."

Waaboo slid from his grandfather's lap and trotted to where Trixie, the O'Connors' ancient pooch, lay on a blanket near her food dish. Trixie lifted her head, and her tail swiped back and forth across the linoleum. In her old age, her pupils had gone cloudy, and there was some concern about her sight going altogether. But her ears and nose still worked well enough, and right now everything about her became suddenly alert as she let out a woof in warning. Only a moment later, the front doorbell rang.

"I'll get it." Jenny left the kitchen.

"A little early for visitors," Rainy remarked.

"Probably John O'Loughlin." Cork was speaking of the neighbor across the street. "Out of coffee again."

"Dad," Jenny called from the front hallway. "Someone to see you."

Although the man standing with her at the front door was a stranger, Cork knew immediately that he had a badge somewhere on him.

"Agent Able Gunderson, FBI." The stranger showed his ID. "Can I speak with you a moment, Mr. O'Connor? And your son and son-in-law as well."

"Is this about the plane crash?"

"Yes, sir."

"Stephen and Daniel are out, but I'm happy to talk with you."

"Can I get you some coffee, Agent Gunderson?" Jenny offered.

"No, thank you." He smiled, polite but steely.

"I'll leave you two to talk then."

"Have a seat." Cork led the way into the living room, and Gunderson took the easy chair.

He was nondescript. Fortyish, medium height and build, sandy hair kept short, eyes whose color was hard to discern or remember. He wore a light leather jacket and jeans.

"Finally getting around to this then," Cork said.

"A lot to be done, Mr. O'Connor. You understand." He took out a small notepad and pen. "What time did you arrive on the scene?"

"Must've been about six-fifteen."

"Who else was there at that time, do you recall?"

"Roy Berg, he's our fire chief." Cork gave the names of the volunteer firefighters he could remember. "Roy would have the full list, I'm sure. Have you talked to him?"

"We have. Any others?"

"Deputy Azevedo. He was coordinating things at the site. Alf Morgan and Joe Riley, they're search and rescue guys, like me."

"I understand there were men from the Iron Lake Reservation."

"Monkey Love, of course. That's Jameson Love. He reported the downed plane. His uncle Ned Love. Daniel English, my son-in-law. Another game warden from the rez, Phil Hukari. And Tom Blessing. He works at the tribal office."

Gunderson wrote down the names. "What was going on when you arrived?"

Cork told him about the flaming fuselage and the firefighters.

"Where were the men from the reservation?"

"Just about to head off to search the woods where some of the debris had come down."

"But they'd been there awhile, searching the area before anyone else arrived, is that correct?"

"Yes."

"And when they went into the woods, you went with them?"

"Not right away. But after the storm began, with all that lightning, Roy made us clear the bog and we joined them then."

"Did any of you find anything?"

"Senator McCarthy's son, still strapped in his seat."

"Did any of you pick anything up?"

"Like what?"

"You tell me. Did you pick up anything?"

"Not that I recall. But as you already know, Daniel and the others were in the woods before us. Have you talked to them yet?"

"We will."

"I have a question for you," Cork said. "Why is the FBI involved?"

"I beg your pardon?"

"I didn't think you guys stepped in unless this was a criminal investigation."

"Senator McCarthy was a national figure, Mr. O'Connor. In these times, when acts of terrorism are possible anywhere, we have to take a close look."

"You think terrorists might have been responsible?"

"I didn't say that. Just that we have to look carefully at a situation like this. I'm sure you understand. These men from the reservation, what's the best way to get in touch with them?"

"Phil Hukari and Tom Blessing live on the rez. Check with the tribal office. They'll point you in the right direction. It's clear you already know that Daniel and Stephen live here. Ned Love and his nephew are a little more difficult. They have a cabin not far from the crash site, but it's pretty hard to find." Cork sat back. "I can't believe nobody's talked to Ned or Monkey Love yet. They were eyewitnesses to the plane going down. The only ones as far as I know."

"We'll get to them, Mr. O'Connor. Is there anything else about the crash site you think we should know, even if it seems inconsequential?"

"To tell you the truth, as soon as your guys showed up on the scene, we got hustled out of there pretty fast, so we weren't a part of the search for very long."

"Our people were preserving the integrity of the site," Gunderson said, as if by rote. He put his notepad and pen away and stood to leave. "Thanks very much for your help. If you think of anything more, feel free to call me." He held out his card.

After the agent had gone, Cork returned to the kitchen.

"What did he want?" Rainy asked.

"Whatever I could tell him about the search at the crash site. But get this. We're almost a week out and nobody's interviewed Ned or Monkey Love. Christ, they saw the plane go down." He took his jacket from where it hung on a peg near the back door.

Rainy gave him a questioning look. "Where are you going?"

"I want to talk to Marsha Dross and George Azevedo."

"Why?" Jenny asks.

"Something doesn't feel right."

Waaboo got up from beside Trixie and hugged his grandfather around the waist. "Watch out for monsters, Baa-baa."

Chapter 9

The entrance to the old logging road along the base of Desolation Mountain was blocked by a wooden barricade. Stephen drove his Jeep slowly past. Two vehicles were parked beyond the barricade, both dark blue SUVs, no official logo of any kind visible anywhere. The plates were U.S. government issue.

Stephen continued two more miles down the main gravel road until he was on the eastern side of the mountain. There was no easy way to the top from there. Photographers and others interested in the view always took a well-worn path that led up from the now-barricaded logging road. He pulled the Jeep off the shoulder and into a flat area among the trees and parked behind a blackberry thicket. He circled the Jeep, satisfied that between its scratched-up, dull olive paint job, the coat of dust and dried mud that it wore, and the leaves of the blackberry thicket it was fairly well hidden. He had no clear idea who he might be concealing it from, but his recurring vision made him cautious.

On official maps, Desolation was the name of the mountain, but the Ojibwe called it Majimanidoo-oshkiinzhig, which meant, more or less, Devil's Eye. Traditionally, it was thought to be a cursed place. Rez elders told children stories about it meant to give them chills. Most modern Shinnobs laughed at the dark tales. Still, Desolation Mountain wasn't a place you were likely to find folks from the rez taking in the view.

Stephen worked his way quietly through the woods to where gray-green rock outcrops, smaller versions of the mountain, began to appear. He wove among the rocks and around a small bog, where the ground began a sharp incline. There was no clear path up the eastern side of Desolation Mountain, and he chose his way carefully. He was in no hurry. Time wouldn't change what drew him to Majimanidoo-oshkiinzhig.

He entered the aspens that ringed the mountain just below the crown. The white trunks around him felt like a host of markers in a vast graveyard, testaments to the dark reputation of the mountain, and Stephen tried to shake the sense of dread that shadowed him.

He broke from the aspens onto a broad, barren stretch that formed the granite apron of the mountaintop. From the edge of the aspens to the crown, the only life-form was simple lichen, which looked like cancer on the rocks. It was a desolate landscape, the reason for the name the whites had given it was easy to see. Above the apron, atop the crest, rose a circular outcrop darker than any of the rock around it. Stephen had seen aerial photographs of the formation and, in them, the justification for the Ojibwe name—Devil's Eye—became clear. That crowning outcrop resembled perfectly a dark pupil set in a gray-green iris, a never-blinking eye staring skyward.

He climbed to the base of the outcrop, a roughly circular formation ten feet high and thirty feet in diameter. If he'd scaled the rock all the way to the top, he would have had a full view of the mountain slope. The landscape was familiar, but not just because he'd been there many times over the course of his twenty years in Aurora. He understood now that each time the vision came to him, this was the place where the scene played out. He looked up. The sky was blue, with a few cotton ball puffs of white. In the vision, the sky was always a boil of dark clouds. The air around him was redolent with the fragrance of the Northwoods, of evergreens and fallen aspen leaves and the mineral smell of the hard rock beneath his feet, and even the clean scent of the lakes he could see from the mountain's crest. In the vision, the air stank of burning fuel and seared flesh.

Stephen was still struggling to understand.

From his vantage, he could make out the bog where the broken wreckage of the plane had come to rest, a bare, circular area among the distant trees. On previous days, he'd tried to make his way there, but the woods continued to be alive with men still searching the crash site. From a case on his belt, he took out a pair of field glasses, put them to his eyes, and adjusted the lenses. The bog came clearly into view, and he saw a few searchers crawling like insects along the edges of the reedy water. The fuselage and other wreckage had been removed. Just a hair to the south were the trees where he'd stumbled upon the boy still strapped in his seat, his face obliterated, all the bones of his body shattered. He lowered the glasses, remembering the horror, the helplessness he'd felt. Time and again since that day, he'd imagined what it might have been like for the boy, his mother, his father, the aide, the pilots, as the plane fell. Through tiny windows, a view of the earth racing at them, the trees looming. The terrible realization, too fleeting to be spoken, of what would happen in the next instant. He'd imagined the mother—not the senator but the woman behind the title—turning her head toward her child, knowing that all she'd hoped for him, had dreamed his life might be, was gone. Worse than her own fate was what she must have understood of his.

Every time Stephen imagined this, he felt anger at the uselessness of his vision.

He put the glasses to his eyes again and moved the lenses to the north. He spotted the oval of blue water that was Little Bass Lake, where Monkey Love and his uncle Ned lived. He could make out the rustic cabin and even the tiny outhouse through whose opened door Monkey had watched the plane go down.

Then he became aware of movement among the aspens ringing the mountain a hundred yards below him. He shifted the field glasses, adjusted the focus. The men who came into view wore military fatigues. They seemed to be conducting a quadrant search, an evidence-gathering technique described to him by his father, in which an area was divided into squares and covered methodically.

A couple of other men in fatigues appeared on the worn path that came up the western slope from the barricaded road. They carried powerful-looking rifles and joined the men conducting the search among the aspens. Stephen couldn't understand why they were searching the mountaintop when the plane had crashed far below. They seemed out of place, especially with the heavy weapons. Something felt terribly wrong.

He continued to scan the trees below. Except for the quadrant where the men in fatigues disturbed the peace, it was a lovely scene. The aspen leaves were shivering gold, the trunks stark white, sunlight breaking among the branches, the ground below dappled with shadows.

Then he spotted the boy. Standing very still. Another shadow among the many shadows beneath the trees. The boy watched the men. Stephen watched the boy. A gentle wind rose up. The shadows of the trees shifted. The sunlight between them danced.

In the next moment, the light faded as a brooding shadow crossed the mountain. Stephen glanced up. The sun had been obscured by a sudden convergence of clouds. When he put his eyes to the lenses again, the boy had vanished.

He moved quickly off the mountaintop and risked a dash down

the bare rock apron, across open ground toward the trees where he'd last seen the boy. As he ran, he heard a shout from the direction of the search area. To his right, two men with rifles rushed from the aspens. His gimp leg was on fire, and the burn ran up his back to the place where a bullet had once entered and lodged against his spine.

The cloud passed and sunlight returned, a dazzle that once again laid down shadows among the trees. He caught a glimpse of something moving there. The boy? *Run,* he wanted to shout. *Run.*

Instead he stopped dead still and turned to face the men with rifles. A decoy so the boy could escape. A sacrifice that deep inside him felt right.

CHAPTER 10

Sheriff Marsha Dross sat in her office, looking up at Cork with eyes so tired they made him want to lie down.

"I'm not running for reelection next year," she said.

"Believe me, I understand."

"Sit."

Cork took the vacant chair on the other side of her desk.

"I thought I'd been through it all. But the senator's plane crash?" She raised her hands in surrender.

"I understood you were out of the investigation."

"We are. Officially. I've still got a line of guys from a zoo of federal agencies coming in constantly, looking for assistance, local info. FBI, NTSB, Homeland Security. The wording I'm supposed to deliver to the media goes something like this: The investigation is out of my hands, but I see nothing to make me question the preliminary determination that the cause of the crash was pilot error."

"A lot of interest among a lot of agencies for a crash caused by simple pilot error."

"In the political environment today, a terrorist is behind every tragic event."

"I was finally interviewed by the FBI this morning."

Her eyebrows lifted. "Only just?"

"They've been busy, the agent said."

"Yeah, fighting among themselves. I can't tell who's in charge."

"Nobody's talked to Monkey or Ned Love yet."

She closed her eyes in frustration. "Is it any wonder we still don't know who really killed Kennedy?"

"Margaret told me at the contact desk that George Azevedo requested a leave."

"Asked for two weeks off. Claimed he couldn't stand the badgering from the feds and the media. They were camped out at his house, following his family. He had to get out of Dodge."

"Not you, though?"

"The buck stops here."

"How would you like to piss off the feds, Marsha?"

"I'd like that quite a lot."

"Put your badge on and follow me."

"Where to?"

"I think it's time somebody talked to Ned and Monkey."

Because Marsha Dross had never been to the Loves' cabin, Cork drove. Also, he liked the idea that his unmarked vehicle wouldn't attract as much notice. They skirted the southern end of Iron Lake and headed east onto rez land, where Cork took back roads he'd traveled all his life. Dross was in her second term as sheriff, but she wasn't native to the area. Like a lot of white folks in Tamarack County, even those born there, when she was on the Iron Lake Reservation, she might as well have been in the Australian outback. Cork kept off the main route to Desolation Mountain, figuring that one or all of the interested federal agencies would still be monitoring the traffic. He eased through a couple of iffy bog areas, and finally Desolation Mountain came into view above the tops of the trees.

"What do you know about Monkey Love?" he asked.

"I heard he was trouble around here when he was a kid, but I've never had a problem with him."

"Nobody's sure who his father was. His mother died when he wasn't much more than a toddler. His uncle took him in, raised him for a long while. Ned Love's a good man, but he's always kept to himself out here in the woods. Monkey grew up comfortable not being around people."

"I can't recall seeing either of them in Aurora more than half a dozen times in the last few years."

"Like I said, comfortable in their isolation. When Monkey was twelve, his aunt, Beulah Love, that's Ned's sister, decided he wasn't being raised right, got Social Services involved. They took Monkey from Ned and placed him with her. She lives in Allouette. A well-meaning woman, I'm sure, but one hell of a Bible thumper. Monkey was an odd kid. Odd looking and socially backward. Threw in with a bad crowd, despite all the preaching of his aunt Beulah. He started using, committed a bunch of petty crimes. Shoplifting, boosting cars, a string of B & Es. Got himself sent to the juvenile detention center in Bemidji. Once he came of age, I ran him in a lot for D & D. Then he tried armed robbery using a pellet gun. Did a couple of years in Sandstone."

"Serving time straightened him out?"

"Not exactly. A guy in Sandstone introduced him to the White Bison program. It's a movement that, among other things, helps incarcerated Native men and women get sober. The program didn't take when he was inside, but it finally clicked for him after he was released. Henry Meloux had a lot to do with that. Monkey moved back in with his uncle five years ago, been there since. Still odd, but he seems a lot more comfortable with who he is."

Cork was following two barely visible ruts. Low-hanging tree branches and the wild undergrowth scraped audibly along the sides of the vehicle.

He finally pulled to a stop in front of the old, one-room cabin that had been home to Monkey Love when he was a kid, and was home to him again.

Dross peered through the windshield. "So, just Monkey and Ned out here?"

"Got themselves an old bluetick hound they call Cyrus, in honor of Monkey's grandfather. Used to be a good hunting dog, but he's old now, years past his prime, arthritic. Mostly he lies in the shade and barks a warning when anyone comes around."

"I don't hear him barking."

Ned Love's old pickup was parked next to the cabin. Beyond it lay the road the Loves took when they came and went, a narrow lane that in winter could be snow-choked and impassable. In the spring melt, when the ground was often nothing but a wet, black mire, it could be just as difficult to traverse. When either Ned or Monkey wanted to go into Allouette, they were often forced to walk, taking the path Cork had just followed, a five-mile trek each way.

Cork and Dross got out of the vehicle and approached the cabin.

Ned Love was a hunter, and beside his front door lay a pile of jumbled deer antlers. Cork knocked, a little surprised that no one had stepped out to see who'd come calling. Cork was pretty sure the Loves got few visitors. At the very least, Cyrus should have been barking up a storm.

"Ned, Monkey, it's Cork O'Connor!"

He glanced at Dross and reached for the door. Few people on the rez used locks, and the door swung open. Inside, the place was furnished simply: an old woodstove at the center, two bunks with their heads against the far wall and between them a chest of drawers, a small table next to the single eastern window with two chairs shoved under, two kerosene lanterns—one on the table and one on the chest of drawers. A wooden counter ran along the south wall; the shelves above it held dry and canned goods and cooking utensils. On the counter itself sat a hand mirror, a white enamel basin, a straight razor. Considering it was the home of two bachelors, the cabin was neatly kept. And empty. Just that. Empty. Nothing sinister. Yet Cork felt something wasn't right.

"Where do you suppose they've gone off to?" Dross spoke just above a whisper, as if their presence was a trespass. Which, technically, it was.

"Hunting maybe. That's mostly how Ned keeps the larder filled."

"They must have taken the bluetick with them."

Outside they checked the shed, which was empty except for the axes, saws, splitter, and other tools Ned and Monkey used to gather and prepare the firewood they sold. The only other structure was the outhouse. Cork walked to it. The door was closed, but he heard a scratching on the other side. He reached for the wooden latch and paused. The scratching ceased. Dross had come up next to him, her sidearm out and in her hand. Cork yanked open the door.

A squirrel shot past them, a blur of gray fur that darted up the nearest pine.

A wooden dock, rickety-looking, jutted out into Little Bass Lake a few yards from the shoreline, just enough to tie up a boat or land a canoe. There was nothing tied at the dock, but Cork strolled out to its end and stood gazing across the lake, which was oval-shaped and only a few hundred yards wide. Reflected on the still, silver-blue surface was the upside-down image of Desolation Mountain, which rose beyond the trees on the far shoreline.

"I didn't see their rifles anywhere," he noted. "So maybe they did go hunting."

Dross bent down and inspected the warped, weathered dock boards. With the tip of her index finger, she touched a spot that had caught her interest, one of a spattering of dark spots at the edge of the dock.

"I wouldn't bet the farm, but I'd wager this is blood," she said.

She stood and looked across the lake, which was as empty as the cabin, and took in the sight of Desolation Mountain, its crown bare and gray against the blue wall of the sky.

"Marsha," Cork said quietly.

She looked where he was looking, into the water just off the end of the dock. The lake was four feet deep there and crystal clear. From the bottom, Cyrus, the bluetick hound, stared up at them with open, dead eyes.

CHAPTER 11

Stephen sat in a chair in the lodge of a resort on Iron Lake, south of Aurora. The resort—North Country Cabins—had been closed for three years. Stephen wasn't sure what the issue was, why exactly it had closed, except that during the recession a lot of resorts in the area had suffered. The cabins had stood empty since. Until now. The lodge room where Stephen sat with a good view of the lake was full of electronic equipment and bankers' boxes containing file folders. Topographic maps of Tamarack County and the Iron Lake Reservation hung on the walls, with pins of various colors stuck in patterns Stephen couldn't decipher.

He was afraid, but not with the kind of fear that always accompanied his vision. It was broad daylight, and the men who'd brought him there appeared to be with the government and bound, he believed, by laws. It wasn't like he was a terrorist.

He'd been questioned, twice. First by the men on top of Desolation Mountain. Hoping they would let him go, he'd told them he was just curious. Instead, they'd brought him down to the lodge. Since the plane crash, there'd been a great deal of activity in Tamarack County, lots of official outsiders poking around. Nobody seemed to know much about the nature of all that effort, beyond trying to get to the bottom of what caused the crash. Which, if you believed the NTSB briefings, had already been pretty much determined to be pilot error.

But if that were the true reason for the crash, Stephen asked himself as he sat, what was it they were looking for among the aspens on Desolation Mountain?

He wasn't alone in the room. A man who called himself Gerard was with him. Gerard was military, Stephen had guessed—because of the man's bearing, which was stiff, his clipped way of talking, the hardness with which he eyed Stephen. Also the camo and the crew cut.

They'd stopped conversing. Stephen had stuck to his story about just being curious. You know, a kid. He'd smiled when he said that. Gerard's reply had been that twenty years old was not a kid. Younger men were in uniform, dying for their country.

In his questioning, Gerard had kept hammering at Stephen about a camera. Was he taking pictures? Stephen had maintained that he wasn't.

In the empty silence after the questions had ended, a woman entered the room. She was tall, blond, and carried herself with the same kind of bearing as Gerard, very military. They spoke in low voices, and Gerard turned to Stephen.

"We've brought your Jeep down. It's parked outside. You're free to go. But, Mr. O'Connor, if we find you in that restricted area again, there will be charges. Do you understand?"

"Yes, sir."

"Show him out, Craig."

Before Stephen left the room, he asked one final question: "Who exactly are you?"

"We are the dead. Short days ago, we lived, felt dawn, saw sunset glow, loved and were loved, and now . . ." Gerard stopped and waited, as if expecting something from Stephen. Then he looked disappointed. "Don't know that poem? 'In Flanders Fields,' a great piece about sacrifice. You want to know who we are, kid? We're the ones willing to put it all on the line so you sleep safe and warm in your bed at night. We stand between you and the enemy."

The woman accompanied Stephen to his Jeep and waited while he got in and turned the engine over. Before he drove away, he gave her a long, deep look. "Craig? Is that your first name?"

She didn't respond for a long time, but just when Stephen thought she never would, she said, "Sandi." From the look on her face, he could tell that she believed he was powerless to use the name against her.

He put to her more or less the same question he'd put to Gerard: "Who are you, Sandi Craig?"

A smile crossed her lips, one as cruel as Stephen had ever seen. The answer she gave him was much more succinct than Gerard's had been. "Your worst nightmare, kid."

It all felt otherworldly to him. As if Tamarack County had been invaded, occupied, and no one could say why. He returned to a deserted house. Daniel and Rainy were at work and Waaboo at preschool. He figured Jenny was at Sam's Place, preparing to open. Maybe his father was with her. In half an hour, Stephen was supposed to be in class, Introduction to Philosophy. He was also on the schedule at Sam's Place that day, from three to closing. If he skipped class, he calculated, there would be plenty of time to do what he believed needed to be done before he went to work.

When he broke from the trees and stepped onto Crow Point, he could see Henry Meloux sitting cross-legged in the middle of the meadow. Only the old man's head and shoulders showed above the tall grass and timothy and wildflowers. The Mide faced him, as if he'd been waiting for Stephen to appear. The sun hung almost directly overhead, and Meloux sat on his own shadow. As he drew nearer Stephen could hear the old man singing softly. At first, he thought Meloux must be singing a prayer, but when he came very close he discerned the lyrics: *Where seldom is heard a discouraging word . . .*

Meloux smiled broadly. "Sit," he invited with his hand held out.

Stephen settled beside him in the grass, which, when he was seated, reached nearly to his chest.

"It is a beautiful moment, is it not, Stephen O'Connor?"

"Henry, we need to talk."

"There is time. For the moment, enjoy this." The old man opened his arms, embracing the beauty of the meadow.

Stephen knew the old Mide would listen only when he was ready.

"Who among us knows how many of these moments we have left? I try to gather them, like a squirrel preparing for a long winter."

Meloux closed his eyes, lifted his lined face to the sun, breathed deeply.

In his presence, in this old man's vast enjoyment of a simple moment, Stephen felt an easing of the tightness in his chest. He breathed, closed his eyes, and like Meloux lifted his face to the warm sun.

"That is all of life," the old Mide said quietly.

"What?" Stephen asked.

"Letting go of the questions. Letting go of the fear that there will be no answers."

"Will there be answers?"

"What we believe we want is like knocking on a closed door. Better to open ourselves to what we have and what we know. The beauty of this moment."

Stephen understood the truth in Meloux's words. But his brain continued to knock at closed doors.

At last the old man gave in with a sigh. "What is troubling you?"

"My vision, Henry. And Dad says you've sensed something bad, too."

"They are different, what you have seen, what I have sensed."

"The vision terrifies me. Dad told me what you sensed frightens you."

"It has concerned me."

"My vision keeps coming back, Henry. I thought with the crash it would stop, but I've had it twice since."

"Is it the same?"

"Exactly. The boy, the bird, the beast at my back. The terror at the end. They have to be connected, what I see and what you sense. Here's another thing. I saw the boy. I saw him on Desolation Mountain."

Stephen related the events of that morning.

"Was he flesh and blood?" the old man asked. "Or like a vision?"

"He was there, then gone. Like a vision, I suppose. But he seemed real enough."

"Have you told anyone this?"

"Only you."

"You should tell your father. And then we will do a sweat."

"You and me?"

Meloux had passed the century mark. Sweats were hard on his body, so Stephen wasn't certain it was a good idea.

"We are the ones who have seen and sensed whatever the spirits of these woods are offering," Henry told him. "Perhaps what they are trying to tell us will become clear. Or we can wait and perhaps time will do the same."

Stephen's chest grew taut again. Time didn't feel like an ally.

"A sweat," he agreed. "But maybe just me."

The old man smiled. "You are afraid my spirit might abandon my body. Let go of that fear. I am not ready yet to walk the Path of Souls. Maybe what I sense and what you see are the same. Maybe they are different. The answer is a closed door now. Maybe a sweat will open it."

CHAPTER 12

"A dead dog and a few drops of blood," Marsha Dross said. "That's not enough to launch an official investigation, Cork."

They were on their way back from Ned and Monkey Love's cabin. Cork burned with a sense of outrage. "The Loves didn't shoot Cyrus."

"It could be the FBI finally sent someone out to interview them. They're off hunting. Only Cyrus is there, and Cyrus does what a good watchdog does. The agent or agents feel threatened and shoot."

"And dump the dog's body in the lake? Come on, Marsha."

"We've both seen stranger things. All I'm saying is that I'm not going to throw a lot of resources at this right now. I'll get those blood samples I took from the dock tested. If they're human, that's different."

"It'll take a while to get results. I'm not waiting."

She leveled a gaze on him, coldly professional in its scrutiny. Her voice was all law enforcement. "What exactly do you intend to do?"

Cork offered no answer. Partly it was because since he'd given up wearing a badge his methods hadn't always been within the letter of the law. But also partly because he wasn't sure how to answer her question.

"When I know about the blood, I'll let you know," she promised, when she got out in the parking lot of the Tamarack County Sheriff's Office. "And if you find out anything, you'll let me know. Right?"

He didn't look at her. "I'll see what turns up."

He drove directly to Allouette, the largest community on the Iron Lake Reservation. When Cork was growing up and hanging out with relatives and friends on the rez, Allouette had been a mixed bag. Like in a lot of reservation communities, unemployment was high, there was poverty and the ills that came with it. Most of the roads in town were still gravel then. The majority of the housing was BIA built, or trailers. Cheap, flimsy. Water and sanitation systems were not always in good operating condition. Tourism was nonexistent. White people kept their distance from Allouette and the rez in general, and complained about old treaties that gave the Ojibwe greater access to fishing on Iron Lake and oversight of areas that still had first-growth pine.

When the tribe built the Chippewa Grand Casino, things changed a good deal, both in Aurora and on the rez. The casino hotel and golf course made Aurora a destination for people who weren't just looking for a gateway to the Boundary Waters. The tribal coffers filled with gambling money. The roads in Allouette were paved. Updated water and sewer systems were laid. A new tribal office complex and a clinic were built. New stands were erected for the powwow grounds. A modern marina was constructed on the lakeshore at the edge of town, and because the cost of mooring was set a good deal less than at the marina in Aurora, a lot of white folks dock their boats there in season. A café had opened, the Wild Rice, with a view of the marina and the lake and the islands. There was a coffee shop in town, the Mocha Moose, and a couple of galleries that offered pieces by Native artists.

The revitalization of Allouette didn't mean that everyone cut their grass regularly. There were still cars up on cinder blocks and some trailers that looked as if a perpetual yard sale was going on, but most folks on the rez seemed to feel a sense of pride in their town, their sovereign nation, and the future they were creating for their children and grandchildren.

On the way, he'd tried the phone number for Beulah Love, Ned's sister, but got only her voice mail greeting: *Hello. This is Beulah. I can't answer the phone, so just leave a message and I'll get back to you. Have a wonderful day and remember that the good Lord's grace and my name end in the same way—with Love.*

Her house was small and yellow, with marigolds still blooming along the foundation. Almost nobody in Allouette had a fence around their yard, but Beulah did, built of little white pickets. Beulah had a head for numbers and worked in the accounting department of the Chippewa Grand Casino. She spent every Wednesday night and most of every Sunday inside the old Cenex building south of Aurora, which had become the Church of Holy Fire, where she was the organist. She had never married, but there had been rumors about her relationship with Rev. Alvin Doyle, the pastor at Holy Fire.

Beulah Love was among the last children from the Iron Lake Reservation to be sent to a government-run boarding school. Cork, who was only a year or two older, could still remember what she was like before she left—a quiet girl, pretty, with a long black braid and fluttery eyes, helping her grandmother make fry bread at tribal gatherings. She'd returned years later, hard, cold, with coiffed hair and a head for calculations. She didn't talk about her experience at the boarding school, but Cork had heard enough horrendous stories from others who'd been torn from their families and forced to go to such places that he understood what her silence concealed.

He stood at the front door and could hear her playing the piano inside. He didn't know much about classical music, but he recognized the Moonlight Sonata and hesitated a moment or two before knocking, reluctant to interrupt the lovely, quiet flow. When he finally put his fist to the door, the music stopped. She opened up and stared at him with eyes like black beetle shells.

"Morning, Beulah."

"Cork." A cold greeting.

"Wonder if I could talk with you a minute."

She checked the watch on her wrist. "I have to be leaving for work soon."

"Like I say, just for a minute."

She stood aside and let him enter.

The unofficial credo of the Indian boarding school system was "Kill the Indian, save the child." Beulah's home reflected nothing of her Native heritage. The paintings on her walls were pastel and pastoral, exactly the kind someone might find in a room at a Comfort Inn. She wore nothing beaded, didn't go to powwows. He believed she was the only Native member of the Church of Holy Fire. As he stood in the sanitized atmosphere of Beulah's home, Cork couldn't help thinking sadly that, in the first part of its mission at least, the boarding school had succeeded.

"What is it?" She crossed her arms over her chest, reminding him of a schoolteacher impatient with a child.

"Have you heard from Ned or Monkey in the last couple of days?"

"I never hear from my brother. I haven't spoken to that wild man in years. Since he took Jameson away from me."

In Cork's understanding, this had worked the other way

around. So he assumed Beulah was speaking of Monkey's decision, once he was grown and sober, to move back in with his uncle.

"What about Monkey? Have you heard from him?"

"I hate that name."

"Jameson then."

"Not since Sunday dinner, after church."

"Sunday dinner with you, is that a regular thing?"

"Yes. We eat, we pray."

"Monkey—Jameson—prays with you?"

"I do the praying."

"Has he talked to you this week?"

"No, but he doesn't need to. We both know he'll be here."

"He might not be here this Sunday."

"Oh?"

Cork explained what he'd found at the cabin. Beulah's face went from dour, its usual cast, to deeply concerned. She sat in a hard, straight-backed chair, staring at one of the pastels on her wall, thinking.

"It's got to be that wild man."

"Ned?"

"When we went to the boarding school, they couldn't keep him there. He'd run away, return to the reservation. They'd send him right back. He'd run away again. We weren't allowed to speak our language. But Ned did anyway. They beat him. Made no difference. He became like an animal. Wild."

But Cork thought the word *free.*

"When Jameson was a boy and I saw that Ned was making him just as wild he was, I took him away, tried to give him a Christian upbringing. But the wild was already there, too deep." For a moment, Cork thought she was going to cry. Instead, her face turned hard. "That wild man has finally gone crazy. Killed his dog and done Lord knows what to Jameson."

"Ned didn't kill Cyrus."

"Who then?"

"I can't answer that, at least not at the moment. Listen, Beulah, if Ned or Jameson contacts you, tell them it's important that I talk to them. Will you do that?"

"Talk to them about what?"

"There's a lot of strange things going on around here since the senator's plane went down. I think Ned and your nephew might know something that other people want to know."

"Like what?"

"That's what I'm hoping Ned or Jameson might be able to tell me."

"They're in trouble? Real trouble?"

"They may be."

"Ned can take care of himself." It was spoken with a grudging assurance. "But Jameson?" She looked up at Cork, her eyes soft and fearful. Family, he understood. Blood love. Even the white boarding school couldn't kill that.

"Let me know if you hear anything, all right, Beulah?"

She nodded. "And I'll pray for them."

He left her in that chair and, before he closed the front door behind him, could hear her supplication.

Chapter 13

The clinic was next to the tribal office complex, which housed a number of the enterprises of the Iron Lake Ojibwe, including the Department of Conservation Enforcement, out of which Daniel and the other game wardens operated. Cork dropped into the clinic first to see Rainy, but she was out making some home calls. In the Conservation Enforcement office, he found that Daniel was out, too.

"He's still trying to chase down them poachers," Clyde Kingbird, the senior game warden, told Cork. "We keep getting reports, and them poachers keep slipping away."

"Native?" Cork was thinking of Monkey Love and his uncle Ned, who hunted on the rez year-round, even though there were restrictions.

"White, nearly as we can tell." Kingbird had a dark mole on his upper lip that had always reminded Cork of a fly, and he'd always had an urge to shoo it away. "But pretty damn smart for *chimooks*. They don't leave nothing behind."

"Poaching deer?"

"Like I said, don't leave nothing behind, so hard to tell what they're poaching."

"How do you know they're poachers?"

"Who else'd be skulking around out there?"

"Where exactly is 'out there'?"

"East." Kingbird waved a hand. "Other side of Devil's Eye."

"Wildlife photographers, maybe. Beautiful, empty country."

"Maybe. They keep coming around, Daniel'll catch 'em eventually. Good man, your son-in-law."

Cork wandered over to the Youth Mentor Program office, where Tom Blessing was the sole employee. The door was closed and locked, no lights on inside. He returned to the Conservation Enforcement office.

"Seen Blessing this morning?"

Kingbird looked up from his desk, where he was reading some kind of official notice. "Nope."

"As far as you know, has anyone interviewed him since the senator's plane crashed?"

"Haven't seen any strange faces around here lately. Unless you count the guy who fills the Coke machine. Reminds me of a bigmouth bass, that one."

Cork had Tom Blessing's number among the contacts on his cell phone. He tried the number, got the message that the user wasn't available.

Tom Blessing shared a house with his mother, Fanny, on a back road a couple of miles outside Allouette. Cork drove down the narrow gravel lane. Marshland lay on either side, full of cattails. Cork had a great respect for the reeds, which his Anishinaabe ancestors had used in dozens of ways—the fluff to line moccasins, waterproof mats woven from the leaves, marmalade made from the roots, bread from the pollen. He pulled into the dirt drive, parked, and waited.

Like many folks who live rurally, the Blessings owned a dog, as much for security as for company. Cork expected Tornado, a bulldog, to come bounding out, woofing a warning. The dog never appeared.

The morning was sunny, but with a few patchy clouds. As Cork sat waiting, the house and the ragged front yard were engulfed in shadow, and a wariness crept over him, a sense that things weren't right. He listened to the red-winged blackbirds calling among the cattails, and he wondered where the hell Tornado was. Which was the same question he'd had about the bluetick hound at the Loves' cabin, and he hadn't liked the answer he'd found there.

He went to the front porch, mounted the three steps, knocked at the door. He tried to peer through a window, but the curtains were drawn. Although Tom Blessing's pickup truck was gone, his mother's big black 1998 Buick LeSabre was parked near the garage.

"Fanny!" he called at the front door. "It's Cork O'Connor."

He considered leaving, but reached for the doorknob instead, gave it a turn, and eased the door open.

"Fanny, are you here? You okay?"

Fanny Blessing had smoked all her life. She suffered from emphysema, and everywhere she went, a little tank of oxygen on wheels followed her. But she hadn't given up her habit, and the odor of cigarette smoke permeated the house, coming off the furniture upholstery, the rug, the curtains. Fanny Blessing had given up housekeeping a while back, about the time the oxygen tank began following her like a puppy. Tom wasn't the neatest of guys, so the place had a messy look. Cork proceeded carefully, as respectfully as possible for a trespasser. All the rooms were empty.

Back outside, he checked the LeSabre. The keys were in the ignition. He wondered if, in addition to everything else, Fanny had become forgetful. He walked to the old garage, where the side door was ajar, and stepped inside. The garage had no windows, and he waited a moment for his eyes to adjust to the dark. When they did, he saw Fanny sprawled on the dirt of the garage floor, the oxygen tank upright on its wheels beside her, like a loyal pet waiting for its mistress to awaken.

"Heart attack, maybe? Stroke?" Bob Arnold, one of the paramedics from the clinic in Allouette, was talking with Cork while they awaited the sheriff's people. "This isn't the first time we've been out here. Fanny's been walking a thin line for years. Refused to give up her coffin nails."

They'd lifted the garage door, and a rhomboid of sunlight fell across the floor and Fanny's bare legs. She wore a housedress, nothing on her feet.

"What was she doing out here?" Cork said this more to himself than to Arnold.

The wood shelves of the garage were filled with cans of power steering fluid and brake fluid, containers of antifreeze and motor oil, a few miscellaneous tools. A couple of tires leaned against one wall. In a corner was an old power mower.

Arnold replied, "Looking for Tom, maybe."

The crunch of tires approaching on gravel pulled Cork to the opened garage door, and he watched Sheriff Marsha Dross arrive in her TrailBlazer, Deputy Dave Foster following in his cruiser. Dross greeted Cork, shook hands with Bob Arnold and Karl Renwanz, the other paramedic, who'd been on the radio, communicating with the clinic.

"You found her and called it in?" she said to Cork.

"Yeah."

She knelt, studied the woman's gray face.

"She's not wearing the oxygen tube," Dross noted. "Why would she take it off?"

"Got me," Cork said.

"Is Tom around?"

"Haven't seen him."

She rose, took in the scene of the woman's death. "What was she doing out here in a housedress and barefooted?"

"Ran out of Wesson oil and was maybe going to cook breakfast with a little ten-thirty?" Arnold offered.

It was clear Dross didn't appreciate the paramedic's black humor. "I gave Tom Conklin a call," she said. Conklin was the county's medical examiner. "He'll be here soon. I want him to have a look at her before we move the body." She turned to her deputy. "See if you can get hold of Tom Blessing."

"I already tried his cell phone," Cork told her. "No answer. And he's not at his office in Allouette."

"Next of kin?"

"Beulah Love is her cousin. I spoke with her this morning. She was just about to head to work at the casino. Could probably reach her there."

"Ned Love must be a cousin, too, then."

"On the rez, just about everyone's a cousin."

"Did you find out anything from Beulah?"

"She hasn't heard from Ned or Monkey in a while. That's about it."

"Check the house," Dross told her deputy.

"Already have," Cork said. "Empty."

Dross looked around, then at Cork. "They have a dog, right?"

"A bulldog. Tornado."

"Where is he?"

"Could be with Tom."

"Like Cyrus was with Ned and Monkey Love? Foster, check the property. See if you can find the dog."

"If he was here, wouldn't he be barking, Sheriff?" the deputy offered.

"Just look."

"Check the marsh," Cork suggested.

Dross studied Cork, then nodded and said to her deputy, "Check the marsh."

CHAPTER 14

It was ten minutes to opening, but his father wasn't at Sam's Place.

"He said he had things to do," Jenny told Stephen. "That's why I called Judy." She swung a hand toward the woman preparing to open the serving windows.

"What things?" Stephen asked.

"Dad found Ned and Monkey Love's dog shot and dumped in the lake at their cabin. The Loves weren't around, so he headed to the rez to see what he could find out. Where have you been all morning?"

"Tell you later." Stephen turned to leave.

"Where are you going?"

"To catch Dad at the rez."

"You don't know where he is out there."

"It's the rez. Somebody'll know."

"Be back at three. You're on the schedule and we'll need you."

Luck was with him. He'd just swung around the southern end of Iron Lake and passed the turnoff to Desolation Mountain when he spotted his father's SUV approaching from the direction of

Allouette. He waved Cork down, pointed to the side of the road, and parked on the shoulder. His father made a U-turn and pulled up behind him.

Stephen was out of his Jeep in a heartbeat and spoke to his father through the lowered window. "Jenny told me about the Loves' dog. Did you find out anything on the rez?"

"Whoa. Hold on a minute. Where've you been all day?"

"You're not going to believe this." Stephen related the details of his morning on Desolation Mountain and his interrogation by the man named Gerard.

"FBI?" Cork asked.

"Military, I think. Did you find out anything about the Loves?"

"Nothing. I went out to see Tom Blessing. He wasn't there, but I found his mother dead in the garage."

"Fanny? What happened?"

"Looks like it could have been a heart attack or maybe a stroke. We won't know until the ME's had a good look at her. But there's a lot not right about it. Any idea what the guys on Desolation Mountain were looking for?"

"None."

"Don't take this the wrong way, Stephen, but the kid you say you saw up there, was he real or another vision?"

Real, Stephen had thought at the time, but as the moment receded, he'd begun to wonder if it wasn't something else, another kind of seeing, not exactly a vision but akin. "He was pretty far away. I saw him through my field glasses. A lot of shadow involved."

"What was he doing?"

"Same thing I was. Checking out the guys in military camo."

His father looked past him, staring at where the lake was visible through a thin line of pines on the other side of the road. Stephen understood that the sparkle of the blue water probably wasn't what his father was seeing.

"I want to check out the mountain," Cork finally said.

"Not without me."

His father shook his head. "They picked you up once and let you go. The next time they won't be so lenient."

"You're not going without me."

Stephen stood with his hands on the vehicle as if intending to hold it there until his father agreed.

"They know your Jeep. We'll take the Expedition."

Three miles up the cutoff to Desolation Mountain, a good mile shy of the logging road that had been blocked that morning, they came to another barricade that hadn't been in place earlier. The two sentries posted there were dressed in military fatigues and wearing sidearms.

"One of them was there this morning with Gerard," Stephen said. "The woman. She'll recognize me."

"Pull the bill of your cap down, turn up your coat collar, and drop your head like you're sleeping. Don't let her see your face."

The woman approached and spoke through Cork's open window. "Road's closed, sir." Except for her sidearm, she wore nothing that signified authority and had no ID badge.

"Because of the plane crash?"

"I can't say, sir."

"Closed for how long?"

"Again, I can't say. You need to turn around and return the way you came."

"Thank you, Sergeant . . . ?"

"Have a good day, sir." The woman stepped back and gave Cork room for a U-turn.

Stephen sat up as they drove off. "What now, Dad?"

"There are other ways to get to the top of that mountain."

He took old logging roads, some so ancient the forest had almost entirely reclaimed the cleared ground. It was slow going, but eventually they found themselves on the far side of Desolation Mountain. Cork parked, and he and Stephen began to make their way through a mix of evergreen, then gradually up the mountainside.

They crossed through the aspens that ringed the mountain near the top. Cork paused before they broke into the open, with a hundred yards of nearly bare rock between them and the dark outcrop that crowned Desolation Mountain. Devil's Eye. For several minutes, he waited to be certain no one was there to see, then moved swiftly up the final bare face of the mountain. They were both breathing hard from the sprint and took a moment to catch their breath. The sky was an azure sea with islands of white cloud drifting across. The wind was gentle, out of the south, cooling their faces. The air smelled of the sun-heated rock against which they rested. To the east, forested hills rolled all the way to the Sawtooth Mountains, sixty miles distant, and beyond that was the great flat blue of the Shining Big Sea Water, Kitchigami, Lake Superior. It was a beautiful vista, and Cork understood why the mountaintop was a favorite destination for photographers. But the stories he'd heard on the rez all his life twisted his perception and he believed he could feel the evil in the place.

He nodded to Stephen, and they went to their knees and eased their way around the wall of the outcropping. What greeted them, Cork could never have predicted.

The man lying there was dressed in camouflage, not military but that of a hunter, the pattern all branches and leaves. He wore a sage-green stocking cap. On the rock beside him lay a firearm, a Sig Sauer, Cork could tell. The man had binoculars to his eyes and was studying the activity in the aspens below.

Stephen looked at his father. Cork put a finger to his lips and motioned for retreat.

Before they could move, the man grabbed the Sig, rolled to his back, and leveled the barrel at them. Then a smile spread across his lips.

"Cork O'Connor," he said quietly. "It's been a long time."

CHAPTER 15

"Best you lie down," the man said. "We don't want them to spot us."

Stephen followed his father's lead and lay on the flat rock beside the man in hunter's camo, who offered his hand. "Bo Thorson."

"This is my son, Stephen," Cork told him. "What are you doing here, Bo?"

"Same as you, I'm guessing. Trying to figure out what's going on down there."

"How's Secret Service involved?"

"I haven't been an agent for a long time, Cork. Went private like you, a few years ago." He put the binoculars to his eyes again. "So, Stephen, when they took you in this morning, did they give you a hard time?"

Stephen was amazed. "How'd you know?"

"Watched it happen. I didn't know who you were then."

"Where were you?"

"In the trees down there." Bo pointed to the aspens where Stephen had seen—or thought he'd seen—the kid from his vision.

"Did you spot anyone in the trees near where you were?" Stephen asked.

"Didn't see anybody up here but you and the searchers."

"Have you been on the mountain all day?" Cork asked.

"A couple of days now. Tried to get close to the crash site, but they've got that bottled up tight. Came up here thinking I might be able to get some kind of view, and that's when I stumbled onto those guys down there. They've been going over the mountainside inch by inch."

"Looking for what?" Stephen asked.

"That's the question, isn't it? I thought maybe the black box."

"There wasn't any black box," Stephen said.

Bo smiled. "You believe everything you read in the papers?"

"There *was* a black box?"

"I can't say for sure. But it's one of the possibilities."

Cork said, "Why would they be looking for it up here?"

"Why would they be looking for anything up here? But clearly they're after something. Whoever they are."

"Maybe it doesn't have anything to do with the plane crash," Stephen offered.

Bo gave Cork a wistful look. "Raised him on fairy tales?" He put the glasses to his eyes again. "We're going to have to move our position pretty soon. They've just about covered the west side of this mountain."

He slid himself back, behind the cover of the crowning rock outcrop, and stood in its lee. Cork and Stephen followed.

"I don't think staying here is going to accomplish anything," Bo said. "And I haven't eaten since before sunup. What say we head somewhere, grab some lunch? We can fill each other in."

Single file and in silence, they descended the eastern slope of Desolation Mountain. Bo had parked his Jeep ridiculously near the place where Cork had hidden his Expedition.

"I had a hell of a time getting here," Bo said. "Hope you know an easier way out."

"Follow me," Cork told him.

Allouette was the nearest town, and they gathered at the Mocha Moose for coffee and sandwiches. Before casino money had helped with the revitalization of the rez community, the building the little eatery now occupied had been a run-down bait and tackle shop. Sarah LeDuc, who owned the Mocha Moose, had completely renovated the place, and instead of fish and worms and leeches, the air was redolent with the scent of fresh-brewed coffee, hot soup, and baked goods.

As they sat waiting for their sandwiches, Stephen took stock of this Bo Thorson. At just over six feet tall, he wasn't imposing, but there was a tough feel to him that made Stephen think of leather. His eyes constantly swept the room, as if scanning for threats. His mind seemed to be constantly calculating, and although he had a ready smile, his face betrayed little of what was really going on in his head. His cheeks were heavily stubbled but his fingernails carefully manicured, which made Stephen wonder if the shadow of the beard was meant to roughen his appearance, make him seem more like a man who might naturally wear hunter's camo.

Cork said, "So, if you're not Secret Service anymore, you must be working for someone."

Bo winked at Stephen. "Your father was always a quick study."

"Who's your client?"

Bo gave Cork a pained look.

"Okay, what can you tell us?"

"The people I'm working for aren't ready to buy the pilot error story."

"What do they believe?"

"They don't want to jump to any conclusions. Right now, they just want more facts."

"And they're getting nothing from the official sources?"

"Is anyone getting anything from the official sources? It's the same story over and over and always shy on details. There are rumors of terrorism, but every time someone advances that possibility, the people in charge crush it like a bug. They continue to pump out the pilot error theory."

"NTSB is supposed to be in charge, but the FBI is definitely involved," Cork said. "Which would make sense if we're looking at some kind of terroristic threat."

"Those men on the mountain weren't FBI," Stephen pointed out. "At least they weren't wearing anything that identified them that way."

"They're very careful about not saying who they are," Bo acknowledged.

"They're the ones who stand between us and them." When his father and Bo looked at him oddly, Stephen explained, "That was the line Gerard fed me this morning when I asked who they were."

"Gerard?"

"The guy in charge. Or one of them anyway," Stephen replied.

"Movie dialogue," Bo scoffed. Which was exactly what Stephen had thought.

"But they probably believe it," Cork said. "You stood between the First Lady and death, Bo. You must have believed in what you were doing."

"I was sworn to protect the First Family. A noble calling, I still believe that. But the downside of that whole affair was that it opened my eyes to what a government really is."

"And what's that?"

"Do you know the Hydra in Greek myth? The many-headed monster?"

Cork didn't, but Stephen, the college kid, nodded.

"The government's just like that. Each head has its own agenda, and God help you if you get in the way."

"That's why you left Secret Service?"

"One of the reasons." He changed the subject, focusing abruptly on Stephen. "Why were you up on that mountain in the first place?" Then his eyes took a swing at Cork. "And why did you go back with him?"

Between them, Stephen and his father explained things: the vision, their time at the crash site, the missing Loves, the missing Tom Blessing, the slain dog, and the woman dead in her garage.

They'd just about finished when their sandwiches arrived, brought by Sarah LeDuc herself. Sarah had been married to George LeDuc, a hereditary chief of the Iron Lake Ojibwe and a longtime friend of the O'Connors. George and Cork's first wife, Jo, had both died under the same black circumstances, a tragedy that had bound Sarah LeDuc and Cork O'Connor ever since. She was a few years younger than Cork, late forties, gone a little plump, filled with a goodness that shone in her broad face and mahogany eyes. But she was clearly concerned when she delivered the food. "I heard about Fanny Blessing. So sad. And I heard that you found her, Cork."

Not much time had passed since his father discovered Fanny Blessing's body, but already word was abroad. The rez telegraph in action, Stephen knew.

She drew up a chair. "Was it a heart attack or something? Her health hasn't been good for a long time." Her eyes took in the stranger. "I'm Sarah," she said to Bo. "I own the Moose."

"Bo," he replied. "Old friend of Cork." His smile was gentle through the rough stubble on his face. "A nice establishment you have here, ma'am."

She looked back at Cork for an answer to her question.

"We won't know for a while, Sarah."

"There wasn't any . . ." She searched for the right words. "Foul play, was there?"

"Why do you ask?" It was Bo Thorson who put the question to her.

"It's just that . . ." Again, she seemed at a momentary loss of words. "It feels like there's something not right out here, ever since the senator's plane went down. I see guys here and all over the rez who aren't tourists and it gives me the willies."

"What do they look like?" Again, Bo's question.

"I don't know. Not abnormal or anything. Just . . . intense. And they're never alone. There's always at least two of them. Sometimes more."

"Where do you see them?" Stephen asked.

"They've been here, around town. And I see them coming in on back roads from the direction of Desolation Mountain. Sometimes they're just parked out in the middle of nowhere. Creepy." She made a shivering gesture with her whole body. "What about Tom? Does he know?"

"I tried calling him," Cork told her. "He's not answering his cell phone."

"Not in his office? You might try Bourbon Lake, there where the Coot River flows out. I heard he's been after a couple of otter poachers. Phone reception is pretty iffy that far out."

"Poachers? Did he report them to Daniel?"

"I don't know. It's just what I heard."

"Thanks, Sarah. I'll give it a shot."

She eyed Bo. "Get your deer yet?"

"Beg your pardon?"

"I figure you must be a bow hunter. That's the only season open at the moment."

Another smile appeared in the rough stubble. "I'm a hunter, Sarah. But not of deer."

As soon as they left the Mocha Moose, they checked at the tribal offices, but still no Tom Blessing.

"Where's this Bourbon Lake?" Bo asked.

"East, along the edge of the Boundary Waters. Not all that far from Desolation Mountain."

"Hard to get to?"

"Follow me," Cork said.

Chapter 16

"You seem to know him pretty well, Dad."

They were following a series of logging roads abandoned long enough ago that nature had reclaimed the ground. Scrub brush clawed the sides and undercarriage of the big vehicle as they maneuvered through. They crossed threads of water, streams nearly dry now, but during the next spring melt they would be impassable. Bo Thorson trailed in his Jeep.

"I met Bo when I was sheriff. This was when Tom Jorgenson was vice president."

Tom Jorgenson was a name probably every schoolkid in Minnesota knew. He'd been a popular governor and then vice president.

"The Jorgensons had a vacation home on Iron Lake for decades. Whenever the vice president was in residence there, I worked with Bo on security. We got on well, and let me tell you that wasn't always the case when I had to work with federal agents of one kind or another."

"So you trust him?"

"Why wouldn't I?"

Stephen shrugged. "Everything feels off. Me, I'm not sure what I can trust."

"Or who? You trust me, don't you?"

"Come on."

"And I trust Bo. Good enough?"

Stephen eyed the trailing Jeep, considered, finally said, "For now."

Cork slowed to a stop and peered through the windshield, studying the ground in front of the vehicle. "Somebody's been this way recently."

"Tom Blessing," Stephen said.

"A lot of damage to the ground cover, more than a single vehicle would have caused."

"He's probably been this way before. Sarah said he's been trying to track down otter poachers out here."

"Maybe."

Cork continued on, but he watched the forest more carefully now. Meloux's cautionary words echoed in his thinking: *There is a beast in these woods that does not belong here. It is huge and it is evil.*

"Over there," Stephen said a few minutes later. He pointed toward two vehicles parked among the pines. Beyond them, thirty yards through the trees, blue water sparkled. Bourbon Lake.

Cork parked near the other vehicles, one of them a big pickup, and Bo pulled alongside.

"That's Tom's Tundra," Cork said.

"What about the other?" Bo asked.

"I don't know. But it has rez plates, too."

They walked over a soft carpet of pine needles to the rocky shoreline. The reason for the lake's name was pretty evident: water the color of bourbon, the result of both the iron content of the soil and the bog seepage along the creeks that fed the lake. Except for the water itself, which shivered a little in the afternoon breeze, making the sunlight on the surface dance, nothing moved.

"Where are they?" Stephen's voice was hushed.

Cork backtracked, carefully eyeing the ground and the bed of needles that covered it. "Here." He went down on one knee and pointed to impressions left in the soft bedding. "They went east, toward the Coot River outlet."

He led the way, one eye to the ground and the other to the trees around them. Stephen and Bo seemed to have sensed his concern. They all walked carefully and didn't speak.

"Hold it right there!" The command came from the trees at their backs.

Cork stopped dead, silently berating himself for leading his son and Bo into this ambush.

"Turn around slowly."

They obeyed.

The man rose from behind the trunk of a fallen pine, a rifle in his hands, the barrel trued on Cork. He wore a green ball cap whose bill shaded the upper part of his face. But a smile slowly spread across his lips and he lowered the rifle. "*Boozhoo,* Cork. Hey, Stephen. What are you doing here?"

"Looking for you, Tom," Cork replied. "What's with the hardware?"

"Poachers," Tom Blessing said, as if the word were dirty. "Otter poachers. You gotta be one heartless son of a bitch to poach a creature as delightful as an otter."

"Good warm fur," Bo noted. "Brings a pretty penny, I bet."

Blessing eyed him with suspicion. "Who're you?"

Another figure rose from behind the blind of the fallen pine. Cork recognized Harmon Goodsky, who was a professional photographer with a gallery in Allouette. His right hand held a camera, to which a powerful-looking lens was affixed.

"*Boozhoo,* Harmon." Then to answer Blessing's question, Cork said, "This is Bo Thorson. A friend."

"Well, friend," Blessing said, "there's more to an otter than its fur."

"I understand," Bo replied. "Just talking about motivation. For some people, it's all about the money."

"Those kind of people we don't need."

"I couldn't agree more," Bo said.

Cork glanced at Goodsky. "I know why Tom's here. What are you up to, Harmon?"

Goodsky was huge, towering. In an earlier time, he'd been an imposing, powerful figure. Now, in a way, he resembled the fallen pine in front of him, a great trunk slowly rotting. He was a veteran of Vietnam and a victim of Agent Orange. He had Parkinson's and was riddled with cancer.

Goodsky held up his camera. "Tom wanted me to document things."

"How do you know they're poaching otters, Tom?" Cork asked.

"There's an otter lodge near the Coot River outlet. With field glasses, you can see it from here. I spotted a couple of guys there a few days ago. I hollered at them and they took off. I've been hanging around since. They came back yesterday and I ran 'em off again. No other reason to be here than those otters."

"Have you mentioned this to any of the game wardens? Daniel's looking for a couple of poachers, too."

Blessing gave a little croak of disdain. "Game wardens'll just hand 'em a ticket. I get hold of these guys, they won't be walking right for a while. I'll make sure they understand the real cost of poaching otters on Shinnob land." A woof came from the other side of the log. Blessing said, "Easy, boy."

"Is that Tornado with you?" Cork asked.

"He's not really a hunting dog, but I brought him along thinking he might help us sniff out these poachers. Or I could sic him on 'em if I had to."

The bulldog showed himself, appearing around the end of the log, his body tensed, as if prepared to attack should Blessing give the word.

What Cork had to do next, he didn't relish. "Look, Tom, I've got some bad news." He gave it a moment, then added, "About your mom."

Blessing waited, but even before he received the word his face reflected an anticipation of the worst. Which is to say, all his features became stone, unreadable. And when he'd heard, his response was a simple nod.

"I'm sorry, Tom."

Blessing's dark eyes searched the woods, the sky, the lake, as if looking for the answer to a question as yet unasked. "All right," he finally said, gathering himself. "We're done here, Harmon. Come on, Tornado." He slipped the rifle strap over his shoulder and began the long journey home.

Goodsky let him walk away a bit, then said to Cork, "Just like in Nam."

"How's that, Harmon?"

He scanned the woods. "You know they're out there. You just don't know when they'll hit you." He followed Blessing and the dog, walking slowly. At every other step, he faltered, as if afraid the bones in that leg might crack under his weight.

Stephen watched him limp away. "It's not just his body." In answer to Cork's questioning look, he explained, "What's eating him doesn't just feed on his flesh and bone, Dad. That man is sick in his soul."

"Think Henry could help him?"

"I'm not sure Harmon wants to be helped."

Cork understood. Some people fed on their anger or their bitterness or their resentment for so long that even though it was poison, it was what they craved.

"Interesting, don't you think, that these poachers seem to have appeared about the same time the senator's plane went down?" Bo said.

"Coincidence?" Stephen suggested.

Bo smiled. "And do you believe in the tooth fairy, too?"

"I think I'd like to talk to Daniel about those poachers he's been chasing," Cork said.

He turned to leave, but Stephen didn't move. He stood at the edge of the lake with his eyes closed. So Cork waited in the quiet of the Northwoods. This was familiar territory to him: the bourbon-colored water, the evergreen-scented air, the rustling bulrushes, the yielding needles underfoot. But something was off.

"Waiting," Stephen said, opening his eyes.

"Who's waiting?" Bo asked.

"The *manidoog*," Stephen replied. "The spirits here."

"Waiting for what?"

On his son's face, Cork saw the shadow of confusion and defeat, which had darkened it so often since he'd first received the vision.

"Hell if I know." Stephen turned and walked away alone.

CHAPTER 17

Bo followed Cork's big SUV west through the woods in the direction of Allouette. He was thinking about the question Stephen had put to him, which was essentially this: Could the appearance of the poachers and the crash of Senator McCarthy's plane be a coincidence? Although he'd sloughed off the question, he knew that due diligence meant he had to eliminate the possibility absolutely. He was hoping once they'd talked with this game warden, this Daniel English, he could put the question to rest.

They weren't far from town when his phone gave a chirp, signaling a text message. Driving along the rugged back roads required his full attention, so he couldn't check it immediately, but he was pretty sure who'd sent it and pretty sure he didn't want to respond just yet.

It wasn't exactly a stroke of luck that Cork O'Connor had stumbled onto him. Bo would have gotten around to him eventually. He remembered Cork from his days with Secret Service, and when he'd agreed to take this assignment, one of his early thoughts was that if he had to, he might be able to tap Cork's local knowledge. Luck came into play when it turned out that the kid he'd seen Gerard's people grab was Cork's son.

Stephen O'Connor was an interesting case. This vision thing. Bo didn't buy into it, but he could see that the young man's father was invested. Maybe it was because of the O'Connors' Native heritage or maybe the man wanted to believe simply because that's what fathers did, supported their children. Bo didn't have children. He'd never really had a father. So what did he know about that kind of relationship? He understood teamwork, however, and that when you've partnered with someone, as he had with Cork that day, you didn't double-cross them. He hoped that in all that might occur going forward, this would be a tenet he could stand by.

Cork parked at the tribal offices. Bo pulled up beside him and took a moment to check the text message he'd received: *Report?* He decided to wait until the day was over before responding. That would be soon enough.

Daniel English wasn't in the Conservation Enforcement office, but the head game warden, a colorful coot with a mole like a tick on his lip, pointed them toward the Mocha Moose, where English had gone for an afternoon break.

They found him sipping coffee and eating a blueberry muffin at the same table where they'd sat earlier.

English was tall, clearly Native, with black hair, dark eyes, high, fine cheekbones, and a steadiness in his gaze, the frank assessment of a law enforcement officer, which Bo could appreciate. Cork introduced them, and they joined English at the table. In an instant, Sarah LeDuc was there with them.

"Did you find Tom Blessing?"

"Out at Bourbon Lake, like you said, Sarah," Cork replied. "Harmon Goodsky was with him."

"Harmon?" Her face showed some pain. "That poor man. What was he doing there?"

"Documenting." Cork looked at Daniel English. "Tom says there are some guys poaching otters at Bourbon Lake. You hear anything about that?"

"Nothing about Bourbon Lake. How does Tom know they're poaching?"

"He spotted them near an otter lodge and put two and two together. He's pretty burned about it."

"Was Harmon there to document the poaching or document the beating Tom was going to give the poachers?"

"Maybe both. And maybe provide a little backup, too."

English looked skeptical. "He's big, but he couldn't provide much backup these days."

"A year to live," Sarah said. "Maybe two. That's the word anyway. Agent Orange. What were those people thinking?"

"People who make that kind of decision think only in the moment," Bo offered. "In my experience, it's an unfortunate hallmark of governments."

"Sarah told me about Tom's mother," English said. "Does Tom know?"

"Yeah." Cork wiped the perfectly clean tabletop with an open palm, as if there was something there that needed to be brushed away. "It's not like it was totally unexpected. She hasn't taken care of herself."

"But something's eating at you," English said.

"If it was just Fanny, that would be one thing," Cork replied carefully. "But add to it the shooting of Cyrus at the Loves' cabin, and it begins to feel questionable."

Sarah finally pulled up a chair. "You think these things are tied together? How?"

Bo said, "I can think of at least one important way. The Loves and Tom Blessing were among the first on the scene of Senator McCarthy's plane crash."

"Why is that important?" Sarah asked.

Although the woman couldn't see the connection, a look of understanding came to O'Connor's face. Then to the face of Daniel English.

It was young Stephen O'Connor who said what they were all thinking. "You were also one of the first out there, Daniel."

English's only acknowledgment of this truth was a slight nod. "Phil Hukari was out there, too."

"Where is he?" Cork asked.

"We came in from poacher chasing because he got a call from his wife," English said. "She was having some pregnancy-related difficulty." He pulled out his cell phone and made a call. He waited, finally spoke into the phone. "Phil, it's Daniel. Give me a call when you get this message."

"Where does he live?" Bo asked.

"They have a small place on Badger Creek, a mile or so outside of town," English replied.

As if of one mind, they all rose, except Sarah, who looked up at them with confusion. "What am I missing?"

"Thanks for the coffee and muffin," English said to her and quickly led the way out.

The caravan sped northeast with Daniel English in the lead. They took the main road for a mile before turning onto gravel and following a stream that threaded among pines and aspens. Bo wasn't a man much given to intuition, but a palpable sense of menace had descended on him. From the glove box, he took the Sig he'd placed there earlier and put it within easy reach.

The cabin was set among pines on the bank of the creek. No

vehicles were visible. English was out of his truck and already at the front door, Cork and his son with him, before Bo had killed the engine on his Jeep. Bo gripped his Sig and stepped from his vehicle, but he didn't join the others. The situation felt precarious to him, and he readied himself to provide cover fire, if necessary. He watched as English knocked, called out, finally opened the door, and disappeared inside. Cork and Stephen followed.

Bo scanned the whole scene. A small garage-like structure stood to the right of the cabin, against which several cords of wood had been stacked. To the left was a big white propane tank. Something moved in the tall grass under the tank. Bo lifted the Sig.

English and the O'Connors emerged from the house and stood talking.

"The propane tank," Bo hollered to them, nodding where they should look.

They saw it then, the movement in the grass. English moved to investigate.

"Easy," Bo called out.

English drew his own sidearm and approached the tank cautiously. When he was very near, the game warden holstered his weapon, knelt, and signaled for the others to join him.

"Noggin," English said, cradling the dog's head.

It was a golden retriever. Dark blood matted the fur on its side, but the animal wasn't dead.

"Easy, boy." Stephen slid his arms under the dog's body and gently lifted. "We need to get him to a vet."

Bo saw the look of indecision on Cork's face, which he interpreted as compassion for the dog competing with an investigator's compulsion to stay with the scene.

"You two go," Bo told him. "Daniel and I will secure things here."

"Keep us posted," Cork said.

"One more thing, Cork. As much as possible, I need to stay off the radar up here. You understand?"

Cork considered his request, then gave a firm nod. He moved ahead of his son to the Expedition, where they laid the dog in the back, then took off.

English eyed Bo. "Cork didn't say what exactly your interest in all this is. I'm guessing you're a cop."

"Former Secret Service," Bo replied. "I do private security work now."

"And you're here because?"

"Representing the interests of a client."

"A client interested in . . . ?" English waited for an answer that never came. "Well, Cork trusts you. That's good enough for me." He studied the scene. "Phil drives a Dodge Ram. Let's check the garage."

It was empty.

"How did things look in the house?" Bo asked.

"Nothing obviously wrong."

English swung his gaze back to the tall grass where they'd found the dog. "I don't think Noggin was shot under the tank. They probably dumped him there thinking he wouldn't be seen." He began to walk a spiral out from the propane tank. After a couple of minutes, he knelt in the wild grass beneath a crab apple tree.

"Here," he said.

Bo joined him. At their feet was a spattering of blood.

"This is where he was hit." English studied the ground and walked slowly toward the stream that ran behind the house. "They came in from this way. Two of them, looks like." At the stream, he paused, then waded across. The water was swift but reached only to his calves. On the other side he knelt, pulled a handkerchief from his back pocket, and picked up something, which he brought back to Bo. Nestled in English's handkerchief was an expended cartridge casing.

"Savage," English said. "Small caliber, probably two-fifty. Mostly for hunting small game or varmints."

"Or watchdogs," Bo said. "When Hukari got that call from his wife, what exactly did he say?"

"Just that she was having trouble, something to do with the pregnancy. She wanted him to come home right away. He said she sounded scared, but he chalked that up to this being their first child." English looked at the blood in the grass. "I'm guessing something else was scaring her."

"Or someone else. Someone who wanted to talk to her husband and wanted leverage."

"Why? What could Phil possibly have that would be worth this?"

When Bo had been with Secret Service and charged, on occasion, with ensuring the safety of someone important, he'd learned to read faces quickly, even in a crowd. He studied Daniel English. What he saw was a man truly at a loss for an explanation, a man hiding nothing.

"Something about the scene of the plane crash," Bo said. "Something these people want, and they believe that you or one of the others who got there early has it."

"Like what?"

Bo looked the whole scene over. The lovely setting at the edge of the stream, the young crab apple tree, the cozy cabin, the pines. All of it idyllic. Except for the splash of blood at his feet.

"That's the question, isn't it?" he said.

CHAPTER 18

Cork pulled his vehicle to the side of the road where Stephen had earlier parked his old Jeep. Just as he got out to help with the wounded dog, his cell phone rang. It was Daniel calling, his voice tense.

"Do you know where Jenny is, Cork?"

"She opened Sam's Place, then she was going to pick up Waaboo from kindergarten. Why?"

"She's not answering her cell phone."

"Did you try the landline at the house?"

"Yeah. No luck."

"What's your worry?"

"We think somebody snatched Phil and Sue. Bo thinks they might go after Jenny and Waaboo, too."

"Why?"

"Still working on that. But I need to know they're safe."

"I'm on my way to the house. You keep trying Jenny."

Stephen was still with the dog, comforting the wounded animal. "What is it?"

"I have to get home, make sure Jenny and Waaboo are okay.

You take Noggin to the vet in the Expedition. I'll take your Jeep."

Driving fast, it was twenty minutes to the house on Gooseberry Lane. Cork was relieved to find Jenny's Forester parked in the drive. He hightailed it inside, called out, received no answer. He checked the first floor, then the second. The house was empty. One of the things that worried him was this: Trixie, the nearest thing to a watchdog that the O'Connors had, was also gone. He thought of Cyrus dead in the lake and Noggin lying shot in the tall grass under the propane tank. He knew that silencing the dogs had made whatever happened to their owners possible. He called Daniel on his cell.

"Have you heard from Jenny yet?"

"Nothing," Daniel replied. "Where are you?"

"At the house. Her car's here, but she's not."

Cork stood in Waaboo's bedroom, staring at his grandson's bed. On the pillow lay a stuffed wolf, a gift Cork had given him on his fifth birthday, a reminder that Waaboo and the O'Connors were Ma'iingan, Wolf Clan. Protectors. Cork closed his eyes.

"I'm ten minutes away." Daniel ended the call.

Cork's heart beat like a fist against his chest, rage and fear battling to control him. He wanted to explode at someone, do something physical and decisive. He grabbed the stuffed wolf and threw it across the room, a useless gesture.

Then he heard the squeak of a hinge as a door opened—or closed—downstairs. He went to the top of the landing, listened, heard only the sound of his own fierce breathing.

"Jenny? Waaboo?"

No answer, and he began to take the stairs, descending slowly, pausing halfway to listen. Outside, a car passed on the street, the soft whoosh like the sound of someone hushing a child. He heard something, or thought he did, coming from the office off the downstairs hallway. He quieted his breathing, crept toward the door, which was slightly ajar, hesitated at the edge of the threshold, and listened again. Someone was inside.

His body went hard, taut. He readied himself, then shoved the door open fully and entered the office, prepared for battle.

"Boo!" His grandson jumped at him and wrapped his little arms around Cork's waist.

"Jesus!" Cork shouted.

"We scared Baa-baa!" Waaboo cried with delight.

Jenny's laughter died when she saw the look on her father's face. "I'm sorry, Dad. Waaboo wanted to scare you. Are you okay?"

She held Trixie's leash in her hand, the old dog sitting on her haunches, tongue lolling.

"Just surprised," Cork managed.

Waaboo released his grip and did a little dance of celebration around his grandfather.

"Where were you?" Cork asked his daughter.

"Taking Trixie for her afternoon walk. What's wrong?"

"Hey, little guy," Cork said. "Trixie looks thirsty. How about putting some fresh water into her bowl?"

"Okay. Come on, girl." Waaboo happily led the dog away.

"Call Daniel," Cork said as soon as Waaboo had gone. "Let him know you're safe."

"What—" Jenny began.

"Just call him, then I'll explain."

She turned to the desk, where one of the landline phones sat.

"What about your cell?" Cork asked.

"It's charging in the kitchen."

She made the call, told her husband that she was fine, listened, then eyed her father. "All right. I'll see you in a few minutes." She set the phone in its cradle. "What's going on?"

As Cork explained their concern, Jenny's face grew pinched. Her eyes moved from her father to the doorway where her son had disappeared with Trixie. She stepped out and down the hallway to where she could see Waaboo in the kitchen.

"What do these people, whoever they are, think Daniel or the others might have picked up at the crash site?"

"Good question. If, in fact, that's what this is all about. At the moment, the only thing we know for certain is that the Loves and the Hukaris are missing."

"And their dogs have been shot and Fanny Blessing is dead," Jenny added.

"We don't know yet what caused Fanny's death. It might have nothing to do with whatever's going on. But it's clear that everyone who was on the crash scene early has been targeted. That means Daniel and you and Waaboo might well be at risk."

The back door opened and Daniel swept in. Waaboo abandoned Trixie and ran to him. Daniel lifted his son and swung him around, and Waaboo shrieked with delight.

Jenny and Cork joined them in the kitchen. Daniel immediately embraced his wife and held her tight for a long while. "I was so worried, Jenny."

"Dad told me." She glanced down at Waaboo, who was watching closely, clearly perplexed, as if he understood that this was far more than a simple display of affection. "What do we do?"

They'd put on a video for Waaboo, *The Jungle Book,* one of his favorites. Now they sat at the kitchen table, talking in low voices, Cork and Daniel explaining everything they knew so far.

"Phil Hukari still isn't answering his phone," Daniel said. "I called the clinic in Allouette and the Aurora Community Hospital, where he might have taken Sue. Nothing. Not that I expected anything."

"Aside from Noggin, there's really nothing to indicate something worrisome has happened to them," Jenny pointed out hopefully.

"Add it up," Daniel said. "The Loves, Fanny Blessing, Phil and Sue. It's a pattern."

"We don't know what happened to Fanny Blessing," Cork reminded him. "We don't know what's going on with Ned and Monkey Love. And, as Jenny says, we don't really know about the Hukaris."

"Are you blind, Cork?"

"Easy, Daniel." Jenny laid a hand on his arm.

"I'm just thinking like the sheriff right now," Cork told him. "We don't have enough evidence for any kind of official investigation. Nobody's been gone long enough yet to be officially missing. As far as we know, nobody's been harmed."

"So we're on our own?"

"Pretty much. At the moment, anyway."

Stephen walked in the back door, took stock of the council going on at the table, and pulled up a chair.

"Noggin?" Daniel asked.

"He'll pull through."

"Thank God for that." Daniel gave Cork a sharp look. "And don't tell me because it was just a dog there's nothing official to be done."

Cork didn't reply. He understood his son-in-law's frustration, which was, he knew, rooted in a very big, very reasonable seed of concern.

"I'll let Marsha know the situation," Cork said. "But we need to canvass the rez, relatives, friends of Sue and Phil, make sure they're really missing before we assume anything."

"Where's Bo?" Stephen asked.

Daniel said, "He told me he had some checking to do on his own. Didn't say what it was. I have his cell phone number, if we need to contact him."

"So once again," Jenny said, looking in the direction of her son, "what do we do?"

"For starters, I'm not letting either of you out of my sight," Daniel told her.

"I'm not sure that's such a good idea," Cork said.

Jenny smiled. "I kind of like it."

"If he's with you," Cork explained, "he's not going be able to get the answers he wants and that we need."

He watched as Daniel weighed the truth of this against the concern for his family's safety. "You have a suggestion?" Daniel asked.

"We get Jenny and Waaboo to a safe place."

"Where?"

"Maybe we could stay with Aunt Rose and Uncle Mal," Jenny suggested.

She was speaking of Cork's sister-in-law and her husband, who lived in Evanston, Illinois.

The idea didn't sit well with Cork. "That's a long way, and I wouldn't feel comfortable unless one of us went along with you. But I don't think we can spare anyone here."

"And they have a new baby," Daniel pointed out. "I'd hate to think we put them all in danger if trouble followed you."

It was Stephen who ended the silence of the next few moments. "Crow Point," he said. "With Henry."

Chapter 19

The cabin sat on a rise above an inlet of Iron Lake, isolated. Bo left his Jeep and unlocked the cabin door. There were no luxuries inside, but the place was well appointed, with a fine view of the lake from its small back deck. Bo took a beer from the refrigerator, stepped onto the deck, leaned against the cedar railing, and breathed deeply.

He was alone, a comfortable state of affairs. For most of his life, he'd been alone. Growing up, he'd spent time homeless, living for a while in an abandoned school bus in a copse of trees on the Mississippi River, within sight of downtown St. Paul. He'd been well on the road to juvenile detention and beyond that, probably, a life that would eventually lead to hard time in a real prison. He'd been saved by a woman, a judge in juvenile court, who'd seen something in him, an ember of goodness, which all the crap that had been piled on him couldn't smother. The road after that had led him into the army, then to college, and finally into the Secret Service, where he'd nearly been killed by an assassin's bullet intended for the wife of the president.

That incident had been a sensational story but one that, for many reasons, had compromised his career. When he left the Secret Service, he'd begun his own agency, a one-man enterprise. He'd never lacked for clients, most of whom were high-profile and demanded total discretion, their interests primarily political. He wasn't sure the juvenile judge would see the same ember of goodness in him now. He often found himself walking a difficult line, one he wasn't always certain of himself. He'd come to understand that there was weakness in even the stoutest of hearts, and that the smallest flaw could be used to crack the moral resolve of the best of human beings. He sipped his beer, drank in the beauty of Iron Lake, thought about the O'Connors and the mess they were in the middle of. And he hoped that what might be asked of him before this whole affair was over wouldn't require that he throw them to the wolves.

He heard the vehicle pull up, set his beer on the railing, and slid his Sig from the belt holster. He entered the cabin and took a position covering the front door. Nothing happened. He edged to the window. Outside, a man stood beside a black SUV, arms crossed.

Bo opened the door.

"Waiting for an invitation?" he called. "That's a new wrinkle."

Gerard approached the cabin porch and paused in the grass at the bottom of the three steps, eyeing the Sig in Bo's hand. "Just wanted to make sure I wasn't going to be shot. You haven't been particularly accommodating lately."

"When have you ever found me accommodating?" Bo holstered his sidearm. "Why the visit?"

"Do I get an invitation or not?"

Bo stepped aside. "Be my guest." Inside the cabin, he closed the door and said, "I was just having a beer. Care for one?"

"I'll pass." Gerard stood in the center of the cabin's living room, assessing the place. "Cozy."

"So," Bo said. "Why the visit?"

"Just wondering whether you're working for me or not."

"I'm doing what I'm being paid for."

"Not exactly an answer."

"The best you're going to get."

"You know how this works. You give me regular updates. You let me know what you know when you know it. I get irritable if I have to track you down to ask."

"Clearly you know where to find me."

Gerard reached into his shirt pocket and drew out a cigar. "Mind?"

"Let's take it outside."

They moved to the deck, where Gerard unwrapped and lit his cigar. As he smoked, he took in the view. "Who gave thee, O Beauty, the keys of this breast, too credulous lover of blest and unblest?"

Bo waited, knowing Gerard would tell him soon enough the source of that poetic line. Quoting poetry and smoking good cigars were two of Gerard's favorite indulgences.

"Ralph Waldo Emerson." Gerard blew smoke toward the sky. "All right, let's have it."

"The men who were first on the scene, most of them Ojibwe, are being hunted," Bo reported. "I don't know why or by whom."

"The black box?"

"They're actually orange now. And according to NTSB, there was no flight recorder on board."

Gerard ignored him, shook his head. "Someone thinks the Indians must have it."

"It was the Indians who searched the woods where the tail section of the plane broke off. So, yeah, maybe it's the flight recorder they're after. Or maybe it's something else."

"Like what?"

"I don't know."

"It's the black box, Thorson. It holds the answers."

"Why would the Indians be hanging on to it?"

"Leverage," Gerard suggested. "Isn't that what everyone wants in a negotiation?"

"Who would they use this leverage on?"

Gerard had no reply.

"If it is the flight recorder, and if, as you say, it holds the answers, and if I'm able to get it for you—a lot of ifs, by the way—what will the people you're working for do with those answers?"

"Not my concern. Or yours."

"Just keeping the lid on things, is that what they're paying you for?"

"That," Gerard said, "and making sure you stay in line."

Bo lifted the beer he was holding in a sign of peace. "No trouble here."

"Let's keep it that way."

"Did you get anything out of your interrogation of Stephen O'Connor?"

For a moment, surprise showed on Gerard's face, then the look vanished. He puffed on his cigar. "How'd you know about O'Connor?"

"Part of what I'm being paid for, knowing that kind of thing."

"Just a curious kid. I reminded him that curiosity killed the cat."

"A lesson I'm sure he took to heart," Bo said wryly.

Gerard ashed his cigar and scraped off the ember along the deck railing. He put what was left in his shirt pocket. "I want to hear from you regularly, understood?"

"I read you loud and clear, Colonel."

Gerard walked back through the cottage and out the front door. Bo remained on the deck, waiting for the sound of Gerard's SUV to fade into the distance. On the lake, just beyond the mouth of the inlet, a boat drifted past, a man trolling. Bo considered what he might really be fishing for. In his life now, he never assumed that anything was what it seemed.

He wondered, were Gerard's men the ones hunting the Indians, or was someone else involved in this game? He shook his head at that thought. It might be deadly, but that's what it was, a game. Like chess, only without the luxury of seeing the whole board or knowing all the players. NTSB. FBI. Gerard and his ghost command. Homeland Security? DoD? Maybe even NSA?

What Bo told Cork O'Connor had been the truth. The government he'd worked for as a member of the Secret Service had never been of one mind. It was, and clearly continued to be, a fractured, barely contained conglomerate of little kingdoms, at war with one another just as often as they were at war with the enemies who threatened. In this isolated county in the North Country, who knew what kind of battle might result and which innocents might be caught in the crossfire?

Bo finished his beer. The sun was dropping and there was still work to be done before the day ended.

CHAPTER 20

Cork held out the baggie into which he'd put the expended cartridge Daniel had found at the Hukaris' cabin. "Same MO as the Loves, Marsha. Shot dog, people missing."

The sheriff took the baggie and studied the contents. "Not a large caliber." She looked up. "How's the dog?"

"He'll make it."

"Any sign of struggle, resistance, a fight? Anything at all at the cabin besides the shot dog?"

"Nothing obvious."

"So it could still be that Sue Hukari was having difficulty with the pregnancy and Phil took her somewhere to be seen. And . . ." She eyed the spent cartridge. "Someone's got a jones on for shooting dogs in Tamarack County."

"Daniel checked at the clinic in Allouette and at the hospital here in town. They didn't show up at either place."

Dross set the baggie on her desktop. "I know it doesn't look good, Cork, but really, what do we have to go on? I need something more than shot dogs."

"I'm not asking you for help, Marsha. Just keeping you in the loop."

She walked to the window. The view beyond was one Cork knew intimately from his own tenure as sheriff: the park, Zion Lutheran Church, the businesses along Oak Street, everything festooned in the red and gold of autumn.

"Something's going on in our county, Cork, something big. I hate to admit it, but I'm feeling helpless against it. Alex Quaker paid me a visit just before you came."

"Should I know him?"

"The number two man with the National Security Branch."

"Which is?"

"Responsible for the FBI's Counterterrorism Division. A courtesy call, diplomatically letting me know that I wasn't to interfere or involve myself in any way with the investigation of Senator McCarthy's plane crash."

"Counterterrorism? So they think the crash wasn't caused by pilot error?"

"He didn't say that. His explanation was simply that in these unsettled times and with someone as highly placed as a U.S. senator, eliminating terrorism as a possibility is essential. He was sure I understood. I told him that we would cooperate in every way we could. To which he said, and I quote, 'Just stay out of our way.'" She turned back. "What I wanted to say to that imperious blowhard was, how would you like it if I invaded your backyard and told you to go screw yourself?"

"Stephen got hauled in this morning and interrogated by someone who wasn't FBI."

"Who?"

Cork related Stephen's story of the men searching the aspen grove on Desolation Mountain and of his questioning by the man called Gerard.

"Military?"

"Certainly military trained. And clearly with authority. But nothing to identify any specific branch."

The sheriff stared at the floor, thinking. "Ned and Monkey Love. Blessing. The Hukaris." She lifted her eyes. "Daniel's next, Cork."

"That's what we figured, too."

"What are you going to do?"

"Put Jenny and Waaboo in a safe place, so they're out of harm's way. That's already happening."

"Daniel's with them?"

Cork shook his head. "I need him with me."

"Risky."

"Maybe so, but he understands."

"Does Jenny?"

That was a question Cork left unanswered as he departed the Tamarack County Sheriff's Office. It was late afternoon, the shadows growing long. He drove a couple of miles out of town to Olson Field, where, in a previously empty hangar, the experts from NTSB continued their business of sorting through the debris from the crash, looking for answers.

Supposedly looking for answers, Cork thought. Because he'd come to understand that at this moment in Tamarack County nothing might be as it seemed. There was plenty of activity at the airfield, vehicles arriving, leaving, NTSB personnel perhaps, but hard to tell because nothing was identified except by government license plates. Cork parked near the airfield entrance and spent an hour writing down the vehicle plates as they passed.

He was just about to wrap up when his cell phone rang. As soon as he answered, he heard the terrified voice of Beulah Love on the other end.

"Someone's after me, Cork. Help me. Please."

She met him at the old Quonset hut, having kept to main, well-traveled roads, as he'd instructed over the phone. When he greeted her at the door, her face was ashen, her hands shaking.

"They're following me everywhere," she said without preamble.

"Sit down and tell me about it, Beulah. Can I get you something? Coffee?"

"Nothing, nothing," she said in a pitched voice. "Just get them off me."

"Sit down," he said again and pulled out a chair for her at the table. He sat, too, and leaned toward her. "I want to know everything. From the beginning."

"After you left this morning, I headed to work at the casino," she began. "The whole way I had the feeling I was being followed."

"You spotted a car?"

"No. Just a feeling. I told myself it was because I knew about Ned and Jameson and poor little Cyrus and I was being silly. But when I got to the casino, I spent a moment in my car, trying to pull myself together, and I saw this pickup truck drive in and park not far away. It just sat there. I finally got out and went into the casino. As soon as I was inside, I looked back through the glass doors. Two men got out of the truck and went to my car, Cork. Right to my car."

"Did they do anything to it?"

"Not while I was watching. They started toward the casino and I took off, hurried up to the office."

"Did they follow you into the casino?"

"I don't know. I thought they would, but I didn't see them. Like I said, I went straight to the office. But I couldn't work. I couldn't concentrate. So I left early. The pickup wasn't there anymore."

"Where'd you go?"

"To church to practice on the organ. I hoped it might settle my spirit. But they followed me there."

"You saw them?"

"After I parked and went inside, I looked out the front window, just to be sure. The pickup drove past."

"The same vehicle, you're certain?"

"It looked the same, big and black."

"Did it stop?"

"Just drove past. I kept watching, but it didn't come back. I was scared, so I didn't stay at the church. I started home, but I stopped at the IGA to pick up a few things first. When I got inside the store, I checked the parking lot, and within a minute, that black pickup was there, parked a couple rows away. That's when I called you."

"What did these men look like?"

Her eyes went distant as she concentrated. Then she shook her head. "Just men."

"How were they dressed?"

She looked down at her hands, which had stopped shaking. "Jeans," she said vaguely. "Flannel shirts. Down vests."

Which could have described half the male population in Tamarack County.

"White, not Native?"

"Yes."

"Did you see any firearms?"

She hesitated. "No. But that doesn't mean they weren't going to hurt me."

"You're safe now, Beulah. Coming to me was a good move."

"Who are they, Cork? What do they want with me?"

"I can't tell you who they are yet. But I think they're looking for something they believe Ned or Jameson might have. Because you're family, I think they're surveilling you, hoping your brother or nephew might try to contact you."

"What can I do? Where do I go? I don't want to be alone."

"Is there someone on the rez you can stay with?"

Her eyes wandered the room. She looked back at Cork, clearly at a loss. The boarding school experience had killed the Indian in her, and she'd burned too many bridges on the rez. Ned and Jameson were her closest kin. She had nowhere to go.

"Let me make a couple of calls," Cork told her. "Are you hungry? Would you like something to eat?"

She gave him a silent nod.

"How about a Waaboo Burger?" To her blank look, he said, "A bison burger. It's good."

In Sam's Place up front, he gave Judy Madsen the order. Judy had been with Cork forever, and she sometimes stepped in to manage when none of the O'Connors were available. "Getting low on the bison patties," she informed him. "That Waaboo Burger's a winner. Will you or Stephen or Jenny be working tonight, or should I bring in some other help?"

They settled things, and Cork returned to Beulah and made a phone call to Sarah LeDuc.

"I have a favor to ask." He explained the situation. When he'd finished, he turned to Beulah. "I'm going to take you back to Allouette, but you won't be alone there. Sarah has agreed that you can stay with her."

Beulah looked even more concerned. "Won't that put her in danger?"

"I don't think you're actually in any danger, Beulah. They're just watching you, hoping to catch Ned and Jameson."

"What if I hear from Ned?"

"Let me know. But don't try to meet him or Jameson anywhere, okay?"

She needed no convincing.

Outside in the parking lot, Cork did a cursory check of Beulah's car, looking for a tracking device the men might have planted. He found nothing obvious but knew that didn't necessarily mean the car was clean. He led the way out of Aurora, Beulah following. He watched the road behind, keeping an eye out for the black pickup, or any other vehicle that might be tailing them. He was pretty certain that despite his best efforts, whoever it was tracking Beulah would know where she'd gone. What he'd told her was what he believed to be true, that she herself was no immediate danger. She would only be in trouble if she had contact with Ned or Monkey.

In Allouette, they parked in front of the Mocha Moose. The coffee shop closed at two every afternoon, but Sarah was waiting and she opened up for Beulah. *"Boozhoo,"* she said in greeting.

"Thank you," Beulah replied, almost in tears. "Thank you, Sarah."

Cork stood in the doorway. "If you have any concerns at all, call me. I mean immediately, Sarah."

"I've got this, Cork." Sarah gestured toward the outside world. "Go do whatever you have to do."

He left the two women, knowing they would go to the living area above the coffee shop, which Sarah had occupied alone ever since her husband was murdered. This thought caused Cork's mind to leap back to the memory of his first wife, Jo, whose death had been caused by the same men who'd killed George LeDuc. For a moment, everything inside him tensed, and he was suddenly uncertain in his belief that Sarah and Beulah weren't in any real danger. How could he know that for sure?

On the other side of Manomin Street, the main route through Allouette, was the little gallery where Harmon Goodsky showed his photographs and those of other Native artists. Cork crossed the street and entered the gallery. A small bell above the door rang, but no one came forward immediately. Then a young man stepped from behind the curtains across a doorway that led to the back area of the gallery.

"*Anin,* Winston," Cork said in greeting.

Winston Goodsky, Harmon's grandson, was fourteen years old, willowy in the way of youths. He was a shy boy, one who didn't often lift his gaze from the floor. In his hand, he carried a framed photograph.

"*Anin,* Mr. O'Connor," the boy replied, studying the wood planks at Cork's feet.

"Is your granddad around?"

"In back. In the darkroom."

Goodsky was a photographer of the old school. He still used film in all his work.

"What do you have there?" Cork asked, indicating the photograph the boy held.

"Nothing." The boy hid the framed photo behind his back.

"Nothing?" Goodsky limped in from the back room. Although he towered over his grandson, he was still bent, resembling an old tree about to fall.

Like many Native children, Winston was being raised by a relative, not his parents. His father was in prison, his mother long dead from a drug overdose. Harmon Goodsky was his legal guardian. Cork knew that with the cancer eating him up inside, Goodsky worried about what would happen to Winston when he was gone. There were other relatives, but Social Services was bound to step in, and who knew what might be the final determination and in whose hands Winston might end up. If it was foster care, then Cork knew Goodsky had every right to be gravely concerned.

"Show him your work, Winston."

Without lifting his eyes, the boy offered up the photograph, a lovely shot of a single aspen leaf fallen on the ground. The leaf was gold-orange, the color of a ripe peach, cut evenly by deep veins, and framed dramatically by the dark soil beneath it. Cork had seen this leaf a million times across decades of autumns, but the photograph made him realize that he'd never taken the time to look closely, to appreciate fully the beauty in that simple image.

"I try to get him to use a good thirty-five-millimeter, like my Nikon, but he's all into digital," Goodsky said.

"It's a great picture, Winston." Cork handed it back.

"And we're going to put it up." Goodsky took the photograph from his grandson's hand, walked to an emptied place on the wall, and hung it. "There, right next to some of my best work."

"It's not as good as yours," the boy said quietly.

"It's promising," his grandfather said. "And it'll sell, mark my words. Something you need, Cork?"

Cork glanced at Winston. "Could we talk in private?"

"How about you start us some dinner?" Goodsky said to his grandson. "There's leftover meat loaf and some scalloped potatoes that can be heated up. Maybe a can of peas along with it."

The boy disappeared through the curtains. Cork heard his steps as he climbed the stairway to the second floor, where he and his grandfather lived.

"So, what's up?" Goodsky asked.

"Some trouble. Beulah Love is staying across the street with Sarah. Somebody's been following her and she's scared."

Goodsky scowled. "Following her? Who?"

"Don't know that yet."

"Why would anyone follow Beulah? You're sure she's not imagining things?"

"I think it has something to do with Ned and Monkey, some people who are trying to track them down."

"Why would anyone be after Ned and Monkey?"

"Again, I'm not sure. But I think Beulah isn't imagining things."

"What do you want from me?"

"Keep an eye on Sarah's place. If you see anything that seems odd, strangers hanging around maybe, give me a call. Will you do that?"

"That's it? Why don't I just go over and take care of them myself?"

Before the cancer began chewing him alive, Goodsky could have handled almost anyone, even a couple of anyones. Cork wasn't sure what Goodsky was or wasn't capable of now.

"Think of me as backup, Harmon. Give me a call and wait. We'll handle it together. Okay?"

"Sure," Goodsky said.

But Cork wasn't at all certain he meant it. "Before you do anything rash and get yourself into trouble, think about Winston."

Goodsky glanced up, where the sound of his grandson's footsteps moved across the floorboards. "Yeah," he agreed soberly.

From the gallery, Cork walked two blocks to the tribal clinic, where he found that Rainy had already left for the day. A few minutes later, as he stood on Manomin Street, which was empty, he remembered the dream Waaboo had related to him that morning, his nightmare about a monster with lots of heads. Which was precisely the way Bo Thorson had described the government, a many-headed Hydra. He considered all the elements at large in Tamarack County, all the agencies named and unnamed, and he wondered if Waaboo, like Stephen, saw things that others could not.

CHAPTER 21

Cork spent over an hour knocking on doors in Allouette, asking friends and relatives of Sue and Phil Hukari if they'd seen the couple that day. He'd spread the word about the shooting of Noggin. Most had already heard about Fanny Blessing. Because he had no answers, only questions, he worked at keeping things calm—his demeanor, his approach, his vague explanations. He decided to say nothing yet about Ned or Monkey Love, or about Cyrus staring dead-eyed up at him from the bottom of Little Bass Lake. For the moment, simpler was better and probably scary enough.

He headed out of Allouette after the sun had set but while the sky was still red, his mind hard at work, trying to find a thread that, if he pulled it, might help unravel the knot of troubling occurrences since the senator's plane went down. He wasn't focused on his own current situation, and the vehicle in his rearview mirror, when he finally became aware of it, was already closing on him.

Because it was dusk, he'd turned on the headlights of Stephen's Jeep. The vehicle fast approaching from behind was running without lights. Cork hit the accelerator, but the Jeep was old and hadn't been made for speed. The SUV—he could see that it was big and black, with tinted windows—continued to gain. A couple of hundred yards ahead of him glowed the taillights of a slower-moving vehicle. Although he knew he might be paranoid—not without good reason—he thought he was about to be put in a squeeze play.

He'd driven that road a thousand times and knew every twist and turn. His mind raced, visualizing what was ahead. The red embers of the taillights in front of him disappeared around the first curve of an *S* in the road. Cork flicked off his headlights and put the accelerator to the floor. He careened around the curve, just in time to see the taillights ahead of him move into the second curl of the *S*. For the next ten seconds, because of the thick woods along the first curve, he would be invisible to the SUV behind him. He hit the brakes and swung onto the gravel access to Wolf Point on Iron Lake. There were no signs for the turnoff. If you didn't know the road, you'd never see it coming. He shot up the first hundred yards, then slowed down. Dark was gathering and speed was a risk. Another hundred yards and he came abreast of the ruins of an old bait shop on a small inlet. He pulled off the road opposite the dilapidated shack, maneuvered the Jeep deep into the trees, and killed the engine. The descending dark was silent all around him, and he waited.

A few minutes later they came, two vehicles moving slowly, tires growling over the gravel, headlights stark and glaring. They approached the old bait shop, shone spotlights on the gray, flaking wood, the glassless windows, the sagging porch. They moved on toward the end of the point, another quarter of a mile west.

Cork considered hightailing it. He could probably be back on asphalt before they were able to swing around in quick pursuit. But he wasn't sure he could outrun them in the old Jeep. He continued to sit and wait.

They returned, their spotlights probing the woods with long white fingers as they crept along. The lights played across the Jeep.

Cork held his breath, hoping the scratched, dull green paint and the dried mud and dust that coated it would camouflage the old heap. The vehicles moved on.

His cell phone rang, and it made him jump.

"Where are you, Cork?" Daniel said on the other end.

"Hiding at the moment."

"Where? Who from?"

"Out on Wolf Point. And I don't know who from. Where are you?"

"At Uncle Henry's. We're all here."

"Rainy, too?"

"Yes."

"I'll come as soon as I can."

"Do you need help?"

By the time Daniel or anyone else reached him, Cork knew it would be too late. "I've got this."

After ten minutes, he eased the Jeep back onto the gravel access and drove to the main road. Both directions, the asphalt tunneled into the empty murk of descending night. He eased back onto the road.

He'd gone less than a mile when the SUV pulled out of the woods ahead and blocked his way. He slammed on the brakes, planning a desperate U-turn, but behind him, the second vehicle cut off any escape. He never carried a firearm, though this was one of those times he wished he did. There was nothing for him to do but sit and see how this played out.

Two men exited the SUV, both dressed in the kind of military fatigues worn by the searchers in the aspens on Desolation Mountain. They walked toward Cork, blinking into the glare from the Jeep's headlights. One was tall, older, craggy, with a silver crew cut, the other much younger, female, with a face set in an expression of iron grimness and a rifle in her hands. Cork lowered his window.

"I warned you already, O'Connor," the craggy one said while

the headlights still blinded him. Then he saw who was behind the wheel. "Who the hell are you?"

"Not the O'Connor you think, Gerard."

"All right, out of the Jeep."

"Not until I see some identification."

Gerard squinted, his face pinched and impatient. "Craig," he said to the woman with him. "Show this man some ID."

The grim blonde in camo lifted the rifle she carried and aimed it at Cork.

"Is that ID enough?" Gerard asked.

"You'd really shoot me?"

"You have three seconds to find out."

Cork opened the door and stepped from the Jeep.

"Who are you?" Gerard asked again.

"Cork O'Connor. You spoke to my son this morning."

Gerard looked past him at Stephen's Jeep. "What were you doing at Olson Field this afternoon?"

"Chalk it up to curiosity. A lot going on around here."

"What's your interest in Beulah Love?"

"I'm interested in her safety. And I'd like to know what's become of her brother and nephew. And while I'm at it, I'd like to know the same about Phil and Sue Hukari. I don't suppose you could enlighten me?"

Gerard studied him. "You were at the site where Senator McCarthy's plane went down. You and your son both. You were a part of the early search."

"Others were there earlier."

"You were with the Indians going over the woods."

"I was one of the Indians going over the woods."

"You're not Indian."

"Because I'm not wearing a headdress and feathers? *Anishinaabe indaaw.*"

The man's eyes were steely, as if he believed Cork was taunting him.

"In the language of my people, that means 'I am Anishinaabe.'"

Gerard made a sound in his throat, a dismissive grunt.

"What is it that everyone is looking for in Tamarack County, Gerard? What is it that you all believe one of us has taken? The black box?"

"There is no black box."

"Then tell me what it is."

"The only thing I'm going to tell you is this: Keep out of our way. I have the power and the authority to see that you're put somewhere you won't like."

"Authority granted by whom?"

"Are you a patriot, O'Connor?"

"I'm an American citizen and proud of that."

"Proud of being a Redskin, too, I suppose," Craig said.

Gerard's head swung around and he snapped, "That's enough, Lieutenant." He looked at Cork again. "Are you a hunter? Of course you are. Every man up here is a hunter. You're after what? Deer? Bear? Grouse? Pretty easy to know what you're shooting at. Me, I'm a hunter of the enemies of our democracy. They are many, O'Connor, and they often look just like you and me. Separating the good guys from the bad isn't such an easy job." He paused, and Cork thought he might go on with his lecture. Instead he said simply, "You're free to go." He signaled the black SUV, and it backed onto the shoulder, clearing the road.

Cork grabbed the Jeep's door handle, but before he got in, he said, "To a man who's really hunting the truth, guys up here like me could be a big help."

"Good night, O'Connor. And a last warning, to you and your son and your friends. Stay out of our way."

As he passed the SUV, Cork tried to get a look at the license plate, but the darkness made this impossible. He kept an eye on the rearview mirror, uncertain if Gerard's dismissal was for real. He couldn't read the man. Which served to drive home Gerard's point about knowing the good guys from the bad. In Tamarack County, that was becoming next to impossible.

CHAPTER 22

Trixie had settled herself comfortably in a corner of Henry Meloux's cabin, which was the spot all of Henry's dogs had claimed for themselves over the years. Henry's last dog, an old Irish setter named Ember, had died quietly a few weeks earlier, and the Mide had decided that was enough. He joked that the next thing he would deliver into Mother Earth's waiting arms was his own body.

"*Mishomis,*" Waaboo said, addressing the old man respectfully, using the Ojibwe word for grandfather. "Baa-baa says that you were a warrior. Did you ever fight white people?"

The child sat at the table in Henry's cabin, along with Stephen and the old man. Jenny and Rainy and Leah Duling were absent at the moment, preparing Leah's cabin to shelter this sudden influx of visitors. Stephen smiled at the innocence of his nephew's question.

"Fight them how?" the old man asked. Henry carved on a stick, his old hands working skillfully, shaking not at all.

"You know. Shoot them with arrows." The boy pointed toward a bow that hung on the wall.

"I never used it to kill anything that walks on two legs," the old man told him.

"Did you use that?" This time the boy pointed toward an old Winchester mounted near the bow.

"Not that either. When I have found it necessary to fight white people, I have used this." The old man pointed at his head. "It has always served me better than any weapon."

"My dad uses a gun."

"He carries a gun," Stephen clarified. "He's never had to use it against anyone, Waaboo."

"What if someone wanted to hurt him? Or Mommy? Or you?"

"I hope that's a bridge he never has to cross."

It was a phrase Waaboo clearly didn't understand and he looked at his uncle with confusion.

"I have something for you, Waaboozoons." Meloux handed the boy the stick he'd been carving.

"A whistle," Waaboo said with delight. "*Migwech, Mishomis.*"

"Not a whistle. A flute."

"What's the difference?"

"A whistle makes noise. A flute makes music."

Waaboo put the little instrument to his mouth and blew, his fingers dancing over the holes, which made Stephen smile. It wasn't music, but neither was it just noise.

"Why don't you show the flute to your mom?" he suggested.

Waaboo was out the door and running through the dark toward Leah's cabin. Stephen shut the door behind him.

"Before the night is out, you might be sorry you gave him that gift, Henry."

The air smelled of the stew simmering on the stove in the middle of the cabin. Leah had prepared enough for them all, if they ate moderately. Stephen wasn't comfortable barging in this way.

"*Migwech,* Henry," he said, his heart full of gratitude. "For taking us in."

"We will fast tonight, you and me," the old man told him. "Tomorrow, we will sweat."

The door opened, and Daniel stepped in with an armload of split firewood. Because of the dark, he wore a headlamp. He restocked the wood box near the stove and turned off the lamp. "I just spoke with Cork."

"Where is he?" Stephen asked.

"Hiding on Wolf Point."

Stephen went rigid. "Who from?"

"He doesn't know."

"We need to go." Stephen was up and moving toward the door.

"He said he could handle it."

"I'm going." Stephen reached for the latch.

"Patience, Stephen O'Connor," Henry said at his back.

"My father's in trouble."

"Your father is hiding. That is one way to avoid trouble."

"What if they find him?"

"He has said he can handle it. Do you trust him or not?"

Stephen stood with his hand on the door latch, torn.

"Wolf Point is far away. Whatever happens there, it will happen long before you arrive."

Stephen lowered his hand. The door opened, and the others came in from the dark. Rainy looked from Stephen to Daniel and finally to her great-uncle Henry. "What's wrong?"

Daniel explained.

"I should go," Stephen told her.

She replied calmly, "Cork said he could handle it."

"What if he's wrong?" Stephen reached again for the door latch.

"If you're bound and determined, we'll go together," Daniel said. "Henry, that old Winchester on the wall, is it in working order?"

"It will do what a rifle does."

"Aunt Rainy?" Daniel said.

She nodded. "I know how to use it, if it comes to that."

Jenny put her hand on Daniel's cheek. "Be careful. Dad wouldn't want you to do anything that will get you hurt. I don't want that either." She hugged him, then Stephen. "Take care of each other."

They moved quickly down the path through the forest, away from Crow Point. Trixie trotted ahead. It was little Waaboo who'd insisted the dog go with them.

"He smells monsters," the boy had assured them.

"Monsters, maybe," Meloux had said. "But also other things a man might not sense. A dog is always good protection on a hunt."

And so the old dog was at their side.

The sky was filled with stars, the moon on the rise but not high enough yet to illuminate the landscape. Daniel's headlamp lit the way. Stephen had always felt a comfort in these woods, but now they seemed to hold only menace. Anything might come at them from the dark, and he was glad to have Trixie along.

He had always wanted to be Mide, like Henry, like Rainy. A healer. A person who understood *ninoododawdiwin,* which was harmony, who lived in the way of *bimaadiziwin,* which was the good life. But since he'd first had the vision of him and the boy and the falling eagle, he'd felt unbalanced, lost. Maybe even unworthy, because although he could usually see the right path with his mind, he hadn't always been able to follow it. Like right now. His father said he could handle the situation on Wolf Point. Henry had counseled patience. And yet there he was, rushing headlong toward a situation he didn't fully understand, dragging Daniel with him.

"You didn't have to come."

"Right back at you," Daniel replied.

"If it was you hiding on Wolf Point, I'd be coming to help."

"Not if I thought I could handle it."

"Why didn't you let me go alone, then?"

"Your dad, when he says he can handle something, knows what he's talking about. You're a good man, Stephen, but you've still got a lot to learn."

"Just because I've never worn a badge?"

Daniel stopped and turned to him. The glare of the headlamp was blinding for a moment, and Stephen lifted his hand to block the light.

"You're not your father and you're not me and you never will be. You aren't *ogichidaa*. You aren't a warrior. You need to be okay with that. You have something Cork and I will never have, and it makes you a kind of man Cork and I will never be. You are *Mide*. Like Uncle Henry."

"He was a warrior once."

"Don't try to be Uncle Henry either."

Daniel continued down the dark path, where Trixie had paused, waiting for them. Stephen followed, twisted inside. But Daniel wasn't the target of his anger. It was Stephen himself. If he'd understood the vision in time, he might have been able to do something to prevent all this upheaval. If he'd understood his earlier visions, maybe his mother would still be alive. Maybe he wouldn't have let a madman put a bullet in his back. Maybe, if he was a little less who he was and a little more like his father and Daniel and even Henry, everything would be different.

Just as they reached the road and the place near the double-trunk birch where they'd parked their vehicles, Daniel's phone rang.

"It's your father." Daniel answered the call. "I'm here, Cork." He listened. "Stephen and I have left Crow Point. Do you want us to meet you somewhere?" He studied the stars. "All right. We're on our way."

He put the phone in his shirt pocket. "Your dad's fine. He wants us to meet him at the house. He's going to try to get Bo Thorson there, too. A little strategizing."

Stephen drove his father's Expedition. Trixie lay on the backseat, tired from the long walk. Daniel led the way, with Stephen following the red eyes of the pickup's taillights. The road to Aurora was a familiar one, but Stephen found himself scanning the dark on either side, wondering what great evil might, even at that moment, be watching him.

Chapter 23

Bo Thorson had been in love, deeply in love, only once in his life. She had been married. More than that, her husband had been the president of the United States. When he saved her life, he understood—they both understood—that they were bound in a deeper way than duty would allow. For both of them, duty dictated separate paths. Bo had found that the heart, once pierced, never fully heals. Sometimes when he was alone on surveillance, as he was now, he imagined a different life, a different duty, a different path. For himself and for her.

He was on a small island in Iron Lake, a hundred yards offshore. The sky was a black plate sugared with stars, the moon still below the treetops. He had a powerful set of ATN night-vision binoculars to his eyes, watching the lodge where Gerard had set up the headquarters for his operation. Much earlier, he'd placed a listening device the size of a postage stamp on the window glass. Gerard wasn't a bad strategist when he believed he was on the offensive, and in Tamarack County, he'd pretty much been bullying his way around. Which meant he probably wasn't watching his back as he should.

The big room with its maps and charts was unoccupied. Gerard had a man posted for security, a young guy who circled the lodge every few minutes on a regular schedule. Rookie mistake, one that had allowed Bo the brief interval he'd needed for placing the bug on the window.

He hadn't figured the truth of Gerard's involvement yet. Nor had he figured exactly who the other players might be. One thing was certain: Gerard believed the crash of Senator McCarthy's plane wasn't the result of pilot error. Who caused it and how were probably what Gerard's presence was all about. He'd brought Bo in, he'd said, to help identify the other interests in this affair. But Bo knew that he'd been told only half-truths, Gerard's modus operandi. Bo, for his part, had responded in kind.

In the period of waiting for something to develop at the lodge, Bo considered the past, the path of his life. He had no real family. He had cultivated many allies but few true friends. He lived alone in a condo high in a building in downtown St. Paul with a view of the Mississippi River, but he was seldom in residence there. More often, he was on a job that took him far from Minnesota.

He considered Cork O'Connor, a man who had built a life in one place and invested his heart in the people there. It was enticing, that comfortable, intimate existence, isolated from the world. Bo tried to imagine what it might have been like for him, had he made other choices. But that wasn't who he was, or who he was ever likely to be. The kind of life Cork led, if it was threatened, became a dangerous entanglement. Once your heart was involved in life-and-death choices, you were vulnerable. Your heart got in the way of your head, clouded your judgment. It was a lesson Bo had learned the hard way. He liked Cork, liked that part of the family he'd met, but he kept the door shut on his heart. In the end, he needed to be prepared to sacrifice Cork. To sacrifice them all, if necessary.

His cell phone vibrated. He checked caller ID. It was O'Connor.

"We need to talk, figure a few things out. Can you meet me?"

"Where?"

"At my house on Gooseberry Lane."

Cork gave directions, although Bo knew the address. When the call ended, he placed the receiver-recorder, which was tuned to the bug on the window, at the base of a pine tree and covered it with needles. He returned to the inflatable kayak he'd come in and paddled a quarter mile to an empty point where he'd parked. He deflated the kayak and stored it in the back of the Jeep. In another ten minutes, he was turning onto Gooseberry Lane.

Before knocking on the door, he stood in the front yard a few minutes, assessing the scene. It was a nice two-story house, with a lovely porch where a swing hung, the kind of house that Bo, when he was a kid living in ratty one-bedroom apartments with his drunken mother, had dreamed of having. But there was no resentment in him. No envy either. A man's life was what it was.

Cork greeted him when he knocked. They went to the kitchen, where Stephen was sitting at the table, along with Daniel English. In the middle of the table sat a cookie jar shaped like Ernie from *Sesame Street*. Stephen munched on a chocolate chip cookie. English sipped from a cup of coffee. To Bo, it felt more like a family council than a war council.

"Have a seat," Cork said. "Can I get you something?"

"Nothing, thanks.

"Where is everybody?" Bo asked, because it was evident that the house was empty.

"We thought it best to move them someplace safe, so they can't be used as leverage against Daniel," Cork explained.

"A good idea," Bo agreed. "Where are they?"

"Safe," Cork said.

Bo held back a smile. Cork was more careful than he'd imagined.

"I just came from a meeting with Gerard," Cork told him. "The man who questioned Stephen this morning."

Bo let nothing show on his face. "How did that come about?"

Cork explained the encounter, then held out a small transmitter. "I found it under the dash of the Jeep after they let me go. Gerard's people must have put it there when they questioned Stephen this morning."

"This Gerard," Bo said. "Think he's in charge of whatever's going on?"

"Here, anyway. Who knows who's pulling the strings and from where?"

"What strings, do you think?"

Cork eyed him frankly. "I thought you might have a better idea than we do. These people who hired you, they didn't give you any information to go on?"

"Just their concerns."

"Family?"

"I can't say, you know that."

"People on the rez, friends of mine, are missing. At this point, they may even be dead. Bo, this has gone way beyond professional courtesies."

"All right." Bo reached into Ernie's head and pulled out a chocolate chip cookie, clearly homemade. He couldn't remember the last time he'd had a homemade cookie of any kind. He took a bite and chewed while he considered what to tell them. "NTSB will continue to put out the story of pilot error. It's the safest explanation for the general public. But as this Gerard hinted to Stephen, there may be other forces involved."

"Terrorists," Stephen offered. "That's pretty much what Gerard said."

"Why would terrorists want to take down Senator McCarthy's plane?" English asked.

"Don't let Gerard or anyone like him fool you," Bo said. "This terrorist thing may be just one of the cover stories."

"You have a better idea?" Cork said.

Bo did have an idea, though not as solid as Cork might be hoping. "Senator McCarthy sits on the Foreign Relations Committee. She's the staunchest opponent of the proposed Manila Accord, which comes up for debate in the Senate in a couple of weeks. If it's passed, it not only makes trade with Southeast Asia easier but also provides for the sale of significant military hardware, much of it to regimes with horrible human rights records. One of the senator's main concerns was the arms part of the accord. She was adamant that we shouldn't try to buy friends with bullets or ignore atrocities because it's convenient for our economic and political interests. One of the inside pieces of information I was given by those who hired me is this: Senator McCarthy had been briefed on threats to her life. It's possible some of those threats came from one of the nations that would benefit from the accord."

"I haven't heard anything about that on the news coverage," Cork said.

"They're probably trying to keep a lid on that."

"Who's they?"

"NSA is the first agency that comes to mind, although I can't say for sure."

"Gerard is NSA?"

"Your guess is as good as mine." The first real lie Bo had told them. "But it would make sense that the government wouldn't want the possibility floated out there that a country we're going to call an ally has assassinated a U.S. senator. That would put an end to any hope of Senate approval."

"You're really saying it might have been agents from the Philippines or Thailand or Indonesia?" Cork said.

"You asked what I thought was really going on. That's my best shot at the moment. If you have a better idea, let's hear it."

The others were sitting back in their chairs. It was as if news of this magnitude had knocked the wind out of them. Geopolitical conflicts intruding on their quiet lives in such a huge and unexpected way. *Foreign agents?* their faces said. *Really?*

"However," Bo went on, offering a nugget of truth, "there are so many interests affected by the Manila Accord that God only knows who might actually be at work here. It doesn't matter who that is, it's in the government's best interest to continue the drumbeat of their story of pilot error. They understand that if you repeat a lie often enough, eventually the public is going to accept it as truth."

"What about the media?" English tossed in. "Newspapers, television. If they got wind of foreign involvement, they'd scream to high heaven."

"Maybe."

"I'd be happy to repeat publicly what Gerard said to me," Stephen said.

"And what, exactly, did Gerard tell you? Did he actually say anything about terrorists?"

"Alex Quaker paid a visit to our sheriff today," Cork said. "The number two man in the FBI's National Security Branch. They oversee the Bureau's Counterterrorism Division."

Bo offered a shrug. "Easily explained. In this day and age, with an accident that kills someone of Senator McCarthy's stature, it's important to eliminate terrorism as a possibility. And they will, mark my words. As long as this is in the news, pilot error will be the constant refrain."

"How do you sort any of this out?" Stephen sounded overwhelmed.

"Exactly." Bo looked to Cork. "Any more word on the reservation about the folks who've disappeared?"

"Nothing."

"That's a place to keep poking."

"We will. What about you?"

"I have a resource I haven't tapped yet but I think it's time."

They waited for him to explain further.

"Sorry," he told them. "Confidential." It was getting late. It had been a long day. Bo could feel the weariness in them all. "Let's call it for tonight and get some rest. It's hard to think clearly when you're tired."

"We're going to do a sweat tomorrow," Stephen said.

"A sweat? You mean like in a sweat lodge?"

"You might find it interesting."

"Is that an invitation to join you?"

"If you'd like."

"Think I'll pass."

Stephen said, "It clears your mind and your spirit. It might help with your thinking."

"My thinking is fine, thanks. But let me know if it helps with yours." Bo stood. "Thanks for the cookie."

"Where are you staying?" English asked.

"The cabin of a friend."

"We know this friend?"

"Confidential. If that sweat clears your thinking, Stephen, and we need to talk, let me know. And remember, Cork, just because you found the transmitter and removed it, that doesn't mean you're not still being tracked somehow, so be careful. Good night, gentlemen."

He left them at the kitchen table and returned to the night. He drove around the block, parked, and walked back to Gooseberry Lane. If he'd known about the transmitter, about Gerard's interest in the O'Connors, he wouldn't have agreed to meet with them. He studied the street. There were only a couple of vehicles parked along the curb. The one that interested him, a black pickup, was half a block from the O'Connors' house, out of the glow of any streetlamp.

Gerard's people? Whoever they were, if they didn't know before that he was working with O'Connor, they knew it now.

Chapter 24

H*e watches the boy on the steep rise above him. He is that boy and he is not.*

The vision played out as it always had: the eagle appearing; the boy shooting it from the sky; the egg and the eagle falling; something huge looming at Stephen's back, so monstrous that he can't look. He and the boy screaming bloody murder.

He woke in the quiet of night, rose from his bed, and walked to the window. Bright moonlight illuminated the landscape, silvering the front yard, making the empty street the color of winter ice.

It wasn't over. He understood this was what the vision was trying to tell him. It wasn't over. Maybe there was still a chance to . . . to what? He lay his forehead against the cool glass of the windowpane. *There must be a way to know,* he thought. *Maybe the sweat.*

He was too restless to go back to bed and stepped into the hallway. The house stood silent all around him, his father and Daniel asleep. He waited for Trixie to come trotting from somewhere. She may have been old, but Trixie still heard everything. When she didn't show, Stephen moved to the top of the stairs. Moon glow through the front door window lit the bottom landing in a ghostly way. He expected to see the dog there, waiting for him to come down, but the landing was empty. He descended, telling himself she was just deep in the slumber of an aged hound. Which was his head talking to him. His gut told him something different, reminding him of the fate of Cyrus and Noggin.

He stood on the carpet of the living room and called, "Trixie," in a hushed voice. "Come here, girl."

He crossed to the kitchen. During the day, Trixie's usual resting place was the corner in the kitchen nearest her food dish. The dog wasn't there. He turned back and stepped on shattered glass. It didn't cut him, but it made him stop dead in his tracks. He saw that one of the panes in the mullioned window had been broken. He walked carefully to the door and tried the knob. It was no longer locked, and he understood that someone who didn't belong there was inside the house.

He listened carefully but heard only his own soft, fast breathing. Gingerly, he stepped around the broken glass and into the dining room. A long, translucent drape was drawn over the patio doors, and against the sheer fabric, the moon cast two shadows, human in shape but exaggerated into things monstrously huge. For a moment, Stephen was unable to move. It wasn't just uncertainty that paralyzed him. It was also fear. The kind of fear that, in his nightmare, kept him from turning to look at the monster at his back. The shadows moved across the drape and disappeared. Stephen forced himself to the patio doors. Hesitated another long moment, and finally pulled the drape aside. The silver eye of the moon stared down at him. The patio was empty.

He crept through the first floor of the house, checking it room by room. He quietly mounted the stairs to his father's bedroom. His father's bed was empty. The squeal of the screen door hinge and the click of the front door handle as it was turned brought him to the top of the stairs, where he caught a glimpse below of someone stealing into the living room. He darted to his bedroom closet, grabbed the Louisville Slugger his father had given him on his twelfth birthday, gripped it with determination, and descended to the first floor. Whoever it was in the house now had moved into the dark of the kitchen. Stephen heard a drawer opened, wood scraping softly along wood. He clutched the bat as he had when he'd played Little League and had bent over the plate, waiting for a pitch. He eased into the kitchen doorway.

"You heard him, too," his father said.

Trixie came trotting, tail wagging, and Stephen lowered the bat. "Where were you?"

"Outside." It was Daniel who answered. Stephen saw him then, near the window above the sink, peering out into the dark.

"Both of you?" Stephen wondered why he hadn't been included.

"Trixie was sleeping in my room," his father said, rummaging in the drawer. "She woke me up with a woof. Daniel was already awake."

"Couldn't sleep," Daniel explained. "Worried about Jenny and Waaboo."

His father closed the drawer, flashlight in his hand. "We both came down to check on things. Someone tried to break in through the back door. We spooked him. He's gone now."

"You saw him?"

His father shook his head. "Got a glimpse of him, but he ran. We followed him to the street, saw a truck down the block pull away. Probably him."

"Who do you think it was?"

"No idea."

Stephen looked at Daniel. "Someone coming for you?"

"Maybe."

"I think that's all the excitement we'll see," Cork said. "I'm going to sweep up that broken glass and hang out down here tonight with Trixie. You two try to get some sleep."

But Stephen lay in his bed, staring up at the ceiling, searching for answers that, like sleep that night, continued to elude him. Along with everything else that troubled him, he wondered why his father and Daniel had gone after the mysterious visitor without him. Did they think he couldn't handle a violent confrontation, if it came to that? In the long hours of dark, he was tortured with doubt, asking himself, *What kind of man do they think I am?* He searched his heart and wondered, *What kind of man am I?*

In his cabin, Bo listened to the conversations the transmitter had picked up in the little war room Gerard had established at the abandoned lodge. There was nothing of substance, mostly Gerard talking with subordinates about the search on Desolation Mountain. They referred to the object of their search in code: bear tracks. As in "We didn't find the bear tracks, sir." And, "Maybe there aren't any bear tracks on the mountain. Maybe the bear tracks are somewhere else." They decided to abandon the search on the mountain and concentrate on something they called the "beach." As in, "Let's hit the beach and see if we can find any evidence of waves."

Bo had himself been a part of covert operations before and knew that this kind of veiled reference was meat and potatoes in any black-ops conversation. Part of the game.

It was late when he finally laid himself out in his bunk. He wasn't sure where the long day had gotten him. Things had only become more complicated. The shot dogs, the missing people on the reservation. Cork O'Connor and his family. They rattled around in his thinking like gravel in a tin can. He needed sleep, but no sooner had his head hit the pillow than his cell phone rang. Not his personal cell phone. One of his burner phones. It was her.

"I just wanted to make sure they haven't killed you yet," she said.

He smiled at the sound of her voice. "I don't kill easy. You know that."

"Doesn't mean I don't worry. Are you all right?"

He rose from his bunk, left the cabin, and stood on the deck in the cool night air. The moon was high overhead, the lake water a mirror.

"Confused, but okay," he told her. "Do you have something for me?"

"Nothing specific. Directives have come down to clamp a lid on any hint of a terrorist attack. A black eye for an administration that campaigned on keeping America safe. On our end, we're sifting through all the threats Olympia received, looking for something specific. Nothing concrete so far. She was on the front line in so many causes. She thought of the threats as proof that she was being heard and insisted they didn't scare her."

She was quiet. He could hear her breathing, soft. Like wind in tall grass.

"Any help from the FBI?" he asked.

"They're not very forthcoming, all the way up the ladder. We're tapping every resource on the inside that we can, but we don't have the leverage we used to. And you've probably heard that the governor's going to be in Aurora tomorrow night for the town meeting about the mine, the meeting Olympia was supposed to attend. It would be good for you to be there, Bo. Take stock of the audience. Maybe someone will stand out."

"Like who?"

"The anti-McCarthy zealots. Someone so rabid they might actually have been motivated to assassinate her."

"In my experience, those people don't tend to be particularly sophisticated in their methods."

"Unless they had help from those who have the wherewithal to be sophisticated or the power to cover up a crude killing."

"Any suggestions in that regard?"

"That's what we're looking to you for." He heard her sigh. "I wish you had someone watching your back up there."

"I've got help, of a sort. A guy who used to be sheriff here. Name's O'Connor."

"Does he know how deep you're in this?"

"That wouldn't be healthy for either of us. As far as he knows, I'm working for an unnamed client."

"The truth," she said. "At least part of it. Tell me about Gerard."

"I'm still not sure who brought him in. Someone's after something that came down with the plane. Maybe the flight recorder, maybe something else. People involved in the early search of the crash site have gone missing. Could be someone thinks they snatched whatever's so important. Gerard might be behind the disappearances, I don't know yet."

"If Gerard gets the recorder, we may never know the truth."

"Then I'll have to find it before he does."

Something jumped in the water, shattering the mirrored surface. Bo watched the dark rings spread out, ripples extending far beyond the point of disturbance.

"You be safe," she said.

"I'll do my best."

The call ended without goodbyes. Bo turned off the burner phone for good. He had many others and she had all their numbers. Only one call per phone, he'd told her, just to be safe. Then he stood a long while, waiting for the lake water to return to glass.

CHAPTER 25

When Stephen, Daniel, and Trixie reached Crow Point early the next morning, the fire had already been prepared and the Grandfathers, the rocks to be used in the sweat that day, were heating. The lodge was on the shore of Iron Lake and surrounded by birch trees. It hadn't always been in its current location. Two years earlier, it was on the other side of Crow Point. In that location, while sweating alone in winter, Stephen had seen the vision of the man who would put a bullet into his back. That shooting had taken place at the sweat lodge not long thereafter.

Following that brutal violation of a sacred place, Henry Meloux had ordered a new sweat lodge built far from the other. Stephen hadn't helped in that construction. He'd had his hands full struggling to walk again. But his injury didn't keep him from participating in sweats, and he was certain that the cleansing rituals had helped his body and his spirit heal.

Trixie trotted ahead, and Waaboo raced to greet her. Then the boy ran to Daniel, who bent, wrapped his son in his arms, and lifted him.

"I helped make the fire," Waaboo told him proudly.

Which was a significant honor, particularly for one so young.

Daniel carried Waaboo piggyback and they continued across the meadow to Henry Meloux's cabin, where the others were waiting. Rainy looked troubled.

"Where's Cork?" she asked.

"Trying to convince Bo Thorson to come out here," Stephen told her. "He thinks Bo might benefit from taking part in the sweat."

"Ah," Rainy said, but looked unconvinced. "An interesting speculation."

"Everything okay here last night?" Daniel asked Jenny.

"Blessedly quiet."

"Where are Henry and Leah?"

"Walking," Rainy said. "They walk together every morning."

"Is he teaching her about the medicine plants?" Stephen asked.

Although he hadn't yet begun his formal preparation to become a Mide, a member of the Grand Medicine Society, Stephen already knew a good deal about the medicines Henry and Rainy used in their healing work.

Rainy smiled. "That's what he says. I think he just likes her company."

Henry Meloux was more than a hundred years old, Leah nearly thirty years his junior. They lived in separate cabins but had joined their lives on Crow Point in a way that someone on the outside might think strange. At twenty, Stephen didn't fully understand the arrangement himself. Was it love? Just companionship? He had never asked Henry to explain what connected them. One day he might broach the subject with the old man, but this was not that day.

"Everything quiet on Gooseberry Lane?" Jenny asked.

Stephen and Daniel exchanged a look.

"What?"

"Waaboo," Daniel said. "Why don't you take Trixie outside to play?"

"Sweats have many purposes," Cork explained to Bo as they traveled north along the shoreline of Iron Lake. "Healing. Cleansing. Visioning. Seeking."

"If I were a religious kind of guy," Bo replied, "I'd say it sounds like praying."

"Prayer is a part of it. It can be about asking. It can be about gratitude. It can be about simply connecting with the sacred spirit that resides in all things, the great spirit that weaves all life together."

Bo studied the lake, which, under the morning sun, shot blinding arrows of light. God was an abstract to him, something he'd discussed only as he might discuss the philosophy of Kierkegaard. He found it almost quaint, the way Cork talked about this belief in spirit.

"So the sweat today, what's that about?"

"Stephen believes he might be given a better understanding of the vision that comes to him."

"'Given,'" Bo said. "'Comes to him.' Cork, I've got to tell you, this is all a little woo-woo for me."

"I understand. I've lived all my life seeing things I can't explain in a rational way. I just ask that you keep an open mind."

They parked along the gravel roadside, behind Daniel English's truck. English and Stephen O'Connor had come out much earlier, Bo knew, probably about the time Cork called to convince him to join them in this Indian ritual. He'd agreed, but not for the reason Cork believed. What Bo wanted to know was the location of the family who might be used as pawns in the game that was afoot in Tamarack County.

"We walk the rest of the way," Cork said.

"How far?"

"A couple of miles."

"I don't do much hiking in the woods. I'm a city kind of guy."

Cork laughed. "You look pretty North Country right now."

The morning was cool, high forties, the air fresh and filled with the scent of pine. The sky was blue and cloudless. Cork talked little as they hiked the trail, and Bo found this to his liking. Although he wasn't an outdoorsman, on such a morning, he couldn't help but believe that any conversation would be a disruption of a quiet that felt, he had to admit, a little sacred.

They came to a stream whose water was red-hued.

"Nibi-Miskwi," Cork said as he danced across rocks to the other side. "That's the Ojibwe name for this stream."

"What's it mean?"

"Blood Water."

"Why the red color?"

"A couple of factors. The iron in all the soil up here, and also tannin from the bog seepage that feeds the stream."

"Nibi-Miskwi. It has a poetic ring."

"It's a beautiful language, Ojibwemowin."

"You speak it well?"

"Not at all," Cork told him. "When I was a kid, it was spoken mostly by elders, but that's changed. More and more children learn to speak it now. We have programs for that. Waaboo's becoming pretty fluent." Cork turned from the red water of the stream. "Still a distance to go before we hit Crow Point." He continued down the path, and the conversation was at an end.

They broke from the trees onto a meadow that began wide but narrowed to the south. The meadow was outlined in birch and aspen trees, and beyond the trees was the silver-blue glitter of Iron Lake. Two cabins stood at the far end of the point. A little to the west rose two outcrops of high rock. Among the trees along the shoreline north of the outcrops was a squat structure with a fire in front sending up white smoke. Several figures were gathered around the fire.

"The sweat lodge," Cork told him. "We'll head over in a bit. First I want you to meet Henry."

They crossed the meadow. The cabin door opened before they arrived, and an old woman stepped out, dressed in jeans and a green turtleneck sweater.

"*Anin,* Cork," she said. *"Aaniish naa ezhiyaayin?"*

"*Nminoyaa gwa,* Leah. This is my friend Bo Thorson."

"Welcome," Leah said with a polite smile. "Won't you come in?"

Inside the cabin was the oldest man Bo had ever seen. His hair was white and long, his face a wrinkled sheeting of flesh. He sat with a boy who was blowing notes on a little handmade flute. The music stopped and the old man and the boy looked up.

"*Anin,* Baa-baa," the boy said to Cork. To Bo he said, *"Boozhoo."*

"Henry, Waaboo, I'd like you to meet Bo Thorson."

The old man rose. He'd seemed bent when he was listening to the boy play the flute. Now his back was straight and his shoulders squared, and Bo saw that the old man was as tall as he.

The old man studied him, eyes dark and penetrating, and Bo felt uncomfortable under their gaze, as if he was being probed. With surprising strength, the old man finally shook the hand Bo had offered.

"You are not what I expected," the old man said.

"Someone taller?" Bo replied with an amiable smile.

"Someone truer." The old man didn't smile nor did he release Bo's hand.

In his time as an agent of the U.S. Secret Service, and as an operative for hire since, Bo Thorson had met many people of high rank—presidents and premiers and CEOs and holders of extraordinary wealth. Standing in that simple cabin in the middle of nowhere, his hand in the grip of the oldest man he had ever seen, Bo realized that he was in the presence of someone whose power was of a remarkably different kind.

CHAPTER 26

Like most white people, Bo had lived with two different images of American Indians. One, perpetuated by Saturday matinee Westerns, was all war whoops and feathered bonnets. The other was of a population beset with a weakness for alcohol, a tendency toward violence, incapable of rising out of poverty, and leading an existence generally bereft of moral grounding; when you were in the proximity of someone clearly Indian, you took stock of your merchandise and you watched your back. His time in Tamarack County had begun to change his thinking.

He sat among the birch trees near the sweat lodge, talking with Daniel English; his wife, Jenny O'Connor; and Leah Duling. Rainy and Waaboo had moved to the lakeshore not far away, Rainy helping the little boy work out some tunes on his flute. From inside the sweat lodge came the sound of low chanting. Bo had opted not to join the two O'Connor men and Meloux in their sweat, hoping he might learn a good deal from conversation with the others that could prove useful to him in getting to the bottom of what was going on.

"She was a great senator," Jenny was saying. "It was like she spoke my thoughts. Cut the defense budget and shift the spending to education, public assistance programs, infrastructure. Keep our wilderness areas wild and safe. Open our arms to the refugees from all the damn wars. Put teeth in all the laws that guarantee civil rights. You ask me, she would have made an ideal presidential candidate in the next election. I'd have voted for her."

"You sound just like her," Bo said with a smile. "But all those ideals put her at odds with lots of powerful people."

"You can't change the world without ruffling feathers," Jenny replied.

"The town meeting that brought her up here was going to be about granting permits for this new mining operation. I know she wasn't in favor of it," Bo said. "But as I understand it, the mine would bring lots of jobs back to the Iron Range."

English stepped in. "The iron mines devastated this area last century, but with time the land has recovered. When rain falls on the tailings from an iron mine, the result is simply rust. This new operation would involve sulfide mining. Do you know what happens when rain falls on tailings from a sulfide mine, Bo? It creates sulfuric acid. Do you have any idea what that would do to the ecosystem here? Or everything downstream of this watershed?"

"The mining company's given assurance that wouldn't happen. I understand there would be lots of checks in place."

"Assurance," English scoffed. "Do you know anything about the Mount Polley Mine in B.C.?"

"Never heard of it."

"A few years ago, a tailings pond, basically a huge reservoir of poison, was breached, releasing over a billion gallons of tainted water into the streams up there. It was an eco-disaster of extraordinary proportion. The mining companies all said this was an incredibly rare occurrence. But the same thing happened in Colorado the following year. And it's happened in hundreds of other places around the world. Mining is about momentary profit. Have you heard of seven-generational thinking?"

"If I'm correct, it's the question of how what we do today will impact the world seven generations from now."

"Exactly. This mine flies in the face of every reasonable consideration of the future."

"Except economic."

"Any gain is only in the short term. If the land and water are poisoned, the long-term effects could be devastating in every way, including economically."

"Well," Bo said, "you've got me convinced."

"I wish our governor was as easily convinced," Jenny said. "He's thrown his support behind the project."

"And if he wrangles an appointment to complete Olympia McCarthy's term, he'll do a lot of damage on a national scale," English added.

"You don't like our governor?" Bo said.

"He owes a lot of favors to big business."

The blanket over the door of the sweat lodge was lifted from the inside and Cork O'Connor crawled out. The old man followed next, and Cork helped him stand. Young Stephen O'Connor was the last to emerge. All of them dripped from head to toe, their hair flat and clinging to their faces, the boxer shorts they wore drenched.

Leah dipped a ladle into a wooden bucket of cold water, and one by one the men refreshed themselves.

"That's it?" Bo asked.

"That's only the first door," English said. "The first round of their sweat."

The old man already looked exhausted.

"Are you okay, Henry?" Leah asked.

The old man sat on a blanket that had been laid on the ground. "A few minutes and I will be fine."

"You two doing okay?" Jenny asked of her father and brother.

"We're good," Cork replied. But Bo could see that both he and his son were looking at the old man with deep concern. "Henry," Cork began.

The old man lifted a hand to stop whatever was about to be said. "I have a heart that is strong and willing and a spirit that whispers 'More.' A few minutes, and I will be ready."

Cork had laid his clothes in a pile near the lodge. Somewhere among all that clothing, a cell phone rang. Cork dug in the pocket of his folded pants.

At the same time, Bo's cell phone vibrated. He stepped away from the others to take the call.

"Where the hell are you?" Gerard demanded. "Why haven't you checked in?"

"Nothing more to report at the moment," Bo said quietly.

"Well, here's something for you. They found the truck that belongs to the missing couple. The Hukaris."

"Where?"

"Some back road out there on the reservation. The truck was pretty well destroyed by fire. No sign of the couple."

"Not the work of your people, I take it."

"If that was meant as a joke, it's not funny. Where are you?"

"You remember the O'Connors, father and son?"

"What about them?"

"They've become my eyes and ears on the reservation. I'll explain later." Bo ended the call abruptly.

When he returned, he found Cork dressing. Rainy and Waaboo had joined the others.

"That was Sheriff Dross on the phone," Cork told Bo. "They've found the Hukaris' truck. Or what's left of it."

"Where?" Bo asked.

"On the rez. It's a burned-out hulk."

English said in a dead voice, "And no sign of Phil or Sue."

"Another thing," Cork said. "The blood we scraped off the dock at the Loves' cabin? It's the same type as Monkey's blood."

"What about the sweat, Dad?"

"The sweat's over for me, Stephen," his father replied. "You have to make your own decision."

The kid looked unhappily toward Meloux. "If I stay, I won't be able to focus, Henry. I'll be thinking about the Hukaris. I'm not sure the sweat would do me any good."

The old man sat on the blanket with his thin legs crossed, his knee bones like doorknobs. When he'd emerged from the lodge, he'd looked done for. But he seemed fine now, recovering quickly from what Bo imagined must be the ordeal of a sweat. More and more this man they called a Mide surprised him.

Meloux gave young O'Connor a wistful look. "An ending for you does not mean an ending for me."

"You're going on with the sweat?" Concern was all over Stephen's face. Except for the old man, they all looked concerned.

"Your path is your path and mine is mine. What I am waiting for has not yet been given. I will wait some more and while I wait I will sweat."

Stephen held himself very still, eyeing the old man, clearly torn.

The choice had been his and he'd made it, but Stephen was angry that the sweat had come to an early end for him. Although he understood that a sweat was about opening to whatever was given, which didn't necessarily mean answers, he'd been hoping the burden of his vision might be lifted somehow.

Now, as he rode with his father and Bo Thorson toward Aurora, he was having real trouble with acceptance. He felt more stuck than ever, as if he were still hammering at a door that wouldn't open for him. Which wasn't, he knew, the way of a Mide. Or the kind of Mide he would like to become someday. The kind of Mide that was Henry Meloux.

Cork and Bo talked up front, discussing the visitor to O'Connor's house the night before.

"Probably the same people who were after the Loves and the Hukaris and Tom Blessing," Bo speculated.

"And who would that be?"

"That's the question, isn't it? I'll do some checking on my end. What about you?"

"I'm going to talk to our sheriff, bring her up to speed on everything."

"Everything?" Bo asked.

"Within reason," Cork said.

They dropped Bo at the house on Gooseberry Lane, where he'd parked his Jeep. Then they headed to Sam's Place.

"Wait here," Cork told Stephen.

He went into the Quonset hut, and a few minutes later, Stephen saw him post a handwritten sign in the serving window that read: CLOSED UNTIL FURTHER NOTICE.

When they walked into her office, Marsha Dross was talking with David Foster, one of her deputies. She put up a finger, signaling them to wait.

"I'm authorizing overtime for every officer, Dave. They're to be in the conference room in an hour. And get hold of Azevedo. His vacation's over. I want him back here. Pronto."

As Foster headed out the door past Stephen and Cork, he lifted his eyebrows in a way that signaled, *Be careful.*

Dross crossed her arms and glared at Cork. "What do you know that I don't?"

"Why do you say that?"

"Sit down." She waited for Stephen and his father to take the two empty chairs. "You know the Iron Lake Reservation and the people out there a lot better than any of us. They whisper things to you that they would never tell me or any of my officers. What I see is that everything that's happened in this last awful week has happened on the reservation. So, tell me what's going on out there that I don't know about."

"For starters," Cork said in a calm voice, "it's not just on the rez, Marsha. Someone tried to break into our house last night."

"Who?"

"No idea. But I'm guessing they're the same people who are responsible for the disappearances on the rez."

"Everyone's okay?"

"We moved Jenny and Waaboo out of harm's way. It's clear that everyone who's been targeted so far was at the scene of Senator McCarthy's plane crash very early, which includes Daniel. We want Jenny and Waaboo safe."

"So they can't be used as leverage?"

"Exactly. That may have been the plan with Fanny Blessing, to use her to get to Tom, except something went wrong. Grabbing Sue gives these people leverage with Phil. Ned Love's sister, Beulah, has been followed, too."

"Where is she?"

"Staying with Sarah LeDuc. I've got Harmon Goodsky keeping an eye on them both."

"What's it all about?"

Cork took a deep breath. "My best guess is that they're trying to find the black box and they believe someone who was at the crash site early picked it up."

"First of all, the official word is that there wasn't a black box. And if there was, why would NTSB lie about it?"

"I'm just guessing here, but maybe the black box would show something they don't want made public."

"That the cause of the crash wasn't pilot error? Hence, the presence of the FBI's number two man from the National Security Branch. But Monkey Love, Fanny Blessing, the Hukaris? That doesn't strike me as the work of the FBI."

"There are other actors involved, but at this point, I've got no idea who they are."

"I called BCA, asked them to come in on this." She was speaking of Minnesota's Bureau of Criminal Apprehension. "I got a song and dance about how they don't have any agents to spare at the moment."

"That's a new one."

"Know what I think? I think the governor's office delivered some kind of directive."

"You'll sound like a conspiracy crackpot if you say that publicly."

"Then I won't say it publicly. But I'm going to get to the bottom of what's going on in this county if it takes every officer I have working twenty-four seven."

"They might not like that."

"My guys?"

"Them, too. But I was thinking about whoever's behind whatever's going on."

"Cork, I need a promise from you. I need to believe you won't keep anything from me that might help in this."

"You've got my word. Can I expect the same?"

"Deal. Oh, and one more thing. The preliminary autopsy finding on Fanny Blessing doesn't show anything unusual. Looks like the cause of death will officially be listed as cardiac arrest. Reasonable, considering the state of her health."

"The timing is interesting, though, don't you think?"

"Is it possible for someone to be scared to death?" Stephen asked.

"I suppose someone whose physical condition is already precarious," the sheriff said, nodding as if she thought the idea had merit. "If anything changes officially, I'll let you know."

Outside the building, Stephen stopped and gave his father a long look.

"What?" Cork asked.

"You promised Marsha that you would tell her everything."

"I did."

Stephen cocked his head. "You never mentioned Bo."

CHAPTER 27

Bo pulled up beside the black SUV. Inside the cabin, Gerard was waiting for him, drinking a Leinenkugel's pulled from the refrigerator.

"I see you didn't stand on ceremony. Just made yourself right at home."

"You know your Robert Service, Thorson? 'Politeness is a platitude in this fair land of gallant foemen.' It's a poem about the cost of chivalry." He sipped his beer. "Here I am tracking you down again. What's this about you and the O'Connors?"

Bo tried to read him. He'd thought the truck that had staked out Gooseberry Lane the night before was Gerard's doing, but maybe not. Maybe Gerard really was as clueless as he seemed.

"I worked with O'Connor years ago when I was Secret Service. He's part Ojibwe, knows the territory. I'm getting good intel from him."

"Yeah? So tell me about the Hukaris."

"The husband was one of the Indians first on the scene of the crash."

"And if someone were looking for the black box, they might think he grabbed it?"

Bo headed to the kitchen area and began to put together a pot of coffee. "That burned-out truck, your handiwork?"

"I wondered if maybe it was yours."

"I don't operate that way. But I wouldn't put it past you. By the way, O'Connor found the transmitter you put under the dash of his son's car. He left it in place, but I doubt they'll be using the Jeep in any way that would be useful to track now. What were you thinking when you bugged the kid?"

"After we caught him up on the mountain and questioned him, it was clear all he was giving me was lies."

"And you thought a twenty-year-old kid might be involved in some grand terrorist plot?"

"Kids younger than him blow themselves up in the name of all kinds of harebrained causes."

"And what kind of harebrained cause do you think he might represent?"

"I was hoping you could tell me. You're the one with an inside line to the Indians around here now."

Bo turned to Gerard as the coffee began to drip. "Someone tried to break into the O'Connors' house last night. Your people?"

Gerard lowered his beer. "Not mine."

Bo opened a cupboard door, took a mug off the shelf. "Your guys up on the mountain, have they found anything yet?"

"Nothing. And nothing in the woods where the tail section broke off or in that muck where the plane crashed or anywhere around it either. Someone grabbed that black box."

"Someone afraid what the flight recorder might say about the true nature of the crash?"

"Maybe."

"Kind of flies in the face of most terrorist agendas, don't you think? A real terrorist would want the cause front and center, blasted all over the headlines. On the other hand, I suppose if someone on the inside were responsible, they wouldn't be eager for things to come to light. So, if the senator was murdered and it wasn't done by terrorists, the question is, who wanted her dead? And also, who has the power to misshape an investigation?"

"Any theories yet?"

Bo removed the pot from the coffeemaker and poured himself what had brewed so far. "The NTSB continues to deliver the same line of pilot error bullshit. The FBI is doing nothing but obfuscating. The BCA here in Minnesota hasn't been brought in, so I'm guessing somebody is sitting on them. Whoever is doing the strong-arming, they've got a lot of clout. And a lot to lose if the truth ever comes out. The assassination of a U.S. senator." Bo blew across the surface of his coffee to cool it and eyed Gerard over the rim of his mug. "You have the clout to misshape this investigation, if you had a mind to. You're looking for the flight recorder, and I still don't know at whose behest."

"Is that important?"

"Only if I find the truth and it gets me killed. Will it?"

"Know the truth and the truth will set you free. Isn't that how it goes?"

"It's not just about the black box, am I right? Did something else come down with that plane?"

Gerard's look was appropriately stony. "What do you mean?"

"Why search the mountain? The flight recorder would have been with the tail section in the woods next to the bog."

"As it came down, the plane clipped trees up on that mountainside. Seemed appropriate to include the area in our search."

"That explanation might read well in the newspapers."

"I'm not one of the bad guys, Thorson. Save your questioning for them." Gerard set his beer, still half full, on the table and started for the door. "I want to hear from you tonight. Don't make me come looking."

Bo waited until Gerard had driven away, then from a case in the bedroom closet, took a radio frequency detector wand and swept each room, searching for bugs. The cabin seemed clean. He stepped outside and ran the wand over his Jeep. Also clean. None of which surprised him. Gerard would have anticipated this move. If Bo were being surveilled, it was in a far more sophisticated way.

He drank his coffee and listened again to the recorded conversations from Gerard's war room. He considered what they might have been referring to when they talked about the "bear tracks" on Desolation Mountain and what they might have meant when they discussed moving their search to the "beach" to look for "waves."

Bear tracks. Evidence left behind that would identify the presence of something on the mountain? If so, the presence of what?

The beach. Waves. A veiled reference to . . . to what? You could see tracks. But waves, not necessarily. Unless they were talking about water, which seemed unlikely, waves couldn't be seen. So airwaves? Radio waves? How would they show themselves on the beach? Electronic detection of some kind?

Bo would have loved to be able to hear what had gone on in the war room since he'd last checked the recorder on the island, but that would have to wait until the cover of dark.

CHAPTER 28

"I made Bo a promise," Cork tried to explain. "He needs to stay off the radar."

They were heading toward home to grab some lunch. Stephen sat stiff on the passenger side, looking disappointed in his father.

"Professional courtesy, one PI to another?" he said.

"That's part of it."

"Marsha's a friend. Seems to me friendship would supersede professional courtesy."

"There are forces at work here that are still very much in the dark, Stephen. With Bo out there in that dark with them, rooting them out, we might have some advantage."

"If Bo can be trusted."

"You don't trust him?"

"I don't know him. How well do you?"

"I worked with him several times. Important work."

"When he was with the Secret Service. That was a long time ago. Is he the same man now he was then?"

"I get the same feel from him now that I got then. A man I can trust."

"He asked you for a promise that made you lie to a friend. I can't remember you doing that before."

"It wasn't a lie exactly."

"If you say so." Stephen looked away, out his window.

"Two things to think about," Cork said. "One, it's clear that Bo knows more than he's telling us, but that doesn't mean he can't be trusted. My guess is that he's made promises he's trying to keep. That's something I understand. Two, Bo risked his life in the line of duty. He put himself between the First Lady and a bullet. That takes a special kind of person."

"You're telling me he's *ogichidaa,* like you, both of you standing between evil and the people you care about. I get that. All I'm saying is that people can change, Dad. Even the best."

Before Cork could argue the point further, his cell phone rang. He pulled to the side of the street. The call was from Daniel English.

"Tom Blessing's gone, Cork."

"Gone?"

"As in missing. He was supposed to meet with the folks at the funeral home this morning to discuss his mother's burial. He never showed. I asked around Allouette. Nobody's seen him since yesterday. I went out to his place. His truck's gone."

"How'd you find out about the funeral home meeting?"

"I was at the tribal building, checking in with Kingbird. We've had more reports of those poachers. While I was there, the funeral home called Tom's office, got no answer, then they called Kingbird wondering if he or anybody else had seen Tom. Considering that his mother died yesterday, he ought to be surrounded by relatives, but like I said, no one's seen him. You add in the missed meeting with the funeral home and what's gone on with Phil and Sue and the Loves, and it seems pretty worrisome."

"Where are you now?"

"Still at the Blessings'."

"Wait there. I'm coming. And, Daniel, you have your sidearm with you, right?"

"You better believe it."

"Who's gone?" Stephen asked when the call ended.

"Tom Blessing."

"Just like the others?"

"That's how it looks."

"What do we do?"

Cork punched in Bo Thorson's number on his cell phone. The call went immediately to voice mail. "Bo, it's Cork O'Connor. Tom Blessing's gone missing. Give me a call when you get this message."

"What do we do?" Stephen asked again.

But Cork was punching in the sheriff's number now. When Dross picked up, he explained the situation, then said, "Stephen and I are heading out to the rez, Marsha. I'll let you know what we find."

He started to punch in Rainy's cell phone number, but Stephen said, "I'm not going with you."

"No?" Then it dawned on him that his son was a college student. "Classes this afternoon?"

Stephen rolled his eyes. "While all this is going on? School can wait. No, you and Daniel don't need me."

"What are you going to do?"

"Head back to Crow Point, finish my sweat."

Cork gave a nod. "All right." He called Rainy and filled her in. "How's Henry?"

"Recovering. The sweat was hard on him."

"Anything good come from his ordeal?"

"He's oddly quiet. It's good Stephen's coming back. Maybe Uncle Henry will talk to him. You take care of yourself."

Cork drove to Gooseberry Lane, spent a couple of minutes removing the tracking device from Stephen's Jeep, and put it in the garage. "We don't want anyone knowing where you're going. Make sure you're not followed, okay?" He reached out his hand to his son. "I hope the sweat gives you what you need."

Stephen's grip was less than firm. "I wish I knew exactly what that was."

Cork watched his son drive away. Among all the weights that had settled on Cork's shoulders lately, one of the heaviest was his concern for Stephen, who seemed so lost. Or maybe not lost but searching desperately for deeper truths. In that search, Cork, who was one kind of man, didn't know how to help his son, who was another. Or maybe Stephen already understood the world in a way that would forever elude his father. So Cork wondered, as he stared at the rearview mirror watching Stephen grow distant in the Jeep, which of them was nearer the important truths. Who was it who was really lost?

His cell phone rang. He figured it was Bo returning his call. It wasn't.

The voice on the other end, electronically altered, said, "What's on the black box will make headlines. You want the black box?"

"Who is this?"

"Do you want the black box?"

"I want the box."

"It will cost you ten thousand."

"What about my friends?"

"First the black box. Then we'll talk about your friends."

"I want to know they're all right."

"Okay, for another ten grand you get them, too."

"Are they all right?"

"They're in one piece."

"How do I know that?"

"Get the money and you'll have proof."

"How do we do this?"

"There's a town meeting tonight. Go to it."

"Then what?"

"You'll be contacted there. I want the money in small bills and in a backpack, the kind a kid might use to carry his schoolbooks. Got it?"

"Yeah, I got it."

"One more thing. No cops. Bring in cops and you'll never see that black box or your friends again."

The call ended and Cork stood for a moment, a little stunned. Then his cell phone rang again. It was Bo this time, finally calling back. Cork explained the two situations: the extortion demand and Blessing's disappearance.

"The money's no problem," Bo said. "Let me handle that. Stupid question, I know, but did you happen to recognize the caller's number?"

"A six-one-two area code. The Twin Cities."

"I'd lay odds it's from a burner phone, but give it to me and I'll have it checked. Where are you now?"

"I'm about to head out to Blessing's place."

"Where is it?"

Cork gave him directions.

"I'll arrange for the ransom money, then meet you there."

Although he'd swept the cabin to be sure there were no bugs, Bo stepped onto the deck to make the call. He stood in the warm autumn sunlight, with gold-leafed birches all around him.

"Twenty thousand?" she said. "That's it? They could have asked for ten times that amount." She was quiet. Then, "O'Connor got the call. Or claimed he did. But he was one of the men searching the woods where the tail section came down. Bo, is it possible he's not the man you think he is?"

"He's the man I think he is, all right. But maybe some of the others aren't."

Bo considered the disappeared Ned and Monkey Love, the vanished Hukaris, Tom Blessing, Daniel English. He'd never met the Loves, so had no idea about them. Ditto the Hukaris. Blessing? He'd seemed a man truly distraught about his mother's death, but that didn't mean he wasn't capable of trying to extort money from wealthy people. English? A family man. Would he jeopardize his family for a mere twenty grand?

"I'll relay this to Olympia's father. We'll get the money to you this afternoon."

"No cops. O'Connor said the guy was clear about it."

"And we'll go with that?"

"For now. One more thing. Could you check the number the call came from? It's probably a burner phone, but let's be sure."

After he'd given her the number, a wind rose, rustling the leaves and branches of the birch trees, a sound like whispering.

"Does he know?" Bo asked. Even though he was sure the phone wasn't bugged, he still used no names. "Does he know about you and me, about all of this?"

"We've kept him in the dark. Plausible deniability. When the money's on its way, I'll let you know. And, Bo?"

"I'm here."

"Thank you. For everything."

"Yeah."

She was gone. No goodbye. He slipped the cell phone into his pocket, listened to the whisper of the golden trees, watched a small sailboat far out drift across the ruffling blue of the lake, and he thought: *Some people lead simple lives. Lucky them.*

Daniel was waiting beside his truck when Cork pulled up. "I checked the house. Nothing apparent. Where's Stephen?"

"He went back to Crow Point to finish his sweat. There's another complication." Cork told Daniel about the ransom call.

"This just gets weirder and weirder. You can get the money?"

"Bo said he'd take care of that. He's on his way here now. I'm going inside to have a look for myself."

He moved through the Blessings' house room by room. Like Daniel before him, Cork found nothing helpful.

When Bo arrived, Cork and Daniel met him in the yard. "Just like the others, Tom's vanished into thin air," Cork said.

"Think we'll find his truck burned out somewhere?" Bo asked.

"At this point, I don't know what to expect. You arranged for the money?"

"It'll be here this afternoon."

"Coming from Jerome Hill, the senator's father? He's your client, right?"

Bo gave him a stony look and said, "How do you figure?"

"Our former First Lady, Kate Dixon, has been with the senator's family since the crash, offering comfort, the media say. You saved Kate Dixon's life. Now you're a hotshot private security operative. If the senator's family wanted Olympia McCarthy's death investigated outside official channels, who would she counsel them to use? And pulling together twenty thousand dollars on the spur of the moment is nothing for someone like Jerome Hill. Tell me I'm wrong."

Bo hesitated, then said, "How long have you suspected?"

"A while."

"This stays between us." He glanced at Daniel, who gave a nod of agreement.

Cork said, "Jerome Hill is a very wealthy man. I imagine he'd be willing to pay ten times twenty thousand for the flight recorder."

"What does that tell you?" Bo said.

"My first guess is that it's someone who thinks twenty grand is a lot. There are plenty of folks on the Iron Range who've been strapped for cash for years. Twenty grand might seem like a pretty big windfall."

"A lot of risk."

"Risk and the Iron Range go hand in hand."

"It's somebody who knows you, Cork, knows you're involved in all this. If they know what's on that flight recorder, it's probably somebody who understands how to read that information. So someone savvy with electronics. Sound like anyone you know?"

Cork and Daniel exchanged a glance.

"Tom Blessing," Cork told him.

"Fill me in."

"Tom was always a smart kid," Cork said. "When I broke up the Red Boyz—that was the gang he was part of on the reservation—he began taking coursework at the community college. Computer technology, programming, electronics. He's the tech wizard for our tribal offices, teaches classes at the community center in Allouette to folks who want to learn more about computers, or any new electronic technology, for that matter. Cell phones, tablets, computers, you name it."

"Another thing," Daniel said. "Tom's been taking flying lessons from Cal Blaine out at the airport. I don't know how that fits in, but I'm guessing it adds to everything he might know about the senator's plane."

Cork scanned the wild landscape that surrounded the Blessings' house—the wide marsh with tamaracks along the edge, the rugged, pine-covered hills. It had been an isolated world once, but no longer. The digital age.

"Tom Blessing?" he said quietly. "It doesn't feel right."

"Easy enough to find out," Daniel said. "Somebody waits here to see if he comes back."

"Could be a long wait," Bo said. "Maybe a waste of manpower."

"Better idea?" Daniel asked.

"Not at the moment. You volunteering?"

"I'll take the first shift anyway."

Cork gestured toward Daniel's sidearm. "Keep that thing handy."

Daniel gave him a two-fingered salute and headed into the house.

"Feels clunky," Cork said. "The paltry amount, me as the go-between."

"If you've never been involved in extortion before, clunky's probably the norm," Bo replied. "If it's a ruse, I can't think of any reason why. We don't have a solid handle on anything, so there's no real investigation to sidetrack."

"You said you had some contacts to check with about our visitor last night. Anything there?"

"Didn't pan out," Bo said. "Sorry."

"You still have anybody inside Secret Service who could check something for you?"

"I still had a lot of friends there when I left."

"If I gave you some government license plate numbers, think you could track down who they belong to?"

"I could give it a try."

Cork tore the sheet from the notepad on which he'd written the plate numbers of the vehicles he'd spotted coming and going from the airport hangar where the crash investigation continued.

"No agency prefix code," Bo noted. "These people want to

remain anonymous. I can't guarantee anything, but I'll give it a shot. So what next?"

"I'm going to track down Cal Blaine, find out about Tom Blessing and his flight lessons."

"So, the regional airport?"

"That's right. Maybe you should come along. That way we're together if instructions for the exchange come."

"All right," Bo agreed.

As he prepared to leave, Cork took a last look at the little house isolated in the great woods. Daniel could take care of himself, but with no idea of what was going on in Tamarack County, Cork was still deeply concerned. The last thing he wanted was for his daughter's husband to join the missing.

CHAPTER 29

The guards in front of the large hangar that was being used to store and sort the pieces of the wreckage made no attempt to interfere with Bo and Cork as they parked in front of a small office a hundred yards away. A sign above the office door read: NORTH COUNTRY AIR ACADEMY.

"Delusions of grandeur," Cork said, pointing toward the sign. "It's just Cal, a one-man operation."

Scrawled on a sheet of paper taped to the office door were the words *Flight Lesson. Back 2:30 P.M.* Cork peered through the glass on the door. "Empty." He checked his watch. "Half an hour to kill. There's a little food place across the road. I haven't had any lunch. You hungry?"

"Come to think of it," Bo said.

At the roadhouse, they ordered burgers and fries and sat on the patio, eating and watching vehicles come and go. Cork was right. Almost all the plates were government issue.

"Must feel like a violation," Bo said.

"The quiet is one of the things I've always loved about where I live."

"Busy in the summer, I imagine."

"Not this way."

"I grew up in the city, but when I was a teenager, I spent time on a farm near Blue Earth. I understand about the quiet. You're a lucky man, Cork."

"Because of the quiet?"

"And the family. And that you have a place you call home."

"You don't?"

"Never have."

"Ever thought of settling down?"

"Lone wolf."

"The strength of the wolf is the pack."

"Is that an Indian saying?"

"Rudyard Kipling, actually. *The Jungle Book.* One of my grandson's favorite movies."

Bo wondered what it would be like to have children and grandchildren, a thread of responsibility that ran through generations. He figured he had enough trouble just worrying about himself.

His cell phone rang. The new burner phone he was carrying.

"I've got to take this." He moved away from Cork.

"The money is on its way," she said. "Olympia's brother is bringing it up by helicopter. He'll call you when he arrives. Any more ransom instructions?"

"Nothing so far. Were your people able to trace the number?"

"Not yet. Like you said, probably a burner phone."

"I might have something for you on this end. One of the Indians who was first on the crash scene is an electronics whiz. He was also a gang member in his younger days. He's gone missing. There's a chance he's behind the extortion. It's possible he grabbed the flight recorder. If so, he may very well know what's on it."

"Name?"

"Tom Blessing. His mother died yesterday, questionable circumstances."

Nothing from her end for a moment. "I worry about you."

"That's something."

And she was gone.

Bo relayed to Cork that the ransom money was coming.

"I keep wondering why the town meeting," Cork said. "It seems way too public."

"Like you said, this feels clunky. Strikes me as someone who's never been involved in this kind of thing before. Would that fit Blessing?"

"Yeah, and me, too. How about you? Ever been in the middle of something like this before?"

"A couple years ago, I was asked to be the go-between in a kidnap ransom that involved the son of an Argentine diplomat."

"How'd that go?"

"Not well. I made the drop. We got the info to locate the boy. Turned out what we paid for was his body."

"Did you find out who was behind it?"

"We knew who was behind it, just couldn't touch them."

"Must have left a sour taste."

Bo heard the sound of a small plane and scanned the sky. "Officially we couldn't touch them. Unofficially? That was another thing. There was payback. But in the end, the taste was still bitter."

Under the cloud of that memory, Bo watched the plane descend and approach the airport runway.

"That'll be Cal," Cork said. Then his cell phone rang. "Yeah, Harmon," he answered. He listened, looked concerned. "I can't be there for a while. Stephen's out on Crow Point. Okay if I send him?" He listened some more. "I'll tell him to make it fast." He ended the call. "Harmon Goodsky, from Allouette."

"The one surveilling Sarah LeDuc and Beulah Love?"

"That's him. He says a couple of strangers have been cruising through Allouette with a particular interest in the Mocha Moose. He took some shots."

"Fired at them?"

"No, photos."

"Have they tried anything with Beulah?"

"Just keeping an eye on the place, sounds like."

"Stephen can handle this?" Bo liked the kid, but he wasn't sure how he might deal with a situation that could easily go south.

"I think he needs to understand that he can." And Cork made the call to his son.

Bo and Cork were waiting at the office when Cal Blaine returned. He was bald, a little heavy, wearing a red flannel shirt. A kid was with him, maybe nineteen. They shook hands; the kid got into one of the vehicles parked in front of the office and drove away.

"Hey there, Cork," Blaine said. "Decided to take up flying?"

"Not me, Cal. Just wanted to ask you a few questions, if I could."

"Sure. Come on in."

Blaine unlocked the office door, and the men followed him inside. It was simply furnished: a gray metal desk, three roller chairs, two file cabinets, a bulletin board with lots of papers tacked to it, a radio set.

"Have a seat." Blaine took the one behind his desk. "Didn't catch the name, stranger."

"Just call me Bo."

"Good enough." He looked to Cork. "So, ask away."

"I understand you've been giving Tom Blessing flight lessons."

"Yeah, he's working on getting his private pilot's license. Say, I heard about his mom. Too bad."

"Did he say anything about why he wanted to fly?"

"Why does anyone want to fly?" Blaine opened his arms. "Freedom."

"Would the instructions you give him or the manuals he reads tell him about the safety equipment that planes are required to carry?"

"Of course."

"Did he ask you questions in that regard?"

"Nothing special, at least that I recall. Why? What's this about?"

"Tom's gone missing. I'm trying to find him. Anything I can learn might help."

"You think he, what, flew away?"

"You never know. And with all this going on." Cork eyed the hangar visible beyond the window, where the NTSB was at work.

"I know. Terrible, terrible."

Bo asked, "Were you out here the day Senator McCarthy's plane went down?"

"I'm always out here."

"Anything unusual about that day?"

"Matter of fact, yeah."

"What exactly?" Cork said.

"The runway lights never came on."

"What do you mean?"

"We're a small airport, no control tower. Planes that want to land have to click the runway lights on."

"Click?"

"The pilot turns to the local frequency and keys the mic. Three clicks for low intensity, five for medium, seven for high. There were low clouds that day, so the runway might have been tough to spot without the lights. Any good pilot would have clicked them on."

"But the pilot in Senator McCarthy's plane didn't?"

"That's right."

"When would the pilot have clicked the lights?" Bo asked.

"On the approach, about seven miles out. A lot of pilots use Desolation Mountain as a visual cue."

"Why wouldn't the pilot have turned on the lights?"

Blaine shrugged. "From what I understand, he knew our airport. So, either an oversight or a misjudgment. Or equipment failure, I suppose."

"Equipment failure?"

"There was lightning in the area that day. Maybe a lightning strike to the plane knocked out the electronics."

"Does that happen a lot?"

"Pretty rare, but it does happen, mostly with small aircraft. As I understand it, after the Duluth control tower gave them their approach heading, there was no more communication from the plane, which wouldn't be unusual unless they sent out a distress call."

"Wouldn't the pilot have done that if they were going down?" Cork asked.

"If he had time and didn't panic."

"And if the radio worked," Bo added.

Blaine sat back. "Too bad there wasn't a flight recorder aboard. Would have answered a lot of questions."

"Yeah," Bo said. "Too bad."

"Did you tell anybody this?" Cork asked.

"Talked to an FBI agent," Blaine said. "He told me it probably wasn't important. Haven't heard anything since. Nobody's followed up."

"Do me a favor, Cal. You hear from Tom Blessing, will you let me know?"

"You got it."

As they walked to their vehicles, Cork said, "I hope the twenty thousand buys us some answers tonight."

Bo made no reply, but he couldn't help seeing in his mind's eye the image of the Argentine boy, his body curled in the trunk of an abandoned Saab and, except for his wrists and ankles bound tightly with white cord and the red gash across his throat, looking as though he might have been sleeping.

CHAPTER 30

Once again, Stephen's attempt at a sweat had been thwarted. The call had come just as he was preparing to enter the lodge. His father had called Rainy, who'd handed Stephen her cell phone. When he'd heard his father's request, what could he say?

Henry Meloux was there, recovered from his own sweat. On his arrival at Crow Point, Stephen had asked the old Mide if the sweat had given him the answers he was hoping for.

"I did not ask for answers," Henry had said. "I asked for understanding."

"Do you understand?" Stephen had asked.

"I understand that an old man's body is not so weak as you might expect." The Mide had grinned. "And I understand that all things come in their time. That includes answers."

Although Henry had seemed satisfied, Stephen found this not helpful at all.

He was on his way to Allouette now, driving the ATV side-by-side Leah Duling kept at her cabin and used when she wanted to go into town. In the winter, she drove a snowmobile. These were new additions to Crow Point, ones that Leah had insisted on when she took up residence there to see to Henry's needs. It was a full five miles into Allouette. For most of his life, Henry had walked to the little rez town, or the farther distance to Aurora, with no problem. The old man seemed just fine letting Leah drive the noisy machines. Stephen suspected it had more to do with Leah's weaknesses at seventy-plus years of age than Henry's at over a hundred.

All things come in their time. A variation on Henry's usual mantra: Patience. So what had the sweat delivered to Henry that he didn't already know?

Then Stephen thought about Rainy, who was also a Mide, and who'd told him many times that one of the things a healer knows is that human beings already have within them an understanding of how to heal themselves. Often, all a Mide did was help guide them to this understanding. A sweat was like that, Stephen decided, and he wondered, *So what do I already know that I need to understand?*

When he reached Allouette, he was still in the dark.

He parked the ATV in front of Goodsky's photography studio. When he entered, the place seemed empty.

"Hello?" he called.

A young teenager stepped through the curtains at the back of the gallery. Stephen had heard about Goodsky's grandson, who'd come up from the Cities to live on the rez, but he'd never met the kid. He seemed fragile to Stephen and skittish, like a small animal in the forest. He didn't look Stephen in the eye. He held a photograph of Iron Lake reflecting the fall foliage, and when he realized Stephen was looking, he turned the photo so the image was hidden.

"I'm Stephen O'Connor."

The kid said nothing.

"You must be Winston."

The kid nodded, still mute.

"I'm looking for your grandfather. He's expecting me."

"Wait here." The kid disappeared through the curtains.

Stephen strolled the gallery, studying the photographs that hung on the walls. He was no art critic, but he knew what he liked, and he liked very much what he saw. The photographs captured the spirit of the land he called home in moments of stunning beauty. Harmon Goodsky's work was well represented, as were the works of other Native photographers. Stephen had never thought of himself as an artist, but the images on the walls in the little gallery made him wish that he were. Then he found himself thinking he'd probably be no better at art than he was at interpreting visions.

"*Anin,* Stephen."

Harmon Goodsky limped through the curtains, all alone. He held a photograph out to Stephen.

"I snapped this shot of one of the men who was watching Sarah's place, and I blew it up."

The photo showed a man framed in the window on the driver's side of a black pickup spattered with dried, rust-colored mud. He wore a jean jacket over a flannel shirt, and a black stocking cap. His face was broad, ruddy, with a diamond-shaped scar at the corner of his left eye.

"You got a photo of only one of them?"

"They were parked down the street from the Mocha Moose for a while, two of them. I walked down to confront them, but they took off. Not before I was able to snap that. I thought maybe your dad could use it to nail these guys before they cause Sarah or Beulah any trouble."

"I think this'll help."

"They wouldn't have something to do with Phil Hukari's burned-out truck, would they?"

"We're trying to find out."

"What is it they want out here on the rez?"

"We don't know for sure, Harmon."

"Government men, maybe?" He pronounced the word as *guvmint* and squinted one eye as if taking aim. "Something to do with the senator's plane crash?"

"Might be."

Goodsky looked beyond Stephen, out the front window of the gallery. Across the street was the Mocha Moose, but Stephen understood that it wasn't the coffee shop Goodsky was seeing. In the way he'd earlier sensed a great sickness in the man that wasn't cancer, Stephen felt now an overwhelming sense of anger and anguish, and he understood that Harmon Goodsky had suffered a deep wound that had never fully healed. Stephen had seen Vietnam vets and, more recently, veterans on the rez who'd returned from Iraq and Afghanistan, men in whom he'd sensed a wounding of the soul and a poisonous festering. He'd witnessed the erratic, often destructive behavior that sometimes resulted. It wasn't PTSD, though clearly some were suffering from that condition. And it wasn't the slow debilitation that came from exposure to toxins like Agent Orange. It was a loss of the connection with the Great Mystery, the spirit that ran through all creation and united all things. Those men, Stephen understood, were lost, disconnected from others and from their true selves. Deep inside him, he felt the call to heal.

"Harmon?" Stephen spoke quietly, but the man didn't seem to hear. "Harmon?" he tried again, with no result.

"Grandpa?" Winston Goodsky stood in front of the curtains, looking concerned. "Grandpa?"

Goodsky stirred, returned from wherever his mind had taken him. "What is it, Winston?"

"The television's having trouble again."

"I'll take a look." Goodsky nodded toward the photograph in Stephen's hand. "Tell your father I want to know what he finds out."

"I'll do that."

Goodsky moved past his grandson, and Stephen could hear his heavy, uneven footsteps as he mounted a stairway out of sight.

"He gets that way sometimes," Winston said. "Kind of lost. I have to watch him."

"If you ever need a hand, you call, okay?"

The kid looked down, studied the floor, mute once again.

Stephen crossed the street and found Sarah LeDuc inside the Mocha Moose, wiping down tables. Beulah Love was there, too, helping behind the counter.

"*Anin,* Stephen," Sarah greeted him.

"*Boozhoo,*" he replied. "My dad sent me to make sure everything's okay."

"All good here. What's that picture you're holding?"

If he showed her, he'd have to explain that Harmon Goodsky was keeping an eye on her and Beulah, and he wasn't certain how that might go down with her. But he didn't really have a choice.

"Harmon snapped this of one of the men who seem to be watching Ms. Love, and now you."

Sarah studied the photo. "Beulah?"

Beulah Love left the counter and joined them.

"Look familiar?"

"Maybe. It's hard to tell."

"Where did Harmon shoot this?"

"Here in Allouette," Stephen said. "They were parked just down the street."

"*Chimooks* thinking they wouldn't stand out on the rez? They're either awfully bold or awfully stupid." Sarah winked at Stephen. "I know where I'd lay my bet. Can we keep this?"

"I'd like to show it to my dad."

"Sure. I'll get a copy from Harmon. Maybe take him some apple pie to thank him for keeping an eye on us. Tell your dad that Beulah and I are doing fine." She turned to the other woman. "Aren't we?"

"We're fine," Beulah said, but not with any certainty.

Back at the ATV, Stephen sat on the photograph so that it wouldn't blow away. He donned his helmet and headed off, intending to return the way he'd come, along a back road that followed the north shore of Iron Lake. The marina parking lot, as he passed it, was almost empty. On a summer day it would have been crowded with cars. This afternoon, only a couple of vehicles were parked there, one of them a black pickup truck spattered with rust-colored mud.

He swung into the lot and stopped near the concession stand, which, in the fall, was open only on weekends. He dismounted from the ATV, removed his helmet, and set it atop the photograph of the man in the black pickup. Trying not to be too conspicuous, he walked toward the marina docks, past the truck, which was empty. The license plates, both front and back, were so mud-covered they were unreadable. He continued to the docks, where the slips were full of sailboats and launches that, in another month, would be dry-docked for the winter. As nearly as he could tell, he was alone.

He figured that if the two men had a boat, they could linger on the water and with field glasses keep an eye on the comings and goings at the Mocha Moose, only a few hundred yards distant. But Stephen saw no boat. The shoreline was rugged, with a mix of hardwoods and tall undergrowth. He considered the possibility that the men had hidden themselves somewhere in the trees or brush and were surveilling the coffee shop that way.

He took out his cell phone and made a call.

"Stay where you are," his father told him. "I'm calling Daniel. He's at the Blessings' place and can get to you faster than I can. But

I'm on my way. Don't, under any circumstances, approach these guys on your own."

Wait for Daniel. Wait for his father. It was clear he wasn't trusted to handle things on his own.

What kind of man do they think I am?

He started into the trees, moving slowly, carefully, keeping low. He followed the shoreline as it edged Allouette. In the end, he found nothing and turned back, disappointed.

They were waiting for him when he broke from the trees on his return to the marina. They flanked him, coming, it seemed, from nowhere. They were taller and broader than he, wearing sunglasses, and with their stocking caps pulled low.

One of them held up the photograph Stephen had left under the helmet in the ATV. "Who are you?" His voice was like the rumble of distant thunder.

Stephen's throat had gone instantly dry and his heart had begun to leap. Maybe it was the surprise of the men's sudden appearance, or maybe the realization that he was in over his head.

"No one," he replied.

The other man said, "Who are you working for?"

"Nobody."

"Where'd you get this?" They shoved the photograph at his face.

"Why are you so interested in Beulah Love?" he fired back, anger taking over his fear.

The man in the photo grabbed Stephen's jacket in his fist and pulled him up to tiptoe. "Who was the old coot that took my picture?"

When Stephen gave no answer, the man released his grip and gave him a hard shove.

His companion's eyes darted all around. "We need to take this somewhere private." He reached inside his jean jacket and pulled out a handgun. "Let's go, kid."

"I'm not going anywhere."

The barrel of the gun clipped his face and Stephen went down. He was pulled immediately back to his feet and shoved toward the marina parking lot. He tried to resist, and the gun barrel again became a bludgeon across the side of his head. Once more, Stephen went down. This time, things went dark, his vision full of sparks, the world muted.

When he came back to himself, he found Daniel English kneeling beside him.

"Don't get up." Daniel put a hand gently against Stephen's chest.

"I'm okay." Stephen could hear the weakness in his own voice.

"You've got a couple of nasty cuts." Daniel drew a clean handkerchief from his back pocket and folded it. "Here, hold that tight against your head."

Stephen pressed it to a place where he could already feel a goose egg forming.

Daniel pulled out his cell phone and made a call. "I'm with him, Cork. They worked him over pretty good. We need to get him looked at. I'm taking him to the clinic here in Allouette. We'll meet you there."

CHAPTER 31

The cut across Stephen's cheek took three stitches. The cut across the side of his head, four more. Mary Gomes, the PA at the tribal clinic, advised Cork that to be certain the blows hadn't done more significant damage, Stephen should be seen at the Aurora Community Hospital for a CT scan or MRI. Cork's son absolutely refused to go but accepted the ibuprofen the PA offered.

They talked in the clinic parking lot—Cork, Stephen, Daniel, and Bo.

"Did you get a good look at them?" Cork asked.

Failure was written all over Stephen's damaged face. "They were wearing sunglasses, stocking caps pulled low."

"I saw the pickup swing out of the marina lot," Daniel told them. "I didn't know it was important until I talked to Stephen, so I didn't get a plate number."

"You wouldn't have anyway," Stephen said. "The plates were covered with mud."

"What about the photo?"

"They took it," Stephen said. "They wanted to know where I

got it." He eyed his father, as if afraid some kind of accusation was forthcoming. "I didn't tell them."

"I'll get another print from Harmon."

"I blew it." Stephen shook his head angrily. "I screwed up."

"Nothing's happened that can't be fixed." Cork put his hand on his son's shoulder, but Stephen stiffened under the touch.

"All right, here's the plan," Cork said. "Daniel, I want you to take Stephen back to Crow Point. Put him into Rainy's care."

"I'm fine," Stephen insisted.

"Your head doesn't hurt?"

"A little."

"I'm sure Rainy can help with that. You need to stay quiet for a while, just to be on the safe side."

"What about Leah's ATV?" Stephen glanced in the direction of the marina.

"We'll see to that later. Okay, Daniel?"

Cork's son-in-law gave a simple nod, and Stephen, zombielike, followed him.

When they'd gone, Cork said to Bo, "I'm going to see Goodsky, get another print of that photo. Then I'll pop into the Mocha Moose and check on Sarah and Beulah. After that, I'm thinking I'll out head to Crow Point."

"I've got some things to see to myself," Bo told him. "I'll have the people I know run those plates you gave me from the airport, see if we can get a better idea who's involved in whatever's going on up here. When the courier delivers the money for the exchange, I'll give you a call and we can figure where to rendezvous."

"Thanks for your help, Bo."

"Goes both ways."

Cork walked the stone's throw to the gallery, where Goodsky was hanging a photograph. The image was of a soaring eagle silhouetted against a cloud. There were only three colors involved. The black silhouette, the white cloud, the blue sky. It was so simple but so stirring in the emotions it evoked in Cork—freedom, flight, release, all of it somehow accompanied by a sense of peace.

"I want that," he said.

Goodsky smiled. "Not for sale. It's one of Winston's. I just put it up so anyone who comes in can marvel at it. I'm good. My grandson? A genius. Did Stephen give you the photo?"

"He didn't have the chance. The man in it beat him up and took it."

Goodsky gave this somber consideration. "Did Stephen tell this thug where the photo came from?"

"No, but he paid a price for his silence. Three stitches across his cheek and more across the side of his head."

"I'm sorry, Cork."

"Not your fault, but I need another print."

"I'll have one for you in a few minutes. Can you wait?"

"I'll come back. I want to talk to Sarah and Beulah."

"I'll have it ready for you."

The women were fine. Cork felt obliged to tell them about Stephen's injuries, mostly so that they understood fully the risks that might be involved.

"I shouldn't stay here," Beulah said to Sarah. "I'm putting you in danger."

"We're seeing this through together, *nimisenh.*"

"Nimisenh?" Beulah's eyes teared up. *"Migwech, nishiime."*

"If we need you, Cork, we'll holler," Sarah assured him.

As he crossed the street to the gallery, Cork thought about what had just occurred. *Nimisenh,* Sarah LeDuc had called Beulah Love. Which meant "my older sister." And in reply, Beulah had called Sarah *nishiime,* which meant "my younger sister." For Beulah, who had separated herself in so many ways from the people of her blood, who'd believed only a day ago that she had no one on the rez to whom she could turn in her time of need, this was a blessing. Once again Cork was reminded of what it meant to be Anishinaabe, a part of this community that, despite its struggle against unrelenting cruelties for generations, had continued to have a strong, welcoming heart. Even in the midst of all the strangeness and menace that had descended on the Iron Lake Reservation, he had witnessed a moment of true beauty.

In the gallery, Goodsky had the print waiting. "These guys mean business."

"I wish I knew what exactly that business is."

"White guys beating up people on the rez. Makes my blood boil. Anything I can do?"

"Just keep an eye on Beulah and Sarah."

"Goes without saying. But I want something in return. When you find out what's going on, who these *chimooks* are, you let me know."

"It's a deal."

In Henry's cabin on Crow Point, Cork found Stephen drinking some kind of tea Rainy had prepared. Stephen looked drained, and there was a sullenness in him that worried Cork.

"How're you feeling?"

"Fine."

"That's surprising," Rainy said. "Those cuts, that knot, most people would be feeling a little pain."

"I've taken a lot more than a little pain before."

"I don't doubt your ability to endure pain," Rainy said gently. "I'm just reminding you that there's no shame in admitting when it hurts."

Cork was pretty sure what hurt Stephen most wasn't his head.

"Where are Henry and Leah and Waaboo?"

"They took Trixie for a little walk," Daniel said.

"There's something we need to discuss."

"That tone always means trouble," Rainy said. "As if we didn't already have enough."

Cork filled them in on the ransom details, at least as they stood.

Rainy looked worried. "Why do they want you to make the exchange?"

Daniel said, "If it is Tom Blessing behind this, it makes a kind of sense. He knows Cork."

"You really believe Tom Blessing would do something like this?" Rainy asked.

"I have to accept the possibility," Cork replied. "If we get the flight recorder back, it doesn't matter who's behind it."

"Why at the town meeting?" Daniel said. "It seems so public."

"The meeting's at the high school. Tom went there, probably knows it pretty well. He may have some special drop site in mind. I like the location. Might be to my advantage."

"How so?"

"Too many witnesses to try something untoward."

"Like shooting you?" Rainy said.

"In a word, yes."

"I should be there with you," Stephen said. "I went to that high school. I know it a lot better than you do, Dad."

"You're staying here. You've already taken enough chances for one day."

Cork saw that this directive didn't sit well with his son, but it was nonnegotiable.

"Tom Blessing." Rainy crossed her arms, clearly unconvinced.

Cork checked his watch. "We'll know in a few hours."

CHAPTER 32

When Gerard answered, he was breathing hard, as if he'd been running or exercising. "Do you have something for me?"

"A question," Bo replied. "Was it your guys who beat up Stephen O'Connor?"

"I've left the locals to you. And why would I have the kid beat up?"

"Exactly. Unless you don't have control over all your operatives."

"You're the only one who ever worries me." Gerard gasped for air. "So, that's it?"

"There's more. It's possible we'll have the flight recorder in our hands tonight."

Gerard was suddenly quiet, as if not breathing at all. Then, "How?"

"O'Connor got a ransom call. Twenty thousand dollars. The exchange is tonight."

"Where's the money coming from?"

"I've arranged for that. My own resources."

"And O'Connor's making the drop?"

"That's right. It's supposed to go down at the town meeting in Aurora."

"I'll have men there."

"Not a good idea. They spot your guys, they might run. Twenty grand isn't much to risk. Leave it to me."

"Right," Gerard said, his voice cold. "And we know how that turned out for you the last time."

Bo ignored the reference to the murdered Argentine kid. "I'll take care of this."

"Who's behind it?"

"At the moment, it's looking like one of the Indians who was on the scene early, a guy name of Tom Blessing."

"Blessing. The one whose mother croaked?"

"Compassionately put."

"Twenty grand. Sounds cheap, even for an Indian."

"Maybe Blessing needs the cash fast. Gambling debt or something."

"Find out."

"Let's focus on securing the recorder first. We can worry about rounding up Blessing later."

"If you get the recorder, there's a bonus in it for you."

A bonus, Bo thought, after he'd ended the call. With Gerard, and depending upon who'd brought him in, that could easily turn out to be a bullet in the brain.

He kayaked to the little island just offshore from Gerard's operations center and downloaded to his cell phone what had been recorded by the voice-activated bug on the window. He reset the instrument, kayaked back to the wooded point where he'd left his Jeep, and listened to the recorded conversations. Mostly they were orders Gerard had delivered to his subordinates and discussions of where to look for what they continued to call the "waves." His name came up. Gerard spoke of him as "our tick on the skin of things up here." That made Bo smile. Then Gerard said something that caused Bo to replay the recording.

"When we get the egg that's dropped, maybe we can shoot down the eagle, too, and close up shop here."

The egg that's dropped. The eagle. These sounded like images straight out of the vision Stephen O'Connor had related, a vision Bo had readily dismissed as Indian voodoo stuff.

He started his Jeep and headed toward the double-trunk birch that marked the beginning of the trail to Crow Point. He needed to talk to Stephen again.

The call came a few minutes later. It was Olympia McCarthy's brother. He informed Bo that he'd just landed at Olson Field.

"I'm on my way," Bo said.

"Look for the chopper. I'm waiting inside."

It was going on four o'clock when Bo had the money in hand, twenty thousand dollars in small bills. Per the extortionist's instructions, it was in a backpack, the kind a high school kid might use to carry books, nothing that would be out of place in a crowd in a high school auditorium. Bo kept the pack on the seat beside him as he continued to the double-trunk birch, then slipped the straps over his shoulders as he began the hike into Crow Point.

He arrived at the old man's cabin to find that all wasn't well. Stephen O'Connor had disappeared. An hour earlier, he'd told everyone he was going out for a few minutes to get some air. He never returned.

"You didn't run into him when you came down the trail?" Cork asked.

Bo shook his head. "And his Jeep wasn't parked on the road either."

"Then he's taken off." Cork was clearly upset.

Meloux, the old medicine man, didn't seem bothered by the kid's absence. "You have put a log across his path, Corcoran O'Connor. He has simply jumped the log."

"It could get him killed, Henry."

"You think he does not know that? And you think he does not understand that you are also willing to put your life in danger? He is his father's son. Would you have him be someone different?"

"Did you try calling him?" Bo asked.

"He's not answering."

"I'm betting he'll be at the town meeting," English said. "With all that bandaging on his head, he'll stand out like a clown. You won't miss him."

"The men who beat him up won't miss him either."

Little Waaboo and his mother sat in the corner of the cabin, the old dog, Trixie, between them. Waaboo looked up from petting the dog. "The monster won't get him. He's too smart."

"What monster?" Bo asked.

"It's a nightmare Waaboo had," Jenny explained.

Which brought Bo back to the reason he'd come to Crow Point. "In this vision your son has, he sees a kid shoot an eagle out of the sky, right?"

"That's right," Cork said.

"And this eagle, as it falls, drops an egg?"

"Yeah."

"The egg has got to be the flight recorder," Bo said. "What about the eagle?"

"I've been thinking it was the senator's plane."

"And the kid?"

"The kid is Stephen," English said.

"And not Stephen," Cork said. "Look, the town meeting's in a couple of hours. I'm heading into Aurora, see if I can track Stephen down before that. Bo, you should probably come with me."

"I'd like to be there, too," English threw in.

Cork shook his head. "I understand, Daniel, but with all the confusion and the disappearances on the reservation, I think it would be best if you stayed. I'd hate myself if I asked you to come and something happened here while we were gone."

"No one knows we're here," English said.

"Maybe. But do you want to take that chance?" He glanced toward Waaboo.

With a nod that was clearly reluctant, English gave in.

Rainy walked with her husband and Bo outside and into the meadow.

"I parked at Crow Point East. That's what we call the parking area nearest Allouette," Cork told Bo. "You came in along the path from the Aurora side?"

"Yeah."

"Let's split up here. I'll meet you at the high school half an hour before the town meeting."

"If you hear anything more, call me," Bo said.

He headed toward the trees where the path to the double-trunk began. Before he left the meadow, he looked back. In the yellow slant of the afternoon light, Cork had his wife in his arms, a long goodbye. Bo felt a deep, painful twist of envy.

CHAPTER 33

Stephen removed the bandaging that covered his cheek. The wound beneath was raw and pink, the stitches black across it. His cheek and eye socket were dark-bruised. Even to himself, he was scary to look at. He'd bought something called Neutrogena Healthy Skin liquid makeup. He tapped a bit onto his fingertip and dabbed the flesh-colored goo over his wound. It wasn't the magic cover-up he'd hoped for, but he did look less like Frankenstein. He applied it to the whole bruised area.

His cell phone rang again. His father. He didn't answer. Next came a text message: *Let me know ur ok*. Stephen replied: *OK*.

He changed his clothes, put on jeans, a long-sleeved T-shirt, a gray hoodie, a black stocking cap. He returned to the bathroom, pulled the hood over his head, and was satisfied. It was hard to tell he'd been injured, and if he kept his head down, hard to tell who he was.

He left the house, figuring that if they were looking for him—his father or the men who put the gashes in his head or the people, whoever they were, who were disturbing the spirits of this place he called home—Gooseberry Lane would be one of their stops. He drove to the Pinewood Broiler on Oak Street, took a seat in a booth next to the window, where he could see who came and went. He had a couple of hours to kill before the town meeting. Coffee and something to eat would do the trick.

"Hey, Stephen."

His waitress was Marlee Daychild, the girl he fell in love with in high school. The only girl he'd ever loved, in fact. Their relationship had been a difficult one, for many reasons, most of them, Stephen knew, because of him, because of all the uncertainty, the restlessness that was such a part of who he seemed to be. Like the town of Aurora itself, Marlee was an element of his life that threatened him because of its comfort.

"When did you start working here, Marlee?"

"Never mind that. What happened to you?"

"Nothing," he said.

Marlee was Anishinaabe and lived with her mother on the rez. Her hair was black and long, tied back in a ponytail. Her eyes were dark brown and warm with concern and caring. More caring than he felt he deserved. She wore a T-shirt with the word RESIST printed across the front.

"You got into a fight?" she asked.

"Just a stupid accident."

"Bullshit." She sat across from him in the booth. "You look terrible."

"Thanks."

"Anything you want to talk about?"

Yes, he thought. But he said, "Let it go, Marlee. It's nothing."

Still, she tried again to break through the shell he'd put around himself. "That stupid accident of yours, it wouldn't have anything do with all the trouble on the rez?"

"Are you going to take my order?"

Her brown eyes became hard and sharp, like little drill bits. "Fine." She stood up and said, "What'll you have?"

"Coffee, a patty melt with fries."

She wrote on her pad, turned on her heel, and left him to his brooding.

When she'd gone, Stephen thought about her T-shirt. RESIST. Resist what? But he could feel it inside himself. A stone of resistance. Which was exactly the opposite of the patience and acceptance Henry Meloux had tried for so long to teach him. Stephen wanted to resist everything. What Marlee was offering him. What his father had taught him. The understandings that Henry and Rainy had tried to guide him toward. He didn't want any more visions. He didn't want to sit waiting for answers to come. He had no patience now. He had only questions, and he wanted to track the answers like a hunter and, like a hunter, bring them down.

He stared out the window of the Broiler. Across the street was Ardith Kane's shop, North Star Notions, the display window already full of Halloween decorations. To the left of it, Pflugleman's Rexall Drugs, to the right Finn's Stationery and Office Supply. Rising behind them was the clock tower of the county courthouse. This was all of a piece, a tableau that hadn't changed across the course of his whole life. He felt trapped. In place. In time. In who he was.

"Here's your coffee."

He was startled out of his angry reverie.

"Are you okay, Stephen? Really?" Marlee had put away her own anger, and once again her eyes were soft with concern. "You jumped like you'd been shot."

"I'm fine. Just need some coffee in me."

She smiled gently. "It's not known for settling nerves."

He managed the ghost of a smile. "You're right. Things are a little tough at the moment. I just need some time to think. And maybe a little food in me."

"That I can help with. Your patty melt will be right up."

He lingered more than an hour, as the Pinewood Broiler filled and Marlee got busy with other customers. The sun was just about to set when he signaled her for the check.

"Call me," she told him.

"I will."

"Promise."

And he did.

At the high school, the parking lot was already nearly full. Two State Patrol officers stood at the front door. Stephen joined a small group entering together, and he passed the officers without incident. A loud murmuring came from the auditorium as people gathered, greeted one another, found seats. As with so many of the gatherings that brought Shinnobs into Aurora, the folks from the rez took seats in back. Stephen stood just inside the door, scanning the crowd. He spotted his father in an aisle seat on the far side. Bo Thorson sat not far away. Stephen lowered his head and sat in the dim light of the back row, where he could keep an eye on his father's movements and Thorson's.

A table and two chairs had been set up in the middle of the stage, two microphones on the table. A few minutes after seven, Renée Legris, the mayor of Aurora, and Governor Arne Johnson walked together from one of the wings and took their seats. The audience quieted.

Stephen knew the mayor. Everyone in Aurora knew the mayor. Stephen had served her burgers through the window at Sam's Place. Her daughter had graduated from high school a year behind him. She was a nice enough person, but he'd always felt an uncomfortable energy coming from her, a relentless push. She introduced the governor and offered him the floor.

Governor Arne Johnson was someone Stephen had never liked. His policies had been at odds with so many of the values Stephen held dear. He came from money, not a sin in itself, but it was clear to Stephen that he'd never understood what it was to struggle. Among the policies that Stephen objected to most was Johnson's stand on the undeveloped resources of Minnesota's North Country. He was an advocate for the proposed mine.

The governor opened with an eloquent portrait of Senator McCarthy, which was a very different depiction of her than he'd painted in the past, when their political agendas had clashed, which had been often. He moved smoothly into the issue at hand, the question of granting permits for the proposed mining operation. He defended his own position, which was that moving forward with the mine would be of tremendous benefit to the Iron Range, an area that, in the wake of so many mine closures, continued to suffer economically.

"I understand Senator McCarthy's concerns about sullying the pristine North Country, but I've studied America Midwest Mining's proposal, and I can assure you that there will be multiple safeguards in place, the most modern techniques available to prevent any spillage that might adversely affect the land or the water here. That's my view, but I'm really here to listen, to let you know that your concerns are being heard."

Right, Stephen thought. *In one ear and out the other.*

Mayor Legris opened up the meeting to comments and questions. And there was a landslide. One after another, the residents of Tamarack County gave voice to their fears.

Finally, Dorothy Heinz left her seat near the back of the auditorium and stepped up to the microphone below the stage. She was an old woman, small, white-haired, a little bent, and Stephen knew her well. She'd been one of his Sunday school teachers at St. Agnes. Born in Turtle Lake, Wisconsin, she'd come to the Iron Lake Reservation as a young child to live with her grandparents. During the Second World War, she'd been a member of the Women's Army Corps, and when she came home to the rez, she'd married and become a strong presence in the community. She loved to bake and had taught classes in traditional cooking and in canning, and her berry pies were legendary. When Stephen camped in the Boundary Waters, he still made bannock bread and wild rice leek soup in the way he'd learned from her. She was a strong woman, who could still be found mowing her own lawn on a riding mower, wearing a Twins ball cap. And as she leaned to the microphone and spoke with grace and authority, Stephen thought there was no better voice for her people, the Anishinaabeg.

"I have lived with the beauty of Mother Earth for more than ninety years," she said. "When I was a girl, I went with my grandfather to catch fish in the lakes and the rivers. We plucked blueberries in the clearings where the bears ate them, too. Every fall, we gathered wild rice on Makwa Lake, watched ospreys dive from the trees, listened to the song of the loons coming from the morning mist. Now that I am *nokomis,* a grandmother, I take my eleven grandchildren and my ten great-grandchildren to the places my grandfather took me.

"The earth isn't just rock and dirt and trees and water. It's one thing, one heart, one spirit. It offers us life and beauty and, if we listen, wisdom. And it asks nothing in return, not even gratitude, because giving is the whole reason for its creation.

"And why are we created? To receive, to honor, and to protect. What you talk about here isn't just the wounding of that beautiful, giving spirit. What you talk about here, in your ignorance, is the wounding of the spirit of us all. We are not separate. To kill the water, to kill the fish, to kill the trees, to kill the birds, is to kill ourselves. That is all I have to say."

To great applause, Dorothy Heinz retook her seat.

Then a shout came from the audience: "When I was a boy my father had a job in the Apex Mine, a good-paying job. We drove a nice car and had a nice house. When the mine closed, all that changed. Hell, look around you. The towns on the Iron Range are sliding downhill, and it won't be long before they hit rock bottom. Ghost towns. It was mining built the Range and it's mining that'll save it. We got plenty of ore still in the ground, plenty of minerals, and plenty of men looking for work. Seems to me a match made in heaven. If the governor says the mine's going to be safe, then the mine's going to be safe. I say let 'em start digging. The sooner they get to work, the sooner the rest of us do, too."

Although the wind so far had been against the mine, this spontaneous outburst was met with more than a little applause. From that point on, the comments flew from advocates on both sides of the issue, and Stephen could feel the mounting tension in the air, a taut spring ready to snap.

Then a man leapt up on the far side of the auditorium, Boog Sorenson, someone Stephen had never liked. "We'd've had that mine up and running a long time ago if it wasn't for people like McCarthy," he hollered. "You ask me, that plane crash was the best thing could've happened up here."

Even in a room so contentiously divided, the comment stunned the crowd to silence.

"Sit down and shut up," someone yelled.

"It's a free country," Sorenson asserted. "I've got a right to say what I think."

"And you've had your say." Mayor Legris's voice was stern. "Now sit down and let others speak."

"Let him talk," another voiced shouted. And chaos threatened to descend.

The outburst had drawn Stephen's attention. When he swung his eyes back to where his father had been sitting, the seat was empty. Bo Thorson was gone, too.

CHAPTER 34

When Boog Sorenson began his rant, Cork wanted to stuff his fist down the man's throat. That was generally the response Sorenson elicited from Cork when he opened his mouth. Boog Sorenson had been a deputy under Cork in his first term as sheriff of Tamarack County and was the only officer Cork had ever fired. He took the action after a number of questionable arrests of people of Anishinaabe heritage, and one particularly nasty altercation on the rez, which Sorenson had handled badly and with clear prejudice. In the next election, Sorenson ran against Cork, and much of his platform had been an angry cry against what he characterized as "a blind eye" when it came to policing Indians, on and off the rez. Cork won the election by a landslide, but the bad blood still ran deep between them.

He was tempted to join those shouting down Sorenson, but his cell phone vibrated and the instructions for the ransom drop came as a text: *The gate of the gravel pit. Now. No funny stuff.* It was from the same number as the call that afternoon.

No funny stuff. Straight out of a bad movie. Cork and Bo rose and left while the rant in the auditorium went on. They headed out to Cork's Expedition to pick up the backpack that held the money.

"An access road a hundred yards that way leads right to the gate of the gravel pit," Cork explained. "Unless I get another instruction, looks like the exchange will go down there."

Bo studied the sky. "Getting dark. Hard to see much of anything. I won't be far behind."

"They said no funny stuff. Direct quote."

"Who are we dealing with, the Three Stooges?"

"I'm about to find out." Cork called the number the text had come from but got no answer. Then he texted, *What about my friends?*

A moment later, he got the reply: *Bring the money. You get them and the black box.*

"You're not going to take any chances, right?" Bo said.

"The flight recorder and my friends, that's all I'm after."

"I won't be more than fifty yards away. Anything goes haywire, I'm right there."

Cork shouldered the backpack and walked toward the access road, leaving behind the bright lights of the school parking lot. In the west, the sky along the horizon still held an ice-blue glow, against which the trees were nothing but silhouettes. He crossed the grass of the school grounds and came to the old asphalt of the gravel pit access road. He turned toward the gate, a black mesh of Cyclone fencing that, against the soft blue of the distant sky, reminded him of a spider's web. He saw no one, but that didn't surprise him. He reached the gate and stood alone, waiting for someone to show or to deliver further instructions.

That's when the shot came.

The round slammed into his chest, dead center, knocking him back. He hit the ground and lay still, staring up at a sky sequined with sparkles, none of which were stars.

Stephen stumbled onto Bo Thorson first, the man in a crouch, a pistol in his hand.

"Down. Get down." Bo's voice was taut.

"Are you hit?" Stephen said.

"No."

"My dad?"

Bo got slowly to his feet. "Stay here."

"I'm coming."

"Then stay behind me."

Bo loped toward the gate of the old gravel pit, Stephen close enough to be his shadow. In front of the gate, a dark figure slowly stood up.

"Dad!" Stephen leapt past Bo and reached his father in time to help steady him. "Are you okay?"

"Feels like a train ran me down."

Bo came up beside them. "You hit?"

"The vest." Stephen's father put a hand near his heart.

"The shot came from the south." Bo used his pistol to indicate a small grove of birch trees a hundred yards away. In daylight, the leaves would have been golden and the trunks stark white. Now they were just a black clustering. "Shooter's probably already bolted."

The three men stood together in a sudden explosion of light.

"Police! Drop your weapons!"

Bo said quietly, "The cavalry."

Sheriff Marsha Dross held up the armor and studied the place where the bullet had hit. "You could have been killed."

Cork said, "Thanks to Bo, the only hole is in the mackinaw I wore over that vest."

Her glare swung to Bo. "You certainly came prepared. What did you bring to my county besides body armor?"

"A license that makes it all legal."

She set the vest on her desk and slid from it one of the ceramic plates. "You were expecting heavy caliber?"

"Best to be prepared," Bo replied.

She turned her attention to the backpack. "Twenty thousand. That's it?"

"I know," Bo said. "Chump change. Pretty sure it was a setup, just to get Cork in the open."

"A setup by who?"

"Wish I could tell you, Sheriff."

"Bo Thorson." She rolled the name around in her thinking. "Bo Thorson." Then a light came on. "Not the Bo Thorson who saved the First Lady?"

"Yeah, that Bo Thorson."

"No longer Secret Service?"

"Left a while back. Private now."

"Working for whom?"

"That's confidential."

She looked toward Cork. "Do you know the answer to that one?"

"Jerome Hill, Senator McCarthy's father." Cork gave Bo a shrug. "Sorry. Not my client."

"He doesn't believe the crash was due to pilot error?" The sheriff's eyes swung back and forth between the two men.

"He has significant doubts," Bo answered.

"And his hope is that the flight recorder will resolve the issue?"

"At least clarify some things."

The sheriff leaned her butt against her desk, crossed her arms, scowled at Cork. "You never mentioned Thorson. I thought we had an agreement." She reached out and tapped the vest. "Don't you think it would have been appropriate to inform me of this at least?"

"Things moved quickly," Cork said, though that wasn't the whole truth.

Dross looked at Stephen, who'd been mostly silent since they were all brought in. "What happened to your face?"

Stephen had been staring at the floor. He lifted his eyes briefly, then looked down again. Cork wasn't sure what to make of this. Nervousness? Shame? Fear?

"Just clumsy."

"And you just happened to be at the town meeting?"

Stephen's voice was quiet but steady. "I wasn't supposed to be. Dad didn't want me there. I went anyway."

"So you knew about this exchange that was supposed to go down?"

"I knew."

Dross breathed deeply, once, twice, thinking things over. "Okay, Cork. If, as Thorson says, the intent was to take you out, it seems to me it had to be someone who knows you're investigating the senator's crash. Who would that be?"

"My family and some of the folks on the rez."

"What about Gerard?" Stephen said. "He seems to know a lot."

"Gerard?" Dross thought for a moment. "The one who questioned you yesterday, right? Who is he?"

Cork said, "He feels military, but there's more to him than that, I'm sure."

Dross left the desk, began pacing. "I had a visit from Alex Quaker, the number two man in the FBI's National Security Branch. He advised me to keep my nose out of this business. Was this an act of terrorism, Thorson?"

"I can't say at the moment. Maybe that's what the flight recorder would have told us."

"You believe someone has it?"

She addressed her question to Cork, and he brought her up to date on what they knew.

"Do you think it was Blessing who shot at you tonight?"

Before he could answer, the phone on the sheriff's desk buzzed. She picked it up, listened. "Send him in." She hung up. "Quaker's here. This should be interesting."

Two men entered. The one in front had red hair and a prognathic jaw that gave him a relentlessly determined look. The man two steps behind was younger, serious-looking in a religiously zealous way. The chill they brought with them reminded Cork of a storm front ushering in a blizzard.

"Sheriff." A one-word greeting from the man in front. He didn't bother introducing his companion. "Which one is Cork O'Connor?"

Cork said, "That would be me."

"And Thorson?"

Bo lifted a hand.

"And you're the son?" the man said to Stephen.

"Yes."

The man's eyes went across the three of them, and Cork thought of a machine gunner taking aim.

"I'll need an interview room, Sheriff."

CHAPTER 35

Gerard leaned against the deck railing of Bo's cabin, smoking a Cuban cigar and gazing out at the black water of the lake inlet. Lights like solitary stars glittered along the far shoreline. A saffron glow over the treetops pinpointed the place where the moon was about to rise. Bo watched the cigar ember brighten, then dim each time Gerard inhaled. He hated the odor of cigar smoke, especially in this place where the scent of evergreen felt calming and healing to the soul.

"So when Quaker asked about your connection with all this, what did you tell him?"

"The truth. That I'm working for the senator's family."

This was clearly no surprise to Gerard. Bo wondered how long he'd known.

"Did you say anything about me?"

"Silence is one of the things you pay me for."

Gerard fixed him with a cold eye. "I guess it was too much to hope that loyalty might be one, too."

"It's a complicated game we're playing."

"What do you tell the senator's family?"

"Everything I tell you."

"Do you tell them things you don't tell me?"

"I tell you everything."

Gerard considered this, probably weighing its truth. "Quaker will be putting two and two together pretty soon, the stiff-jawed bastard. I'll take care of him eventually, but we need to keep him in the dark awhile longer." The cigar ember bloomed red, and smoke exploded gray above the deck railing. "I wonder if they really have it."

"They?"

"Whoever tried to take O'Connor out."

"If they had the recorder, they wouldn't care about O'Connor. As far as I can tell, we've gotten nowhere. Quaker thinks it's domestic terrorism, thinks the Lexington Brigade might be behind it."

"The Lexington Brigade?" Gerard gave a grunt that passed for a laugh. "Bunch of wackos out of South Dakota."

"The name Cole Wannamaker mean anything to you?"

"He heads up the brigade. He's got himself a compound in the Black Hills."

"Quaker says Wannamaker dropped off the radar a couple of weeks ago. Quaker thinks he might be around here somewhere."

Gerard faced Bo, the cigar ember like a gaping red hole in the center of his pursed lips. "Why?"

"A guy stood up at the meeting tonight and basically hailed the senator's demise. Got some applause among the folks in that auditorium. The guy was Boog Sorenson, commander of the local chapter of the Lexington Brigade. He's got a few followers in the North Country."

"Wacko enough to assassinate a U.S. senator?"

"Think Oklahoma City."

"Why now?"

"Maybe the brigade up here has taken strong exception to the senator's opposition to this mine proposal. Another possibility might be the bill banning assault rifles she was about to introduce. That bill's got a lot of press, and it's looking like it might actually have some good bipartisan support. It certainly has the NRA worried. Or maybe the Manila Accord. The alt right likes it because they hope it'll contain China without America having to confront the Red Dragon directly. The senator made it clear she was going to do her best to defeat the accord."

"How does he think the plane was brought down?"

"Didn't say, but if he's thinking domestic terrorism, it had to be something like a ground-to-air missile."

"The brigade?" Gerard ashed his cigar beyond the railing. "I don't buy it. What about this Blessing?"

"I'll check him out some more, but he doesn't feel right for any of this."

"Did you fill Quaker in about Blessing and the other missing Indians?"

"Yeah. He told me and O'Connor to back off, he'd take things from here."

"You keep doing what you're doing. I'll take care of Quaker." Gerard studied his cigar, which he'd smoked almost to its end. "You're sure there's nothing you haven't told me?"

Bo thought about Stephen's vision and the boy bringing down the eagle, but said, "You know what I know."

When Gerard had gone, Bo made a call. "It was a setup."

"We heard. And we heard that you're okay. The news is reporting it as a flare-up because of the contentious town hall meeting up there. One shot fired, but not at the governor. No one hurt. Nothing else official at the moment."

"Alex Quaker is here keeping a lid on things."

"You've seen him?"

"Had a long conversation this evening. His story is that it's the Lexington Brigade."

"We've suspected that some of the threats Olympia received came from the brigade."

"So when he puts it out there, it'll be a story that will carry weight, a good diversion."

"You don't buy it?"

"There are things about it I like. If it is the brigade and they do have some membership up here, that might explain the disappearance of the Indians. The locals might have the kind of information that would make it possible for them to locate and grab these folks." Bo thought for a few moments. "And there've been reports of white poachers on the reservation. Could be the brigade scoping out the territory."

"It could be anybody scoping out the territory, even Gerard's people. Bo, is it possible Gerard was behind the setup tonight?"

"With Gerard, anything is possible. But I don't know how getting O'Connor out of the picture would benefit him. It could be someone on the rez who doesn't want him asking questions. And there are still players involved in this that I haven't identified yet."

"Players?"

"O'Connor wrote down a bunch of numbers from government plates out at the airport where NTSB is running their investigation. They were all vehicles from a pool, no agency prefixes. I have a friend looking into who checked them out from the pool. That might prove enlightening."

At the other end, she sighed. "I'm beginning to wonder if we'll ever know the truth. There's so much smoke."

"I'll do my best to clear it away, I promise."

"I know."

The odor of Gerard's cigar still lingered in the air. Bo moved to the far end of the deck, where the scent of evergreen was strong. "Gerard knows I'm working for the senator's family."

"How?"

"I told him, but it was clear the news came as no surprise. Surveillance of some kind, probably. He might even have somebody on the inside on your end. You be careful."

"I will."

Bo breathed in the scent of pine, which made him feel oddly refreshed, even hopeful. "When will he be arriving for the memorial service?"

"The day after tomorrow."

"He's kept a low profile during all this."

"When we have answers, he'll speak out. You know that."

"And you'll be right there beside him."

"That's where I belong." When he didn't reply, she said, "Is that all for tonight?"

"No rest for the wicked. Still a little cleanup work to do."

When the call had ended, he returned in the dark to the wooded point where he'd sequestered his kayak and paddled to the island offshore from Gerard's command center. He downloaded the most recent recording. Back at his cabin, when he listened, he was more convinced than ever that Gerard wasn't behind the setup that night. In what was clearly a conference between Gerard and a couple of his top people, the suggestion arose of salting the audience with their own men. Gerard nixed that, giving Bo a compliment: "One good man is all I need there."

Gerard was a piece of work, one Bo had never been able to pin down completely. It was clear the man appreciated his abilities, but Bo also understood that if Gerard had to, he'd feed an operative, any operative, to the wolves. The game they were all playing was deadly, and it had no rules.

Chapter 36

They'd gathered around the fire ring on Crow Point. The air was still, the moon on the rise, midnight sapphires sparkling on the surface of Iron Lake, only a stone's throw away. Waaboo slept on a blanket on the ground, his little arm thrown over the old dog, Trixie, who wasn't asleep but lay blinking in the firelight.

"Thank God for that vest." Rainy sat close beside Cork, her fingers laced in his and resting on his thigh. He felt her concern in the intensity of her grip. "No more heroics, promise me."

"Nothing heroic about it. I just walked into a setup."

"And you," Jenny said to Stephen. "What were you thinking?"

"That I might be more useful there than sitting around here." His voice remained sullen.

"From now on," Cork said, "nobody acts alone. We're in this together. Clear?" He'd addressed his remarks to them all, but his eyes were on Stephen.

"It wasn't Tom Blessing," Daniel said. "I'd stake my life on it."

"I think you're right. But that probably means Tom's in the same boat as the Hukaris and the Loves, and what boat that is God only knows. There's a clock ticking in my head. I'm thinking that if we don't we get some answers soon, Phil and Sue and Tom and the Loves are . . ." He couldn't quite bring himself to finish, to say the word. *Dead.*

Leah Duling sat next to Henry Meloux, who had said almost nothing since he'd asked for the fire to be built. When Leah had offered a mild objection—"It's late, Henry"—the old Mide had replied, "We are in the dark, and fire illuminates." Now she asked, "Do you sense death?"

The old man looked toward the dark where the forest lay beyond the firelight. "Something is here. It is huge and it is evil and it is meant for killing. That is what I sense."

"The monster at Stephen's back?" Jenny asked.

But Cork was also remembering that Waaboo had had a nightmare of a many-headed monster.

Trixie stood suddenly and eyed the gap in the outcrops where the path from Meloux's cabin came through. In the firelight, the rocks quivered red-orange, the gap between them murky black. The dog gave a low, menacing growl. Cork freed himself from Rainy's grip and stood. Daniel rose, too, reaching for the sidearm holstered at his waist.

What stumbled into sight surprised the hell out of Cork, probably out of them all. Ned Love stood illuminated in the firelight, supporting the weight of his nephew Monkey, whose jacket was black with old blood.

"We're on the dock," Ned explained, "just getting into the canoe to cross Little Bass for some hunting. Cyrus sets up a ruckus like I ain't heard from him in a long while. Then the shot comes, takes out Cyrus. The next shot catches Monkey. I spot two men at the cabin, get my rifle to my shoulder, squeeze off a couple of rounds. I drag Monkey into the canoe and paddle like hell for the far side of the lake. Had to leave Cyrus behind. Near broke my heart."

They were in Meloux's cabin, Monkey Love on the bunk, where the old Mide and Rainy tended to him. They'd opened his shirt to expose the bullet's entry wound.

"I tried to clean that best I could," Ned said. "Put some moss on it, but I knew it needed better looking after. Why I brought Monkey here."

"The wound looks clean, Ned," Rainy said. "That moss was a good idea. But Monkey's lost a lot of blood. We need to get him to the hospital."

"Nope. In a hospital bed, Monkey'd be like a fish in a barrel."

"Did you get a look at them?" Cork asked.

"Not a good enough look."

"Two of them, you say?"

"That's all I saw. Could've been more, I suppose. But if there was, they weren't shooting."

"Two," Cork said. He glanced at Daniel. "Your poachers?"

"Could be."

"Or the guys who did this," Stephen said, pointing to his stitched cheek.

"That bullet's still in Monkey's shoulder," Rainy said. "Ned, we really have to get him to the hospital."

"Ain't going to happen."

"Who knows what damage that bullet's done?"

"I put him in that hospital, I got a feelin' he ain't coming out."

"Ned—"

"Remove his shirt," Meloux said.

Rainy made no move to comply. "Why?"

"Remove his shirt and you will see."

With Ned's help, Rainy stripped off the bloodstained shirt. Monkey Love's torso was like a human game of tic-tac-toe, long scars crisscrossing his skin.

"What happened to him?" Rainy asked.

"Prison fights, mostly," Ned Love replied. "He didn't do so well inside."

"Turn him over," Meloux said.

Monkey, who'd seemed only vaguely aware of things since his arrival, gave a long, painful groan with the repositioning. Like his chest, his back was remarkable for the number of scars it bore. Meloux sat on the bunk and ran his hand lightly over Monkey's back near the right shoulder blade.

"There," he said. "Feel it, Niece?"

Rainy touched where Meloux had indicated. "The bullet."

"We will take it out."

"Uncle Henry, a procedure like that should be done in an operating room."

"You have cut human beings before."

"Minor things. This is way beyond my capability."

"You will not do it?"

"I can't, ethically."

"Fetch my knife, Leah," the old Mide said.

Rainy's dark brown eyes grew huge with surprise and concern. "You're not going to cut it out, are you?"

"I have cut out bullets before."

"I'm not even going to ask about that, but it had to have been in a time when those hands of yours didn't shake."

"I'll cut it out," Cork offered.

"No." Meloux was firm. "This is work for a healer." He looked to Ned Love. "You are his uncle, his closest family. What do you wish?"

"He ain't going to a hospital. He's been sliced up before, and not by anyone who gave a hoot about him. He'll survive another cut or two."

"What about all that lost blood?" Rainy said.

"He is not the first human being to lose blood to a wound.

When the bullet is out, if the wound stays clean, his body will make more blood in time."

"Uncle Henry—" she began but once again was cut off.

"I will take the bullet out," Meloux said.

"No." Rainy turned to Leah. "My medical bag is in your cabin. Could you bring it to me? And, Stephen, I'll need clean towels, lots of them. Go with Leah."

As a public health nurse, Rainy made all manner of calls on the rez, and she always brought her medical bag. She did the same, Cork knew, whenever she visited her centenarian great-uncle on Crow Point. She was a woman always prepared. Now she closed her eyes and steeled herself for what was ahead.

When it was over and Monkey was resting, Rainy said, "I'm going to get some air."

She went outside into the night, and Cork started after her.

"She needs to be alone, Corcoran O'Connor," Meloux advised.

Cork had seldom argued with Meloux, but he said, "I should be with her."

"To tell her that she is a fine healer, that she is loved, that you understand the difficulty in what she has done? Do you think she does not know these things?"

"To comfort her, Henry."

"The comfort of a healer is the healed. Give her the honor of her time alone with herself."

It was hard accepting the advice of the old Mide, but Cork lowered himself back into his chair.

"Who were they?" Ned asked. "Them men who shot my nephew."

"We don't know," Daniel replied. "But we think we know what

they were after. We think they're looking for the flight recorder from the plane that crashed."

"What's it look like?"

"They call it a black box, Ned, but it's really orange."

"Orange?" Ned Love squinched up his face. "A little orange box? I know where it is."

Cork sat suddenly erect in his chair. "You picked it up?"

"Nope, just know where it is. Would have told somebody if I'd known they were looking for it, but we got shoved away from that crash so quick. And nobody came around later to ask us. Then those guys showed up and started shooting."

"Where is it?"

"In the woods by the bog where the plane came down."

"People have been over that area a hundred times, Ned. How come they haven't found it?"

"Them searchers, I'm guessing they were looking at the ground. Me, I hunt squirrels, so I look up."

CHAPTER 37

He woke and lay in his sleeping bag, which he'd unrolled in the tall grass of the meadow on Crow Point. The moon was full and, like a ravenous god, had devoured the stars around it. The two cabins nearby were dark, everyone inside asleep. The breeze was out of the southwest, soft and unseasonably warm. The grass stalks around him swayed, and he could hear the voice of that gentle wind whispering to him. He didn't hear the menace Henry Meloux seemed to have heard the spirits speak. To Stephen, the sound was a hopeful crooning: *Soon, soon, soon.*

It was the vision that had awakened him, the same visitation played out in the same way. His inability to understand its meaning had eaten at him, an acid on his soul. But tonight was different. Tonight there was promise. In the wind. In the voice. In the way the tall grass yielded.

He heard the creak of the door on Henry Meloux's cabin, watched as the old man came his way, bent ever so slightly, like the grass. In the moonlight, the old man was silver.

Without a word or an acknowledgment of his presence, Henry

sat beside him. It was as if, to the old Mide, Stephen was just another of the wild things that grew tall in the meadow.

"It's coming." Stephen spoke in a whisper no louder than the voice of the wind.

"The great evil?" the old man said.

"The meaning of the vision."

"Ah."

Stephen sat up. The upper half of the sleeping bag fell to his waist. He wore a long-sleeved T-shirt, which was enough to keep him comfortable in that fall night. Henry had put on his old mackinaw.

"There's more than evil out there," Stephen said. "There's promise. The flight recorder Ned Love saw lodged up in a tree, that was the egg falling from the eagle. I think the full meaning of the vision is unfolding."

Not far away, the grass shifted suddenly as something darted through it, an animal who believed there was safety in the night.

"It's been hard, Henry. This knowing and not knowing."

"What in life is not hard, Stephen O'Connor?"

There was another creaking door, this time from Leah Duling's cabin. Rainy stepped into the moonlight and crossed the meadow. She was barefoot but wore sweatpants and a light jacket. She sat on the other side of Stephen. The gray-white streak in her long black hair gleamed like a vein of silver.

"You were amazing with Monkey Love," Stephen told her.

"I was scared shitless."

"Your hands did not shake, Niece," the old Mide said. "Not once."

"My heart was doing a tango, Uncle Henry."

"Jameson Love has a spirit of stumbling luck. This wounding is not the last scar he will bear in his life, I think."

Another voice spoke, and a ghost-white figure appeared beside them. "Monkey's luck may be on the clumsy side, but that spirit of his has got leather in it. My nephew's tough."

"You scared me, Ned," Rainy said. "I didn't hear you coming."

"I learned a long time ago hunting that if I make noise, my supper runs away." He sat beside Rainy. "Thank you for what you done for Monkey tonight. *Chi migwech.*"

"He's resting well?"

"Whatever it was Henry here gave him to drink put him out good. Don't know how I'm gonna repay you."

Stephen didn't say it, but he was thinking that the black box was payment enough.

Ned turned to him. "Your dad told me maybe the same guys who shot Monkey gave you that face."

Stephen touched the stitches on his cheek. "Maybe."

"What do they want with that recorder?"

"We think they want to hide the truth of what caused the plane to crash."

"Monkey said it was flying all crooked when it came down this side of Desolation Mountain, like a sick bird."

"Did it look like it had been hit with something?" Stephen asked, thinking of his vision and the boy with the powerful bow.

"Monkey didn't say nuthin' about that."

A subtle cough announced another arrival.

"Couldn't sleep, Cork?" Rainy asked.

"Guess I'm not the only one." Cork plopped down beside her. "I called Bo Thorson. He'll be ready first thing in the morning. We'll be going after that flight recorder, although I didn't tell him that. Best to keep it quiet for the moment."

"The egg that dropped from the eagle," Stephen said.

"That seems pretty clear," his father agreed. "Anything else becoming clear?"

"Not yet, but I think it will. I'm going with you tomorrow."

Cork shook his head. "I've got another mission for you. I want you to head into Allouette and bring Ned's sister out to Crow Point."

"Beulah?" Ned said.

"She's been worried about you and Monkey."

"Monkey, maybe. She never had much use for me."

"We may need to build another cabin, Corcoran O'Connor," Henry said.

They all rose and drifted back to their beds and their blankets, leaving Stephen alone again. He lay under the watchful eye of the moon, thinking about his vision, about the full meaning slowly revealing itself, which was good, except for one thing. The vision always ended with a beast at his back so terrible he couldn't force himself to turn and look at it. Even awake, the idea of facing that monster terrified him.

In the early hours of the morning, long before sunrise, Cork left Crow Point, in the company of Daniel English and Ned Love. Cork had arranged to meet Bo Thorson outside Allouette, though over the phone he hadn't explained why. From there, they'd go to Ned Love's cabin, then walk to the bog where the plane crashed. The site was still closed to the public and periodically patrolled. He was hoping to slip in and out at first light without being spotted.

Bo was waiting for them beside his Jeep. Cork introduced him to Ned Love and recapped the story Love had told the night before.

When Bo heard about the flight recorder Love had seen caught in the top of a pine tree, he said, "I'll be damned." Then he looked up at the sky, which was still full of stars. "I hope you can find it in the dark. They're patrolling the area from dawn to dusk."

"We'll be there at first light and, with any luck, gone before anyone else shows up," Cork told him.

By the time they parked at Ned's cabin, the whole eastern horizon had gone powdery blue. Before they started for the bog, Ned walked to the end of the dock on Little Bass Lake, whose surface reflected the image of Desolation Mountain, a hard black shape against the soft, vague blue of the predawn sky. He knelt and stared into the water.

"After we get that box, I'm coming back for Cyrus. And then I'm gonna find the men who shot him and Monkey."

"We'll give you a hand with that, Ned," Cork promised.

"Will you give me a hand shootin' 'em? 'Cause that's what I intend to do."

"How about we cross that bridge when we come to it?"

The man rose and began to lead the way. They moved through the woods in the thin, early light. In fifteen minutes, they'd reached the north side of the bog. Cork saw where the undergrowth all along the edge and well into the trees had been crushed by the constant trample of the searchers' boots. They paused in the cover among the tamaracks, listened, heard nothing. Without a sound, Ned crept around the bog to the place where, soon after the crash, Cork and Stephen and Daniel and the men from the reservation had found the broken tail section and the dead boy still strapped in his seat. Ned walked without hesitation to a red pine whose crown, like many of the others around it, had been sheared off, leaving only a ragged, white tip of trunk resembling the end of a broken bone. Cork followed Ned's gaze upward. Fifty feet above them, a small chunk of plane debris was caught among the remaining pine branches, and within it was a dash of orange.

"Damn," Daniel said. "We're going to need climbing spurs or spiked logger boots to get up there."

"Got anything like that at your cabin, Ned?" Cork asked.

"No use for 'em. When I cut firewood, I bring the whole tree down. Squirrels and possums, when I shoot 'em, they just fall to the ground."

"I'll give it a try," Bo said.

He stepped up to the pine trunk, which had a diameter of roughly three feet, felt for handholds, pressed himself against the rough bark, and tried to find purchase for the soles of his boots. It was hopeless from the get-go. He stepped back, swearing under his breath.

"We'll need to come back with climbing spurs," Cork said.

Bo gave the pine trunk a light kick. "I hate being this close and having to walk away."

"We'll have to wait until dusk," Daniel said.

Cork eyed the patch of orange above them. "At least we know where it is. We're getting somewhere."

Except for the call of birds, the woods were quiet. But from the distance came the diesel rumble of a heavy engine approaching on the logging road.

"That's it for this morning," Cork said. "Let's go before we're spotted."

When they dropped Bo at his Jeep, they made arrangements to meet in the late afternoon. Cork promised to bring climbing spurs. Bo waited until the vehicle was well gone, then made his call.

"I know where it is."

"The flight recorder? You have it?"

"Not yet. Tonight. It's a little tricky." Bo explained about the pine tree. "The recorder might not have any of the answers," he cautioned.

"We'll know soon enough. Thank you, Bo."

He was being paid for his work, but even if he weren't, the sound of her thank-you would have been enough.

CHAPTER 38

Stephen walked with Rainy to the logging road that led toward Allouette. Daniel's pickup truck was parked in a bared pull-off, an area most folks referred to as Crow Point East. They drove the three miles into town, and Rainy dropped him at the marina, where he'd left the ATV side-by-side the day before. The plan was for him to use the little machine to take Beulah Love back to Henry Meloux's cabin. Rainy stuck around only long enough to make sure there was no problem with the ATV. As soon as Stephen kicked the engine over successfully, she headed to the clinic, just to check in.

It was still early and Allouette was quiet. Stephen pulled up in front of the Mocha Moose, where Sarah LeDuc and Beulah Love waited for him inside. The café smelled of sweet, freshly baked dough.

"*Boozhoo,* Stephen." Sarah greeted him with a smile and a white pastry bag. "Donuts to take back to everyone on Crow Point."

"How is Jameson?" Beulah asked, her face pulled tight with worry.

"He's doing fine, you'll see."

"And Ned?"

Stephen filled them in on the mission of the men that morning.

"It's all about a black box stuck up in a pine tree?" Sarah said. "That's why Monkey was shot? Any more word on Sue and Phil and Tom?"

"Dad's still working on that, Sarah."

"Let him know that everyone on the rez is willing to beat the woods to find them."

"If Dad knew what part of the woods to beat, I'm sure he'd say go for it."

"I heard you were at the town meeting with the governor last night when somebody fired shots."

"Only one shot, Sarah. And I heard it was just a couple of rowdies." The lie he'd sworn to tell. "No one hurt. You ready, Ms. Love?"

"Call me Beulah."

Across the street from the Mocha Moose, several teenagers from town had gathered where the bus would pick them up and take them to the high school in Aurora. Stephen spotted Harmon Goodsky's grandson, Winston. He stood apart from the other kids. Stephen wondered if that separation was his choice or theirs. The kid had been looking at the ground. Now he lifted his eyes and they locked on Stephen. There was something about him that set a hook in Stephen's thinking. Maybe it was that Stephen, too, knew what it was to be different.

Beulah settled herself beside him in the ATV. "I've never been in one of these before."

"Here, put this on." He handed her a neon yellow helmet and grabbed the other for himself. "The ride's a little rough, but it'll get you there."

A mile outside Allouette, Stephen swung off the pavement

onto the dirt road he would follow back to Crow Point East. The ATV kicked up a rooster tail of red dust. A few moments later, he felt prickles climb his spine, and he glanced back. Nearly cloaked in the dust behind him and closing fast was a black pickup.

"Hold on!" he hollered to Beulah.

He gunned the ATV and began a rapid calculation. Half a mile ahead was the cutoff for a logging road unused for years and overgrown. If he was able to keep ahead of the pickup, he figured he could swing onto that track, which would take them into low hills, where he might be able to lose whoever was dogging them.

Although she'd buckled into a harness, Beulah held to the roll bar for dear life. Her eyes were riveted to the road ahead, and when Stephen looked her direction, he saw that her lips were moving. A prayer, he figured. What could it hurt?

He slowed, took the turn, and plowed into undergrowth two feet high. The trees were close on both sides. He shot a quick look over his shoulder. The cutoff was choked with a swirl of red dust, and a dim black shape flew past. They'd missed the turn, but only for a moment, Stephen knew. As soon as they broke from that dust cloud, they'd double back.

The little ATV bounced along the narrow track, leaving a clear trail of crushed vegetation behind. There were hundreds of old logging roads in the woods of Tamarack County, and this was one Stephen had never traveled. He had no idea where exactly it would take them, but at least he'd bought some time. Beulah was still praying up a storm.

Then they hit a dead end. The track simply stopped. Tall pines boxed them in on three sides. The only way out was the way they'd come. Stephen had no time to consider options. He pulled off his helmet and threw it down.

"Out," he shouted to Beulah.

Her face was a mask of horror and she didn't move.

"We have to get into the woods. Now!"

He reached out and unbuckled her harness, then leapt from the ATV. She was slow to follow, as if dazed. Stephen grabbed her arm and pulled her into the woods. In the quiet after he'd killed the engine, he heard the grind of the big truck engine coming. He ran through the pines with Beulah in tow. They were among hills with lots of gneiss outcrops. Stephen made for a low rise with a crowning of rock where he hoped they'd leave no footprints. They struggled up and made the summit just as the black pickup roared up behind the ATV. Stephen yanked Beulah down beside him and they lay prone. Through the pines, he watched two men exit the truck. He recognized them as the ones who'd beat him the day before. They were dressed for the North Country—jeans, flannel shirts, boots, ball caps—and carrying rifles. They checked the ATV, then scanned the woods. One of them walked in a slow circle, studying the ground. He said something to his companion, and they started in the direction Stephen and Beulah had fled.

"We have to go," Stephen whispered.

He slid back, staying low until he was sure the rise hid him. Beulah followed suit. He began at a lope through the woods, searching for good cover somewhere ahead. Beulah did her best to keep up, but she wasn't a woman used to running, especially in the wilderness. Twice she fell, tripped by underbrush. She didn't say a word of complaint, simply pulled herself up and ran on. Stephen made for a long ridge whose gray-white rock stood out through the trees. When they reached it, he glanced back, looking for the men on their tails. He didn't see them, but that didn't mean they weren't coming.

Beulah stared hopelessly at the rock face, which rose thirty feet above them. "Climb?" she said, as if that would be asking the impossible.

"Not here. This way."

Stephen led her north fifty yards to a place where a natural crease cut up the ridge at an angle. It would still require a climb, but one he hoped Beulah could handle. "Follow me."

Good shrub cover grew in the crease, Juneberry bushes whose leaves had gone red with the season. Beulah used the thin branches to help pull herself up. They'd made it halfway to the top when she cried out and fell and lay holding her ankle.

"Twisted," she said through gritted teeth.

Stephen crouched beside her. The men had topped the rise where he and Beulah had first hidden themselves and stood surveying the woods.

"Stay down and keep still," he told her.

He hoped the men would come no farther into the forest. But his hope died almost immediately as they began in the direction of the ridge.

Stephen wore light green khakis, a tan chamois shirt, a brown, quilted vest. Not bad camouflage for the woods. Beulah was another story. She had on blue jeans, a red jacket, and was still wearing the neon yellow crash helmet he'd given her in the ATV. Because of the red leaves on the Juneberry shrubs, the jacket might be okay, but that helmet had to go.

The men veered south. Although Stephen hoped that they wouldn't follow the ridge to the crease with the Juneberry thicket, he decided hope wasn't enough.

"Give me your helmet. Stay here and stay quiet. I'll come back for you," he promised.

"No." Beulah grasped his arm, her eyes wide with fear. "Don't leave me."

"I have to. You'll be fine if you just lie still." He pulled free. "Go ahead and pray," he advised before he left. "But silently."

He slid down the crease to its base and jumped into the open. The men were bent, focused on studying the ground. Stephen loped in the opposite direction along the rock face until he was well away from the crease. Then he stood tall, donned the bright yellow helmet, and waited until the men spotted him and leapt to the chase. Although the place where a bullet once lodged in his back burned like a forge on which every step hammered out pain, Stephen put his whole body into running, and his heart as well.

On their way back to Crow Point, Cork and Daniel made a stop in Allouette at the home of Dennis Vizenor, a man who'd logged timber all his life, and they left with a pair of spiked logger boots. When they reached Meloux's cabin, Cork was surprised to find that Stephen hadn't returned with Beulah Love. He called Sarah LeDuc, who assured him that his son and Beulah had left together a couple of hours earlier. Rainy also hadn't returned from checking in at the clinic. He called her cell and was relieved when she answered.

"I'm sorry, Cork. I got held up here. They were a little overwhelmed this morning, so I stayed to give a hand."

"Have you seen Stephen?"

"Not since I dropped him at the marina. Why?"

"He and Beulah have gone missing."

She was quiet on her end, then spoke the words Cork had thought but hadn't said. "Like all the others."

"I'm going to find them," Cork vowed. "But Daniel and I are coming to get you first. I don't want you traveling back to Crow Point alone."

"If you're looking for my sister, I'm going with you," Ned Love insisted.

Henry Meloux, who had listened to all the conversations without comment, offered this as they departed: "What your head believes you are looking for is not always what your heart is seeking, Corcoran O'Connor."

Which, Cork thought with frustration, was no help at all.

They double-timed it to Crow Point East, where Cork had parked his Expedition, then followed the logging road that ran along Iron Lake into Allouette and rendezvoused with Rainy at the clinic. They split up—Daniel and Rainy to the safety of Crow Point, and Cork and Ned to the Mocha Moose, where Sarah told them that the last she'd seen of Stephen and Beulah, they'd been headed back to Meloux's cabin.

As they left Allouette behind, Ned said, "If I was going to bushwhack 'em, I'd do it somewhere down that logging road toward Crow Point. Not much traveled, so less chance of anybody seeing what they're up to."

Cork sped to the logging road cutoff, but as he headed toward Crow Point, he began to go more slowly. Several other tracks led off into the woods, old logging accesses, but nothing caught his eye.

"There," Ned finally said. "See them wheel marks?"

Cork turned onto the cut into the woods, a narrow track he'd never followed before. The tall weeds had been pressed down along several lines; multiple vehicles had recently passed this way. They came to a dead end, and there sat the ATV, abandoned. One of the crash helmets lay on the ground in the tall grass. Cork scanned the woods, but saw no sign of his son or Beulah.

"Over here." Ned had moved to the far side of the ATV and was studying the ground cover. "A bunch of folks went this way."

Cork saw where the wild grass had been trampled, and he and Ned followed the trail into the trees. Cork had always been a hunter and wasn't a bad tracker. But for most of his life, Ned Love had fed himself on wild game, and he could follow a track as if it had a voice and called to him. Cork followed Ned to a rocky rise and then beyond, where they paused.

"They separated here. A couple of 'em went that way." Ned pointed toward a place where the gray-white rock of a low ridge was visible through the trees. "And a couple took off that way." He pointed toward a line that went a bit to the south.

"Let's check the ridge," Cork said. "That's where I'd go if I was trying to lose somebody."

"I'm with you on that one."

They went another hundred yards, then Ned stopped abruptly and studied the ground. "Another trail crosses here. Looks like the two who headed south changed their minds and cut north, going fast."

"Which trail do we follow?"

Ned considered, gave a nod toward the low ridge, and moved on. At the base of the rock face, Ned turned north, moving quickly and confidently, until he came to a fold in the ridge full of Juneberry bushes, where a small voice stopped them.

"Ned? Is that you?"

"It's me, Beulah. You can come on down from there. You're safe now."

"I can't," she said. "I think I've broken my ankle."

"Hold on," her brother told her. "We'll come get you."

She lay in a place well concealed by the thicket, and when they reached her, she offered them a huge smile of relief.

"Stephen?" Cork asked.

Her smile vanished. "He led them away hours ago. He promised he'd come back for me, but he never did."

"Them?" Ned said.

"Two men. They chased us here."

"Did they come back?" Cork asked.

"I haven't seen them since they took off after Stephen."

"We're going to get you to safety, Beulah," Cork promised her.

Using a two-man chair carry, they carted her to the Expedition and drove her to Crow Point. A vehicle like Cork's was a rare sight in front of Henry Meloux's cabin. When people came to Meloux, they made that pilgrimage on foot. The big SUV seemed so out of place that as he parked, Cork felt a little sacrilegious. They carried Beulah Love inside and Cork explained the situation. Daniel and Ned both insisted on returning with him to search for Stephen.

It was well into the afternoon by the time Ned Love picked up Stephen's trail at the crease in the rock face and followed it north, where it was joined by the trail the two men had left. For a mile or so, Cork could easily see the signs. Then they came to a bare, rocky slope and Ned paused.

"They split up here. Only one kept after Stephen."

"The other?" Daniel asked.

"Headed back toward where they left their truck."

Cork studied the ground but saw nothing. "Which way did Stephen go, Ned?"

Ned gestured toward the top of the broad, barren rise. "He's staying north. Smart boy."

"Why smart?" Daniel asked.

"Bunch of rock rises for the next half mile. Me and Monkey, we call this area the Hungry Hills. Never can track deer here. We always go home hungry. It'd be hard for anyone to follow Stephen in these rocks, me included."

"We've got to try," Cork said.

"Yeah, we gotta try." But Ned's voice held little promise.

They spread out and moved separately, yards apart. Wherever there was soil between the rocks, Cork looked for prints. On the stone itself, he searched for patches of lichen that might have been scarred by boot soles. He found nothing. Ditto Ned and Daniel.

"We could maybe keep going north," Ned said. "But once Stephen hit this area, he coulda took off in most any direction. Me,

I'd circle back, but maybe Stephen done something different. You know him better, Cork."

The honest-to-god truth was that Cork didn't have a clue. He couldn't put himself inside his son's thinking, particularly in this uniquely terrible situation. He felt deficient, like there was something essential lacking in him, especially as a father. Christ, why didn't he know his son better?

Daniel said, "We have a good hour of sunlight left. We can keep looking. But there's the flight recorder."

Cork stood on the rocky ground, which had yielded nothing, thinking for a hopeless moment that his son, like the others, was gone.

Then he remembered Henry Meloux's advice, which he'd discounted as nonsense: *What your head believes you are looking for is not always what your heart is seeking.*

"Let's get the flight recorder," he said, turning back.

"What about Stephen?" Daniel asked.

Cork walked ahead of the others, saying as if it were a prayer, "Stephen can take care of himself."

CHAPTER 39

"You just left him out there?"

Jenny looked stunned. In Meloux's cabin, they all looked a little nonplussed. Except perhaps for Meloux. The lines on his face gave away nothing but the fact that he was practically as old as creation itself.

"Dad, you can't just abandon him." Jenny was furious.

Daniel said, "We didn't have time to search anymore. We need to get the flight recorder." He looked out the window at the setting sun, which was balanced on top of a distant pine like a yellow ball on the nose of a seal. "And your dad's right. Stephen can take care of himself."

"Like Ned and Monkey?" Jenny threw back at him. "Like Sue and Phil and Tom?"

"This is different," Daniel said. "Stephen was on the run."

"On the run? How far do you think that gimp leg will get him?"

Ned spoke up, a little hesitantly, as if unsure he should intrude. "He's not alone out there."

Jenny turned her anger on him. "No, he's out there with men who probably want him dead."

"That's not what I meant."

"I made my decision, Jenny," Cork said. "It's too late to go back now. It would be too dark to see anything."

"You're going after that damn recorder in the dark."

Daniel said, "It'll only be dark if we don't leave right now."

"Fine," Jenny said. "I'm going to look for Stephen."

Meloux said, "Ned is right. He is not alone out there."

Probably because it was Meloux who'd spoken, Jenny took a deep, calming breath. "I don't understand what that means."

"Monsters," Waaboo said fearfully.

Meloux reached out and placed a reassuring hand on the boy's shoulder. "Not monsters, Little Rabbit. Spirits. Energies. Guides."

"That's sorta what I meant," Ned said. "If you know the woods, you pick up on things. Spirits maybe, but I was thinking more about things like that Juneberry patch Stephen hid my sister in."

"We just stumbled onto it," Beulah said.

"Might've seemed that way to you," Ned said. "I look at it different."

"If we're going to get that recorder, we have to go now," Daniel told them.

"Stay here, Jenny," Cork said. "We don't need you lost out there in the dark, or maybe running into the men who are after Stephen."

He could tell there was more his daughter wanted to say, but it was also clear that he'd gotten through to her.

Meloux walked the men out and looked deeply into Cork's face. "You found what your heart was looking for."

Cork eyed the solid line of trees at the edge of the meadow to the north. Stephen was somewhere in the wilderness a few miles beyond, and the dark would soon be descending. He looked back at Meloux and repeated, as if it were a mantra, "He can take care of himself."

"And," Meloux added, "he is not alone."

Bo Thorson was waiting for them in the place where they'd met that morning. He had a pair of climbing spurs with him. "Bought these this afternoon. I'm ready."

Daniel held up the spiked logging boots. "We borrowed these this morning."

"Then let's go get some answers."

They parked at Ned Love's cabin and began their hike to the crash site as the light in the sky was fading. When they arrived at the bog, the area was deserted.

"Like I told you," Bo said. "They only patrol dawn to dusk. They've become a little predictable. That's good for us."

They quickly made for the tall red pine where they'd spotted the flight recorder caught in the high branches. At the base of the tree, they gazed up. Cork saw the green of the needles, the brown of the branches, the pale blue of the sky beyond. But nothing orange-colored.

"Where is it?" Daniel asked.

"Wrong tree?" Bo scanned the nearby pines.

"This is the tree," Ned assured him.

Cork ran his hand over the bark. "Holes from climbing spurs. Someone beat us to it."

"Who knew about this tree but us?" Daniel said.

Cork, Daniel, and Ned eyed Bo Thorson and the pair of climbing spurs he'd brought.

Bo said coolly, "We've got some talking to do."

Henry Meloux insisted they build a fire. It was dark night, and the blaze in the fire ring illuminated the rock outcrops with a dancing yellow glow. Except for the convalescing Monkey Love and Leah, who'd offered to stay with him, they were all gathered there, even little Waaboo, sitting on cut sections of log. Meloux had smudged and said a prayer, asking for clear minds and clear hearts and true tongues. And now they were silent, listening to the pop and crackle as the flames consumed the wood.

Cork chewed on anger, on doubt, on guilt. The recorder was gone. Phil and Sue Hukari and Tom Blessing were still missing. Stephen was out in the wild with God knew what—assassins maybe—and Cork was beating himself up for not continuing the search for his son. He doubted everything now, especially his trust in Bo Thorson.

Thorson continued to insist that he wasn't responsible for the missing flight recorder, but what did Cork really know about the man? When Thorson was Secret Service and Cork was sheriff of Tamarack County and they'd worked together on security, Thorson had seemed not just competent but accomplished. And trustworthy. But that was years ago, and people could change. He didn't really know who Thorson might be now. His sense had been that the heart of the man was still good, still decent, but at the moment, he wasn't sure he could trust in his own sense of anything.

Meloux said, "Speak the truth." He was looking at Thorson.

"I didn't take the flight recorder. That's the truth. All of it."

"What'd you do today after we split up?" Daniel asked.

"Picked up that pair of climbing spurs."

"Took you all day?"

"I made my report to the people who hired me."

"Who exactly is that?" Daniel said.

"I've already told you."

"Olympia McCarthy's father. Would you object if we called to check that out?"

"You can call. I doubt that he'll admit to it. It's a delicate matter, a man in his position questioning the veracity of the NTSB and the FBI."

"How can we be sure you're not working for Gerard?"

Bo said, "Cork, do you really think I might be working for Gerard?"

Cork gave the question serious weight, and finally shook his head. "I still think you're one of the good guys."

"Thanks," Bo said. "Now let me ask a question. Did you tell anybody about the flight recorder?"

"Only the people around this fire," Cork said.

Beulah Love, who'd been carried to the fire ring because of her swollen ankle, said, "Ummmm."

Ned cocked his head. "Something to say, Beulah?"

"When Stephen came to get me this morning, he told Sarah and me about the recorder in the tree."

"Sarah LeDuc," Cork said. "Christ. So much for secrecy. I'm sure the whole rez knows by now."

"Are you suggesting someone on the rez is working with those goons, Cork?" Rainy gave him a doubtful look.

"Unless Bo told someone."

"I didn't say a word to anyone," Bo protested. "But there's another possibility."

"What's that?" Daniel asked.

"Bugs," Bo said simply. "Maybe in the Mocha Moose or someone's phone's been tapped or there are a dozen other ways of listening in. The technology of surveillance would amaze you."

"The bottom line," Cork said with a dismal sinking of his heart, "is that we're right back where we started."

Trixie, who'd been lying at Waaboo's feet, lifted her head and gave a little woof. Henry Meloux's face went intent as he listened. "Maybe things have moved farther ahead than you think, Corcoran O'Connor."

In the next moment, a figure stumbled between the rock outcroppings and into the firelight, a stranger in ragged pants and with his hands tied behind his back. Then another figure appeared.

His heart singing, Cork said, "Good to see you back, Stephen."

Bo listened with the others as Stephen O'Connor recounted his ordeal. He'd been chased by the two strangers and had headed north from the low ridge where he'd hidden Beulah Love.

"Why north?" Ned Love asked.

"I don't know. It's just the way I went."

"If you wanted to lose those guys, north was the way to go."

"I found that out when I reached all that rock."

"The Hungry Hills," Love said.

Stephen described how he'd mounted the rocky slope and had hidden himself and watched as the two men who came after him stopped to talk things over. One headed back and the other continued trying to find Stephen's trail.

"My leg was killing me, and it was pretty clear he knew how to track, so I decided my best shot was to take him out."

"With what?" Jenny said.

"The thing those Hungry Hills has the most of. A rock. I was lying low behind a big boulder. He was studying the ground, walked right past me. I caught him in the back of the head. As soon as he was down, I pulled the gun from his holster. He had a knife on his belt, and I took that, too."

"How come his pants are all raggedy?" Waaboo asked.

"I cut strips so I could tie his hands."

"Any ID on him?" Cork asked.

"I didn't look."

"Stand up," Cork ordered the stranger. He checked all the pockets, found nothing, and shoved the man back down to the ground.

He turned back to his son. "We looked for you at the Hungry Hills."

"We didn't stay there. I thought his partner might come back, so I pushed him north across all that rock. When I thought we were clear, I cut west, then finally south, making for Crow Point."

"So," Cork said to the stranger, whose hands were still tied with strips cut from his own pant leg. "Who are you?"

The man's eyes flicked toward Cork, then back to the flames, and not a word came from his mouth.

Bo, who so far had been silent, said, "Gerard sent you?"

The man showed no sign of recognition.

Cork said, "Rainy, Jenny, Waaboo, join Leah and Monkey back at Henry's cabin. We'll be along shortly."

Jenny stood, took Waaboo's hand, and walked away between the rocks with Trixie at their heels. Cork's wife had risen, but she didn't follow. "What are you going to do, Cork?"

"Question him."

"I know how you question people."

"We need to know what he knows, Rainy, especially if he knows about Sue and Phil and Tom."

"You're going to hurt him."

"Only if necessary. The choice is his."

"Cork—"

"Stay, Niece," Meloux interrupted her. "Sit." He said to the stranger, "My niece is a healer. It may be that you are going to suffer much. When we are finished with you and you have told us what you know, we will allow her to do what she can to ease your pain."

In the firelight, Rainy's face was a blaze of surprise. Or was it dismay?

"Sit, Niece," Meloux said again.

Bo had been studying the stranger, who'd seemed unmoved

until the old man spoke. The way such menacing words came so soothingly from those ancient lips made them even more chilling. The man eyed Meloux, then the others, and Bo saw cracks in his stolid veneer. He'd begun to understand what even decent people might be capable of when protecting those they cared about.

"I am Ojibwe," Meloux said to the stranger. "Do you know what that word means?"

The stranger made no response.

"In the language of my people, it means 'to pucker.' Do you know where that name comes from? I will tell you what I have heard. It comes from the way in which my people have been known to treat their enemies. We roast them until their skin puckers." The old man waited for his words to sink in. "There is no glory in giving a man pain. There is also no glory in hurting those who have done nothing to you." His dark eyes held the stranger's gaze. "There is only one thing we ask. What has become of the people we care about? Have they been harmed?"

Although the stranger didn't speak, Bo could see that his brain was working, worrying itself over the old man's words.

"Bring me fire," Meloux said to Cork.

"Wait," the stranger said. "We weren't supposed to hurt nobody, just bring them in."

"What about these stitches?" Stephen said.

"You'll heal," the stranger said, as if the beating were nothing.

"You shot Monkey Love," Daniel pointed out coldly.

"Wasn't me. There's others out there."

"You killed people's dogs."

"The dogs got in the way. And they was just dogs."

"Just dogs?" Ned Love rose, huge and menacing. "I'll pucker you, you son of a bitch."

"Hold on, Ned." Cork stepped between Love and the stranger.

"Let him talk. You said you brought them in. Brought them where?"

"The Op Center."

"Where's this Op Center?"

The man stared into the fire. "I want immunity."

"What?"

"I want immunity. I don't want to go to jail. I remember when you was sheriff, O'Connor. I figure you still got some clout."

"Immunity," Cork said. "All right, I'll do what I can."

The stranger looked up at Cork. "Then I guess I'll tell you."

CHAPTER 40

The stranger's name was Wes Simpson. Once they got him talking, he told them much. He came from Yellow Lake, a community fifteen miles south of Aurora. He was a member of the Lexington Brigade mostly because his cousin had recruited him.

"Axel says our country's going to hell in a handcart. The government's been taken over by big money and special interests. He says a war's coming, but it ain't going to be between us and the Russians or the Arabs. It's going to be us against the government. He gets real worked up. Me, I kinda like the maneuvers we sometimes go on during weekends. Get to pretend we're at war for a while, then have us some steaks and brews. Honest to god, I never thought we'd be tapped to do anything."

He claimed he didn't know much about what was going on. He and his cousin had been called up a day before the senator's plane went down. That's when he met Cole Wannamaker for the first time.

"I knew about him, course. We all got pictures of him. But meeting him in person, that was something. I mean, he's a celebrity."

"Was he the one giving orders?"

"Yeah, him and Boog Sorenson. He's our local colonel."

"I know Sorenson," Cork said, with an unpleasant taste in his mouth. "You were called up before the senator's plane went down. What for?"

"Boog put Axel and me at a barricade on the road to Desolation Mountain. Gave us hard hats to wear, like we was working road construction. Told us to keep anybody out who was headed toward the mountain that afternoon. He spread the others out in them aspens up there on the mountain. Said a plane was going to be coming down somewhere around there. When it crashed, our job was to get rid of the barricade, get to the wreckage along with the other guys, and pull out the flight recorder. He showed us a picture of what it would look like. Told us it would be somewhere in the debris of the tail section."

"Did you know whose plane was going to crash?"

"Not until after, when I heard it on the news."

"But you didn't get the recorder," Bo said.

"Didn't have no chance. That plane came down way past where any of us was. When we got there, them Indians was already all over the place. By the time we assembled ourselves enough to maybe run 'em off, fire trucks and police cars and you name it had showed up, and we had to get our asses out of there."

"Did Boog tell you to round up the people from the reservation?" Cork asked.

"Them orders came from Wannamaker hisself."

"Your cousin, was he the man with you when you went after my son?"

"Look, I'm sorry about that beating, kid," he said to Stephen. "That was Axel's doing. He's always been on the impulsive side."

"What about my dad?" Stephen said. "Someone took a shot at him. Was that you?"

"Not me. Nels Jensen, one of the other guys in the brigade. Boog's orders."

"Why me?" Cork said.

"Boog was real worried about you interfering. You know, you being this hotshot investigator and all. Plus, I guess he's never liked you much. Jensen was supposed to take you out at your house, but he blew it."

"The break-in," Daniel said.

"After that, you were bouncing around so much, we couldn't get a bead on you. Wannamaker suggested Boog set you up somewhere Jensen could take a good, clean shot. Boog came up with the ransom idea. Guess he didn't count on you wearing body armor."

"Why'd you and your cousin split up today?" Stephen asked.

"Got a cell phone call from Boog. Surprised the hell out of me that we could even get service out here. Something big was going down. He wanted us all back at the Op Center. By then we figured the woman must be hiding somewhere behind us. Axel went to look for her. I kept after you. He was supposed to come back for me. The son of a bitch musta just took off. Or maybe he was under orders."

"Something big?" Cork said. "Did they tell you what it was?"

"Uh-uh. Just ordered us to come back."

Cork saw a look in Bo's eyes that told him they were both thinking the same thing. It was Bo who spoke. "They have the flight recorder."

"Where's this Op Center?" Daniel asked.

"Bout five miles west of Aurora on a little lake called Celtic."

"Because the water's green," Cork said. "I know the place. An old hunting lodge, the only structure on the lake. Pretty well isolated. Used to belong to Casper Ferguson before he died. Don't know who owns it now."

Rainy spoke for the first time since the questioning of Simpson had begun. "What about the people from the rez you rounded up?"

"Got 'em locked in an old smokehouse at the Op Center."

"They're okay?" Cork asked.

Simpson was slow to answer. "The men, their faces are going to look kinda like your boy's. Nothing that time won't take care of."

"What's the plan?" Bo said. "Any idea what they're going to do with those people?"

"I don't know."

"Think about it for a moment, Wes," Bo pressed him. "Those people were kidnapped. That's a felony, maybe a capital crime. If they can identify you and the others, that's prison, at the very least, for all of you."

"Not me. I got immunity promised."

"My point is this," Bo said. "Now that they have what they wanted, they can't just let those folks go."

"Kill 'em?" Simpson said, as if it was the first time the thought had occurred to him. "Naw. Axel is a little hotheaded, but he wouldn't just kill somebody."

"Maybe not him," Bo said. "But the others. Wannamaker or Sorenson or that Nels Jensen who took a shot at Cork."

Simpson mulled it over. "Yeah, I guess I could see Wannamaker or Boog or Jensen doing something like that. Or maybe even one of the other guys. They really buy this resistance shit."

"How many are there?"

"Seven locals and Wannamaker."

"We need to get our people out of there now," Cork said.

Daniel spoke the unthinkable. "Maybe it's already too late."

Henry Meloux, who'd been silent for a long while, staring into the fire and listening, said, "And maybe it is not. There is only one way to know."

Before leaving Crow Point, the men discussed bringing in Sheriff Marsha Dross, but Cork was deeply concerned that every passing minute placed the prisoners in greater danger, especially if the brigade had the flight recorder in its possession. If the sheriff was brought in, too many agencies would want a hand in mounting an assault, and the time it would take to mobilize them might make it too late to save the Hukaris and Blessing. At the very least, it would be wise to confirm the truth of the things Simpson had told them before bringing in the authorities.

It was well after midnight when they got to the cutoff to Celtic Lake. The moon was up, casting shadows. Cork pulled the Expedition off the road and into a grove of aspens. Simpson's hands were bound with duct tape substituted for the strips cut from his pant leg.

"Just keep away from the road and you should be good," Simpson advised. "About that promise?"

"I'll make sure you get immunity," Cork said, a lie that fell easily from his lips.

On foot, they paralleled the lane through the forest, keeping their distance because of the motion sensors Simpson had claimed were placed along the way. In the moonlit night, it took them fifteen minutes to reach the lodge, which was perched on a rise overlooking the small lake. A light shone in a window on the first level; otherwise the building was dark. Several vehicles had been parked in front.

"Yep, Axel's there. See that big black Ram pickup? That's mine. We was driving it today."

Cork said, "Where's the smokehouse they've got our people in?"

"Among them trees to the right of the lodge. Can't really see it in the dark like this."

"Is it guarded?"

"Just locked. But the brigade's got itself an armory," Simpson cautioned. "Heavy-caliber stuff. They hear us coming, they'll cut us down in seconds."

Cork prayed they could do this thing without any shots being fired. Bo had drawn his Sig and Daniel his service sidearm. Ned Love carried his rifle. But from what Simpson said, this was nothing compared to the armaments inside the lodge.

They moved slowly, carefully. The building was surrounded by birch trees whose leaves were so newly fallen that they'd created a soft bedding on the ground, which muted the men's footfalls. At the edge of the birch trees lay a wide, barren space, the parking area for the brigade vehicles. Some twenty yards to the right, just as Simpson had said, stood a squat log structure, dappled with silver moonlight breaking through the branches of the trees. The men made their way around the yard to the smokehouse. Again, just as Simpson had said, the door was padlocked.

"Who has a key?" Cork asked.

"Wannamaker and Boog. That's it."

"We'll need to pry that hasp loose."

"I got a crowbar in the toolbox in the back of my truck. I can get it," said Simpson.

"No, I'll get it," Cork told him.

"There's a combination lock." Simpson gave him the numbers.

He stole across the yard to the big Dodge Ram and climbed into the bed. He unlocked the toolbox and dug as quietly as he could for the crowbar. Just as his hand wrapped around the cold metal, the door of the lodge swung open, and a man stepped onto the porch. The opened door allowed light to spill across the yard, and Cork was no longer in the dark. He froze, pressed himself against the back of the cab, the crowbar clutched in his hand. The man walked to the edge of the porch, a figure black against the light from inside. There was something odd about the silhouette. Then Cork understood he was carrying a rifle on a strap, and the long barrel was like a single antenna jutting up from his shoulder. The man struck a flame, illuminating his face for a moment as he lit a cigarette. Cork didn't recognize him. The man smoked for a while, then flicked the butt and its ember onto the ground.

"Time to take care of business," he mumbled to himself, but loud enough that Cork heard.

Business? he thought. His hand tightened around the crowbar. He calculated quickly. If the man headed to the smokehouse, he'd have to be taken out, and taken out quietly. It would require a leap from the truck bed and a sprint, a significant risk, but one that couldn't be avoided.

The man moved across the yard toward the smokehouse. He brought the rifle off his shoulder and cradled it with both hands. Cork tensed, ready to leap.

Then the man stopped. He set the rifle on the ground. Cork heard the sizzle of a zipper being lowered, followed by the dull sound of urine on dirt, a sound that went on for a while. The man zipped back up, lifted his rifle, and returned to the porch, where he paused, eyeing the night one last time before he slipped back inside, closing the door behind him.

Cork loped to the smokehouse.

"Thought he was coming this way for sure," Daniel said, his firearm in his hand.

"Keep those guns ready," Cork said. "This might be noisy."

He worked the teeth of the crowbar between the hasp and the wood of the door, which had softened with age. He wedged the two teeth deeper until he got some force behind the pry. The wood gave a loud creak. He stopped, waited. Nothing from the house. He resumed the prying and in a minute, had broken the hasp free. He opened the door, and the smell of burned wood washed over him. There was no sound from the utter dark inside, and he tried to prepare himself for the worst. Bodies, maybe. Or maybe nothing. Because if you killed someone in the North Country and you wanted to get rid of the evidence, there were plenty of bogs that would swallow a body whole.

He slipped out his cell phone and used the light to illuminate the dark.

They sat on the dirt of the smokehouse floor, their backs against the wall. Sue Hukari was positioned between her husband and Tom Blessing. Her eyes were white circles of fearful anticipation. Her hands, and her husband's and Blessing's, were bound at the wrists with disposable plastic restraints.

"It's Cork O'Connor," he whispered. "We're getting you out of here."

Ned Love and the others joined him, and they cut the restraints. They helped the prisoners to their feet and, because their ordeal had weakened them, offered support.

In half an hour, they were back at the Expedition, and Cork made the call.

"Marsha, we've got a situation."

CHAPTER 41

"I had to bring Quaker in, Cork. Domestic terrorism is out of my jurisdiction. Quaker made that abundantly clear to me."

They waited with Marsha Dross at the Tamarack County Sheriff's Office—Bo and the O'Connors and Daniel English. The others—Wes Simpson, Ned Love, Phil and Sue Hukari, and Tom Blessing—were all still being questioned by the FBI. Assistant Director Alex Quaker had come and gone, taken with him the information they'd supplied, as well as diagrams of the exterior and interior of the lodge that Wes Simpson had sketched. Quaker assured them that agents were preparing an assault at Celtic Lake. Dross had put a call out to all her deputies to assemble and stand by.

"They better get there soon," Cork said. "If those lunatics see that broken hasp on the smokehouse door, they'll scatter like flies." He stood at the window of Dross's office, staring where the streetlights of Aurora shone in bright circles on the empty thoroughfares.

It had been a long day for Stephen O'Connor, who sat in the common area visible through the door of Dross's office, his feet propped on a table, eyes closed and, despite all the activity around him, napping. English had gone outside to talk to his wife on his cell phone.

Bo sat in a hard wooden chair in front of the sheriff's desk, drinking bad coffee from a cardboard cup.

"The Lexington Brigade shot down Senator McCarthy's plane." Dross sat at her desk, looking as tired as the others, her words sounding leaden. "I would have said that's nuts, except for Oklahoma City and Ted Kaczynski and the bomb at the Atlanta Olympics."

Bo could have offered other examples of patriotism gone horribly awry, many of which were completely unknown outside a relatively small circle of D.C. national security experts.

"What did they hope to accomplish?" She spoke more to herself than to the others.

"Maybe they'd finally had enough of her political agenda," Bo said. "It certainly ran contrary to everything the brigade espouses. But there's still the question, why now?"

"The mine?" Dross offered. "It's generated a lot of anger up here, from all sides. And Senator McCarthy was outspoken in her opposition to the project. Maybe Wannamaker convinced Boog Sorenson this was the time to make a stand."

Cork was still looking through the window at the dark night. "A stand. Shooting down a civilian plane? Now there's true American heroism for you."

Bo said, "If they were the ones who got to the flight recorder before us, I'd love to know for sure how they understood where to look. The rez telegraph you talk about, Cork?"

Cork looked over his shoulder. "No telling who's tapped in."

"Boog Sorenson is a horse's ass," Dross said bluntly. "But he's got a lot of feelers out there in Tamarack County, and some of them, I'm sure, extend into our Native community. And, Cork, somebody must've let the brigade know you were involved and helped set you up for that shot at the town meeting."

"There are lots of people with Native blood who share the brigade's distrust of our government," Cork said. "But I have trouble believing they'd go along with any of this. I'm inclined to think Bo was on the right track. Someone bugged us."

"The brigade?" Dross said.

"If they have the flight recorder, I guess it had to be them." Cork put his hand to the window glass as if trying to touch the night outside. "We'll know in a while."

Not long after, a sudden commotion arose in the common area, and Alex Quaker entered the sheriff's office, flanked by two men looking just as grim as he. Daniel English and Cork's son came in behind them, escorted by another agent.

"Close the door," Quaker ordered one of the agents.

It was a crowded room now, and Quaker moved to the center.

Dross said, "Well?"

Quaker focused on Cork. "Tell me again what went down while you were out there."

"We arrived at Celtic Lake and proceeded to the lodge, then to the smokehouse, where I pried off the hasp. We freed our friends, left the scene. I called Sheriff Dross and brought everyone back here."

"You were armed?"

"Bo, Daniel, Ned, they had firearms. No one else."

"What kinds of firearms?"

"A Sig Sauer, a Glock, a hunting rifle."

"Did you discharge them?"

"Are you kidding? From what Simpson told us, they had an arsenal in that house. If we'd fired a shot, they would have cut us down. What's going on? When are you going to make your assault on the lodge?"

"The operation is finished."

"Finished?" Dross sounded astounded. "So soon?"

"We encountered no resistance. What we found were seven bodies inside the lodge. They'd been lined up and executed."

"Wannamaker?"

"He wasn't among them."

"Boog Sorenson?"

"Dead, like the others."

"What about the flight recorder?" Cork asked.

"We retrieved the flight recorder."

"Executed," English said. "By whom?"

"That's the question, isn't it?" Quaker sat on the edge of the sheriff's desk. "It's going to be a while before you folks go home."

They were all interrogated again and, as the sky began to show the first light of day, finally allowed to go. The Hukaris and Tom Blessing had been taken to the Aurora Community Hospital to be checked over before they were officially released. Wes Simpson was being held, pending charges. The others piled into Cork's Expedition and headed toward the reservation. They were silent, drained, each lost in thought or in the drowse of exhaustion. They arrived at the place where Bo had left his Jeep the evening before, and they prepared to separate.

"Guess that's it," Cork said.

"Are you kidding?" Bo gave a short laugh. "The press is going to descend on you. You're heroes."

"I don't feel like a hero," Stephen said.

"As I understand it, heroes seldom do," Bo told him. "I don't know about the rest of you, but I need some shut-eye."

"Thanks for your help." Cork extended his hand.

"Any time."

Bo stood on the roadside and watched as the Expedition

headed toward Allouette and beyond that the dirt road that would take them all back to Crow Point East. He believed that for them, this incident was over. He still had miles to go before he slept.

She was quiet on her end.

"Quaker will release an official statement soon, I'm sure, at least outlining the operation and what came of it," Bo told her.

"The Lexington Brigade. Fanatics. And all this death." She sighed, a sound like a hand smoothing satin. "What about Cole Wannamaker?"

"If what Wes Simpson told us was correct, he was at the lodge earlier. But he wasn't among the dead. The speculation at the moment is that he executed them all."

"Why?"

"A case could be made, I suppose, that he was just trying to cover his tracks."

"Or he was just as crazy as he's always sounded."

"They'll grab him. Maybe not right away, but he can't stay underground forever. Once they have him, they'll get the whole story."

"Remember Jack Ruby? Someone arranged for him to kill Oswald before the man could talk."

Conspiracy theory, he thought. But she, of all people, was entitled to believe in conspiracies.

"How did they do it?" she asked.

"What?"

"Bring Olympia's plane down?"

"Quaker said they found a couple of Stingers among the armaments at the lodge."

"A Stinger?"

"A manually operated ground-to-air missile system. Looks like a fancy bazooka. Quaker believes that the flight recorder and the NTSB investigation will verify that's what brought the plane down."

"So. End of story."

"Maybe. I'm not letting go yet. There are still some loose ends."

"Like what?"

"Like how the brigade knew where to find the flight recorder."

"Didn't you say that word got out on the reservation?"

"That's one possibility. It's also possible someone involved was bugged."

"But you're not buying it?"

He waited a moment, then, "Who did you tell on your end?"

"You still think Gerard might have somebody on the inside here?"

"I'm just trying to consider all the possibilities. Who did you tell?"

"Olympia's father, that's it."

"Who did he tell?"

"I don't know."

"Ask him."

"All right," she agreed, but she didn't sound happy. "What about you? What are you going to do?"

For the first time since she'd brought him into this situation, he wondered if he should tell her the truth. "Get some sleep, then get back to work."

Bo brewed himself some coffee, sat at the table in his cabin, and as the sun began to peek above the trees along the inlet on Iron Lake, listened again to what he'd just downloaded from the recorder hidden at Gerard's command center. It was nothing but static, which could have been the result of defective equipment. Bo sipped his coffee, watched the sun ease itself into the day, and didn't for an instant think that defective equipment was the reason.

Chapter 42

The news, when it broke the next day, was big, and Aurora swelled once again with media people thick as summer tourists. Just as Bo Thorson had predicted, the O'Connors and the folks on the reservation became the targets of significant and unwanted attention. When Cork attempted to reopen Sam's Place, reporters descended like locusts, and he shut down again. Stephen tried to return to his classes at the community college but was dogged even there by reporters and barraged with questions from his classmates, so he stopped going. He'd begun texting regularly with Marlee Daychild and found her company, even in a virtual way, comforting. Mostly, the O'Connors hid out on Crow Point, waiting for things to quiet down.

Allouette was overrun. Phil and Sue Hukari took off to stay with relatives in Oregon until things died down. Tom Blessing muddled along in the preparations for his mother's funeral. Ned and Monkey Love, whose cabin was nearly impossible to find, were the only lucky ones.

Although the FBI had reported that the flight recorder recovered in the lodge on Celtic Lake was wiped clean by the brigade, word had leaked that the NTSB's investigation confirmed the senator's plane had, indeed, been shot out of the air by a missile. A national manhunt for Cole Wannamaker was under way. Members of the Lexington Brigade were being rounded up and questioned. The president, in a news conference, praised the work of the FBI and vowed that protecting the nation against terrorism, both domestic and from abroad, was a top priority. At the Capitol, the Senate prepared to begin debate on the Manila Accord.

The nightmare should have been over. But Stephen's vision continued to plague him.

Three days after the rescue of the Hukaris and Blessing at the lodge, Stephen sat with Henry Meloux, Leah Duling, and Beulah Love on the shoreline of Iron Lake. It was a perfect morning, the lake a mirror reflecting the powder blue of the sky and the trees along the shoreline full of autumn fire. Beulah Love had shown no inclination to return to her home in Allouette or to her former existence. A woman Stephen had always seen as cold and aloof had undergone a remarkable transformation. She'd formed a deep friendship with Leah Duling and was constantly expressing her appreciation for Stephen's heroic effort in saving her from the men of the Lexington Brigade. She'd just finished weaving a wreath of wildflowers, and she leaned far forward and studied her reflection in the mirror of the water.

"I used to make these when I was a girl. A long, long time ago."

"Before boarding school?" Leah said.

"The end of my childhood," Beulah noted with sadness.

"But you have found again the child in your heart," Henry told her.

"I would never have thought something good would come from all this."

"I think there is still more good on the horizon," Henry said. "More good before the storm."

"Storm?" Stephen turned his gaze from the far islands that lay like sleeping dogs on the mirror of the lake.

"These woods," the old Mide said. "They still speak of a great evil."

"The monster at my back," Stephen said.

"Maybe at the backs of us all."

"You're scaring me," Leah said.

"And me," Beulah chimed in. "Are you afraid, Henry?"

"Unsettled." To Stephen, the old man said, "I would like to see this monster that does not show itself to you. When you face this thing, and I think you will, I would like to be with you."

Stephen was torn. If he ever confronted this terrible thing, he would like his old mentor at his side. But he was also afraid for Henry, who sometimes seemed so frail that a strong wind could blow him over.

"It might show itself when you're not with me, Henry."

The old man thought about that. "Then I will stay with you."

"I'm not sure that's feasible."

"Then we must flush this beast from its hiding."

"I'd love to. Any idea how?"

"I will think on it."

Henry rose slowly and began to make his way back to the cabin. Beulah stood and followed, but Leah remained seated beside Stephen. "I'm afraid for him," she confessed.

As the old man moved away, he seemed to grow smaller. Stephen said, "So am I."

That same day, Daniel and Rainy returned to work. Daniel took his truck, but Stephen shuttled Rainy in his old Jeep. In Allouette, he dropped her at the clinic, then passed the stop where the kids from the reservation waited for the school bus. Winston Goodsky wasn't among them. Stephen parked and went into Harmon Goodsky's gallery. The place felt empty. He prowled, admiring the photographs on the walls, and came to one of a familiar scene, a gray-green outcrop crowning a hill of stone. Desolation Mountain. The photo made the rock outcrop look like a castle keep, a foreboding structure against a threatening sky, a powerful and disturbing image.

Harmon Goodsky stepped from the curtains that closed off the back rooms. "*Boozhoo,* Stephen." He walked like a man teetering at the edge of a precipice, doing his best not to fall. Looking at him, the healer in Stephen understood that he was beyond the help of even Henry Meloux. "What can I do for you?"

"Just looking. I like this photograph. Did you take it?"

"One of Winston's. My grandson's got a natural eye for drama. I forgot about that one." He removed it from the wall.

"You should leave it up. It's good."

"He's shot better."

"I didn't see him at the bus stop this morning."

"Isn't feeling well. I've been keeping him home. Things okay with you and your family now? That was some big stuff went down."

"Not quite back to normal, but we're headed there."

Stephen left, but Winston Goodsky's photo had nudged him in a direction he hadn't thought of in a while. He decided to make a visit to the place where everything had begun.

The road to the base of Desolation Mountain was clear and empty. Stephen hiked the path that most people took to the top and made his way through the ring of aspen trees. The path was blanketed in fallen gold leaves. He walked in stillness until he came to the end of the aspens and stood at the edge of the wide, bare apron of rock that lay around the base of the crowning outcrop.

It was a golden day. The sun sat atop the mountain like a king on his throne, and Stephen shielded his eyes against the brilliance. Under the shade of his hand, he saw a figure fifty yards up the slope. The figure was turned toward the mountain crest. To Stephen it appeared as if one of the figure's arms was pointed toward the crowning outcrop, and the image shook loose a startling recognition.

At the sound of Stephen's approach, the kid spun, his face full of surprise and fear.

"Easy, Winston," Stephen said. "Just me."

The kid held a camera, to which was affixed a long telescopic lens.

"I thought you were sick," Stephen said. "That's why your grandfather's keeping you out of school."

The kid looked down at the hard rock beneath his feet. "He wants me to stay home for a while, until everything settles down."

"Does he know where you are?"

Winston shook his head. "I told him I was going to shoot along the lakeshore. He doesn't want me coming up here."

"Why?"

"He's afraid."

"Of what?"

"I should go."

"Wait. I'll make you a deal. There's something I want to tell you about this place, something that might sound pretty strange. If it makes sense, you tell me why. Okay?"

"Really, I have to go."

"It's important."

The kid let a few seconds pass. Stephen wondered what he was weighing in his thinking. Then the kid gave a simple nod.

Stephen told him about the vision in which they both played a part. When he finished, he said, "I see this night after night. Does it mean anything to you?"

The kid looked away from Stephen. His eyes settled on the outcrop that topped the mountain. "There's something you should see."

He tipped his camera and, in the shade of his own shadow, studied the LCD display screen as he scanned through images. He stopped and handed the camera to Stephen. The image showed the crown of Desolation Mountain, that outcrop like a castle keep. But to the right was something else, something smaller and squarish in design. Stephen squinted but could make out only that he was looking at a vehicle of some kind. "I don't understand."

The kid took the camera, zoomed in on the image, and returned it to Stephen. Now what Stephen saw was a military-looking truck painted in camouflage. From the open bed in back rose a huge device that, with its hood and forked tongue, reminded Stephen of a cobra about to strike. Three men seemed to be attending to the device.

"What is it?"

"I don't know," Winston said. "But look at this."

He shifted the focus on the LCD display to a bird in the sky above the vehicle and zoomed in even farther on the display. Now Stephen could see that it wasn't a bird at all.

"Is that Senator McCarthy's plane?"

Winston didn't reply, but his face said it all.

CHAPTER 43

The final meeting with Gerard went, as Bo had suspected it would, with all the emotion and formality of an exchange of chips at a casino window. He was paid in cash for his services, and Gerard didn't even bother to shake his hand. It took place at Bo's cabin, and as Gerard headed toward the door, Bo said, "What about my bonus?"

"Bonus?" Gerard turned back. "What bonus?"

"You told me if I got the black box, there'd be a bonus in it."

"The FBI got it in their sweep of the lodge on Celtic Lake."

"Ah, but how did it get there?"

"Search me."

"That wouldn't do any good. You'd be clean as a new bathtub." Bo was sipping a beer, Leinenkugel's. He lifted the can in a toast to himself. "I didn't do a bad job of sorting out the players. NTSB and FBI, they were obvious. I tracked a lot of vehicles up here back to DoD, several different departments. The Lexington Brigade, of course. Elements of the Ojibwe community. But I still have no idea who hired you."

"Is that important?"

"The FBI may have the black box, but the information that was on it? That went to whoever brought you in. Then you wiped the recorder clean."

"The Lexington Brigade wiped it clean."

"That's certainly the story."

"I know another story, Thorson. One about a man hired to do a job. Then he sells himself out to another employer. What do you think of a man who'd do that?"

"Like everything that happens in the world, Colonel, it all depends on the reason."

"In this story, if I were a romantic, I'd say the reason was affection."

"Maybe you wouldn't be entirely wrong. But the truth is more complicated."

"Truth?" Gerard's face was a gray slate on which nothing was written. "We float on a sea of lies. There is no solid ground called truth."

"What poem is that from?"

"No poem. Just the way it is."

"And that's where we differ."

Gerard turned back toward the door. "I'll expect you to leave this county today."

"Always a pleasure dealing with you, Colonel."

For the next couple of days, Bo lived out of his Jeep, staying off Gerard's radar, avoiding communication with everyone. Communications had clearly been monitored. He was almost certain that, from the beginning, Gerard had known about *her*. The bug, he suspected, was probably on her end the whole time. Without knowing it, she had been compromised from the get-go, or Olympia McCarthy's family had been.

Although the man had made it quite clear that Bo was not to stick around, Gerard himself made no move to leave, which led

Bo to believe there were still loose ends to be tied up. The knots Gerard used to tie up loose ends were often of a lethal kind. Bo was concerned about the safety of the O'Connors and the people on the reservation. He was also concerned about getting to the truth. A U.S. senator had been assassinated, and her family killed along with her. As corny as it sounded, Bo wanted justice for them.

He practically hijacked Cork O'Connor. He'd been waiting half a day near the double-trunk birch that marked the path to Crow Point. When Cork finally showed and began the hike, Bo stepped from the cover of the trees.

"Jesus!" Cork jumped back and tensed as if for a fight. "What the hell, Bo? I thought you were gone."

"We need to talk."

"I'm heading to Crow Point. Why don't you join me? You'll be welcome there."

"Maybe not after you hear what I have say. There's something I need to explain."

Cork waited. Everything around them was quiet. Bo felt as if the forest, too, was listening. After all he'd heard the old Mide say, he'd come to accept that the forest might have eyes and ears and spirit. That it might already know the truth.

"That ransom I told you about, Cork? The Argentine diplomat's son? It was Gerard who brought me in. I've worked with him a few times over the years."

Cork looked stung, then wary. "Why didn't you tell me sooner?"

"It's complicated."

"Were you working for him up here?"

"Yes. And no. After the senator's family contacted me, Gerard did the same. I knew if he was involved, something definitely wasn't right. I accepted his offer, thinking that what I learned from him, I could pass along to the senator's family."

"Like some kind of double agent?"

"More or less."

"And you couldn't tell me?"

"Safer for you and for everybody if I didn't. I'm sorry about that, but I hope you understand."

"So who is this Gerard?"

"An operative of sorts for the government. A kind of fixer."

"A fixer?"

"He's brought in to manage delicate situations."

"Like the assassination of a U.S. senator?"

"Let's walk," Bo said.

As they made their way toward Crow Point, Bo explained to Cork about the bug he'd placed at Gerard's headquarters and that Gerard had eventually discovered and disabled.

"They talked about looking for bear tracks on Desolation Mountain and looking for waves on the beach. Code, of course, but code for what?"

"The flight recorder," Cork said, as if it were obvious.

"Bear tracks? I don't know. And waves on the beach? I get a different feel."

"Maybe he's talking about evidence of the brigade's missile attack. Bear tracks could, I suppose, refer to the trail they left up on the mountain."

"What about waves on the beach?"

Cork thought for a bit. "Got me."

"Waves," Bo said. "It sounds electronic to me."

"So how do you want to proceed?"

"I'm not sure. Mostly I wanted to warn you. Gerard hasn't left Tamarack County. If I were a betting man, I'd lay odds that he got to the flight recorder ahead of us. I think he downloaded the info he wanted from it, wiped it clean, then planted it at the lodge on Celtic Lake."

"Planted it?" Cork stopped and stared at Bo. "Are you saying Gerard killed all those men?"

"I wouldn't put it past him."

"How did he know about them?"

"I don't know if he was aware of them from the beginning, or if he picked up that information along the way. There are still a lot of unanswered questions. But one of the reasons I wanted to talk to you was just to alert you to the fact that he's still around, maybe still monitoring you and your family and those folks on the reservation. Be very careful what you say and who you say it to. And keep watching your backs. There must still be some loose end, and until he's tied it up, Gerard won't leave."

They'd come to the creek Cork told him was called Blood in the language of the Ojibwe. Bo paused there.

"Don't tell anyone you saw me. But, Cork, if you learn anything of value, anything that might point us toward some answers, let me know."

Cork studied him, and Bo knew that he was making a difficult decision. The man understood the whole truth now and had no reason to trust him.

"A call?" Cork finally said.

"That's fine. But let's use a code word to let me know without saying it."

"*Migwech,*" Cork said.

"*Migwech?*"

"It means 'thank you' in Ojibwe."

"All right. *Migwech* it is."

"If we need to meet, how about the fire ring on Crow Point? A good, safe place."

The two men shook hands, and as Cork walked away in the early afternoon shadows, Bo looked after him, thinking how wrong

Gerard had been. In every sea of lies, there were always islands of truth.

On his return to Crow Point, Cork found Jenny and Daniel at Meloux's cabin. Daniel seemed in a particularly good mood.

"We finally tracked down those two we thought were poachers," he told Cork. "Tom Blessing reported them at Bourbon Lake again, near the otter lodge. They were still out there when I arrived."

"Thought were poachers?" Cork said. "They weren't?"

"They were pretty reluctant to talk, but when I threatened them with the poaching charge and told them it could carry a sentence of up to two years in prison and a ten-thousand-dollar fine each, they spilled the beans."

"Two years in prison? Ten thousand dollars? And they bought that?"

Daniel laughed. "Clearly not hunters."

"So what are they?"

"They call themselves 'prospecting geologists.' "

"Prospecting for what?"

"They were hired to find the limits of the Duluth Complex, this mother lode of heavy metals."

"On the rez?"

"They think the bulk of the resources may be under reservation land."

"Who hired them?"

"A company called PolyOre Exploration. They were supposed to keep this on the QT. That's why they were so elusive."

"PolyOre Exploration? I'm thinking we should know more about these people."

"I already do. As soon as I finished interviewing the geologists, I got on the Internet. PolyOre Exploration is a subsidiary of Intercontinental Minerals Inc., which, if you follow the difficult track back, is owned by America Midwest Mining."

"What do they think? That in the end they can mine anywhere they want? That land belongs to the Anishinaabeg."

"All of the Black Hills belonged to the Lakota once," Jenny pointed out.

"Did you keep them in custody, Daniel?"

"No reason. They weren't poaching."

"Where is everybody?" Cork asked, because except for his daughter and son-in-law, Crow Point was deserted.

"Rainy's still at the clinic," Jenny replied. "Henry, Leah, Beulah, and Waaboo are out gathering herbs. Trixie trotted along with them."

"Stephen?"

"We haven't seen him since he left with Rainy this morning. He should have been back by now."

Bo's warning—*Keep watching your backs*—returned in a powerful rush.

"Try his phone, Jenny."

She used her cell, waited. "He's not answering."

"He could just be out of cell phone range," Daniel said. "Hit and miss out here. But if you want to look for him, I parked my truck out at Crow Point East. I'll drive."

The two men moved quickly down the path that headed east from Crow Point and along the lakeshore. Cork went over in his head all the safe possibilities: Stephen was, as Daniel suggested, out of cell phone range; his phone was out of juice; he was involved in something important and had simply missed the call. At the same time, he had to consider the more dire possibility: just as Bo Thorson had speculated, there was more going on in

Tamarack County, and Stephen was caught in some deadly, new threat.

"Cork," Daniel said, pulling him out of his dark reverie. "Listen."

They stopped near a copse of birch. A stiff wind shoved through the trees, and at first Cork heard only the loud liquid sound of the leaves rustling in its passage. Then he heard what Daniel's younger ears had already picked up, the sound of an approaching vehicle. With all the uncertainty that had been the norm of late, they took to the trees to wait. In half a minute, Stephen's dusty old Jeep appeared, carefully following the narrow path. Stephen wasn't alone, and the kid in the passenger seat was quite a surprise to Cork. He and Daniel stepped into the open.

"You've been gone a long time," Cork said, approaching the driver's side. "And you aren't answering your phone."

"Sorry, Dad. It's on vibrate, hard to feel in the Jeep." Stephen took the phone from the pocket of his jacket and made the switch.

"Afternoon, Winston," Cork said.

The kid stared down at his feet.

"What's up, Stephen?"

"Dad, there's something you've got to see. Show him, Winston."

The kid had a camera in his lap, a fine-looking Nikon with a powerful telescopic lens affixed. "You . . . you need to come over here," he said.

Cork moved around to the other side of the Jeep. The kid held out the camera in a way that made the display screen visible. What Cork saw appeared to be a military vehicle mounted with some kind of dish being operated by men in camo.

"What is this?"

Stephen answered: "Winston took that on Desolation Mountain the day Senator McCarthy's plane crashed. Show him what's in the sky, Winston."

The kid took the camera, shifted the image on the display, enlarged it, and handed the camera back to Cork. After a long moment, Cork said, "We've got a lot of talking to do, son."

Fresh in his mind was Bo's warning of the possibility of surveillance bugs everywhere, even in the cabins on Crow Point, and Cork herded everyone to the safety of the fire ring to hear Winston Goodsky's story. The young man was clearly uncomfortable with such a large gathering. Cork suspected he would be uncomfortable regardless of the size or makeup of the group. He was like an animal of the forest, a deer maybe, harmless, whose best defense was stillness and second best was flight.

"After school, I went to take some pictures on the mountain. My granddad lets me use his truck as long as I don't leave the rez. I couldn't get to the mountain that day. There was some work going on and the road was closed."

"Roadwork?" Daniel looked to Cork and Stephen. "Wes Simpson and his cousin at the barricade."

"Let him finish," Cork said.

"I know lots of old logging roads, so I drove around to the north side, and parked near Little Bass Lake and hiked up from there. I wanted to get some pictures of those rocks at the top against the clouds. I thought it was, you know, a dramatic setting."

"I saw one of your photographs of Desolation Mountain at your grandfather's gallery today," Stephen told him. "I thought it was awesome."

The kid's face lit up at the praise. "What I wanted to do was make a series across the whole fall, then winter and spring and summer. My granddad said I should call it the Desolation Series."

"Go on," Cork said.

"I was standing just where the trees end, that ring of aspens, you know. I liked the long shot up the bare slope, nice foreground stuff. I put on my AF lens." He tapped the powerful attachment on his camera. "I did a couple of shots, then that truck or whatever showed up. It parked at the top of the mountain and those guys started working with that thing in back. They ruined the whole scene. But I thought what the heck and kept shooting anyway."

"Did they see you?"

"Not then. I was still in the cover of the trees. But I heard the plane coming and then, it was really strange because the sound of it cut out. Like the engines just died. I could see it starting to fall from the sky and I took shot after shot. I got so caught up that I moved out of the trees to follow it as it fell. That's when they saw me."

"What did they do?" Cork asked.

"I don't know. As soon as they saw me, I ran. I got down to my granddad's truck and took off and went back to Allouette as fast as I could."

"Did you tell your grandfather what happened?"

The kid nodded. "And I showed him the pictures. He told me not to say anything to anyone until he decided what we should do. Then everybody started disappearing on the rez, and he got real scared for me. He made me promise never to say a word. And never go to the mountain. But I've sneaked back a couple of times and watched them searching. I never could figure what for."

"I saw you there," Stephen said.

"I know. When you came into the gallery, I was afraid you would recognize me and tell my granddad." The boy looked at the others in a guilty way, thinking, perhaps, that what he'd revealed to them was a breach of his promise.

"You've done the right thing," Cork assured him.

What he didn't say was that he understood now Bo Thorson's concern regarding Gerard. Winston Goodsky was the loose end that needed tying up.

CHAPTER 44

The call came much sooner than Bo had expected.

"Just wanted to say thank you for all your help, Bo. In the language of the Ojibwe, that would be *migwech*."

"No problem, Cork. You folks up there in Tamarack County, you take care of yourselves. I'm sure our paths will cross again someday soon."

He turned his Jeep around and headed back to the double-trunk birch, then along the trail to Crow Point. It was late afternoon when he found Cork and the others gathered around the fire ring. With them was a teenager he'd never seen before.

O'Connor introduced Winston Goodsky and explained all.

"Let me see the picture."

Winston showed Bo the image on the camera display.

"EW, I'm guessing," Bo said.

Cork gave him a look of incomprehension. "EW?"

"Electronic warfare. A weapon that fires an electromagnetic pulse, an EMP. They're designed to take out electronic systems. Shooting planes out of the sky is one of the potential uses." He glanced at the kid. "Which might explain why you heard that plane's engines go suddenly quiet." Bo studied the image again. "I've only seen pictures, so I don't know for sure. I have a friend in the Pentagon, a guy who used to work Secret Service with me. He might be able to help us out. Can I get a copy of this?"

"I'll have to download it first," Winston said. "My laptop's at my granddad's."

"We need to talk to your grandfather," Cork told the teenager. "He should know all of this."

The kid didn't look happy about it.

"Okay if I go along?" Stephen addressed this to Winston, not to his father.

The kid looked so relieved he almost smiled. "Thanks."

In the end, it was Bo, Winston, Cork, and his son who headed into Allouette. Stephen led the way, ferrying the Goodsky teenager in his old Jeep. Cork and Bo followed. On the way to town, they went over the pieces, trying to fit things together.

"An EW, that would be a military weapon, right?" Cork said. "So, how did the Lexington Brigade get its hands on something like that?"

"They sure as hell didn't buy it off the Internet," Bo said. "Stole it, maybe."

"If it was an electronic weapon that brought the senator's plane down, why is the word from NTSB that a missile was responsible?"

"This sounds like that rare bird, multiple agencies of the government actually working together, in this case to cover up the truth."

"Which brings us to Gerard," Cork said. "If he's this fixer, who's he working for and how does he fit in?"

"He keeps the hands of important people clean. Very important people. Who is that in this case? You could cover him in red-hot coals and he wouldn't tell you."

"Might be a good man to have on your side," Cork noted.

Although he couldn't disagree, Bo added, "But one hell of an adversary."

On the way to Allouette, Winston was quiet, staring straight ahead as if looking into a dismal future.

"Don't worry," Stephen told him. "My father will square things with your granddad."

"He worries about me. A lot." The kid sat slumped, as if under a heavy burden. "He won't talk about it, but everybody knows he's dying. He's worried what'll happen to me when he's gone."

Not an unreasonable concern, Stephen knew. Across the course of his life, living so near the rez and being of mixed heritage himself, he'd seen the frightening pitfalls of the foster care system firsthand, especially when it came to Native kids.

"No family left on the rez?" he asked.

"No one interested in taking me." Winston's hands gripped his knees, as if trying to hold himself down. "I grew up in the city. Feels strange on the rez. I'm not like the other kids there. And I'm not like the kids in town."

Not Ojibwe enough for the Ojibwe or white enough for the whites, a feeling Stephen knew well, one that had plagued him, too, for most of his life. And he thought about his vision and Winston's part in it. *Him and not him.* Kindred spirits, he understood.

In Allouette, Winston lingered in front of the door to his grandfather's gallery, gathering strength to face the music.

"It'll be okay," Stephen assured him.

Stephen's father put his hand on the boy's shoulder. "Telling us was the right thing."

"Convince my granddad of that," the kid said hopelessly.

Inside, Winston led them through the curtains into the back

area of the gallery, where his grandfather sat at a bench, building a frame of lacquered birch for one of his photographs. Goodsky looked up from his work, clearly surprised to see his grandson in all that company.

"What's going on, Winston?"

"Okay if I explain things?" Cork asked, and Winston looked grateful.

When he'd finished the story, Cork said, "It's a good thing he told us, Harmon. There are still people out there trying to track him down."

"And they're the kind of people who won't stop until they find him," Bo added.

Goodsky stood up. In the wake of his conversation with Winston, Stephen was struck by how all the man's ailments threatened to topple him. "Go on," Goodsky said to his grandson. "Put that photo on your laptop. I want a few words with these men."

Winston headed upstairs.

"Wish you didn't know any of this," Goodsky said. "A secret never keeps long on the rez." He looked toward the ceiling. "I fear for him."

"With good reason," Stephen's father said. "But maybe the best way to protect him is to make sure the right people hear what he knows."

"And who would that be?"

"Why don't we start with talking to the sheriff?"

"I don't want to talk to the sheriff." Winston stood at the bottom of the stairs. He held his laptop and a cable connection. "Can't you just show them the picture?"

"It's on the laptop now?" Bo asked.

Winston nodded and handed over the computer. They spent a couple of minutes together, transferring the image to Bo's cell phone.

When they'd finished, Bo said, "What do you think, Cork? Once we get confirmation about the EW, we can take everything to Sheriff Dross. I think in the meantime we could leave Winston out of this." He eyed the boy. "You understand that you'll have to tell your story eventually."

Winston looked as if he were suffering from a toothache.

"We'll be there with you," Stephen assured him.

The rest of the day they waited on Crow Point. Dusk came, and still no word from Bo's contact at the Pentagon. After dark, Stephen walked out into the meadow, unrolled his sleeping bag, and lay down, staring up at the stars. Daniel and Jenny had erected a big tent next to Leah's cabin, where, until the craziness in Aurora had passed, they would sleep with Waaboo. Cork and Rainy shared the cabin with Leah. Bo Thorson had accepted the loan of a good thick blanket and had thrown it out in the meadow near the tent. Stephen, too, preferred to bed down under the open sky, but he'd moved far away from the others. He should have felt satisfied because at last he'd been able to divine much of the meaning of a vision in time for it to be useful, at least where protecting Winston Goodsky was concerned. He understood the element of *him and not him* now. Winston, a kid of mixed heritage, unsure of his future, whose eyes saw the world in a way others did not, and who was somehow able to capture that vision with his camera. Stephen, who often felt like an outsider, too, and had his own unique way of seeing. But there were still two significant elements of the vision that remained a mystery. He didn't understand the part he'd played—or may have yet to play—in the bird shot from the sky. And, maybe most important, he had yet to face the monster at his back.

Dog-tired from another long day, he was asleep before he knew it. And the vision visited him again.

He woke with a start and sat up. A glow came from beyond the rock outcrops where the fire ring lay. He slipped from his bag, put on his boots, and headed toward the fire. Except for Henry, all the men were there: his father, Daniel, and Bo Thorson.

"What's up?" Stephen said.

"We thought you were sound asleep," his father told him.

"I was. What are you all doing here?"

"I got a message from my friend in the Pentagon," Bo said. "He's onto something. I'm waiting for the next communication."

"We're all waiting," Stephen's father said. "Have a seat."

Stephen sat between Bo and Cork and stared into the fire.

"I've been meaning to ask you about this vision of yours," Bo said. "I know the general outline, but I don't know the specifics. Mind going over it with me?"

Although he'd told it many times now, Stephen told it again in detail.

"The eagle shot from the sky? You think that's the senator's plane?"

"What else?"

"Hmmm." Bo tossed a stick onto the fire. "Why, in this vision, does Winston shoot the eagle out of the sky? It wasn't him operating that electronic weapon on the mountaintop."

"I don't know."

"Tell me about this eagle."

"It's just an eagle. Except there's something odd about its tail."

"Odd how?"

"It's not like a regular eagle's tail, which is all white. This one has other colors mixed in."

"What colors?"

"Blue and red."

Bo looked at him, wide-eyed. "Red, white, and blue? The eagle's tail is red, white, and blue?"

Stephen said, "I've been thinking that must be because the plane was carrying a U.S. senator."

Bo pulled out his cell phone, keyed in something, then said, "Does your bird look like this?"

The image was of an eagle in flight, wings spread, talons sharp, as if preparing to grasp some prey. The tail feathers, like those on the bird in Stephen's vision, were red, white, and blue.

"That's it," Stephen said.

Bo tapped in something else on the phone and showed Stephen the screen again. This time the eagle was part of a commercial logo.

"American Byrd Industries," Stephen read aloud. "Never heard of it."

"The name William Byrd doesn't mean anything to you?"

"William Byrd?" Cork said. "As in the Black Bird?"

"The Black Bird," Bo confirmed.

Stephen said, "Wait a minute. Who's this Black Bird?"

"William Byrd, a very wealthy Kansan with a finger in a lot of pies," Bo replied.

"What does he have to do with my vision?"

"You don't know anything about him?"

Stephen gave a shrug. "I don't pay a lot of attention to the news."

"This guy's a heavy hitter in American business and has bullied his way into politics. His family made its fortune manufacturing drilling equipment early last century. During World War Two, they shifted to military production of all kinds, including weaponry. Which made them even richer. After the war, they got into mineral extraction, agribusiness, railroads, trucking, you name it. William Byrd has an interest in more commercial enterprises than you can imagine, but he's still heavily invested in developing weapons for the U.S. and building much of the expensive armaments that we supply to our friends overseas."

"Why did you call him the Black Bird?"

"It's how he refers to himself."

Bo tapped on his cell phone again and showed Stephen an image of a man with a dark complexion and a thick mane of hair the color of an obsidian knife.

"His mother was Italian, I think. Maybe even Sicilian. That's probably where the dark skin comes from. Byrd's somewhere in his eighties, but he keeps that hair as black as coal dust. His nickname probably comes from that. But I've had a couple of brushes with him, and it also describes the color of his heart. Calls himself a patriot, but if you ask me, what he stands for is what's good for William Byrd."

"What kind of brushes?" Stephen's father asked.

"The first was up here, back when you were sheriff and I was Secret Service. He made a visit to the vice president at his vacation home on Iron Lake."

"I don't remember him coming."

"It was very hush-hush, at Byrd's insistence. The man was an asshole, behaved abominably to everyone, including the vice president and his family."

"What about the second brush?" Cork asked.

Bo shook his head. "That one I can't talk about. It's the only job I ever walked away from."

"How would he be involved in what's gone on up here?" Stephen asked.

"For starters, the Senate begins debate on the Manila Accord next week. That's an agreement Senator McCarthy was leading the charge against. Passage would facilitate trade with much of Southeast Asia. It's aimed at taking away some of China's economic influence there. Byrd Industries would certainly benefit from that. But a lot of the accord is about selling military armaments to these nations as well. I'd bet my bottom dollar there's plenty of money earmarked for Byrd Industries. So that's a possibility. I've got to tell you, the Black Bird's a man who feels privileged right down to the marrow of his being. If he wanted someone dead, no matter the reason, he'd see that it was done." Bo gave Stephen a long look of careful appraisal, one that made Stephen uncomfortable. "I've had my doubts about all this vision stuff. But like the man said, there's clearly more in heaven and earth than I've dreamed of in my philosophy."

"You really think Byrd might be behind all this?" Cork asked.

Bo said, "I'm hoping my friend at the Pentagon can enlighten us." Once again, his eyes settled on Stephen. "But you know that monster at your back in the vision? If there are real monsters in this world, William Byrd is one of them for sure."

The night wore on, and the men finally split up and returned to their sleeping places. Stephen sat cross-legged on his sleeping bag in the meadow and thought about the eagle shot from the sky in his vision. He was relieved that it wasn't a sacred eagle, but instead an evil thing that had taken an eagle's form. He used his cell phone to explore further the monster named William Byrd. He wondered what could turn a man's heart to such darkness. He wondered if there was any ceremony that could heal that damaged spirit. He might have spent the rest of the night caught up in the electronic web, which offered him information but no answers, except that his phone chirped at him and shut itself off, and he realized he'd emptied the battery.

Probably for the best, he decided. He lay down and gazed up at the stars, which were beautiful but, like the Internet, gave him no answers.

Chapter 45

The text from Bo's contact in the Pentagon came in the dark hours long before dawn.

This is big. Meet contact 0400 hours. Fly silent. Code word: Eagle. The GPS coordinates followed.

In the meadow not far from where Stephen O'Connor was sleeping, Bo threw off his borrowed blanket. He couldn't see the young man, the grass was so high. It had been a long time since Bo had spent a night like this, under the stars. Hiding out from Gerard, he'd slept in his Jeep. Under the night sky, it was as if something wonderfully clean and whole had been shared with him, a feeling he couldn't recall experiencing since his days on the farm down in Blue Earth, when he was a delinquent teenager trying to become someone better.

He tapped at the door of Leah Duling's cabin. Cork opened up.

"My friend at the Pentagon finally got back to me."

"What did he say?"

"Nothing except that it's big. He's set me up with a meeting, one of his people. I'm on my way."

"Where?"

Bo gave him the coordinates, then said, "When I map it, that's the junction of County Roads Eight and Seventeen."

"South end of Iron Lake. Reasonable if he's coming up from the Cities," Cork said. "Want company?"

"I'll take this one alone."

"Be careful."

"You sound like someone's grandmother."

Bo had parked his Jeep near the double-trunk birch. When he reached it, he was still an hour away from the meeting time. The headlights of the Jeep illuminated a tunnel in the dark, and as Bo headed toward the rendezvous, he considered again the players in this game.

NTSB, FBI, DoD, the Lexington Brigade, maybe William Byrd and Byrd Industries. And Gerard. Were they working at odds with one another, Bo wondered, or in concert? The most recent word from NTSB had confirmed that the Stinger found in the brigade's lodge was probably what had brought down the plane, so all the official lips were saying the same thing. But Winston Goodsky's photograph told a different story.

Bo came back to Gerard. He was pretty sure the man's job was to keep a lid on the truth, to eliminate any evidence that contradicted the official story. Why? Who needed protecting? Gerard was a floater. He and his team worked for no one, and for everyone. So, who was he working for this time around?

Bo's contact at the Pentagon, Max Freeman, had begun his career in the Secret Service, training with Bo. Then he'd moved on, taken a position with DSS, the Defense Security Service, and been assigned to the Pentagon. They'd remained friends and in touch. But this was the first time Bo had tapped Max for something more than a few beers together whenever his own work took him to D.C. He hadn't been certain Max would be willing to help but was grateful his friend had come through. As Bo approached the rendezvous point, he was still puzzling, hoping the information from his contact might help.

He was still a few minutes early and parked well shy of the junction of the two isolated county roads. He checked his Sig Sauer, slipped it back into the holster on his hip, and got out. He kept to the trees that edged the road. The moon was a deflated yellow balloon but gave enough light for Bo to see his way. There was no sign of anyone at the lonely intersection, and he hunkered among the trees, as still as one of the trunks, waiting.

The vehicle came slowly, two bright eyes in the distance, then a broad beam of headlights that illuminated the crossing. An SUV, dark blue or black. It pulled to a stop on the shoulder. The engine died, then the headlights. A door opened, closed. A figure separated itself from the vehicle and moved to the middle of the intersection. Bo couldn't tell a thing about it in the faint moonlight.

Then the figure struck a match and lit a cigar and Bo understood.

He didn't even turn when he heard the click of the cocking hammer at his back.

"The Colonel would like to see you." It was a woman's voice, as cold as he'd ever heard.

The smoke Gerard blew was dark gray against the waning moon. The cigar ember was a third eye low in his face. Two of his people were with him—one just behind Gerard, and the woman with the weapon still in Bo's back.

"I'll take it from here, Lieutenant Craig," Gerard said, and Bo sensed the woman retreat a step or two. Gerard held up a photograph, and Bo didn't have to look to know what it was. "You should be more careful who you trust, Thorson."

"So much for friends," Bo said.

"In our business, friendship is a luxury we can't afford. Which is too bad. In a different world, I think you and I might have had something."

"That's a world I can't even imagine," Bo replied.

"I offered you a chance to get out of this cleanly. That was partly because of our relationship. Not exactly friendship, but about as close as I ever come."

"What's your relationship with the Black Bird?"

"I have none."

Bo thought about this, then said, "You're a fixer. You were called in to fix a fuckup. His?"

"William Byrd has always been a shrewd businessman, but in his old age, he's chosen to wade into areas well beyond his expertise. He used to be satisfied just giving a shitload of money to both sides of the aisle in Washington, currying favors, which we both know is pretty much the norm. But the Black Bird is a little cantankerous these days and impatient with Congress. He finally decided to take things into his own hands."

"And get rid of Senator McCarthy?"

"Not a bad idea when you think about it, with the Senate poised to debate the Manila Accord and Senator McCarthy the very vocal leader of the opposition. And then there's that pesky assault rifle legislation she was about to introduce. If she's out, your governor steps in to fill her shoes, and he's made his own sympathetic views on the accord and his opposition to gun control quite clear. There's one other interesting intersecting consideration here, probably not even on your radar. That mine that's got everybody so worked up in these parts? If you follow the very convoluted trail of ownership, who do you think it leads back to?"

"William Byrd."

"Turns out all those heavy metals in the ground under our feet are necessary to the production of sophisticated military weaponry. A kind of beauty in the synchronicity of all this, if you look at it in the right way. Do you know your Keats? 'A thing of beauty is a joy forever.' "

"Byrd brought in the brigade to do his dirty work?"

"Not exactly. You remember General Buck Cushing? Well, if you don't, he was removed from his command in Iraq because of his very public criticism of how our commander in chief was conducting things over there. After Cushing's forced retirement, Byrd, whose sympathies were much in line with the general's, hired him to head up research and development in Byrd Industries' military weaponry division. Now, guess who was Cushing's chief adjutant. Colonel Cole Wannamaker. He took retirement along with Cushing and got himself a ranch in South Dakota, where he raises horses and continues to play at being a soldier with the Lexington Brigade."

"Cushing supplied Wannamaker with the weapon in the photograph?"

"Cutting-edge electronic warfare, Thorson. It's the Vulcan N-17X, still in the test phase. It has the capability of sending out a powerful EMP, yes, but it's also a neutron cannon."

"Which is what?"

"Remember the neutron bomb? Kills a whole city without damaging any of the superstructure. This is a big gun that does the same thing. It fires a directed neutron beam. Imagine being able to take out a whole cadre of terrorists deeply embedded in the buildings of a city block without reducing that block to rubble. Humanitarian in its way. Keeps homes and businesses intact for the return of the citizenry. Think what most of Syria might be today if we'd been able to use it there. The beauty of employing it to assassinate the senator is that everyone on board was dead before they hit the ground. No chance of survivors telling a tale."

"Senator McCarthy and her family weren't deeply embedded terrorists."

"Of course not. No one would ever consider what the Black Bird and Cushing did a reasonable action. But the kind of weaponry Byrd Industries is developing, now that's worth protecting."

"Have you known it was him from the beginning?"

Gerard blew smoke toward the stars. "Pretty much. Three weeks ago, someone inside Byrd Industries leaked to the Pentagon that one of the N-17X prototypes had gone missing from Byrd Industries' test facility in Utah. That kind of weapon doesn't just go missing. None of this was ever made public, of course. When the senator's plane came down, I was sent to check it out. Hell, everyone was sending someone to check it out. It was a mess of bureaucracies stumbling over one another. Nobody was sure of all the details. That's where you came in. You and your friends up here, you've been very helpful. I didn't know the territory like you do. I didn't have the local contacts. Once you gave me the lay of the land, I passed that along and things finally began to be coordinated. From very high up."

"How high?"

"You have no idea, Thorson."

"All to protect the Black Bird?"

"If you blow that photo up enough, what you see is that one of the men operating the N-17X prototype is Cushing himself, no doubt acting on orders from Byrd. If I could, I'd just put a bullet in those nutcases. But Byrd Industries is important to our national security."

"What happened to the N-17X?"

"Two days after the plane crash, some of my people intercepted it on its way back to Utah, along with Cushing. He claimed they'd done a field test in Wyoming and denied any involvement in the senator's death, but what we got off the black box was pretty damning. We thought that was it, the end of it. Then you and O'Connor led us to Wannamaker, and he told us about the photographer on the mountain. If that photo of Cushing and the N-17X ever got out, there was no controlling the damage." Gerard smiled around his cigar. "Thanks to you, that's not a problem now. Cushing and the prototype have been returned safely to the Utah test facility. The NTSB's report, when it's finally made official and public, will confirm the Stinger story."

"You planted the Stingers and the flight recorder?"

"It's what I do."

"And the massacre of the brigade, that was your work, too. What about Wannamaker? Did you kill him, dump his body somewhere he'll never be found?"

Gerard gave his head a shake. "He still has work to do."

"And me? I'll just disappear?"

"Not quite yet." Gerard threw the butt of his cigar to the ground, crushed the ember with the heel of his boot, and said, almost sadly, "I need some answers from you first. Then I have another massacre to arrange."

CHAPTER 46

Trixie barked.

Cork, who was in a sleeping bag with Rainy on the floor of Leah Duling's cabin, woke in the dark. The old mutt was up, teeth bared, growling at the door. Cork's first thought was that a black bear had come prowling. Then another possibility set in, and he rose quickly, but too late.

There was no lock on the door. Meloux had no need of locks in his little piece of paradise. The door was thrown open and banged against the wall. Cork crouched, his hands empty but fisted, ready to throw blows. The light from the doorway blinded him.

"Hold it right there, O'Connor, or I'll shoot you where you stand!"

Rainy had risen and stood shoulder to shoulder with her husband. She was dressed in gray sweatpants and a blue T-shirt and held herself tense. Behind them, bunk springs creaked.

"What's happening?" Leah said.

"We need you folks to come with us."

You folks, as if this were a friendly invitation, but the voice was icicle sharp.

"Who are you?" Cork demanded.

"Everything will be explained."

"Let me put on something warmer," Leah said.

"We've got a fire going. It'll be plenty warm."

Trixie continued to growl and bare her teeth, the hackles on her neck raised. No one moved yet.

"Maybe this will help," said the voice behind the blinding light.

Little Waaboo, looking confused and scared, was shoved into the beam of the flashlight. Cork lunged for him protectively, but a black-gloved hand grabbed the child and pulled him back into the dark.

At that Trixie, in full protective mode, gathered herself and launched her old body with a youthful vigor toward the source of the light. But the automatic rifle barked several times. Trixie fell short of her mark and lay sprawled on the cabin floor, perfectly still.

"No!" Rainy cried and tried to move toward the dog.

Cork held her back because the barrel of the automatic rifle was trained on his wife now. But Waaboo somehow broke free and ran to the dog and laid himself on Trixie as if trying to protect his beloved pet from further harm.

"Get the boy," the voice behind the beam ordered. "Get him up and let's get going."

Cork eased Waaboo gently from the still body. "She won't feel any more pain, little guy. Trixie's with the angels now."

The T-shirt his grandson had slept in was stained with blood, and tears streamed down little his cheeks. Waaboo turned toward the light beam and growled, "Monster!"

They were ushered outside, where they joined Daniel and Jenny, who'd already been rounded up. Jenny hugged her son to her. "Oh, God, I heard the shots and was so afraid."

"Trixie," Cork told her, his voice as sharp and jagged as a saw blade. "She tried to protect our little guy."

They stood in a loose group and watched as Henry Meloux was brought from his cabin. Although the old man walked slowly, his back was straight, his shoulders squared. When he was with the others, he said to the men who surrounded them, "Weasels and thieves come in the dark."

"It's clear you've never been in a war, old-timer." The man who spoke wore camo and his face was painted shades of black and dark blue. "Okay, folks, move out. Follow the flashlight."

Cork and Rainy walked directly behind Jenny and Daniel, with Waaboo between them, each holding one of his hands. They were all barefoot, the ground cold against their soles. Cork's brain was going a thousand miles an hour, trying desperately to figure a way to bring a moment of chaos into this situation, some ploy that might help those he loved break free. But the men who herded them held all the cards. It was clear they were disciplined. From the very first order delivered in the cabin and reinforced by Trixie's death, Cork understood that whoever was in charge had given permission to shoot to kill.

They were taken to the fire ring, where flames from the earlier blaze had been rekindled. Another man with an automatic rifle was already there. Seated with his back against one of the rock outcrops that isolated the ring was someone Cork recognized immediately from all the recent news stories: Cole Wannamaker, national leader of the Lexington Brigade. His hands were cuffed with a plastic restraint, and duct tape sealed his mouth. His eyes followed Cork and the others as they were paraded past and, like him, seated with their backs against the rocks.

There were four guards in all. Cork watched as they spoke quietly among themselves, then he asked, "What now?"

One of them responded simply, "Now we wait."

Far out in the meadow, Stephen crouched. He'd watched the lights play across the cabins and the tent, had heard the angry voices, the shouted orders, the shots. He didn't know what was happening but understood that something terrible was going down on Crow Point. He slipped his boots on and began to crawl on all fours through the high meadow grass toward the two rock outcrops that sequestered the fire ring. East of the rocks, he crept among the birches along the shoreline of Iron Lake, where the moon created a yellow path across the surface of the black water. He darted from the cover of one white birch trunk to the next, until he could see the fire ring.

Four men with powerful-looking rifles stood guard over his family and Henry Meloux and Leah Duling. It took Stephen a moment before he recognized the man seated with the others: Cole Wannamaker, whose face had been all over the newspapers. What he was witnessing made no sense to him. But he understood that there was nothing he could do alone that would change the situation.

He carefully retraced his steps to the meadow and took the cell phone from his pants pocket. He tried to turn it on, then remembered to his profound dismay that his Internet search earlier that night had drained the last of its power. His phone was dead.

He looked back to where the glow of the fire rose above the rock outcrops. He could put together no plan to save his family and the others. He had nothing to match the automatic weapons. His only hope, he decided, was in Allouette. He dug into his pants pocket and made sure he had the key to his old Jeep, which was parked at Crow Point East. Then he began to run.

He'd reached the edge of the meadow and was just about to

take the path that led along the lakeshore when, in the dim glow of the waning moon, a figure stepped from the shadow of the trees and blocked his way. He couldn't see the figure clearly. What he could see was the rifle the figure held and the long barrel that was pointed at his chest.

CHAPTER 47

When Bo Thorson stumbled into the flickering light around the fire ring, Cork saw the damage that had been done to him, at least the damage that showed. His face was a bloody mess. Because it was hard for him to walk, he was supported between two of Gerard's people. They threw him roughly against the rock wall, and he slumped beside Cork, his chin on his chest, his breathing labored.

Gerard strode into the firelight. He looked down the line of all those who'd been taken prisoner.

"Craig," he snapped. "Where's the kid?"

"This is everyone," the woman told him.

"No." He stepped to Cork and leaned down. "Where's your son?"

"I don't know."

Gerard spoke to them all, "Anyone care to answer?" When no one did, he moved to Waaboo and crouched in front of the boy. "Do you know where your uncle Stephen is?"

"You're a darkpoople," Waaboo threw at him.

"A what?"

"You're a . . . a muggymonster."

Gerard smiled. "That sounds about right. Now, son, I need to know something. I need to know where your uncle is. It's important to me."

"I don't care."

"I understand. But if you don't tell me, this is what I'm going to have to do. I'm going to have to hurt your mommy. I don't really want to do that. But I will if I have to."

"You hurt my mommy and I'll kill you."

"He was sleeping in the meadow." Bo raised his head wearily. "I doubt he's still there."

Gerard gestured to two of his men, who headed into the dark.

Gerard pulled a photograph from under his jacket, the photo Winston Goodsky had shot and Bo had sent to his friend in the Pentagon.

"I want to know who took this." When no one responded, Gerard nodded to another of his people. "Bring Thorson."

The man yanked him to his feet and marched him to where Gerard stood.

"I asked Thorson the same question I just put to you," he said to Cork and the others. "This is what his silence got him. Crude methods, but in the field, you do what you have to." He clapped Bo on the shoulder, as if they were comrades. "Thorson's a tough son of a bitch, I'll give him that. I didn't get an answer from him." His gaze shifted to Cork. "One by one, I'll question your family, O'Connor. Even little—what do you call him? Waaboo?"

"Gerard," Bo said. "I'll make you a deal."

"I don't think so." Gerard hadn't taken his eyes off Cork. "I think I'll get what I want."

Meloux said, "These woods have eyes and ears and spirit."

Gerard shifted his attention to the old Mide. "You're the shaman, right?"

"I am just an old man. But old men understand many things younger men do not."

"Like who took this photograph?"

"I was thinking more that among human beings there is sometimes a sense of order that is not true."

Gerard looked interested. "I have time, old man. Explain."

"One thing leads to another. Is that how you believe it works?"

"That's how it's always seemed to me."

The old Mide gave his head a single shake. "All things happen at the same time. What was, what is, what will be. Nothing comes before. Nothing comes after. Everything is."

"This is important to me how?"

"The spirits of these woods are part of the eternal. To a man who knows how to listen, they speak. Of what was, what is, and what will be."

"You're talking nonsense, old-timer."

Meloux's face was cracked and hard. Like the ancient rock that crowned Desolation Mountain, Cork thought.

"Nonsense only because you do not understand. But you are about to." Then Meloux smiled almost beatifically. "Things fall apart. The center cannot hold."

Gerard was clearly taken by surprise. His eyebrows lifted, he studied Meloux and added, "Mere anarchy is loosed upon the world."

"Yeats," Jenny murmured.

Gerard stood pondering this as the two men he'd sent to look for Stephen returned. Cork felt a flood of relief to see that all they brought with them was Stephen's sleeping bag.

"Well?" Gerard said.

"This was it. No kid."

"He's out there somewhere. This time don't come back until you find him. Take Craig and Edwards with you."

Before any of them could act on his order, a shot splintered the quiet. The sound of it came from somewhere along the lakeshore. It kicked up dirt at Gerard's feet. Gerard and his men scattered like roaches into the dark at the edges of the firelight.

"Stephen?" Rainy asked.

"Maybe," Cork replied. "Where's your Winchester, Henry?"

"It was hanging on the wall in my cabin." The old man spoke calmly, as if none of this was surprising to him, and Cork thought: *What was, what is, what will be.*

Another shot cracked the night. This one came from a different direction.

"If it's Stephen out there," Daniel said, "he's not alone."

With the fire ring deserted by Gerard and his people, Wannamaker pushed himself up and made a run for the lake. He hadn't gone but a few steps before a burst of automatic weapon fire from the dark cut him down.

Cork had been considering the same thing but thought better of it now. He stayed where he was seated, waiting to see how this sudden turn of events played out, wondering if it was Stephen out there with the rifle, and if not Stephen, then who?

For half an hour there were no more shots, then Gerard stepped suddenly into the firelight, pushing someone before him as a shield. Monkey Love. Gerard held the barrel of a big pistol pressed to the back of Monkey's head.

"You out there!" he hollered. "Come into the firelight or I'll put a bullet through this man's head."

Monkey looked at Cork and the others. "Sorry," he said.

"Shut up," Gerard snapped. "You out there! You have two minutes before I shoot!"

Gerard was the only visible member of his squad. The others

were still out there, looking for the second shooter. Because it was Monkey whom Gerard had snagged, Cork knew the other shooter had to be Ned Love. How they had come to be on Crow Point, God only knew.

"Did you hear? Two minutes!" Gerard called out.

Another rifle shot came from beyond the rocks, followed by the staccato of an automatic weapon. Then silence, broken only by the crackle of the fire in the ring.

"One minute!"

Cork watched as Monkey Love pulled himself proudly erect. His arms were every bit as long and awkward-looking as they had always been, but there was a noble aspect to him in this moment as he prepared, Cork understood, to die.

"Gerard," Cork said.

"Shut up, O'Connor." Gerard hollered toward the night, "His death is on your hands!" He cocked the hammer on the pistol. "Ten seconds!"

Into the firelight from the direction of the lake stepped Ned Love. In front of him was one of Gerard's people, the woman, Craig. Ned carried a rifle with the barrel pointed at her back. "You okay, Monkey?"

"Put the rifle down," Gerard ordered.

"Let's barter," Ned suggested.

"You have nothing to barter with."

"This woman's life isn't important?"

"Lieutenant Craig is a soldier. Dying is what soldiers do."

"Colonel?" the woman said, clearly not on the same page.

"How about you call the others in and we do some dealing?" Ned said.

"I don't have to call."

At the edges of the firelight, his men appeared. They ringed Ned, weapons trained on him from every direction.

"Winning hand," Gerard said. "Put your rifle down."

Ned hesitated a breath or two, then lowered his rifle to the ground.

Gerard holstered his sidearm and shoved Monkey. "Both of you over there with the others."

Ned and Monkey sat against the rock, and Cork thought how they were all lined up now, as if readied for an execution.

Gerard walked to where Wannamaker lay dead and stared down at the man, a disgusted look on his face.

Bo said, "Can't use him now. A second massacre perpetrated by a man with a dozen bullet holes, that just won't fly."

Gerard spun, crossed with a determined step to Waaboo, lifted the boy in a rough grasp, and hauled him toward the fire. He held up Waaboo with the boy's bare soles only two feet above the flames, his little legs kicking ferociously at Gerard.

"Who shot the photo? Ten seconds before the boy burns."

Bo said, "Do this and you become everything you claim to fight against."

Gerard seemed not to hear. There was a demonic blaze in his eyes that had nothing to do with the reflection from the fire, and Cork made his own desperate calculations: ten feet to Gerard; knock him and Waaboo away from the fire; if he was lucky, he might make it before he was cut down; if he wasn't lucky, maybe it would create enough distraction that someone else could grab Waaboo.

"Five seconds."

"Winston Goodsky," Jenny shouted. "He shot the photograph. Now put my son down, you bastard."

But Gerard didn't seem inclined to keep his promise. He lowered little Waaboo so that his kicking feet were only inches above the flames. "Who is Winston Goodsky?"

"No," Jenny screamed.

"Winston is my grandson, and a better man than you'll ever be, you son of a bitch."

The words were spit out from the dark beyond the firelight.

The moment Gerard looked in that direction, Daniel and Cork both shot up, launching themselves toward Gerard and Waaboo. Cork hit the man and spun him away from the fire. Daniel grasped his little son and wrested him from Gerard's grip. Gerard stumbled to the ground with Cork all over him, and they grappled. Gerard was made of iron, a soldier. But Cork was full of bitter fire, and the blows he threw were fast and angry.

"It's over, Cork!"

He felt hands pull him off Gerard, and he stood breathing hard, glaring down at the man. Gerard slowly brought himself into a sitting position. The blaze in his eyes had died, replaced by a cold understanding of his situation. His people made no move to help him, because they were in need of help themselves. Behind each one of them stood at least two Shinnobs from the Iron Lake Reservation, who had emerged from the dark, holding hunting rifles.

Harmon Goodsky strode fully into the firelight. Stephen flanked him on one side, Winston on the other. Cork smiled at his son, then turned slowly, recognizing all the faces of these reservation folks he'd known his whole life. Sarah LeDuc was there. And Tom Blessing. And Clyde Kingbird, with the mole above his lip like a blackfly. And Isaiah Broom and Sonny LeBanc and Dennis Vizenor and so many others. Some were his cousins by blood, others he simply called by that name.

"Chi migwech, niijikiweyag," he said to them. Thank you, my friends.

CHAPTER 48

They sat around the fire ring, the O'Connors and Bo. Little Waaboo, exhausted, lay sacked out on his mother's lap. Sarah LeDuc had stayed, but the other Ojibwe had gone. The sun was little more than a promise on the horizon, creating a long ribbon of pink sky. Sheriff Marsha Dross was with them, too. Her people and Quaker's agents had taken Gerard and his squad and had removed Wannamaker's body. The FBI's initial round of questioning had been completed, but there would be others. A mountain of paperwork was waiting, yet Dross had taken this time to be alone with the O'Connors, who were more to her, Bo understood, than just constituents. Like so many others in Tamarack County, she was a good friend, one far truer than the last friend Bo had chosen to trust.

"When I ran into Ned and Monkey Love lurking out there at the edge of the clearing, my cell phone was dead. And you know Ned and Monkey," Stephen was explaining. "They live outside the twenty-first century. So no cell phone with them. Taking my Jeep into Allouette for help was the only option."

"What were they doing out there?"

"Ned told me he and Monkey had been keeping tabs on Crow

Point since the raid at Celtic Lake. With Cole Wannamaker still at large, they were concerned about our safety."

"So they just lurked around here?"

"Pretty much."

Cork looked to Meloux. "Did you know?"

"There is little about these woods that I do not know."

Which made Bo remember how calm the old man had seemed in the face of all Gerard's threats. And he remembered the old man's words: *These woods have eyes and ears and spirit.*

"Why didn't you say something, Uncle Henry?" Rainy asked.

"Because I am a better keeper of secrets than some around this fire." He didn't look at anyone particularly.

Stephen went on: "Ned told me that he and Monkey would do their best to keep Gerard and his people busy until I came back from Allouette with reinforcements."

"And then you ran the whole way to the Jeep, all two miles to Crow Point East, with that leg?" Jenny said this as if it were a kind of miracle.

Stephen shrugged it off. "I didn't have much choice."

"Didn't it hurt?" English asked. "Your leg?"

"Are you kidding? It hurt like hell. But I wasn't alone out there."

"The spirit of the woods?" Bo smiled when he said this.

Young O'Connor looked at him steadily. "The spirit of all things. It's all connected."

In this, Bo heard wisdom, the kind he might have expected from the old Mide, and although it would be a long time before he fully accepted that there were mysteries which could never be solved, in that moment, in that intimate circle around the fire, he was willing to embrace the truth of Stephen O'Connor's words.

"What happens from here?" Rainy asked.

Dross said, "It'll be complicated, I'm sure. There are still a lot of missing pieces. It's clear that much of what's gone on was manipulated from high up."

"They'll get nothing from Gerard or his people," Bo said.

"But the truth will come out, yes?" Rainy looked to him with hope.

Bo spoke carefully. "There will be a lot of smoke. There will be a lot of accusations designed to misdirect, obfuscate, confuse. There will be a lot of finger-pointing that will get no one anywhere. It's how our government operates when all the disparate heads are trying to cover their asses. It's never about getting to the truth."

"The many-headed monster of Waaboo's nightmare," Jenny said. She ran her hand gently over her son's cheek. "Maybe you're not the only one who has visions, Stephen."

"But *we* know the truth," Sarah LeDuc insisted. "We can speak out."

"Who takes the word of an Indian seriously?" English said bitterly.

"Marsha knows the truth," Stephen said.

"I'll do what I can," the sheriff promised, then, after a pause, added with a dour note, "But they've taken all the evidence."

"What about Winston's camera and laptop?"

Bo said, "By the time the sun is up, Quaker's people will have confiscated that, too."

"There's your cell phone," Cork pointed out. "You used it to send the photo to your Pentagon friend."

Bo shook his head, which still hurt from the beating he'd taken when Gerard tried to get information from him. "They grabbed that when they nabbed me at the crossroads."

"They can't just make Wannamaker's body disappear," English said.

"He was a dangerous, wanted man, a domestic terrorist. They

caught him. He tried to run. They shot him." Bo shrugged. "Who knows? In the end, Gerard might end up the hero of this story."

"They beat you," Jenny said.

"That's my story. Did any of you see it happen?"

"You sound like one of them," Sarah LeDuc said.

"Believe me, I'm not, Sarah. But I know how they work."

"They can't just cover all of this up."

"They've done it before," Bo told her. "This won't be one of Gerard's finer moments, but whenever you try to pin him down, he's like an eel. And he'll get all kinds of protection from above." He threw a stick into the fire, watched it burn. "Doesn't matter who's in the White House, the truth about our government, any government for that matter, is that protecting its citizens is never its first priority. Its first priority is protecting itself."

Around the fire, the mood had taken a sour turn. It was the old man, Meloux, who lifted their spirits.

"This is not a time for heavy hearts," the Mide said. "Death was our shadow, but that shadow is gone. Justice? We will pray this comes with the light of day. In this moment, here and now, we celebrate the spirit of what is good in each of us and in those friends who stood with us in the dark and chased away death's shadow." He lifted his eyes to the night sky. "We give thanks to the Creator and we pray that in the battle between love and fear, which is always raging in the human heart, love will triumph." He lowered his eyes and, one by one, fixed each of them around the fire with his steady gaze. When he came to Bo, he smiled. "Love will win," he said gently, as if the words were meant for Bo especially. "In the end, love always wins."

CHAPTER 49

The memorial service for Olympia McCarthy and her family was held in the Twin Cities at the Cathedral of St. Paul on a rainy autumn afternoon. The broadcast was carried live on all the local network stations. The governor was there and other politicians. A number of the senator's colleagues from D.C. had flown in to attend. The huge sanctuary was packed, every pew filled shoulder to shoulder. During the service, the governor spoke. He praised the work of the FBI and never mentioned Gerard's name when speaking of the death of Cole Wannamaker, a man he called a wild-eyed, misdirected fanatic. Gerard's name, in fact, had never come up in any of the journalistic accounts of what occurred in Tamarack County. Wannamaker's death was always attributed to very nonspecific "U.S. security personnel."

Alone in his condo in St. Paul, Bo watched the service on the television. Every so often the camera angle shifted to the cathedral's front pew, where Olympia McCarthy's father sat, along with other members of the family. With them was the most illustrious of the memorial's attendees: former President Clay Dixon. His wife, the lovely former First Lady, sat at his side.

The media had made much of the fact that Olympia McCarthy and Kathleen Jorgenson Dixon had been college roommates and lifelong best friends, and how, after the tragedy, the former First Lady had been with the senator's family constantly, offering her support. She didn't speak at the service, but Bo could still hear her voice, the sound of her soft breathing, like wind across tall grass. He thought about how she'd kept their conversations from her husband, so that, should things go south, he could claim plausible deniability. He wondered what she intended to do with the photo he'd sent her from his cell phone, moments after he'd sent that same photo to the man he'd believed was his friend in the Pentagon. It had been his last communication with her before Gerard nabbed him and beat him and prepared to stage another massacre. Bo never told Cork O'Connor or his family about that final communication. He didn't want to raise their hopes only to have them dashed on the rocks of some necessary political cover-up.

When the service had finished, under an awning erected outside the cathedral to protect the podium from the rain, former President Clay Dixon, as promised, addressed the media. He was flanked by his wife and by Olympia McCarthy's father. In a surprise move, he opened his remarks by displaying a photograph, which he said had been taken by a young Native American atop Desolation Mountain the day Olympia McCarthy died.

Cork sat with Rainy in front of the television in the house on Gooseberry Lane. They'd watched the service, had heard all the lauding of a woman who, in the end, had sacrificed everything in her fight for the ideals she believed in. They'd both shared their story with reporters, but they'd never seen any of the truths they told make it into print.

Waaboo and Jenny came from the kitchen, bringing coffee and cookies.

"A little something to brighten a dark day," Jenny said.

Waaboo settled himself on the sofa next to his grandfather. He lay his head against Cork's shoulder. "I miss Trixie, Baa-baa."

"She died trying to protect us. A good death."

"Do dogs go to heaven?"

"Why wouldn't they?"

"They're not people."

"Do you think only people are in heaven?"

Waaboo took a bite of the chocolate chip cookie in his hand. "I guess I'll find out someday."

Cork put his arm around his grandson. "That day is far, far away, little guy."

On the television, the service had finished and former President Clay Dixon was stepping up to a microphone under a canvas awning that dripped rain, preparing to speak.

"Just for once," Jenny said, "I'd like to hear a politician say something meaningful and true."

"Give the man a chance," Cork said and reached for a cookie.

It was night and Stephen was alone with the old Mide. They sat before a fire burning in the stone ring at the edge of Iron Lake. The sky had spit rain all day, and there was still a brooding overcast, so that the only light came from the dance of flames in the fire ring.

"He told the truth," Stephen reported. "In front of television cameras, he showed the photograph Winston Goodsky took, and he told what happened up here."

With a nod of approval, the old man said, "*Debwewin.*" Which, Stephen knew, meant "truth" in the language of his people. "One of the gifts of the Seven Grandfathers." Then the old man said,

"I hear that you have befriended Winston Goodsky." He nodded in approval. "He is a young man who will need guidance and a friend."

"He knows his grandfather's death isn't far away and he's afraid of what will come after that. It's important for him to know he won't be alone."

Small drops of rain hit lightly on Stephen's face. He had come to the old man with a heavy heart and he hadn't spoken yet the real truth that brought him. He summoned all his strength of spirit. "Henry," he said. "I had the vision again."

The old man waited. The fire popped. Embers flew like glowing bits of a shattered dream toward the black night sky.

"This time I found the courage to look at the great, terrible thing at my back. It had nothing to do with what happened on Desolation Mountain."

The old man turned his face to Stephen, his skin cut by the lines from a century of erosion, his eyes like ancient stones. "And what did you see?"

Stephen looked long and deep at this man who had taught him so much about life, whose spirit was the truest he had ever known.

He said at last the words, which nearly broke his heart: "I saw you dead."

Henry's smile was comforting. His old hand when he placed it over Stephen's was more warming than the fire. He let silent moments pass before he spoke in the soft voice of acceptance, "I know."

AUTHOR'S NOTE

Like Athena from the head of Zeus, Cork O'Connor first leapt from my imagination more than a quarter of a century ago. He came to me as a man with a history in law enforcement. He'd been a police officer in Chicago, a deputy, and finally sheriff of Tamarack County. But in *Iron Lake,* the initial entry in the series, his law enforcement career was behind him. Across the course of the sixteen subsequent novels, I've given readers an occasional glimpse of the time Cork wore a badge, but I've never lingered long on his history.

The short story you're about to read offers another look at Cork in his time as sheriff. Sam Winter Moon and Henry Meloux, two characters important in the Cork O'Connor stories, play significant parts as well. They're younger men in this tale, and I enjoyed immensely the opportunity to render them as they might have been.

I have it in mind at some future point to write a whole novel about Cork set entirely in the past, and these occasional journeys to an earlier time help stir the pot of my imagination. I hope you enjoy reading "Butcher Bird" as much as I enjoyed writing it.

Turn the page for "Butcher Bird,"
a bonus short story by William Kent Krueger

BUTCHER BIRD

It happened in *Manidoo-Giizisoons,* the month of the Small Spirit Moon, December.

The trail Sheriff Cork O'Connor followed with his Maglite was clear on the new-fallen snow. The footprints showed bare feet. The other searchers had spread out behind him, Sam Winter Moon to his left, Deputy Ed Larson to his right, and at his back, Henry Meloux, the eighty-year-old Mide. A deep quiet had settled over the great Northwoods after the snowfall, and as they walked, the men made almost no sound in the fresh powder. The moon, nearly full, cast sharp shadows, and the snow was like a canvas painted in bold, black strokes. The men didn't speak, hadn't spoken since they'd left the torn-apart trailer, but they were all of the same mind: Find her.

They'd walked for half an hour when the trail came to an abrupt end. In the middle of a small clearing, the footprints simply stopped. Cork shone the beam of the Maglite in every direction, but the surface of the snow was unbroken.

The Mide said, "She is smart, this little one."

"She doubled back," Cork said. "Gave us the slip."

"And anyone else who might have been after her," Sam Winter Moon said.

Ed Larson took off his gloves and blew into his cupped hands. "We don't find her soon, she'll freeze to death out here."

"Then we will find her," Meloux said. He turned back the way they'd come.

They'd been careful not to disturb the girl's prints. Meloux and Sam Winter Moon walked ahead, her trail between them, reading it with eyes practiced across a lifetime of hunting in the great Northwoods. They halted at the same time, in a place where they had to bend a little in order to proceed under the broad boughs of a white pine.

Meloux spoke to the tree: "*Ondaas, waawaashkeshiins.*" Come here, little deer.

The tree didn't answer.

"*Booske giin,*" he said. It's up to you.

They stood waiting, puffing out clouds that were silver in the moonlight.

"*Gigawabamin nagutch,*" Meloux said—See you later—and he started away.

The tree spoke: "Don't go."

She dropped from the branches and fell to her knees in the moonlight. She wore only a T-shirt and jeans.

"I can't walk," she said.

Sam Winter Moon lifted her in his arms.

"Wrap her in this." Cork shed his fleece-lined leather jacket.

"Her toes look like strawberries," Ed Larson said. He pulled his knitted scarf from around his neck and swaddled the girl's feet.

"Let's go," Cork said and quickly led the way.

She thought she was six years old but wasn't sure. She also wasn't sure of her real name.

"Mama called me Giji. She said it was short for *gijigaaneshii*."

"Chickadee," Sam Winter Moon said.

"I told her it was a funny name. She said it was because I was a funny girl."

She sat on the sofa, her feet in a plastic tub of tepid water, a heavy blanket around her shoulders, while they waited for the EMTs. They were all there, the men who'd tracked and found her. It was crowded in the tiny trailer, but she made a great fuss whenever any of them tried to leave.

"He might come back," she said. "*Ningotaaj*." I'm afraid.

Her eyes were amber, her hair black and cut short in the way of a boy.

"Do you know his name?" Cork asked.

"Where's Mama?" she said.

Cork said, "He took her."

"No! He's a *windigo*. He'll eat her heart."

"That's why you have to help us find her. Do you know his name?" he asked again.

"I want Mama. I want Mama."

Meloux, who sat next her, leaned and whispered into her ear. She listened, and when he straightened, she wiped away her tears, looked up into his face, into his warm, almond eyes, and nodded.

She said, "Mama told me to call him Papa."

Later, when Cork replayed the 911 call, he could hear the banging on the trailer door and the man's voice shouting incoherently. He also heard the girl crying and pleading, "Mama! Mama!"

"He's going to kill us," the woman had screamed into her phone.

"Where are you, ma'am?" The dispatcher had kept her voice calm.

"A trailer on Little Wolf Road. A mile down the County Seventeen turnoff. Hurry! He's crazy. He'll kill us."

"Stay on the line, ma'am. Officers are on their way."

But she hadn't stayed on the line.

The trailer was located on the Iron Lake Reservation, and as luck would have it, when Cork got the call from dispatch, he was talking with Sam Winter Moon and Henry Meloux outside the community center in Allouette, where he'd met with the tribal council to discuss security for the casino they were proposing to build.

"I know that trailer," Winter Moon had said, and he and Meloux had gone with Cork.

When they'd arrived, twenty minutes later, they'd found that the door latch had been broken, the trailer destroyed inside, blood on the floor, but the place was empty. By the time Ed Larson pulled up in his cruiser, they'd discovered a broken window in the bedroom, and in the snow beneath, a trail showing where small bare feet had run off into the woods.

As they waited for the EMTs, Cork took Winter Moon aside and asked quietly, "What do you know about her mother?"

"Not much. Her name's Hannah LeBeau. Came to the rez maybe a month ago, rented this old tin can from Cubby Broom. Keeps to herself. Doesn't work, as far as I know. I didn't even know she had a daughter. She kept that little girl a secret." Winter Moon eyed the destruction inside the trailer. "Guess I know why."

"Family on the rez?"

"I think she might be a cousin of Charise Kingbird. But she's not from Iron Lake."

"Charise Kingbird? Is that Bobby Kingbird's little sister?"

"Yeah. She has her problems, but nothing like Bobby."

"God, I hope not. Best news I had this year was that after his stretch in Stillwater, he stayed in the Twin Cities. Another cop's problem now." Cork glanced out the tiny window of the kitchen nook. "That El Camino parked in front has North Dakota plates. Why come here?"

"Maybe because it's pretty far from everything and everyone," Winter Moon said.

Cork looked at the wreckage around him. "Not far enough."

While they waited, Winter Moon sang a song to the little girl:

Gigikenimaag ina Dasher miinawaa Dancer miinawaa Prancer miinawaa Vixen,
Comet miinawaa Cupid miinawaa Donner miinawaa Blitzen.
(You know Dasher and Dancer and Prancer and Vixen,
Comet and Cupid and Donner and Blitzen.)

She laid her head against his shoulder, closed her eyes, and in a short while, was sound asleep. By then, it was nearly midnight.

In the only bedroom, Cork found a framed photograph that showed mother and daughter against an urban background. He gave it to Ed Larson with instructions to have it faxed to the sheriff's departments in all adjacent counties, along with a BOLO.

When the EMTs arrived, the little girl refused to leave with them unless Winter Moon and Meloux went with her. In the end, they did.

Cork stayed until Ed Larson and his evidence team had gone over the trailer. By then, the plates on the El Camino had been run and dispatch had reported back that the car had been stolen in Fargo six weeks earlier. Cork was the last to leave the scene, and from there he headed to the Aurora Community Hospital, where he found the girl asleep between clean sheets, Winter Moon and Meloux in chairs at her bedside.

"She didn't want to be alone," Winter Moon said.

"And who could leave a child this way?" Meloux said.

"Need anything?" Cork asked.

"The true name of the man called Papa," Winter Moon said.

Cork handed him a brown paper bag filled with clothes for the girl, which he'd taken from the trailer, along with the only pair of shoes he could find, sneakers worn down to almost nothing.

"I'll pick up new shoes for her in the morning," he said.

It was 2:00 A.M. when Cork climbed the stairs of his house on Gooseberry Lane and stood in the doorway of Annie's bedroom. He didn't look away from his sleeping daughter until he heard the soft approach of Jo's feet on the carpet.

"You okay?" his wife asked. She was carrying their third child, a boy the ultrasounds had shown, and her rounded belly brushed gently against him.

"The little girl doesn't even know how old she is. Six, she thinks. Annie's age. And she was barefooted out there in that cold, running from a monster."

"Any word on her mother?"

"Nothing." He leaned against the doorframe, feeling weak, inadequate. And angry. "Help me here, Jo. You keep telling me God is merciful. Where's the mercy in this?"

"You," she said. "And Sam and Henry and Ed. You found her. You saved her."

"We haven't found her mother or the monster who took her."

"If I were that woman, you know what I would want? To know that my daughter is safe."

"I'd love to tell her that myself."

"Come to bed," Jo said. "You're not going to find her tonight."

When Alice Growe, from Tamarack County Child Protection, arrived at the hospital the next morning, the little girl's face went hard.

"Mama told me about you. You take kids away and you give them to mean people."

"Sweetheart," Alice said, "I won't give you to anyone who would hurt you."

"Give her to me," the Mide said.

"I don't think so, Mr. Meloux. From what I hear, you don't even have plumbing at your cabin."

"But it is safe."

"I won't place her anywhere that isn't, I promise. And it's just until we find her mother."

Cork stood at the window, looking out at a morning that had delivered a sharp, blue sky and sunshine that exploded blindingly off the snow-covered North Country, and he wondered if they were ever going to find her mother, and if they did, would she still be alive.

"I'll take her," he heard Sam Winter Moon say. "I've got water and indoor plumbing."

The girl grabbed Meloux's hand. "I want you to go, too."

"I have room for you both," Winter Moon said.

The social worker shook her head. "A bit too unorthodox."

"But safe." Cork turned from the window. "The man who took her mother may return, Alice. You want him coming after the nice family you might give her to?"

On her discharge that afternoon, little Giji left in the company of the two men and Cork. By then, he'd canvassed the rez. Charise Kingbird, when he finally tracked her down, didn't seem happy to see him, which because of his badge, wasn't unusual on the rez. She barely looked at him while they talked. But she did confirm that Hannah LeBeau was a distant cousin. When she was a girl, Hannah had spent time on the Iron Lake Reservation, staying with grandparents, both deceased. Charise hadn't seen her for years. She'd heard someone was living in that old dump of a trailer but didn't know it was Hannah until a week ago, when they bumped into each other at the IGA. And a little girl? That was news.

"Ever hear from your brother?" Cork asked.

"Last I heard, Bobby was raising hell in Minneapolis." She lifted her eyes to Cork for an instant with a hostile look, then glanced away. "Guess if he knows what's good for him, he'll stay there."

Cubby Broom, who'd rented the trailer to Hannah LeBeau, told Cork he didn't know anything about her except that she'd paid a year's rent in advance. "Hell, for a year's rent in advance, I'd've let Custer live there, no questions asked."

The rent, Broom told him, was three hundred a month. A year in advance meant nearly four thousand dollars. Where, Cork wondered, did a woman who lived in an old tin can of a place and didn't have a job get four thousand dollars?

Nothing had come yet from the BOLO or the circulated photograph, but late in the day, Cork got a call from Winter Moon. "Something you need to see."

"She's never gone to school," Winter Moon told him. "Her mother taught her how to read. She's smart, this little Chickadee, and speaks pretty good Ojibwe."

They stood outside Winter Moon's cabin, which he'd built in a stand of aspen on the shore of Iron Lake, north of the rez town of Allouette. The aspen were bare and the lake frozen. By then the sun had become a weary, red eye on the western horizon, and as the men talked, the cold air condensed their breath, the gray hanging between them.

"What did you want me to see?"

Winter Moon held up a sheet of white drawing paper with a charcoal sketch of a man's face. "This is Papa."

"You drew that?"

"From what Giji told me. She says it looks like him."

"Shinnob?"

"Indian anyway. She said he has a tattoo on his forearm. A turtle. It could be his clan, but that would mean he's not Anishinaabe. Maybe Mohawk. In the teaching of the Seven Grandfathers, the turtle represents truth. But given what we know about him, I'd say that's an unlikely inspiration."

"Maybe it's just in honor of a pet turtle he had when he was a kid," Cork said.

"Maybe," Sam said. "But when she speaks Ojibwemowin, that little girl speaks it with a Cree accent. There's lots of Cree among the Turtle Mountain people. I'm thinking maybe this guy is a Turtle Mountain Shinnob."

"North Dakota," Cork said, thinking about the stolen El Camino at the trailer. "Mind if I take that sketch, Sam? I'll fax it to the police in Belcourt, see if we get anything." He looked at the cabin, where the windows showed bright light within. "How's she doing?"

"Come inside and see."

The cabin smelled of sage and sweetgrass, and Cork knew Meloux had been smudging it to cleanse the space. On the walls hung drawings and paintings Sam Winter Moon had done over the years. Winter Moon was many fine things, among them an artist. Meloux and Giji sat on a braided rug in front of the fireplace with a checkerboard between them. When the door opened, she looked up, her face drawn taut with fear. But when she saw it was only Cork, she relaxed.

"Is everything okay, Giji?" he asked.

She smiled at Meloux. "*Mishomis* is funny." Grandfather, she'd called him. Her eyes lifted to Winter Moon. "And Uncle is nice. Did you find Mama?"

"Not yet, but I will."

"Can I have Chester?"

"Chester? Who's that?"

"My teddy bear."

"Where is he?"

"Under my bed. I put him there so Papa wouldn't hurt him."

"I'll bring back Chester."

"Promise?"

"Promise."

Cork and Winter Moon stepped outside. It had been warm in the cabin, and the cold of the day stung Cork's face.

Winter Moon said, "You know the butcher bird?"

"Yeah, another name for a shrike. Eats other birds."

"We're not going to let this butcher bird get our little Chickadee."

"No," Cork said. "We're not."

He stood in the middle of the tiny trailer, eyeing the destruction wrought by the man with the turtle tattoo. The cushions had been cut into and ripped apart. The cupboards of the kitchen nook had been cleared, and the drawers had been dumped, their contents scattered on the floor. In the bedroom, everything from the dresser and the little closet had been tossed. In anger, perhaps. But Cork wondered if there was more to it than that.

He found Chester under the bed, just as little Giji had said, an old stuffed toy, the fur rubbed bare in places, both button eyes reattached loosely with white thread, one arm sewn back on, a little cotton stuffing still poking through the haphazard stitching. He thought of *The Velveteen Rabbit,* one of Annie's favorite books. The story of a simple thing, loved to death.

On his way to Winter Moon's cabin, he got a call from dispatch. The police in Belcourt were familiar with the man in Winter Moon's sketch, one Charles Richard Grandbois, a.k.a. Goose Grandbois. He was, indeed, from the Turtle Mountain Band and had been linked with the Red Bloodz. He'd dropped off their radar a long time ago, but they promised to do some more checking and get back with what they found. Cork knew about the Red Bloodz, a Native American gang originally operating out of the Twin Cities but recently, he'd heard, with strong ties to Fargo. He'd been watching for the spread of its influence but hadn't yet seen evidence of it in Tamarack County. Only a matter of time, he figured.

"It's a little on the ratty side," he said, when he delivered the bear to Winter Moon. "You might reinforce some of those stitches before you give it to Giji."

"Maybe I can even figure a way to thicken up that fur coat," Cork's friend said. "How's the investigation going?"

"We still don't know much, but it hasn't even been a full day yet."

"To that little girl's mother, it probably feels like forever."

If she can still feel, Cork thought grimly, as he headed to his Bronco.

He was on his way back to Aurora when he got another call from dispatch. Winter Moon wanted to see him ASAP. Cork turned his Bronco right back around.

The little girl was sleeping when he stepped into Winter Moon's cabin. Henry Meloux stood over her like an old guardian spirit. Winter Moon held out his hand. A key rested in his palm.

"Found this stuffed in the bear when I went to restitch that loose arm."

"Looks like a key to a locker," Cork said. "Bus station or train, maybe."

"I'm thinking the butcher bird wasn't after our Chickadee or our Chickadee's mother."

"That's why he tore the place apart. But Hannah's nine-one-one call didn't give him much time." Cork looked at the child, who clutched the stuffed animal as she slept. "The shrike, Sam, think it's a night bird?"

Under the full moon, the world was only two colors, black and white. A pickup truck came without headlights, the tires making a sound on the snow like the growl of a hungry animal, loud in the quiet of the Northwoods night. Fifty yards distant, it slowed and stopped for a full minute, then came forward again and parked. The driver's door opened. A man got out, pulling someone much smaller with him, someone who gave a cry of pain. She fought, and he needed both hands to corral her and shove her forward. The door swung open, and she stepped into the dark of the trailer, a small black shape against the moonlight outside. A much larger silhouette loomed at her back.

"Where's the damn switch?" the man said.

She reached out, and the light blazed on, illuminating the unexpected presence of Sheriff Cork O'Connor.

The woman, who wasn't much more than a girl, broke and ran to safety behind Cork and his drawn sidearm. The butcher bird turned to run, only to find that two of Cork's deputies had come from their cover and stood blocking his escape. He spun back, his eyes burning with defiance. But to Cork's surprise, it wasn't the man with the turtle tattoo.

"Bobby Kingbird," he said with a heavy sigh. "I was afraid it was only a matter of time."

"Grandbois gave her the money. Ten thousand. She says there's almost five still left in a locker at the Greyhound depot in Duluth. Ed's on his way down to pick it up now."

The little girl hadn't awakened, and Chester was still in her arms.

"Grandbois couldn't get himself out of the gang," Cork went on, "but he wanted Giji and her mother out. That ten grand he stole from the Red Bloodz was their ticket. When she hit Duluth, she used a pay phone to call him at the house they'd been living in, but he wasn't the one who answered. The voice on the line belonged to One Crow Diderot, the guy who heads up the Red Bloodz in Fargo. He told her if she didn't come back with the money, he'd kill Grandbois. In no uncertain terms, she told Diderot to go screw himself. She heard a gunshot, hung up, and never tried to contact

Grandbois again. Cass County Sheriff's Department is checking out the house even as we speak. I'm sure the Red Bloodz dumped the body a while ago, but her testimony might go a long way to getting an arrest."

"And Bobby Kingbird? He's with the Red Bloodz?" Winter Moon said.

"Yeah, and proud of it, Sam. They're here now," Cork said, feeling angry and weary at the same time. "In Tamarack County, on the rez."

"They won't be here long," Winter Moon vowed. "And we'll make damn sure they don't hurt Giji or her mother."

"Stay with her," Meloux said to Winter Moon and indicated for Cork to follow him.

Outside the cabin, the night was quiet and moon-silvered. Cork and the Mide stood together a long while without speaking.

"Cold out here, Henry," Cork finally said.

"It should be. *Manidoo-Giizisoons,* the month of the Small Spirit Moon."

"Small spirit. That's certainly mine."

"You have reason to celebrate. The little Chickadee and her mother are safe."

"For how long? The shrikes are here now. More will be coming."

"The butcher bird is a small creature with a small heart. There is room in it only for anger, and anger will be its undoing. It is also wise to remember that a bird can change its feathers."

"How?"

"You have already seen it. The man with the turtle tattoo. He was a butcher bird and then he was not. He became someone with a different heart, and because of that different heart, he made a great sacrifice. What changed him?"

"Chickadee, I imagine. And her mother."

"There is your answer." Meloux breathed out a silver cloud. "Good night, Corcoran O'Connor."

The old man returned to the cabin, but Cork stood in that December night for a very long time, the moon and the cold his only company. He knew there was a lot of dark ahead, but he didn't feel so weary now, his spirit so small. And when he walked away from the cabin, there was room in his heart for hope.

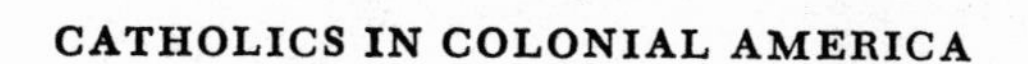
CATHOLICS IN COLONIAL AMERICA

CATHOLICS IN COLONIAL AMERICA

By John Tracy Ellis

Professor of Church History

In the

University of San Francisco

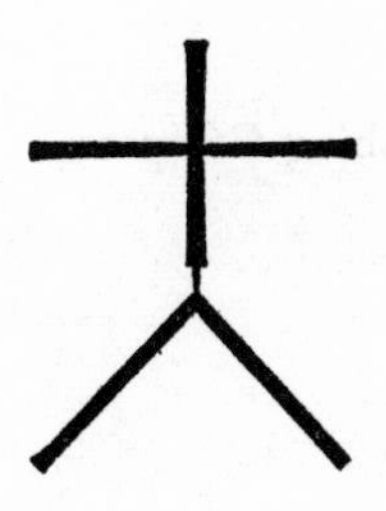

BENEDICTINE STUDIES

HELICON: BALTIMORE · DUBLIN

Nihil obstat:
Louis A. Arand, S.S.
Censor Deputatus

Imprimatur:
✠ Patrick A. O'Boyle
Archbishop of Washington
February 8, 1963

The *Nihil Obstat* and *Imprimatur* are official declarations that a book or pamphlet is free of doctrinal or moral error. No implication is contained therein that those who have granted the *Nihil Obstat* and *Imprimatur* agree with the content, opinions, or statements expressed.

This volume is the eighth in a series entitled *Benedictine Studies* sponsored by the American Benedictine Academy and published by Helicon Press, Inc., Baltimore, Maryland 21202.

Library of Congress Catalog Card Number 64-10920

Typography and design by Frank Kacmarcik

Printed in St. Paul, Minnesota
by the North Central Publishing Company

TO

THE MOST REVEREND PAUL J. HALLINAN

ARCHBISHOP OF ATLANTA

DISTINGUISHED PRELATE OF THE
CHURCH UNIVERSAL

FEARLESS LEADER OF MEN

ABLE HISTORIAN OF THE AMERICAN CHURCH

WITH DEEP RESPECT AND SINCERE AFFECTION

PREFACE

This is the first time that I have written a book that I had not intended to write. Having been granted a sabbatical leave for the academic year 1959–1960, I had hoped that by the end of that time I would have finished a one-volume history of the Catholic Church in the United States. Instead, the autumn of 1960 found me with a manuscript of several hundred pages with the English colonial missions as yet untouched. By the time that I realized how much I had over-written the account of the missions of Spain and France for the purpose of a general history, I was reluctant to set aside the result of many months of labor. I decided, therefore, to proceed with the missions of English America in the same detail and proportion as I had given to those of the Spaniards and French. Completion of the work was delayed quite beyond what I had at first anticipated, and whether or not my determination to stay with the colonial period as long as I did was a wise one, I must leave to others to decide.

There is no work of comparable content and length on the subject, but I am not unaware that some may reply that there was little need for such. While I grant that there is no pressing need for a detailed treatment of the missions of the Catholic Church throughout that part of North America that later became the United States, it is over a century since John Gilmary Shea published his volume on the Catholic missions among the Indians, and it is seventy-seven years since there appeared his last extended account of the missions in his four-volume history of the Catholic Church in this country. I trust that a work of this kind will, therefore, be thought to have fulfilled a useful purpose. It will serve to acquaint students with an aspect of the American colonial past that is no more than adumbrated in most histories of the period. Moreover, it will afford the general reader a knowledge of the extraordinary efforts put forth by numerous European missionaries from the time of Columbus' discovery of America to the American Revolution to plant the Catholic faith among the savage tribes that roamed the vast continent from the Atlantic to the Pacific Oceans on east and west and from the Rio Grande on the south to the Saint Lawrence River on the north.

In the mission history of the three major European powers one meets with numerous men of heroic courage, deep piety, and marvelous perseverance in the face of seemingly insuperable obstacles. But as is true of virtually every human undertaking, mingled among these attractive figures were ruffians, adventurers, and other evil characters whose conduct and policies often cast somber shadows over the colonial settlements. There are unpleasant features in that history, for example, the white man's cruelty to the native Indians, the latter's barbarous retaliations, and the exhaustive wars between European rivals striving for the mastery of the new world—all these in addition to the wasteful and debilitating quarrels of civil governor against military commander, of merchant against trader, and at times of friar and priest against them all. Yet amid these struggles there emerge majestic figures like Francisco Eusebio Kino in what is today Arizona, Junípero Serra in California, and Jacques Marquette in the Mississippi Valley, to mention only the three missionaries whose exploits have recommended them for a place in Statuary Hall of the national capitol.

Although it was not these Catholics of colonial America who fixed the pattern from which the principal social and cultural institutions of the United States took their rise, it was from among their number that there were drawn the agents who were responsible for the indelible mark of Christian faith left on the souls of countless Indians, and it was to the missionaries, more than to any other group, that the native peoples owed whatever knowledge and training they had in the arts and skills of civilized living. From the colonials there came, too, the names of dozens of cities, counties, rivers, valleys, and mountains that dot the national landscape and that have become part of the national heritage of all Americans. And since Americans, as well as many outsiders who study their history, have a special predilection for the history of the West, it should be mentioned that some of the most stirring pages of "the epic of America," to paraphrase Herbert Eugene Bolton's happy phrase, were written by the sons of Saint Francis of Assisi and Saint Ignatius of Loyola.

The narrative has been accompanied by footnote references that give the essential bibliographical data for the leading collections of printed sources and secondary accounts, and thus it seemed unnecessary to add a formal bibliography. As is the case with practically every undertaking of this kind I incurred obligations to many friends and acquaintances during the course of its preparation. Among these were the members of the staffs of the Mullen Library of the Catholic University of America, the Library of Congress, and the Gleeson Library of the University of San Francisco. In particular I am grateful to two friends at the Catholic University of America, namely, the Reverend Antonine Tibesar, O.F.M., associate professor of Latin American history, for the constructive criticisms that he offered after his reading of the section devoted to the Spanish missions, and the Very Reverend Louis A. Arand, S.S., retired associate professor of dogmatic theology, to whom I am once again indebted for a careful reading of the entire manuscript and for offering, as he has often done for me in the past, many suggestions that have helped to clarify and to improve the work. Finally, I wish to thank my faithful and devoted former secretary, Mrs. Ruth K. Carney, for the many helpful tasks she performed without ever counting the cost.

JOHN TRACY ELLIS

February 8, 1963

CONTENTS

CATHOLICS IN COLONIAL AMERICA

CHAPTER ONE

THE CHURCH IN THE AGE OF DISCOVERY

As is true of other institutions in the United States, the Catholic Church traces its origins to a remote past outside the national frontiers. In fact, by the time that the first acts of Christian worship were performed on land that would come to be known as the American Republic, the Church had already nearly fifteen centuries of life behind it. Born in Palestine with the first Pentecost, during the first years it witnessed its doctrines carried by the apostles and their associates over portions of Asia Minor and into Egypt before their advent to Europe. The entrance to the European continent came as a direct consequence of a vision of St. Paul in which he saw a man who called out to him, "Come over into Macedonia and help us." [1] The apostle to the Gentiles set out immediately for Macedonia where at Philippi the teachings of Christ were heard for the first time in Europe. From Philippi St. Paul later proceeded westward and at Athens, center of the ancient and rich culture of Greece, he dared to address these cultivated pagans in the Areopagus. Keen observer that he was, Paul remarked that he had noticed the objects of their religious worship, and he added, "I found also an altar with this inscription 'To the Unknown God.' What therefore you worship in ignorance, that I proclaim to you." [2]

Thus was the missionary career of the Catholic Church begun on the soil of Europe. Through nearly 300 years its members remained a pro-

[1] *Acts of the Apostles*, XVI, 9.
[2] *Ibid.*, XVII, 23.

scribed and persecuted minority until Emperor Constantine I joined with Emperor Licinius at Milan early in 313 in issuing the famous edict by which the Church was accorded official toleration and placed on a basis of equality with the pagan cults. Having, as they said, put other matters pertaining to the common welfare in order, the emperors believed that among the things that would profit their subjects was the cultivation of religion. With that in mind, therefore, they had decided to

> give both to Christians and to all others free facility to follow the religion which each may desire, so that by this means whatever divinity is enthroned in heaven may be gracious and favourable to us and to all who have been placed under our authority.[3]

By the age of Constantine the decline that had overtaken the Roman Empire was well advanced, accompanied as it was by a deterioration in pagan worship. Thus during this period of transition the Catholic faith gradually emerged as far more than the religion of a despised minority of men, and from a position of toleration granted by the State at Milan the Church became the institution of greatest strength and stability in a day when the invasions of the barbaric tribes were hastening the end of the old empire and inaugurating a new era in the history of Europe.

For example, Pope Leo I proved a tower of strength to Italy's bewildered inhabitants in the crisis that befell them with the invasion of Attila and his cruel Huns, and as time passed and more and more of the barbarians embraced the Christian religion the prestige of the Church was enhanced. The striking ceremony of the coronation of Emperor Charlemagne by Pope Leo III on Christmas Day of 800 in St. Peter's Basilica at Rome was the adumbration of something more than the revival of the Roman Empire in the West. It was a manifestation of the leading role which the Church had come to play in the public life of Europe, and it was also an outward sign of the gradual emergence of that social unity which we have long identified as western Christendom.

Prior to the formal organization of the Church in the more remote areas of Europe, there had arrived the vanguard of countless missionaries who carried the cross of Christ beyond the frontiers of the old Roman Empire. They brought to these barbaric peoples – and this was

[3] "The Edicts of Toleration and of Milan, 313," Colman J. Barry, O.S.B. (Ed.), *Readings in Church History* (Westminster, 1960), p. 77.

especially true of the monks of St. Benedict—not only the light of a supernatural faith, but likewise the finest features of ancient learning and civilized living. Then in the eleventh century there was inaugurated a tremendous expansion of the Christian culture of western Europe in all directions, and in the succeeding centuries it was that culture, nurtured and matured by the Church, that transformed Europe from what a distinguished philosopher of history of our day has called "a barbarian hinterland into a centre of world culture which equalled the older oriental civilizations in power and wealth and surpassed them in creative energy."[4]

The creative energy of the culture fostered by the Catholic Church has rarely shown to better advantage than it did during the twelfth and thirteenth centuries. Missionaries won new conquests for Christianity by bringing Prussia within the orbit of the Church, and the heathen inhabitants of lands as far away as Lithuania and Livonia had the gospel preached to them. The papacy attained the peak of its political power in the days of Innocent III when princes often received their kingdoms from the hands of the pope as the arbiter of European affairs. Out of the early monastic and cathedral schools there had meanwhile evolved some of the greatest of Europe's centers of learning, and there was no more distinct bond among the new universities at Paris, Oxford, and Salamanca than the curriculum of scholastic theology and philosophy which they taught in Latin, the language of the Church and of all educated men in the West. Christian art and literature flourished as never before; to this time we owe such gems as the cathedrals of Rheims, Chartres, and Amiens. Toward the end of the period the wonderful artistic genius of Giotto anticipated tendencies in religious sculpture and painting which were to find their full expression in the Renaissance. And before the fourteenth century was far advanced Giotti's fellow Florentine, Dante Alighieri, produced the *Divine Comedy*, the poetic masterpiece of the Middle Ages, wherein was mirrored so much of the life and thought of Catholic Europe.

The high Middle Ages were remarkable likewise for a great number and variety of saints and new religious orders. St. Bernard of Clairvaux spread the fame of the Cistercians far and wide at a time when his contemporary, St. Norbert, was enriching the life of western Europe with his canons of Prémontré. Even more famous was the man who

[4] Christopher Dawson, *Understanding Europe* (New York, 1952), p. 33.

became so general a favorite, St. Francis of Assisi who, with St. Anthony of Padua and St. Clare, in time made the Franciscan name universally beloved. St. Dominic founded his Order of Preachers for the suppression of heresy only a generation before St. Simon Stock introduced the Carmelite friars to the great university cities of the West. Nor was holiness confined to monasteries and convents, for it was this same age which witnessed in St. Ferdinand III, King of Leon and Castile, St. Louis IX, King of France, and St. Elizabeth of Hungary, notable examples of sanctity among the rulers of Christendom.

Yet at no time in all the thousand years that separated the pontificate of Pope Gelasius I – the first to proclaim the papacy's independence of the State in spiritual matters – from the age of Columbus, had the Church attained a complete and unchallenged mastery over the affairs of men. It was, indeed, true that by 1492 virtually every section of western Europe paid homage to the successor of St. Peter at Rome. But through the intervening centuries western Christendom had been the scene of intermittent struggles with stubborn heresies and schisms that at times had rendered forfeit parts of the pope's spiritual domain. Moreover, from time to time ambitious princes had waged war upon the papacy in seeking either to curtail the spiritual power of the pope over their subjects or to lessen his status as the political ruler of central Italy. Nor were the losses suffered by the Church in the medieval centuries always brought on by forces outside its official household. Corruption and abuse in the governing councils of the Church had on occasion aggravated attacks and contributed to the scandal and loss by which the luster of its exalted mission had been diminished. More than once in that thousand years a spirit of worldliness had overtaken large segments of the clergy, and it was only the forceful action of reformers like Pope St. Gregory VII that had again restored the clerical state to its proper dignity and decorum.

Probably more important, however, than all these factors in the final disruption of the unity of Catholic Europe was the gradual emergence of a phenomenon which is considered as relatively modern, namely, nationalism. Modern it is, but as one of the ranking historians of nationalism has said,

> this is not to say that certain of its elements, and a good deal of its spirit, are not very old, or that the Church has not been repeatedly plagued during its long history by spasmodic surges of national sentiment and patriotic egotism,

which in combination have represented at least an embryonic or nascent nationalism.[5]

One of the most acute surges of nationalist feeling against the Church occurred at the opening of the fourteenth century when King Philip IV the Fair sought to bend the Holy See to the interests of the French monarchy. In the quarrel which followed between Philip IV and Pope Boniface VIII the pontiff met defeat, and with the death of Boniface and the election of the Frenchman, Bertrand de Got, Archbishop of Bordeaux, as Pope Clement V there began an exile of the papacy in France which was to last for seventy-two years and which was to have seriously detrimental effects upon the Church's universal mission. Out of the maelstrom which had been created by the jealousies and bitterness of the residence of the popes at Avignon there ensued in 1378 the great schism of the West when rivals for the papal throne divided Catholic Europe into warring camps, a condition which found no remedy until that November day of 1417 when Pope Martin V was elected at the Council of Constance. The protracted sessions at Constance — more than any previous council in the history of the Church — had demonstrated the severe damage which resulted to the cause of Catholic unity by the clashing interests of national groups. The catastrophic events which followed the pontificate of Boniface VII lend weight, therefore, to the view that his death marked the end of an epoch and the beginning of a new age in which the papacy and religion gradually ceased "to be taken into account as factors in the public life of the Christian nations."[6]

The tragedy which this dismal chain of events entailed for the Catholic Church was, in a certain sense, symbolized by the condition in which Martin V found the city of Rome upon his entrance there in the last days of September, 1420. Many of the artistic monuments that were once the glory of Rome was now in ruins, the streets were overgrown with grass, and sections of the city walls were broken down so that at night wolves came out of the Campagna, invaded the gardens of the Vatican, and dug up the corpses of the dead buried in the Campo Santo.[7] It was true that under the patronage of the papacy the Rome of

[5] Carlton J. H. Hayes, "The Church and Nationalism — A Plea for Further Study of a Major Issue," *Catholic Historical Review*, XXVIII (April, 1942), 2.

[6] Philip Hughes, *A History of the Church* (New York, 1947), III, 57.

[7] Ludwig Pastor, *The History of the Popes* (St. Louis, 1923), I, 216. Hereafter this work will be referred to as: Pastor, *History of the Popes*.

the Renaissance would rise from its ruins later in the same century and would produce artistic splendors never before realized. But in the intervening time since St. Thomas Aquinas and St. Bonaventure had won such splendid achievements for scholastic theology and philosophy at the University of Paris, a serious change had come about in the world of learning which, insofar as it related to the spiritual mission of the Church, was in time to reveal the artistic effulgence of the Renaissance as a kind of brilliant façade behind which there lay concealed the elements of a deep decay.

One of those who figured prominently in this decline in Christian thought was William of Ockham, a lecturer in theology at the University of Oxford, who introduced into his teaching and writings, a strange theory of knowledge which came to be called nominalism and which when followed logically to its conclusion, led to an hostility between faith and reason. Although Ockham's ideas were condemned by Pope John XXII, they lingered on in certain circles during this age of decadent scholasticism, and the affinity which was later shown between the thought of the English Franciscan and that of Martin Luther served to emphasize its damaging character.[8] A contemporary of Ockham's, Marsiglio of Padua, was even more radical in his break with the dominant theories of medieval Christendom in the realm of politics. In a work entitled *Defensor pacis*, which appeared in 1325 and which has been characterized as, "perhaps the most mischievous book of the whole Middle Ages,"[9] Marsiglio frankly aimed at the elimination of the papacy and—what was even more extreme—at the destruction of the notion that religious ideas, independent of the State, were the ultimate norms of man's conduct either in public or private life.

If it is recalled that these were likewise the years when Petrarch and Boccaccio, as precursors of the humanist movement, were establishing the vogue for the pagan authors of classical antiquity, one can better appreciate how men's minds were gradually weaned away from the medieval ideal of living as a child of God for the next world and focused upon the pleasures and accomplishments of the present life. Thus had the seeds of rebellion against the Church been planted in

[8] Hughes, *op. cit.*, III, 21, says: "From Ockham to Luther is indeed a long road, and the Franciscan's thought doubtless suffers many losses as it makes the journey along it. But it is a road whose trace is unmistakable, and the beginning of that road needs to be noticed."

[9] Philip Hughes, *The Reformation in England* (New York, 1951), I, 331.

the fourteenth century, and 200 years later they were to bear their harvest in the Protestant Revolt when the increased powers of secular rulers over both Church and State had received fresh impetus in a famous work called *The Prince*, begun in 1513 by Nicolò Machiavelli.

In the myriad economic and social changes that had meanwhile transformed the crude feudal society of the early Middle Ages into the flourishing commercial and industrial life of the growing urban centers, the Church had, of course, played only a secondary role. Yet the revival of trade and industry, the introduction of coined money, and the rise of the towns had profoundly affected the Church by reason of its vast property holdings, the movement of thousands of people into the towns, and the mounting spirit of secularism among the rich bourgeoisie who dominated the new urban society. Thus from a largely rural institution it had become, perforce, an important element in the rising cities with their numerous parishes, schools, charitable enterprises, and religious fraternities.

These changed conditions offered to churchmen a severe challenge, for it was far more difficult to hold men to their religious duties amid the highly prosperous and organized life of the fifteenth century than it had been to draw them to God in the fifth century when the Church alone stood between them and the disorders of that troubled age. In fact, the very prosperity which became so marked a feature of the life of western Europe was itself one of the causes for the weakness which had overtaken the Church as the Middle Ages drew to a close. The increased wealth which had accrued to ecclesiastical nobles, as well as to their lay counterparts, caused the spiritual ideal to grow dim in their lives, and the worldliness of many a bishop and abbot was the occasion for the decline of religious values among those whom they ruled. And yet the age was not without those who kept alive a keen sense of the Christian virtues, for as St. Catherine of Siena and St. Vincent Ferrer had battled valiantly for the unity and welfare of the Church in the sad days of the Avignon Papacy and the great schism of the West, so Catherine's fellow townsman, St. Bernardine, and his Franciscan companion, St. John of Capistrano, aroused widespread enthusiasm for reform by their striking success as preachers of the word of God.

One of the principal factors that accounted for the enrichment of Europe in the years before the discovery of America was the tremendous expansion of its business interests beyond its own frontiers. It was a development that had had a long history. Although there had never been a complete isolation of Christian Europe from the East, it was the crusades, organized for the purpose of rescuing the Holy Land from the Moslems, that had opened the eyes of admiring Europeans to the splendors of the Orient. And in this movement, too, the Church had played an important part. From that day in November, 1095, when Pope Urban II fired his vast audience at the Council of Clermont with so strong an urge to deliver the Christians of the East that the cry "God wills it" was heard on all sides, many churchmen had actively engaged in the crusades. To be sure, the high goal of permanent conquest of the Holy Land was not accomplished, but the repeated attempts of Christian Europe through the next two centuries brought countless western men into close contact with their eastern neighbors.

In this vast movement of peoples the spiritual aim of delivering the Holy Land was often lost to view, but the profits to be derived from trade were not. As a consequence, interest in the Orient was quickened and, as in many other places and times, the cross was frequently associated with the flag and the caravans of trade. It was in the years when men's minds were so strongly directed toward the East that Pope Innocent IV in 1246 sent the Franciscan friar, John of Piano di Carpine to the court of the Mongol rulers of China in the hope that they might be converted to Christianity. Other missionaries followed later, the most notable of whom was John of Montecorvino, who succeeded in establishing a promising mission and was named Archbishop of Peking by Clement V. But the prospect which this Franciscan effort held out in its earlier stages was never realized. The friendly Mongols were overthrown in 1368 by the Ming dynasty, which again adopted the policy of exclusion of foreigners, and the intrepid missionaries were left to face persecution without any effective support from the papacy which by now found itself caught up in the whirlpool of events that heralded the great schism of the West.

The busy traffic with the Orient over both the land routes and the sea lanes of the eastern Mediterranean provided a strong incentive to geographical and nautical science, and as devices like the compass and the astrolabe came into general use the sailing ships were set in motion in all directions. As a consequence, navigation took on increased importance in the West as well as in the East. The Portuguese, for example, sent out numerous early exploring parties along the west coast of Africa and to the adjacent islands such as the Canary, the Madeira, and even as far away as the Azores. Thus the way was prepared for the career of the famous Prince Henry the Navigator, whose patronage not only advanced cosmography and discovery to a marked degree, but whose every endeavor was motivated by a deep desire to convert the native peoples to the Catholic faith. Missionaries appeared along the African coast soon after the explorers, and as early as 1351 Pope Clement VI named a Carmelite friar as the first bishop in the Canary Islands. Slowly the mysteries of the African coastline yielded before the persistence of the Portuguese seamen, and in 1488 Bartolomeu Dias succeeded in rounding the Cape of Good Hope four years before the discovery of America.

As Europe's explorers, traders, and missionaries had, therefore, maintained relations with Asia and Africa which stretched far back into the Middle Ages, so, too, the old continent's first contacts with what was to be recognized in time as the western hemisphere were of a very early date. In the various enterprises which marked the initial and tentative efforts to establish European settlement in the islands of the north Atlantic, the Church was in the foreground. An example can be found in the Irish monks who, in search of new missionary fields, reached Iceland a century or more before the Norsemen settled there in 874.[10] But these early visits and settlements of Irish Christians in Iceland yielded nothing of a lasting character to the Church, and it was only after the Norsemen under Eric Thorwaldsson (the Red) had discovered Greenland in the late tenth century, that there appeared a prospect of permanency for Catholicism in those remote and forbidding lands. The early history of Iceland and Greenland is shrouded in considerable uncertainty. There is no doubt, however, that, with the aid of missionaries from England, the Catholic faith was greatly advanced in Norway and in its colonies under Kings Olaf Trygvesson and

[10] Even though the alleged voyage to America of St. Brendan (c. 435–c. 583) belongs in the category of legend, the widespread belief accorded to it exerted a strong influence among medieval seafarers. Samuel Eliot Morison speaks of Brendan as one "whose saga of ocean voyaging was one of the most popular stories of the Middle Ages." *Admiral of the Ocean Sea. A Life of Christopher Columbus* (Boston, 1942), I, 41. It was also characterized as "one of the moving causes that led Columbus to the discovery of the New World," by Joseph Dunn, "The Brendan Problem," *Catholic Historical Review*, VI (January, 1921), 470. Hereafter the Morison work will be referred to as: Morison, *Columbus.*

St. Olaf II, and it was under the first of these rulers that Iceland and Greenland accepted Christianity about the year 1000. Subsequently the Church was organized in both countries under bishops with the See of Skalholt erected in Iceland in 1056 and another diocese established at Holar in 1106. Likewise in Greenland about 1112 the name of Eric, Bishop of Gardar, entered the records of that country for the first time.[11]

The Norsemen were a sea-faring people, and it was in the first years of the eleventh century that Leif Ericsson and Thorfinn Karlsefni inaugurated a series of voyages to what Ericsson called Wineland (Vinland) which was probably Nova Scotia. How long the Norsemen continued to visit America and how far inland they penetrated, it is impossible to say. The intriguing possibilities suggested by the discovery of the Kensington Stone near Kensington, Minnesota, in 1898 and of similar remains in other places, have led some investigators to conclude that the Norsemen's American contacts were far more extensive and lasting than had originally been believed. But the data so far uncovered to support this theory have not been sufficient to inspire general acceptance among scholars.[12] What is certain, is that the extension of European settlement and of the Catholic religion into the western hemisphere took place nearly 500 years before Columbus' famous voyage of 1492.

But it was not the Norsemen and their religious institutions that were to give character and form to the Catholic Church as it developed in

[11] Laurence M. Larson, "The Church in North America (Greenland) in the Middle Ages," *Catholic Historical Review*, V (July–October, 1919), 184. These northern dioceses maintained an irregular line of bishops up to the opening of the modern era. The last Bishop of Gardar to be named was Vincent Kampe, a Dane, who was appointed in 1519 by Pope Leo X. The succession of bishops in Iceland came to an end after the appointments c. 1520 of Jón Arason for Holar and Oejmundr Pálsson for Skalholt. In 1961 Danish archeologists discovered in Greenland the foundations of a small church that had been built around 1001–1002, the first in the new world. It was founded by Tjodhilde, wife of Erik the Red, who was buried in the churchyard with her son. It was their son, Leif Ericson, who came to Greenland accompanied by two missionaries. Cf. Michael Wolfe, O.M.I., "Thjodhild's Church. The Cradle of Christianity in Norse Greenland," *American-Scandinavian Review*, LI (Spring, 1963), 55–66.

[12] Both sides of the question can be read in the following articles, the first of which rejects the claim of authenticity while the second accepts it: Milo M. Quaife, "The Myth of the Kensington Rune Stone: The Norse Discovery of Minnesota, 1362," *New England Quarterly*, VII (December, 1934), 613–645; and Hjalmar Rued Holand, "A Review of the Kensington Stone Research," *Wisconsin Magazine of History*, XXXVI (Summer, 1953), 235–239; 273–276.

the new world. It was rather the men of western Europe who were to transplant across the seas not only their civil laws and customs but, too, the peculiar ecclesiastical regulations and traditions that had become identified with Catholicism in countries like Spain and France, and at a later date with the new Protestantism and beleaguered Catholicism in England. In the case of some types of office and organization, common to the Church in the era of discovery, no permanent roots were struck in what later became the United States. This was true, for example, of cathedral chapters of canons which, aside from a relatively brief history in places like New Orleans, played no part in the development of Catholicism in this country. In other cases, however, the ecclesiastical regulations introduced into the American colonies of the European powers had a lasting effect upon the Church. And among these there were few which proved to be more important — and troublesome — than that of the manner of holding church property. In fact, one of the most entangled problems faced by the American government as late as the defeat of Spain in 1898 revolved around the difficulty over the Church's lands in places like the Philippine Islands, Cuba, and Puerto Rico. For that reason it is necessary to know something about the way in which the properties of the Church in Europe were held in the early modern era, if one is to understand the problems which later developed around that subject in America.

The Church, as we have said, was the sole stabilizing factor in society during the period when the old Roman Empire was breaking up and the barbarians were roaming at will over its far-flung provinces. Its principal mission, to be sure, was to instruct these untutored peoples in the truths of the Christian religion. But if that were to be accomplished, a settled existence would first have to be provided for them, and the best means available to introduce discipline and order was to establish a fixed abode on the land. In this way ecclesiastics entered into the complicated system of land tenure which evolved under feudalism, and a situation developed in which the bishops and higher clergy acquired large tracts of land upon which they settled numerous tillers of the soil. As the monastic movement expanded in the West, the same was true of abbots and other superiors of religious orders whose communities assumed a leading role in the process of civilizing the barbarians and of instructing them in Christianity. Not only were numerous properties secured directly in this manner to the Church, but it likewise became the beneficiary of many gifts of land from lay princes and nobles who often gave over their properties to ecclesiastical hands as an act of charity or in reparation for their sins.

In an age when towns were few in number and rural isolation was very real, it frequently happened that members of the feudal nobility and their families wished to have the religious ministrations of a priest in their own household. In a case of this kind the lord would build a church on his estate and then seek the permission of the local bishop to have it recognized as a place of worship. The bishop, in turn, would demand that a sufficient provision of worldly goods be secured to support a priest in the office. This was the lay lord's responsibility, but in fulfilling that responsibility it was not unnatural that he should consider himself as having certain rights in the choice of the man to be named to the post. The lay lord owned the soil upon which the church stood and the land or goods set apart for the sustenance of the priest who served it. He was, therefore, its patron, and as such he demanded the right to present the name of the priest of his choice to the bishop for the benefice. Here in essence was the *jus patronatus*, the right of patronage or advowson, as it was called.

The importance of lay patronage of clerical benefices need hardly be emphasized, if it is kept in mind that the practice gradually spread throughout the whole Catholic world until it embraced some of the richest churches and religious foundations of western Europe. Although it would be untrue to say that all ecclesiastical properties were held in this manner, a very great number were so held, and long before the end of the Middle Ages it had become an accepted norm in both canon and civil law. In some instances, indeed, the right of patronage was so firmly fastened upon parish churches, monasteries, cathedrals, and other forms of church lands or buildings that for generations single families held the power of presenting the ecclesiastics for their chief offices.

In the increasingly secular atmosphere of the late Middle Ages the vast properties of the Church came to be more and more an object of contention. This was due to a number of factors, of which the chief were: 1) the movement toward centralization of political power in the hands of the kings; 2) the rising tide of nationalism; 3) the cupidity aroused by the maturing capitalist system; and 4) the corruption and abuses existing among so many of the higher clergy. As the kings secured a greater mastery over the old feudal nobility and succeeded in centralizing more of the power of the state in their own hands, they eyed with much less favor the papacy's control over so many important offices and possessions within their realms.

Nor were matters pertaining to clerical benefices improved as a consequence of the great schism of the West and the period of attempted rule of the Church by general councils in the early fifteenth century. In fact, the spirit of nationalism took the ascendancy so effectively in gatherings like the Councils of Constance and Basel that the supranational power once exercised by the pope over the Church's lands and offices was never again the same as it had been before these councils met. It was largely as a result of the inspiration afforded by the anti-papal decrees of Basel that King Charles VII of France summoned his clerical and lay nobles to meet him at Bourges in May, 1438. There in the following month was issued the pragmatic sanction, a royal edict which gave the force of law to a limitation of the Holy See's right in the nomination of candidates to French benefices, prohibited the payment of certain taxes to Rome, and forbade appeals from the French courts to the papal tribunals. The following year the Diet of Mainz, held under the auspices of Emperor Albert II, accepted the Basel program for the German world, even if it stopped short of an administrative ordinance such as that adopted at Bourges.

These measures marked notable advances in the displacement of the papal by the national power over ecclesiastical goods and offices. They likewise served as precedents for further encroachments in a later period when, for example, a monarch like Francis I of France won from Leo X in the Concordat of Bologna of August, 1516, the right to present to the pope for confirmation royal candidates for the ninety-three bishoprics of France, as well as the names of the abbots and other superiors of over 500 French religious houses. The significance of an act of this kind for the future of Catholicism in colonial America may be better appreciated if it is recalled that by the time François de Montmorency de Laval was consecrated as the first Vicar Apostolic of New France in December, 1658, the kings of France had enjoyed the right of presentation to such benefices for nearly a century and a half. And in this instance it is rendered more pertinent by the fact that Bishop Laval – who was to exercise episcopal jurisdiction over vast areas of what is today the United States – experienced one of his earliest and most unpleasant conflicts at the hands of the Archbishop of Rouen, François de Harlay-Chanvallon, and the parlement of that city. The Rouen authorities, supported in their pretensions to jurisdiction over the Church in New France by King Louis XIV, sought to incorporate the future bishopric of Canada into the French hierarchy and to reduce Laval to the status of a mere vicar general of Rouen. It was only after a long and arduous struggle that a compromise was effected when Pope Clement X on October 1, 1674, erected Quebec into a diocese and made it directly subject to the Holy See. Thereafter Bishop Laval succeeded in securing at least a partial relief from the interference of the French ecclesiastical and lay officials in the business which related to his apostolic labors for the Church in the new world.

But at no time were the ecclesiastical benefices in France's North American possessions really free of the hampering restrictions of the lay authorities, as the history of the French missions of the seventeenth and eighteenth centuries makes abundantly clear. On the contrary, that history, as we shall see later, is filled with the record of almost constant tension between the officials of the crown and the missionaries who were working among both the white and Indian populations. The disastrous results which followed from the lay domination of the affairs of the Church – hastened by the growth of rationalism and irreligious thought in French official circles during the eighteenth century – were never more strikingly illustrated than in the sad episode which terminated the long and valiant efforts of the Society of Jesus to convert and civilize the American Indians. Those who were intent upon the destruction of the Jesuits in France gained their first victory in 1761, and, as we shall see, they soon found ready imitators in the colonies.

The secular control of the Church which, in the case of France, was to influence so strongly the course of the missions of that nation in the regions of the Great Lakes and the Mississippi Valley, had an even more direct bearing on the history of the missions established under the crown of Spain in what has been called the Spanish borderlands of the United States. Ten years before the discovery of the new world Pope Sixtus IV, deeply embroiled in the wars of the Italian states and in need of the good will of the Spanish sovereigns, was forced to yield to the pressure of King Ferdinand II of Aragon and Queen Isabella I of Castile by granting to them extensive concurrent rights over episcopal nominations within their domains. Having won the right of patronage at home, it was not surprising that after they had acquired an overseas empire the Spanish rulers should seek the same privileges abroad. In the next decade one of Sixtus' successors, Alexander VI, a Spaniard, had become even more dangerously involved in the politics of the Italian peninsula, and the support of Spain was every bit as necessary to his purposes. Further concessions followed, therefore, and in 1493 the pope granted to the rulers the right to name all the missionaries who should go to the new world, and in 1501 he conceded to them all the ecclesiastical tithes in Spain's American possessions to be used for the building and support of churches in the colonies.

But the most sweeping and enduring of the papal grants of ecclesiastical power to the kings of Spain came under Julius II. In the bull, *Universalis ecclesiae*, of July 28, 1508, the pontiff commanded that no church, monastery, or religious house should be built in the colonies without the royal assent having first been obtained. Moreover, the *real patronato*, or the right of the rulers to nominate to all ecclesiastical benefices without exception and in perpetuity, was made over to them. At that time the dignities and property holdings of the Church in the West Indies were, of course, insignificant, but the action of Julius II took on enormous importance after the conquests of the Spaniards on the mainlands of North and South America.

The disadvantages associated with lay patronage were quickly demonstrated when the same pope attempted to set up the first episcopal sees in the Spanish colonial empire. In November, 1504, Julius II issued a bull in which he erected a metropolitan see with two suffragan dioceses in Española (Haiti). But as soon as King Ferdinand learned that the pope had assigned part of the tithes on gold, silver, and precious stones to these bishops, he protested vehemently that this entailed a violation of the right which he possessed from Alexander VI. The king refused, therefore, to allow the bishops to leave for their dioceses and the whole affair came to nothing. Some years later the pope and the king reached an agreement and on August 8, 1511, Julius II erected two dioceses at San Domingo and Concepcion de la Vega in Española and at San Juan in Puerto Rico, all three to be suffragan sees of the Archdiocese of Seville.

It was under Ferdinand's grandson, King Charles I of Spain, however, that the *real patronato* was first felt directly in the area which later came to be the United States. It was at the instance of the young king that Pope Adrian VI in April, 1522, erected the Diocese of Santiago de Cuba, and it was from that see that authority was exercised over the Church in Florida after the Spaniards had settled there. But it was in the origins of the diocese from which there was derived the Church's jurisdiction over the American Southwest that the incongruities of the system of lay patronage were especially noteworthy. In this case the first bishop in Mexico was chosen solely on the authority of Charles I. He was a Spanish Franciscan, Juan de Zumárraga, who sailed for Mexico in August, 1528, and governed the diocese for five years without even having received episcopal consecration. Only after that time did this otherwise worthy friar return to Spain to receive the bulls of election and to be consecrated in April, 1533, at Valladolid.

Situations such as these evidence how far-reaching was the power of the Spanish crown in the affairs of the Church. The rights conceded by the papacy were, as one might expect, often broadly interpreted, and ultimately the Church in the Spanish colonies came to be almost as completely subordinate to the crown as the army itself. To be sure, for these concessions the Spanish sovereigns, as was also true of the French kings, promised to promote and support the conversion of the native peoples to Catholicism. But the inheritance which this system bestowed, by way of problems relating to ecclesiastical properties and offices in the colonial missions of the future United States, proved to be a very troublesome one. Tradition and precedent frequently showed themselves to be stubborn barriers to ecclesiastical control over the Church's possessions, and the evil effects of lay patronage continued to be felt in the regions of Spanish and French settlement as late as the mid-nineteenth century.

In matters pertaining to the patronage of ecclesiastical benefices in the medieval and early modern Church, whether that patronage was in the hands of clerics or laymen, the spirit of avarice nurtured by the maturing capitalist system played at times a significant part. As capitalism took a firmer grip upon the business world of Europe there evolved a stronger desire for riches, and one of the most effective ways of adding to one's fortune was to acquire more land or to establish a profitable interest in someone else's properties or business enterprises by means of loans and mortgages. Through this means there arose large banking companies or houses such as the Bardi and Peruzzi of Florence. Not only did they loan enormous sums to lay princes, but they also financed popes, bishops, and others among the high clergy in undertakings like the crusades and the wars in which these churchmen engaged against their local enemies. The bankers of Siena in the fourteenth century, for example, grew very rich from the exorbitant rates of interest which they were able to collect on their loans to the papacy. But to no bankers were the popes more beholden than to the Medici of Florence. This famous firm flourished and spread to such an extent that it had branches in almost all of the large cities of Europe, and as the popes of the fifteenth century became more deeply immersed in secular concerns, the Medici influence increased at Rome.

Naturally transactions of this kind, often involving excessive rates of interest or commissions, were the source of deep resentment and scandal to ordinary men. It was a sordid arrangement along these lines, entered into with the German banking firm of the Fuggers of Augsburg by Archbishop Albert of Brandenburg less than a quarter century after the discovery of America, that provided Luther with an occasion for revolt against the Church in 1517. In this instance the Fuggers advanced the money to the Archbishop of Magdeburg to cover the cost of the fees necessary to satisfy Albert's ambition to hold simultaneously Magdeburg, the See of Halberstadt, and the Archdiocese of Mainz. To this plan Leo X gave his assent by allowing a crusade of indulgences to be preached in Saxony, half of the income from which would go to the pope for the building of St. Peter's in Rome and half to the archbishop to discharge his debt to the bankers. It was not strange, therefore, that such clerical abuses, which were so widespread in the age of discovery, should have led not only to a loss of confidence in the high clergy, but to a loss of faith on the part of many who were aware of what was taking place.

The leadership of the Church in this critical period was anything but what one had a right to expect of an institution whose main business it was to improve men's morals and to advance their eternal salvation. In the half century that lay between the election of Sixtus IV in 1471 and the death of Leo X in 1521, five of the six pontiffs who occupied the chair of Peter not only did little to arrest the moral decline, but they actually hastened it by their preoccupation with secular pursuits. Among them were, it is true, men of very high intelligence who were endowed with superior gifts as administrators, but there was entirely lacking either a genuine awareness of the absolute necessity of radical reform or a firm will to push through a serious reform program in the face of fearful odds that had accumulated during so many years of moral laxity. The outrageous nepotism of Sixtus IV, the indecision and incompetence of Innocent VIII, the gross immorality of the Roman court under Alexander VI, and the dynastic wars or artistic extravagances that marked the pontificates of Julius II and Leo X provided a fitting stage for rebellion from the authority of popes who had proven so unworthy of their exalted office.

The curious inconsistencies to be found in the papacy at this time are well illustrated by the case of the sixth of these pontiffs, Pius III, who lived less than a month after his election on September 22, 1503. This Piccolomini pope was a man of blameless character and sincerely determined to undertake reform, but the ecclesiastical oddities of the age are revealed in the fact that for over forty years he had been Archbishop of Siena – at the gift of his uncle, Pius II – without ever having been consecrated a bishop. It was only after his election to the papacy that Pius III received priesthood and episcopal consecration. In an atmosphere of this kind it was little wonder that the fiery sermons of the Florentine Dominican, Girolamo Savonarola, which had begun in the summer of 1490, should have made so slight an impression upon the curia of Innocent VIII, and that the friar's insistent demands for clerical reform should have ultimately encountered the wrath of Alexander VI. Savonarola perished, therefore, in May, 1498, without having effected any real cure of the vices that were slowly corroding the power and influence of the papacy over the souls of men.

The impression which one receives from a study of the late medieval Church with its prevalence of abuses of lay patronage, questionable finance, and clerical corruption is, indeed, a depressing one. And yet these unhappy features of ecclesiastical rule do not tell the whole story of the religious life of those years, for the Church is not limited to what can be seen of it from without. Even amid the moral decay which accompanied the Renaissance, and which made such deep inroads upon the lives of many churchmen, the spirit of piety and high sanctity were not extinguished. For example, the same France of Charles VII that had struck at the papal prerogatives in the Pragmatic Sanction of Bourges in 1438, had been a witness only a few years before to the striking holiness and purity of life of St. Joan of Arc, who in May, 1431, had sacrificed her life at Rouen in testimony to the truth of her heavenly voices. And two generations later St. Jeanne of Valois, the despised daughter of King Louis XI and the humiliated wife of Louis XII, demonstrated extraordinary virtue at a royal court that was notorious for its profligacy and worldliness. Far to the north in Poland a priest professor, St. John Cantius, shone before his students at the University of Cracow by the luster of his holiness as much as by the brilliance of his mind, and this in the same years that a Polish prince, St. Casimir, was winning souls to God by the good deeds which he performed at the court of his father, King Casimir IV.

Many Spaniards, too, remained untouched by the sordidness of the age. Among the early settlers in the Canary Islands there appeared the devout Franciscan lay brother, St. Didacus, who left a lasting mark upon the Catholic life of those islands as he was later to edify men in the cities of Rome and Alcalà. So, too, during the early reign of King Ferdinand of Aragon, St. John of Sahagún, an Augustinian hermit, effected tremendous changes in the social life of Salamanca and its environs by his fearless preaching of reform. Nor was Italy devoid of saints who held firmly to the ideal of personal sanctity during this turbulent period. Mention has already been made of the two great reform preachers, SS. Bernardine of Siena and John of Capistrano. It was likewise during the period of confusion that characterized the conciliar movement in the Church, when the authority of the popes was severely challenged by general councils and anti-popes, that a woman such as St. Frances of Rome serenely pursued the spiritual ideal and drew around her others of a similar disposition to start a new religious community, the Benedictine Oblates of Tor de' Specci. St. Francis de Paola is another case in point, a man whose holy life attracted many disciples and enabled him to found the new order of Minim Friars which received the approval of Sixtus IV in 1474.

Neither had the corruption in high places altogether deprived the Italian episcopate of its saints, for the nobleman, St. Laurence Giustiniani, who in 1451 became the first Patriarch of Venice, not only governed his see with exemplary virtue but found time to write mystical treatises which won the praise of discerning minds. Another Italian bishop who, like Laurence Giustiniani, accepted the miter with the greatest reluctance was the Dominican, St. Antoninus. This learned theologian left his Florentine convent of San Marco very much against his will to spend the last thirteen years of his life as Archbishop of Florence in the very period when Cosimo de Medici was enhancing that wealthy city's prestige as a center of the arts and solidifying the domination of his family over its civil life.

The episcopal careers of these two saintly bishops offer an interesting study in contrasts with that of their contemporary, Pope Nicholas V. Both Laurence and Antoninus were conspicuous for the austerity of their personal lives and for the great liberality with which they dispensed assistance to the poor and afflicted among their diocesan charges. At the same time Nicholas V, who is generally regarded as the first of the humanist pontiffs, was definitely identifying the Holy See with the revival of classical learning, and in his enthusiasm for the movement the pope did not hesitate to lavish huge sums of money on some scholars and artists whose philosophy and morals were seriously detrimental to the welfare of religion.

Thus did the Church in the fifteenth century, as in every other age, reveal simultaneously the lights and shadows which the moral rectitude or laxity of those who composed its membership cast over its history. Saints there surely were in these days of clashing and discordant elements in ecclesiastical life, but it is significant that of the seventy-six persons either canonized or beatified who lived in the half century between Sixtus IV's accession to the papal throne and Leo X's death in 1521, fifty-five of them belonged to the mendicant orders. The number of canonized bishops and secular rulers had noticeably declined since the thirteenth century, and it was apparent that extraordinary piety was no longer associated with those of high station in the same degree that had been true of an earlier day. The stronghold of holiness was now more closely confined to the seclusion of the monasteries and convents of the religious orders.

Meanwhile what is one to say of the religious faith of the common people? Obviously it is impossible within so brief a space to offer even an adequate sketch of the true depth and extent of the faith of the ordinary man. But these facts concerning the religious attitudes of the general population, we do know. First, the third orders, which were begun by the mendicant friars in the thirteenth century, continued to flourish two centuries later, and thousands of devout laity were still being enrolled in their ranks and by this means brought to a higher level of personal holiness. Secondly, there was a tremendous multiplication of religious books after the invention of movable type around the middle of the century. Thus the *Imitation of Christ*, commonly attributed to Thomas à Kempis, became almost as widely read as the Bible. It was the most famous product of the so-called *Devotio moderna*, a movement which had its origins in the Low Countries with Gerard Grotte as a pioneer, and was largely a reaction against the formalism which in many places the more social and liturgical forms of religion seem to have been promoted. Moreover, the *Imitation of Christ* was only the best known of a large number of devotional books which were widely diffused in the vernacular languages through the new invention of printing.

In addition, the fact that there continued to be repeated and insistent protests against clerical abuses and demands that they be reformed, was itself evidence that the traditional Catholic faith of western Europe was still very much alive. Throughout the fifteenth century pleas of this sort were constantly reaching the papal curia. We have already spoken of the efforts of reformers like St. John of Sahagún in Spain and Savonarola in Italy. Other countries, too, had leaders in this cause, men who, like the learned chancellor of the University of Paris, John Gerson, and the German cardinal and philosopher, Nicholas of Cusa, were deeply aroused by the moral decline and who were determined to correct it. These leaders and their followers were, it is true, a small minority among the great masses, and their ultimate failure to win the papacy to a serious reform program made the explosion of the Protestant Revolt seemingly inevitable. One of the saddest consequences of this failure to arrest the moral laxity was the fact that the accompanying ignorance of theology among the clergy reflected itself in a lack of proper instruction of the common people in the essentials of their religious belief. The improvement in clerical discipline and learning which resulted from the introduction of regular seminary training for aspirants to the priesthood had to await the salutary legislation of the Council of Trent.

And yet at the time that Columbus set forth upon his famous voyage the vast majority of men in western and central Europe were still being born and raised within the Church as their ancestors before them had been for centuries. Every professed Catholic was expected to give at least outward conformity to the doctrines and moral precepts of the faith, and the Church itself was not merely a private and voluntary organization but an official and public institution. The canon law of the Church was equally respected with the civil law of the State and the jurisdiction of the ecclesiastical courts over subjects such as matrimony and wills was recognized throughout western Christendom. Church and State were closely united, and each government interested itself actively in religious questions and undertook to enforce obedience on the part of its subjects to the Church. It was still the prevailing belief that heresy to the Church was the practical equivalent to treason to the State. The time honored theology of scholasticism, despite the decline it had undergone since the period of St. Thomas Aquinas, embodied as before the principal teachings of Catholicism, the faithful were still nourished by divine grace through the sacraments, and they continued to accept the spiritual rule of the bishops of their dioceses and the pastors of their parishes who, like their predecessors for centuries before them, represented to the minds of the Catholic laity the central authority of the See of Peter.

The Catholic Church had, then, unquestionably suffered grave losses as it neared the dawn of the modern era, and if extremists among the first Protestants of Luther's day believed that death was finally at hand for the old Church that they had been brought to hate, it was understandable. But such had been its history through all the 1500 years that separated it from the apostolic age; yet in spite of reverses it had moved on, losing here and gaining there. The early followers of Luther, Calvin, Zwingli, and the rest could not foresee the fresh vigor and new life that would rise from within the Church in the Catholic Reformation of the later sixteenth century to regain many of the souls who had been led astray. Neither could they foresee that as the Catholic Church in countries like northern Germany, Scandinavia, and England was crushed out of existence, unknown lands across the sea like Mexico, Peru, and New France would rear themselves to redress in part the balance that had been lost. Less than twenty years after Luther's death in 1546 the Spaniards planted the cross at St. Augustine, Florida, in August, 1565, to found the first parish in what would one day be the United States. New areas of spiritual conquest opened before the Church, therefore, at the very time that it had sustained its heaviest defeats in Europe. Thus was there illustrated again the truth expressed by one churchman when he said:

> Where those outside the Church see an agony, believers, without any risk of error, discern a renaissance. If the Church is the tree grown from the mustard seed, it is normal that she experience, like it, the succession of seasons – autumns and springs.[13]

[13] Emmanuel Cardinal Suhard, *Growth or Decline? The Church Today* (South Bend, 1948), p. 27. For a thoughtful essay on the Church in this period cf. Wallace K. Ferguson, "The Church in a Changing World: A Contribution to the Interpretation of the Renaissance," *American Historical Review*, LIX (October, 1953), 1–18.

PART ONE

THE SPANISH MISSIONS

CHAPTER TWO

FLORIDA

More than thirty years ago an American historian stated, "It is of prime significance for the life of America today that the first white men to settle on these western shores were Spaniards and Roman Catholics, representatives of a powerful nation that was the citadel of a united faith."[1] The story of Spanish discovery, exploration, and colonization of the new world has been told often and well, and there is no need to retell it here. Not so well known, however, is the part played in that dramatic and colorful movement by the numerous Spanish priests who marched at the side – and sometimes ahead – of the military and civil officials as they gradually enlarged the frontiers of the American empire of the kings of Spain. That the missionary was at times in advance of the explorer and the soldier in the vast enterprise of charting the unknown wastes, in opening up the wilderness for the first time to civilization, in exploring the rivers and traversing the mountains and plains, is indeed true. But that was not his primary objective. Uppermost in his mind was the ideal of a herald of the gospel, of a searcher after souls, and of an agent who would plant the Catholic faith in the untutored minds and hearts of the native peoples. Such was the compelling motive that activated his life in the new world. It is with the achievements of the Spanish missionaries in causing the Catholic Church to take root in the regions of what would later be recognized as the southern arc of the United States that we are here concerned.

[1] Herbert Ingram Priestly, *The Coming of the White Man, 1492–1848* (New York, 1930), p. 1. Hereafter this work will be referred to as: Priestly, *Coming of the White Man.*

That the discovery of America should have come at the time that it did proved especially fortunate for the advancement of the Catholic faith in the new world. It was a period of high religious fervor in Spain when the reforms of the great Franciscan cardinal, Francisco Ximénes de Cisneros, Archbishop of Toledo, Primate of Spain, and Grand Inquisitor, would soon produce through his University of Alcalá and other measures an enlivening effect upon the religious spirit of the people. Moreover, less than a year before Columbus set foot on American soil the combined armies of Aragon and Castille had succeeded in January, 1492, in dislodging the Moslems from Granada, their last great stronghold in the peninsula. It was not surprising, therefore, that this culminating act in a religious warfare that had been waged off and on for over seven centuries should have stirred the Spaniards so deeply. For if the various kingdoms of the peninsula were not as yet fully united in political rule, they were very much united in their religious faith. And that the spread of that faith motivated much of their thinking during the age of discovery that was then breaking upon them, there is ample evidence. For example, among the reasons assigned by Columbus for his epochal voyage of 1492 was the hope that through contact with the native princes and peoples of what he believed would be India there might be observed what he termed "the manner in which may be undertaken their conversion to our Holy Faith. . . ." [2]

Once the preliminary voyage had been completed and Columbus had returned to Spain plans were laid for a second expedition. Among the royal instructions that were issued for this second voyage it was stated that the prime object of the undertaking was to be the conversion of the natives who were to be treated with consideration. And in order to carry out this directive Bernardo Buil, at one time a Benedictine and later a member of the Order of Minims, Ramón Pane, a Jeronymite friar, and three Franciscans were appointed to accompany the expedition of seventeen caravels carrying around 1,500 men when it sailed in September, 1493. The necessary equipment for setting up the first church had been supplied through the gift of Queen Isabella and it was these furnishings that were employed when on the feast of the Epiphany, January 6, 1494, Mass was said for the first time in the

[2] Morison, *Columbus*, I, 204. After quoting the original entry Morison says, "So begins the most detailed, the most interesting and the most entrancing sea journal of any voyage in history" (I, 205).

temporary church erected at Isabela, the tiny settlement on the island of Española [Santo Domingo-Haiti].[3] But the inauguration of the Catholic Church in the western hemisphere encountered difficulties from the outset. Buil proved to be a troublesome and discontented fellow who quarrelled with Columbus and who not long after returned to Spain filled with complaints against the great navigator. It was Pane, a modest and tractable priest, who accomplished the baptism of the first Indian convert in Española in September, 1496, and with this the Church's long and often painful history among the native peoples was begun.

The quickened tempo of discovery and exploration that marked the next half century, and that was to witness a large part of the globe brought within the knowledge of European men, is a familiar tale. Even though Columbus may have retained to the time of his death in relative obscurity in 1506 the conviction that what he had discovered were the outlying parts of Asia, the opinion of many experts was already strong that the world that he had opened was entirely new. Thus restless navigators sailing under other flags soon made the Spaniards realize that they would have to vie with Portuguese, French, and English competitors if they were to hold their primacy of place. But the Spaniards of this generation were equal to the task, for within thirty years of the original discovery they had not only fanned out from their settlements in the West Indies to the coasts of South America, but Balboa had crossed the Isthmus of Panama and became the first white man to gaze upon the Pacific Ocean, Cortés had conquered the Aztec empire of Mexico, and by 1522 one of the vessels of Magellan, who had sailed under the auspices of the Spanish crown and discovered the Philippines where he met his death, had circumnavigated the globe.

Wherever the navigators and explorers had gone the missionaries were either to accompany them or to follow soon thereafter. And that

[3] There has been considerable controversy over the question of whether or not there was a priest with Columbus on his first voyage. According to Father Fidel Fita, S.J., who at the time of writing was one of the leading authorities on the Columbus explorations, a secular priest, Pedro de Arenas, accompanied the navigator in 1492, said the first Mass in America, and remained in the new world after Columbus had returned to Spain. Cf. "La Primeria Misa en América," *Boletin de la Real Academia de la Historia*, XVIII (Junio, 1891), 551–554. Morison, on the other hand, maintains that there was no priest on the first voyage and remarks, "Certain pious souls, worried by the absence of a priest, have tried to invent one" (*op. cit.*, I, 193).

not much time was lost in providing for regular ecclesiastical government is seen by the fact that in 1511 two dioceses were erected in Española along with the See of San Juan in Puerto Rico, and by 1522 the Diocese of Santiago de Cuba, from which there would derive the jurisdiction over the first Spanish settlements in the future United States, had been established.

Even an age as accustomed as our own to scientific marvels can still read with a sense of wonder the extraordinary achievements of these Spanish pioneers — whether lay or cleric — and feel a temptation to follow them through the course of their amazing exploits. But it is a temptation that has to be resisted, for the development of Catholicism in Latin America and in the Far East belongs to other chapters of the Church's absorbing history. We must confine ourselves here to what took place in that portion of North America that was later to be the United States. In tracing that history, insofar as it relates to Spain's American colonies, we shall limit our discussion in the main to what American historians have frequently termed the Spanish borderlands, that is, to Florida, the Southwest (New Mexico, Arizona, and Texas), and California.

In general one can for convenience think of the development of the Spanish mission system in the future United States with the present location of New Orleans as a center with all east of that point expanding up to about the year 1700 and contracting thereafter, and all west of that point expanding after 1700. Florida, of course, belonged to the former area and period, and its permanent colonization by Spain proved to be a prolonged and uncommonly difficult task.

During the more than half a century that elapsed from the time when Juan Ponce de Léon discovered the peninsula in 1513 to 1565 when the first successful settlement was made at St. Augustine five or six attempts were launched to bring Florida within the confines of Spain's American empire but they all ended in failure. In these colonizing efforts, as was true of practically all Spanish expeditions of a like character throughout the new world, provision was made for priests to accompany the colonists with all their expenses and necessary equipment supplied by the crown. For the spiritual needs of the white settlers normally diocesan or secular priests were appointed, while members of one or other of the religious orders were engaged for the purpose of converting the native peoples. Thus priests were among the company of about 200 settlers with whom Ponce de Léon landed on the west coast of Florida in 1521 only to have their hopes dashed by a series of Indian attacks that forced them to abandon the project. Somewhere, therefore, along Florida's west coast in that spring of 1521 Mass may, indeed, have been said for the first time on the soil of the future United States, although we have no certain details, nor do we even know the names of the priests involved.

Five years after this original failure a second attempt to settle was made by Lucas Vásquez de Ayllón who sought to implement his patent of June, 1523, for a colony in the region of Cape Fear. In that patent the King of Spain had declared "our principal interest in the discovery of new lands is that the inhabitants and natives thereof . . . may be brought to understand the truths of our holy Catholic faith . . . and this is the chief motive that you are to bear and hold in this affair. . . ." Since this would require the presence of ministers of religion Ayllón was commanded to take priests with him, and it was specified that their transportation, support, and the supplies needed for divine worship were to be paid "entirely from the rents and profits which in any manner shall belong to us in the said land." [4] If union of Church and State in Spanish America had its real difficulties at times for the propagation of the Catholic faith, as it certainly did, it also had its advantages. Numbered among the more than 500 settlers, therefore, were three Dominican friars of whom one, Antonio de Montesinos, had raised a storm in Española shortly after his arrival in 1510 by being the first to denounce the enslavement of the natives by their Spanish overlords.[5] Presumably Montesinos and his companion priest, Antonio de Cervantes – the third Dominican was a lay brother – would have said Mass during that harsh winter of 1526–1527 and would thus be among the earliest priests to have offered the eucharistic sacrifice in this country. But a combination of difficulties, including the death of Ayllón, internecine quarrels, epidemics, and attacks by the Indians quickly depleted the ranks, and

[4] Quoted in John Gilmary Shea, *History of the Catholic Church in the United States* (New York, 1886), I, 105–106. Hereafter this work will be referred to as: Shea, *History*.

[5] It was in late December, 1510, that the famous sermon of Montesinos was preached in which he charged the Spaniards with living and dying in mortal sin because of their cruelty toward the Indians. "Are they not men?" he asked. "Have they not rational souls?" Cf. Silvio Zavala, *The Political Philosophy of the Conquest of America* (Mexico, D.F., 1953), p. 67.

in the spring of 1527 the colony of San Miguel de Guandape was abandoned by the 150 survivors who returned to Española.

Scarcely a year had passed before Pánfilo de Narváez appeared near Tampa Bay in April, 1528, with an expedition of several hundred colonists among whom were several secular priests and five Franciscans headed by Fray Juan Suárez, who was named a bishop and protector of the Indians by Charles V and commanded to leave for America before he received episcopal consecration. Narváez' heart was set on gold and after a northward march to the neighborhood of the present Tallahassee had failed to uncover more than a squalid Indian village the party set sail in September for Mexico. Ultimately shipwreck, which was followed by disease, starvation, and exposure, left only four survivors of the original company. After enduring six years of slavery at the hands of the Indians, Alvar Núñez, Cabeza de Vaca and his three brave companions managed to escape and to complete an amazing overland journey on foot which brought them to Mexico City by April, 1536. The Narváez expedition left no trace in Florida, although Cabeza de Vaca's intriguing account of his great trek through the American Southwest and northern Mexico with its tales of the fabulous riches of the cities of Cíbolá was later the inspiration for the preliminary explorations of what is today New Mexico with their accompanying attempts to bring the Catholic faith to its inhabitants.

The next Florida undertaking in 1539, that of Hernando de Soto, had many of the same characteristics as that of Narváez such as the desire to repeat the exploits of Cortés and Pizarro by discovering silver and gold, the long and futile marches through parts of Alabama, North Carolina, Mississippi, and Arkansas with their constantly mounting losses of lives and provisions until de Soto's own death in May, 1542, and his burial in the Mississippi River. Here, too, eight secular priests and four friars were in the company, but most of them lost their lives before the remnants of the expedition emerged into the settled parts of Mexico under Luís Moscoso de Alvarado, de Soto's successor, in 1543.

Four major attempts, then, to secure a foothold in Florida had nothing to show for their pains, although the careful preparations, the numbers involved, and the arms supplied for protection might well have warranted them in anticipating success. The fifth enterprise was of an entirely different character. For some years a group of Spanish Dominicans had been having considerable success in pacifying and converting the Indians of Central America without benefit of the military and civil officials. Like their confrère, Montesinos, these friars were highly critical of the Spaniards' abuse of the natives, and following the principles of their most famous member, Bartolomé de las Casas, they had endeavored to keep the Indians apart from the Spaniards as far as possible so as to reduce to a minimum the latter's often degrading practices on the redmen. They were hopeful, therefore, that these same methods might work elsewhere.

Among these Dominicans was Fray Luís Cancer de Barbastro who in 1546 conceived the idea of extending their missionary apostolate in Florida. On a trip to Spain in 1547 he won Charles V to his scheme and returned to the new world armed with a royal decree that instructed the Viceroy of New Spain to supply the missionaries with everything they might need for the undertaking. Sailing from Vera Cruz in the spring of 1549, Cancer and his little company of four friars and a few laymen touched first at Havana where they secured as an interpreter a Florida Indian woman by the name of Magdalena who had been converted to the Catholic faith. Arriving at a point near Tampa Bay, the unarmed vessel coasted for a time in search of a favorable place to land. The first landing resulted in the mysterious disappearance of Fray Diego de Tolosa, a lay brother, and a sailor, all of whom, it was soon learned, had been killed by the Indians. Although warned of the dangerous mood of the local savages and urged to abandon the area, Cancer would not be put off from carrying out the mission to which he felt committed in conscience. On June 26, 1549, therefore, he insisted upon landing alone and was promptly fallen upon and murdered within view of his confrères and the sailors who had remained on board ship. The experiment of a totally religious and unarmed settlement among the natives, such as had yielded favorable results in Central America, was not, therefore, so much as given a chance to show what it might do in Florida. The swift fate that had overtaken Cancer and his associates served to re-enforce the belief that the Church's missions among the Indians could not safely be advanced except in union with the protecting arm of the Spanish military.

Reports of these early expeditions with Florida as a goal must have made dismal reading in Madrid, as would likewise that of the costly colonizing project under Don Tristán de Luna y Arellano which had been urged by the Archbishop of Mexico, the Bishop of Santiago de

Cuba, and others. The party of 1,500 colonists, accompanied by Fray Pedro de Feria, O.P., as superior of a group of Dominicans, set out from Vera Cruz in June, 1559. But the dilatoriness and inefficiency of the commander, the grave internal dissensions, and the waste of lives and resources, to say nothing of the fruitless efforts of the friars to inaugurate a mission among the Indians, once again spelled ruin and after two years the enterprise was abandoned in 1561. In fact, so discouraged had the Spanish government become over the losses in Florida that in September of that year Philip II issued an order barring any further colonizing measures in the peninsula.

And yet if Spain was to hold securely its vast commitment in the new world Florida could not be counted out. Since the treasure fleets from South America and Mexico were accustomed to gather at Havana and then take the gulf stream which passed by the Florida coast, it was vital that Spain should not allow Florida to fall into rival hands that would find there an ideal place from which to attack the fleets. Not only had the treacherous tropical storms – from which there was no relief at hand in a strong outpost on land – made the Florida coasts a graveyard for the treasure ships, but the steady encroachment of Spain's rivals in the area soon forced a reconsideration of the entire matter at Madrid. The losses incurred by the storms at sea were serious enough, but the threat from the French and English offered even a greater peril. The sixteenth century was an intensely religious age, and it has probably not been sufficiently recognized how important a part religion played in the moves and countermoves of the European powers for overseas settlements. At the moment France was torn by civil war over religious differences and the French Protestants (Huguenots) were still strong and filled with ambitious plans to establish colonies in the new world. As for the English, the marauding expeditions of privateers in the first years of Elizabeth's reign yielded sufficient profit and excitement to attract imitators. Thus a decade or more before Richard Hakluyt's *Discourse of Western Planting* (1584) had furnished a spur to English bias against Catholicism second only, perhaps, to John Foxe's *Book of Martyrs* (1563), there was already shaping a series of assaults that would enrich their promoters and at the same time strike a blow against Catholic Spain. To men like John Hawkins, Francis Drake, and their contemporaries the enticement of booty from Spanish treasure ships was very real, but they likewise kept to the forefront of their minds the prospect of extending the Protestant faith among the heathens and of saving the new world from the papists. That was the idea with which many of the advocates of an overseas empire sought to win the English ruling circles, and as one historian has said, "Certainly it was an excellent item of propaganda in a country emotionally aroused against Spain and the Catholics." [6]

But it was the French who offered the most immediate threat to Spanish claims in Florida. If there had been any lingering doubts in Madrid concerning the reality of the danger from this source they were dispelled when the colonizing parties of Jean Ribaut and René de Laudonnière, Huguenot leaders, finally succeeded in 1564 in establishing a settlement at the mouth of the St. John's River. To have French Protestants occupying Fort Caroline at a point that commanded the homeward route of the Spanish treasure ships was an intolerable situation in which Philip II's government realized that it could not acquiesce.

Once having determined upon the expulsion of the French from Florida, plans went forward under the capable direction of Pedro Menéndez de Avilés, whose years of commanding the fleets in the Caribbean waters made him an ideal choice. This time the Spaniards met with success. During the months of preparation for assembling the ships, soldiers, and supplies Menéndez likewise kept in mind the missionary aspects of the undertaking. In the agreement which he entered into with Philip II in March, 1565, he assumed all the costs of the project, including that of transportation and maintenance of priests of his choice and, as the royal document read, "likewise four others of the Society of Jesus, so that there may be religious instruction in the said land, and the Indians can be converted to our Holy Catholic Faith and to our obedience. . . ." [7] Sailing from Cádiz in late July, 1565, Menéndez put in to a harbor on the northern coast of Florida on August 28, the feast of St. Augustine, whose name he gave to what was soon to be the first permanent white settlement within the limits of

[6] Louis B. Wright, *Religion and Empire. The Alliance between Piety and Commerce in English Expansion, 1558–1625* (Chapel Hill, 1943), p. 14. Hereafter this work will be referred to as: Wright, *Religion and Empire.*

[7] "Agreement between Philip II and Pedro Menéndez de Avíles for the Conquest of Florida and the Assignment of Jesuit Missionaries, March 20, 1565," John Tracy Ellis (Ed.), *Documents of American Catholic History* (Milwaukee, 1956), p. 14. Hereafter this work will be cited as: Ellis, *Documents.*

the United States as well as the first parish of the Church in this country. During the next few days the commander searched out the French, and following the code of warfare that then generally obtained, he wreaked a swift vengeance upon the Huguenot colony by putting its inhabitants to the sword. By September 6 he was back in the harbor of St. Augustine where two days later he landed in a ceremony that included a *Te Deum* and the celebration of Mass in the formal taking possession of the land in the name of God and the King of Spain. In token of the action the spot was given the name of Nombre de Dios and there Martín Francisco López de Mendoza Grajales, a secular priest, began to function as the first pastor of the parish.

For the better part of the next three years the Spaniards were preoccupied in establishing military posts both inland and along the coasts as well as engaging in a series of mutual slaughters with the Huguenot remnants of Fort Caroline and those who were sent out to retaliate for the losses the French had suffered. But the missionary cause did not wait upon the outcome of hostilities. As a result of an agreement between Menéndez and St. Francis Borgia, General of the Society of Jesus, in 1566 the first contingent of Jesuits arrived that year for the opening of their first organized missionary effort in the new world which proved to be about as disastrous a failure as the Society was to experience in colonial America. The Jesuit misfortunes began before the year was out with the killing of Father Pedro Martínez on an island near the mouth of the St. John's River. While the arrival of ten more Jesuits in 1568 under the leadership of Juan Baptista Segura enabled them by the end of 1569 to extend their activities to the tribes living within the future States of Georgia and South Carolina, nowhere did they meet with anything but the most severe reverses at the hands of the redmen.

Yet Segura refused to admit defeat and he decided to head personally an even more distant mission in the region of Chesapeake Bay. The party sailed from Santa Elena in August, 1570, with five Jesuits, several lay catechists, and Luís de Velasco, a convert Indian guide who gave reassuring information concerning the natives in the area. In view of the tragic outcome of the venture a letter of Luís de Quiros, S.J., from Virginia in mid-September to a friendly Spanish official in Havana, was especially pathetic. He said, "I am convinced that there will be no lack of opportunity to exercise patience, and to succeed we must suffer much. But it has seemed good to expose ourselves to that risk and this especially so, since in your kindness you might be able to send us a generous quantity of corn to sustain us and to let all this tribe take some for sowing."[8] Lacking sufficient supplies for the winter, surrounded by unfriendly Indians, and unfamiliar with the terrain, the Jesuits' hopes were given the final blow when their guide turned traitor and brought on an Indian attack in February, 1571, that wiped out the entire group. Thus thirty-six years before the founding of Jamestown there ended the initial attempt in what was soon to be known as Virginia to plant a white settlement and to bring the Catholic faith to its native people.

The tragedy at Ajacan in the Chesapeake district only confirmed the General of the Jesuits in the wisdom of an action that he had been contemplating for some time as a result of the losses sustained by his subjects in their Florida assignments. It was futile to waste any more lives of badly needed missionaries in this area, for as he told Menéndez in a letter of March 20, 1571, "They have worked and suffered in Florida with a constancy that has been manifest and yet they have seen little or no fruit of their labors, which is the greatest suffering of all for those who seek only the good of souls for the greater glory of God."[9] The Jesuits were removed from Florida, therefore, and sent to Mexico where their efforts were destined to yield a rich harvest of converts for the Church. The recall of these religious was, of course, a serious setback for Menéndez and the hopes that he held out for his colony. While in Spain in 1573, however, he received a new commission from the king which ordered him to continue the conquest and likewise to engage Franciscans to accompany the settlers who were intended for the venture that was now projected.

In no sense was it an inviting prospect that confronted the sons of St. Francis in Florida. True, the Spaniards had traversed and brought under claim an immense territory that embraced not only Florida proper but large portions of the future States of Georgia, South Carolina, and Alabama with lines extending into Mississippi, North Carolina, and as far as Virginia. But the conquest was more apparent than real.

[8] Luís de Quiros, S.J., to unnamed Spanish official, Ajacan, September 12, 1570, Clifford M. Lewis, S.J., and Albert J. Loomie, S.J., *The Spanish Jesuit Mission in Virginia, 1570–1572* (Chapel Hill, 1953), p. 90.

[9] "St. Francis Borgia withdraws the Jesuits from the Florida Missions, March 20, 1571," in Ellis, *Documents*, p. 16.

Plagued by many handicaps, the colony had not prospered, for in addition to a lack of mineral resources that had quickly enriched other Spanish settlements there were deficiencies in administration. The governors failed to develop a consistent and enlightened policy toward agriculture, the colony's sole hope of economic progress, and the introduction of Negro slaves from the West Indies in 1581 by an English ship did not make up in any basic way for the general economic weakness. In general Florida was treated like a stepchild by Cuba, the center of Spanish power and influence in that part of the Spanish dominions, and was thus denied the assistance that might otherwise have been furnished from that source. To a certain degree this was likewise true in the spiritual realm where frequent shifting of personnel between the Caribbean islands — or Spain — and the mainland was disruptive of the Church's work and often made it difficult to determine how many priests were available at a given time.[10]

Yet these obstacles did not deter the Franciscans who began their Florida venture in 1573, and for nearly two centuries until the English occupation of 1763 it was these friars, and the secular priests in the white settlements, who constituted the spiritual force in the colony. For the first two decades the friars remained few in number as, for example, in 1578 when there were only two members of the order then engaged as chaplains to the military forts at St. Augustine and Santa Elena. Good was accomplished even during this somewhat barren period, however, for both the whites and the growing number of Indian converts. Men like Fray Alonso de Reinoso, the active promoter of missionary recruits, assisted the advance of religion as was also the case with Fathers Balthasar López and Pedro de Corpa, two notable friars, after they came upon the scene in 1587. The same was true of Fray Francisco Marrón who after he arrived in June, 1594, served not only as commissary and superior of the missions but also as pastor of the parish of St. Augustine until relieved of that duty three years later by the secular priest, Don Ricardo Artur.

But it was only with the arrival in September, 1595, of eleven additional Franciscans under Fray Juan de Silva that missionary work could be begun in earnest. Without much delay the new recruits were

[10] The historian of the friars speaks of the "confusing and even contradictory" character of the documentary evidence of these early years. Cf. Maynard Geiger, O.F.M., *The Franciscan Conquest of Florida, 1573–1618* (Washington, 1937), p. 36.

given their assignments and soon they were fanning out in all directions from the central convent at St. Augustine to their distant stations. Among this group was Francisco Pareja, who during his twenty years of fruitful service to the Timucuan tribe mastered their language and wrote a number of catechisms and books of devotion in that language, the first of which was published in Mexico City in 1612. The initial contacts of the new missionaries with the Indians were encouraging, and when Marrón made a visitation of the missions late in 1596 he was able to report the natives' friendly reception of the friars, the latter's eager attempts to learn the Indian languages, a cessation of tribal warfare, and the amicable relations then existing between the Franciscans and the Spanish soldiers who had been sent for their protection.

Nevertheless, there was more than had met the eye of Father Marrón at some of the missions of his tour. Crude and unlettered as they were, the American redmen were often shrewd, canny, and masterful in their deception, and at this point there occurred one of those episodes which are so frequently met in the history of the colonial missions, namely, a sudden and unexpected uprising. To the freedom-loving savage who for generations had roamed the wilderness at will, the efforts of the Spanish friars to settle them permanently and to initiate them into the arts of civilization were exceedingly irksome. Even more unwelcome was the code of Christian morality introduced by the missionaries with its restrictive measures that demanded a sacrifice and self-denial that were entirely alien to the natives' pagan cults. The Guale tribe, for example, had long practiced polygamy, and when the Franciscans rebuked one of their leaders for having more than one wife he stirred up a rebellion in September, 1597, that cost the lives of five friars, the capture and enslavement of Fray Francisco de Ávila, and the destruction of all the Guale missions except San Pedro on Cumberland Island. By 1600, it is true, the revolt had been brought under control by the Spanish military and thereafter the Franciscans renewed their labors; but here as elsewhere in colonial America the factor of sudden rebellion was overlooked only at the white man's peril and on numerous occasions it proved to be a deadly deterrent to the missionary cause.

In spite of this handicap, and of drawbacks such as the recurring jurisdictional disputes between the friars and Governors Gonzalo Méndez de Canzo and Pedro de Ybarra who ruled the colony between 1597 and 1609, the work went on. As early as 1594 there were enough whites of Spanish or mixed blood, in addition to the growing number of Indian converts, to raise the question as to how these Catholics were to receive the Sacrament of Confirmation. For this sacrament a bishop was the proper minister, and after an attempt to have Florida erected into a diocese with its own bishop had failed, those who had the matter at heart looked to Santiago de Cuba whose bishop had jurisdiction over the colony on the mainland. At length the ordinary of that see, Juan de las Cabezas de Altamirano, O.P., undertook the task and arrived in St. Augustine in March, 1606, where on Holy Saturday he ordained more than twenty young men – probably to minor orders – and on Easter Sunday he confirmed 350 persons in the first ceremonies of ordination and confirmation to be performed within the present limits of the United States. During his stay Altamirano also visited the missions and before his departure he had confirmed 2,444 of whom only 370 were whites. In general the prelate had words of praise for the colony's civil and military personnel as well as for the missionaries, even if the hope that he might be able to settle the jurisdictional differences between the friars and the government had been left largely unrealized.

As time passed more Franciscans were assigned to the Florida missions and by August, 1618, there were thirty-eight in the colony. In 1633 they extended their apostolate to the Apalachee tribe, and by the middle of the century they were in charge of approximately forty missions with an estimated 26,000 Indians who had been either wholly or in part converted to the faith. Apart from the Indian mission stations the little capital of St. Augustine, while no more than an ill fortified village of several hundred inhabitants with relatively few comforts, had its parish church, a Franciscan convent, a hospital, a school for boys, and a number of religious fraternities all of which helped to relieve the drabness of the pioneer community. On the whole these years of the mid-century marked the high point of both the Spanish occupation and of the missionary advance with generally peaceful conditions and some measure of material advance, although the colony never acquired the status of the rich and self-sustaining settlements in other parts of Spanish America.

Following this period which has been characterized as the golden age of the Florida missions there was never again the same prosperity. The decline that set in toward the end of the seventeenth century was due to many causes. First, Florida was never self-sustaining but had to be subsidized from the outside, and the amount of the subsidy was determined by the number of employees of the crown on the payroll in Florida. This worked a hardship on the missions since the crown's policy was to hold down the number of missionaries. For example, some time before the visit of Bishop Altamirano the Franciscans had opened a novitiate in St. Augustine. In 1608, however, the crown asked the friars to transfer their novitiate to Cuba in order to lessen the obligation of subsidizing so many clerics. This was done and thus passed the first religious novitiate – and probably the first seminary – on the soil of the future United States.

A second factor was closely related to the first. The missions were organized on a coastal basis, and although they stretched north, south, and west from St. Augustine about a day's journey, the Spaniards were unprepared for the type of attack that was mounted in 1661, for example, by the Westoe Indians who were armed with rifles from the Virginians and who attacked the northern missions. And then with the founding of Carolina in 1670 the English multiplied the attacks with the result that more Spanish soldiers had to be brought into Florida to protect the colony, with the consequence that the far flung missions were greatly contracted and the number of missionaries lessened in favor of a greater number of soldiers.

Added to these obstacles was the inherent difficulty of trying to convert large numbers of unlettered tribesmen to the Catholic faith and the ways of European civilization which, of course, was not a situation peculiar to Florida. Here as elsewhere the contacts of the Spanish civil and military personnel with the Indians also created a serious problem for the missionaries since at times they were guilty of practicing abuses toward the natives that made the latter draw away from all white men. When the friars asserted themselves in an effort to protect their neophytes from forced labor or immoral practices, dissensions arose, and in some cases prolonged disputes over the question of jurisdiction created a further disadvantage for the missionary cause. Moreover, as time passed the idealism of some of the Franciscans cooled, influenced no doubt by what must often have seemed a hopeless task, and there was evidence of neglect of duty on the part of some of these friars.

For situations of this kind a remedy was sometimes found in the superior authority of a bishop. For example, when Gabriel Díaz Vara Calderón, Bishop of Santiago de Cuba, came in August, 1674, for a visitation that lasted for eight months he met with signs of this relaxation. He promptly commanded the friars under severe penalties to give instruction in the catechism on Sundays and holy days and, too, to learn the native languages in order that this might be done more effectively. While Bishop Calderón discovered a number of things that called for correction, that he should have been able to confirm 13,152 persons during his stay and to ordain a half dozen or more youths to minor orders – presumably students of the boys' school that the Franciscans had continued to maintain at St. Augustine – would indicate that there was still a fairly wholesome religious life in the colony.[11]

The bishop had been favorably impressed with the Indian converts, and in his report to Queen Mother Marie Anne of Spain he commented on their faithful attendance at Mass, their devotion to the Blessed Virgin, their presence at the Christmas Mass when they came "with offerings of loaves, eggs and other food," and the extraordinary penances which the redmen performed during Holy Week when for twenty-four hours on Holy Thursday and Good Friday "they attend standing, praying the rosary in complete silence, 24 men and 24 women and the same number of children of both sexes, with hourly changes."[12]

But except at long intervals – and then usually for only a brief time – Florida did not enjoy the advantage of a resident bishop during the colonial period. And when the Bishop of Santiago de Cuba attempted

[11] That there were some native born youths who studied for the priesthood would seem to be clear, although the records do not furnish much authenticated data on them. One was Francisco de Florencia, S.J., who was born in St. Augustine in 1619 and received his early training there at the Franciscans' school for boys. De Florencia later had considerable fame in Mexico as a professor and writer. It has been said of him that he was the first native American to become a Jesuit and that he was also the first priest born in what later became United States territory, "unless perhaps preceded by Franciscans of the same school" that is, at St. Augustine. Michael Kenny, S.J., *The Romance of the Floridas* (Milwaukee, 1934), p. 332.

[12] "Report of Bishop Caldéron of Santiago to Queen Mother Marie Anne on the Florida Missions, August 14, 1674," Ellis, *Documents*, p. 23.

to exercise his authority through a secular priest appointed as a delegate to represent him it aroused the resentment of the friars. Bishop Diego Evelino de Compostela tried this in 1688, but the Franciscans protested, as they had done on previous occasions, and an appeal was made to the crown against what they regarded as an unwarranted interference in their affairs from one who was neither a bishop nor a member of their own order. During the eighteenth century the colony was visited by episcopal superiors from Cuba on four different occasions, and in 1735 Francisco Martínez de Tejada, Auxiliary Bishop of Santiago de Cuba and himself a Franciscan, arrived and remained for ten years, the longest stay made by any of these prelates. The last visit of this kind was something of an accident. In the English siege of Havana in 1762 Bishop Pedro Augustín Morell de Santa Cruz was captured, carried off to Charleston, South Carolina, and after being held a prisoner for several weeks was sent to St. Augustine where between December, 1762, and the late spring of 1763 he confirmed over 600 persons and performed other useful services in this part of his diocese.

Long before Spanish sovereignty over Florida had been ceded to Great Britain by the Treaty of Paris of February, 1763, however, the missions had in good measure been destroyed by the English and their Indian allies. At no time in the history of the colony had there been a sufficient number of Spanish troops to hold effectively the claims made to distant areas west and north of Florida proper. After the advent of the French to Louisiana in 1699 the Spaniards' western frontier around Pensacola was subject periodically to attacks and pressure from their new neighbors. And in the north the Indian tribes that had been brought under Spanish surveillance could easily be induced to change their allegiance at the prospect of material gain or greater freedom. Thus when the English settled permanently in Carolina in 1669 the proximity of a hostile force became a real peril to Florida. Realizing the danger to both the national interests and the missions of Spain, Governor Juan Marques Cabrera endeavored, therefore, in 1684 to move the Catholic Indians southward. But the inept manner in which he tried to carry out his objective not only destroyed any hope of success but was the occasion for some of the tribes in the Guale region going over to the English.

As early as the Peace of the Pyrenees in 1659 it had become evident that Spain had passed its peak as a great power, and these intermittent skirmishes with France and England during the remainder of the century only hastened its decline on both sides of the Atlantic. When the War of the Spanish Succession broke in 1701, therefore, it was the signal for open warfare on Florida by its northern neighbors, attacks that were at first led by Colonel James Moore, Governor of Carolina, who with the aid of Indian allies wiped out the Guale missions. In December, 1702, the campaign was carried to St. Augustine when the colonial capital was plundered and burned, although its fort held out against the invaders. Two years later the fate that had overtaken the Guale missions was visited upon those of the Apalachee tribesmen where the English forces destroyed thirteen Apalachee villages each with its mission. In the spring of that year Moore reported to the lords proprietors of Carolina that he had captured 300 men and 1,000 women and children and had either killed or reduced to slavery 325 men and seized as slaves 4,000 women and children. "All of which I have done," said Moore, "with the loss of 4 whites and 15 Indians, and without one penny charge to the publick."[13]

In terms of England's imperial and Protestant interests it had been a notable victory, and the missions of the Franciscans among these tribes were never again revived. Yet the spirit of the friars had not been broken by their heavy losses, for as seven of their number told Philip V in a joint letter in May, 1707, which described the murder of their confrères, they were ready to suffer further hardships even to exposing themselves to a similar fate "in the joy of obedience in the service of Our God and Lord." They would persevere, they said, "to the last moments of life, as to the present we have done, in obedience to Your Majesty and in the government and instruction of the few Christians that remain, without shrinking from the severity and tyranny of the enemy."[14] Given a spirit such as this it is easier to understand how Florida's missions endured for nearly two centuries against the heaviest odds.

Upon the cession of the colony to England the Florida subjects of Charles III of Spain were offered a refuge by the crown in either Cuba or Mexico. As a result the white inhabitants of St. Augustine and Pen-

[13] Moore to the Lords Proprietors, April 16, 1704, Mark F. Boyd, Hale G. Smith, and John W. Griffin (Eds.), *Here They Once Stood. The Tragic End of the Apalachee Missions* (Gainesville, 1951), p. 94.

[14] Franciscans to Philip V, St. Augustine, May 7, 1707, *ibid.*, p. 89.

sacola emigrated practically *en masse* and with them went their secular priests and the ten Franciscans who were left in the colony by 1763. For the next few years Catholic activity came to a standstill until the arrival in the summer of 1768 of around 1,200 colonists from the island of Minorca, then under English rule, who were mostly of the Catholic faith. The Protestant promoter of the new colonizing project, Dr. Andrew Turnbull, a Scottish physician who had married a Catholic wife, provided for the Minorcans' spiritual needs by engaging Father Pedro Camps, a secular priest, and Bartolomé Casanovas, an Augustinian, who accompanied the group and settled with them at New Smyrna about seventy-five miles down the coast from St. Augustine. New Smyrna failed after a few years and in 1778 Camps led the 600 survivors of the original colonists to St. Augustine. In the main it was these indentured servants from Minorca who managed amid the gravest hardships and reverses to keep the Catholic faith alive until Florida had once more passed to Spain after the peace treaties of 1783.

Catholic life among the Indians, as has been mentioned, had long since been obliterated, but with the Spaniards' return, it was revived in the old towns of St. Augustine and Pensacola. Relatively little has been written about the part played in the history of these communities by the succession of secular priests which began with Martín Francisco de Mendoza Grajales who came with Menéndez in 1565 and continued down to the English occupation of 1763 when Father Juan José Solana brought to a close a nine-year tenure of the pastorate of St. Augustine. While there were intervals when the friars were in charge by reason of the absence of the regular pastors, the parishes for the white settlers were for the most part in the hands of the secular clergy, and the ancient parish registers of these colonial towns bear witness to the dutiful manner in which their ministrations were conducted. The Franciscans have been more fortunate than the secular clergy in their Florida historians and hence their story is well known. Yet what the friars did for the Indian converts, that the diocesan clergy did for the Spanish civil officials, the military personnel, and their families. And during the difficult transitional period from 1763 to 1822 when the number of English-speaking settlers was on the increase it was principally secular priests of Irish birth who gave to Catholicism in Florida whatever vitality it had. For example, in the two decades from 1784 to 1804 twenty of these Irish priests, most of whom had been trained at the Irish College in Salamanca, were sent out by the Spanish government and almost as many more volunteered for these missions.[15]

Twenty years before Florida became a Spanish colony for the second time Louisiana had likewise come under Spanish rule and in 1793 the province was erected into a diocese at the request of King Charles IV. During the nearly forty years of Spain's second period, therefore, it was Louisiana that furnished most of the priests who ministered to Florida's few and widely separated Catholics. Such remained the condition of the Church there until the United States took possession in 1821. By that date there was already near at hand an organized ecclesiastical government in the recently erected Diocese of Charleston. Thus with the departure of the Spaniards for the last time the jurisdiction that for nearly three centuries had been exercised over Florida by the bishops of Cuba was transferred to a prelate in Louisiana who assumed the responsibility – with assistance from the Bishop of Charleston to whom powers of a vicar general were given – until more permanent arrangements could be made for the future of the Church in Florida.

[15] Cf. the chapter, "Immigration and Irish Priests: 1784–1804," in Michael J. Curley, C.SS.R., *Church and State in the Spanish Floridas, 1783–1822* (Washington, 1940), pp. 164–211.

CHAPTER THREE

NEW MEXICO AND ARIZONA

NEW MEXICO

As Florida had been settled either directly from the mother country or from the West Indies, so the occupation of New Mexico was carried out from the Viceroyalty of New Spain with its center in Mexico. In addition to the difference in the base of operations there was a difference in the native populations of the two areas. While the Florida Indians could not in the strict sense be classified as savages or lower nomads since they lived in villages and had recourse to agriculture for part of their food supply, they were a very crude people whose manners and customs afforded little foundation for the arts of civilization. In New Mexico, on the other hand, the tribes were heirs of an ancient way of life that was related to that of the Aztecs and the Indians of Yucatán. They grew maize or Indian corn, engaged in some grazing, raised cotton from which they made articles of clothing, and lived in towns or pueblos which contained along with their dwellings the *estufas* or community buildings for civil and religious ceremonies. Here the Spaniards found at least an elementary social structure on which to build a civilization, and in this respect these tribes of the Southwest offered a brighter prospect for missionary efforts than was probably true of any other part of what would one day be the United States.

Following the conquest of the Aztec empire of Mexico in the 1520's, Cortés and his successors were eager to extend the periphery of Spanish power over the adjacent regions. And of no area in the new world, perhaps, were there more intriguing stories than those told of the lands that lay to the north of Mexico. In this instance legends, such as that of the bishop from Lisbon who departed from the Iberian peninsula after the Moslem invasion and founded seven cities (Antilia) on islands in the Atlantic, along with the fanciful tales of travellers – with their implied riches at the end of the trail – formed the dominant motivation for the early Spanish advance. We have already mentioned how Cabeza de Vaca, reaching Mexico in 1536 after his journey through the American Southwest, had excited Spanish imaginations with stories of what he had heard concerning large cities to the north of his route. And one of the most attentive of his audience was Antonio de Mendoza, the able viceroy, who determined to know more about these cities of Cíbolá as they were called. Mendoza had arrived in April, 1535, as the first viceroy in a land where his lawyer's training was at a disadvantage in comparison with the heroic feats of men like Cortés and Guzmán. It was a matter of paramount importance for Mendoza, therefore, to anticipate these military leaders who were looking for fresh exploits, in the discovery of new lands. When his appeal to Cabeza de Vaca and others to lead an exploratory expedition to the north was unsuccessful he purchased Cabeza de Vaca's Negro slave, Estévan, who had accompanied his master across the Southwest, and engaged an experienced Franciscan, Marcos de Niza, who had already seen service in Peru and Guatemala. In this way the initiative remained in the viceroy's hands. In March, 1539, Fray Marcos left Culíacán, northern outpost of Sinaloa, with Cabeza de Vaca's Negro, another friar, and a few Indians. After several months of difficult and dangerous travel during which the Negro was killed by the natives, the friar returned to Mexico with glowing accounts of the cities and their prosperous state.

Fray Marcos' report of what he had seen in Cíbolá has been the subject of serious controversy among historians. While one need not subscribe to the harshness of some of the judgments concerning the friar's veracity, there was no doubt that Marcos de Niza had exaggerated the extent and wealth of the Zuñi pueblos in western New Mexico which he had observed from a neighboring hill. In any case, he was the first white man to make known the relatively advanced state of these Indians, and it was on the basis of his report that Mendoza decided to outfit an expedition that would explore the region in more detail and establish Spain's dominion over it. To lead the expedition Francisco

Vásquez de Coronado was chosen as commander of the large company which included Fray Marcos and four or five other Franciscans.

Coronado set out from Compostela in February, 1540, with about 200 horsemen, seventy foot soldiers, and almost 1,000 Indian allies and retainers upon an enterprise that would consume two and a half years and that would ultimately take rank as one of the greatest explorations of the century. This is not the place to detail the commander's disappointment over the failure of the Zuñi pueblos or the distant country to the northeast, called Gran Quivira, to yield the riches that he had anticipated. To Coronado the whole undertaking offered slight consolation since he could not foresee the lasting importance that would attach to his personal explorations through the Texas Panhandle and into Kansas as also to those of his lieutenants who discovered the Colorado River, the Rio Grande, the Grand Canyon, and hitherto unknown lands as far west as Lower California. The exploration had, indeed, more than justified itself even if it had not brought the gold that the too fervent imaginations of the Spaniards had located in Cíbolá and the Gran Quivira.

But it is with the fate of the missionaries who accompanied Coronado that our principal interest lies. When the commander gave orders for the return to New Spain in April, 1542, three of the friars decided to remain behind in the hope of converting the natives to the Catholic faith. Their initial contacts with the Quivira Indians had led them to the belief that these tribes might offer a fruitful return for their labors. It was a highly courageous choice for the Franciscans to make since they thus exposed themselves to the whims of the redmen hundreds of miles away from any source of protection. Sensing the risk they were taking, Coronado sought to lessen it as much as possible when, according to one of his company, he "ordered the soldiers to let any of the natives who were held as servants go free to their villages" lest if they should be carried away it might afford an excuse for an attack on the friars.[1] But the precaution was without effect, for Juan de Padilla was murdered somewhere in eastern Kansas soon after his return to Quivira, and in his death the Catholic Church in this country received its protomartyr and the Franciscan Order the first of forty-two

[1] "The Narrative of the Expedition of Coronado by Castañeda," Ellis, *Documents*, p. 11.

friars who gave their lives during the succeeding two centuries in the Province of New Mexico. Nor were Fray Juan de la Cruz and the other brother ever heard from again. During the time that the temporary chapel at Tiguex in the neighborhood of modern Bernalillo had been in use the Franciscans had ministered effectively to the soldiers, but no permanent foundation for the Church had resulted from the great expedition. Nonetheless, all was not loss since the area was now known for something approximating its true worth and at least an opening had been made for the conquest that would come a half century later when the friars would return to New Mexico to plant the faith for which their confrères had given their lives.

For the next forty years, however, nothing was done to bring the lands traversed by Coronado under subjection. But in the meantime the Spaniards were expanding northward from Mexico through the Province of Nueva Vizcaya as well as increasing their activity along the Pacific Coast. In the course of these developments mineral deposits were discovered in some sections of the territory with the result that the Spaniards' desire to conquer more Indian tribes was quickened in the hope of enlisting them as a labor force to work the mines.

It is here that one encounters one of the most unhappy aspects of Spanish rule in the new world. From their advent to America there had never been a sufficient number of European colonists to exploit fully the natural resources. Consequently both the Indians, and the Negroes once the trade in blacks had been recognized in the West Indies in the early sixteenth century, were reduced to a state of slavery. It was the Spaniards' cruel exploitation of the native peoples that, as we have seen, had aroused the protests of the Dominican friars and other churchmen at an early date, and ultimately word of the situation reached the Holy See. As a consequence in June, 1537, Pope Paul III issued the bull *Sublimis Deus* in which he championed the human nature of the American redmen and maintained that they were capable of conversion to Christianity. In an effort to save them the pontiff declared that regardless of what had already been said or done to the contrary

> the said Indians and all other people who may later be discovered by Christians, are by no means to be deprived of their liberty or the possession of their property, even though they be outside the faith of Jesus Christ; and that they may and should, freely and legitimately, enjoy their liberty and posses-

sion of property; nor should they be in any way enslaved; should the contrary happen, it shall be null and of no effect.[2]

Unfortunately, enough pressure was brought by Charles V against the provisions of *Sublimis Deus* to prevent their being carried out in his overseas dominions so that while the pope did not retract what he had said regarding the Indians' capacity for conversion, he felt compelled to nullify the ecclesiastical censures and penalties imposed by the missionaries for the Spaniards' ill treatment of the natives. Yet it would be unfair to infer that the crown did nothing to improve the Indians' lot. In 1542 there was passed the so-called 'new laws' which sought through a detailed set of regulations to prepare the redmen to take their place ultimately as integral and useful members of colonial society. Here, too, the ideal was never attained, but such regulations as those forbidding exploitation of the Indians, the cancellation of the *encomienda* system which had enabled the Spaniards to take advantage of the natives' labor, and the charging of the crown officials with the Indians' welfare brought a mitigation of the abuses. It was a welcome change in policy, to be sure, but it was felt only after vast and irreparable damage had been done to many natives and to the white man's reputation among them. While it is true that the Spaniards' methods of dealing with the tribesmen in later years fell short of outright enslavement, through the entire colonial period there were frequent occasions when their arbitrary treatment constituted a grave deterrent to the advance of the Catholic faith among the Indian population.

Not until 1581 was another attempt made to conquer New Mexico, and on this occasion it was an old Franciscan lay brother, Agustín Rodríquez, resident near Santa Bárbara, Mexico's northernmost outpost, who supplied the impetus for the renewal of Spanish effort. Rodríquez was encouraged to believe that the northern tribes were in a mood for evangelization and with that in mind he travelled to Mexico City to plead their cause with his brethren. The devout lay brother won a favorable hearing and two young priests of his order, Francisco López and Juan de Santa Maria, were appointed to return with him.

[2] "The Bull *Sublimis Deus* of Pope Paul III, June 2, 1537," *ibid.*, p. 9. One writer has maintained that since the reversal of papal policy was not widely known, *Sublimis Deus* "lived on as a force to be reckoned with in the endless disputes over the true nature of the American Indians. . . ." Lewis Hanke, "Pope Paul III and the American Indians," *Harvard Theological Review*, XXX (April, 1937), 97.

It was these particular friars, incidentally, who gave to the region its permanent name of New Mexico. After some initial success had indicated the need for more missionaries, Fray Juan set out for the south to secure further recruits but was killed on the way by a band of Tigua Indians. Meanwhile hostile natives invaded the village where López and the lay brother were living and when the former rebuked them he, too, was killed and Brother Agustín was soon thereafter the victim of a similar fate. The prolonged silence of their distant confrères alarmed the Franciscans in Mexico and Bernardino Beltrán, O.F.M., championing a search party, was joined by Don Antonio de Espejo, a rich and pious layman, who gathered a small company and started north from the valley of San Bartolomé in November, 1582. Although they failed to find the missing friars, Espejo's men visited several of the neighboring tribes and were sufficiently attracted by the prospects of the region to request permission to occupy New Mexico.

But Espejo's influence at the viceregal court was not equal to winning the important assignment and he was recalled, with the result that a number of years passed before the viceroy gave official sanction in August, 1595, to Don Juan de Oñate to undertake the conquest. After further delays and also false starts Oñate's expedition, which numbered around 400, including 130 soldiers, some with their families, and nine Franciscans under the leadership of Fray Alonso Martínez, finally got underway and by April, 1598, they had reached the Rio del Norte. Here on the feast of the Ascension a solemn Mass was sung and a sermon preached after which there was held the formal ceremony of Spain's taking possession of New Mexico. During the summer Real de San Juan, the first white settlement in the colony, was laid out and by September 8 the church was finished and dedicated. Thus thirty-three years after the founding of St. Augustine in Florida and fifty-six years after Padilla's murder on the northern plains, the pioneer colony of the American Southwest got its first Spanish town.

During the ensuing months Fray Alonso spread his priests out through the surrounding pueblos with a view of contacting the natives and inaugurating among them instruction in the Christian faith. Meanwhile the Spaniards were busily engaged in investigating the possibilities for mining and agriculture in the area, as well as in establishing on the adjacent lands the more than 7,000 head of cattle and sheep that they had driven up from Mexico. In the spring of 1599 the governor decided to send a military officer to report to Mexico City and to seek further recruits and supplies, and Father Martínez and another friar went with him with the same intention in mind. The appeal for more missionaries brought eight new friars in 1600 who were escorted on their journey by 200 troops intended as a reinforcement for Oñate's military contingent.

Like most pioneering enterprises the first settlements in New Mexico encountered their share of setbacks, and on one occasion the absence of Oñate on an exploring expedition and the incursion of unfriendly Indians prompted some of the colonists, joined by a few of the missionaries, to lose courage and start back to Mexico. If some of the Franciscans had grown discouraged during their first years in New Mexico they had ample reason. Added to the governor's lack of interest in the future of the colony was the absence of natural resources to make it self-sustaining, and a dry season now and then contributed to the dismal picture by causing a scarcity of food. In fact, talk of abandoning the project had become serious. In order to head off that possibility Fray Lázaro Ximénez and another friar were delegated in 1608 by the more determined colonists and missionaries to go to Mexico to plead the colony's case with the viceroy. Ximénez' principal argument was that the King of Spain could not in conscience abandon several thousand baptized Indians, and it was sufficiently cogent to carry the day and win a decision to continue to finance the New Mexico settlements at royal expense as an investment in the advancement of the Catholic faith. This action on the part of the viceregal government was proof that Spain's moves in the new world were not always tinged by greed for gold, and as one historian of New Mexico has said, it was a case that offered "an excellent example of the effectiveness of the religious motive in Spanish colonial enterprise." [3]

In the end the missionaries had their reward, for by 1608 the tide of sentiment had turned among the natives and around 8,000 baptisms were counted for the New Mexico tribes. The changed situation naturally warranted further hands for the work, and when Alonso Peinado arrived as superior with eight more friars in the winter of 1609–1610 they were among the first to occupy the Franciscans' new missionary headquarters at Santo Domingo some miles to the southwest of the new

[3] France V. Scholes, "The Supply Service of the New Mexican Missions in the Seventeenth Century," *New Mexico Historical Review*, V (January, 1930), 114.

colonial capital of Santa Fe, a town that had been founded in the spring of 1610, three years after the English had established Jamestown in Virginia.

For the course of the next quarter century the missions of New Mexico showed a remarkable advance, and that in spite of frequent clashes between the ecclesiastical authorities on the one hand and the civil and military rulers on the other. In 1616 the Franciscan Order raised its New Mexican houses to the status of a custody at a time when twenty-five friars were caring for around 10,000 Christian Indians in eleven missions. In January, 1626, Fray Alonso de Benavides arrived in Santa Fe to assume the office of custos, and with his advent the conflicts between Church and State were for a time mitigated and the missions now entered upon their golden age in the province.[4] At the expiration of Benavides' term in 1629 he was succeeded by Fray Estévan de Pedea who returned for a second period as custos with twenty-nine additional Franciscans. During the next decade these men continued the earlier efforts of their confrères to solidify the conversion of tribes such as the Pecos, Taos, and Jémez as well as to try to win the more difficult Moquis and Zuñi nations to the Christian faith.

But about 1632 missionary achievement began to taper off and there set in a slow decline that was to be climaxed a half century later by a violent rebellion of the Indian population. The change was due to many causes and came about only very gradually. By the very nature of the missonary process the Indians' traditional way of life had to be thoroughly uprooted if they were to be made lasting Christians. It was a fundamental point, for the obligations laid upon the natives by the rules of a new and strange religion not only imposed severe restraints upon their natural appetites, but they aroused the smouldering hatred of the medicine men whose strong pagan influence over the Indians would be destroyed if Christianity were to prevail. Moreover, the Indians were expected to labor for the white man—be he governor or

[4] It is to this friar that historians of the Southwest owe two of the best contemporary descriptions of New Mexico in the form of reports which he prepared with a view to enlisting the interest and help of Philip IV of Spain and Pope Urban VIII. Cf. *Benavides' Memorial of 1630* translated by Peter P. Forrestal, C.S.C., with an introduction and notes by Cyprian J. Lynch, O.F.M. (Washington, 1954), and Frederick W. Hodge, George P. Hammond, and Agapito Rey, *Fray Alonso de Benavides' Revised Memorial of 1634* (Albuquerque, 1945); the second is a more detailed version of the report of 1630.

friar — and that, too, went very much against their natural bent. And, of course, in New Mexico as elsewhere in the Spanish Empire the missionaries encountered the customary difficulties over language, the natives' reluctance to stabilize their lives along Christian lines, and the casting aside of traditions — both religious and social — that had been with them for generations.

A further factor in holding back the missionary advance were the intermittent feuds between the Spanish representatives of Church and State. That these quarrels were a real stumbling block to the ultimate success of the Church's work in the province was true, although their detrimental results should not be exaggerated since the over-all number of converts made among the Indians during these years would belie an altogether devastating effect on the missions. But since the history of these conflicts is better known, perhaps, in New Mexico than in other Spanish areas of the future United States, it may be of profit to dwell on them a bit to get a better understanding of these clashes of the ecclesiastical and civil-military authorities. Both sides were at times to blame. For example, in the days of Governor Pedro de Peralta (1610–1614), who was himself not without fault, the conduct of Isidro Ordóñez as Franciscan superior was so arbitrary that serious complaints were lodged against his administration by even his own friars. Later the coming of Juan de Eulate as governor from 1618 to 1625 introduced a character who has been described as "a petulant, tactless, irreverent soldier whose actions were inspired by open contempt for the Church and its ministers and an exaggerated conception of his own authority as the representative of the Crown."[5] Again in the 1660's the regime of Governor Diego de Peñalosa, a notorious adventurer whose abuse of power involved a betrayal of his country, resulted in a condition bordering on civil war when he had Alonso de Posadas, the Franciscan custos, arrested and imprisoned. Peñalosa was finally summoned to Mexico City to stand trial before the Holy Office of the Inquisition where in 1665 he was removed from office, condemned, and ordered to make reparation for the damage he had done in New Mexico.

The root of most of the trouble in New Mexico and elsewhere lay in the claims of both parties to jurisdiction over the Indians. Since New Mexico's unprofitable economic character had dictated that it should

[5] France V. Scholes, *Church and State in New Mexico, 1610–1650* (Albuquerque, 1937), p. 70.

be chiefly a missionary project of the crown rather than the customary mixed enterprise of lay and clerical effort, it was natural that the friars should maintain that the natives whom they had succeeded in converting to Catholicism should remain exclusively in their charge. But ambitious lay governors and rough military commanders were not disposed to sacrifice the chance of turning to personal profit their time in New Mexico, aware as they were, that their counterparts elsewhere in the Spanish dominions were enriching themselves at the cost of Indian labor. There were repeated violations, therefore, of the laws forbidding the governors to engage in trade, grave exploitation of the Indians, and even organized slave raids against the nomadic redmen of the plains. And when the missionaries interposed with objections to this type of conduct the seeds of a fresh conflict were sown. This bickering, needless to say, had a deleterious effect upon the natives, and it is little wonder that it should at times have contributed to their state of bewilderment and demoralization.

If more summary action was not taken by the crown to end these controversies it was probably due to the fact that the royal officials were anxious that neither the ecclesiastical nor the secular authorities in the distant provinces should grow too powerful, and thus appeals to the crown should be fostered so as to keep both groups aware of the source of ultimate authority and final decision in these matters. But to the crown's credit it must be said that after 1670 a higher type of official was named to the governorship and relations between that office and the friars greatly improved. As a consequence there was more efficiency in hunting out elements of discord for both groups, for example the medicine men. The latter were apprehended and brought to book, and it was one of these who had been hauled up but later released whose desire for revenge started the disastrous rebellion of 1680.

The civilization which the Franciscans introduced into New Mexico was, to be sure, far superior to that which the natives had known before their coming. Each pueblo had its church which was durably constructed and usually elaborately decorated in a way to catch the Indians' fancy for bright colors. Each little community also had a convent for the friars and a school in which they taught not only Christian doctrine but the elements of reading, writing, music, and certain rudimentary social obligations which the Indians owed to their fellows. The Indians had mastered the art of weaving before the Spaniards' arrival, but workshops were set up by the friars wherein they instructed their neophytes in other crafts and trades. More important, perhaps, than these changes was the Spaniards' introduction of horses and herds of cattle and sheep which in many ways virtually revolutionized the lives of the Indians since the domestic animals not only gave the natives a highly useful element for their daily living but often served as an object of excitement and entertainment as well. There were, too, the improved methods of agriculture such as the *acéquias* or irrigating trenches that helped to moisten the soil so that it would yield a more bountiful return of grain. All of these improvements, of course, demanded a greater amount of work than that to which the Indians had been accustomed, and it was especially the men who resented the increased labor since it had been their practice to leave work assignments to the women and children while they spent their time seeking fish and game and making war. Amid these changes, moreover, the friars had adopted a daily program of spiritual exercises which the Indians were expected to follow, a regime which Fray Alonso de Benavides described in part for Pope Urban VIII in 1634 when he wrote:

> Promptly at dawn, one of the Indian singers, whose turn it was that week, goes to ring the bell for Prime, at the sound of which those who go to school assemble and sweep the rooms thoroughly. The singers chant Prime in the choir. The friar must be present at all of this and takes notes of those who have failed to perform this duty, in order to reprimand them later. When everything is neat and clean, they again ring the bell and each one goes to learn his particular specialty; the friar oversees it all. . . . After they have been occupied in this manner for an hour and a half, the bell is rung for mass. All go into the church, and the friar says mass and administers the sacraments. . . . Mass over . . . all kneel down by the church door and sing the *Salve* in their own tongue. . . .[6]

Given the previous carefree existence of the Indians, it is not difficult to understand how this new order of work and prayer should have provoked them to several futile attempts at armed rebellion in the very years when the missions were seemingly making progress.

Although these revolts between 1645 and 1675 were suppressed, the basic causes of discontent continued to simmer beneath the surface

[6] "Alonso de Benavides' Description of the New Mexico Missions, February 12, 1634," Ellis, *Documents*, p. 17.

of pueblo life. And the periodic forays of the savage Apache who would fall quickly upon the villages of the Christian Indians, murder the inhabitants, destroy the crops, and then flee to the neighboring mountains and canyons only served to emphasize the more in the minds of the mission Indians the freedom that they had forfeited. But more important than any other cause was the persistence of their weird pagan rites in the *estufas* or community halls. Upon discovery they were energetically hunted out and the *estufas* closed by the missionaries, only to have them reopen secretly when the friars' vigilance had relaxed. Here in subterranean fashion the Indians' smoldering hatred of the white masters was whipped up by the medicine men whose hold upon many of the tribesmen had still endured after they had submitted to Christian baptism.

By the summer of 1680 the entire province had become a hidden network of conspiracy, even to the extent that plots were hatched with the dreaded Apache in order to rid themselves of the Spaniards. Friendly Indians warned the friars of the danger and they, in turn, alerted Governor Antonio de Otermín. The latter's initial reluctance to credit these stories caused delay and by the time that he had called for reinforcements it was too late for them to reach their goal, for at a signal from a Tejua medicine man by the name of El Pope, the Indians struck on August 9. At the time there were approximately 2,800 Spaniards in New Mexico with thirty-two Franciscans spread through the pueblos where they were ministering to around 35,000 Christian natives. The whites and those Indians who remained loyal were hopelessly outnumbered and within a few days 400 Spaniards, including twenty-one Franciscans, were murdered, many of the women carried off for a worse fate, the missions destroyed, and the entire region laid in ruins. With Otermín directing a retreat of the survivors southward toward El Paso, New Mexico's Christian vestiges that had taken three-quarters of a century to imprint were no more. Added to the loss of life and property were the cruel tortures to which the captives were subjected, the desecration of the churches and their sacred vessels, El Pope's order that the names of Jesus, Mary, and the saints were never to be heard, the banning of rosaries and crosses as well as of the Spanish tongue, the freedom given to the men to put away their legitimate wives, and even so minute a detail that none but native crops were to be planted. The annihilation of everything for which the missions had stood was complete.

For the next twelve years New Mexico presented a desolate picture with the Apache striking again when they knew the former mission Indians were at their weakest and with renewed suffering and misfortune visited upon those friars who had the courage to attempt a return. The first efforts of the Spanish military also failed, and it was only in February, 1691, when Don Diego de Vargas took command at El Paso that any real hope dawned for the recovery of the lost province. Vargas directed the campaigns with real energy and by the end of 1694 his success made him hopeful that the enemy had been vanquished. But the friars, more experienced in dealing with the Indians, were less sanguine and their doubts were more than confirmed when two years later a fresh uprising caused the murder of five more of their number. By June, 1697, however, the reconquest had at last been accomplished and resistance reduced to minor skirmishes. Yet in spite of the reinstatement of Spanish power, the missions were never again what they had been before 1680, and the permanent defection of the Moqui and Zuñi destroyed the prospect that had once been held out for their conversion to Catholicism. This fact left the sons of St. Francis to face into the new century with these dangerous neighbors as a grim reminder that the earlier and happier chapter of their history in New Mexico had definitely closed.

As Spanish control was once more established the missionaries slowly made their way back and by 1706 twenty-one friars were serving the nearly 9,000 Christian Indians who had been gathered about the eleven missions and the seven *visitas* or churches without resident priest. Additional recruits continued to arrive from the missionary colleges in Mexico and by 1750 the peak strength of the eighteenth century was attained with twenty-two missions having resident friars in charge of around 17,500 Indians. In general life on this distant frontier resumed many of the features that it had known in former times, and though there was still friction between Church and State, the perils from native conspiracies and outside attack tended to draw the representatives of the two authorities closer together with the result that in comparison to the previous period the new century was relatively free of these feuds.

The history of the Spanish colonies can never be divorced from that of the mother country since the course of events in the latter often accounted in good measure for developments in America. For example, the early eighteenth century was a period of serious disruption and uncertainty in Spain with Louis XIV of France putting forth the claim of his grandson to the Spanish throne after the death of Charles II in November, 1700. This threat of further French aggrandizement threw western Europe into a state of crisis which led to the outbreak of the War of the Spanish Succession in the summer of 1701, a conflict that lasted until the Peace of Utrecht in April, 1713. Not only was Spain's internal economy weakened and its manpower drained by the war, but the center of government itself was torn by rival factions supporting the Bourbon prince, Philip V, and the Hapsburg heir, the Archduke Charles.

Amid this kind of turmoil it was exceedingly difficult for officials in the new world to know who were the responsible parties at Madrid to whom they should appeal and from whom they should take directions. And the prolonged fighting in Europe made it more and more difficult to supply the recruits that were needed for the military forces in America, a factor that was keenly felt in Florida, for example, when the English stepped up their attacks from Carolina, and in New Mexico, too, where a full military quota was a matter of paramount importance to protect the advancing frontier. If, therefore, there was relatively little solid progress to show in New Mexico and elsewhere in these years, the situation was as much due to a harassed and unstable home government as it was to local causes such as the stubborn and rebellious Indians. Not until about 1720 were conditions in Madrid stabilized so that once more order began to emerge and the improved situation was reflected in the colonies.

Early in the eighteenth century a new element entered the ecclesiastical life of the province with the visitation of the missions by bishops from Mexico. From the outset New Mexico, unlike Florida, had known no distinction between parochial and missionary clergy. The Franciscan superior possessed faculties for conferring the Sacrament of Confirmation, and since Pius V's bull *Exponi nobis* had in 1567 given missionaries the right to serve both Indians and whites in those areas not subject to a parish priest, the friars had acted as pastors of the parishes in Santa Fe, Albuquerque, and the other Spanish towns.

Such being the case, the Franciscans had felt free to proceed with their ministrations with little reference to the Bishop of Guadalajara whose see, erected in 1548, embraced New Mexico.

When the province passed to the new See of Durango in 1620 the situation remained substantially the same, except for the resistance offered by the Franciscans when the ordinaries of Durango attempted *in absentia* to extend their authority over the missions. In the 1630's the friars themselves had taken the initiative in seeking to have New Mexico given its own bishopric, but this proposal of Fray Alonso de Benavides, later repeated on several occasions, came to nothing. Differences of this kind adumbrated the trouble that was to follow, although during the century that elapsed between the establishment of the Diocese of Durango and the first visit in person of one of its bishops, these early controversies were fought out largely on paper. But in 1725 the Bishop of Durango, Benito Crespo, determined upon a personal visit and with that the stage was set for a series of prolonged and often bitter jurisdictional quarrels between the contending ecclesiastical parties.

The first visit of Bishop Crespo, which was confined to the El Paso region, passed off peacefully enough with the prelate making a gesture toward the friars by appointing their custos and vice-custos as his vicars and ecclesiastical judges for the province. But the Franciscans were not to be deflected from the main point at issue, and in the meantime they appealed the jurisdictional question to their higher superiors in Mexico and were sustained in their views so that when Crespo arrived for his second visitation in July, 1730, the missionaries, led by Fray Andrés Varo, the custos, were prepared to offer serious resistance. In spite of their remonstrances, however, Crespo proceeded on his way and after a confirmation tour during which he observed conditions at first hand he wrote a damaging report to the viceroy. He commented on the friars' prolonged absence from certain missions, on their failure to show real energy in trying to convert the Moqui and other pagan tribes, and on their neglect in collecting the tithes. But the bishop's principal criticism was reserved for the Franciscans' failure to learn the native languages which, in his judgment, was the root cause of the spiritual stagnation that he had witnessed in the province. After referring to several of the friars by name, Crespo told the viceroy that as for the rest, there were many who had been in residence eighteen or twenty years of whom, he said, "not one has dedicated himself, and they are as alien as if they had had no dealings with the said Indians." [7]

These were grave charges, surely, and the missionaries were at pains to repel them in the reports that they forwarded to Mexico City and Madrid. During the course of the lengthy litigation that ensued numerous and often contradictory documents poured in from both sides, and it has been difficult for historians of the Church in the Southwest to sift the charges and counter charges in such a way as to arrive at a satisfactory judgment on all particulars. Yet about one charge there was no doubt, namely, that the friars had failed to learn the native languages. On that point both friend and foe were agreed, for even the more objective Franciscans admitted the defect and lamented the handicap that it had caused to their work. It had not always been thus in New Mexico, for in the early seventeenth century one of their number, Jerónimo de Zárate Salmerón, had distinguished himself by his mastery of the Jémez tongue and had written several very useful books in that language. But that day had long since passed. Beyond the fact of the variety and complexity of the tribal languages of the Southwest, and that the crown preferred to have the natives learn Spanish rather than the missionaries learn the Indian tongues, it is not easy to account for the failure of the New Mexico friars to stress this basic technique which their brothers elsewhere had employed to such good effect. The problem of language was a troublesome one in all the Spanish colonies. For example, in Baja California in the mid-eighteenth century it was present, and the guardian of the College of San Fernando in a circular letter of June 8, 1756, wishing to clear up a number of doubts on various points, told his men that he had consulted the Archbishop of Mexico in whose jurisdiction the missions were about their doubts on the score of language, and "his answer was that the missionaries could employ the best method suited for the advancement of the Indians." In other words, they might use either Spanish or whatever Indian language was pertinent for the prayers and the *doctrina*.[8]

[7] Crespo to Viceroy Juan Vásquez de Acuña, El Paso, September 25, 1730, Eleanor B. Adams (Ed.), *Bishop Tamarón's Visitation of New Mexico, 1760* (Albuquerque, 1954), Appendix I, p. 103. Crespo's successor in Durango, Martín de Elizacoecha, visited New Mexico in 1737 but little is known about his findings.

[8] Maynard J. Geiger, O.F.M., *The Life and Times of Fray Junípero Serra, O.F.M. or The Man Who Never Turned Back, 1713–1784* (Washington, 1959), I, 134. Hereafter this work will be referred to as: Geiger, *Serra.*

On the broader front of official reaction to the ecclesiastical rivalry over jurisdiction, while the judgments of the crown's representatives were never so decisive as to put an end once and for all to the disputes, the general tenor of the government's policy, such as the decree of the Council of the Indies of December, 1738, was to support the bishops' right of visitation but to deny their right to appoint vicars and ecclesiastical judges for New Mexico. Yet the crown's decision, too, often went unheeded as, for example, in the case of Don Santiago Roibal, a secular priest, who for forty-four years was upheld as vicar and ecclesiastical judge at Santa Fe by several of the ordinaries of Durango.

Nor was Roibal's lengthy tenure of these offices disturbed when Pedro Tamarón y Romeral, Bishop of Durango, arrived in April, 1760, to make the final eighteenth-century visitation of the province. Bishop Tamarón's tour lasted several months during which there were reenacted many of the episodes that had occurred during the visits of his predecessors. The detailed report which the bishop later drew up showed that he had inquired closely into conditions both in the Spanish towns and at the Indian missions, and as in the case of Bishop Crespo thirty years before, his impressions were not flattering to the friars. Tamarón was particularly emphatic about the unhappy effects that followed from the superficial religious instruction of many of the natives which, he said, amounted to scarcely more than their outward conformity to certain religious exercises without any true comprehension of what they were doing. The bishop's second most important complaint had to do with New Mexico's grave weakness arising from the officials' failure to work out a systematic defense against the repeated raids of the pagan Indians. Once again the government was told of the evils stemming from the friars' ignorance of the native languages, a condition which Tamarón illustrated from his observations concerning the Pecos pueblo about which he wrote:

> Here the failure of the Indians to confess except at the point of death is more noticeable, because they do not know the Spanish language and the missionaries do not know those of the Indians. They have one or two interpreters in each pueblo, with whose aid the missionaries manage to confess them when they are in danger of dying. And although they recite some of the Christian doctrine in Spanish, since they do not understand the language, they might as well not know it.

This point saddened and upset me more in that kingdom than in any other, and I felt scruples about confirming adults. I remonstrated vehemently with the Father Custos and the missionaries, who tried to excuse themselves by claiming that they could not learn those languages. In my writs of visitation I ordered them to learn them, and I repeatedly urged them to apply themselves to this and to formulate catechisms and guides to confession, of which I would pay the printing costs.[9]

Although intermittent attempts were made during the last years of the century to arrest the decline of New Mexico's religious life, the prosperity that it had once known was never regained. For example, in 1775 the Franciscan superiors in Mexico appointed Fray Francisco Atanasio Domínguez to make a tour of inspection of the province, but his efforts at reform were not well received and a few of his disgruntled confrères tried to discredit his mission by forwarding adverse reports about him to headquarters.[10] Domínguez arrived in Santa Fe in March, 1776, where he found 2,014 Spaniards in the capital and its neighboring ranches among whom, as he noted, there were still functioning the Third Order of St. Francis, the Confraternity of the Blessed Sacrament, and the devotion to the Poor Souls. In the interior missions the Franciscan visitor counted at that time 18,344 natives under the care of twenty friars,[11] but the proportion of Indians to whites steadily decreased thereafter so that by the end of the century there were less than half that number in the mission pueblos.

Whatever hope there may have been for a religious revival from investigations such as that of Domínguez was largely dissipated in succeeding years by the political upheavals arising out of Mexico's revolt from Spain. With the winning of Mexican independence in 1821 the frontier province followed suit and in January, 1822, Santa Fe celebrated the new republican regime with an enthusiastic festival. In the same year Spanish colonial policy was reversed and New Mexico was thrown open to American trade. Before long, therefore, the population of Spanish, Indian, and mixed blood was augmented by the influx of immigrants from the United States among whom were nu-

[9] Adams, *op. cit.*, p. 48.

[10] Eleanor B. Adams and Angelico Chaves, O.F.M., *The Missions of New Mexico, 1776. A Description by Fray Francisco Atanasio Domínguez with Other Contemporary Documents* (Albuquerque, 1956), p. xvii.

[11] *Ibid.*, pp. 12–43, 217.

merous rowdy characters who had come to make their fortune from the traffic that passed over the famous Santa Fe Trail.

Meanwhile the Church garnered little advantage from the new order of things. The republican government at Mexico City refused to be bound by the precedent of the viceroy's furnishing financial aid to the Church, and its imposition of an oath of allegiance upon the populace thinned the ranks of the clergy, both secular and regular, since a number of the priests departed rather than promise fealty to a government which they could not in conscience support. As the Indians gradually drifted away from the mission pueblos most of the friars went back to Mexico so that by the time of the American occupation there existed scarcely more than the broken and neglected fragments of these once populous centers of Christian life. On several occasions after 1823 the Mexican Congress discussed the question of a separate diocese for New Mexico, but nothing came of the proposals. In the meantime the province continued as part of the Diocese of Durango. The visit in 1830 of the vicar general of that see, and those of José Antonio Zubiría, Bishop of Durango, in 1833 and 1850, produced only more somber reports of religious conditions in both the old Spanish towns and in the missions. Now that the State no longer supported the Church in the fashion that had been true of the viceregal regime, the population who had grown up under the old system felt no obligation to come to the rescue of religion. Thus without financial support, a sufficient number of worthy priests, and the growing chaos in regard to ecclesiastical government, it was not difficult to envision a complete eclipse for Catholicism in New Mexico.

It was not until the province had again passed under a new sovereignty that there was any substantial hope of rectification of these evils. But the outbreak of war between Mexico and the United States in May, 1846, was destined to alter the entire course of New Mexico's future. One of the immediate effects that followed from the war was for the Mexicans to foster the belief that the Americans would destroy the Catholic Church. Aware of this propaganda, President James K. Polk gave instructions that every consideration was to be shown to the religious sensibilities of the people. Upon Santa Fe's capitulation in August without the firing of a shot, therefore, Colonel Stephen W. Kearny, the commander, was at pains to let them know that his government had given orders, as he said, "to protect the property of the church, to cause the worship of those belonging to it to be undisturbed, and their religious rights in the amplest manner preserved for them."[12] This promise was fully honored so that when Bishop Zubíria came in 1850 for his final visitation — two years after the territory had been ceded to the United States — he was shown every courtesy.

The dismal picture presented by the New Mexico Church at the time of the cession should not be permitted, however, to dim the achievement of the missionaries during the previous two and half centuries. By virtue of their zeal thousands of souls among the native population had received the grace of baptism and had died in the Christian faith. It was due to their ingenuity as well that these Indians had risen to a higher civilization and that many among them had become equipped to serve themselves and their families in a useful way by their improved knowledge of farming, grazing, weaving, and other occupations. There had, indeed, been heart-breaking defections in their ranks, but a sufficient number had always responded to the spiritual and material advantages offered by the friars to warrant nearly 300 of these religious in New Mexico and the neighboring area that was to become Arizona giving all or a part of their adult lives to their care. On their part, some Franciscans had likewise at times fallen short of their lofty ideals, but when one considers the almost insurmountable difficulties involved in these mission stations, and the true nature of the Indians and their forbidding country, it is scarcely an exaggeration to speak of New Mexico's missions as having shown "a permanence and stability rivaling that of any other frontier institution."[13] What Christian faith there was in the province at the time of its transfer to the United States was Catholic, and for that the friars were to be thanked. Thus when the Holy See in July, 1850, acted in response to the American hierarchy's petition for an ecclesiastical government by erecting the Vicariate Apostolic of New Mexico, the first vicar apostolic, John B. Lamy, upon arrival in Santa Fe in August, 1851, found at least some kind of tradi-

[12] Quoted from *House Executive Documents*, 30th Congress, 1 Session, No. 60, Arnold L. Rodríquez, O.F.M., "New Mexico in Transition, 1830–1860," unpublished master's thesis, The Catholic University of America (1948), p. 79.

[13] Cyprian J. Lynch in *Benavides' Memorial of 1630*, p. xxi.

tion upon which to rear a new structure for the Catholic Church in this historic land.

ARIZONA

To the west and south of New Mexico there stretched a vast region of which parts had been traversed in the sixteenth and seventeeth centuries by several Spanish exploring expeditions. Deriving its name of Pimería Alta from the Pima Indians who inhabited the territory, its northern limits remained for all practical purposes during the colonial period the Gila River with the Gulf of California forming the western extremity. Within this area, which today forms the northern part of the Mexican State of Sonora and the southern portion of the State of Arizona, the first missionaries had been the Franciscans who had won some of the Moqui Indians to Christianity, but in the great rebellion of 1680 they fell away and were never fully retrieved for the faith.

Following the Franciscan pioneers in Pimería Alta there came the Jesuits who worked intermittently in this region for the better part of a century before their expulsion in 1767. As we have seen, in 1572 the Society of Jesus had withdrawn from Florida and had transferred its men to Mexico. For the next two decades they engaged in a variety of activities the most important of which was the conducting of colleges. But with Gonzalo de Tapia, S.J., crossing the Sierra Madre Mountains in 1591 to begin the northward advance, the Jesuits entered seriously into the mission field. And in spite of tremendous losses – such as the Tepehuán uprising of 1616 that destroyed the missions and claimed the lives of eight Jesuits – the advance continued. By the late seventeenth century the Black Robes' twin columns on either side of the Sierra Madre extended from Durango to northern Chihuahua and from Culiacán to the border of what is today Arizona. The cost was often high, and yet by 1645 there were on the western side of the mountains more than thirty missions with their subsidiary stations.

At the time that the Jesuits approached Pimería Alta in the late 1680's the population there was estimated at about 30,000 natives composed of an agricultural people who raised maize, beans, wheat, and melons on their irrigated lands in the river valleys as well as grew cotton for their clothing. They were not the primitive savages that had been encountered elsewhere, therefore, but the hardships attending their attempted evangelization were nonetheless real. The first three Jesuits arrived in March, 1687, and established the original mission to which they gave the name of Nuestra Señora de los Dolores which was located in Sonora many miles to the south of the present international border.

Among the three Jesuits who gave northern Sonora its first mission in 1687 was one of the most remarkable personalities in American colonial history. Eusebio Francisco Kino (Kuhn), born at Val di Nou near Trent in the Tyrol forty-three years before and graduated from the University of Ingolstadt where he had shown a flair for mathematics, had already spent six years in America when he received his new assignment. The spirit in which Kino set about the business of saving souls is well illustrated by an incident that occurred at Guadalajara in December, 1686, on his way north. Having been informed that the Spanish officials in Nueva Vizcaya had been guilty of grave abuses against the Indians by forcing them to work in the mines before they had even been baptized, Kino petitioned the *audiencia* of Guadalajara that the natives should not be employed by the Spaniards until five years after their conversion, and that those Christian Indians who voluntarily worked in the mines and at other occupations for the white men should be paid a fair daily wage for their toil. Kino's petition came at a favorable moment since a royal *cédula* had just been received from Spain that new converts might not be taken off for this kind of labor for twenty years after their conversion. The *audiencia* gave a quick decision in Kino's favor, therefore, ordering that the Indians were not to be obliged under any pretext to work in the mines or on the *haciendas* for twenty years after they had accepted the Christian faith. Armed with this order Kino proceeded with more assurance. for he was wise enough to know that if the Indians were to be enslaved by the white men there was little prospect of any lasting effect to what he and his confrères hoped to do for their souls.[14]

From the time that Kino reached Pimería Alta until his death in 1711 this extraordinary man distinguished himself not only as a zealous priest who by the time he died had baptized over 4,000 souls, but he excelled as well as an explorer, cartographer, historian, and rancher. To his thorough explorations and careful map-making in both Cali-

[14] Herbert Eugene Bolton, *Rim of Christendom. A Biography of Eusebio Francisco Kino. Pacific Coast Pioneer* (New York, 1936), pp. 233–235.

fornia and Pimería Alta – carried out by thousands of miles of travel on horse or mule back – there was added the establishment of missions on both sides of the Sonora-Arizona line, the introduction of stock raising into five or six river valleys, and the setting up of ranches at nearly twenty different locations. "He was easily," says his biographer, "the cattle king of his day and region."[15] When one recalls that these grilling tasks were accomplished amid periodic Indian mutinies that had to be quickly combatted lest the mission natives revolt and drive off the stock, as happened in 1695, and amid the ever-present danger from the Apaches who more than once struck devastating blows at the settlements of the Christian Indians, the marvel of his varied achievements is all the more striking. Besides his tireless efforts to instruct the neophytes in their catechism and to minister to them through the Mass, the sacraments, and other religious exercises, Kino found time to write extensive accounts of these northern missions, and his *Favores Celestiales*, as he entitled it, is recognized as the historians' best source of information for the area in Kino's time. Moreover, his elaborate maps of Lower California, Pimería Alta, and the Jesuit missions of New Spain were sufficiently expert in several instances to make them the subject of serious plagiarism by European geographers.

Of the colonial missions in what was to become Arizona, the most famous was founded by Kino. In April, 1700, he began the construction of a church at San Xavier del Bac about nine miles south of the present city of Tucson. It was at a location about a mile from the present church which was completed in the late eighteenth century by the Franciscans and which remains one of the most beautiful historical monuments of the Southwest. Kino sent repeated calls back to Mexico for more missionaries, and shortly after the arrival of four Jesuits in 1701 in response to his request there came into existence two more missions at San Gabriel de Guévavi and San Cayetano de Tumacácori.

For another decade after the founding of San Xavier del Bac the intrepid Kino continued his ceaseless activity. In all of this, to be sure, he had the assistance of his fellow Jesuits and his faithful Indian converts. But Kino remained the soul of the enterprise, and some notion of the sweep of his accomplishments is conveyed in the account of his work to which he put the finishing touches the year before he

[15] *Ibid.*, p. 589.

died. He stated that from the mother mission at Dolores in Sonora he had made over forty expeditions to the north and west which varied in length from fifty to more than 200 leagues, a league being 2.63 miles. On these journeys he was sometimes accompanied by other fathers, but as he said, "most of the time with only my servants and with the governors, captains, and caciques of different rancherías or incipient pueblos. . . ." And by reason of these expeditions and the missions founded along the way there had been brought into the Catholic fold over 30,000 souls. "I have solemnized more than four thousand baptisms," said Kino, "and I could have baptized ten or twelve thousand Indians more if the lack of father laborers had not rendered it impossible for us to catechize them and instruct them in advance. . . ."[16] By this time one would think that Kino might have been entertaining ideas of a leave from his strenuous labors. But it was not his nature to rest, and it was while on a visit to Magdalena to dedicate a new church to his patron, St. Francis Xavier, that death came quite suddenly to the great missionary in March, 1711, at the age of sixty-six.

When the historian meets a character like Father Kino, or the Franciscan Serra whom we will see later in California, there is a temptation to view an entire movement through their striking and remarkable deeds. But it would be misleading to do so, for Kino's achievements in Pimería Alta, extraordinary as they were, did not endure insofar as the permanent establishment of the Catholic faith was concerned. For one reason the Jesuits' practice of not accepting native whites as novices meant that all recruits for their missions had to be imported, and as a consequence they were always handicapped by a shortage of manpower. Moreover, the nature of the area, and that of its Indian inhabitants, was unprofitable for Catholicism; as its subsequent history was to show, it never yielded anything like a satisfactory return for the amount of time and labor expended on it by the missionaries whether they be Franciscan or Jesuit. And as has been mentioned, during the reign of the last Hapsburg ruler, Charles II (1665–1700), Spain suffered severe reverses which were not overcome by any marked revival of Spanish energies under the first of the Bourbon kings, Philip V, who was only seventeen years of age at his accession in 1700. Conse-

[16] "Report of Eusebio Francisco Kino on the Missions of Pimería Alta (Arizona) in 1710," Ellis, *Documents*, p. 27.

quently, with mounting pressure on the weakened mother country, it was not surprising that relatively little material aid in support of the missions found its way to distant Pimería Alta.

Yet the frontier was not altogether abandoned. A report by Bishop Crespo of Durango describing the neglect in which he found the missions on his visit in 1725, plus a military inspection the following year, helped to convince the government at Madrid that something should be done. In 1722 a royal decree had ordered a renewal of missionary activity at the king's expense, and as a result of Philip V's action a group of German Jesuits, headed by Ignacio Xavier Keller, reached the north in 1732. The old missions were now reoccupied, several new ones were founded in Sonora, and after the fashion of Kino, explorations along the Gila and Colorado Rivers were once again undertaken by Keller and his fellow Jesuit, Jacob Sedelmayr.

But in the end the barriers to lasting success proved too formidable. During the thirty-six years between the coming of Keller and his companions and the final expulsion of the Jesuits from the Spanish dominions one obstacle after another thwarted their hopes for subjecting the pagan tribes to the Catholic faith. And even if the tribesmen had been less hostile, as previously mentioned, there were never enough Jesuits to man these missions properly. To add to the difficulties the Black Robes, like the friars, also had their troubles with bishops over jurisdictional matters. Among the objectives of the Jesuits had been the warlike Moquis whom they desired to convert. Two centuries before the Franciscans had made their first contacts with this dangerous people and they had tried unsuccessfully a number of times since to bring them to accept Christianity. Now that a rival band of missionaries was at hand the friars rekindled their zeal, and they volunteered to make a new effort without the benefit of the military. After an initial success full responsibility for this tribe was assigned in 1745 to the friars by a government that was anxious to be freed from the obligation of providing military protection such as the Jesuits had demanded. It was a situation that might have developed into a healthy rivalry between the two orders had it not been that before long the obstinacy of the Moquis and the banishment of the Jesuits completely wiped out the prospect. Far more serious was the uprising of 1751 among the northern Pimas who destroyed several missions and killed two Jesuits. The revolt had at least the good effect of demonstrating the validity of the missionaries' repeated requests for greater military protection, and as a result two new presidios were established at Altar and Tubac near the mission of San Xavier. Even this advantage was in part dissipated, however, by the effects of a quarrel that ensued between the Black Robes and Governor Diego Parrilla after the Pima uprising.

But the really fatal blow to Jesuit hopes in Pimería Alta was the execution in 1768 in New Spain of Charles III's decree of March, 1767, ordering the expulsion of the Society of Jesus from all his dominions. Unlike the populous provinces to the south, there were no thriving colleges and parishes for the Jesuits to surrender here, for it was not until after the founding of Tucson in 1776 as a presidio that any sizeable Spanish town was known in the future Arizona. There were only the three missions which by orders of the government were to be handed over to the Franciscans, and by this time San Xavier del Bac and its sister missions at Guévavi and Tumacácori were in a sad state of enfeeblement.[17]

With the removal of the Black Robes there came to Sonora and the north a band of friars from the College of the Holy Cross at Querétaro who found sixteen pueblos in the Pimería Alta district with about 180 Spaniards intermingled among the widely scattered and thinly populated Indian settlements. These Franciscans were in general conscientious and hard working men, but the colorful career of one of their number, Francisco Garcés, has caused us to know more about him than we do of the others. Garcés was assigned to San Xavier del Bac where his stature as a missionary, explorer, and writer made him a worthy successor to Kino who had founded the mission sixty-eight years before. Garcés was convinced that New Mexico would make a better base for California than Sonora, and in his efforts to prove the validity of his theory he undertook a number of overland journeys – often without military escort – from the Colorado and Gila River Valleys west-

[17] That the friars or other Spaniards had no chance to do anything for the Jesuits was evident from the order of Carlos Francisco de Croix, Viceroy of New Spain. Since he had been threatened with death if even a dying Jesuit remained in New Spain once the embarcation of the religious order had been completed, it is small wonder that he should have given instructions to all Spaniards not to speak of the matter "for the subjects of the great monarch, who occupies the throne of Spain, must henceforth know once and for all that they are born to keep silent and must obey but not to discuss or to judge the lofty affairs of government." Quoted by Geiger, *Serra*, I, 182.

ward to California. Exploration was not, however, his main objective; it was rather the hope that along this new inland route the friars might establish a chain of missions that would be linked up with those of their confrères in California. Thus for over a decade this intrepid Franciscan journeyed back and forth across the vast expanse laying plans for missions and trying to devise ways by which the friars might bring the Moquis and Yuma Indians under Christian influence. In the sequel Garcés' explorations proved of capital importance to official undertakings such as the expeditions of Juan Bautista Anza in the 1770's, but it was otherwise with the cause that the friar had nearest to heart. As had happened so many times before, the arbitrary conduct of the white men ruined whatever prospect there was of adding the Yumas permanently to the Christian fold. Seizure of a part of their lands and the arrest and public punishment of one of their chiefs provoked a rebellion in July, 1781, in which Fray Francisco and three of his fellow friars lost their lives.

While the tragedy at Yuma was the most costly experience of these years for the Franciscans, they were able to make only slight progress farther east in Primería Alta proper. Tucson, it is true, had been established in 1776 as a Spanish settlement and Garcés had had a church and a priest's house erected in the village. But aside from the completion in 1797 of the new church at San Xavier del Bac, an impressive structure that had taken the Papago Indians many years to build substantially in the form we know it today, there is little to recount of the religious life of the late eighteenth and early nineteenth centuries. Mexico's declaration of independence from Spain broke more of the old ties and caused a further deterioration to the Church as, for example, in 1828 when the government at Mexico City demanded an oath of allegiance from the inhabitants. Practically all of the remaining priests — like their confrères in New Mexico — felt too strong a loyalty to the mother country to forswear it for an uncertain future in the new republic and were thus compelled to depart.

With the Franciscans no longer on the scene many of the mission Indians either drifted away or lapsed into their former pagan practices and the missions themselves fell into decay and ruin. The wild Apache continued their periodic forays through the region and, in fact, it was these fierce tribesmen who offered as late as the 1850's the most serious challenge when the Americans, in search of gold, began to appear in considerable numbers. In 1853 what was to become southwestern Arizona was secured to the United States as part of the Gadsden Purchase and the erection of military forts and mining camps followed in due course. The troops stationed at places like Forts Yuma and Buchanan kept the Indians at bay, but neither the soldiers nor the swarm of gold prospectors who now descended upon the area were of much help to the moral tone of the frontier communities. From the first gold strike in 1853 to the exhaustion of the Arizona mines in 1864 quick fortunes were made – and lost – but in the process religion suffered further reverses in settlements like Gila City which for a time was regarded as the most wide-open town in the West.

In the intervening years Arizona saw little formal ecclesiastical organization save for the ministrations of a few priests – mostly French-born – of the Diocese of Santa Fe who served as itinerant missionaries in this western extremity. Among these were Joseph Machebeuf, a future Bishop of Denver, who visited the white settlements and the remnants of the Indian missions in 1858 and again in 1859. In September, 1868, five years after Arizona had been organized by Congress as a territory, it was given its first bishop with the appointment of John B. Salpointe who assumed control the following year as first ordinary of the Vicariate Apostolic of Arizona. But for another generation the Church remained exceedingly weak and little could be done by the bishop and his handful of impoverished priests to render viable the Catholic life of a land that two centuries before had seen the advent of Kino and his fellow Black Robes.

CHAPTER FOUR

TEXAS

Of all the areas of missionary effort of the Catholic Church in colonial America that in the expanse of territory that stretched eastward from New Mexico and that ultimately came to bear the name of Texas was, all things considered, the least successful. There were manifold reasons why the missionaries failed to bring the Texas tribes in any numbers into a lasting union with the Catholic faith. First, the tremendous distances that separated the area from the Spaniards' base of operations in Coahuila was a serious deterrent; secondly, although the Indians here – with the exception of the Apache and Comanche – were in general probably no more intractable than the tribes elsewhere, they were on the whole a fickle lot and they offered a special difficulty by reason of the bewildering variety of their tribal languages which proved a major stumbling block for many a Texas missionary. A third factor was the growing weakness of the mother country. From the time that Spain became involved in war with France in 1622 there were few prolonged periods of peace during which the nation could recoup its strength for further expansion. With each succeeding peace settlement from that of the Pyrenees in 1659 to the Treaty of Paris that ended the Seven Years' War in 1763 more and more of the empire was lost until by the late eighteenth century Spanish power was hardly more than a shadow of what it had been 200 years before. As a consequence the resources at the disposal of the Madrid government to support the ambitious undertakings of its overseas representatives in Texas were meager and, in truth, the mother country had little interest in the area beyond that of securing the northern and eastern limits of the Viceroyalty of New Spain against attacks from the French. Moreover, there was also present here the familiar pattern of friction between ecclesiastical authorities and civil and military officials with costly mistakes in judgment made on both sides. The situation was such, therefore, that the disillusionment and discouragement induced by so many unsuccessful attempts to plant the faith in the hearts of the Texas Indians finally led to the gradual undermining of the spirit of the missionaries themselves.

While the lasting effects of the Spanish occupation of Texas were in the end slight it was the scene of numerous activities on the part of the white man between 1519 when Alonso Álvarez de Pineda sailed along the gulf coast and the establishment of a permanent settlement in the region of El Paso nearly a century and a half later. For example, Cabeza de Vaca crossed Texas in the 1530's, Coronado was there in 1542 in search of the Gran Quivira, and in 1553 a Spanish fleet was shipwrecked on the Texas coast and most of its crew and passengers were lost, including five Dominican friars who were murdered by the Indians.

But the most unusual event of these early years were the appearances beginning about 1620 of Mother María de Jesús de Agreda, superior of a convent in the little town of that name on the border between Aragón and Castile, to the Jumano and Tejas Indians. The historian is naturally sceptical of stories of bilocation, but there would seem to be little doubt that someone whom the natives called "the woman in blue," did visit these tribes on a number of occasions during which she instructed them in Christian doctrine and directed them to seek missionaries from whom further enlightenment could be had about the faith. It was from a group of about fifty Jumano Indians who came to Isleta near present day Albuquerque in July, 1629, in search of a priest that the first news of this phenomenon was learned, and similar instances were met in later years among the Tejas tribesmen in eastern Texas. In any case, the "woman in blue" figured prominently in getting underway a number of missionary enterprises in behalf of the Indians of New Mexico and Texas during the seventeenth century.[1]

[1] On María de Agreda cf. Carlos E. Castañeda, *Our Catholic Heritage in Texas, 1519–1936* (Austin, 1936), I, 195–215. This six-volume work is the best general history of the Church in colonial Texas. By reason of an abundance of new source materials Castañeda was able, as he stated in the preface to Volume I, to expand the history of the area. "The traditional eight or ten expeditions into Texas

When at length the first missions in the present State of Texas were founded their location was in the region of El Paso, eastward in what is today Edwards County, and southward along the Rio Grande in the Del Rio-Eagle Pass neighborhood. In each case the initiative for these undertakings was due to the zeal of the Franciscan friars to whose order belongs the credit for the spread of the gospel among the Texas tribesmen. Once the Spaniards had occupied New Mexico under Oñate it was natural that the white men should frequently traverse El Paso on their way to and from New Spain. Thus the friars' contacts with the neighboring Manso and Zuma Indians in the early years of the century gradually grew more steady and finally led in December, 1659, to a permanent foundation when Fray García de San Francisco de Zúñiga erected on the site of the present Mexican town of Ciudad Juárez across the river form El Paso the mission of Nuestra Señora de Guadalupe de El Paso. In time this mission gave rise to others nearby and by the last decade of the century there were fourteen Indian pueblos each with its church and ten friars in charge of these natives. When the great rebellion took place in New Mexico in 1680 it was the settlements around El Paso that afforded the safest haven for the survivors of that disaster. After a good deal of controversy a presidio was ultimately located at El Paso by 1685 and Spanish settlers in places like Real de San Lorenzo were compelled to move closer for their own protection so that by 1691 there were over 2,000 worshippers who used the El Paso church.

As for the missionary activities to the east of El Paso, it was a friar by the name of Fray Juan Larios who was largely responsible for their beginning. During his travels in Coahuila in 1670 Larios had encountered representatives of northern tribes who were seeking a priest, and with a view to meeting their need he carried the story to his superiors. After the customary delays an expedition was in consequence finally fitted out which set off in April, 1675, for the north. Fernando del Bosque was in command of the soldiers who escorted Larios and his confrère, Fray Dionisio de San Buenventura, with about 120 Indians also in the company. By early May they had crossed the Rio Grande and had reached a point which they called San Ysidro which was probably on one of the branches of the Nueces River in Edwards County. Here on

up to 1731," he said, "have been enlarged to ninety-two, and the list of missions expanded from an equal number to more than fifty" (I, ix).

May 16 there was sung the first Mass of which we have record on Texas soil. After the Mass the Indians, who were found to number 1,172 at this place, asked to be baptized. But the Franciscans showed their prudence and good sense by declining to receive the natives until they had been properly instructed in the Catholic faith, and as del Bosque remarked in his diary ". . . when they were given to understand by him [Larios] through an interpreter that he could not baptize them until they knew their prayers, to console them he baptized fifty-five infants, the Spaniards acting as their godfathers."[2]

At the very time that these settlements were being made in western Texas a menacing situation was developing elsewhere for Spain due to the aggression of the French, English, and Dutch in the West Indies, the English raids on Florida, and the French penetration into the lower Mississippi Valley. It gradually became apparent that if the Madrid government intended to have its claims to the area stretching eastward from Florida to New Mexico taken seriously it would have to do more than merely assert them. In the commercial wars in which the powers of western Europe were then engaged theoretical claims counted for little, and the only overseas possession of which a European state could be certain was one that it could protect by force of arms. Moves such as those of Jolliet and Marquette in descending the Mississippi in 1673, and La Salle's exploration of the great river to its mouth nine years later, finally convinced the Spaniards that they had better take action before it was too late.

It was the same Robert Cavelier, Sieur de La Salle, who, in fact, became the immediate spur to Spanish efforts in eastern Texas. After his exploratory trip down the Mississippi, during which he had formally laid claim for France to all the territory drained by that river and its tributaries, he had returned to Europe in 1683 just as war was again breaking between France and Spain. La Salle's proposals for occupation of the Mississippi were heard, therefore, with more than ordinary interest, and by the spring of 1684 he had won a commission from Louis XIV to head an expedition and by late July of that year it was ready to sail. In his company were three Sulpician priests, of whom one was his brother, and several Franciscan friars who were intended to evangelize the natives. The little fleet sailed past the mouth of the

[2] "Fernando del Bosque's Account of the First High Mass in Texas, May 16, 1675," Ellis, *Documents*, p. 24.

Mississippi and in February, 1685, it put in at a point on Matagorda Bay on the Texas coast. Thus was begun a two-year stay that was to prove disastrous to the French and the source of great anxiety to the Spaniards.

During the course of their time in Texas the French encountered about every conceivable misfortune, culminating in serious internal dissension that finally led in March, 1687, to the murder of La Salle by one of his own men. All during this time the Spaniards kept sending out — both by land and sea — one search party after another in an effort to track down the French and expel them. It was not until April, 1689, however, that Alonso de Léon the younger, Governor of Coahuila, who was in command of the operations came upon the ruins of Fort St. Louis a short while after the Indians had massacred the surviving French and burned the fort. With de Léon at the time was Fray Damian Massanet, a Franciscan missionary, whose zeal was quickened when he learned from a neighboring chief of the Tejas tribe that the Indians were desirious of having a priest. Moreover, to Massanet's astonishment it turned out that some of the natives had a vague knowledge of the Christian religion which had been passed on to them by their ancestors who, they said, had been taught by the "woman in blue." Here, surely, was an ideal situation for the friars, and when de Léon's party departed in early May for Coahuila Father Damian promised the Tejas that he would return to teach them more about the white man's God.

Massanet had no great difficulty in convincing his superiors that the prospects in eastern Texas were worth the price of a major effort, and thus when de Léon's company set off for the north again in March, 1690, it included six friars from the college at Querétaro with Massanet in the office of commissary. The long journey took two months, but by May 25, the feast of Corpus Christi, they had reached their goal and formal possession of the region was taken in the name of God and Charles II of Spain with the first mission, called San Francisco de los Tejas, established on San Pedro Creek near the present town of Weches some miles west of the Neches River.

But there was a fundamental difference of approach between de Léon and Massanet, and it was not long before this conflict manifested itself and imperiled the future of the entire enterprise. There is no need to enter into the complicated story in detail. Suffice it to say, to the civilian mind the only feasible plan was to establish a series of presidios and Spanish settlements that would guarantee protection against both the French and hostile Indians and keep open the communications with Coahuila. But this policy was altogether unacceptable to Massanet who was intent upon constructing a group of missions among the natives with only enough troops to afford protection for the friars. Between the two contrary points of view the viceregal government acted as arbiter and at Mexico City the paramount problem was to keep the French at bay and to do that at the least possible expense. In the end de Léon lost out, in part because of his failure to allay the suspicions of the viceregal officials concerning what they believed were the continued activities of the French in eastern Texas and along the gulf coast. In the sequel it was finally determined to erect Texas into a province with the major authority, however, in the hands of the missionaries, and in January, 1691, Domingo Terán de los Rios was appointed governor of a jurisdiction to which there was applied for the first time the name of Tejas, or Texas as we know it.

Meanwhile the Franciscans had received further recruits and were proceeding with the task that had brought them to eastern Texas. In the autumn of 1691 a new mission was founded about five miles to the east of San Francisco de los Tejas to which they gave the name of Santísimo Nombre de María and others followed in due course. And while the friars busied themselves in an attempt to reach the minds of the natives Governor Terán was energetically exploring the surrounding country. His series of difficult journeys were climaxed in late December, 1691, when he returned to San Francisco de los Tejas without having discovered any trace of the French to find that Father Damian was unwilling to loan him any of the mission horses for further travels. By this time the breach between Terán and Massanet had widened and, indeed, in the interval the attitude of the Indians had so changed toward the missionaries that a number of the latter, thoroughly discouraged, decided to abandon their posts and return to Coahuila with the governor in January, 1692.

Were it not for missionaries like Massanet and Francisco Hidalgo the missions would probably have been abandoned before this, for the Tejas or Asinai tribesmen were by now showing more and more resistance to their presence, even going so far as to utter veiled threats of what might happen if the friars did not clear out entirely. In spite of overwhelming odds, however, Massanet persisted for nearly two years, but by then his spirit was broken by virtually complete failure to make any headway with the Indians. In October, 1693, he finally bowed to the inevitable and with a saddened heart personally set fire to the Mission of San Francisco de los Tejas and left with his few remaining confrères for the south. Spain's first attempt to plant colonies in eastern Texas by means of the mission system ended, therefore, in a dismal failure and two decades were to pass before the effort would be seriously renewed. In the second instance, however, the presidio which de Léon had advocated and which experience had proved was necessary — not only for Spain's political interests but also for the success of the missionary cause — was from the outset an accepted feature of the undertaking.

If the Spaniards could have satisfied themselves that they had seen the last of the French in the lower Mississippi Valley that would in all likelihood have been the end of the mission story in east Texas. Indeed, after their withdrawal from that area in the early 1690's their sense of security led for a time to a general decline of interest, and requests of missionaries like Francisco Hidalgo for support to renew the attempt to convert the Asinais met with little response. But the closing years of the century witnessed a changed situation among the European powers and with it the prospects for missionary work brightened once more. At the Treaty of Ryswick in 1697 Spain lost Haiti to France and in the following year Louis XIV joined with England and Holland in a treaty for the partition of Spain's vast possessions. The new alignment was made real for the Spaniards when early in 1699 the enterprising Pierre Le Moyne d'Iberville arrived to establish a French colony at Biloxi in the present State of Mississippi. From here — and from St. Louis on Mobile Bay to which the settlement was moved in 1702 — the French exploring parties penetrated the interior and were successful in making friends with a number of Indian tribes. The selection by the childless Charles II of Spain of the grandson of Louis XIV to succeed him and Charles' own death in November, 1700, did not radically alter affairs in the Texas-Louisiana area. True, the two Bourbon monarchies were allies in the War of the Spanish Succession, but within five years thereafter a clash of interests brought them to war in 1718. In fact, the *pacte de famille* between Madrid and Versailles in 1733 and its renewal in 1761 only involved the weakened Spain in further conflicts, and there were few years between the outbreak of the War of the Spanish Succession in 1701 and Spain's entry into the final stages of the Seven Years' War in 1762 in which the mother country was not engaged in armed conflict in Europe with grave detriment to its overseas empire.

It was a strange combination of circumstances that led to the renewal of missionary efforts in eastern Texas. In its first years France's Louisiana colony was a commercial venture, and among the designs of its managers was the opening of trade relations with the Spaniards as well as with the Indians. After the failure to establish contact with the former by sea, the French began to think in terms of an overland route through Texas. About this time Lamothe Cadillac, Governor of Louisiana, received a surprising letter from a Spanish missionary. Fray Francisco Hidalgo, eager to return to the Asinai tribesmen among whom he had spent three years, and having met with no success in his appeal to the government at Mexico City, decided in January, 1711, to write the Louisiana official to ask him to interest himself in the spiritual welfare of these Indians. Cadillac seized upon this unexpected turn of events as an excuse to send Louis Juchereau de St. Denis the younger, an active and important Canadian-born member of the colony who had been in Louisiana since 1700, to seek out Hidalgo and probe the possibilities of this odd approach for trading advantages with New Spain. St. Denis was naturally suspect by the Spaniards, and after he and his three companions reached the Presidio of San Juan Bautista beyond the Rio Grande in the fall of 1714 they were arrested and held until instructions were received from the viceroy that they should be sent to Mexico City where they arrived in June, 1715. It was a compliment to St. Denis' diplomacy that he overcame the suspicions of the viceroy and his officials and ended by convincing them of the desirability of outfitting an expedition for the permanent settlement of eastern Texas.

Through the autumn and winter the preparations were hastened and by February, 1716, the expedition was ready to depart from Saltillo. The full company ultimately numbered seventy-five persons with Captain Domingo Ramón in command of the soldiers intended for the presidio, a group of Spanish civilians, and St. Denis with two other Frenchmen. The ecclesiastical personnel consisted of a dozen friars from the colleges at Querétaro and Zacatecas who were to divide the mission territory between them. The goal was reached in June and on June 5 Ramón gave over formal possession of the re-established Mission of San Francisco de los Tejas to Father Isidro Felix de Espinosa, of the Querétaro friars. Knowing that for nearly a quarter of a century the veteran missionary, Francisco Hidalgo, had been praying and working for this day, it was a courteous gesture for Espinosa to appoint the old friar as minister at San Francisco. During the late summer similar ceremonies were held at four other missions and by the autumn Ramón and the Zacatecas friars had worked themselves as far east as the region of Natchitoches, Louisiana, where the last of the six missions, San Miguel de Linares, was erected at a site near the present town of Robeline and its care given over to another Franciscan destined to win fame in Texas, Fray Antonio Margil de Jesús.

But this second attempt to plant permanent colonies in eastern Texas proved to be as ill-starred as the original effort almost thirty years before. In spite of all that the friars did they could not induce the Indians in any numbers to come in to the missions and to remain long enough to enter upon serious religious instruction. Moreover, the soldiers were an undisciplined lot and before long a number of them deserted and rode away on the badly needed horses. Added to the customary difficulties experienced on a venture of this kind, the tremendous distance between these outposts and Coahuila, the base of supplies, entailed an acute hardship. After a few weeks this fact was brought home to the leaders when the magnitude of their undertaking began to dawn upon them. On July 22, 1716, a letter was sent off to the viceroy in which they outlined their precarious position with only a very limited manpower and a meager amount of supplies at their command amidst thousands of Indians on whose continued friendly disposition it was scarcely prudent to count. In despatching his urgent request for assistance it must have been a sobering thought for Ramón and the mission superiors to calculate the months that might be consumed before their emissaries could complete the journey and return with the aid that was so badly needed.

It was this distance of 800 miles or more between the missions in eastern Texas and the nearest outpost in New Spain that was largely responsible for the next advance in Texas' mission history. Reports of increased French activity in the region of the lower Mississippi were again coming through, and it became evident that if they were to be held off from making alliances and entering upon illicit trade with the Texas tribes, Spain would have to secure its interests by a greater military force than that of the presidio in east Texas and those along the Rio Grande. Once again it was the zeal of a Franciscan for the souls of the redmen that provided the chief impetus for a decision taken by the viceregal government. Fray Antonio de San Buenaventura Olivares, an experienced friar, who had first conceived the idea of missions in the region of the San Antonio River in 1709 during a trip to the Colorado, arrived in Mexico City in September, 1716. Olivares brought with him a lengthy report which detailed the advantages of the San Antonio area both for missions and for winning Indian allies for Spain. The new viceroy, the Marquis de Valero, was soon won to Olivares' proposals and in early December he authorized a colonizing expedition and appointed Don Martín de Alarcón as captain general and governor. Alarcón was instructed to take with him fifty soldiers to establish a presidio as well as to furnish at royal expense all the supplies that would be needed for Olivares' mission.

With the additional promise of ten soldiers to guard the projected mission it was thus a bright prospect that opened before Fray Antonio de San Buenaventura in the early winter of 1716. Before long, however, that prospect was clouded by a series of differences between the friar and the governor over the latter's failure to move with the speed that Olivares thought both possible and necessary and, too, over the soldiers destined for the mission, the Franciscan insisting that they should be married men, as the instructions had directed, rather than the unmarried troops who were assigned to him. Through these conflicts in policy the two leaders drew farther apart and by the time the group was ready to move forward from the Rio Grande in the early spring of 1718 their quarrels had rendered friendly co-operation between them all but impossible.

In spite of this handicap the expedition at length got underway and the military and civilian contingents – numbering seventy-two in all – arrived at the site of the present city of San Antonio on April 25 and ten days later Alarcón took formal possession in the name of Philip V and gave to the settlement the name of San Antonio de Béxar. Meanwhile Olivares, traveling apart from the main company, had reached the San Antonio River on May 1 where he met Alarcón. The governor handed over to him formal possession of the new mission which was called San Antonio de Valero – later known as the Alamo – which was located about two miles down the San Pedro Spring from the military post. At first the Indians were slow to come in to the mission, but by the winter they had congregated in such large numbers that Alarcón felt justified in organizing an Indian pueblo near the mission. The early days of 1719 found the new colonists digging the irrigation ditches and soon the grains, vegetables, and fruits were planted and provision was being made for the new supply of cattle, sheep, goats, and pigs that had been driven up from Coahuila.

It was the viceregal government's intention that the Alarcón expedition should likewise make the relief and protection of the hard pressed Spanish settlements in east Texas one of its major objectives. Alarcón, it is true, visited them in October-November, 1718, but the hopes to which his visit had given rise, that it would mean an increased number of troops, assurance of ample supplies, and the bringing of the Indians in to the mission compounds were not realized. From the time of their re-establishment these six missions, along with the presidio, had been plagued by the prevalence of disease, desertion among the military, persistence of idolatry, and aloofness on the part of the redmen, as well as the failure of re-enforcements and supplies to come through. How long the missions would have been able to hold out, it is impossible to say. In any case, their tenuous position was soon terminated when a fresh outbreak of war occurred between Spain and France in January, 1719. At the time Jean Baptiste Le Moyne de Bienville was Governor of Louisiana, and as soon as he learned the news he prepared to attack the Spaniards at Pensacola, the Bay of Espíritu Santo, and in east Texas. Weakened as they already were in the last named place, they were no match for their enemies, and when a small party of Frenchmen suddenly descended on the Mission of San Miguel de los Adaes in June, 1719, it was the signal for the beginning of a general retreat that continued through the summer and fall. By December of that year the presidio and the six missions had all been abandoned and their inhabitants, both clerical and lay, had found refuge at San Antonio. Thus a year and a half after the Spaniards had settled there its usefulness for their harassed brethren to the east had been clearly demonstrated.

No man can witness the destruction of an enterprise to which he has devoted his best talents without a pang of regret, and that is no less so when the principal motive has been a love of God and one's fellowmen. It was understandable, therefore, that as the Franciscans made their way across Texas in the last months of 1719 they should have done so with heavy hearts. And yet the catastrophe that had overtaken their eastern missions did not dampen their resolve for very long. It was here at San Antonio that Antonio Margil, who was in temporary residence from December, 1719, to May, 1721, made what was, perhaps, his most enduring contribution to Catholicism in Texas by founding in February, 1720, the Mission of San José about five miles distant from San Antonio de Valero. Here, too, there was opposition and this time from his confrère, Father Olivares, who felt that it was a mistake to congregate Indians hostile to those at San Antonio de Valero so close to the latter. But Margil secured the support of the Marquis de San Miguel de Aguayo, Governor of Texas, and his lieutenant general, Captain Juan Valdez, and thus succeeded in founding at San José what turned out to be the most beautiful of all the missions of colonial Texas and one of the most prosperous. Actually Margil was only marking time at San Antonio until the way would be open again for him to return to eastern Texas. The thoughts that were uppermost in the mind of this beloved friar during this period were conveyed to Antonio Andrade, a Franciscan confrère in Guatemala, in a letter of September, 1720. Margil said:

> It was necessary for us to gather our vestments and things and retire to this mission of San Antonio . . . where we came a year ago on the eve of the feast of Our Father St. Francis, awaiting the help to restore the said six missions and proceed with our plans. Although the Viceroy assigned 225,000 pesos to get 500 men ready at once, so that with the 106 who already were here, there would be 600 . . . the local alcaldes mayores pressed them into service; until now not only have they not arrived but the majority of the 106 men have deserted; others, after having been abandoned, killed themselves. . . . We here are quietly hoping for the opportune time to return to our enterprise, for God and for souls, in the first place; and secondly, that they may not say it was lost, because of us or that it was not recovered by us.[3]

That Margil and his fellow friars were sincerely intent upon the restoration of the missions soon became evident. A full year before the French invasion of east Texas the King of Spain had issued orders in June, 1718, that all the frontier communities were to be securely defended against the French and that no trading with them was to be

[3] Eduardo Enrique Rios, *Life of Fray Antonio Margil, O.F.M.*, translated and revised by Benedict Leutenegger, O.F.M. (Washington, 1959), pp. 122–123.

permitted. In pursuance of this royal command which was long in reaching New Spain, and now with the added stimulation of armed conflict, the viceroy set in motion the preparations for a new expedition. He named as leader the Marquis de Aguayo, and since the re-establishment of the missions was a major part of the over-all plan Aguayo took counsel with Father Espinosa. After the inevitable delays that attended so large an undertaking were overcome the expedition was ready by November, 1720, to depart from Monclova, the capital of Coahuila. Traveling with Aguayo were not only Fray Espinosa and a fellow Franciscan but two diocesan priests, José Codallos y Raval, Vicar General of the Diocese of Guadalajara in which Texas was then included, and the expedition's official chaplain and chronicler, Juan Antonio Peña. By the following spring they had reach San Antonio where they were cheered by the news that another part of the general plan of campaign had been successfully accomplished in the occupation on April 4 of the Bay of Espíritu Santo by a force under Captain Ramón.

No one received the new arrivals at San Antonio with more enthusiasm than Margil and his confrères who had been waiting for so long a time for a chance to resume their labors in the east. After a stop-over of some weeks the expedition set out again on May 13 with the added friars in the company and by the first week of August it had reached the Neches Rives where there was re-established the Mission of San Francisco de los Tejas. They then proceeded with the refounding of the other missions and by late September the extreme limit of the settlements had been reached in the land of the Adaes nation several miles from where Robeline, Louisiana, stands today. Here a fort was constructed and plans laid for a mission nearby, and here for the next half century was to be located the residence of the governors of the province until it was moved to San Antonio in 1772.

The month of August, 1721, was a full one for Antonio Margil. In less than three weeks he had the joy of witnessing the refounding of four missions and of being the celebrant of the high Mass at each ceremony. His labors were increased when news reached him that Francisco Estévez, prefect of the missions for the Congregation de Propaganda Fide, had died on May 25, for as second in command he became prefect *ad interim* and was soon exercising his faculties in that capacity. This famous friar would have asked nothing better than to remain among these Texas Indians until death. But that was not to be, for early in 1722 there came word that he had been elected guardian of the College of Our Lady of Guadalupe at Zacatecas which he himself had founded in 1707. He was compelled, therefore, to wind up his affairs at his distant station and set out for his new assignment which he reached in June of that year. It had been nearly forty years since Margil had arrived in the new world where in the early part of his missionary career he played a significant role in the evangelization of Yucatan, Nicaragua, and especially of Guatemala where in 1692 he had established a college for the training of missionaries. At the time of his recall from Texas he had spent eight years working for the northern tribes amid heart breaking disappointments and frustrations. Yet in spite of all obstacles he had managed to advance the faith in this region and to leave his stamp upon the colonial history of Texas. After serving a term as superior at Zacatecas the old friar was appointed to a Franciscan house in Mexico City where death overtook him in August, 1726, in his seventieth year. His sanctity made a deep impression on all who came in contact with him and it was no surprise, therefore, that his body should have been enshrined in 1778 by the Archbishop of Mexico and that in 1836 Pope Gregory XVI should have declared his virtue to be heroic.

It is not necessary to trace in detail the developments in either the older missions or in the numerous Texas foundations that were made by the Franciscans after 1722. Suffice it to say, the handicaps that had been encountered in earlier years, such as the multiplicity of Indian languages, the struggle to get the natives to remain within the pueblos and to accept regular habits of industry, and the periodic outbreaks of smallpox and other diseases – all these continued as fairly constant factors to the end of the century. Moreover, here as elsewhere the feuds between civil and military officials on the one hand and the ecclesiastical authorities on the other were costly to the missionary cause. In many of these quarrels it was the selfish policies and conduct of the civil and military commanders that was to blame. But neither were the missionaries always free from guilt, and at times the mistaken policies or prejudices of a friar proved to be a grave impediment to the spread of the faith among the redmen.

An example of this kind was Fray José González of the Mission of San Antonio de Valero who in March, 1724, made serious charges to the viceroy against the presidio commanders and who likewise reflected unfavorably on the governor, the Marquis de Aguayo. González had set his heart on winning the Apaches and to his mind it was on this major objective that the Spanish efforts in Texas should be concentrated, even if it meant giving up the commitments in the eastern part of the province. At first he was highly successful and as a result of his representations his principal foe, Captain Nicolás Flores y Valdez of the Presidio of San Antonio de Béjar, was removed in June, 1724, for his alleged abuses of the Apaches during a campaign, and this in spite of the governor and Father Margil and Miguel Núñez de Haro of San José Mission who sought to sustain Flores. Within a year's time, however, the viceregal officials saw their mistake and ordered the reinstatement of Flores and the recall of Father González.

Yet the recommendations contained in the friar's reports continued for some time to affect Spanish policy. A case in point was Colonel Pedro de Rivera who in 1727 conducted an official tour of inspection of the presidios and missions and whose report of the following year showed the González influence in its recommendation that the troops of the eastern military posts should be reduced. Since the three missions of the Querétaro friars were dependent on these soldiers for protection it was natural that the Franciscans should protest their removal. But their appeal addressed to the viceroy in July, 1729, was of no avail, and as a consequence the missions were compelled to move and by May, 1731, they were again functioning in the neighborhood of San Antonio. The case is an instructive one in that it shows how the troubles that so frequently engulfed the missions were not always the fault of arbitrary governors, rapacious soldiers, or fickle Indians; at times they were traceable to the missionaries themselves. It further illustrates a problem that was especially acute in Texas, namely, the repeated removals from one part of the vast province to another which, needless to say, were disruptive of the work that had brought the Franciscans on the scene in the first place.

For the first seventy years or more of the Spanish regime Texas remained almost exclusively a missionary and military enterprise. Yet the desirability of a civil settlement had been expressed as early as 1716, although it was March, 1723, before the crown finally issued the official orders for a foundation of this kind to be made by colonists from the Canary Islands in the vicinity of Espíritu Santo. Seven more years were to pass before the plan was put into execution and the first ten families, numbering fifty-nine persons in all, arrived at Veracruz in June, 1730.

Meanwhile the site for their future home had been shifted from the coast to near San Antonio which the little band of immigrants reached only in March, 1731, after the long and very trying march from Mexico City.

In the plans for the new community both the spiritual and material needs of the settlers were kept in mind. Since the town's inhabitants would be confined to the whites, its ecclesiastical jurisdiction would derive from the Bishop of Guadalajara to whom the viceroy applied for a priest. The parochial records of San Fernando, as it was called, were begun by Father José de la Garza, the first pastor, and date from August, 1731. During the early years the Canary Islanders worshipped in the chapel of the presidio, and it was not until around 1750 that they had their own parish church which was the forerunner of the present parish of San Fernando Cathedral of the Archdiocese of San Antonio. This oldest canonical parish in the State of Texas followed for almost a half century the diocesan regulations of Guadalajara until the erection in 1777 of the Diocese of Linares. Among the Guadalajara decrees that were in force at San Fernando was that of Bishop Juan Gómez de Parada who in March, 1746, fixed the number of holy days of obligation at eighteen, besides Sundays. Some years later another was added when an entry in the parish register for December 12, 1759, noted that day also as a holy day of obligation. It had come about as a result of the request of several of the bishops of New Spain to Pope Benedict XIV who had instituted the feast of Our Lady of Guadalupe to commemorate the miraculous appearance of the Virgin Mary to the Indian Juan Diego near Mexico City in December of 1531.

On the material side the land survey was complete at the site chosen for the new town in the summer of 1731, and on August 1 there was held the first election when nine of the principal citizens voted for two *alcaldes ordinarios*, or justices of the peace, the choice of whom was approved by the viceroy several months later. The original band of immigrants were joined in 1744 by about fifty more families from the Canary Islands. The lot of these islanders, however, remained a hard one and they were destined to experience a great many trials, both great and small, including disputes with the missionaries over the hire of the Indians and the divisions of the land and cattle. It was to the islanders, therefore, that Spanish Texas owed its first civil community, the predecessor of towns like Dolores and Laredo which were part of the ambitious plans of José de Escandón carried out between 1749 and 1755 for the conquest and colonization of the lower Rio Grande Valley.

While San Fernando was thus gradually emerging as a center for white settlement the Franciscans continued their labors for the Indians of the neighborhood. True, the friars and the Canary Islanders had their points of friction, but they were mild in comparison to the trouble that was experienced at the hands of an official like Governor Carlos Franquis de Lugo. During his brief tenure of a year he managed not only to tamper with the missionaries' mail, to order the mission guards removed, and to claim the right to remove the missionaries from their posts, but he also called into question the fundamental honesty and integrity of the Franciscans. They must have sighed with relief, therefore, when the contentious fellow was removed from office in September, 1737, and even the sore trial of the smallpox and measles epidemics that followed in 1739 were in many ways a lighter cross to bear than the rule of a Franquis and his kind.

Feuds of this kind, and the complaints against the friars to which they gave rise, were in part responsible for the superiors of the college at Querétaro deciding in 1745 to launch a full investigation of the four missions maintained by them in the San Antonio area. For this task Fray Francisco Xavier Ortiz was appointed and he went about his job in such a thorough and systematic way that his findings provide the historian with as reliable a body of data as is extant on conditions at the mid-century. Between 1718 and 1745 these missionaries had baptized 2,282 Indians of whom 1,349 had persisted until death and received the last sacraments and Christian burial. Of the 885 neophytes then living in the four missions 744 had already been baptized and the others were under instruction. The natives likewise showed substantial progress under the supervision of the friars in a material way, for when Ortiz ordered an exact count of the livestock it turned out that there were 5,115 head of cattle, 2,661 sheep, 664 goats, and 257 horses. Moreover, the Indians were raising about 8,000 bushels of corn a year, over 300 bushels of beans, and 2,000 pounds of cotton, not to mention fruits and vegetables such as melons, sweet potatoes, pumpkins, etc. Fray Ortiz was not content to take evidence solely from his own men; he submitted a series of searching questions to the civil and military officers to gain their reactions to the work of the missions.

Their answers constituted virtually a unanimous vote of confidence in Ortiz' confrères from men like Captain Toribio de Urrutia, commander of the Béjar presidio, and from others at both the military post and the town of San Fernando. In view of the results shown by the Ortiz investigation the friars' historian was warranted in stating:

> Taken as a whole, the figures, when added together, are a remarkable revelation of the success attained by the patient and painstaking missionaries, whose work has so often been thought a failure by those who have not taken the trouble to examine the fruits of their labors.[4]

Conditions in the Texas missions of the friars of the college at Zacatecas, however, were not as happy as those among their Querétaro brethren, although San José Mission near San Antonio which belonged to Zacatecas outranked all the Texas foundations in prosperity. As a result of inquiries from Madrid and Mexico City concerning their work in Texas the Zacatecas superiors prepared a detailed report in 1749. It was drawn up by Fray Ignacio Antonio Ciprián who confessed that the three missions in the eastern part of the province had been largely a failure due to the Indians' persistent suspicion of Christian baptism, their wide dispersal which made it extremely difficult for lone missionaries to reach them, the Indians' illicit trade with the French from whom they secured firearms, and the distance of the presidio from all these eastern missions except that of San Miguel. From their foundation in 1716 up to 1748 there had been 1,318 baptisms among these tribesmen, but these were mostly children or adults who were *in articulo mortis*. Ciprián likewise admitted that at times the missionaries had to bribe the parents to overcome their reluctance to have their children baptized, and in places like the Mission of Nuestra Señora de Guadalupe the warriors still continued to have two and three wives.

Far to the south along the coast at La Bahía was the Mission of Espíritu Santo de Zúñiga which was also a Zacatecas foundation, and here the more than 400 persons living in the mission pueblo were divided between the Tamiques who were practically all baptized and the Xaranames among whom a few were still under instruction. This, in brief, was the condition at La Bahía shortly before the mission was moved in 1749 for the third and final time to the site of the present town of Goliad, Texas. In contrast to the dismal conditions that ob-

[4] Castañeda, *op. cit.*, III, 110.

tained in the eastern Texas stations and the indifferent success attained at La Bahía, San José presented a very bright picture. Here over 200 neophytes were living in stone houses in the mission pueblo with likewise a stone residence for the friars and a church which, according to Ciprián, was capable of holding 2,000 persons. The missionary presented a clear idea of both the spiritual and material prosperity of San José when he told his superior:

They not only comply with the duties of the church but many of them frequent the sacraments during the year. On Saturday they say the rosary outdoors and sing it very sweetly with much devotion. They are all dressed in cotton and woolen cloth from the mission where they weave it themselves in their modest looms. They have two thousand head of cattle and one thousand sheep. Of corn they harvested fifteen hundred *fanegas* (three thousand bushels) each year, and if they planted more, they could raise more. When the Indians in this mission are administered the sacrament of Baptism, they resign their practice of polygamy and after they choose one wife, they are duly married by the church.[5]

As one reads Texas' mission history he is struck by the slender prospects of success with which the Franciscan friars at times pursued their high goal. More than once costly ventures of a doubtful character were set on foot because a missionary's zeal for souls had been fired by contact with redmen who had requested instruction in the Catholic faith, and in the sequel the missionary was sustained by the crown officials in Madrid or Mexico City. Fray Mariano Francisco de los Dolores y Viana was such a man. As early as 1734 he had made the acquaintance of the Indians who lived along the Brazos River and who roamed as far as the Trinity River Valley and southward to the coast. He had tried to draw them toward Christianity, but it was not until June, 1745, that his approaches seemed to offer any hope of success. At that time seventeen members of the Deadoes, Mayeye, and several allied nations came to San Antonio to visit Fray Mariano and to ask for a priest. The friar responded as speedily as the circumstances would permit, and by February, 1746, the beginnings of the Mission of San Francisco Xavier had been made and within the next three years it was followed by those of San Ildefonso and Nuestra Señora de la Candelaria.

From the outset these San Xavier missions, as they were called,

[5] Ignacio Antonio Ciprián to Fray Juan Antonio Abasolo, October 27, 1749, in Castañeda, *op. cit.*, III, 124.

encountered formidable obstacles. To the difficulties common to all the missions there was added in this case the almost constant harassment from the Apaches. But the peculiarly evil genius that haunted this latest undertaking of the Querétaro friars was a combination of a hostile governor, Jacinto de Barrios y Jáuergui, who assumed office in December, 1750, and Captain Felipe de Rábago y Terán, commander of the San Xavier Presidio, who took charge of his post a year later. From that time on to the end of their brief history these missions knew little peace. There is no need to recount the dismal catalog of annoyances and frustrations which the friars suffered at the hands of Barrios, or the abuses to which they were submitted by Rábago's arbitrary conduct and overbearing manner. Suffice it to say, the latter's administrative deficiencies were capped by his liaison with the wife of Juan José Ceballos, one of the men he had recruited for the presidio while in San Antonio. On Christmas eve of 1751 the outraged husband managed to escape the eye of the presidio guards and to take refuge in the chapel of Mission Candelaria, only to have Rábago ride in to the chapel on his horse the following morning, seize Ceballos, and take him back to the presidio. The friars were naturally grieved at this violation of the right of sanctuary, and when Rábago showed no signs of repentance either for this or any of his other scandalous actions Fray Miguel Pinilla, the chaplain of the presidio, excommunicated the commander and his garrison on February 19, 1752. The decree was read to the astounded soldiers by Fray José Ganzábal, and it had a sufficiently sobering effect that within ten days they sued for pardon and the ban was lifted on March 1.

But the ecclesiastical censure did not change Rábago's ways, and two months later he was the cause of a new crisis. Two of the Cocos Indians at Mission Candelaria went to the presidio on May 1 with their bows and arrows and were subjected to a severe beating by the commander who had forbidden the natives to enter the presidio with arms. The injured redmen aroused the ire of their fellow tribesmen and that night the entire group fled from the mission and disappeared. But the worst of the tragic situation was yet to come. Ceballos, the wronged husband of Rábago's mistress, had meanwhile come to live with the friars at Candelaria. On the night of May 11, 1752, they were taking their meal near an open doorway because of the warmth of the evening. Suddenly a shot rang out and immediately thereafter a second one found its way through the doorway and struck Ceballos who fell to the floor. While Father Miguel bent to the dying man his confrère, Fray Ganzábal, went to the door with a lighted candle to try to detect the culprit, only to have his heart pierced with an arrow from the darkness beyond.

During the investigation that followed the murders a Sayopin Indian by the name of Andrés was apprehended and confessed to having killed Father Ganzábal after reaching the mission in the company of four soldiers from the presidio who, he said, were intent on doing away with Ceballos and the friars. Rábago's attempt to throw the blame on the Cocos, who had fled from Candelaria ten days before the crime, was not successful, for as the friars pointed out, these Indians never used guns. Although the affair contributed to Rábago's removal from office in the spring of 1753, conditions did not greatly improve, for there was not enough really viable material left at San Xavier to enable the missions to get a fresh start. Severe drought was followed by excessive rains which, in turn, bred malignant fevers that took a heavy toll at both the presidio and the missions. Under conditions of this kind it was not surprising that sentiment should have grown stronger for abandonment of the entire project and for removal to a healthier and more hopeful location.

In August, 1754, there arrived at San Xavier an official investigator in the person of the commander of the Presidio del Sacramento, Captain Pedro Rábago y Terán, who was as able and conscientious a servant of the crown as his nephew had been the reverse. After some weeks of firsthand observation Rábago recommended removal to the viceroy, but due to contradictory recommendations reaching Mexico City the final decision was delayed. Meanwhile matters grew so desperate at San Xavier that both the soldiers and the missionaries pleaded with Rábago to permit them to be gone. Lacking authority to give an order of this kind, he finally yielded to their pleas to the extent of taking responsibility for an *ad interim* removal until the viceroy could be heard from. Thus by August, 1755, the San Xavier colony was assembled on the San Marcos River about midway between San Antonio and its original location. Here it remained for about a year and then moved again to the Guadalupe River near the present town of New Braunfels where, as Pedro Rábago had suggested in his report of September, 1754, the missionaries and soldiers might be employed in the solution of a problem that was preoccupying the Spaniards very much of late, namely, that of the Apache Indians.

For years the Spanish settlements in New Mexico and Texas had suffered from the depredations of the Apache warriors, and yet the crown officials had not formulated any clear and decisive plan as to how the menace should be met. Many would doubtless have favored a war of extermination if the whites had had the strength, but lacking that the jagged course continued with periodic raids from the Indians and haphazard counterattacks by the Spaniards. It was again a veteran missionary who was the first to suggest a radical change in official thinking about the Apaches. Shortly before he died Fray Francisco Hidalgo in 1725 strongly advocated the adoption of a policy of conciliation in the belief that these natives might be won for the Church. After Hidalgo's death one heard little more of this approach until the early 1740's when Fray Benito Fernández de Santa Anna championed the Apache as suitable material for evangelization. Fray Benito's personal efforts to bring them around, however, were in no way encouraging, and had it not been for a crisis that had come upon the Apaches from another source they would in all likelihood have shown no change of heart. They had earlier been driven out of New Mexico by the Comanches, a tribe of superb horsemen who were now pressing them hard for possession of the south plains of Texas. These invaders had so terrified the Apaches that the latter were brought to making a bid for peace with the Spaniards in the hope of gaining their protection and support. With that in mind they sent delegates to San Antonio in November, 1749, and after a series of conferences there took place the strange ceremony of burying a hatchet and a live horse to signify the peace that the Apache now pledged themselves to observe.

During the next few years the Indians' conduct was such as to inspire confidence with the peace carefully kept and the trade relations maintained. Gradually the feasibility of founding missions among these people began to impress itself more strongly on the minds of the Spaniards. At this point a 'lord bountiful' entered the picture in the person of Don Pedro Romero de Terreros, a rich cousin of Fray Alonso Giraldo de Terreros, who had been one of the foremost advocates among the friars for an Apache mission. Don Pedro's generous offer to pay all expenses for three years hastened matters and it served, too, to unify the diverse plans that the Spaniards had been pursuing for some time in regard to the Apache. In the end the idea that had originally grown out of the explorations of the Apache country in 1753 by Lieutenant Juan Galván and later by Pedro Rábago and others, and that by 1756 had won the viceroy's approval, was merged with that of Fray Alonso and his wealthy cousin; it was decided to locate a presidio and mission on the San Sabá River about 125 miles to the northwest of San Antonio.

Those Franciscans who had long been urging a more positive approach toward the Apaches were in high spirits at the prospect of finally bringing these redmen who had been the cause of so much of their grief within the pale of Christianity. The spiritual aspect of the undertaking was made the joint responsibility of the missionary colleges of Querétaro and of San Fernando in Mexico City, while Colonel Diego Ortiz Parrilla, who from the outset was sceptical of the Apaches' sincerity, was placed in charge of the presidio and its garrison. By April, 1757, the company had arrived near present Menard, Texas, where they set up the Mission of San Sabá and the Presidio of San Luis de las Amarillas. But every attempt to get the Indians to congregate so that their religious instruction and the mission tasks might begin was unavailing. Just when it seemed that something might be accomplished the Apaches would ride off again to the buffalo hunt and leave the friars for weeks at a time with little to do but pray and try to smother their growing anxiety. In the end the San Fernando missionaries proved to have the greater patience, for the Querétaro men became convinced that the situation was hopeless and withdrew. Their departure left the three friars from Mexico City with a guard of four or five soldiers, eight or ten faithful Tlascalteca Indian families, and a few native servants at the mission, while at the presidio there were from 300 to 400 Spaniards of whom 237 were women and children.

As the months passed and the Apaches continued their stubborn resistance to conversion there was an increase of tension with the insistent rumors of a coming attack. On March 16, 1758, the rumors were made all too real as the Comanches suddenly fell upon the mission, and Fathers Alonso and José Santiesteban were both killed, along with eight Spaniards, and the mission was looted and burned. The surviving missionary, Fray Miguel Molina, managed after a harrowing experience to escape with several others to the presidio. Conscious that the countryside was alive with Comanches, the garrison at San Luis de las Amarillas was frozen with fear and even the runners who got through to San Antonio were not successful in rounding up a relief force so terrified were all the Spanish settlements of the Comanches. The Spaniards had to endure a long siege, therefore, before the threat of the Comanches wore off. When word of the disaster reached the viceroy he informed the wealthy patron of San Sabá, and it was a tribute to Romero de Terreros' deep faith and generosity that he should have offered to finance a new group of missionaries and to pay for the rebuilding of the mission. The viceroy's appeal for more friars also met with success and in August, 1758, the San Fernando superior agreed to send two more men to replace the fallen heroes at San Sabá. It is interesting to note that the two whom he designated were Junípero Serra and Juan Palóu; had not the plans been changed, therefore, San Sabá would have deprived the California missions of both their famous founder and their first historian.

The subsequent history of the San Sabá missions was a checkered one. Their re-establishment at the site of the massacre of 1758 was a dubious move at best and it was not long before the leaders were casting about for a more favorable location. But before action could be taken the Apaches launched an attack in March, 1759, that proved how little their word could be trusted. Angered at this treachery, Colonel Parrilla determined upon a punitive expedition into the northern territory of the Apache, and for this purpose he gathered a force of 360 presidial soldiers and volunteers with 176 Indian allies and over 1,500 horses and mules along with ample provisions. The Spaniards' high hopes were quickly dashed, however, when the Indians administered a humiliating defeat on Parrilla's men in October, 1759. Just about this time Felipe Rábago y Terán was cleared of all guilt for the murders in east Texas seven years before and was restored to his command and now replaced Rábago at San Sabá. With the aid of Fray Diego Jiménez the new commander—without authorization from the viceroy—proceeded to move the presidio and missions southward about 100 miles to the Nueces River in a valley generally known as 'El Canón.' Here the Missions of San Lorenzo and Nuestra Señora de la Candelaria were opened early in 1762, and had the chiefs of the approximately 800 Apaches whom these missions were intended to serve given heed to the advice of the friars there might have been a fair chance of success in this region. But the redmen insisted upon trying to avenge themselves on the Comanches by forays into their territory with the result that they provoked a series of retaliatory attacks that began in 1764 and continued for the next three years which largely dissipated the hope of any lasting success in 'El Canón.' Rábago in the meantime grew discouraged and when his request to abandon the presidio went unanswered he took it upon himself to withdraw the troops in June, 1768, leaving the missions in a more exposed position than ever before.

By reason of the repeated reverses and misfortunes that overtook the Texas missions, such as those of San Sabá, many have concluded that the propagation of the Catholic faith in that remote colonial province was largely a lost cause. That there were, indeed, numerous failures is altogether true. Yet a closer examination of the results attained reveals that the missions in Texas had, too, a considerable measure of success. From time to time the good that these foundations were able to accomplish was set forth in detail in reports drawn up by the friars as, for example, that covering the missions of the San Antonio neighborhood which was made in response to the order of October, 1761, issued by the Commissary General of Missions in New Spain. Acting upon the directive of their superior, Fray Mariano Francisco de los Dolores and his confrères stationed in and around San Antonio completed by March, 1762, an account that furnished a full picture of these foundations. During the period of forty or more years since the establishment of the five missions they had witnessed the baptism of 5,115 Indians, and the friars had performed 751 marriages and given Christian burial to 3,322 of the natives. For these services the missionaries had after 1760 the manual of instructions for administering the sacraments in the language of the most commonly used dialect of the redmen, the work of Fray Bartolomé García which he finished during his time at the Mission of San Francisco de la Espada. The number of Indians living in the mission pueblos had been in a state of almost constant flux and by the late eighteenth century it had undergone a serious decline; yet at the time of the report in question there were still 1,242 Indians in residence who represented twenty-three different nations and tribes. When, therefore, one remembers that it was for the purpose of saving souls and bringing them into the Catholic Church that the Franciscans had originally come to Texas the over-all results as summarized in 1762 made it evident that the friars had not failed in their objective.

Moreover, besides the spiritual aspects of the natives' lives there was likewise their material welfare in which there was clear evidence of advancement under the missionary regime. Whereas the Indians had been largely nomadic and in possession of few if any of the arts of civilization when the friars first came on the scene, it was a measure of the latter's success in training these crude people that the report of 1762 should have noted nearly 10,000 bushels of corn and over 700 bushels of beans in the mission granaries, products of the Indians' labor which they had planted and raised under Franciscan tutelage. And on their surrounding *rancherías* the redmen had 5,487 head of cattle, 17,000 sheep and goats, over 600 saddle horses, almost 1,000 breeding mares, more than 100 donkeys and almost as many mules. In addition sixteen looms were in operation for weaving the wool and cotton goods which the Indians had either gathered from their sheep or raised in their fields, and there was even a tailor shop for the manufacture, sale, and repair of clothes.

In fact, life had generally progressed better in the missions than it had in the white settlements of Texas. In the latter the Catholic faith met with drawbacks of another kind than those experienced among the redmen, and when the Franciscan Bishop of Guadalajara, Francisco de San Buenaventura Martínez de Tejada, concluded his visitation of these settlements and reported to the viceroy in December, 1759, he did not conceal his disappointment with the wretched conditions that he had observed in some of these Texas towns. Almost a half century later the episcopal visitation of Primo Feliciano Marin de Porras, Bishop of Nuevo León, to San Antonio, La Bahía, Nacogdoches, and other Spanish centers did not uncover in 1805–1806 conditions that were essentially different from those described by Tejada in 1759. The territory was altogether too large to be governed – either by Church or State – in an efficient manner, a factor that constituted a major obstacle well into the nineteenth century. At the time that Louisiana was ceded to Spain in 1763, a change which altered considerably Spanish policy toward Texas, there were twenty-one missions and four *visitas*, or stations without a resident missionary, as well as seven formal presidios and an additional military post. But these widely separated settlements, together with the half dozen towns, were a feeble instrument with which to enforce the Spanish authority over so immense a territory. The Texas missions and presidios were costing the King of Spain over 100,000 *pesos* a year to support without any return to the royal treasury by way of profit from these outposts of empire. Yet fears of French and English aggression, and of illicit trade and military alliances between the Texas Indians and these rival powers, was deemed sufficient warrant for the expenditures needed to maintain the friars and their military protectors.

With Spain's entrance into the Seven Years' War, and the treaties that ended that conflict, however, there ensued major changes in both the ecclesiastical and the civil-military life of the province. Although defeated in the war and compelled to cede Florida to Great Britain in order to recover Cuba, Spain secured Louisiana from France in the peace settlements of 1763. With that action Texas, as its missionary historian has expressed it, "had ceased to be a bulwark against foreign aggression and had automatically become an interior province."[6] During the reorganization that followed there eventually emerged for the governance of New Spain the so-called 'new regulations' of September, 1772, by which the presidios were reduced in number and the troops concentrated in a few strategic places.

The time was now at hand, too, for a decision that would settle the fate of the troublesome area of east Texas. Between Charles III's demand for the occupation of both Louisiana and Alta California—which would require a heavy outlay of both manpower and money—and the continuance of the Comanche attacks in the east, there was good reason why the crown should have ordered the abandonment of a remote region that was no longer needed as a bastion against the French. Instructions to this effect were issued in March, 1773, and by the late summer the four missions of the Zacatecas friars in east Texas had been suppressed, the presidio destroyed, and the governor's residence moved to San Antonio. A number of Spanish families that had made their homes in and about these eastern settlements were reluctant to leave, however, and after receiving an indirect permission from Mexico City they established a new settlement about midway between San Antonio and Natchitoches in Louisiana which they called Pilar de Bucareli. For the first few years all seemed to go well and friendly relations were maintained with the neighboring Indians. But in 1778 the Comanches began to assail the Spaniards' Indian allies and soon Bucareli was in sore straits with its parish priest, José Francisco Mariano

[6] *Ibid.*, IV, 204.

de la Garza, reporting conditions of starvation by January, 1779. Encouraged by the hope of protection from the friendly Tejas tribesmen who lived near Margil's old mission of Nacogdoches, a number of the settlers fled there early in 1779. Thus at the site of a mission that had maintained a precarious existence since 1716 this little band of about 350 Spaniards established at Nacogdoches what proved to be an important outpost on Texas' eastern frontier and a center of Spanish-Indian trade up to the time of the coming of the first Anglo-Americans.

The year 1772 was also an eventful one for the missions. Ever since their advent to Texas the Querétaro friars had been restive and unhappy over the burden they had been compelled to assume for the material welfare and protection of their native converts. Had the civil and military men done their duty the Franciscans would not only have been able to concentrate on the spiritual aspects of their assignment but they would also have escaped much of the criticism of their fellow whites who frequently charged them with being more interested in enriching themselves from the Indians' labors than in saving their souls. Actually, the avarice and ambition practiced against the natives forced the missionaries to oppose what has been described as "the wanton destruction of the mission herds, the encroachment upon the cultivated fields of the neophytes, and the unscrupulous dealings of the neighboring settlers."[7] As a consequence the Franciscans incurred the resentment of their own countrymen, and it was against a background of this kind that Fray Mariano de los Dolores made a formal offer in February, 1769, to resign the temporal administration of Querétaro's six missions. A factor that strengthened their resolve to be quit of Texas was the effect upon their own missionary college of Charles III's drastic order of 1767 expelling the Jesuits from his dominions. Querétaro was asked to assume responsibility for Jesuit missions of Pimería Alta and the college was hard pressed to find sufficient men to fill all the vacancies. In spite of opposition from civil authorities anxious to preserve the status quo, the viceroy accepted the Querétaro proposal and in July, 1772, he issued a decree transferring their Texas missions to their fellow religious of the college of Zacatecas and of the Province of Guadalajara, a measure that was carried out early in 1773.

Another step in the general direction of closing out the missionary regime in Texas came about as a result of the abandonment of the

[7] *Ibid.*, IV, 259.

settlements in the eastern part of the province. The *Adaesanos*, as the displaced Spaniards from Los Adaes were called, had sacrificed their homes at the order of the king only to find themselves with little or no prospect of making a living in the San Antonio region. Their plight suggested to the civil officials the possibility of settling some of these refugees on lands belonging to the Mission of San Antonio de Valero which was now largely depopulated because the Indians had become Catholics and had attained sufficient stability to be left on their own. In other words, the mission had fulfilled the object for which it had been founded. When, therefore, Fray Pedro Ramírez de Arellano, the superior, was approached in March, 1778, by Governor Domingo Cabello he stated that he would be glad to assist the *Adaesanos* by letting them take up lands on a temporary basis. But this the refugees refused to do, and ultimately a plan was worked out by the government whereby the mission would be secularized for the refugees' use and at the same time full justice would be done to the Indians' land claims, a plan which received the royal assent in May, 1782. Although the secularization of Valero did not take place at this time, this first serious proposal for the secularization of a Texas mission was a foreshadowing of the approaching end of the age of the missions.

By the 1780's the strength of the old order had been pretty well spent among the Zacatecas friars as well, and in January, 1780, the governing council of their college asked the Commandant General of the Interior Provinces, Teodoro Caballero de Croix, to relieve them of all temporal administration of the missions as being unsuited to their sacred calling. It had only been because the missionaries had recognized that the Indians were quite incapable of initiating themselves into the customs and manners of the white man's civilization that they had assumed charge of their temporal interests in the first place. And in this, surely, they had been right, a fact that was proven by the painfully slow pace with which the friars were able to bring the natives to a point where they could manage their own affairs as members of a civilized community, and the speed with which many of these Indians reverted to their primitive ways once the guiding hand of the friar was removed. Now that a considerable number of the neophytes had reached a measure of stability, however, the Zacatecas Franciscans felt no desire to continue as managers of farms, supervisors of herds of cattle and sheep, and overseers of the weaving industry of the

Indians. Yet in making their proposal to withdraw they were careful, as was likewise true of their Querétaro brethren, to lay down specific and detailed directions in an effort to safeguard the redmen's interests by such means as an equitable distribution of the common property. All they asked to retain for themselves were the churches, the priests' residences, and the supplies and furnishings necessary for the conduct of divine services. And since, as has been mentioned, the missions had been a severe drain on the royal treasury, it was to be expected that the crown's representatives in New Spain would eagerly seize on proposals of this kind in the hope that they might help in reducing the costs of the viceregal government.

In the end the actual secularization of the Texas missions came about as the result of a number of converging policies in both Church and State. In the San Antonio area, for example, it was not only the Valero mission that had declined in Indian population; the same was true of the other four missions which were suffering from a lack of active hands to maintain them in a prosperous condition. At this point a new commissary and prefect of the Zacatecas missions was elected in 1790 in the person of Fray Manuel de Silva. Not only was he aware of the problem, but for some time he had been hoping to see a new mission field opened up by the friars of his college for the coastal Indian tribes who, he believed, were promising candidates for conversion. After a tour of inspection of the northern missions de Silva was prepared by March, 1792, to make definite proposals. He suggested that San Antonio de Valero be secularized completely and that the four remaining missions in that region be reduced to two. In this way friars could be freed for the projected mission on the coast without the need of bringing others up from Mexico. Fray Manuel's idea met with the hearty approval of Governor Manuel Muñoz and in April, 1793, a decree was issued for the secularization of San Antonio de Valero. This old mission set the pattern and Muñoz lost little time in proceeding to the others, for a year later, on April 10, 1794, the remaining San Antonio foundations were secularized, while those of the La Bahía group were given a further lease on life when the governor found that their Indians were as yet quite unready for an independent status.

The thinking of the Spaniards was at this time strongly colored by revolutionary France's declaration of war upon their country in February, 1793. They naturally feared for their American possessions, and especially for the sprawling colony of Louisiana which had been taken over from France only thirty years before and where there still were many colonists whose sympathies lay with their former masters. Madrid and Mexico City were intent, therefore, that a stronger link be forged between Louisiana and Texas so that the former might be defended in case of an attack from the French. It was a policy that fitted very well into Father de Silva's plans to bring the coastal Indians like the Karankawas and Jaranames into the Christian fold. The result was that in February, 1793, the Zacatecas friars, with the active assistance of the civil and military authorities, founded in the vicinity of Matagorda Bay the Mission of Nuestra Señora del Refugio, the last to be established in Texas under the Spanish auspices. In January, 1795, it was moved to a spot near the present town of Refugio where, it was hoped, a healthier climate might overcome the illness with which the whites had been plagued at the original location.

By the time that the friars had settled down at Refugio, however, events were moving so fast on both sides of the Atlantic that there was little prospect of a prolonged and peaceful period of evangelization of the natives either at Refugio or elsewhere. The Americans, whose independence had been recognized by Great Britain twelve years before, were now moving south and west in considerable numbers and they had begun to be active along the frontier. The mysterious goings and comings of adventurers like Philip Nolan, a protege of General James Wilkinson, were a source of worry to the Spaniards as early as 1791, and they continued to give concern even after Nolan was killed a decade later in a fight with Spanish troops. If this sort of activity augured ill for the peace of the frontier it became still more uncertain when Spain was compelled in 1801 to cede Louisiana to Bonaparte who, in turn, two years later suddenly sold it to the United States. Confronted after 1803 by the Americans as next door neighbors, the Spanish regime in Texas tried valiantly to keep them at bay by legal restrictions on immigration. But the frontier was too long and the manpower too meager to maintain an effective watch with the result that as early as January, 1804, sixty-eight foreigners were reported in Nacogdoches, a group that included Frenchmen, English, Irish, and Americans. Within a few years, in fact, the eastern part of Texas was so overrun by those from outside that the Spaniards were hopelessly outnumbered.

But the American infiltration was not the only cause for loosening Spain's hold upon Texas. The white population had always been scarce, and the 2,819 whites of 1783 did not noticeably increase, for as late as August, 1810, Governor Manuel Maria Salcedo reported a total of only 4,155 whites in the province of whom 1,033 belonged to the military contingents. And there were at this time but 343 Indians left in the six missions that were still operating, a fact which lent plausibility to Salcedo's view that they should be abolished as an outmoded institution. Moreover, numerous tribes were still swarming over the plains, and even San Antonio was not immune from attack by the red marauders.

It was into a situation such as this that there came the exciting news of Mexico's revolt from Spain and the declaration of an independent republic. By October, 1810, the revolt had moved into the northern provinces and as a consequence Texas lost more of its white population who left out of fear and uncertainty concerning the future. The few remaining missionaries held on for a time, but it was not long before they, too, gave up and departed. During the next few decades the Texas Church declined to a point where it all but disappeared, and when Father John Timon, C.M., who was sent to investigate conditions in the new Republic of Texas, reached there in December, 1838, there were but two priests of Mexican origin left in the entire region, and their manner of life was more a source of scandal than of spiritual uplift to the inhabitants. A new start was clearly called for. After the Holy See had had time to acquaint itself with matters a vicariate apostolic was erected for Texas in April, 1841, and a French-born Vincentian confrère of Timon's, Jean Marie Odin, was consecrated in March, 1842, and became the first resident bishop. The Church had thus received a formal organization three years in advance of the annexation of the young republic to the United States.

CHAPTER FIVE

CALIFORNIA

Of all the states of the American Union upon whose early history Spain left an imprint it is that of California, perhaps, that is best known because of the charm and fascination that have surrounded its missions. In little more than a half century after 1769 the Franciscan friars established twenty-one of these foundations between San Diego and San Francisco Solano. Yet California was very much a late comer to Spain's North American empire, so late, in fact, that by the time the first permanent settlements were made along its coast Spanish power in Florida had for some years been extinguished and in Texas, New Mexico, and Arizona it had undergone a decline. The reason for the Spaniard's tardiness in settling Upper California was due in part to their preoccupation elsewhere, as well as to the fact that by the middle of the eighteenth century, when once more it began to occupy their attention, ambitious new ventures of this kind came with increasing difficulty to a nation now weakened by recurrent wars and outdistanced by its European rivals. The Spaniards had, of course, been in Lower (Baja) California for over seventy years where the Jesuits had thirteen missions by 1767, the year that they were expelled from the peninsula.

Spain had, needless to say, long known about Upper California, for as early as 1542 – the year that Coronado reached Kansas – Juan Rodríguez de Cabrillo sailed up the coast and the next year his lieutenant, Bartolomé Ferrelo, got as far north as Oregon. That their possession of those territories, however, was by no means an established fact was illustrated in 1579 by Francis Drake who cruised along the coast of

California and claimed the region for Elizabeth I. But Drake sailed off across the Pacific and the Spaniards' uneasiness was again allayed. During the years that followed they periodically explored along the coast, but not until 1602 was a really major effort made to establish a permanent base in California. In the spring of that year a little fleet of three ships containing about 200 men under the command of Sebastiáno Vizcaíno sought to establish a port for the Philippine trade vessels somewhere on the coast of California. It was on this occasion that the name of Monterey, after the viceroy in Mexico City, was given to the bay, and several Carmelite friars who had accompanied the expedition said Mass at the site and named the river that flowed into the bay the Río de Carmelo after their religious order. With a new viceroy, however, there came a change of plans and Vizcaíno's expedition led to no enduring results. There then ensued a long interval of over 160 years during which the Spaniards were content to leave Upper California to the wild and indolent natives who roamed its vast expanse. Only the projection of an entirely new element into the rivalry for that distant coastline served to awaken Charles III's government to order the permanent occupation of California.

It was fear of Russia—and its growing friendliness with England, a major enemy—that in the end proved to be a greater spur to activity in Upper California than the maneuvering of Spain's traditional foes. Beginning about 1725 there took place a series of stupendous explorations by Vitus Bering, and by the early 1740's the Russians were reaching down the coast from Alaska in a way that aroused fears in Madrid. The order was issued, therefore, in 1768 to occupy the territory in the king's name, and a resolute commander was at hand in the visitor-general, José de Gálvez, to see to it that the will of the royal government was set in motion. The plan was to establish garrisons at San Diego and Monterey and to establish missions under the protection of these troops for the conversion of the natives. For the military side of the enterprise Gálvez chose Don Gaspar de Portolá, and for the missionary aspect of the future settlements he encountered in Lower California the man he wanted in Fray Junípero Serra, a Franciscan friar, who for the previous six months had been superior there of his order's missions. Serra was then in his fifty-sixth year and had already spent over twenty years on the missions in the new world, traveling upwards of 7,000 miles throughout the Viceroyalty of New Spain. Here, then, was a seasoned missionary who not only matched Gálvez in enthusiasm and drive but who likewise was possessed of a profound religious sense that was equal to any hardship that might arise in this new campaign to spread the faith of Christ among the native pagans.

Governor de Gálvez and Fray Junípero worked at top speed and by the early days of 1769 the first contingent was ready to depart by sea while others were preparing for the overland journey. The *San Antonio* reached San Diego on April 11 with two Franciscans on board, and between that date and July 1 the other friars and soldiers arrived either by land or sea. Serra traveled overland with Portolá and the way was at times so rough that it put a frightful strain on the chronic injury that he had been carrying in his leg for twenty years. At one point his suffering was so acute that Portolá suggested that he turn back. The true measure of the friar's character was revealed when he replied, "Even though I should die on the trail, I shall not turn back. They can bury me wherever they wish and I shall gladly be left among the pagans, if it be the will of God."[1] With this man in command of the mission enterprise during the next quarter century one can understand why the Franciscans showed the progress they did!

At length the full company was assembled and on July 16 there was held the ceremony of erecting the first mission to which was given the name of San Diego. Portolá now set out with sixty-five of his men to take formal possession of Monterey while forty some Spaniards remained behind, including three friars who spent their time trying to figure out the best approach to the neighboring Indians and providing religious services for the Spaniards. As it turned out Portolá's party missed Monterey and got as far north as the present San Francisco when the provisions running short, the command was given to return south and they trudged back into San Diego late in January, 1770, after their long and strenuous march.

In the meantime their countrymen had undergone their own trials at the hands of hostile Indians around San Diego, and when Portolá announced that if relief were not forthcoming by the end of March the entire enterprise would be abandoned, there were probably few who strongly dissented from his view. But the commander had not reckoned with Serra. The latter was determined to exhaust every possibility before he would admit defeat and he, therefore, enlisted his men to join

[1] Geiger, *Serra*, I, 220.

him in a novena to Saint Joseph for relief to the hard pressed colony. Whether or not it was in response to the friars' petitions we do not know, but in any case on March 19, the feast day of Saint Joseph, the *San Antonio* sailed into port with new recruits and fresh provisions. Serra was convinced that Saint Joseph had directly intervened to save the day, the entire company was filled with joy, and with this no more was heard about abandoning California.

Strengthened by the reinforcements, Portolá now decided upon a second try for Monterey and a few weeks later they set off with Serra this time in the company. A more watchful eye was now kept out for the intended goal and Monterey Bay was not passed by. Formal possession of the site was taken in the name of the King of Spain, and on June 3 the humble little chapel was dedicated to Saint Charles Borromeo to bring into existence California's second mission. It was apparent, however, that if this vast land and its crude inhabitants were to be made subject to Spanish rule and the Catholic faith more men would be needed. With that in mind Serra appealed to the authorities of the College of San Fernando in Mexico City, the official sponsor of the California missions, and by April, 1771, ten more Franciscans appeared at Monterey and put themselves at the disposal of Fray Junípero. He could now proceed to implement his plans for future foundations with something approaching the pace dictated by his ardor and zeal, and it was not long before these new recruits found their place in Serra's schemes for the spiritual conquest of California's native tribes.

Fortunately, Junípero Serra's first year at San Diego, during which he did not succeed in winning a single Indian to the Christian faith, was not an accurate gauge of future developments. In fact, once the Franciscans got fully underway their success attracted the attention of others and their fellow friars, the Dominicans, were soon seeking to enter Upper California. It was wisely decided, however, that the Californias should be divided between the two mendicant orders with the Dominicans taking full charge of Lower California and the Franciscans being assigned complete responsibility for Upper California, an agreement to that effect being signed in April, 1772. Meanwhile Serra and his confrères were busy reaching out to the tribes whose habitat lay to the north of San Diego. They lost no more time than was necessary and by the date that Serra left on a business trip to Mexico in September, 1772, there were already five missions: San Diego (1769), San

Carlos Borromeo (1770), San Antonio (July 14, 1771), San Gabriel (September 8, 1771), and on the way south in 1772 the mission president founded the fifth mission, San Luís Obispo (September 1). He had early determined upon San Carlos as his headquarters, and shrewd fellow that he was, he moved the mission, on the pretext of lack of water and good soil, from the original site at Monterey to the valley of the Río Carmelo a few miles away. In reality Serra's concern was more to avoid contamination of his neophytes by the Spanish soldiers than worry over the water supply. True, there was need of the white man to demonstrate to the Indians a permanent agricultural civilization and to protect them and the friars from the pagan tribes, but the example which they often gave was such as to scandalize the Indians under instruction and thus to make the work of evangelization all the more difficult.[2]

[2] Serra's biographer gives the following summary of the mission superior's complaints against the commanders and their troops, or more particularly against the latter:

> Though the guard was strengthened, satisfactory conditions did not prevail at the mission [the time was May, 1773, in Serra's report to the viceroy]. Serra described the soldiers with their corporal as an unfortunate group. The soldiers were idle and refused to work; they became bored and discontented because of dissatisfaction with Fages [the military commander]; they frequently fought with each other even to the point of the dagger; they were impudent toward the missionaries. At the same time they were commanded by a "useless corporal" whom they neither respected nor obeyed. As if the unfortunate incident of the Indian chief had not been sad enough, soldiers in companies of six or more would leave the mission in the morning, with or without the permission of the corporal, and go to distant rancherías where they lassoed Indian women as they would cows or mules and seized them to dishonor them. When their men tried to defend the women, several were killed by musket fire. Serra states he received these facts from the missionaries in repeated complaints. The Indians themselves complained to the padres.
>
> The soldiers brought their immorality close to the mission. One of the missionaries caught a soldier *in flagranti* with an Indian man who had come to the mission. Young boys coming to the mission were likewise molested by the soldiers. Knowledge of these happenings caused Father [Pedro Benito] Cambón to become so ill that he had to take to his bed and, at the advice of the other padres, he retired to San Diego. [Antonio] Cruzado, [Antonio] Paterna, and [Angel] Somera preached on morality from the pulpit; they spoke to individual soldiers, they appealed to the corporal. The only answer the Fathers received from the corporal was: "If the pagans say that, let them prove it." Serra was informed by letter of these matters, which lasted about a year. How any conversions were effected under such circumstances is little short of a marvel. (*Ibid.*, I, 307–308).

In time a fixed pattern of separate establishments of this kind for the religious and military personnel emerged in Upper California as it had elsewhere. Ultimately four presidios were located at San Diego, Monterey, San Francisco, and Santa Barbara with a supposed contingent of 250 troops at each, although the full complement was rarely ever attained. In addition to these military posts which neighbored the missions there were three small self-governing Spanish towns at San José (1777), Los Angeles (1781), and Branciforte (1797) whose religious life was also in charge of the Franciscans, although the friars had no such authority over the white inhabitants as they had over the mission Indians. Moreover, these Spanish settlements never grew to any size. At one time there were high hopes for white colonization in California, especially after Captain Juan Bautista Anza – with Father Francisco Garcés as his guide – succeeded in 1774 in the difficult task of opening a land route from Arizona to California which, had it endured, would have offered a much cheaper and easier access to the coastal region than the voyage by sea. Anza, it is true, achieved further notable explorations in 1776, assisted by Father Pedro Font, as did likewise the Franciscans, Francisco Domínguez and Silvestre de Escalante, who explored as far as the Utah basin about the same time.

But an insurmountable obstacle to making Anza's route a permanent one had arisen in consequence of the revolt of the Yuma Indians. In July, 1781, they suddenly fell upon Fray Garcés, his three confrères, and a group of Spaniards consisting of about twenty families in the two recently built missions at the junction of the Colorado and Gila Rivers and most of the men were massacred, although the women and children were spared. And in spite of the fact that the Yumas were severely punished in the following year by Pedro Fages and his soldiers, this revolt proved to be the death knell for the land route to California. This was partly the explanation why the white population of California never reached any sizable proportions, there being only 970 in 1790 and not more than about 1,200 at the opening of the nineteenth century. The Spaniards' success in California, therefore, was confined almost exclusively to the Indians, and for that, of course, credit was owed to the friars.

In spite of the undoubted progress, Serra and his brethren had their share of troubles. There is general agreement that the Indians of the coastal area were culturally below those of New Mexico and Arizona, to say nothing of those of Mexico, and a recent writer has gone as far as to say that the California natives "were as primitive and backward as any in the western hemisphere."[3] Needless to say, this was one of the major causes for slowing down the work of the Franciscans. Yet Fray Junípero had many reasons for rejoicing. Three years after his coming to Upper California he told his friend, Fray Francisco Palóu, that the friars' consolation was the knowledge that as a consequence of their presence numerous souls were then in heaven from Monterey, San Diego, and San Antonio. True, they had been warned that the natives might turn on them at any time, and Serra did not deny that this might, indeed, prove to be the case, but as far as those of Monterey and San Antonio were concerned he maintained that "with each passing day they improve."[4] If all those Indians with whom they had come in contact were not as yet Christians it was due principally, in Serra's judgment, to the missionaries' ignorance of their languages and the natives' slowness in learning Spanish. As for himself, he had always felt that his own lack of facility in learning languages was, as he said, "because of my many sins." There was need for many more missionaries, surely, but as he told Palóu, those who elected these missions must anticipate hardships. "Those who come," he remarked, "should be provided with a good stock of patience and charity, and their stay will be one of delight to them. It will enable them to amass riches – a wealth of sufferings."[5]

Troubles there were aplenty, and among them the military commander who succeeded Portolá, Captain Pedro Fages, was the cause of much of the friars' grief. Fages alienated many of his own men by his arbitrary conduct, and he encroached upon the missionaries' province by taking the punishment for the Indians' small offences into his own hands, refused to remove dissolute soldiers from the mission guard, and even tampered with the Franciscans' mail. Since Serra was anxious, in any case, to learn the dispositions toward California of the new viceroy, Antonio Bucareli y Ursúa, and, too, to get more recruits from his Franciscan superiors, he decided to go to Mexico City in person where he could place before the viceregal government the differences between

[3] Kurt Baer, "California Indian Art," *The Americas*, XVI (July, 1959), 23.

[4] Serra to Palóu, Monterey, August 18, 1772, Antonine Tibesar, O.F.M. (Ed.), *Writings of Junípero Serra* (Washington, 1955), I, 267. Hereafter this work will be referred to as: Tibesar, *Writings*.

[5] *Ibid.*, I, 269.

himself and Fages. He set out by ship in the fall of 1772 and reached San Blas by boat without incident, and from that seaport he traveled the 600 miles to the capital where he arrived in the early days of 1773. Fray Junípero was at pains to give both the civil and ecclesiastical officials as full an account as he could of the California missions, detailing the grievances of the friars and outlining the pressing needs of the missions that must be met if they were to fulfill their high promise.

The five missions then had nineteen friars with a guard of six or seven soldiers at each place. As yet there were no mission pueblos for the Indians and the baptisms to date were less than 500 while the marriages had numbered only sixty-two. The reason, as Serra explained, was that the friars had used great caution lest they should admit to the sacraments those who were not yet fully instructed and, too, because to date there had not been sufficient food and clothing to keep great numbers of the natives at the missions. More ambitious agricultural projects, larger herds of live stock, and extensive irrigation were called for, and for this more men and money would be necessary.

It was a compliment to the little friar's skill in pleading his case that he won on practically all counts, and his biographer maintains that the most significant point of his victory was contained in the clause of Bucareli's decree which stated that "the government, control, and education of the baptized Indians should belong exclusively to the missionaries."[6] Moreover, the viceregal government ordered an increase in the number of troops with each mission to receive servants who would be paid from the royal treasury, the military commander was told to remove those guards who had become *persona non grata* to the missionaries, the latter's mail was to be forwarded separately, and the friars were to be given full charge of the missions which they were to manage as the father of a family. The increased expense which these improvements would entail was to be met from the income of the salt mines at San Blas, from the Pious Fund which had been taken over by the government from the expelled Jesuits,[7] and if these sources did

[6] Geiger, *Serra*, I, 383.

[7] The Pious Fund was begun in 1697 from sums of money given by devout persons to help finance the Jesuit missions in Lower California. In time it grew very large and by the end of the eighteenth century was yielding about $50,000 in annual income. When the Jesuits were expelled in 1767 it was taken over by the government and used to assist the missions of other religious orders. The

not yield sufficient revenue then the royal treasury would make up the difference. Morover, the missionaries were to receive an annual wage of $400. A way was likewise found to get the troublesome commandant out of California and in May, 1774, Fages was replaced by Captain Fernando Rivera y Moncada.

Further evidence of Fray Junípero's resourcefulness was his application to the Holy See, through his Mexico City superiors, for permission to confer the Sacrament of Confirmation, a faculty which was granted in 1774 by Pope Clement XIV for a period of ten years. During his lifetime Serra confirmed over 5,300 persons and his successor, Fermín Lasuén, was granted the same faculty and confirmed around 9,000 before the privilege lapsed. This faculty of confirming, which was normally granted only to bishops, was the occasion of dissension between Governor Felipe de Neve and Serra on the score of its having been employed without permission of the Spanish government, Neve going as far as to forbid its use until in 1781 an order came through from Mexico City instructing the governor to desist from interfering with Serra.

As in other areas of the Spanish colonial empire, the civil and ecclesiastical authorities were often at loggerheads in California over matters of this kind. Mention has already been made of the difficulty with Commandant Fages, and Governor de Neve's troubles with the friars were not confined to the question of confirmation. He likewise tried to insist that the Indians be organized on a pueblo or village basis, a policy to which the Franciscans were strongly opposed because they were convinced that the Indians were not yet capable of even the moderate self-government that this implied. Although the record shows numerous instances when the two groups co-operated for the advance of the interests of both Spain and the native peoples, there were likewise many charges on the part of the civil and military officials con-

Mexican republic claimed as successor to the Spanish regime the right to administer the fund, and in 1848 when the United States defeated Mexico and took California there ensued a series of lengthy legal disputes until finally the two governments agreed to submit the matter to the Permanent Court of International Arbitration at The Hague. In the first decision handed down by that tribunal in October, 1902, the sum of $1,420,682.67 was awarded in annuities for the years 1869–1902 and an annual sum of $43,050 in perpetuity. Mexico paid these sums up to and including 1913, but they ceased to pay thereafter and efforts to bring about further payments ended in failure. Cf. James Brown Scott (Ed.), *The Hague Court Reports* (New York, 1916), pp. 3–54.

cerning the friars' refusal to sell their mission produce to the presidios at government prices, their spiritual neglect of the presidios, and their trips to and from Mexico without permission.

In spite of these differences real progress was made in taming the fickle and irresponsible natives of the California coast. Before the death of Serra, which occurred at San Carlos Borromeo on August 28, 1784, he had personally founded nine missions and after he was gone twelve more were added before 1823 by his successors. At their peak these twenty-one missions witnessed around 30,000 Indians engaged in farming, weaving, raising live stock, and other profitable occupations which had been taught to them by the friars. Within each mission compound, which was normally a quadrilateral structure of about 600 feet in length, there was a church, a convent for the missionaries, a school, shops wherein to teach the various trades, and storehouses for the produce from the fields which for fifteen or twenty miles around were cultivated by the Indians under Franciscan supervision. One gets a clear impression of the California mission system from Serra's detailed reports. A good example is the final report he drew up on his beloved *San* Carlos de Monterey which he signed on July 1, 1784, less than two months before his death. Here, he stated, there had been 1,006 baptisms since the mission was opened in June, 1770, along with 936 confirmations, 259 marriages, and 356 Christian burials. At that time San Carlos possessed 500 head of cattle, 220 sheep and goats, 128 horses and mules, twenty-five pigs, and, as Serra put it, "One old ass that may be with foal." As for the natives' daily routine and the variety of work performed by them, the superior of the missions remarked:

> They pray twice daily with the priest in the church. More than one hundred twenty of them confess in Spanish and many who have died used to do it as well. The others confess as best they can. They work at all kinds of mission labor, such as farm hands, herdsmen, cowboys, shepherds, milkers, diggers, gardeners, carpenters, farmers, irrigators, reapers, blacksmiths, sacristans, and they do everything else that comes along for their corporal and spiritual welfare.[8]

In this way did the sons of St. Francis gradually effect the civilizing of thousands of California Indians in the sixty-five years between their coming in 1769 and the secularization of the missions in 1834. During

[8] "Junípero Serra Makes His Final Report on the Mission of San Carlos de Monterey, July 1, 1784," Ellis, *Documents*, p. 45.

that period in the immense territory stretching for more than 600 miles between San Diego and San Francisco Solano upwards of 100,000 natives had been baptized, of whom many were likewise taught by the friars how to earn their living. The number of Franciscans involved varied from year to year, and in 1805, the year in which they reached their greatest strength, there were forty-five in California of whom thirty-eight were regular missionaries. In the seventy-six years between the founding of San Diego and 1845, the year before the coming of the Americans in force, 146 Franciscans had given all or a portion of their mature lives to these missions of whom sixty-seven died at their posts and of these several deserve to be ranked as martyrs to the faith.

The principal objective of these religious was, of course, the Indians' spiritual welfare. But in the process of acquainting them with the Catholic religion they likewise introduced them to at least the rudimentary arts of civilized living. It was the friars who brought from Mexico the first horses, cattle, sheep, and swine that were to make the mission ranches so prosperous. And it was they who taught the neophytes how to weave cloth, to construct buildings and roads, to irrigate the fields, as well as other skills that added to their comfort and physical well being. Removed by more than a century from the mission era, one can still get a fairly vivid impression of the success attained by these institutions when he recalls that at the height of their prosperity there were in these twenty-one establishments over 230,000 head of cattle, 268,000 sheep, 8,300 goats, 3,400 swine, to say nothing of the 34,000 horses and 3,500 mules that served the friars and Indians to such good advantage in easing the burden of the heavier tasks. Moreover, the mission farms at one time were yielding around 125,000 bushels of grain a year along with rich returns from the orchards, gardens, and wine presses. In the light of these achievements – and their striking contrast to the treatment meted out to the redmen by the English colonists on the Atlantic Coast during the same period – it is not surprising that a leading authority on the history of early America in surveying the work done by the mission should have reached the conclusion that, "Its accomplishment challenges the result of any other system of control of dependent people developed in the field of modern colonization."[9]

But the life span of the colonial mission was all too brief for it to bring the simple Indians to civilized maturity. The chain of events set

[9] Priestly, *Coming of the White Man*, p. 127.

off in March, 1808, by the invasion of the Spanish peninsula by 100,000 French soldiers under the standard of the Emperor Napoleon was due in less than a generation to be felt in California and to lead to the ruin of the mission system. The political confusion that overtook Spain in these years is well known and needs no repetition here. Obviously the disruption of the internal life of the mother country could have only an adverse effect upon its overseas empire. Even before the end of the year 1808 rumblings of unrest were heard in New Spain, and soon there rose to political prominence the parish priest of Dolores, a town to the northwest of the capital, by the name of Miguel Gregorio Hidalgo y Costilla, who by 1810 had helped mightily to light the fires of revolutionary fervor. Although the break with the mother country was a decade or more in working itself out, by the summer of 1821 the uncertain situation had finally crystallized in favor of complete independence of Mexico from Spain. From that time on the friars in California, as those elsewhere in the former provinces of the Spanish Empire, had to deal with a bewildering variety and succession of rulers at Mexico City and the other capitals, many of whom were unfriendly to the Church's interests, especially in education, and some of whom were inspired in their hostility by Masonic ideals.

During this hectic period the instability of the central government was visited upon California as, for example, in the confiscation of the Pious Fund for the missions, the neglect to pay the presidios' soldiers who, in turn, borrowed heavily from the missions, the failure of ships to call regularly at the ports, and the menacing threat that outright secularization of the missions might come at any time. In fact, as early as September, 1813, a decree of secularization had been passed by the Spanish Cortes, but in the general turmoil of the period it had not been enforced. As for the Mexican government, it was so preoccupied with other matters that it did not get around to the secularization question until a decade or more after independence. Finally, however, in August, 1833, the Mexican Congress passed a law which secularized the missions, and on August 9 of the following year this law was formally promulgated at Monterey by Governor José Maria Echeandia.

For the most part the Franciscans were not opposed to the idea of secularization because they felt they had gone about as far as they could with the Indians of the missions, and they hoped, too, to go inland and build a new chain of missions for the less civilized natives. But they did remonstrate against the manner in which the Mexican officials set out to do the job, feeling that it entailed a grave injustice to the Indians who were the real owners of the mission properties and goods. Moreover, they were fully aware that most of their Indian wards were not ready for the mature and independent status that secularization implied, namely, complete freedom as members of regular canonical parishes which would be in charge of the secular clergy. That they were right was proven by the fact that as soon as the friars' supervision was relaxed many of the redmen took to the hills and by 1842 the Catholic Indians had been reduced from their once proud total to less than 5,000. Meanwhile the Indians' mission property in live stock and grain offered a tempting invitation to some politicians to enrich themselves and much of this wealth was stolen from the mission compounds. At the same time the Franciscans, who had been responsible for bringing the natives to this relatively high state of civilization, were in many cases either chased out or left to fend for themselves, and those who requested to remain to minister to their former neophytes were often compelled to endure ignominy and insult. The majority of the friars departed, however, when they were confronted with the demand that they take an oath of allegiance to the Mexican government of which as Spaniards they did not approve. The Church in California was, then, face to face with complete destruction and for a time there did not seem to be any way to avert it.

Yet amid the shifting political currents in Mexico City the politicians had not completely forgotten about the problem of ecclesiastical life in the far off province. The Mexican Congress finally got down to the business of discussing a bishopric for California, and after lengthy and somewhat awkward negotiations with the Holy See an agreement was reached. Pope Gregory XVI acceded to Mexico's request by erecting the Diocese of the Two Californias on April 27, 1840, and he approved the selection as first bishop of the Franciscan friar who had been superior in California, namely, the Mexican-born Francisco García Diego. The latter was an experienced missionary attached to the college in Zacatecas which in 1833 had assumed responsibility for the California missions from the College of San Fernando. The government promised to pay for the expenses of establishing the new see as well as to give the bishop an annual salary of $6,000. García Diego was consecrated in October, 1840, at the National Shrine of Guadalupe and in December, 1841, he arrived and took up his residence at Santa Barbara as California's first resident bishop. The prelate's efforts to build a seminary, cathedral, and bishop's house were greatly hampered, however, by the government's failure to live up to its pledge of financial assistance, and García Diego struggled on for four and half years more until his death in April, 1846, without having been able to accomplish any really lasting benefits for the Church.

But apart from Bishop García Diego's unhappy situation, California was now on the eve of radical changes that were destined to transform the entire course of development for the Catholic Church as well as for every other institution in the province. Two weeks after the bishop's death the United States and Mexico went to war and on July 7 Commodore John B. Sloat seized Monterey and proclaimed possession of California for the United States, and two days later Captain John B. Montgomery took San Francisco. With the signing of the peace treaty at Guadalupe Hidalgo in February, 1848, the regime of Spain and its daughter republic was ended and the future of California now belonged to the Americans. As for the Church, the uncertainty and disorder continued for another two years until a Spanish-born Dominican, Joseph S. Alemany, after nine years of missionary work in the United States, was consecrated in June, 1850, to be California's bishop. The area was already filling up rapidly with thousands attracted by the discovery of gold at Sutter's Fort in January, 1848, and three months after Alemany's consecration the old province of New Spain entered the American Union as a state on September 9. With the arrival of Bishop Alemany at San Francisco on December 6, 1850, therefore, the American chapter in California's Catholicism may be said to have begun.

With the passing of California and the Southwest to the United States there came to a close over three centuries' of Spanish activity along the southern borderlands of this country. Today there is little evidence to indicate the importance of Spain's influence in those areas other than the place names that one meets within the immense arc that stretches from St. Augustine in Florida to Sacramento in California. Yet these names tell of who first settled there and who brought to the region the arts of European civilization. If the thousands of native

Indians who once peopled the missions of the Franciscans and the Jesuits have disappeared, it was through no fault of the friars and the Black Robes, their first white masters. For as one of the leading authorities of the period has remarked, "the missions were a force which made for the preservation of the Indians, as opposed to their destruction, so characteristic of the Anglo-American frontier." [10]

It was the element of compassion for the Indian as a child of God that motivated the missionaries to forfeit every comfort – often their lives – for his welfare. Fired as they were by the conviction that the redman had a soul worth saving, it was that goal that inspired their extraordinary sacrifices, and that alone explains the dogged persistence with which these Spanish religious pushed on frequently in the face of almost insuperable odds and, indeed, at times of stark tragedy. With thousands of the natives they succeeded, and with still more thousands they failed. But the consolation of knowing that they had been the instrument of salvation for so many was reward enough. As Serra once told Palóu, "we all feel the weight of the vexations, hardships and contradictions we have to face; but none of us wishes, or intends to leave his mission. The fact is that, hardships or no hardships, there are many souls sent to heaven . . . ," [11] and for Serra and his confrères that was sufficient return. Such was the spirit that kept them at their posts when many men of equal strength, but with a less exalted ideal, would quickly have abandoned the dull and fickle Indians.

Aside from the instruction in the Catholic faith, which was their greatest gift to the redmen, the missionaries also helped to evolve a distinct style of architecture that is still in favor as especially well adapted to these regions. Moreover, it was these Spanish priests who first introduced domestic animals, plants, and grains, so much a part of civilized living, to the natives. When, therefore, the Americans began to arrive they found at least the rudiments of the kind of life that they had previously known. For some years to come the whites were still to endure severe trials at the hands of the warring tribes; but they were also to experience contact with many Indians whose memories of the Black Robes and the friars' training made them receptive to the new-

[10] Herbert E. Bolton, "The Mission as a Frontier Institution in the Spanish American Colonies," *American Historical Review*, XXIII (October, 1917), 61.

[11] Tibesar, *Writings*, I, 267.

comers in a way that would not otherwise have been true. By the 1840's when American immigration into these former provinces of New Spain swelled to the proportions of a major movement, the Catholic Church was only a feeble remnant of what it had been in the days of high missionary endeavor. But the light of faith had not entirely gone out, and in more than one community in-coming American Catholics were able to satisfy their religious obligations at the same locations where the missionaries to the Indians had once performed their difficult ministry. The age of the missions had passed, but with its passing there was transmitted to the new order the foundation stones of a structure upon which to build the civilization of another era.

PART TWO

THE FRENCH MISSIONS

CHAPTER SIX

MAINE

It had been one of Spain's distinct advantages that during the era of the new world exploration and early colonization a fundamental religious and political unity obtained at home. It was an advantage that France did not at the same time enjoy. From the outset of Martin Luther's revolt against the Catholic Church in 1517 that movement won active sympathy from many of the French nobility and the better educated and well to do middle class. The religious division within France which was thus foreshadowed even before John Calvin had in 1534 quit his homeland for the safer haven of Switzerland, was accelerated under the weak kings who followed Francis I, and during the entire second half of the sixteenth century a major share of the national energies was expended in what came to be called the religious wars. These conflicts between Catholics and Protestants were, indeed, religious in character, but they were also political, civil wars fought between parties headed by Catholic Guise and Protestant Huguenots with the crown as the supreme prize. The civil strife that engulfed France in these years saw little abatement until the triumph of Henry of Navarre in 1589 had ultimately led to the Edict of Nantes of April, 1598, a settlement that granted to the Huguenots equal political rights with the Catholics, although it did not secure them complete freedom of religious worship.

Given a background like this it was not to be expected that France would keep pace with Spain in the new world, even though the Florentine navigator, Giovanni da Verrazano, had as early as 1524 provided

Francis I with the basis for his claim to parts of North America, and the native Frenchman, Jacques Cartier, had followed up with extensive explorations between 1534 and 1542. As a result of what he learned of the new world and its inhabitants from Cartier, the King of France became temporarily enthusiastic about the idea of an empire beyond the seas. Two Indians whom Cartier had brought back from his original voyage served as a further incentive to the royal zeal for the conversion of the North American natives to the Catholic faith. In a new commission which Francis I issued early in 1540 to Cartier, therefore, the religious motive showed up rather strongly when the king spoke of the Indians who had been brought to France so that they might be instructed and taken back, as he said, "in company of a goodly number of our subjects of good will in order more easily to induce the other peoples of those lands to believe in our holy faith." This permanent colony envisioned by Francis I would advance the royal intention of doing something pleasing to God and, as it was termed, "to the satisfaction of his holy name, the augmentation of our Christian faith, and the growth of our mother the Holy Catholic Church of whom we are called and named the first son."[1] The economic and territorial considerations that had hitherto dominated the new world activities of the French were now joined by a religious motive which continued as a part of official policy until their major defeat and expulsion from the North American continent in 1763.

The lofty sentiments expressed in the commission to Cartier were not realized in the king's lifetime. Cartier did, indeed, cross the Atlantic for his third voyage in 1541, but the renewal of hostilities the next year between Francis I and the Emperor Charles V prevented the promised recruits and provisions from being sent and in April, 1542, Cartier abandoned this first French attempt at a colony in North America and sailed home. For the next twenty years nothing further was done. Then in 1562 one of the Huguenot leaders, Admiral Gaspard de Coligny, launched a scheme for checkmating Catholic Spain by way of a colony in Florida; but within three years, as we have seen, Fort Caroline on the St. John's River was destroyed by the Spaniards and the Huguenot colony dispersed. Not until sixty years after Cartier's

[1] Francis I to François de la Rocque, Seigneur de Roberval, January 15, 1540, in *Collection de Manuscrits contenant Lettres, Mémoires, et Autres Documents Historiques Relatifs a la Nouvelle France* (Quebec, 1883), I, 31.

final voyage, therefore, was a permanent colony planted by the French, and this time it was under the leadership of Samuel de Champlain, soldier, courtier, and enthusiastic Catholic, who acted as the agent of Pierre du Guast, Sieur de Monts, who was himself a Huguenot.

Before Champlain's colony had been firmly fixed at Quebec, however, a brief and ill starred venture had brought the first French priests to the new world at another location. The colonial interests of Monts were placed in 1603 in the hands of Jean de Biencourt, Sieur de Poutrincourt, who in the following year established a colony at Port Royal in Acadia or present day Nova Scotia. At the time France was still in the throes of bitter internal dissension over religion, and the Gallican party among the Catholics—which sought to limit papal authority within the kingdom—as well as the Huguenots were both arrayed against the growing influence of the Society of Jesus. In spite of this opposition, by 1608 the Jesuits had sufficiently won their way with Henry IV that he determined to found a mission of their Society in Acadia. To offset the criticism that his colony had neglected religion, and to head off the Jesuits, Poutrincourt in 1610 engaged the services of the Abbé Jessé Fleché of the Diocese of Langres for Acadia. During his time in the colony this secular priest instructed more than 100 of the Micmac Indians and brought about among a number of them a rather superficial conversion to Christianity.

The Jesuits were not to be put off, however, and through the influence of the king's confessor, Pierre Coton, S.J., they won the friendship and patronage of Antoinette de Pons, the Marquise de Guercheville, lady-in-waiting to the queen mother. The wealthy marquise bought a ship, the *Grâce de Dieu*, arranged with the son of Poutrincourt for the passage of the first Jesuits, and soon thereafter began to negotiate for the purchase of the rights to the entire colony. The two original missionaries were Pierre Biard, S.J., and Ennémond Massé, S.J., who arrived in Acadia in May, 1611. Although they made some progress with the local redmen, by 1613 the tension between Poutrincourt and the marquise led to a decision to locate the projected new mission of Saint Sauveur near the present city of Bangor, Maine. It was with this in mind that a ship from France carrying two more Jesuits, Father Jacques Quentin and Brother Gilbert du Thet, called at Acadia, picked up Biard and Massé, and started south to begin anew. But the party never reached its intended goal, for while at Mount Desert Island they were surprised by Captain Samuel Argall from Virginia who was under orders from England to chase out the French. During the ensuing fight Brother du Thet was killed, the others were taken captive, and their Indian neophytes scattered by the English. Thus there came to a sudden and violent end the first mission of the French Jesuits in North America.

Five years before this temporary blighting of Jesuit missionary hopes on Mount Desert Island the foundation of Quebec had been laid by Champlain in July, 1608. For a quarter century or more it remained only a tiny settlement that served as a trading post and fort, but the choice had been a wise one. Not only did the site command the entrance to the Saint Lawrence River and the Great Lakes beyond, but the western portages gave relatively easy access to the Mississippi and the heart of the continent, while to the northeast of Quebec lay the Gulf of Saint Lawrence and the Atlantic Ocean. It was an ideal location for a fur trading center which was the principal object in the minds of the French merchants who held the patent.

From Quebec the energetic Champlain, with nearly twenty years of exploring experience in the western hemisphere already behind him, soon set out for the West in search of new fur-bearing regions and the further geographical knowledge that they might yield. Since the Huron Indians controlled the routes along which the French would have to pass, Champlain made friends with this tribe and in 1609 an alliance was concluded. Unfortunately, the Hurons had a mortal foe in the Iroquois who probably did not number more than 40,000, but who were the terror of the northern tribes, and in a scuffle with a band of Iroquois near Ticonderoga in July, 1609, Champlain killed one of their chiefs. The encounter, a natural sequel to the alliance with the Hurons, proved to be one of the most costly in France's colonial history. From that day forward the Iroquois vowed vengeance upon the Hurons and their white allies, and for over a century the aftermath of the action on the shores of the lake that bears Champlain's name was felt in a steady toll of lives. And in the course of this sacrifice to Iroquois fury no group was more prominent than the Jesuits who again and again braved almost certain death in order to reach the souls of the Hurons and the other western Indians.

Until his death in 1635 Samuel Champlain remained the soul of the French enterprise in North America, and had it not been for his determination and organizing ability the feeble colony might well have perished. Support from France was often half-hearted when it came at all, and with the assassination of Henry IV in May, 1610, Champlain lost a strong defender of his colony. The government at Paris passed into the uncertain hands of Marie de Medici who acted as regent for her little son, Louis XIII, and the court became a nest of intrigues centering around the Italian favorites of the queen mother. Yet upon his visit to France in 1612 Champlain did not permit himself to be daunted by these unfavorable circumstances. He had come to enlist further political and economic aid and, too, to engage missionaries to carry out his religious policies, and he intended to succeed. And succeed he did, for it was on this trip that he won the assent of the Franciscans, or Recollets as the French called them, a reformed branch of the Friars Minor with contemplative tendencies, to send missionaries to the new world. The first four friars reached Quebec in the summer of 1615 and on June 24, the feast of Saint John the Baptist, Father Denis Jamet, the superior, said the first Mass in the colony, a circumstance that accounts for the patronal feast of the French Canadians to the present day. That same summer another Franciscan, Joseph Le Caron, anticipated Champlain in reaching Georgian Bay and there on August 12 he celebrated the first Mass in the future Province of Ontario in a cabin built for him by the Indians.

During the course of the next decade the Franciscans exerted every effort to convert the pagan Indians as well as to afford the few French an opportunity to practice their religious duties. They were found all across eastern Canada from the fishing and trading post of Tadoussac on the east to Lake Nipissing on the west with Father Jean d'Olbeau seeking out the Montagnais tribe on the lower Saint Lawrence, Le Caron working among the Hurons and Wyandots west of the Ottawa River, and after 1619 a new group of friars establishing missions in New Brunswick and Gaspé as well as ministering to the French and the Micmac Indians in Acadia. Yet a decade of serious toil left them with little to show for their pains. The Franciscans' limited numbers were not sufficient for so large an undertaking, and their semi-contemplative way of life was unsuited to missionary work among the primitive natives. By 1624 – the year before they received their first martyr in the drowning of Nicolas Viel by a Huron Indian in the rapids of the Rivière des Prairies –

it had become apparent that some radical step must be taken to arrest their falling fortunes, and they determined to invite the Society of Jesus to come to their assistance.

The call for service in the new world came on the eve of one of the greatest periods of religious zeal in the annals of the French Church, and the Jesuits lost no time in responding to the plea for help. Six Black Robes, with Charles Lalemant at their head, sailed for Quebec in 1625, and among them were Ennémond Massé, hopeful that the new assignment would prove more rewarding than his earlier experience in Acadia, and Jean de Brébeuf, son of a Norman noble, who was destined to bring enduring fame to the missions by his heroic sufferings and martyr's death. For the first few years little progress was made by either Jesuits or Franciscans for the reason that in addition to the obstacles and setbacks that characterized every missionary endeavor of this kind the infant colony's life was then disrupted by repeated alarms and threats of foreign invasion and attack. The state of undeclared war between France and England which periodically marked these years – with the English pledged to help the Huguenots against Cardinal Richelieu, the powerful minister of Louis XIII – was also extended to the new world. It is true that in the meantime Brébeuf made headway in learning the language of the Montagnais tribe during a five months' stay among them, and through the nearly three trying years that he dwelt with the Hurons he gained valuable firsthand knowledge for himself and his confrères concerning the sacrifices and hardships that awaited them, although he did not make a single convert.

Experience of this kind, valuable though it proved to be in the years ahead, seemed for the moment to have been gained for naught when an English naval force seized Quebec in July, 1629, and dispersed the French inhabitants. For a brief time, in fact, there was not an inch of North America in French hands. But the deepening conflict between King Charles I and Parliament came more and more to occupy the first place in English minds, and in the Treaty of Saint Germain-en-Laye of March, 1632, England restored all the captured territory in North America. A boon likewise resulted from Richelieu's decision that the missionary cause would be best served were it entrusted to a single religious order. He first invited the Capuchins to accept the assignment, but when they declined he turned to the Jesuits. Entrusted with sole responsibility, therefore, three Jesuits made ready to depart with the group of about 100 agents and colonists who sailed in April, 1632, and this time it was Paul Le Jeune, a former Huguenot, who was the superior with Father Anne de Nouë and Brother Gilbert Burel as his subjects.

The constant bickering of the rival trading groups that had ruled the colony up to this time had been a sore handicap both to the trade itself and to colonization, and once the masterful mind of Richelieu found time to focus upon the situation a drastic change was in the making. Intent that New France should be not only a source of profit to the crown but an attraction for future colonists, the cardinal reorganized the entire management in 1627 and gave it over to the so-called Company of the Hundred Associates. In the charter which was issued to this body in the name of Louis XIII the religious clauses were given a prominent place as, for example, the duty of converting the Indians to Christianity. Moreover, residence in the colony was restricted to Catholics, and the company undertook to maintain three priests for fifteen years in each future community to be founded. Under the new charter supreme authority was vested in Samuel Champlain as Governor of New France. In the brief span of life that remained to him Champlain, now sixty-three years of age, was by no means to be freed of grave problems, but at least some of the chief stumbling blocks had been removed and the colony could proceed to a fresh start.

On board the *Saint-Pierre* as it carried the new governor into Tadoussac in May, 1633, were also Fathers de Brébeuf and Massé returning once more to the work from which they had been cut off by the English invasion. Three years before de Brébeuf had confided to his private journal that he was fearful lest his soul might be lost since God had dealt too kindly with him, and at that time he had expressed a desire to suffer for Christ. "Only then, happily," he had written, "shall I hope for my salvation when occasions of suffering shall present themselves."[2] Yet even the invincible spirit of de Brébeuf could hardly have foreseen the atrocious torments that lay in store for him and which he endured, along with Father Gabriel Lalemant, with almost unbelievable courage before he succumbed to the tortures of the Iroquois in March, 1649. But we are anticipating our story. With the small but able band of Black Robes now in control of the missions in New France there opened the

[2] Quoted from the manuscript of de Brébeuf's spiritual notes in the archives of Collège Sainte-Marie, Montreal, by Francis Xavier Talbot, S.J., *Saint Among the Hurons. The Life of Jean de Brébeuf* [Image Books edition] (Garden City, 1956), p. 96.

period of the Jesuits' highest achievements, and from this date to their expulsion from the French dominions in 1764 theirs was the major—although, as we shall see, by no means the only—contribution made to the spread of the Catholic faith in France's American possessions.

As Mexico and the West Indies provided the base from which there was launched the Spanish missionary drive on American soil, so it was Canada that furnished the starting point for the advance of the French missionaries into what is today the United States. Likewise as there were five principal areas wherein the Spanish missions occupied a major role in American colonial history so, too, there were five regions of this country whose earliest civilized settlements owed much to the French missionaries, namely, Maine, New York, the Great Lakes, the Illinois Country, and Louisiana. The mission history of these areas differed, of course, from place to place. Yet in the span of 170 years from the ill fated attempt of 1613 to plant the cross on Mount Desert Island in what is today Maine to 1783 when Great Britain formally acknowledged the independence of the United States, and with it American sovereignty over the Great Lakes and the Illinois Country to the eastern boundary of the Louisiana colony, the religious life of both the white inhabitants, and those Indian tribes who were brought within the pale of Christianity, was fashioned more or less along the same lines. As the Spaniards had held sway in the huge arc or borderlands stretching from Florida to California, so French rule made itself felt in varying degrees and at different times from the northeast corner of the future republic through the system of great inland lakes and on to the valley of the mighty river that divided the continent along its lengthy course to the Gulf of Mexico.

There is no need to trace the zig-zag course of Maine's colonial missions in detail. The territory, regarded for many years as part of Acadia, was a highly controversial one during the seventeenth and eighteenth centuries, situated as it was between the French in Quebec and the English in Massachusetts, with a widespread ignorance of geography contributing to the confusion. The fact that the area changed hands nine times in a century and a quarter is sufficient evidence of its instability and of the deleterious effects that these constant military and political changes had upon the Catholic missions. It was in 1604 that the first priest set foot in the future State of Maine when Nicolas Aubry, a member of de Monts' company, came to Saint Croix or what is now known as Holy Cross or Dochet's Island. But, as we have seen, neither de Monts' expeditions nor the Jesuit mission of 1611–1613 had any lasting results for the Church. Following the expulsion of the Jesuits from Mount Desert Island, missionary activity consisted chiefly of visits made after 1619 at irregular intervals to the tribes of northern Maine by the Franciscan friars from their headquarters on the Saint Jean River, and in the next decade an occasional Jesuit attached to the fort and settlement called Sainte Anne also visited these Indians.

It was rather the Capuchins – like the Society of Jesus one of the new orders that had emerged during the Catholic Reformation – who more than the Franciscans and Jesuits figured as missionaries in Maine during the first half of the seventeenth century. It was a period of great prestige for these friars. In the slow evolution at Rome of a policy and organization for spreading the Catholic faith in missionary lands the Capuchins had taken a leading part, and when Pope Gregory XV in June, 1622, established the Congregation de Propaganda Fide by the bull *Inscrutabili divinae* they were among the new congregation's first effective agents.[3] At the time the Capuchins held a rather unique position in both France and England as well. One of their number, Joseph du Tremblay, was the principal adviser to Cardinal Richelieu, and not long after the marriage of Charles I of England to the Catholic Henrietta Maria, sister of Louis XIII, they became chaplains to the queen and in 1630 eight friars crossed to London when it was against the law for a Catholic priest to enter the kingdom. When, therefore, peace between France and England was restored by the Treaty of Saint Germain-en-Laye and Propaganda wished to establish a prefecture apostolic in Acadia, it was to the Capuchins that the new jurisdiction was entrusted. After their arrival in 1632 they eventually erected seven

[3] England's American colonies were first brought to the attention of the new Congregation de Propaganda Fide by an English Discalced Carmelite, Simon Stock Doughty (Dawson). As a consequence of his prompting in November, 1630, Propaganda erected the Prefecture Apostolic of New England and named the French Capuchin, Joseph du Tremblay, as first prefect. Before any practical steps could be taken, however, the restoration of peace between France and England in March, 1632, changed the plans and eventually brought about the Prefecture Apostolic of Acadia with which that of New England was merged in September, 1632. While the ecclesiastical jurisdiction bearing the name of New England never existed except on paper, it is of interest as the first action of that kind taken by the Holy See in specific relation to part of what became the United States. For this episode cf. John M. Lenhart, O.F.M. Cap., "The Capuchin Prefecture of New England, 1630–1656," *Franciscan Studies*, XXIV (March, 1943), 21–46.

permanent missions over a large area that included Acadia (Nova Scotia), New Brunswick, and Maine as far as the Kennebec River. One of these was located on a peninsula jutting into Penobscot Bay and was called Fort Pentagoet now Castine, Maine. This mission continued for nearly two decades until a renewal of war made it a victim of English seizure in 1654, and in the next year the Capuchins' missions in this part of North America came to an end. During their period of service, however, about forty friars had labored in Acadia and the adjacent regions, and it was thanks to them that the faith was implanted and kept alive in the hearts of a small number of Indians who constituted a nucleus about whom the Capuchins' successors were able to develop a Christian community after they had withdrawn.

The principal group with whom most of these missionaries had worked from the early seventeenth century were the Abenaki Indians, a branch of the Algonquin tribe, who first met the French when Pierre Biard, S.J., visited the region of the Kennebec River in 1612. The Abenaki were a superior type to many of the native tribes encountered by the missionaries in that they had an interest in agriculture and were, therefore, less nomadic than many other Indians, and they likewise displayed qualities of docility and loyalty that made them much easier to handle. The fact that they were enemies of the Iroquois drew them naturally to the French, although their trade relations with the English created a conflict of interests that was at times a source of trouble. In an effort to save the Abenaki from the Iroquois the French missionaries had induced a number of the tribe to come to Sillery, a Christian Indian village established in 1636 several miles above Quebec. Here they were instructed in the elements of the Catholic faith and prepared to return to their fellow tribesmen in the capacity of forerunners, so to speak, of the missionaries. On the whole the Indians seemed favorably impressed with the Frenchmen's religion – as they were probably not unmindful of their value as an ally against their traditional foe – and in 1646 they made a formal request for a priest to come and reside among them.

As a consequence of this appeal Father Gabriel Druillettes, S.J., set out from Sillery in August, 1646, with a group of the Abenaki for their village of Norridgewock on the Kennebec River where he spent nearly a year trying to learn their language, nursing their sick, and preparing the minds of the natives for the reception of the faith. Druillettes soon saw that if there was to be any genuine conversion among these Indians they would have to relinquish certain of their customs such as the use of liquor, the inter-tribal wars, and, too, belief in the manitous or pagan spirits. These were, of course, heavy demands to make of a primitive people, but Druillettes insisted that such were the conditions if a priest was to remain permanently among them, and the fact that he succeeded in eliciting a prayer for forgiveness of the Iroquois, their arch enemies, seemed to offer a favorable omen for the future.

In June, 1647, Father Druillettes returned to Quebec to report to his superior, and the latter would probably have despatched missionaries to the Abenaki sooner had he not received a protest from the Capuchins against what they regarded as an invasion of a territory that belonged to them. After a visit to Quebec and Sillery in 1648, however, the new Capuchin superior, Cosme de Mantes, reversed his confrères' policy and sent a warm invitation to the Jesuits to join them on the Kennebec. It was an odd set of circumstances that occasioned Druillettes' second visit to the Abenaki in the autumn of 1650. Massachusetts Bay colony had requested a reciprocal trade treaty with the French, and the latter were receptive to the idea on condition that the English colonists would agree to enter a military alliance against the Iroquois. For more than a generation this fierce tribe had warred on the Hurons until by 1650 they had been practically obliterated. In fact, for some years the French and their Indian allies had known little or no security and it was now hoped that they might enlist their southern neighbors in a common cause. In order to make known its position the government at Quebec asked Gabriel Druillettes to act as its emissary and he spent a brief time with the Abenaki on his way to Boston.

It was somewhat ironic that a Jesuit should have been chosen for any kind of a mission to a colony that three years before had enacted a law against the entrance of Catholic priests with special uncomplimentary references to members of the Society of Jesus. But the law that declared a priest's second unauthorized entrance into Massachusetts punishable by death carried an exception for, as it was termed, "any such as shall come in company with any messenger sent hither vppon publick occasions. . . ."[4] Upon his arrival, therefore, Druillettes was cordially received by Major Edward Gibbons who provided hospitality and a room

[4] "Massachusetts Bay Passes an Anti-Priest Law, May 26, 1647," Ellis, *Documents*, p. 114. The strong anti-Catholic sentiment of the English colonies was the cause of a good deal of legislation of this type as, for example, Massachusetts and New York's later act against Jesuits and 'popish missionaries' of June, 1700. (*Ibid.*, pp. 121–123).

in which he might conduct his private devotions, Governor Thomas Dudley gave a dinner in his honor, Governor William Bradford of Plymouth was courteous when he called, and even the formidable John Endecott entertained him at Salem. Try as he might, however, he could not convince the Puritan leaders of the advisability of an alliance that would entail a break with the Iroquois, and he returned to Quebec in June, 1651, without a commitment. A second trip was undertaken by Druillettes in September of that year – this time in the company of Jean Godefroy, a member of the governor's council, and Jean Guérin, a Jesuit lay assistant – to New Haven where a meeting of the New England Confederation was in session. But the second journey proved to be no more successful in its objective than the first, and it now became apparent that the friendship of the Iroquois, whom the English recognized as their strongest bulwark against the advance of the French, was more highly valued than any advantage that might be gained by trade with the latter.

Very early in their days in New France the Jesuits had seen the wisdom of concentrating the Indians in separate villages where they would be relatively free from the contamination of the rough French traders. Here, it was hoped, the natives could be gradually brought to a state where they would be well instructed Catholics and permanent residents whose mastery of the elements of civilized living might eventually make them self-supporting. The first of these villages, Saint Joseph at Sillery, as we have seen, was begun in 1636 near Quebec, and after a generation or more of cultivation had practically exhausted the soil it was moved in 1699 to the Chauvière River. The following year this location gave way, in turn, to the mission of Saint François on the Saint François River, and in 1708 a formal grant of land was made for another village under the patronage of Saint Francis Xavier at Becancourt. During the second half of the seventeenth century when the present area of Maine was marked by so much fighting between the English and French and their Indian allies there was little or no missionary effort. But considerable numbers of the Abenakis found a safe haven from these conflicts in Sillery and the other villages where they became devout Catholics.

If the Jesuits could have had their way about these Christian villages for the natives of New France they would have developed along the lines of the reductions of Paraguay where at this time their Spanish confrères were establishing some remarkably strong settlements far to the interior of the country. But the French laymen, whether traders or civil and military men, were in general no more co-operative in the matter of segregating the natives for religious purposes than were the Spaniards in South America. The missionaries frequently found themselves thwarted, therefore, by their countrymen's desire to use the redmen as a barrier between themselves and their enemies, as well as to retain them as the best channel through which the rich fur pelts from the hunting expeditions would reach French hands. And if these objectives could be furthered by enticing the natives with liquor, so much the worse for the Black Robes' hopes to keep them free from a vice to which they were all too prone.

In spite of these handicaps two of these villages, Saint François and Becancourt, persisted through the whole of the French regime and were the scene of many native conversions to Catholicism with the faith passed on to their descendants down to our own time. In these settlements men like Jacques Bigot, S.J., and Joseph Aubréy, S.J., gave their best efforts for the redmen's spiritual welfare, and the latter, who was stationed at Saint François for nearly half a century, likewise found time to compile an Abenaki dictionary, to compose hymns in their dialect, and to keep copious journals on the Indians' customs and way of life.

As for the original habitat of many of these transplanted natives, it was not until the late 1680's that active missionary work was resumed in what is today Maine. The murder of La Salle in 1687 while trying to establish a French colony in the lower Mississippi Valley had a lasting effect on missionary activity in New France. It was at this time that the Jesuits decided to consolidate their commitments along the watershed of the Saint Lawrence River with only secondary importance given to the western missions. As a part of this policy Jacques Bigot, S.J., intensified his labors in the Christian Indian villages and extended his travels as well to the Abenaki on the Kennebec River. But the Jesuits were not alone in re-entering Maine. About the same time the Abbé Pierre Thury, a secular priest of the Quebec seminary, opened a mission at Nanransouock on the Penobscot and the Franciscans also re-appeared in the person of Père Simon who before long had 100 or more neophytes at Medoctec at the mouth of the Saint John. The two latter groups did not last long under their respective masters, however, and within a few years both the seculars and the Franciscans had given way in these missions to the Jesuits.

The Black Robe whose presence among the Abenaki on the Kennebec was to be more felt than any other was Sebastian Rale who arrived in Maine in 1694 after several years in the Illinois Country and who remained until his death at the hands of an English partisan thirty years later. Rale tried hard to make the Abenaki a sedentary people in which he was only partially successful. They were committed both by tribal custom, and by what they regarded at times as necessity, to the hunt, and Father Rale not infrequently had to move off with them to the gaming area with his portable altar and Mass equipment as part of his baggage. On the whole, however, these natives were loyal to the Church once they had been baptized, and far from running away from the missionary, as so often happened elsewhere, on the eve of the hunt they would tell him, as Rale wrote to his brother, "It would be hard for us to give up our Prayer; therefore we hope that thou wilt be disposed to accompany us, so that, while seeking for food, we shall not interrupt our Prayer." [5]

The most trying – and, as it proved, fatal – chapter in Father Rale's life in Maine opened with the renewal of war between France and England. The American counterpart of the War of the Spanish Succession broke in May, 1702, with England's declaration of war upon France. The conflict created a difficult situation for the Abenaki torn, as they were, between the French whose religion they had adopted and with whom they had been friendly, and the English with whom they had continued to trade. The fighting was largely confined to periodic raids into each other's territory, but the fierceness and brutality of these forays made life a nightmare for the inhabitants of the borderland settlements through most of a decade. Some notion of the character of the struggle can be gained from the fact that both the English and the French indulged in the practice of paying their Indian allies for enemy scalps. Even before the outbreak of hostilities fear and suspicion had been widespread, which would account for the anti-priest laws passed by the assemblies of both Massachusetts and New York in 1700 under the inspiration of the notoriously anti-Catholic Richard Coote,

[5] Rale to his brother, Narantsouak, October 12, 1723, Reuben Gold Thwaites (Ed.), *Jesuit Relations and Allied Documents* (Cleveland, 1900), LXVII, 215–217. Hereafter this work will be referred to as: *Jesuit Relations.*

Earl of Bellomont, who was governor of the combined colonies. These measures were intended to rid the colonies of the imagined priest-spies in their midst who, it was said, were stirring up the Indians against the white settlers. As for English policy toward the redmen, zeal for their conversion to Christianity had never enjoyed much consistent support or emphasis, and when France's Indian allies fell upon their outlying towns and spread havoc, as in the savage raid on Deerfield, Massachusetts, in February, 1704, where even women and children were not spared, it stiffened English determination to have done with methods of conciliation and to liquidate the Indians once and for all time.

One of the curious results that followed from these French and Indian wars, as they are called in American history, was that they provided the first group of Anglo-American converts to Catholicism in New France. In the period between 1680 and 1760 approximately 1,200 captives were seized in the New England settlements and taken to New France. Of these about 250 – among whom were many children – remained and were later converted to the Catholic faith, and of their number was Martha French, the maternal grandmother of Joseph Plessis, Bishop of Quebec from 1806 to 1822, who as a child of eight had been taken captive with her family in 1704 in the raid on Deerfield.

The damage done to the English cause in these raids was slight, however, in comparison to the more important fighting areas where Great Britain had much the better of the war. And in the Treaty of Utrecht that ended the conflict in 1713 the English secured Hudson's Bay, Newfoundland, and Acadia (Nova Scotia), as well as won an acknowledgement of their wardship over the Five Nations of the Iroquois Confederacy. It was especially unfortunate for the Abenakis that the language of the treaty was so vague in regard to the limits of Acadia, for the contrary interpretations put upon the phrase, "according to its ancient boundaries," led to further confusion and acrimony. The French contended that it meant the Saint Croix River which would leave them the area between that stream and the Kennebec, while the English insisted that it meant the latter river which, of course, included the Abenaki homeland.

The repeated meetings and disputes among the boundary commissioners made the Indians very restive, and finally they revolted against the inroads of the English, a revolt in which the Quebec government backed them up. Nor were matters improved when Massachusetts sent the Reverend Joseph Baxter to Maine in the hope of converting them to Protestantism. Rale protested this attempt to alienate his neophytes from their religious faith, and when Baxter cast aspersions on Catholicism the situation became so tense that he was practically forced to withdraw. Father Rale protested directly to Governor Samuel Shute of Massachusetts in August, 1717, against the moves of the latter's subjects in Maine, but his letter remained unanswered. Meanwhile matters steadily deteriorated and in July, 1720, the Massachusetts government, in a fit of exasperation at the one whom they believed to be the chief source of their troubles, voted a reward of £100 for the Jesuit's capture. Although the English had continued to consolidate their position by crossing the Kennebec line and setting up trading posts, all efforts to woo the Abenakis to their side had ended in failure.

Previous to one of the attacks on Father Rale's community he and his Indians had been warned in time to escape, but not soon enough to enable them to take all their personal effects. Rale's papers were seized, including his dictionary of the Abenaki language which later found its way to the Widener Library at Harvard, some letters of Philippe de Rigaud, Marquis de Vaudreuil, Governor of New France, in which the latter had urged Rale to incite the Indians against the invaders, and a letter of the Jesuit to the redmen telling them to resist the encroachments on their religion and their rights. On this evidence Governor Shute declared war on July 25, 1722, and it was these same documents that later furnished the basis for the case against Rale as a warmonger and intriguer, an opinion that endured for generations in the minds of New Englanders. During the ensuing two years several expeditions were sent to apprehend Rale, but it was only in August, 1724, that a band of about 160 troops fell on Norridgewock, and before the Jesuit could be captured—which was what the instructions called for—a partisan of the English, Lieutenant Stephen Jacques, shot and killed him. His scalp, along with those of about twenty others, was brought to Boston and there high holiday was proclaimed and a procession marched through the streets exhibiting these pitiful remnants of the victims.

Before his death Father Rale had foreseen that the bloody raids of the Indians on New England towns would be likely to bring reprisals. Fearing that his converts might not be equal to these contests, he urged them to move to New France in order to prevent their annihilation, a suggestion followed by a considerable number, even though Governor Vaudreuil was not happy to have them. Not only had the old mission of Norridgewock been wiped out during the fighting, but other Maine missions suffered as well, for example, the settlement on the Penobscot which was attacked in March, 1723, and set on fire with the loss of the church that had been built by Father Etienne Lauverjat, S.J.

Although the Maine missions were reactivated after the restoration of peace in 1726, there was little marked progress made in the area during the balance of the eighteenth century. The reasons for this are not difficult to understand. First, the peak of French missionary fervor had been passed and fewer missionaries were coming to the new world. Secondly, the Quebec government remained as opposed as ever to the missionaries' policy of segregating the natives, while at the same time urging them – in the interests of colonial defence – to keep as close as possible to the Indians. Thirdly, in Maine, which after 1713 was regarded by the English as an extension of Massachusetts, the anti-priest laws might at any time be invoked against those missionaries who sought to serve the natives on the Saint John and Kennebec Rivers. While these handicaps were sufficient to prevent any genuine advancement of the missionary cause, they did not prevent the Jesuits from holding much of what had previously been gained. Thus Lauverjat returned to the Penobscot and rebuilt his church, Jacques Sirenne came to Norridgewock with the reopening of that mission in 1730, Charles Germain established Sainte Anne on the Saint John near present day Fredericton, New Brunswick, and Jean-Pierre Daniélou served in the same region where in 1730 he took up a census of its inhabitants. At the same time those Maine Indians who had settled in the native Christian villages in New France had priests in regular attendance, Father Germain ending his life at Saint François du Lac in 1779 and Simon-Pierre Gounon, S.J., serving at Becancourt until 1764 after which date the Franciscan friars shared in the religious care of these Indian villages.

The missions were destined to suffer further reverses with the opening in the summer of 1755 of the final phase of the Anglo-French struggle for the mastery of North America. Through the next five years as the British gradually advanced toward ultimate victory and the overthrow of France's last strongholds at Montreal and Quebec, the mission personnel was slowly depleted by the withdrawal of many French priests to their homeland, the total for the colony of 181 in 1758 dropping to 138 by 1766. To make matters worse, in December, 1764, King Louis XV decreed an end to the Society of Jesus in all his dominions, and although New France had by this time been in English hands for four years it came as a severe blow to those French Jesuits who had stayed on in their missionary posts. With the Treaty of Paris of February, 1763, therefore, the Indians' one time friends and coreligionists were eliminated as a controlling factor in continental affairs. Henceforth the Catholic redmen would have to deal with the English with whom they were familiar enough in the realm of trade but not in matters relating to their religious faith.

Vigorously opposed as were most of the officials of both Canada and New England to the Church of Rome, they refrained from any campaign of oppression of the French and Indian Catholics who inhabited the new territories that had now been added to the crown. Instead they sought to wean the native converts from their religious allegiance by indirect methods. In the years after 1760 the principal concern of these Indians was a supply of priests to minister to their spiritual needs. With the passing of New France to Great Britain that colony came under the ecclesiastical jurisdiction of Richard Challoner, Vicar Apostolic of the London District, but it would have been futile to have appealed to Challoner even had the Indians known of him, or if he had been aware of their plight, for he had not enough priests to man his own stations. Where, then, were the Indians to find priests? Since they had been accustomed to look to Quebec in matters of this kind it was natural that in 1764 they should have appealed to James Murray, Governor General of Canada, who referred them, in turn, to the Governor of Massachusetts on the score that they were now residents of the latter's province. An appeal to Boston proved to be equally barren of results, for there were no Catholic priests at the command of the Puritan authorities even if they had been disposed to furnish one. But the redmen would not give up, and in September of the same year a Penobscot delegation met with Sir Francis Bernard, Governor of Massachusetts, to whom their spokesman stated:

> . . . we want a Father to baptize our Children, & marry us, & administer the Sacrament to us, & confess us, & shew us the way to Heaven; That is, to keep us from what is bad, correct our lives, & absolve our Sins. It is a few years since Canada was taken, & since we have had no father among us; our

People grow loose & disorderly, drink too hard, & run into many bad practices, which a Father (if we had one among us) would remind us of & correct. It is usual to help the poor; We are poor, & therefore help us in the matter of Religion.[6]

It would be difficult to imagine more eloquent testimony to the constructive role that the Catholic missionaries had played among these simple people than this touching petition. But Bernard was concerned with the political implications of the appeal, reminding the Indians of the danger of having a French priest reside with them lest he stir up trouble. And in an effort to quiet them, and at the same time to bring them closer to their new masters, he tried to get them to accept a minister of the Church of England. But the Indians were not to be beguiled by Bernard's attempt to distinguish between the Anglican and the Puritan divines, and when twelve years later a delegation of the Micmacs and the tribes from the Saint John River region met with a similar disappointment at Watertown, Massachusetts, they just as resolutely declined the offer to provide them with Protestant ministrations. In fact, when the Reverend Daniel Little appeared in Maine several times during the 1770's he only created confusion and made matters more complicated than they had been before.

With the dawn of the American Revolution the demands of the Abenaki Confederacy for Catholic priests took on a new aspect. The division of allegiance that then ensued between the subjects of the crown in Canada and in New England made the loyalty of these tribes a matter of more than ordinary importance, located, as they were, in between the two groups. Thus in April, 1778, Governor William Arbuthnot of Nova Scotia (Acadia) asked the Governor General of Canada to have Bishop Joseph Briand send a priest to quiet the Indians of his jurisdiction. In response to this appeal the Abbé Joseph-Mathurin Bourg, grand vicar of Acadia, was appointed, and by October of that year Richard Hughes, Arbuthnot's successor, was able to report that the Indians had been induced to sign a treaty of friendship and had returned peacefully to Fort Howe under the English flag. In acknowledging his obligations to those who had assisted in bringing about this turn of events Hughes

[6] Report of conference between Bernard and Indian chiefs, Fort Pownall, September 26, 1764, James Phinney Baxter (Ed.), *Documentary History of the State of Maine* (Portland, 1909), XIII, 368.

mentioned Bourg as "the priest to whom we owe the success of this treaty. . . ."[7]

Meanwhile in January, 1777, the Massachusetts government had appointed as superintendent of the eastern Indian tribes a sensible and intelligent officer, Colonel John Allan, who took a realistic attitude toward the redmen's desire for a priest. Yet nothing resembling a permanent solution to the problem came about until after the Revolution. In 1790 the Penobscots addressed appeals to both Bishop Jean François Hubert of Quebec and to the Catholic authorities in New England. As a consequence a French priest then resident in Boston, Louis Rousselet, went to them in October and administered the sacraments, baptizing sixty-five and marrying twelve couples. Early in 1791 the Passamaquoddy Indians, who lived on the border of Canada and who had been less fortunate than their fellows in finding a priest, asked Colonel Allan to intercede for them. By this time the whole of the nascent republic of the United States had been constituted the Diocese of Baltimore, so Allan assisted the Indians in drawing up a petition to Bishop John Carroll. Carroll replied in early September that he would try to send them priests just as soon as they were available. When the early months of 1792 brought to Baltimore six French Sulpicians who had fled the revolutionary assault on the Church in their own country, the bishop asked one of their number, Father François Ciquart, who had already had some missionary experience among the Indians in Canada, if he would undertake the Maine assignment. Ciquart accepted readily enough and after arriving at his new post he worked in close co-operation with Allan, the Indian superintendent, and ultimately he succeeded in getting the Massachusetts General Court to grant the Passamaquoddy Indians a permanent home at Pleasant Point. The Sulpician spent two years in Maine before returning to Canada in August, 1794, after which the natives were again at the mercy of periodic visits from itinerant clergymen.

The Passamaquoddys were not easily discouraged, and in June, 1797, a delegation of their chiefs traveled to Boston to renew their request for a resident priest. This time they had the good fortune to receive Jean de Cheverus, future first Bishop of Boston, who was not yet a year in New England. In Cheverus the redmen found a devoted

[7] Arthur Melançon, *Vie de l'Abbé Bourg, Premier Prêtre Acadien . . . 1744–1797* (Rimouski, 1921), p. 100.

spiritual guide who during the extended visits that he made to them on his annual tours was able to solve most of their religious problems. At length in July, 1799, Cheverus was relieved of the responsibility by the arrival of another French refugee, Jacques-René Romagné, who continued to be the main stay of the religious life of the Indians of Maine until his return to France in August, 1818.

By the time of Father Romagné's departure the Diocese of Boston, which included Maine, was already a decade old and Maine itself was nearing the end of its territorial status. Time had taken its toll on the Indians and by 1820, the year that Maine became a state, they had been reduced in number to about 750 of whom roughly 350 lived on Indian Island near Oldtown while the remainder were located at Pleasant Point in the region of Eastport. The Indians' persistence in the Catholic faith through all the hardships and disappointments they had encountered was a tribute both to the sincerity of their religious convictions and to the thoroughness with which the original missionaries had instructed their ancestors. At the time of Maine's separation from Massachusetts – unlike many other new members of the American Union – it found no vexing problems with its Indian inhabitants. The loyalty and relative docility which had characterized the loose confederacy comprising the Abenakis, Micmacs, Penobscots, and Passamaquoddys from the white man's earliest contacts with them had continued through the years and now made their contribution to the peaceful transition of Maine to statehood. Nor did these tribes present any special difficulty to the authorities of the Diocese of Boston, except their distance from the see city and the perennial problem of finding priests to serve them. Once they had a priest they remained content, and in the later history of these Indians there were no serious defections or scandals. Thus when the Catholic Church in Maine reached a point of development that warranted the erection of the Diocese of Portland in July, 1853, the redmen and their families were among the most loyal and peaceful Catholic communities to greet David W. Bacon when he came to Maine as the first resident bishop of the state.

CHAPTER SEVEN

NEW YORK

The history of the Catholic missions in colonial New York is inseparably linked with that of New France, and to be properly understood it is necessary to have some knowledge of developments as they transpired in the valleys of the Saint Lawrence, Richelieu, and Ottawa Rivers and in the area stretching westward to the Great Lakes. Long before the appearance of the Europeans there had existed a deep enmity between the Huron Indians, numbering between 20,000 and 30,000, who lived in the northern part of this extensive territory, and the Iroquois Confederacy, comprising the Mohawk, Oneida, Onondaga, Cayuga, and Seneca tribes – in all about 17,000 – who inhabited the southern shores of Lakes Ontario and Erie, extending from a line near Schenectady to the Genesee River in what is today the State of New York. Both groups followed a semi-agricultural type of life and dwelt in their stockaded villages on a somewhat permanent basis. Although the Hurons were the more numerous, the Iroquois were reckoned as, perhaps, the most intelligent, daring, and cunning of all the North American tribes, and it was they who first came into possession of European firearms through the Dutch.

When the French, the Dutch, and later the English came upon the scene in seventeenth-century New York they had necessarily to contend with the Indians and to adjust their policies and actions to conditions as they found them among the native inhabitants. As we have already seen, it was a costly day for France when in 1609 an Iroquois chief was killed by Champlain, for it brought down upon the French the undying hatred of that powerful confederacy. And, unfortunately, it was as a consequence of the alignment that followed from this incident that the fate of much of the Catholic missionary effort in this part of the French colonies was decided. The presence here of members of the Society of Jesus—for it was almost exclusively a Jesuit undertaking—was primarily by reason of their zeal for souls, although simultaneously they acted as agents for French interests. The coming of the French laymen, however, as well as the Dutch and English traders, was for the most part prompted by an eagerness for monetary gain. It was the desire for profit, especially from furs, that made the possession of these river routes and shorelines of the lakes a paramount concern and a frequent cause for war. And in this situation the Church's missionary goals could rarely be pursued without reference to the laymen's objectives, for at times the very lives of the clergy were dependent upon the protection afforded by those who were in the hire of the trading companies or of the king.

It was as a result of a meeting in the summer of 1641 of some missionaries with delegates of the Chippewas and other western tribes who had come east to the Huron country for the ceremonies surrounding the feast of the dead, that the sanguinary chapter of the Jesuits' history in New York was opened. For some years they had been laboring among the Hurons and that, of course, made them marked men in the eyes of the Iroquois. But their determination to evangelize the western Indians was strong enough to overcome their fears, and two of their number, Charles Raymbault and Isaac Jogues, seized the chance of an opening from the Chippewas to return west with them in the autumn of 1641. In doing so they became the pioneer priests of the future State of Michigan when they stopped at the place to which they gave the name of Sault Sainte Marie, a name which it still retains. After a winter and spring among the Chippewas the Jesuits left with a group of Hurons in early June to return to Quebec in order to get supplies and to enable Father Raymbault to recover his health.

Following Jogues' stay of some weeks in the colonial capital where he secured the needed supplies and recruited two lay assistants, René Goupil and Guillaume Coûture, as well as several Christian Hurons, he and his companions set out for the West again in early August, 1642. But on this occasion they had not gone very far before a party of Mohawks fell upon them about thirty miles from Three Rivers and took them captive. They were brought to the Mohawk villages where they were submitted to cruel tortures, and in the following month at Ossernenon near the present Auriesville, New York, the Mohawks murdered Goupil. Jogues and Coûture were enslaved and for more than a year they endured frightful abuse and insult at the hands of the savages. In August, 1643, Jogues contrived to escape with the aid of the Dutch commander at Fort Orange (Albany) who had him taken down the Hudson to New Amsterdam where as the first priest in the future New York City he found only two Catholics, a Portuguese woman who was the wife of an ensign and an Irishman who had come up from Virginia. He was kindly treated by Governor William Kieft and after an interval of several months he was put on board a ship bound for his homeland whose shores he reached on Christmas Eve of 1643.

It was a period of high religious fervor in France and the young Jesuit missionary from the new world, with hands mangled by the tortures of the savages, became something of a sensation. The Queen Mother, Anne of Austria, insisted on receiving him at court and Pope Urban VIII granted a dispensation for him to say Mass with his mutilated hands. But Jogues was in no way beguiled into prolonging his stay by these attentions, for he was intent upon only one thing and that was a return to the missions. He lost no time and in the spring of 1644 he sailed again for New France. In his absence further fighting had occurred between the Iroquois and the Hurons during which several Iroquois braves had been captured by their enemies. The successor of Champlain, Governor Charles Huault de Montmagny, was hopeful that these captives might be made the occasion for a peace settlement. A message to this effect was despatched to the Iroquois and in response a delegation arrived at Three Rivers in early July. By this time Jogues was back in the colony and he was invited to participate in the conference. Although peace terms were agreed upon and gifts exchanged between the Iroquois and the Hurons, the Jesuit was uneasy in not finding among the former's delegates any representative of Ossernenon which he knew to be one of the principal villages of the Iroquois Confederacy. Nonetheless, the French officials felt that a return embassy was worth the risk and Jogues was selected to go as ambassador. Accompanied by Jean Bourdon, an experienced hand in the colonial government, the Jesuit set out in May, 1645, and after a week spent in concluding the negotiations he was back in Quebec by July 3 to report his success and to make ready for another trip to the West, this time on a purely religious mission.

The omens for what proved to be Isaac Jogue's final journey to the western country were not favorable. Notwithstanding the peace treaty of the previous year, the Iroquois were not reconciled to ending their historic feud with the Hurons, even if they might have been willing to go along with the French. An epidemic had lately broken out among the natives, and they had likewise experienced a season of poor crops. When, therefore, there was discovered a box of religious articles – left behind by Jogues when he was at Ossernenon the year before – it became the occasion for firing the imagination of the superstitious and hostile Mohawks with tales of the evil spirit in the Black Robe's box as the cause of their misfortunes. Into this kind of atmosphere, then, came the news that Jogues was again heading in the direction of the Mohawk country. As a consequence the redmen were lying in wait and when Jogues' little band, consisting of himself, the lay assistant, Jean La Lande, and several Huron converts, reached a point not far from Fort Richelieu they were attacked, taken captive, and brought the long distance to Ossernenon. Here after a lengthy discussion a council of the tribe finally determined to set the prisoners free. But a group of Mohawk fanatics of the Bear Clan nullified the tribal decision by treacherously ensnaring the Jesuit and his companions. On the evening of October 18, 1646, Father Jogues was tomahawked as he entered an Indian cabin, and the next day the same fate was visited on Le Lande and the Huron guide who had loyally adhered to the missionaries. Three French Jesuits had now shed their blood for the Catholic faith on the soil of northern New York.

With the killing of Jogues and his companions the fragile peace of 1645 collapsed entirely and the Iroquois opened a war to the death on the Hurons until the latter were virtually exterminated. The Iroquois' early success emboldened them to make forays near Montreal, Three Rivers, and Quebec in order to wreak their vengeance on those Hurons who had taken refuge in the neighborhood of these French towns. During one of these raids Father Joseph Poncet was captured near Cape Rouge not far from Quebec, taken to the Mohawk villages, and submitted to the same kind of torture that they had practiced on Jogues.[1] In addition to the Iroquois Confederacy's general enmity for the Hurons there was a keen rivalry between the Mohawks and the Onondagas to seize the remnants of the doomed tribe and incorporate them into their respective groups. In this the Onondagas had the edge because of the Christian Hurons already in their hands whom they correctly reasoned the Jesuit missionaries would not entirely abandon. At the time the Five Nations were at war with the Eries in the west and the Susquehannas in the east, and they were anxious to eliminate one or other of these battle fronts. With that in mind a party of about sixty Onondagas appeared at Montreal to sue for peace. The French agreed on condition that Father Poncet should be freed, a point on which the redmen were prepared to yield, and the missionary was set at liberty and returned to Montreal in October, 1653.

To the Jesuits the captive Hurons held by the Iroquois offered a hope that through the medium of these Christian cells within the pagan tribes a possible opening might be found for the conversion of all these native peoples. In order to test the sincerity of the Onondagas it was decided, therefore, to send an embassy and Father Simon le Moyne was chosen as their representative. He started in July, 1654, passing through the upper Saint Lawrence and Lake Ontario to the mouth of the Oswego where he was received with signs of joy by the deputies of all the Five Nations except the Mohawks who were missing. On his way down le Moyne found some of his old Huron converts to whom he administered the sacraments, and upon his return he carried back to the Jesuit headquarters at Quebec two precious relics, the New Testament of Jean de Brébeuf and the prayer book of Charles Garnier

[1] The sufferings of these French Jesuits were among the most frightful in the missionary history of the Church. Like Poncet, a number of them endured severe tortures but were finally liberated. For example, the Italian-born Giuseppe Bressani was captured by the Mohawks in the spring of 1644, tortured, his hands mutilated, and he was made to run the gauntlet; but like Jogues ahead of him, he was rescued by the Dutch and shipped back to France where he arrived in November of that year; but in 1645 Bressani returned to his Huron mission station. Of the eight Jesuits who were canonized as martyrs to the faith by Pope Pius XI on June 29, 1930, three met their deaths in what is today New York State: René Goupil (1642), Isaac Jogues and Jean Le Lande (1646), while the other five were murdered in the present Province of Ontario: Antoine Daniel (1648), Jean de Brébeuf, Gabriel Lalemant, Charles Garnier, and Noël Chabanel (1649). Their combined feast day is September 26.

both of whom had fallen victim to the Iroquois savagery five years before. Le Moyne brought news that the Indians wished the French to establish a colony among them, a suggestion that met with an enthusiastic reception, although the French desired that first a mission and then a colony should be planted on Lake Ontario. Fathers Pierre J. M. Chaumonot and Claude Dablon were selected to make the start and they left Quebec early in the autumn of 1655. After preliminary investigations at Onondaga, Chaumonot became convinced that no peace would hold unless the French were at hand, and he sent Dablon back with this advice.

When Father Dablon reached Quebec the question was discussed at length by Governor Jean de Lauzon and the Jesuit community and they ultimately decided to follow Chaumonot's counsel. A party of about ten soldiers, between forty and fifty colonists, and four Jesuit priests with two lay brothers was fitted out with Dablon named superior of the religious among whom were François le Mercier, René Ménard, and Jacques Frémin. Upon their arrival in the early summer of 1656 they were well received by the Onondagas who allotted them a tract of land on what is now Lake Onondaga. The location was a good one, central as it was to the Cayugas and Senecas on the west and the Oneidas and Mohawks on the east. Aside from the aloofness of the Mohawks, who were still eyeing the Hurons, matters at first went very well, and the Onondagas seemed to take to the Catholic faith even more readily than had the Hurons. The presence of the Christian members of the latter tribe helped considerably and soon the women began to come over, and women exerted a powerful influence among the Iroquois braves.

With this promising beginning a small bark chapel was erected at Onondaga, the first Catholic church in New York State, to which the name of Saint John the Baptist was given, and in the following year it had to be enlarged. So flourishing, in fact, had the Onondaga mission become that before long three sodalities of the Blessed Virgin had been formed among its inhabitants. Meanwhile the missionaries worked out from that center to the other tribes with Chaumonot going to the Senecas, Ménard to the Cayugas, and visits made as well to the Oneidas. After some time, however, the Jesuits began to receive warnings that a plot was being hatched against them, and it turned out that the rumors were true, for the Mohawks and the Oneidas, jealous of the trade passing through other hands, had incited the Onondagas against the French. As usually happened among the redmen, the coming break was preceded by a mounting number of unpleasant incidents, and the governor at Quebec, made aware of these storm signals, decided to strike first by ordering all the Iroquois within his jurisdiction to be seized, put in chains, and held as hostages for the safety of the French who were resident in the country of the Five Nations. At the same time he sent a message to the colonists concerning the danger that now surrounded them.

The warning from Quebec was promptly heeded and the colonists hurried within the palisade where small boats were built with which they might elude their threatening hosts at the first opportunity. It was an Indian superstition that gave the key for the escape. A young *coureur de bois*, Pierre Esprit Radisson, who had been adopted into the Onondaga tribe had a dream calling for a banquet. In Indian ritual if one were invited to a feast it was expected that he would eat everything put before him. The French, therefore, invited the Indians and obliged by providing a staggering meal after which the redmen fell into a drunken stupor. Under cover of night the colonists and missionaries then carried their boats to the Oswego River and escaped through the broken ice. Thus ended in April, 1657, the first attempt to introduce the Catholic faith among the Iroquois of the future State of New York.

The escape from Onondaga was but an episode in what proved to be the most acute crisis that the French had yet encountered from the Iroquois, and of the effects of that struggle on the missions we shall speak later. At the same time the colony was on the eve of radical changes in the government of both Church and State. During the more than fifty years that they had held power in New France the successive trading companies had demonstrated that profits in furs was their overriding preoccupation, and that the duties attached to the civic welfare and increase of colonization—with which they had been charged in their respective charters—were often either badly performed or neglected entirely. With the current running so strongly toward centralization of power in the mother country it was to be expected that Paris would seek to eradicate the abuses, still the complaints, and heighten the commercial importance and attraction of its distant colony by applying remedies fashioned along absolutist lines. In 1663 New France was made a royal province with authority vested in a superior council consisting of the governor, the bishop, five appointed councilors – ultimately increased to twelve – an attorney general, and a secretary. But more significant than any of these officials in the governmental reorganization was the man who held the newly created post of intendant.

With this basic change in political rule the monopoly in trade, on which Louis XIV's great minister, Jean Baptiste Colbert, had set high hopes, was given over to the state corporation of the Company of the West Indies. Within the next two years the new appointees arrived to assume their posts with Daniel Rémy de Courcelle as governor, Jean Talon as intendant, and Alexandre de Prouville, the Marquis de Tracy, as commander of the armed forces. The bishop, about whom we shall speak presently, had already been established in Quebec for some years, the population was practically doubled by the new colonists brought over by Talon, and the regiment of over 1,000 officers and men under de Tracy now afforded adequate protection. Thus as a recent historian has remarked, "The old order was swept away and New France was made over in the image of Louis XIV's France." [2]

The changes in the ecclesiastical life of the colony were equally fundamental. From the outset the question of canonical jurisdiction had been met in only a rather tentative and uncertain manner with the missionaries of the religious orders usually receiving faculties from their respective superiors general. Since most of the ships sailing for New France had left from ports located within the Archdiocese of Rouen, it was thought by many that canonical jurisdiction was the prerogative of the occupant of that see. For example, in 1647 a request was made of François de Harlay, Archbishop of Rouen, to regularize the situation and both he and his successor had granted the faculties of vicar general to the superior of the Jesuits at Quebec. For some years after 1632 the Jesuits were practically the only priests in the colony and while this remained true the arrangement proved satisfactory enough. But the Company of Montreal, a group of pious persons organized in Paris who established the settlement of that name in 1642, later applied to Jean Jacques Olier, founder of the Sulpicians, for priests of his Society. In response to this request four Sulpicians arrived in New France in 1656 under the leadership of Gabriel de Thubières de Quéylus. It was now an altered situation, and when it was learned that de Quéylus was being

[2] Mason Wade, *The French Canadians, 1760–1955* (Toronto, 1955), p. 17.

talked of for bishop of the colony the seeds of conflict had been sown.

Behind the ecclesiastical feud that now broke over New France fell the shadow of party alignments in the French Church of the period. In official circles Gallicanism, with its emphasis on the State's control of the Church, was exceedingly strong; on the other hand, the Jesuits and their followers — called ultramontanists by their enemies — stood firmly for the rights and independence of the Holy See in its dealings with the Church in France. If there was to be a bishopric at Quebec — something the colonial government had envisioned as early as 1647 — it became a matter of supreme importance on whose initiative it would depend and from which party the bishop would be drawn. In other words, would the Paris government succeed in bringing the bishopric under the terms of the concordat of 1516 that gave the king the upper hand, or would the Ultramontanists move in time to assure one of their own number and thus maintain the paramount position of the Holy See?

There is no necessity for entering into the details of the complicated negotiations and maneuvers that now ensued between Quebec, Paris, and Rome before a final settlement was reached that proved acceptable to the parties concerned. Suffice it to say, the Holy See and the French court ultimately agreed on a former student of the Jesuits, François de Montmorency de Laval, who was consecrated by the papal nuncio as titular Bishop of Petraea *in partibus infidelium* at the Church of Saint Germain-des-Près in Paris on December 8, 1658. In naming Laval a vicar apostolic rather than a bishop with proper or ordinary jurisdiction — which the government had sought — the Holy See scored a point, for it was easier to keep in line a missionary prelate who depended for his authority on the Congregation de Propaganda Fide than it was an ordinary who had been sponsored by a powerful lay source like that of the French crown.

Bishop Laval's appointment brought a vigorous protest from the Archbishop of Rouen who felt that it was a violation of his canonical rights, a position in which the Gallican-minded *parlement* of Rouen sought to sustain him by forbidding Laval to exercise his episcopal powers in the colony. But the archbishop's objections were upheld by Rome only to the extent of confirming all acts performed under his authority in New France up to the arrival of Bishop Laval at Quebec in June, 1659. And when Rouen attempted to continue the new world jurisdiction by granting the Abbé de Quéylus the powers of vicar general, it caused a prolonged quarrel that ended with Laval winning complete jurisdiction. Finally in 1674 he was granted the title of Bishop of Quebec when the vicariate was raised to the dignity of a diocese.

If we have dwelt on this subject at some length it is because the episcopal jurisdiction of François de Montmorency de Laval and his successors was exercised far beyond what we today call Canada. With the extension of French power through the Great Lakes region and the Mississippi Valley the authority of the Bishop of Quebec reached a large part of the future United States as well. Of the formidable prelate whose policies were to leave so deep an imprint in the new world it has been said:

> In all, Laval guided the destinies of the Church in New France for thirty-four years, ruling in a more authoritarian and absolute fashion than any representative of the all-powerful Sun King. He left more of a mark upon the colony than any governor except the great Frontenac with whom he had quarreled violently. . . .[3]

The success with which Laval asserted his authority against the representatives of the crown took much of the edge off the State's control of the Church, and for that reason the union of the two, though real, was never as close and effective in New France as it was in New Spain. Laval's insistence upon the principles that insured his liberty of action frustrated the men of Gallican sympathies as well as helped to establish a tradition of freedom for the Church in the new world such as it did not know in France. By the same token, to be sure, the bishop's close adherence to papal policy fostered an ultramontanist spirit, as his stern discipline and strict interpretation of the moral code were responsible for a somewhat severe tone in the ecclesiastical life of his jurisdiction, even though he escaped the doctrinal excesses of that contemporary Jansenistic movement.

To return to the Jesuits' missions among the Iroquois, the decade of warfare that followed the French retreat from Onondaga was almost entirely a Canadian rather than an American affair and needs only

[3] *Ibid.*, p. 39. A recent biographer of Frontenac, speaking of the close control maintained by the State over the Church in France at the time, has stated: "This made the king and his ministers very sensitive and suspicious; the slightest manifestation of independence by the clergy appeared to them to be an attempt to challenge the authority of the state. It was this climate of opinion that was transplanted to New France by officials of both church and crown." W. J. Eccles, *Frontenac. The Courtier Governor* (Toronto, 1959), p. 51.

to be summarized here. Like all Indian wars it took its tool in lives needlessly sacrificed, for example, the two Sulpician missionaries, Jacques Lemaître and Guillaume Vignal, who were murdered by the redmen in 1661. In the early stages the fighting at times ran dangerously near to an Indian victory, but with the coming of de Tracy and his seasoned troops in 1665 the tide turned in favor of the French. In 1667 the Indians sued for peace whereupon there took place the Jesuits' strongest bid for the souls of the Iroquois. By the end of 1668 they had established missions in all five cantonments of the Confederacy, and ultimately each had a unit of the Confraternity of the Holy Family which had been founded at Montreal by Father Chaumonot, Marguerite Bourgeoys, and others.

During the succeeding decade the Black Robes counted over 2,200 baptisms, although by no means all of these became permanent Catholics. The customary obstacles were met, of course, such as the general unreliability of the Indians – and the special fickleness of the Senecas – the intrigues of the medicine men, and the difficulty with the native languages. But the major stumbling block in these Iroquois missions was the liquor traffic which Parkman called "the most potent lure and the most killing bait." For, as he said, wherever it could be found, "thither the Indians and their beaver-skins were sure to go, and the interest of the fur-trade, vital to the colony, were bound up with it." [4] The French, the Dutch, and the English – all used brandy to win the savages to their side and to keep them there. In fact, it was not only the natives' pagan practices that prompted the missionaries to move their neophytes to the Christian Indian villages along the Saint Lawrence; their determination to save them from the effects of the white man's fire water was often just as strong a motive.

True, a majority of the Iroquois Confederacy never accepted the Catholic faith as a permanent thing in their lives, but many of them did and among these were some striking instances of virtue that had a lasting effect among their fellow tribesmen. For example, Daniel Garakonthié, a relative of an Onondaga chief sachem, was deeply impressed by the wholesome influence of Christianity that he observed in the converts of his own tribe, and as a consequence he became a powerful protective force for the missionary cause, although only late

[4] Francis Parkman, *The Old Regime in Canada* (Boston, 1910), II, 124.

in life was he personally baptized. In the same manner Saonchiogwa, a Cayuga chief, and Pierre Assendasé, a former Mohawk medicine man, were of great assistance in bringing relatives and friends into the Church and in exercising a generally uplifting influence.

The most famous converts, perhaps, were among the women. Katharine Ganneaktena, of the Erie tribe, was the instrument of much good before her death in 1673, and it was to her that there was chiefly owed the establishment of the Christian Indian village of La Prairie near Montreal, a community that for many years afforded not only a refuge for the Catholic Indians who could not live in safety in their own tribes, but also something of a model of sedentary life for the redmen. And Katharine Tekakwitha, the Mohawk girl whose mother had been a Christian Algonquin, gave an extraordinary example of sanctity among her people. When the menacing treatment of her pagan uncle made life in her native village intolerable, Katharine was counseled by Father Jacques de Lamberville, S.J., to flee to La Prairie which she did in the autumn of 1677. There the pious girl who lived with her brother-in-law was the source of deep edification to all in the community. Upon her death in the spring of 1680 at the age of twenty-four Katharine was buried at a spot she had chosen some years before, and the fame of her virtues traveled far and wide and became a source of pride for the Christian Indians of both New France and northern New York.[5]

Some years before Katharine Tekakwitha had left for the safety of La Prairie a major change had taken place in the rule of the colony where she had been born and raised. In March, 1665, King Charles II of England had made a grant to his brother James, Duke of York, of an immense tract extending south from Maine to embrace the islands off the cost of New England and stretching from the western boundary of Connecticut to the eastern shore of Delaware Bay. The duke moved quickly to take possession by appointing commissioners with Colonel Richard Nicolls at their head and an armed force to capture New

[5] In 1884 the bishops of the Third Plenary Council of Baltimore petitioned the Holy See for the beatification of Katherine Tekakwitha, and again in 1935 both the American and Canadian hierarchies asked for this favor. On the subject of her virtues cf. Robert E. Holland, S.J. (Ed.), *The Positio of the Historical Section of the Sacred Congregation of Rites on the Introduction of the Cause for Beatification and Canonization and on the Virtues of the Servant of God Katharine Tekakwitha, the Lily of the Mohawks* (New York, 1940).

Netherlands from the Dutch. Nicolls executed his commission with remarkable ease in September, 1664, and in the same month the English took the place of the Dutch in an alliance with the Iroquois Confederacy.

From this point on the Anglo-French rivalry that we have already met in Maine and New England was to include New York, as the former Dutch colony was now called. And one of the most critical and sensitive areas was the territory along the southern shores of Lake Ontario where the Iroquois had many villages, territory that was obviously of prime importance to both the French and the English for the fur trade as well as for defense. In the foreshadowing of the contest between the two powers in the 1660's the inequality between them was not nearly as marked as it later became, for the French had the advantage of centralized control, a growing string of forts in the western country, an excellent fighting force, and a series of treaties of friendship with most of the Indian tribes from the Abenakis of Maine on the east to the Algonquins of Wisconsin on the west, to say nothing of the detailed knowledge and experience of the western wilderness possessed by their *coureurs de bois* which could not be matched by any other white men. On their side the English had overwhelming numerical superiority with around 200,000 Anglo-Americans in 1689 when the contest broke in earnest to the 10,000 French Canadians. Moreover, they had the Iroquois alliance and marked superiority at sea as well as in trade and finance.

To men like Jean Talon, able and resourceful intendant of New France, and after him Louis de Buade, Count de Frontenac, whose policies as governor after 1672 were those of Talon, the fur trade was the all important factor, and every move on the political chessboard was made with a view to keep the pelts moving along the Saint Lawrence to the French depots and prevent them from being syphoned off on the opposite side of Lake Ontario and down the Hudson to the English. It was this policy that dictated the construction of Fort Frontenac on Lake Ontario in 1673 where Kingston now stands, as it was the motive behind La Salle building Fort Niagara four years later. In order to maintain the fur routes in the hands of friendly Indians it likewise meant that the French had to espouse their red allies whenever the Iroquois attacked them, and that was true for distant tribes like the Eries and the Miamis as well as for the Illinois on Lake Michigan and the Algonquins on Lake Superior. In the prosecution of this major objective the missionaries were also made to serve as instruments of the State's policy insofar as Frontenac and his successors could bring that about. If, therefore, one is to understand the troubled history of the missions of New York and the western country this background must be kept constantly in mind.

Through the first two decades of English rule in New York there was relatively little friction along the ill-defined boundaries of the two European powers. The early governors were noted for no outstanding accomplishments and they did not seriously challenge the French, even when the latter invaded northern New York in pursuit of their Iroquois enemies. But with the coming of Colonel Thomas Dongan in August, 1683, who was Governor of New York until the summer of 1688, English policy assumed a more aggressive tone. To Dongan incursions into what he regarded as part of the territory of his colony were not to be tolerated, although he was careful not to make open war because England and France were then at peace. Nonetheless, when the Iroquois vowed vengeance on the Illinois for the latter's killing of a Seneca chief and the French took the side of the Illinois, Dongan served notice on Quebec in June, 1684, that he considered the Iroquois Confederacy under English tutelage and any invasion of their lands would be regarded as an unfriendly act. At a meeting with the Iroquois chiefs at Albany in the same summer the governor accepted their offer of friendship and from that time on they remained firmly in the English camp until France was finally compelled to acknowledge that fact in the Treaty of Utrecht in 1713. While he continued as governor Dongan maintained a vigilant attitude and at times even provided powder and guns to the Iroquois tribesmen. At a time when the penal laws against the English Catholics were very much a reality it was slightly ironic that this far-seeing policy that prepared the way for a stronger English position when open hostilities broke in 1689 should have been owed to a Catholic official. As one authority expressed it:

The English governor who saw most clearly the strategic possibilities of the New York frontier, whether for trade or politics, was not an Englishman at all, but the Irish Catholic, Thomas Dongan. In an era of intense religious partisanship, when the loyalty of Catholics was sharply questioned, this Catholic governor was probably the most persistent and aggressive defender of British interests in North America.[6]

More pertinent to our purpose was Dongan's attitude toward the Church's missions. As a Catholic he did all he could to provide for the ministrations of the faith in New York by bringing out with him Father Thomas Harvey, an English Jesuit, approving the building of a small church and the opening of a Catholic school, and welcoming two other English Jesuits, Henry Harrison and Charles Gage, when they joined Harvey several years later. But it was one thing to assist the Church in his own colony; it was quite another to be expected to foster the missions of the French Jesuits among the Iroquois. To Dongan these priests were agents of a rival power that might at any time become an active enemy of his own sovereign. For that reason he refused to be drawn in by Frontenac's successor, Jacques Réné de Brisay, the Marquis of Denonville, when he suggested that the New York governor join the French against the Iroquois on religious grounds. Dongan made clear to Denonville, as he did later to Father Jean de Lamberville, that he would protect the missionaries in northern New York, but joining up against his Indian allies was another matter. That he was as good as his word about affording protection we know from the letter of Claude Dablon, superior of the French Jesuits, in which he told Dongan that his men on the Iroquois missions had informed him that, as he expressed it, "you spare no pains to procure for them the repose necessary for the exercise of their functions, furnishing them also the means to send many souls to Paradise."[7]

[6] Evarts Boutell Greene, *The Foundations of American Nationality*, rev. ed. (New York, 1935), p. 161. That Dongan could have reached the office of governor at this time was owing to the fact that the proprietor, the Duke of York, had himself become a Catholic sometime before 1672 and had among his objectives to rehabilitate his coreligionists as far as circumstances would allow. Dongan's contribution has been recognized by all the leading authorities on the subject. For example, Edward Channing stated that France's acknowledgement of English dominion over the Iroquois in 1713 was equivalent to a recognition of British sovereignty as far north as Lake Ontario. "Such an outcome," said Channing, "was the direct result of the firm stand that Dongan had taken. To him must be given the credit for first seeing the importance of the position of New York and of the Iroquois in the international politics of North America." "Colonel Thomas Dongan, Governor of New York," *Proceedings of the American Antiquarian Society* [New Series], XVIII (1907), 345.

[7] Dablon to Dongan [undated, probably late 1685 or early 1686], Hugh Hastings (Ed.), *Ecclesiastical Records. State of New York* (Albany, 1901), II, 905.

While they continued to reside in these missions Governor Dongan respected the French Jesuits, although he frankly wished that they would be gone since he regarded them, altogether rightly, as agents of France's interests among the savages as well as missionaries. He would neither recognize their presence as an argument for French hegemony over the Iroquois nor would he reconcile himself to their policy of sending away the Christian Iroquois to New France. In the summer of 1687 he informed Denonville that he was aware of what had happened – and was still happening – in directing the converts to the villages along the Saint Lawrence, and the French governor would pardon him, therefore, if he stated frankly that "that is not the right way to keep fair correspondence."[8] Dongan estimated that the loss already suffered by his colony through this means amounted to between 600 and 700 Indians and, as he told the Committee of Trade in London, "and more like to doe, to the great prejudice of this Goverm^{t} if not prevented."[9]

When the Jesuit superior sought the permission of the Governor of New York to have his men resume their work among the Iroquois, therefore, Dongan firmly refused since, in his judgment, they were being used to establish a French foothold within Iroquois territory. As a Catholic he was not indifferent to the souls of the savages, and he had a plan to provide for their religious needs by importing English priests on whose political loyalty he could count. Thus upon Denonville stepping up operations by sending an expedition against the Senecas in the summer of 1687 the New York governor reacted energetically. He met the Iroquois chiefs at Albany in early August where he submitted a number of recommendations of which two related directly to the missions. Dongan suggested that they despatch messengers to their Catholic tribesmen in New France with a request that they return, assuring them that he would see that they were furnished with lands to begin life anew. Moreover, he asked them not to receive Father de Lamberville or, as he said, "any French Priests, any more, having sent for English Priests whom you can be supplyed with, all to content."[10] The redmen agreed to get rid of the French mission-

[8] Dongan to Denonville, June 20, 1687, *ibid.*, II, 938.

[9] Dongan's report to Committee of Trade, February 22, 1687, E. B. O'Callaghan (Ed.), *The Documentary History of the State of New York* (Albany, 1850), I, 99.

[10] Dongan's Propositions to the Five Nations, Albany, August 5, 1687, John Romeyn Brodhead (Ed.), *Documents Relative to the Colonial History of the State of New-York* (Albany, 1853), III, 440.

aries, and they stated that if any of the Five Nations should desire English priests in their place they would inform Dongan.

The Governor of New France professed to be scandalized by so callous an attitude on the part of a Catholic official who would not hesitate to sacrifice the conversion of the natives to serve his political purposes. Actually, at the time there were no missionaries among the Iroquois. The war between the French and the Five Nations had forced several of them to withdraw in 1683, Father Etienne de Carheil was driven out by the Cayugas in the following year, and with the recall of Jacques de Lamberville to New France in 1686 there was left only his older brother Jean. If Dongan needed any further evidence of the way in which the Quebec government used the missionaries for political purposes, he found it in Denonville's deceitful employment of Father Jean de Lamberville as an intermediary to induce the Iroquois to accept an invitation to a peace conference. Confiding in the priest's integrity, the chiefs kept the appointment only to find themselves seized, thrown into chains, and sent to France to become galley slaves. The Jesuit had not been let in on the governor's secret plans, and it was a tribute to the Indians' regard for him that after they learned of what had happened he was not summarily killed. Instead the older chiefs, uncertain of how the young braves would react to de Lamberville's part in the incident, had him escorted to the nearest French post where they handed him over and thereupon prepared for war.

Thus the French missionaries were compelled to abandon their Iroquois missions before Dongan had English priests to replace them. As it turned out the three English Jesuits, Fathers Harvey, Harrison, and Gage, never worked among the Five Nations. Their own time in the colony was, of course, brief, for with the revolutionary disturbances of 1688 they became themselves hunted men. Precisely why they did not undertake work among the natives, it is impossible to say, but it may well have been because the Iroquois never gave any indication of having accepted Dongan's offer of English priests as missionaries.

With Father de Lamberville's departure the most fruitful twenty years of missionary labor among the Five Nations came to a treacherous and inglorious end with this Jesuit's betrayal and compromise by New France's Catholic governor. In the years that followed the Society of Jesus made little or no headway. During the time that Pierre Milet,

S.J., was a prisoner of the Oneidas before his release in October, 1694, he had the consolation of ministering to some Christian converts and of rendering spiritual aid to the captives who were sentenced to death. The devastating campaigns of Count Frontenanc, back again as governor, through the Onondaga and Oneida lands in 1696 frightened the redmen into suing for peace the following year. Peace was also made between England and France at Ryswick in September, 1697, although it brought no real settlement of the rival claims of the two powers in North America.

Thus during the interval that led up to England's renewal of war on France in May, 1702, border warfare continued to take its toll in lives and property. A further evil circumstance for the missions in this year 1697 was the appointment of the notoriously anti-Catholic Richard Coote, the Earl of Bellomont, as Governor of New York. With the English colonies in a state of excitement over tales of papist spies stirring up the Indians, Bellomont had no difficulty in having the assembly pass a law in August, 1700, that made it punishable by perpetual imprisonment for any Catholic priest to come into the colony or to perform any religious ceremony of the Church of Rome; and any colonist who received or harbored a priest was liable to a fine of £200 and to be put in the pillory for three days.[11]

In spite of this threat, however, the Jesuits dared to return. Father Jacques Bruyas came back to Onondaga in June, 1701, and when the Indians appealed for additional missionaries six of his confrères followed within the next few years. At the outset of what was called Queen Anne's War in America the Iroquois were neutral, but when they threw in their lot with England it sounded the death knell for the missions. The Anglo-Americans, suspecting the influence that the priests had over the natives, were intent on clearing them out as part of their preparations for what proved to be an abortive attack on New France. With that in mind Colonel Peter Schuyler, American-born militia officer, came to Onondaga in 1709 where at the time there were two Jesuits, Jacques de Lamberville and Pierre de Mareuil. Feigning peaceful intentions, he first prevailed on de Lamberville to act as an emissary to Quebec, but he had hardly left before Schuyler secretly

[11] A similar measure was enacted in Massachusetts, of which Bellomont was also governor, on June 17, 1700. For the text of the Massachusetts law cf. Ellis, *Documents*, pp. 121–123.

inspired a group of drunken Indians to plunder the mission church and residence and then set them on fire. He next turned his blandishments on Father de Mareuil by pretending that his life was in danger and warning him that he should seek safety from the savages. The missionary believed what he was told and accompanied Schuyler to Albany, not knowing that on June 29 the New York assembly had issued a warrant for his arrest; thus he walked into a trap and was detained until 1710. In this fashion there was acted out the final episode in the history of the Jesuit missions within what is today New York State.

Thereafter, aside from the Franciscan friars whom the French maintained as chaplains beyond the middle of the century at their military posts like Niagara and Crown Point, the only other contact worth mentioning that New York had with Catholicism before the American Revolution centered around the site of the present city of Ogdensburg. When the French troops were marching to attack Fort Edward in May, 1745, they had with them as their chaplain the Sulpician, Father François Piquet, who conceived the idea of a mission at this spot similar to Saulte Saint Louis or Caughnawaga, a Christian Iroquois village a few miles above Montreal. Piquet succeeded in interesting the Governor of New France, Clement de Taffanel, the Marquis de la Jonquière, who went with him in May, 1748, to select a site. Construction of a palisaded fort and chapel were soon underway in the settlement to which Piquet gave the name of La Présentation in honor of the patronal feast of the Sulpicians, the presentation of the Virgin Mary in the temple. Considerable sums were spent on the fortifications and dwellings and Piquet traveled widely contacting the natives and recruiting settlers as far away as Niagara. But the bright prospect soon faded when a sudden raid by the Mohawks in October, 1749, delivered La Présentation to the flames. Had the Sulpician been a man of less resolute character that would have been the end of the story. But he refused to be daunted and with a little group of five or six families a new start was made, and in about two years the community had grown to nearly 400 families with around 3,000 souls drawn mostly from the Onondagas and Cayugas.

The success that Father Piquet had achieved in enlisting help for his mission from friends in Montreal, its stable government vested in twelve chiefs, and the steady rise in its population by recruiting among the neighboring tribes, eventually brought a pause to critics who had ridiculed Piquet's folly. In May, 1752, La Présentation was visited by Bishop Henri-Marie de Pontbriand of Quebec who baptized 120 Indians and confirmed a large number on this first visit of a Catholic bishop to New York. A few years thereafter, however, the flourishing community faced a new crisis with the outbreak of the French and Indian War in 1755. The Indian braves were called up for military service, and as the war turned more and more against the French the position of La Présentation became a hopeless one to defend and it had to be abandoned. Father Piquet and his neophytes settled for a time at Grand Isle aux Galops, but that, too, finally gave way before the sweep of the Anglo-American and Iroquois victories, and on May 10, 1760, Piquet wrote the final entry in his parish register and set out for France by way of Louisiana. A Sulpician confrère, Jean Pierre Besson de la Garde, chaplain at Fort Levis, at first cared for Piquet's converts, but La Présentation's community was ultimately scattered with a number of them being absorbed into the Christian villages of Canada.

In the 118 years between Jogues' first capture by the Mohawks and Piquet's departure the present State of New York was the scene of repeated attempts to bring its Indian population to an acceptance of the Catholic faith. In general those attempts failed, for at no time was more than a minority of the Five Nations enrolled as practicing Christians. Moreover, some of the missionaries had to endure from the savages of this region tortures that were almost without parallel in the history of the new world. Yet the story of the New York missions was not one of complete failure, for several thousand Indians were made stable Catholics, and there were likewise hundreds of children and adults who were baptized before their deaths. That the evangelization of many of these redmen had been effective, was evident from the fact that as late as 1905 there were over 2,000 of their descendants in the town of Caughnawaga alone, to say nothing of those who lived in other Indian settlements of Canada. But in New York itself at the end of the French regime scarcely a trace remained of the supreme efforts that had been put forth save the charred ruins of the missions and the scattered remains of the missionaries who had given their lives for the faith that they had so bravely preached to these savage people.

Aside from the purely spiritual aspects of the New York missions there were the secular interests of the missionaries. Here as elsewhere some of their number acted as explorers, and during their travels they assembled much important data on the plants, minerals, and animals of the regions that they traversed. In the early years these secular interests were more marked, although at all times the principal attraction for these cultivated Frenchmen living in the midst of a wilderness with a primitive people was the Indians themselves. As a consequence of their varied interests the annual reports to their superiors in France, the famous *Jesuit Relations*, constituted more than the mere chronicle of the spiritual progress or retrogression of the savages; they also became a prime source of information about the natives' way of life.

Beyond the personal interests that lay outside the individual missionary's spiritual duties there was no time, of course, when the missions in general were free from ties of one kind or another that bound them to a civil and military administration from which they derived real advantages in physical protection and material support. As Father Barthelemy Vimont, the Jesuit superior at Quebec, told his provincial as early as 1643, his current report contained the usual examples of virtue and notable increase of the faith, but these had to be tempered by "the bitterness of manifold evil tidings" caused by the Iroquois who, as he said, "had we not some help from France, would undoubtedly ruin here both the faith and commerce."[12] And as time went on this need for protection increased, becoming especially acute in the 1680's during the weak administrations of Governors Denonville and La Barre when the Iroquois grew bold enough to massacre the inhabitants of Lachine near Montreal. Nor were the missionaries independent of the government for the material support of their work. Father Martin Bouvart, the Jesuit superior, made that clear in his financial report of October, 1701, which revealed that nearly half of the total annual income of a little over 13,000 livres had come from the crown in the form of a pension of 5,000 livres for the general missions plus 1,500 livres as a donation from Louis XIV for the poor and indigent among

[12] Relation of Barthélemy Vimont for 1642–1643 [undated, but in early autumn of 1643], *Jesuit Relations*, XXIII, 269. A similar comment on the military may be found in the report of François Le Mercier, S.J., dated November 3, 1665, where he rejoiced at the arrival of de Tracy and his regiment some months before. (*Ibid.*, XLIX, 215).

the Abenaki and Iroquois converts.[13] On the basis of both defense and financial support, therefore, the missions gained important advantages from the co-operative action of Church and State.

There were likewise distinct disadvantages from the close association of the two powers in New France. The priests constantly complained about the demoralizing effects of the liquor and firearms furnished by the white men to their Indian neophytes, as well as the liberties that at times were taken with the Indian women. Moreover, the government officials' calls upon the priests for diplomatic and political tasks, especially in relation to the Indians, was a further distraction from their main business. In their role as agents of His Most Christian Majesty the missionary not infrequently found that the purposes of the crown were difficult to reconcile with his prime objective of saving souls. The union of the spiritual and temporal powers was, then, at best a mixed blessing. Given the circumstances of life in the wilderness colony, however, it was inevitable, for had the French removed their protecting arm the missionaries would often have been in danger of annihilation. And by the same token the civil and military personnel had no more effective instruments at hand for quieting the natives and for acting in the role of peace emissaries than the Catholic missionaries.

Finally, situated as it was between the Great Lakes and the Saint Lawrence Valley, the heartland of the French enterprise, New York could not escape becoming a bone of contention, whether that be between the French and the Iroquois or between the French and their European rivals.

Thus the missions among the Five Nations rarely, if ever, enjoyed a prolonged period of unbroken peace during which the Indians were not being either wooed or warred upon by one or other of the principal powers. In this sense these missions were even more unhappy in their location than those of Maine situated between Acadia and New England. Willy nilly, then, New York became a part of the great struggle that shaped the history of this part of North America in the late seventeenth and eighteenth centuries, a struggle that was finally determined only in September, 1760, when the last French strongholds on the Saint Lawrence were surrendered into British hands.

[13] "Revenues of the Jesuits in Canada," *ibid*, LXV, 181–187. The livre was roughly equivalent to 25¢ in American money.

CHAPTER EIGHT

THE GREAT LAKES

But if the Iroquois goes thither, why shall not we also? If there are conquests to make, why shall not the faith make them, since it makes them in all parts of the world? Behold countless peoples, but the way to them is closed; therefore we must break down all obstacles, and, passing through a thousand deaths leap into the midst of the flames, to deliver therefrom so many poor Nations. We have not spared ourselves for any of them, nor have we let slip a single opportunity that has presented itself for hastening to their aid; and we are running to succor them again at the present time. . . .[1]

It would be easy to dismiss these words from the Jesuit mission report for 1659–1660 as the perfervid rhetoric of a religious enthusiast were it not that they offer a true description of what really happened when the French missionaries seriously turned their attention beyond their familiar haunts along the Saint Lawrence and northern New York. Behind this zealous exhortation from the Jesuit superior at the end of the 1650's there lay a series of developments in Indian warfare and the fur trade that conditioned the new advance of the cross into the West, and it is necessary to understand that background first before one attempts to chart the course of the missionaries' invasion of the western country.

As has so often been said of New France, the very life of the colony depended on the trade in furs. Before many years had passed most of the fur-bearing animals in the Saint Lawrence region had been killed off and the French were compelled to look elsewhere, and it was here

[1] Relation for 1659–1660 credited to Jerome Lalemant, S.J. [n.p., n.d.], *Jesuit Relations*, XLV, 239.

that the Ottawa River offered the natural route to a new source of supply. As early as 1634 Jean Nicolet had explored the Ottawa, traversed Georgian Bay, and had gone as far south as Green Bay at the request of Champlain who had heard of a great waterway in the West and thought that it might be a route to China. It never occurred to the French, therefore, to doubt their claim to the western country, and had it not been for the enmity of the Iroquois their access to the furs of that region would not have constituted too great a problem. As French allies the Hurons and the Ottawas had acted as middlemen for the furs which the tribes in the upper Great Lakes area brought down to barter for the knives, needles, and other utensils furnished by the French. But the Five Nations were relentless and by 1650 the Hurons and the Ottawas were beaten and dispersed, and the gravity of the situation was brought home to the French in 1652 when not a single fur reached Montreal from the western country.

In spite of the Iroquois triumph the white men held on and after several years they had secured the Ottawa route to a reasonable degree. In order to eliminate the middlemen and to lessen the hazard and cost of transportation new trading posts at Michilimackinac, Green Bay, and Sault Sainte Marie were established which ultimately superseded those on the Saint Lawrence. And as the West gradually opened up it brought the heyday of the colorful and daring *coureurs de bois* who numbered between 500 and 600 in 1679, and whose dangerous occupation was lucrative enough to draw men off from the land to the alarm of the authorities of both Church and State. To the latter it meant a lessening of the colony's badly needed tillage, to say nothing of the loss to the spare white population of the colony which totaled only 7,500 in 1675; to the former it meant not only a similar loss to the ecclesiastical land holdings, but the consciousness that this line of work usually led to the *coureur de bois'* relinquishment of whatever moral code he had when he met the Indians – to their mutual contamination – in the inland forests.

Nearly two decades before Father Lalemant had written his stirring lines on the West as a mission field Charles Raymbault and Isaac Jogues, as we have seen, had been the first of the French Jesuits to penetrate that country. And their lack of success in the early 1640's was repeated by that of their brethren who came after them. For example, in 1656 Léonard Garreau and Gabriel Druillettes thought to return west with a group of Ottawas only to be overtaken by a Mohawk war party that killed Garreau and put the Ottawas to flight while Druillettes managed to escape. Yet despite these reverses the Jesuits never allowed their gaze to be diverted from the missionary potentialities of the West as they watched the feverish activity of the French for traders and the turmoil of Indian warfare. Not only was it their hope to bring new tribes to the faith, but they were also intent on keeping in touch with the Hurons whom they had instructed and baptized and who had subsequently fled westward before the vengeance of the Iroquois.

In the summer of 1660 a fresh opportunity seemed to present itself when a flotilla of Chippewas came to Montreal under the guidance of that remarkable pair, Médart Chouart, Sieur de Groseilliers, and Pierre Esprit Radisson, brothers-in-law whose careers offered about as strange a mixture of exploration, trading, and political manouvering as one will find among the wilderness adventurers. On this occasion Fathers Réné Ménard and Charles Albanel were appointed to return with the Chippewas along with seven other Frenchmen, but as it turned out the Indians in the canoe to which Father Albanel had been assigned refused to take him and in the end they departed with Ménard as the only priest in the party. The latter had a presentiment of what awaited him, for in a letter written to a fellow Jesuit before leaving Three Rivers he said:

> This is probably the last word that I shall write to you, and I wish it to be the seal of our friendship until eternity. . . . In three or four months you may include me in the Memento for the dead, in view of the kind of life led by these peoples, of my age, and of my delicate constitution. In spite of that, I have felt such powerful promptings and have seen in this affair so little of the purely natural, that I could not doubt, if I failed to respond to this opportunity, that I would experience an endless remorse.[2]

During the long journey Father Ménard was compelled to endure all kinds of sufferings and insults from the Chippewas who delighted in such tricks as throwing his breviary into the water and in setting him on shore and then rowing off to a place that forced him to clamber over sharp rocks in order to catch up. But the missionary's will power was equal to the test and by October 15 they reached a point on the

[2] Ménard to an unnamed Jesuit, Three Rivers, August 27, 1660, Relation of 1659–1660, *ibid.*, XLVI, 81.

south shore of Lake Superior on Keweenaw Bay probably a few miles from the present town of L'Anse, Michigan, where he had the consolation of saying Mass. It was a grim prospect for the cultivated French priest who at the time was fifty-five years of age and in delicate health, knowing that he was almost 1,000 miles from any other priest and that the crude savages were to be his chief companions through the long winter months.

But Ménard spent the time profitably by concentrating his catechetical instructions on a few natives who had the proper dispositions for, as he said, "I was unwilling to admit a large number, contenting myself with those who, I judged, would continue firm in the faith during my absence."[3] That his judgment had not betrayed him was proven when his Jesuit confrères later visited the area and discovered that these Indians were still faithful to Ménard's teaching. In the spring of 1661 he heard of a band of Catholic Hurons to the southwest and he decided to go to them. He and a single companion set out on their dangerous journey on July 13 during which in some mysterious manner the two became separated and the missionary was never heard from again. When it became known to Ménard's brethren that he had forfeited his life somewhere in present day Wisconsin it quickened their resolve to replace him, and in 1664 Claude Jean Allouez was appointed, a priest who was destined to become one of the most famous of the missionaries of the West.

The appointment of Father Allouez came at what seemed an opportune moment for an enterprise such as the western missions. Upon the death of Cardinal Mazarin in 1661 the young Louis XIV had assumed personal charge of the government of France and had reversed the policy of neglect which the mother country had for so long a time practiced toward its new world colony. Thoroughly in sympathy with the mercantilist philosophy of Colbert, his great controller-general of finances, the king was anxious to advance France's power in North America, and the penetration and acquisition of the heart of the con-

[3] Ménard to unnamed correspondent [n.p., n.d.], Relation of 1663–1664, *ibid.*, XLVIII, 273–275. For example, the Relation of 1666–1667 signed by François Le Mercier at Quebec, November 10, 1667, incorporated portions of the report of Claude Allouez, S.J., wherein he spoke of having stopped at the place where Ménard spent the winter five years before and of encountering there, "some remnants of his labors, in the person of two Christian women who had always kept the faith, and who shone like two stars amid the darkness of that infidelity" (*ibid.*, L, 269).

tinent were admirably suited to serve that objective. In the attempt to extend French dominion over the western country the missionaries were prominently associated along with the explorers, traders, and soldiers. For every new mission placed on the Great Lakes was an additional source of strength since the Black Robes were frequently able to exert a pacifying influence over the Indians even where they could not accomplish their religious conversions.

At the time of his new assignment Claude Allouez was forty-two years of age and had been a missionary in New France for six years. His initial start proved abortive when he reached Montreal only to find that the annual flotilla of the Ottawas had already departed for the West. But he had better luck the following year and with six Frenchmen and over 400 savages he left Three Rivers on August 8, 1665, and reach Sault Sainte Marie early in September. During the course of that month they cruised along the shores of Lake Superior until on October 1 they reached a place on Chequamegon Bay where Allouez erected a bark chapel to which he gave the name of the Holy Spirit. Thus was there begun the mission that came to be known as La Pointe du Saint Esprit near present Ashland, Wisconsin. It was a good location, for the abundant supply of fish helped to attract a variety of Indians, and some time later the Jesuits reported that they had met at La Pointe twenty or thirty 'nations,' all with different languages, customs, and policies. Here, then, in October, 1665, Allouez inaugurated a western career that was to be terminated only with his death in August, 1689, in what is today northern Indiana. During nearly a quarter of a century he traversed the present State of Wisconsin from one end to the other, founded missions at Green Bay and Sault Sainte Marie, traveled south for a mission on the Miami River, and worked with Jacques Marquette among the Illinois at Kaskaskia. Early writers have spoken of Allouez in superlative terms, likening him to a second Francis Xavier, and crediting him with having instructed over 100,000 and baptized more than 10,000 savages. Allowing for exaggeration, it was still an impressive record, and among France's seventeenth-century empire builders he deserves an honored place.

In his new location Father Allouez was more than a missionary, for in July, 1663, Bishop Laval had appointed him his vicar general for the western country with jurisdiction over the French inhabitants as well as the Indian neophytes. He spent his first two years in the West traveling widely and acquainting himself with the area, one trip taking him as far as the extreme western shore of Lake Superior where he had his first contact with the terrible Sioux who were as much of a scourge to the western Indians as the Iroquois were to those farther east. In early May, 1667, Allouez made a journey to the Lake Nipigon region where he sought to revive the faith of the Nipissings who had been among those evangelized in the days of the Huron mission. It is interesting to note how often the missionaries returned to the subject of these earlier converts and with how much warmth they referred to the manner in which they had held to the Catholic faith. It was in that vein that Allouez spoke of his experience at Lake Nipigon when he described the Mass that he had said in a "Chapel of foliage" and how the Nipissings listened with "as much piety and decorum as do our Savages of Quebec in our Chapel at Sillery"; and he added, "to me it was the sweetest refreshment I had during that Journey, entirely removing all past fatigue."[4]

It was a distinct benefit for the missionaries to meet these refugees from the Huron mission in the West since it helped to dull the edge of disappointment that they experienced from some of the tribes of that region. It so happened that the Ottawas had been the first Indians from the upper lakes to trade with the French, and as a consequence it was their name that was given to all the tribes of that vast territory. But the Ottawas proper were a deeply depraved lot about whose vices Allouez would write some vivid passages, and the proud and cruel Sacs and Foxes did not suggest very promising material on which to work. But the Black Robes' spirits were buoyed up by even minor successes as, for example, an entire year's labor that resulted in the baptism of eighty children of whom several had died and gone to heaven. As the superior remarked, "That mitigates all their hardships, and fortifies them to undergo all the labors of that Mission."[5]

But there were bright spots, too, of which the Pottawatomies offered one, although it was the Illinois who seemed to furnish the finest prospect for future conversions. A band of this southern tribe had come to La Pointe shortly after Allouez' arrival and he had preached to them with such promising results that he became a champion for a mission among these people. As he told his superior about the Illinois, "I con-

[4] Relation of 1666–1667, *ibid.*, LI, 67.
[5] *Ibid.*, LI, 261.

fess that the fairest field for the Gospel appears to me to be yonder. Had I had leisure and opportunity, I would have pushed on to their country, to see with my own eyes all the good things there of which they tell me." He had been intrigued by the Indians' account of the warm climate of their homeland, the absence of forests, and the vast prairies "where oxen, cows, deers, bears, and other animals feed in great numbers." Even the Illinois' forthright admission that their country was infested with rattlesnakes that caused many deaths, and for which there seemed to be no remedy, did not discourage him.[6]

In all his early travels in the West Father Allouez had kept his eyes opened for everything about the land and its inhabitants that might tell for or against his prime objective. Of one thing he had become convinced: if the Jesuits were to have any lasting success in this western land suitable buildings such as lodgings and chapels would have to be constructed. And for this type of work there was needed either a number of lay assistants, men who though in the lay state gave their services to the Society of Jesus, or laymen whom they would hire. His realization of the price exacted of even the most vigorous and robust men by long and fatiguing trips through the forest and over the rivers and lakes, was confirmed by his own experience which had taught him that even a "body of bronze" could not withstand the wear and tear of this continuous traveling, especially if a man had to labor in construction work or if he had no fit place to which to retire for rest and recuperation.[7] With a mind crowded with ideas of this kind, as well as with much useful data on physical aspects of the country and the characteristics of its native peoples, by the summer of 1667 Allouez was ready to accompany the annual Indian flotilla when it left for Quebec, there to report to his superiors and to seek new recruits and fresh supplies.

Whenever the missionaries traveled with the redmen they were, of course, at the mercy of the latter's timetable, and on this occasion Allouez found that he would have only two days in which to transact his business in the colonial capital. But he made the hours count, and when he boarded the Ottawa canoe for the return he had the consoling thought that Father Louis Nicolas, S.J., was in the company and that now Jesuit headquarters was adequately informed of what the

[6] *Ibid.*, LI, 51.
[7] *Ibid.*, LI, 71.

missionaries were likely to face on the opposite side of the Great Lakes. But on the matter of his lay helpers and supplies he met with a heartbreaking reverse, for at the last minute the Indians refused to accommodate the four Frenchmen and the baggage in their canoes. While in Quebec it was also Allouez' duty to report to Bishop Laval as his vicar general for the West. Word of the abuses practiced by the French traders had probably reached Laval long before this and in all likelihood Allouez had only confirmed it. In any case, on his return he carried a pastoral letter, signed August 6, in which the bishop forbade Frenchmen to be present at those Indian feasts which were "manifestly idolatrous," and granted full authority to Allouez to impose ecclesiastical penalties on those who refused to obey, as well as on the impenitent who were given "in an extraordinary degree to scandalous impurity."[8] It was open to question how much a weapon of this kind could curb the unruly impulses of the *coureurs de bois*, but the name of Laval was one to be conjured with by Frenchmen of that generation, and the pastoral letter might, indeed, be of some effect even at so remote a distance.

In the two years that Allouez had been the sole missionary at La Pointe he had not, as we have seen, been able to make any noticeable headway with the redmen on the score of their religious beliefs. Yet he had not despaired, and it was in behalf of the spiritual interests of the tribes served by this mission that he had undertaken the long and arduous trip to Quebec, which by the water route was over 1,000 miles each way. Upon their reaching the West in the early autumn of 1667 Father Nicolas went to the Sault and Allouez resumed his post at La Pointe. But after another largely fruitless year the latter finally announced to the heedless Indians that he was leaving them for good. Thereupon occurred a sudden *volte-face* on the part of one group which caused the missionary to change his plans. The chiefs of the Kiskakon clan of the Ottawas held a council and decided to abolish polygamy and the sacrifices to their pagan deities, as well as to decline hereafter to attend the superstitious ceremonies of other tribes in the vicinity. Moreover, by way of showing that they meant what they said, they moved their residence near to the chapel so as to facilitate the Jesuit's instructions for the women and children. With this turn of

[8] Quoted in Shea, *History*, I, 271.

events Allouez spent the winter of 1668–1669 giving instructions and in the following June he reported that among the Kiskakons there had been about 100 baptisms – adults and children – with thirty-eight baptisims of Huron refugees and over 100 among other tribes of the neighborhood.

The Kiskakon converts did not detain Allouez indefinitely, however, for in the summer of 1669 he was off once more for Quebec. On this occasion he had the good fortune of effecting a truce between the Five Nations and the western tribes through the instrumentality of several Iroquois prisoners whose rescue he had been able to bring about. During the same summer the Jesuit superior at Quebec made a series of new appointments in the western missions. Claude Dablon, a veteran of the Iroquois country, was made superior in Allouez' place with residence at the Sault, Jacques Marquette, who had been serving there since he came west in 1668 with Brother Louis de Boesme, was now transferred to La Pointe, and Allouez was designated to found a mission at Green Bay.

Marquette arrived at his new post on September 13 to find between 400 and 500 Hurons, almost all baptized, in a repentant mood for their share of blame in Allouez' withdrawal of some months before. Marquette's assignment to La Pointe was only a temporary one since he had been told to prepare himself to open a mission among the Illinois. While attending a sick man among the Kiskakon neophytes the stricken Indian presented the young Jesuit with a gift in the form of a slave who had recently been given to him by the Illinois, and it was with this boy that Marquette began his tutoring in the Illinois language. It was the apparent interest in Christianity manifested by the Illinois braves who came to La Pointe to trade that first focussed the attention of the missionaries on their southern homeland and its great river about which they spoke. It was this river that was to provide Marquette with his strongest claims to an unsought fame, and about which at the time he was so little informed that he conceived the Mississippi as reaching the sea in California.

The ignorance of Father Marquette concerning the mouth of the Mississippi was matched by his lack of knowledge of the Sioux who inhabited a part of its northern course, a tribe which, as he soon learned, constituted an important element in the lives of all at La Pointe. By way of trying to establish contact with these fierce warriors, he sent them some religious pictures in the hope that what he could not communicate in person in their own language he might demonstrate in another way. But his attempt to reach the Sioux was of no avail due to the mounting tension between them and the Hurons and Ottawas, a situation for which these tribesmen were themselves largely responsible. After the Sioux had been thoroughly aroused by the Huron-Ottawa attacks and had sent back Marquette's pictures, they declared war. The Hurons and Ottawas realized too late that they had brought upon themselves a contest to which they were in no way equal, and in deadly fear of capture by the Sioux, they now began frantic preparations for flight. There was nothing for Marquette to do, of course, but to follow them, and thus in the spring of 1671 he had the melancholy experience of witnessing the abandonment of the mission that Allouez had begun five and a half years before. For over a century and a half thereafter La Point was the rendezvous of only Indians and white traders, for not until Father Frederic Baraga came that way in July, 1835, was the word of God again preached in the vicinity of the Mission of the Holy Spirit.

In their anxiety to get away the Hurons and Ottawas headed their canoes eastward along the shores of Lake Superior until they reached Sault Sainte Marie where Father Gabriel Druillettes, whom we met earlier in Maine, had been stationed since the preceding autumn. After a stop at the Sault the two tribes parted company, the Ottawas proceeding east to Manitoulin Island where Louis André, S.J., awaited them, and the Hurons, with Marquette in their company, steering west toward their old haunts around Michillimackinac Island. Here, at a spot about fifty miles from the Sault as the crow flies, Father Dablon had in the previous winter founded the Mission of Saint Ignace which had the double advantage of proximity to the route taken by the Indians who used the straits and an abundance of fish in the surrounding waters. Between the date of its founding and 1765 when it was finally abandoned by the Jesuits, Saint Ignace moved several times from island to mainland and back again, but in the period of which we were speaking it enjoyed what were, perhaps, its most flourishing days. Marquette and his lay assistants worked here from the summer of 1671 until the missionary left on his historic trip to the Mississippi in the spring of 1673. That their labor had not been in vain was evident from the approximately 1,800 Christian Indians who were at Saint Ignace in 1677 and who pretty well filled its commodious church which was equipped with fine vestments and other furnishings provided by benefactors of the missions.

While his confrères were thus engaged in the region of Sault Sainte Marie, Father Allouez had not been idle. Upon receiving the assignment to found a mission on Green Bay he began his preparations and in November, 1669, the departure from the Sault of a group of Pottawattomie traders afforded him the chance for the first of three trips that he made to Green Bay before the mission was finally founded. Allouez spent two winters in this area, preaching to the natives, studying their customs, and trying to familiarize himself with their dialects. Then when river navigation opened each spring he began his travels anew. In this fashion he reached at various times the Foxes, Mascoutens, Miamis, Menomonees, and Winnebagoes among whom he endeavored to prepare the way for more permanent missionary effort at a later date. In the autumn of 1671 Allouez came for the third time to Green Bay, accompanied by Father André, and it was during the early months of this winter that there was built the bark chapel of Saint Francis Xavier in the Indian village where today there stands the town of De Pere, Wisconsin. A number of the natives showed a disposition to follow the missionaries' instructions, and some time after Allouez had left to preach to the tribes in southern Wisconsin, André counted about 500 souls who frequented the enlarged chapel that was built at Saint Francis Xavier. That the latter was not altogether devoid of refinement in its religious services, we know from a monstrance about fifteen inches in height that was dug up in 1802 at De Pere and which bore an inscription stating that it had been given in 1686 as a gift to the chapel by Nicolas Perrot, French commandant of the West.

The year 1671 was likewise notable for a further step taken by France to consolidate and extend its sovereignty over the interior of the continent, a policy that owed its most energetic expression among the Quebec officialdom to Jean Talon, the intendant. But before treating that event it will be well to take note of the rising feeling in France against the Society of Jesus and its relation to the Church in the new world. Talon belonged to the growing number of civil and military servants of the crown who felt an antipathy for the Jesuits, and who entertained a suspicion that their activity in the western country was motivated by a desire for material gain as well as anxiety to save the souls of the savages. This anti-Jesuit sentiment had already reached serious proportions in France, and since the broader issues out of which it evolved were to color ecclesiastical developments up to the early years of the nineteenth century in the later United States as well as in Canada, it will be helpful to understand something about its origins.

In the realm of ideology there were two movements within the French Church of this period that had their reflection in the colonies, even if they did not manifest themselves here to the same degree as they did in the mother country. One of these was Jansenism which centered about the interpretation given to the working of divine grace upon the individual soul. This bitter controversy broke over France in the early 1640's and split the upper class Catholics into warring camps that were arrayed against each other for generations. In this struggle the Jesuits vigorously opposed the theological pessimism of the Jansenists with its harshness and moral rigorism, only to have their opponents, in turn, assail them with equal vigor as laxists. The second movement had to do with the relations of the French Church to Rome and to the State in what came to be called Gallicanism. Briefly, the Gallicanists would make the Church in France virtually independent of the Holy See and almost completely subservient to the French monarchy. To this position, which was substantially contained in the propositions that were published in 1663 by the theologians of the Sorbonne, the Jesuits were again the prime opponents. It was in the French members of the Society that the Holy See, and the Ultramontanists generally—as they came to be called—found the staunchest defenders of the papacy's traditional position as the supranational authority for world Catholicism.

There were other reasons for enmity toward the Jesuits that had little to do with either theological principles or political theories, the principal one of which was probably their very success in France. In less than a quarter of a century after 1610 the Jesuits' numbers had almost trebled from the 1,135 of that year to the 3,350 members of 1643. Not only were there five flourishing provinces in France proper, but they maintained seven large missions in the French colonies as well as missions in places as remote as Persia and China. Moreover, the succession of nineteen Jesuits priests who served as confessors to the King of France gave them an influence at court, the true extent of which could not be known. But what their enemies could not measure, they proceeded to imagine or to suspect with often little scruple shown about circulating stories of secret Jesuit manipulations behind the scenes with the king and other members of the royal family.

This influence of the Jesuit confessors, whether real or imagined, became the object of envy and intrigue on the part of rival contenders for the royal favor, and for well over a century—at least from the accession of Cardinal Richelieu as prime minister in 1624 to the death in 1764 of the Marquise de Pompadour, the mistress of Louis XV—it remained a fairly constant factor in the arguments of the anti-Jesuit party. Finally, there was the wealth of the Society of Jesus. An organization of its size and multiple commitments, particularly when it had enjoyed such spectacular success, could hardly escape accumulating corporate wealth in the form of lands, buildings, and investments of one kind or another, the income from which was used to finance their vast undertakings in education, the foreign missions, and other enterprises of a parochial or scholarly character. But here, too, the enemy found material for unfavorable comment in the form of reports concerning Jesuit profits and the reasons that allegedly lay behind the ceaseless industry which they displayed in the pursuit of their varied activities.

When the scene is shifted from these religious tensions of the old world to America, the influence that they exercised in shaping the development of the Church in the colonies becomes fairly clear. And in no individual figure was that better demonstrated than in Bishop Laval. He was not only a former student and friend of the Jesuits, but a man whose entire temperament and turn of mind fitted him for casting his lot with the champions of Rome against the Gallican tendencies of the colonial officials. The result was that not long after his landing in June, 1659, Laval was engaged in a series of feuds with intendant, governor, and anyone else who ran afoul of the high concept he had of his episcopal prerogatives and of the obedience that was owed by all Catholics to the directives of the Holy See. The conflict centered about such questions as the regulation of the brandy trade which Laval and the Jesuits were determined to check as detrimental to the natives, and in the support which the bishop gave to the missionaries in their attempts to segregate the Indians from the whites, to the grave annoyance of the government which felt that the best way of handling the Indian problem was to bring them closer to the French and gradually fuse the two races into one community.[9]

For a decade or more Bishop Laval battled strenuously with the lay officials over issues of this kind, refusing as well to acknowledge the jurisdiction of the Archbishop of Rouen which the government sought to impose on him as a suffragan of that ecclesiastical province. In November, 1671, he sailed for Europe a second time to seek a solution to some of the problems that beset him, and this time he was gone for three years. But for Laval it was time well spent, for after prolonged negotiations the crown finally gave way in its insistence on regarding the new world bishopric as subject to the terms of the concordat of 1516. Once Louis XIV had relaxed his grip, Rome moved with greater ease and on October 1, 1674, Pope Clement X issued a bull erecting the Diocese of Quebec and making it immediately subject to the Holy See. Laval had won his principal point, and this latest triumph of his unshakeable will was to have a lasting effect, for as a recent writer has said, "ultramontanism was built into the very fabric of the Church in Quebec, which assumed a position very different from that which it held in gallican France."[10]

We are now in a better position to understand Talon's insistence that the power of the French government should without further delay make itself felt in the West in order not only to frighten off foreign rivals and impress the Indians, but, too, to rein in, as it were, the missionaries before they had secured a stronger hold on the area and its inhabitants and created there a sort of *imperium in imperio*. For these reasons the intendant organized two expeditions, one to the northwest under Simon-François Daumont, Sieur de Saint-Lusson, and another to the southwest under the command of René-Robert Cavelier, Sieur de La Salle. Needless to say, both commanders shared Talon's distrust of the Society of Jesus and its intentions. But all these men were realists enough to know that it would be an extremely short-sighted policy to ignore the Jesuits; it would be far better to associate them with the civil and military

[9] Most authorities are agreed about the deleterious effects that followed from the Indians and whites living near to each other. For example, in mentioning the failure of the efforts of various religious groups to assemble the Indians near the white settlements, Eccles stated that both the Jesuits and the Sulpicians "had learned to their cost that when the Indians lived in close contact with the French, each race quickly acquired the worst habits of the other" (*op. cit.*, pp. 56–57).

[10] Wade, *op. cit.*, p. 37.

undertakings and thus reap the benefit of their undoubted influence over the Indians, while at the same time keeping them mindful of the superior authority of the crown.

In preparation for the ceremony of taking formal possession of the country, which Talon had ordered Saint-Lusson to hold, the Indians for miles around were invited to meet the French at Sault Sainte Marie in the early summer of 1671. There on June 4 representatives of fourteen tribes gathered for the most important event in the colonial history of the Sault when the symbols of Church and State, the cross of Christ and the standard of Louis XIV, were raised aloft with elaborate flourishes before the puzzled gaze of the natives. The four Jesuits who were present – Dablon, Druillettes, Allouez, and André – joined in leading the prayers for the king after which the redmen's eyes became riveted on the firearms as the French discharged their muskets with all the thunder of which they were capable.

At this point Father Allouez stepped forward to begin his speech in which he called the Indians' attention to the cross and dwelt upon it as the symbol of Him about Whom they had so often heard him preach. The Jesuit then launched into a eulogy of Louis XIV, emphasizing the tremendous power which the king commanded, how superior he was to the strongest Indian chief, how his armies had put to rout the formidable Iroquois, and how in contrast to their canoes which held only four or five men the king's ships held 400 to 500 or even 1,000 men. By reason of his great power, therefore, other rulers feared and respected the King of France. Moreover, he was fabulously rich, and he had a house that was longer than the distance from the spot at which they stood to the head of the Sault, higher than the tallest trees in their forests, and contained more families than the largest Indian villages could accommodate. And then, as Dablon concluded his account of Allouez' part in the ceremony, "The Father added much more of this sort, which was received with wonder by those people, who were all astonished that there was any man on earth so great, rich, and powerful." [11] At the conclusion of Allouez' speech Saint-Lusson, in "martial and eloquent language," addressed the Indians and told them that he had been sent to take possession of the country and to receive them under the protection of his king so that in the future their land and that of France would be one. The final portion of the program came toward

[11] Relation of 1670–1671, *Jesuit Relations,* LV, 113.

evening when a huge bonfire was lighted around which they all gathered for the singing of the *Te Deum* as a hymn of gratitude to God that the Indians were now the subjects of the King of France.

The ceremony of June, 1671, was about as interesting an example as one will find in the history of the French regime in what was to become the United States of a working arrangement between Church and State. Here was union of the two powers at a time and in a place where the one could survive without the other only at a grave risk. The Indians had undoubtedly been impressed by the white man's colorful display of pomp and power at Sault Sainte Marie. But how much their unsophisticated minds took in concerning the gratuitous protection held out to them by Louis XIV's lieutenants, and the cavalier manner in which the lands which they had freely possessed for generations were now declared to belong to France, we have no way of knowing; nor will we ever know how much of the deeper significance and meaning of other aspects of the event reached the redmen's consciousness.

Another way in which the colonial officials sought to counterbalance Jesuit influence was to encourage other religious communities to interest themselves in the Indians, and here the Sulpicians and the Franciscans were the most important. As previously mentioned, the four pioneer Sulpicians had come to New France in 1656, and for the first few years their activities centered almost exclusively about Montreal. What especially endeared the followers of Jean Jacques Olier to men like Governor Courcelles and his aids was their willingness, in contrast to the Jesuits, to co-operate with the government's aim of concentrating the savages near the white settlements where the Sulpicians attended to their spiritual needs. In their missionary labors these priests also had their martyrs, having, as we have noted, lost two of their men in 1661 at the hands of the Iroquois. In the late 1660's they began to venture farther afield as, for example, Fathers François de Salignac de Fénelon and Claude Trouvé, who set off in October, 1668, to found a mission on Lake Ontario, and Michel Barthélemy who at the same time went to the Algonquins.

A more ambitious Sulpician undertaking was launched in July, 1669, when a small expedition of a half dozen or more canoes left Montreal under the leadership of La Salle, who had a Sulpician brother, and Father François Dollier de Casson who took with him the deacon, René de Bréhant de Galinée. La Salle's principal aim was to reach the Mississippi for exploratory purposes, while the Sulpicians thought in terms of a mission for the savages somewhere along its course. By mid-August they had attained the lands of the Senecas where they were warned of dangerous territory ahead. Crossing the Niagara River below the falls, they met Louis Jolliet who was coming down from his first western trip that had taken him to the copper country around Lake Superior, and who recommended that they proceed by way of Green Bay and the Wisconsin River. La Salle, differing with his companions over the route to be taken, pleaded illness and turned back. But Dollier de Casson, de Galinée, and their lay assistants persisted and spent the winter on the northern shore of Lake Erie where during a storm their chapel equipment and many of their personal belongings were lost. In the spring they began their travels again and by late May they had advanced as far as the Sault where they stopped for three days with Dablon and Marquette. In addition to the other factors which militated against their going on, the Sulpicians learned here that the Jesuits would not welcome the competition of outsiders in the Ottawa missionary territory, so they decided to abandon their original plans and return to Montreal which they reached on June 18, 1670.

CHAPTER NINE

THE ILLINOIS COUNTRY

Two months after the Sulpicians had come home from their abortive efforts to establish a mission in the West there arrived at Quebec the ship that carried Talon, who was back from France with his re-appointment to the post of intendant, and who had with him six Franciscan friars. Nearly forty years had passed since the latter had been recalled at the time that Richelieu had given the colonial missions over to the sole charge of the Jesuits. In Talon the Franciscans had a powerful friend who had been instrumental in their return, and from this time on to the end of the French regime, as we shall see, they were to figure in the history not only of New France proper but of the Great Lakes, the Illinois Country, and the Mississippi Valley as well. They were welcomed by Bishop Laval and by the people, and even the Jesuits who, in a sense, they had been brought out to curb, manifested a cordial spirit. Privately, however, the Jesuits had some misgivings about the purpose that lay behind the appearance of the friars, as their superior, Jerome Lalemant, hinted in a letter to the general in Rome a month after their arrival.[1] As for the civil officials, there was little doubt about the pleasure they felt at having the Franciscans at hand to implement their plans for curtailing Jesuit power. As Colbert later reasoned to Frontenac, both the Sulpicians at Montreal and the Franciscans at Quebec should be accorded all the protection he could give, "these two ecclesiastical groups having to be supported in order to balance the

[1] Lalemant to Paul Oliva, September 19, 1670, in Camille de Rochemonteix, S.J., *Les Jésuites et la Nouvelle-France au XVIIe Siècle* (Paris, 1896), III, 90, n. 1.

authority that the Jesuit Fathers might assume to the prejudice of that of His Majesty." [2]

The policy that had inspired the ceremony at the Sault in the summer of 1671 was not unrelated to that lying behind the historic voyage down the Mississippi two years later. When one considers the extensive exploration that had taken place in the new world during the nearly two centuries since Columbus' initial voyage, and that De Soto had discovered the river as early as 1541, it may seem strange that in the 1670's it was still generally believed that the Mississippi River emptied into the south seas whence one might reach the Orient and its riches. Yet such was the case, and it was with that hope in mind that Louis XIV and Colbert issued an order for the river to be explored. The Quebec government took up the directive from Paris, and one of the last acts performed by Talon before he left office was to join with the newly arrived governor, Count Frontenac, in commissioning the young Quebec-born explorer and trader, Louis Jolliet, to undertake the assignment.

Unlike his employers, Jolliet, who was twenty-eight years of age at the time, was not of the anti-Jesuit party; in fact, he had not only been educated at the Jesuit college in Quebec but he had joined the Society of Jesus and had advanced to minor orders before he dropped out, lured like so many others, by the more exciting prospects of a career in the wilderness. At Talon's instance he made a trip to the West in 1669, and it was on that occasion that he had met Marquette. It was likewise while returning from this venture that he had encountered the Sulpician party and had informed them of the new route—disclosed to him by an Iroquois Indian—via the Detroit River into Lake Erie. In 1671 Jolliet travelled west again in the company of Saint-Lusson and was present at the Sault for the ceremony enacted in June of that year. It was not surprising, then, that his experience should have recommended him, and that he should have been chosen by agreement of Talon and Frontenac for what the latter described to Colbert as, "the discovery of the South Sea, by the country of Mascoutens and the great river which they call the Mississippi which is believed to disembogue in the

[2] Memoir of Colbert to Frontenac, Versailles, April 7, 1672. Pierre Clément (Ed.), *Lettres, Instructions et Memoires de Colbert* (Paris, 1865), III[2], 537. A recent writer has said: "One reason why Frontenac was anxious to have Recollets at these posts was that they made no difficulties over the trading of brandy to the Indians, for if they had, they would very quickly have lost favour with both Frontenac and Colbert." Eccles, *op. cit.*, p. 72.

sea of California."[3] Such in brief was the background of the man who headed his canoe westward for the third time in the autumn of 1672. Jolliet arrived at Saint Ignace on December 8 where for the following five months he and Marquette carefully laid their plans for the expedition that would permanently link their names in American history.

That Jolliet should have arrived at Saint Ignace on the feast of the Immaculate Conception would have more than ordinary significance for Marquette, for he had a special love for the Mother of God under that title, and mention of the 'Blessed Virgin Immaculate' was frequently made in his writings. No one has written more majestically of this personal devotion of Marquette's than Parkman who, although in no way sharing his beliefs concerning Mary, appreciated, nonetheless, the elevation of his thoughts and how much the heavenly Lady meant to the young Black Robe amid his missionary trials. Of this devotion, Parkman stated:

> He was a devout votary of the Virgin Mary, who, imaged to his mind in shapes of the most transcendent loveliness with which the pencil of human genius has ever informed the canvas, was to him the object of an adoration not unmingled with a sentiment of chivalrous devotion. The longings of a sensitive heart, divorced from earth, sought solace in the skies. A subtile element of romance was blended with the fervor of his worship, and hung like an illumined cloud over the harsh and hard realities of his daily lot. Kindled by the smile of his celestial mistress, his gentle and noble nature knew no fear. For her he burned to dare and to suffer, discover new lands and conquer new realms to her sway.[4]

Much has been written on the expedition of 1673 of a controversial character, involving such points as the respective merits of the two principals, the titles of each to be called the leader, and the nature of the written evidence of the expedition. These problems, however, need not detain us here.[5] Suffice it to say, Jolliet was the only one officially

[3] Extract from an undated letter of Frontenac to Colbert, Pierre Margry (Ed.), *Mémoires et Documents pour servire à l'histoire des origines françaises des pays d'Outre-mer* (Paris, 1879), I, 255.

[4] Francis Parkman, *La Salle and the Discovery of the Great West* (Boston, 1910), pp. 59–60. Parkman's use of the words 'adoration' and 'worship' to describe Marquette's devotion to our Lady are misleading. These words are properly applied only in describing man's relationship to God.

[5] Francis Borgia Steck, O.F.M., *The Jolliet-Marquette Expedition, 1673* (Washington, 1927), treated these controverted questions in detail in three final chapters (pp. 192–310).

designated by the government to undertake the work and Marquette went along through the friendly intervention of his superior, Claude Dablon, with Jolliet. The two men seemed to have been admirably matched and to have recognized in each other kindred spirits, for to his primary objective of saving souls the young Jesuit added a real flair for observation of the country through which he passed. And when it is remembered how enthusiastic the Jesuits at the Sault had become about the friendly Illinois tribesmen, and the bright prospect that the latter seemed to offer for conversion, one can understand how eagerly Marquette seized the chance to combine the dual objectives of touching the souls of these savages and of exploring their great river.

It was on May 17 that Jolliet and Marquette left Saint Ignace with their five French oarsmen in two canoes. Coming down the western shore of Lake Michigan and into Green Bay, where they made a stop at Saint Francis Xavier Mission, and then on to the Fox River, they were in relatively familiar territory. But when they had completed the portage to the Wisconsin and embarked on that stream it became a stranger land. At this point Marquette remarked that before embarking they had begun "all together a new devotion to the blessed Virgin Immaculate, which we practiced daily, addressing to her special prayers to place under her protection both our persons and the success of our voyage. . . ."[6] A month to the day after they left Saint Ignace they had their first view of the Mississippi where the Wisconsin flows into the former several miles from Prairie du Chien. For a week thereafter they saw no one, but then they met up with a band of Illinois who displayed their customary friendliness and offered hospitality for an overnight stay during which the guests were entertained by a variety of dances and songs. For several weeks more they continued on their course, noting where rivers like the Ohio and the Missouri met the Mississippi, and by July 17 they had become convinced that they had the answer to the question that had inspired their commission. About where the Arkansas meets the Mississippi all signs pointed to the fact that the latter reached the sea at the Gulf of Mexico, and one of the most interesting of these signs were the firearms of the Arkansas Indians which told the Frenchmen that they were approaching the colonial possessions of Spain. Having carried out their instruc-

[6] Marquette's account of the expedition, as composed by Claude Dablon, S.J., from the former's notes [Baye des Puants, 1674], *Jesuit Relations*, LIX, 107.

tions to their satisfaction, the canoes were turned northward for the more difficult ascent of the Mississippi.

On the return homeward the exploring party took the Illinois River as the easier route to Lake Michigan and a few miles below where Ottawa, Illinois, stands today they met a band of Kaskaskia Indians with whom they tarried for three days while Marquette instructed them in the Christian religion and sought to satisfy their request for a mission by a promise to come back later. Going by portage to the Chicago River and thence once more to Lake Michigan, the great adventure that had lasted for four months and covered about 2,700 miles came to a close at the hospitable mission of Saint Francis Xavier. Here the party spent the winter with the two principals composing their respective accounts, Jolliet to the Governor of New France and Marquette assembling his notes for Father Dablon, his superior. The experience had taken a heavier toll on Marquette's health than he realized, for he never fully recovered from the dysentery contracted on the trip, and it was this disease that carried him off a year and a half later.

But the wasted young Jesuit would not hear of giving up, for he only awaited the permission of the superior at Quebec until he would head back for the Kaskaskia village to fulfill his promise to evangelize them. By the autumn of 1674 the dysentery had improved to the point where he believed he had been cured, and shortly after word came from the superior that he might proceed, Marquette started on October 25 from De Pere with his two trusted aides, Pierre Porteret and Jacques Le Castor. From mid-December until late in March of 1675 Marquette's weakened condition, as well as the frozen streams, kept them encamped at the site of the future city of Chicago, a stay that proved a severe trial to the three Frenchmen who had no adequate protection against the winter cold. Yet Marquette's cheerful description gave little hint of all this, and here again the heavenly patroness received the credit when he said:

> The blessed Virgin Immaculate has taken such care of us during our wintering that we have not lacked provisions, and have still remaining a large sack of corn, with some meat and fat. We also lived very pleasantly for my illness did not prevent me from saying holy mass every day. We were unable to keep Lent, except Fridays and saturdays.[7]

[7] Marquette's unfinished journal [n.p., 1675], *ibid.*, LIX, 181.

With the coming of spring Marquette and his companions proceeded down the Illinois, and on April 6 he made the final entry in his diary, a signal, perhaps, of his growing weakness. Two days later they came to where the present village of Utica, Illinois, stands where he opened the Immaculate Conception Mission in fulfillment of his promise to the Kaskaskias who were assembled to the number of between 500 and 600 families to hear him. He would have rejoiced to have continued with his instructions and to remain with these Indians until they were ready for baptism. But his physical discomfort and increasing weakness gave warning that there would not be time. In the hope of either gaining relief, or of dying among his own, the missionary, still two months short of his thirty-eighth birthday, made the reluctant decision that they should start north.

Going by way of the Saint Joseph River, they began the ascent of Lake Michigan on the eastern shore, Marquette all the while endeavoring to concentrate on his prayers when he was not giving instructions to his aides as to what they should do when his end should come. In the detailed description of these last days, written by Father Dablon from accounts furnished by Marquette's companions, it was noted that they came upon a river emptying into the lake on the shore of which stood a little knoll. This Marquette "deemed well suited to be the place of his interment, [and] he told them that That was the place of his last repose." [8] It was May 18 and here, near the present Ludington, Michigan, Marquette breathed his last. After burying the body his companions marked the grave, and two years later a party of Kiskakons, whom Marquette had made Christians at La Pointe du Saint Esprit, came upon it, disinterred the remains, and reverently brought them to Saint Ignace. Here the solemn procession was met by Fathers Henri Nouvelle and Philippe Pierçon who conducted the funeral service for their departed confrère and then buried his bones once more on June 8, 1677, beneath the log chapel of the mission. In time Saint Ignace Mission was abandoned, and it was not until September, 1877, that the grave beneath where once had stood the old chapel was discovered by Edward Jacker, the priest then stationed at Point Saint Ignace, who caused a fence to be built about the spot.

Despite the importance of the Jolliet-Marquette expedition, there

[8] Claude Dablon's Account of Marquette's Voyage and Death [Quebec, 1677], *ibid.*, LIX, 195.

was no immediate follow up by the French due to the involvement of the mother country in a European war and the colonial government's lack of resources. It was only in the generation after Jacques Marquette's death that the conflicting interests of the European powers became gravely involved over the great river that he had helped to explore. Meanwhile, however, the Anglo-French rivalry did not in any way abate, and the contest for the mastery of North America grew progressively sharper and broke out in new places. In May, 1670, Charles II of England had issued a charter to a trading company for Hudson's Bay with the view, as the English hoped, that the fur trade could be diverted from the Saint Lawrence to their own profit. In the region of Hudson's Bay, therefore, in the islands off the northeast coast, in the West Indies, in fact, wherever the French and English encountered each other, trouble ensued. And as one moved into the eighteenth century the struggle for the continental heartland, through which ran the Mississippi and its numerous tributaries, took on increasing importance, first as between France and Spain and later between France and Great Britain.

Mention has frequently been made of the close association of French ecclesiastical and lay interests in the new world, and it is not necessary to emphasize it further. Nonetheless, it should be stated that the course of missionary development through the late seventeenth to the middle of the eighteenth century around the Great Lakes, in the Illinois Country, and in the lower Mississippi Valley was shaped in good measure by France's eagerness to secure a firm hold on all this territory and to counter the moves of Britain and Spain. In doing so the personnel, location, and ultimate success or failure of the missions in a given area often depended as much, if not more, on the relation they bore to the political and economic aspects of this dominant consideration of international policy than they did on the response of the Indian neophytes and the zeal of the individual missionaries.[9]

In the career of no prominent lay figure of French colonial America was the influence of secular policies on the affairs of the Church more marked than in the case of Robert Cavelier, Sieur de La Salle. Close collaborator of Frontenac as he was, he shared the governor's dislike of the Jesuits as well as his prejudice against Bishop Laval.

[9] Recent research bears out this interpretation, e.g., Gustave Lanctôt, *Histoire du Canada: des Origines au régime royal* (Montreal, 1959).

When La Salle sought to carry out his ambitious schemes for the western country, therefore, it was not to the Jesuits that he turned for religious to accompany his expeditions, but to such communities as the Sulpicians and the Franciscans. As for the latter, during Louis XIV's war against the Spanish Netherlands in 1667–1668 the French had overrun a good part of Flanders, and in the sequel a number of the Flemish Franciscans had been forced to attach themselves to the French province of their order. It was mainly from among these Flemish friars that Talon had recruited the contingent for New France, and with their arrival at Quebec in 1670 La Salle now had at hand religious who were congenial to his purposes. It was in these circumstances, then, that the Franciscans made their entrance into the West.

As it turned out the principal work of these friars in New France was to minister to the white settlements along the Saint Lawrence and to act as chaplains for the military posts in the western country. This fact, together with their close association with the ill-starred ventures of La Salle, left them little time to accomplish anything of note for the native population, although they had a few missions for the Indians for brief periods. Their patron enjoyed an advantageous position on many counts, for La Salle had not only received a seigniory at Lachine near Montreal from the Sulpicians, but his friend, Count Frontenac, had granted him further lands and a patent that insured a monopoly of the fur trade at Fort Frontenac, a post the governor had built in 1673 on the northern shore of the outlet of Lake Ontario near modern Kingston. But La Salle's restless nature could not be at peace either on his estates or as an overseer for the trade in furs. Instead his imagination carried him away with dreams of French expansion over a good part of the continent, and in a number of these visionary projects the Franciscans were linked in a way that at times cost them dearly.

One of the ideas that La Salle had, and it was basically a sound one, was to construct ships on the Great Lakes in which the furs could be moved to the eastern depots and thus provide a cheaper and safer means of transportation. It was in pursuance of this plan that the first of the Flemish friars came upon the western scene when Louis Hennepin, destined to have a notable career in exploration, joined the group at Fort Frontenac that had been commissioned by La Salle to establish a post on Lake Erie and to build there a ship for navigation on the lakes. Under the leadership of Pierre de Saint Paul, Sieur de la Motte-Lussière, they left Fort Frontenac on November 18, 1678, and after having overcome a number of serious perils on the way they arrived at the Niagara River in early December. Here Fort de Conty was constructed along with a bark chapel and residence built by Father Hennepin. It was Hennepin who was to furnish the world with the first published description of Niagara Falls in a work which was translated into English at the close of the seventeenth century with the title, *A New Discovery of a Vast Country in America.* His first book was published in Paris in 1683 and by the time that his third work appeared at Utrecht in 1698 he had become the center of a heated controversy over the authenticity of the claims which he made to various discoveries in America, a controversy that has lasted down to the recent past.[10] While scholars are generally agreed that Hennepin's claims to having explored the lower Mississippi were false, his descriptions of the upper portion of the river are for the most part regarded as genuine.

But to return to the French at Niagara. In January, 1679, La Salle arrived and took charge and during the winter they constructed a trading vessel to which was given the name *Le Griffon.* Four other Franciscans soon reached Niagara from Fort Frontenac: Gabriel de la Ribourde, Zenobius Membré, Melithon Watteaux, and Luke Buisset. In May a grant of land was made to the friars at Niagara by La Salle for a residence and a cemetery, and when the expedition sailed later that summer Watteaux and Buisset remained behind, the one as a missionary to the Indians and the other as chaplain for the fort. De la Ribourde had been named superior for the expedition and Hennepin and Membré were also aboard when *Le Griffon* sailed from Niagara in early August. The ship first passed through Lake Erie and then into Lake St. Clair, a name which these Frenchmen gave to that body of water since they entered it on the feast day of the holy nun of Assisi. They continued through the Strait of Detroit and on to Michilimackinac where they made a brief stop with the Jesuits and then proceeded on Lake Michigan to Green Bay. It was at Green Bay that *Le Griffon* was loaded with furs after which it set sail never to be heard from

[10] Among the more recent critical works on this subject is Jean Delanglez, S.J., *Hennepin's Description of Louisiana* (Chicago, 1941). Delanglez concluded that the first two-thirds of Hennepin's narrative on Louisiana was a plagiarism of the first third of the *Relation des déscouverts* of the Abbé Claude Bernou who, in turn, had taken ninety-five percent of his account from three letters of La Salle.

again, the fate of this first sailing vessel on the Great Lakes having ever since remained a mystery.

Fired by the grandiose idea of exploring and laying claim for France to the interior of the continent, La Salle soon started off with his companions and pushed south until they came to the mouth of the Saint Joseph River. Some years before the Jesuits had a mission here of brief duration, and it would again be the scene of missionary activities in the years ahead. While the laymen were constructing Fort Miami the friars were engaged in building a chapel which they named Saint Anthony, a crude structure which was used both for preaching to the Indians and for ministering to the whites, and which was the first Catholic church in the lower peninsula of Michigan. From Fort Miami a party of thirty or more Frenchmen under La Salle's leadership departed in early December, using first the Saint Joseph River and then passing by portage to the Kankakee and thence to the Illinois. As they glided down the latter stream they came upon a large deserted village of some 460 cabins below what is today called Starved Rock. The local natives were away on the hunt and the Frenchmen made a stop during which the priests said Mass on new year's day of 1680, and the course was then resumed down the Illinois to Lake Peoria where they met another village of around eighty cabins.

It was near this spot, a short distance below the present city of Peoria, that La Salle had built in early January a fort to which he gave the name of Crêvecoeur. Here the friars again erected a simple chapel, although they were unable to say Mass as they had run out of wine. The reception accorded the French by the Peoria Indians was agreeable enough, but their apparent friendliness was no indication of any attraction for the Christian religion and its self-denying ordinances as Father Membré was soon to learn. While de la Ribourde ministered to the whites and tried to make some headway with the Indian dialect and Hennepin prepared for his exploration of the upper Mississippi, Membré endeavored to reach the natives by catechetical instruction, only to meet with virtually complete failure. He found the Peorias a bad lot, and he later described them as "wandering, idle, fearful, and dissolute . . . irritable and thievish."[11] They not only

[11] Christian Le Clercq, *First Establishment of the Faith in New France*, translated by John Gilmary Shea (New York, 1881), II, 134. Le Clercq incorporated the account of his fellow friar and contemporary into his own work.

practiced polygamy but unnatural vice, and aside from baptizing several dying children and two or three dying adults who had shown the proper dispositions, the friar found little outlet for his ministry. As he made clear, it was not due to lack of communication since he had mastered their language sufficiently well to make himself understood in all that he wished. But, as Membré maintained, "there is in these savages such an alienation from the Faith, so brutal and narrow a mind, such corrupt and anti-Christian morals, that great time would be needed to hope for any fruit."[12]

In February, 1680, La Salle dispatched a party of three men, Michel Aco [Accau], the leader, Antoine du Gay Auguel, and Father Louis Hennepin, to explore the upper reaches of the Mississippi. Shortly thereafter the explorer himself, uneasy of mind over the lack of any news about *Le Griffon*, the disappearance of a number of deserters from his service, and word that his creditors had seized Fort Frontenac and were stopping the supplies, set out for the northern post. The overland journey made during the breakup of winter entailed severe personal suffering, but La Salle made it in sixty-five days. With these departures there were left about fifteen men under the command of La Salle's faithful lieutenant, Henry de Tonty, including the two friars, de la Ribourde and Membré. It was a trying summer for those at Fort Crêvecoeur, too, with difficulties raining upon them from all directions. More men deserted, the fort remained unfinished, and late in the season the surrounding area became an Indian battleground. Through it all the Franciscans carried on their labors, de la Ribourde ministering to the whites while making some headway with his study of the Indian language and Membré still hopefully preaching to the Indians. But the latter's visit to the Miami tribe was of scarcely more profit than his earlier attempts with the Peorias, and about the only ray of light that shone in the lives of the two friars was the ripening of the grapes in late August which enabled them once more to have wine for Mass.

All the troubles of that summer of 1680 were overshadowed, however, by the appearance of the Iroquois intent upon the annihilation of the Illinois. At the cost of incurring several serious wounds in an encounter with the Iroquois, Tonty braved their camp to protest the attack upon these allies of the French, but it was all in vain and he was fortunate to escape alive. With the Illinois now terrified and in

[12] *Ibid.*, II, 137.

full flight there was nothing for the little band of six Frenchmen to do but to get away as soon as possible. They made off hurriedly up the Illinois River, therefore, in a battered bark canoe on September 18 without provisions or food. The next day, at a point a few miles west of where the town of Seneca now stands, they put ashore to repair their leaking vessel. Father de la Ribourde, who was seventy years of age at the time, went into a nearby grove of trees to read his breviary. The friar was never seen again. Later it was learned that he had been murdered by some young Kickapoo braves who stripped his body and threw it into a hole, while his breviary and ordo, relics of this latest martyr to the redman's fury, were after a time retrieved from the Indians by a Jesuit missionary.

After searching and waiting in vain for the missing priest until the following afternoon, at Tonty's insistence the party pushed on. They had a harrowing three months before them, and by the time they met a company of hospitable Indians, as Membré said, "Not one of us could stand for weakness; we were like skeletons, the Sieur de Tonty extremely sick. . . ."[13] At the end of the year the weary and beaten travellers finally reached Saint Francis Xavier Mission at De Pere where the Jesuits extended to them every comfort within their power. The rest of the winter was spent in rest and recuperation from the ordeal and in June, 1681, Tonty and Membré moved on to Michilimackinac, arriving just a day late for Tonty to meet his cousin, Daniel Greysolon Duluth, but a day in advance of La Salle who rejoiced to learn that his friend was not dead as he had begun to fear. At Michilimackinac fresh plans were laid by La Salle and his associates about which we shall see presently.

As for the other Franciscan friar, Louis Hennepin, after leaving his confrères at Fort Crêvecoeur in February he and his two companions met their own share of troubles during the balance of that year 1680. They first followed the Illinois to its confluence with the Mississippi and then turned north on the latter, exploring far into the interior of the future State of Minnesota, although not as far as the river's source. In mid-April they were taken captive by a band of Sioux Indians, and for the next five or six months they spent most of their time traversing a fair portion of Minnesota with their captors. Apparently Hennepin made no serious attempt to convert the savages, for his account of his

[13] *Ibid.*, II, 150.

days among them is chiefly notable for feats of exploration such as the discovery and naming of Saint Anthony's Falls at the site of the city of Minneapolis. In fact, of all the descriptions of the American aborigines written by Catholic missionaries his is one of the most emphatic on the well nigh insuperable obstacles to be overcome in bringing the Indians to a knowledge of the Christian faith.[14]

Fortunately for Hennepin and his companions, Duluth was in the region at the time of their capture and was on good terms with the Sioux with whom he had made a treaty some time before. When he learned of the plight of his countrymen, therefore, he abandoned his own plans for exploration in order to effect their release. Once they were free of the Sioux, the little group started toward New France via Wisconsin and Michigan with Duluth as their escort. They spent the winter at Michilimackinac and then the Franciscan proceeded on to Montreal and Quebec whence he sailed for France in the fall of 1681 never to return. Within two years Hennepin's first book of American travels had appeared and he had become the focal point of controversy that he was to remain for the rest of his life.

More than a year had elapsed between the time that La Salle had parted from Tonty and Membré at Fort Crêvecoeur and their reunion at Michilimackinac in June, 1681. In the interval the explorer's interests had sustained staggering reverses, and yet he had not lost heart. Allowing for La Salle's undoubted defects – as also for the Franciscan bias in his favor – it is, nonetheless, difficult to withhold admiration for the man whom Membré's memoir described at this point, or to deny assent to what the friar said. After recounting how they had exchanged stories concerning the misfortunes that had befallen them since last they met, Father Zénobe continued:

> . . . . yet never did I remark in him the least alteration, always maintaining his ordinary coolness and self-possession. Any one but him would have renounced and abandoned the enterprise; but, far from that, by a firmness of mind and a constancy that has seldom been equalled, I saw him more resolute that ever to continue his work and to carry out his discovery.[15]

His troubles had, indeed, failed to shake La Salle's conviction that the Mississippi could be made the lifeline of a French domain in the in-

[14] For his description of the difficulties in converting the Indians cf. Reuben Gold Thwaites (Ed.), *Louis Hennepin. A New Discovery of a Vast Country in America* (Chicago, 1903), II, 457–474.

[15] Le Clercq, *op. cit.*, II, 156–157.

terior through a chain of forts that would be supported by the fur trade. And in Tonty and the Franciscan he had sympathetic listeners who readily entered into his plans for a new expedition. The summer was spent in making preparations, and by early November a company of twenty or more Frenchmen and about thirty Indians, including ten women and several children, had assembled at Fort Miami whence they proceeded early in 1682 by portage and stream to the Illinois River. On this occasion La Salle decided to locate a fort on the upper part of the river at what is today called Starved Rock rather than at the old location of Fort Crêvecoeur farther down stream. It was his hope that a number of the western tribes might be concentrated at this spot and made into a powerful force that would be able to withstand the attacks of the Iroquois.

It was from the new fort, named Saint Louis, that La Salle, Tonty, Father Zénobe, and the others set out in the spring to begin the descent of the Mississippi to its mouth. They reached their goal on April 9, 1682, a date that marks the climax of La Salle's career when he took formal possession of the immense valley for his king, and the friar joined in signing the act that gave it the name of Louisiana in honor of Louis XIV. On the return La Salle took seriously ill and was tenderly cared for by Membré which helped to solidify the bond between the two men, and upon the explorer's recovery he asked the priest to accompany him first to New France and then to Europe. In addition to the physical handicap of that summer of 1682, La Salle suffered the further blow of having his friend Frontenac recalled as governor and Antoine Lefebre, Sieur de la Barre, a man of the Jesuit party, appointed in his stead. The latter ordered the explorer to surrender Fort Saint Louis and summoned him to Quebec to answer for his conduct. The first command La Salle honored by sending Tonty to deliver the fort to the governor's representative; but the second he ignored by proceeding directly to France without reference to de la Barre.

The Europe to which La Salle and Membré returned in late December, 1682, was filled with an air of excitement. Three months before John Sobieski had repulsed the Turks at Vienna, and the western powers were eyeing with growing anxiety the aggression of Louis XIV and his Chambers of Reunion as they snuffed out the independence of one important city after another along France's frontiers. Spain felt especially aggrieved at the incursion into the Netherlands, and in

December, 1683, war was declared on France. The homecoming of La Salle was well timed, therefore, since he brought glowing tales of the prospects that awaited the French on the Mississippi where he pictured the promise of a future empire that would at the same time checkmate the Spaniards to the west of the great river. As a consequence he was not only restored to all his honors and rights, but the king received him in audience, listened with interest to his proposals, and then gave authority for the outfitting of a fleet for the purpose of planting a permanent colony in Louisiana. By late July of 1684 the four ships, carrying around 280 persons and large quantities of supplies, were ready to sail with La Salle now invested with the proud title of Viceroy of North America and command over all the territory from Illinois to the borders of the Spanish colonies.

Ample provision had been made for the religious aspects of the expedition with six priests in the company, of whom three were Franciscans, namely, Anastase Douay, Maxime Le Clercq, and again Zénobe Membré, whose provincial had secured them faculties from the Congregation de Propaganda Fide. There were also three Sulpicians, Jean Cavelier the explorer's brother, and the Abbés Chefdeville and d'Esmanville, who had faculties from the Archbishop of Rouen with which they hoped to fulfill the wish of their superior general, Tronson, to establish a Sulpician mission in Louisiana. After losing one of the ships to the Spaniards in the Caribbean, by some odd circumstance the other vessels missed the mouth of the Mississippi and by February, 1685, found themselves in the region of Matagorda Bay on the Texas coast. A landing was made and a fort constructed, to which again the name of Saint Louis was given, and thereupon ensued one of the century's most disastrous episodes for the French colonies. The contemporary accounts leave one uncertain about many details of the ill fated settlement, although it is clear that internal dissension was one of the major deterrents to success. By March 12 the discouraged and disgruntled, led by La Salle's second in command, the Marquis de Beaujeu, boarded the *Joly* and sailed for France, and with them was Father d'Esmanville who declared after hearing that La Salle thought of attacking the Spaniards, that he had come to the new world to fight demons, not Christians.

By the fall of that year the anomalous situation had become too much for the restless La Salle, and in October he started out with a group of about fifty men on the first of three trips into the interior on none of which his goal seemed to be entirely clear, but on none of which did he either find the Mississippi or encounter the Spaniards. And each of these inland journeys, of course, was the cause of further losses in men and supplies. In the meantime the colony itself steadily declined. With hostile Indians roaming the environs and competing Spaniards to the west and north, the less than fifty persons at Fort Saint Louis could hardly avoid recognition of the fact that little short of a miracle could now rescue them from this distant and unfriendly outpost. Following two fruitless exploratory trips La Salle finally determined on a last desperate overland effort to gain assistance in New France. There accompanied him when he departed in early January, 1687, his Sulpician brother, the Franciscan friar, Anastase Douay, La Salle's two nephews, and about twenty others. But the explorer was never again to see New France, for they had not gone very far when the ill will of several of the men turned to mutiny against the leader and near the banks of the Brazos River in southeastern Texas La Salle was murdered on March 19. His nephews suffered the same fate, although the two priests, Cavelier and Douay, finally managed after many trying experiences to reach France in October, 1688.

For almost two years after La Salle had departed from Fort Saint Louis the pitiful little band of twenty some men and women and a few children continued their struggle for survival under constantly mounting odds. The three priests, Chefdeville, Membré, and Le Clercq, ministered to their spiritual needs in the chapel of the fort, and the Franciscans even tried to start a mission among the Cenis Indians until the hostility of the savages drove them away. The sword that for so long a time had hung over the heads of the colonists finally fell early in 1689 when the fort was attacked by the Indians and, except for two or three who made good their escape, the French were all massacred. Thus when the Spanish captain, Alonso de Léon, came on the scene in April of that year there was nothing but ruins to indicate what for four years had been the site of the French colony.

La Salle's tragic end might, indeed, have been anticipated, given that authority never sat lightly with him, and that the exasperating circumstances of his final march – coming after two years of frustration and failure – were such as to drive unthinking men to extremes. The explorer was a man of genuine breadth and vision, but, unfortunately, these qualities were neither matched nor moderated by tact and good judgment. Consequently, in spite of the twenty-one years that he gave to France's interests in America, the final record was quite barren of the achievements that his good qualities might otherwise have brought about. As for the missionary aspect of La Salle's numerous undertakings, it scarcely ever emerged beyond the planning stage. The fate of the Franciscans was intimately linked with that of La Salle himself, and after his death one heard little more of them save as chaplains at several of the western military posts.

The activities of these priests in the future United States between 1673 when Hennepin first appeared at Niagara and 1689 when Membré and Le Clercq were killed by the Texas Indians, netted nothing of any lasting character for the Catholic faith among the native population. Yet one must not judge the Franciscans by that fact, for their principal duty was always to the whites, and that they performed with complete fidelity. In fact, the only cloud that passed across their good name during these years was owing to the falsifications of Hennepin about his explorations and discoveries. But they made no pretense to missionary prowess, and what Father Zénobe Membré wrote of the friars' effect on the Indians of the Illinois Country might be applied to their relations with all the natives with whom they came in contact. He said:

> With regard to these nations, perhaps, some one, by a secret effect of grace, has profited; this God only knows. All we have done has been to see the state of these nations, and to open the way to the Gospel and to missionaries. . . .[16]

If the special character of the Franciscans' assignment in America accounted for their meager accomplishments in the conversion of the savages of the Great Lakes and the Illinois Country, the missions of their Jesuit contemporaries in these same areas suffered an eclipse for other reasons. By the mid-seventeenth century France's splendid religious revival had passed its peak, and in consequence the American missions experienced a decline in recruits. Moreover, the renewal of war by the great powers in 1689 brought its American counterpart during which the Iroquois were stimulated to further attacks on the French and their allies of the semi-Christian tribes, and French policy itself underwent a shift that had adverse effects on the missions. Finally,

[16] *Ibid.*, II, 194.

among the principal causes for the Black Robes' reverses was the ascendancy of the anti-Jesuit party in France's colonial officialdom and the behavior of the French traders who mingled with the Indians. Together these factors constituted a formidable combination, and by the opening years of the eighteenth century it had worked a noticeable change in the fortunes of the Jesuits in the Great Lakes and the Illinois Country.

At this time Jesuit activity was concentrated mainly in the territory extending from the Illinois missions on the south to Saint Ignace on the north while in between were Saint Joseph in southwestern Michigan and Saint Francis Xavier at De Pere in Wisconsin. Upon the death of Marquette the Jesuit superior appointed Father Allouez to continue his work, and after a number of delays he reached the Kaskaskia village in the spring of 1677. Allouez was well received and on this occasion he spent several months giving instructions and prospecting for a permanent mission site. He returned again in 1678 and, except for brief intervals, the remaining eleven years of the great missionary's life were spent between the Mission of the Immaculate Conception, as Marquette had named it, and Saint Joseph Mission for the Miamis among whom he died in August, 1689, at the age of sixty-seven. Almost a quarter of a century had passed since that summer of 1665 when Allouez inaugurated his labors in behalf of the western Indians along the shores of Lake Superior. After his death his superior estimated that during his time in the West he had given instructions to over 100,000 and had baptized more than 10,000 savages. Allowing, as has been said, for possible exaggeration in Father Dablon's figures, Allouez had, nonetheless, a remarkable missionary career, and one can understand why Dablon would have been prompted to refer to him as "a second Xavier." [17]

As much as the successors of Allouez deserve to have their story told in similar detail, it is not possible to do more here than to summarize the principal happenings in the Illinois Country from the close of the seventeenth century to the period when the area became a battleground, first between the French and the English in the French and Indian War and then between the English and the Americans dur-

[17] Dablon, to 'Mon Révérend Père, Quebec, August 29, 1690, Pierre Margry, *Découvertes et Etablissements de Français dans . . . l'Amérique septentrionale, 1614–1698* (Paris, 1879), I, 63.

ing the latter's revolt from the mother country. With Allouez' passing a fairly steady procession of Black Robes entered the area between the time of his immediate successor, Jacques Gravier, and the death in February, 1777, at Prairie du Rocher of Sébastien Louis Meurin, the last of the many French Jesuits to give all or a portion of their adult lives to this work in the Illinois Country. Among them Gravier was outstanding. His special apostolate was to the Kaskaskias whom he served at three different locations: Starved Rock, Lake Peoria, and at their settlement near the confluence of the Mississippi and the river which came to bear their name. At first Gravier had considerable success with this tribe, baptizing Chief Rouensa and over 200 of his followers in 1693. As time went on, however, the Indians cooled toward all Frenchmen, and although the Jesuit returned to them after a term at Saint Ignace as superior of the western missions, he accomplished relatively little. Nor was there much likelihood that Father Gravier would have found his position substantially improved had he been given a longer span of life. Wounded by an Indian in the summer of 1705, he sought medical treatment in Louisiana, and from there he made a trip to France in the hope of recruiting more men to assist the three Jesuits then in the Illinois Country. Although he returned to America in mid-February, 1708, with the idea of resuming his work, his health must have been more seriously undermined than he realized for in about two months he was dead.

Before Father Gravier had been called away from the Peoria mission in 1696 to serve as superior, he had enjoyed for two years the assistance of Sébastien Rale whom we have previously met in Maine. Father Rale later stated that while the Illinois Indians permitted their children to be baptized, and even attended the instructions themselves, the real stumbling block to permanent conversion was the practice of polygamy which they refused to give up. It was no less an obstacle to the Jesuits who came to take the places of Gravier and Rale, to men like Julien Binneteau, who was to die an early death, and François Pinet and Jean Mermet who established and served the short lived Mission of the Guardian Angel for the Miamis on the site of the present city of Chicago where they worked from around 1696 to the abandonment of the mission in 1702.

It was Father Pinet's departure from Chicago for the village of the

Cahokia Indians on the Mississippi that occasioned a conflict over ecclesiastical jurisdiction that further weakened the missions. As we have seen, Bishop Laval had made the Jesuit superior in the West his vicar general for that region not long after he came to New France, and the practice continued until a new group of missionaries appeared in the upper Mississippi Valley in the closing years of the century. These men were secular priests who owed their organization to the Bishop of Quebec. While still a priest in France, Laval had been a member of the group whose apostolic zeal had given rise to the famous Seminary of the Foreign Missions, and it became one of his most cherished hopes to found a similar institution in the new world. In 1663 he succeeded in getting a seminary underway at Quebec in which the students were trained along missionary lines, and although Laval resigned his see in 1688, he lived on for twenty years and took a lively interest in all that pertained to this favorite enterprise. In June, 1698, Jean Baptiste de Saint Vallier, second Bishop of Quebec, granted authority to the seminary priests to open a mission among the Tamaroa Indians on the Mississippi which, of course, was part of his diocese. The three pioneers were François de Montigny, who was named superior and vicar general, Antoine Davion, and Jean François Buisson de Saint Cosme.

The new missionaries left Quebec at mid-year of 1698, stopping en route with the Jesuits, first at Saint Ignace and then at Chicago, and from the latter Fathers Pinet and Binneteau accompanied them down the Illinois River. By early December they had reached the Cahokia and Tamaroa villages on the Mississippi, but the three secular priests continued south on the great river in search of the most advantageous locations to begin their work. Having finally determined on how they would divide the labor, they parted company in January, 1699, de Montigny taking up residence with the Taensas, a tribe allied to the Natchez, between where Natchez and Vicksburg stand today. Davion going to the Tonica village then located on the Yazoo River, and Saint Cosme returning up the Mississippi to the Tamaroas. They were not long in realizing that if their expectations were to be fulfilled more priests would be needed, and de Montigny's appeal to Quebec for recruits was answered not long after by the arrival of several more priests among whom was Father Jean Bergier.

At the time the Jesuits had three missions in the area, namely, Holy

Family for the Tamaroas and two others for the Peorias and the Kaskaskias. It was the first named that was to prove the principal source of trouble since it was there that the secular and Jesuit jurisdictional claims suffered a direct clash. The representatives of the two missionary groups, Pinet, the Jesuit, and Bergier, the secular priest, arrived among the Tamaroas within a month of each other, and during the next two years the awkward situation became increasingly embarrassing and tense. Meanwhile de Montigny, realizing that serious difficulty on this score was unavoidable, sailed for France to represent the seminary clergy's interests, and Saint Cosme replaced him at the Taensas mission near Natchez. But the French Jesuits were not without firsthand evidence, for Father Gravier had also gone back to France after a stay in the new colony of Louisiana where he had made the acquaintance of the governor, Pierre Le Moyne, Sieur d'Iberville, whose plans for the future he had been anxious to probe.

Although the case had been referred to Quebec by the respective contestants, the ultimate authority on both sides was in the mother country, and it was only there that a final decision could be rendered. Louis XIV appointed a royal commission headed by the Archbishop of Auch which numbered the Bishops of Marseilles and Chartres, along with Saint Vallier of Quebec who was also in France at the time. Their judgment on the Tamaroa mission was made known in June, 1701, in favor of the seminary priests, although it was another year before Gravier returned from France to Louisiana and came up the river to inform Pinet. In the meantime Bergier had declared to the Jesuit that he was ready to take over the mission, and when Pinet refused to yield, the secular priest, acting in his capacity as vicar general of the Bishop of Quebec, had placed the Jesuit chapel under interdict. Once Gravier had delivered the decision of the royal commission, however, Pinet withdrew to the Kaskaskia Indians on the other side of the Mississippi where he died in August, 1702, and Bergier, his erstwhile rival, officiated at the funeral.

Up to about 1770 secular priests from the seminaries of either Quebec or Paris continued to be sent to the Illinois Country where they exercised their two-fold ministry among both the natives and the white settlers. They were able and conscientious missionaries, even if several of their numbered failed to measure up to their society's high standards. Some insight into the work of these men can be gleaned from a rapid glance at the principal personalities and happenings at Cahokia, the name that finally fixed itself on the Tamaroa Indian village. After the death of Father Bergier in November, 1707, an interval of some years elapsed before another seminary priest appeared, and during this time Cahokia was attended by the Jesuits from their Kaskaskia mission. Upon Bergier's death the office of vicar general passed to Dominique Marie Varlet, French-born doctor of the Sorbonne, whose name was inscribed in the records of various settlements between Mobile and Cahokia up to 1718 when he returned to France. Although the former missionary was not long after made a bishop, his reputation in orthodox circles was soon compromised by his Jansenist sympathies, and when censure from the Holy See failed to bring a remedy he broke with the Church. Varlet was ultimately the instrument through which the Jansenist schism in Holland was perpetuated in the Old Catholic Church when he illicitly consecrated several recalcitrant priests and himself died excommunicated in 1742.

A seminary priest of a quite different stamp was the Canadian-born Jean Baptiste Mercier who came to Cahokia in 1718 and during his first term of five years as pastor here mastered the Illinois Indian language thoroughly. One of the most colorful episodes of the thirty-five years that this zealous priest spent on the missions was his chaplaincy of the expedition of 1723 led by Etienne Veniard de Bourgmond for the exploration of the Missouri River. Mercier remained with the party for several years and was present at the building of Fort Orleans in the present Carroll County, Missouri, as well as being the clergyman who officiated at the *Te Deum* in November, 1724, when de Bourgmond returned there from his adventurous march across the plains of the future State of Kansas. It had been the hope of Mercier and the other seminary priests that they might evangelize the Missouri River tribes, but the hope was never realized. They had, of course, only very limited resources, and the fact that the Company of the Indies, leaseholder of the Louisiana colony at the time, had promised to pay Mercier an annual salary of 600 livres for his services on the de Bourgmond expedition and in the end had paid him nothing, would indicate how little support the missionaries could expect from the secular authorities.

Like the Jesuits before them, the seminary priests strongly protested against the French selling liquor to the Indians, and it was in consequence of a remonstrance from Mercier on this head that the royal order forbidding the traffic was renewed. But it was one thing to issue an order from Versailles; it was quite another to enforce it in the Illinois Country. At the end of his time at Fort Orleans on the Missouri, Father Mercier resumed his pastorate at Cahokia where he earned the highest commendation from all who came in contact with him. And the memory of his good deeds lived after him, as one traveler who visited the village nearly three years after Mercier's death made clear when he described how well he had known him and how great an influence he had exercised among the savages whose language he spoke fluently and whose confidence he had won completely by his probity and disinterestedness. The natives had consulted him on all matters, and as this French naval officer remarked, "Because of the good a man of this type does for the Indians, his life always seems to be too short regardless of how long he lives." It was stated that at the priest's death both the French and Indians were inconsolable, and the latter came in swarms, as was their custom, to mourn for Father Mercier at his tomb. "The Indians," said Bossu, "whom we call savages, recognize true virtue in a man. The Abbé had worked for their salvation almost all his life, and they called him their father or the 'prayer chief.'"[18]

Fortunately, by the mid-century the unpleasantness that had marked the transfer of the Cahokia mission from the Jesuits to the seminary priests fifty years before had passed, and in 1750 Father Louis Vivier, S.J., of the Kaskaskia mission reported to his superior in the most favorable terms concerning Father Mercier and the two other seminary priests who were in the region at the time. "Nothing can be more likeable than their character, or more edifying than their conduct," he said. "We live with them as if we were members of the same body."[19]

[18] Jean-Bernard Bossu to the Marquis de l'Estrade, 'Among the Illinois,' July 21, 1756, Seymour Feiler (Trans. and Ed.), *Jean-Bernard Bossu's Travels in the Interior of North America, 1751–1762* (Norman, 1962), p. 93. The anti-Jesuit bias of many Frenchmen at this time was well illustrated in Bossu. Writing to de l'Estrade from New Orleans on July 1, 1751, he said: "The Capuchins were the first monks [*sic*] to go to New Orleans as missionaries in 1723. The superior of these good monks, who are concerned solely with their religious work, is vicar of the parish. The Jesuits settled in Louisiana two years later, and these shrewd politicians managed to exploit the richest plantation in the colony, obtained through their intrigues." (*Ibid.*, p. 24). And in another letter to de l'Estrade he said the Indians spoke of the Jesuits as "men in black dresses," which prompted the remark, "They say that they are not like other men and laugh at them as though they were women." (*Ibid.*, p. 168, n. 4.)

[19] Vivier to an unnamed Jesuit, Among the Illinois, November 17, 1750, *Jesuit Relations*, LXIX, 223.

It was understandable, therefore, that when death took the beloved pastor of Cahokia on March 30, 1753, the grief should have been general throughout the river settlements. With the exception of the strife that arose between the two groups around 1749 over Saint Anne's Chapel of Fort de Chartres and which lasted for some years, the peace was not marred again during the French regime.

The work of the Black Robes in this neighborhood is probably seen to the best advantage at Kaskaskia, which for some decades served the Illinois Country as its principal center. The mission for the Indians of this name had been begun by Marquette when the natives were resident on the Illinois River near the present village of Utica. As we have seen, the Jesuits stayed with the tribe when they moved to the Mississippi. Even before Father Pinet had lost out at Cahokia in June, 1702, to his seminary rival a considerable number of this tribe had crossed the Mississippi and located anew on the Des Peres River at a spot that today lies within the confines of Saint Louis. It was natural, therefore, that the Jesuit should have followed them when the order came for him to yield to Father Bergier. In fact, Pinet's death less than two months later on August 1 was the occasion for the first recorded Christian burial in the future State of Missouri.

But the vacancy created by Father Pinet's death did not cause an interruption in the Kaskaskia mission. Several years previous Pierre Gabriel Martes, S.J., had worked among these redmen on the Illinois River, and he was now at hand to continue the Immaculate Conception Mission, as Marquette had named it. The Kaskaskias did not remain long in Missouri, however, for fear of the Iroquois and a desire to be within easier reach of the new French colony in Louisiana decided them to abandon the Des Peres settlement in April, 1703, and to cross the river once more. This time they located some miles from where the river of their name then flowed into the Mississippi. Marest accompanied his neophytes to their new home where the ministrations of himself and his confrère, Jean Mermet, yielded fruitful results during the next few years. Having mastered the Kaskaskia language and compiled a catechism in that dialect, Marest must have used it to good advantage, for by 1707 he estimated that all the Kaskaskia tribe, numbering over 2,000, were Christians. The veteran missionary continued on at Kaskaskia until his death in September, 1714, just a month short of his fifty-second birthday, and soon after Kaskaskia's new church was finished his remains were transferred there in December, 1727.

In the case of Kaskaskia, as in that of all the other settlements in the Illinois Country, the immediate future was to be strongly influenced by the changes in France's military fortunes and in the civil administration of its overseas colonies. The Treaty of Utrecht of April, 1713, ending the War of the Spanish Succession, had brought immense losses to the French in North America, and the succeeding decades were to witness strenuous efforts on their part to strength their defenses against the English and, through the medium of a chain of military forts, to tighten their hold on the great arc that stretched from the Saint Lawrence to the Gulf of Mexico.

Figuring prominently in these changes was a new element in France's North American projects, namely, the infant colony of Louisiana where the first permanent settlement was planted in 1699. The original effort at Fort Maurepas on Biloxi Bay did not prosper, however, and Louis XIV, still hoping that the colony might be made to yield a profit, granted in 1712 the exclusive privilege of exploiting it to Antoine Crozat. But Crozat was no more successful than his predecessors, and in 1717 he surrendered his charter. By this time the financial exigencies of the government of Phillipe, Duke of Orleans, who was ruling as regent for the child King Louis XV, made it impossible for the government to act directly, and it was this situation that opened the way for a man whose grandiose schemes were to embrace Kaskaskia and its neighboring villages as well as lower Louisiana. That man was John Law, a Scotsman whose financial prowess had made a deep impression in France. The regent now granted a charter to a group organized by Law under the name of the Western Company which ultimately came to be called the Company of the Indies. Control of Louisiana passed to the company on January, 1718, and for the next two years feverish activity over the colony's prospects was prevalent in Europe where colonists were recruited and shipped out and where the price of the company's stocks soared to amazing heights. But the whole undertaking was constructed on a speculative basis, and in 1720 with Law's bankruptcy the bursting of the Mississippi Bubble, as it was called, not only put an end to the Scotsman's financial adventures, but ruined hundreds of French investors and created a highly uncertain situation for the numerous colonists who had been scattered along the banks of the Mississippi from below New Orleans to the settlements in the Illinois Country.

It is with the increase of population in the latter area that we are mainly concerned here. It is impossible to tell exactly how many people were involved in Law's schemes, although it is safe to say that few of the nearly 2,000 Rhinelanders and German Swiss who were brought to Louisiana by the company ever reached as far north as Illinois. This region did, however, receive some of the 800 French who arrived in 1718. In any case, the Louisiana venture of John Law had one good effect – besides focusing France's attention once more on its colonies and overseas trade – in that it added a considerable number to the sparsely populated upper Mississippi villages, even if the character of some of these newcomers made them a rather doubtful acquisition.

Before Law's colonists had come upon the scene, however, an administrative change had occurred that turned the eyes of the Illinois inhabitants southward and away from Quebec. With a view to a more efficient military and civil administration, these towns were transferred in 1717 from the government of New France to the Louisiana district, and thus they were already a part of the province when Law's colonists began to arrive. The increase in the number of whites accentuated, of course, the differences between them and the surrounding Indians, and at Kaskaskia the changed situation was reflected in the order of the military commandant, Pierre Dugué, Sieur de Boisbriant, in 1719 that the whites and Indians should be separated into two villages. Knowing how hard the missionaries had fought to keep the races apart out of fear of the whites' unwholesome influence on their neophytes, this must have come as welcome news. In the following year Kaskaskia's French congregation was formally erected into a canonical parish of the Diocese of Quebec, and the Jesuits remained in charge of both the parish and the Indian mission. A further racial complication presented itself for Kaskaskia and its neighbors in 1720 due to French eagerness to exploit the lead mines of Missouri. A mining company was formed of which Philippe François de Renault was director, and he brought a large company of miners, including a group of Negro slaves from Santo Domingo, up the river from Louisiana to work the mines. With the advent of Negro slavery to Illinois and Missouri – some of the Indians had already been enslaved – there was an added responsibility for the priests whose task was aggravated at times by the unscrupulous manner in which some of the whites used the slaves for immoral purposes.

It was in the middle decades of the eighteenth century that France's upper Mississippi settlements enjoyed their most flourishing life. Partly as a result of the increase of colonists brought in from New France as well as from lower Louisiana, and partly due to the traders and military personnel whose business centered around these posts, the inhabited areas on both sides of the river gradually extended until by the time that they were ceded to Great Britain in 1763 there were five villages in Illinois along with Sainte Genevieve on the Missouri side of the river. Fort de Chartres, for example, was built in 1720 with its chapel dedicated to Saint Anne around which there slowly evolved a little congregation that was at first under Jesuit care but which, after a lengthy dispute with the seminary priests, passed to the latter about 1759.

It was the colonists introduced by de Renault who were responsible for the next village, begun about three years after Fort de Chartres and located five miles to the northeast, to which was given the name of Saint Philippe. The final settlement on the Illinois side of the river during the French regime owed its origins to Saint Joseph's Mortuary Chapel which was erected near a cemetery in 1734, and its higher ground attracted an increasing number of families living along the river banks in the years that followed. One of the major hazards of this region, in fact, was the river whose influx often played havoc with the settlements and was responsible for the ultimate abandonment of Fort de Chartres in the 1780's. It was around 1788, therefore, that Saint Joseph's at Prairie du Rocher, as the village was called, became the parish of the district, it being the only one that has preserved its identity to the present day as a thriving rural congregation of the Diocese of Belleville. Although from 1715 on there was considerable French activity in the region of the original site of Sainte Genevieve on the Missouri side, the exact date of the founding of the village there remains uncertain. What is certain is that by 1749 the Catholic Church was organized in the community as the records of Philibert Watrin, S.J., attest. Like its Illinois neighbors, Sainte Genevieve felt the encroachments of the Mississippi and ultimately the original site was abandoned for the higher ground some three miles to the north where the town is at present located.

Even in their best years the over-all population of these villages was not large. In a letter from the neighborhood in June, 1750, Louis Vivier, S.J., spoke of there being five white villages in which, he said, there might be 1,100 whites, 300 blacks, and about sixty "red slaves," as he termed them, while he did not think that the three Indian villages of the area would have more than 800 inhabitants of all ages.[20] All were agreed on the marked decline in the area's Indian population once the whites had settled in any number. In a description which Father Vivier sent to a friend late in 1750 he mentioned that the Kaskaskia Indian village then numbered 600 of whom all but five or six had been baptized. But the Jesuit was under no illusion about the true state of their religious life, in explanation of which he emphasized one of the major factors for the decline in population among the Christian redmen when he said:

the brandy sold by the French, especially by the soldiers, in spite of the King's repeated prohibitions, and that which is sometimes distributed to them under the pretext of maintaining them in our interest, has ruined this Mission, and has caused the majority of them to abandon our holy Religion. The Savages—and especially the Illinois, who are the gentlest and most tractable of men—become, when intoxicated, madmen and wild beasts. Then they fall upon one another, stab with their knives, and tear one another. Many have lost their ears, and some a portion of their noses, in these tragic encounters. The greatest good we do among them consists in administering baptism to dying children.[21]

It was a pathetic picture to have to paint after nearly a century and a half of Jesuit effort for the North American natives, but the Illinois Country could scarcely hope to escape the evils of the brandy trade when it was an almost universal phenomenon.

In 1763, the year that the French settlements passed under British rule, their population was estimated rather closely. Starting with Kaskaskia, the largest village and the one farthest south, there were at that time about 500 whites and 500 Negroes; seventeen miles to the north Prairie du Rocher counted about 100 French and about an equal number of slaves; still moving northward Fort de Chartres was reckoned to have about forty families, while five miles farther on Saint Philippe

[20] Vivier to an unnamed friend, Among the Illinois, June 8, 1750, *ibid.*, LXIX, 145.

[21] Vivier to an unnamed Jesuit, Among the Illinois, Novemger 17, 1750, *ibid.*, LXIX, 201–203.

was said to number only twelve or fifteen families. Lastly, forty-five miles beyond Saint Philippe lay the oldest of the villages, Cahokia—the original site of which is now within the limits of East Saint Louis—and here in 1763 there were about 300 whites and eighty Negroes. As for Sainte Geneviève across the river, it profited by the cession of the Illinois Country to England since large numbers of the French inhabitants refused to live under British rule and moved elsewhere, most of them going to New Orleans or to the new settlement begun in February, 1764, by the enterprising Pierre Laclede Ligueste and Auguste Chouteau which was to become the city of Saint Louis. But Sainte Geneviève, too, got a portion of these Illinois people, and by 1772 it counted 404 whites and 387 slaves which was a notable increase over the twenty-two inhabitants reported for the village twenty years before.

Life in these pioneer river communities centered largely around the village church, the fort, and the trading post. The inhabitants' living was made principally from two sources, namely, cultivation of the land and trade in furs. While the settlers were on the whole possessed of relatively little of this world's goods, there was individual ownership of land and little necessity for dire poverty for those who were willing to work. The soil was rich and in normal years the yield in maize, wheat, fruits, and vegetables was more than enough for their needs and left a good margin to be shipped out. It was the Jesuits who introduced wheat into the region, and it became the chief product along with the maize with the trade of furs a close rival, the service in which was leased to individual traders at the various posts. In communities of this type it should not surprise one to find that the priests earned most of their income from the land in the same way as their parishioners. True, the government promised to pay each priest 600 livres a year, as well as to give 200 livres as a gratuity for five years for each mission founded. But as one historian has remarked, "the stipends were often in arrears and frequently were defaulted altogether, so that the church was largely sustained by its own faith and the love of its people." [22] After 1716 the Jesuits had their own large farm at Kaskaskia which consisted of a little over 180 acres, while at Cahokia after 1722 the seminary priests had four leagues square of property on which the village largely grew up. All landowners were, indeed, supposed to pay a tax of one twenty-sixth from their annual earnings for the support of the parish church,

[22] Priestley, *Coming of the White Man*, p. 279.

but these payments were often quite irregular, and the priests – Jesuits and seculars alike – found their most dependable source of income from their farms which were worked either by hired hands or by slaves.[23]

In this rather primitive society the highest social caste were the military officers with the priests occupying their own unique position. There were no schools as such, although the priests taught catechism to the children. With educational facilities generally lacking, it was understandable that as late as 1796 two-thirds of the population of Vincennes could neither read nor write, a condition that was matched in the Mississippi River villages to the west. After the first quarter of the eighteenth century military service became a universal obligation which was almost a necessity in a country that was never long without the Indian peril. The Illinois Country's settlements had one advantage, however, on those of New France in that they had a voice in the conduct of their own local affairs through the medium of a democratic procedure which evolved in the village meeting. The people elected syndics to represent them in civil matters, and in ecclesiastical affairs they likewise elected *marguilliers* or wardens. And for both groups the place of meeting and of reporting to their constituencies was generally at the church door after Mass on Sundays or holy days. Here the local *curé* presided over the *marguilliers* and the elder syndic over the civil gathering in a system that had about it many of the features of the famous town meetings of New England.

In selecting sites for settlement in the western wilderness for obvious reasons the accessibility of water communication was a primary concern of the white man. Thus within the immense military commandery that the French centered at Fort de Chartres on the Mississippi, there were remote posts such as Fort Arkansas, the earliest white settlement in the lower Mississippi Valley, which Tonty built on the river of that name in 1686. The Jesuits opened a mission here three years later and it was attended intermittently by the missionaries for many years, but the Catholic faith did not prosper among the Indians of the region and during the French regime Fort Arkansas' chief importance was as an administrative and commercial center for the extensive district which

[23] In his letter of November 17, 1750, Vivier in speaking of his order's sources of income in lower Louisiana, mentioned the Jesuit plantation as "a considerable settlement," and remarked that the revenues from the plantation, "added to the pensions given us by the King, supply the needs of the Missionaries." *Jesuit Relations*, LXIX, 203.

the fort commanded. A second post of this kind was Fort Orleans on the Missouri River which was constructed in 1723 with the idea of holding the line of the river against Spanish incursions from the Southwest and, too, of opening trade with Santa Fe. As we have seen, Father Mercier, the seminary priest, made a stay of several years at Fort Orleans after it was first established, but here, too, there was no development of religious life and activity.

Such was not the case, however, with the easternmost fort of the commandery, Post Vincennes, which was located on the Wabash River about 240 miles east of the French villages on the upper Mississippi Vincennes owed its origin to François Bissot, son of Jean Baptiste Bissot, Sieur de Vincennes, both of whom served simultaneously in the French military forces. The exact date of establishment of the fort, as well as of the mission that followed, is not known, but the former was begun about 1732–1733, and the first priest of whom there is definite evidence, Father Xavier de Guienne, S.J., of Kaskaskia, visited the post in 1734. Two years later the founder of Vincennes, along with Father Antoine Senat, S.J., also of Kaskaskia, met a tragic end when they were captured and burned to death in May, 1736, near the present town of Pontotoc, Mississippi, by the Chickasaw Indians who were at war with the Illinois.

In the shadowy early years mention was found now and then of priests at Vincennes, but the first resident missionary of whom there is certainty was Sébastien Louis Meurin, S.J., whose entries in the parish register began in April, 1749, and who probably gave to the village church its name of Saint Francis Xavier. Through the next decade and a half the settlement was served without interruption by a succession of three Black Robes until the banishment of the Society of Jesus from the Illinois Country resulted in the arrest of Father Julien Devernai in October, 1763, his transportation to the Mississippi, and the seizure of the mission property at Vincennes. Of the Jesuits who were assembled at New Orleans for deportation at that time only Father Meurin was permitted to return to the Illinois Country where he attempted to care for the spiritual welfare of the French villages and the remnants of the Indian missions. In March, 1767, he described for Joseph-Olivier Briand, Bishop of Quebec, the plight of the settlements now largely deprived of priestly ministrations, and he made special mention of his former charge on the Wabash when he told of the difficulties at Vincennes. "Some come here [Kaskaskia] to be married, or make their Easter duty," he said, but "the majority do not wish to, nor can they do it." [24] As badly as the Mississippi villages needed priests, Vincennes, he thought, needed one even more.

As a consequence of Father Meurin's appeal, late in 1768 there arrived on the Mississippi the newly ordained Canadian-born priest, Pierre Gibault, who was to prove a great assistance to the aging missionary during the last eight years of his life. For the first year Gibault remained on the Mississippi, but early in 1770 he undertook the long and hazardous journey overland to Vincennes. What he found was not a pleasant picture. During the seven years that had passed since there had been a resident priest at the post religious practice had steadily declined, license had become widepread, and some of the *habitants* had begun to despair of ever seeing a priest again. Yet their faith was not extinct, for as Gibault told Bishop Briand, upon his arrival the whole town turned out to welcome him at the river bank. The moving scene was described by the young missionary when he wrote:

> Some threw themselves upon their knees and were quite unable to speak; others spoke only by their sobs; some cried out: Father, save us, we are nearly in hell; others said: God has not then utterly abandoned us, for it is He who has sent you to us to make us do penance for our sins; and others again exclaimed: Ah! Sir, why did you not come a month ago, then my poor wife, my dear father, my loved mother, my poor child would not have died without the sacraments! [25]

On this occasion Gibault remained two months, and he came back again in 1771 and 1773.

It was the priest's visit in the summer of 1778, however, that made history for the West as we shall see later in more detail. Suffice it to say here, Father Gibault proved very helpful to George Rogers Clark and his Virginia militiamen when they reached Kaskaskia in early July, 1778, and revealed their intention of advancing on the Post Vincennes. Once having satisfied himself that the Americans would respect the freedom of worship of the *habitants*, Gibault came over to their side and

[24] Meurin to Briand, Kaskaskia, March 23, 1767, Charles H. Metzger, S.J., "Sébastien Louis Meurin," *Illinois Catholic Historical Review*, III (April, 1921), 376.

[25] Gibault to Briand [n.p., n.d., probably the spring of 1770], Lionel St. George Lindsay (Ed.), "Letters from the Archdiocesan Archives at Quebec, 1768–1788," in *Records of the American Catholic Historical Society of Philadelphia*, XX (1909), 414.

when they set out on July 14 for the long trek overland to Vincennes the priest was in the company. Upon arrival Gibault assembled the people, assured them of the good will and intentions of the Americans, and within two days the Vincennes *habitants* had taken the pledge of allegiance to the new government and raised the American flag for the first time on the soil of the future State of Indiana.

Meanwhile, of course, the British had not abandoned hope of retaining the area, and with a view to strengthening their hold and of forestalling moves such as those of Clark, they sent an army of over 500 men from Detroit which in December took the fort with ease. We are not concerned here with the daring mid-winter march from Kaskaskia to Vincennes of Clark and his little force of less than 200 followers in February, 1779. Actually, they surprised the British and captured the fort to find a local population of whites and neighboring Indians who were glad to receive them. Formal execution of the terms of surrender took place at Saint Francis Xavier Church where the villagers were accustomed to gather for their public meetings under the syndics as well as for their religious services. For years thereafter Gibault continued to protest to Briand his innocence of any political motive for his trip of 1778, insisting that it had been made solely in the line of his missionary obligations. But his statements at this time were anything but consistent, and one gets the impression that fear of the bishop prompted him to deny having done things that clearly he had done.

In any case, Father Gibault was to see a good deal more of Vincennes, for he returned there in 1785 and this time remained for four years. The interval of six years during which the village had been without a priest had taken its toll on the people's religious life, and in describing for Briand the unhappy spiritual conditions in a letter of June, 1786, the missionary deplored especially the lack of morals among the youth who, he said, "have been raised like the savages in the midst of whom they live." But there had also been improvement through the catechism classes which he held twice a day, after Mass and in the evening before sundown. A year and a half before he had found only one European who could serve Mass, and when he was not available, there was no Mass. But, said Gibault, now "the smallest boys in the village know not only how to serve Mass, but also the ceremonies of festivals and Sundays and the entire catechism, small and large. . . ." Moreover, he was then in the midst of building an adequate church for which he had gained the unanimous support of the parishioners once they learned that the Cahokia congregation had made an attractive offer to their pastor if he would return to the Mississippi. At that, said Gibault, the Vincennes flock, "just fearful lest I abandon them," hastened to lend their support to the project for the new church.[26]

Thus Vincennes passed through the transition period between its status as a military outpost and mission, first in French and then in British hands, and the time when immigrants from Virginia and Kentucky began to arrive in the neighborhood bearing land warrants for service they had performed during the Revolution. Inevitably, there was at first tension and ill feeling between the representatives of the old and the new orders. But gradually the frontiersmen of English blood and the descendants of the original French *habitants* began to mingle, and in this manner there was laid the foundations for the American community that numbered around 2,500 people in the town and environs when it became the capital of Indiana Territory in January, 1801, a distinction it was to enjoy for only twelve years. In 1834, however, Vincennes again took on added prominence in being chosen as the see city of one of the oldest western dioceses of the American Church.

The new world missions, as we have seen, were never free to develop independent of international politics, a fact that was clearly demonstrated in the late seventeenth and early eighteenth centuries in what the Jesuits called the Ottawa Mission. The fall of King James II and the succession of William of Orange to the English throne early in 1689, the formation of the Grand Alliance against Louis XIV in May of that year, and the renewal of war between France and England in that same month, was just such a chain of events as multiplied and aggravated the difficulties of the missions centered at Michilimackinac. At that time Father Jean Enjalran was the general superior at Saint Ignace and Etienne de Carheil, S.J., was stationed with him, while Henri Nouvelle was at Saint Francis Xavier on Green Bay, and Sault Sainte Marie had Fathers Charles Albanel and Pierre Bailloquet. More recently, Saint Joseph Mission for the Miamis had been founded about 1693 as a dependency of Saint Ignace near the present Niles, Michigan, where Claude Aveneau, S.J., served after Allouez' death, and in south-

[26] Same to same, Vincennes, June 6, 1786, *ibid.*, XX, 426–427.

western Wisconsin. Father Joseph Marest, brother of the Kaskaskia missionary, had tried his hand with the Dakota Indians on the banks of the Saint Croix River.

The increased dangers for all these missions from the English and their Indian allies, once war had been declared, were obvious, and even at Michilimackinac the military commander thought it wise in 1691 to enclose the church and the priests' residence within a palisade. In addition to the anxiety created by the war, the missions suffered a further setback when Antoine de la Mothe Cadillac was appointed as commandant at Michilimackinac in 1694. Cadillac was about as hostile to the Jesuits as were Frontenac and La Salle, and during the three years he held the office he showed by his strongly mercenary views that he would not hesitate to reduce the religious aspects of the post to a mere instrumentality of his economic policies. Of late the French had become aware of the strategic importance of the Detroit River, and in June, 1687, formal possession was taken of the site where Detroit stands today. Convinced of the desirability of occupying this location, Cadillac drew up a report on the service that the Detroit River could render the western fur trade by way of protection from the English. His proposal won the endorsement of Governor Louis de Callières at Quebec, and late in 1698 Cadillac arrived in France where he laid the plan before the government and finally gained the approval of Louis XIV. Thereupon Cadillac was given a grant of Detroit, made head of a company that had a trade monopoly, and had bestowed on him the title of lieutenant of the king.

Returning to America in a triumphant mood, Cadillac still had to overcome a good deal of opposition from the Jesuits and the intendant who was favorable to their interests. But by the spring of 1701 he believed that he was strong enough to proceed, and on June 5 he left Montreal with a band of fifty soldiers and about as many *coureurs de bois*. In the company were two priests: Constantin Delhalle, a Franciscan friar, who was to be the chaplain of the troops and pastor of the white settlers, and François Vaillant de Gueslis, S.J., whose presence has never been satisfactorily explained but who, in any case, remained only a few months and then returned to New France. Arriving at their destination, the settlement was formally founded on July 21, construction was begun on Fort Pontchartrain, and on July 26, the feast of Saint Anne, work was started on the chapel where the friar was soon to inaugurate the first permanent religious services for white men in the West.

Cadillac's plans envisioned the assemblying at Detroit of the Hurons and Ottawas from Michilimackinac as well as the Miamis and the Potawatomies from Saint Joseph, and from these tribes he expected to create a strong defense post and trading headquarters for the inland part of France's empire somewhat after the fashion that Quebec and Biloxi were then serving the extreme ends of the water route of the continent. Behind this plan lay his further hope that he might woo the northern Indians away from the habit of taking their pelts to the English on Hudson's Bay or to the Hudson River, a practice that the redmen followed because they received goods at a cheaper rate in exchange from the English as well as acquired more readily the much desired brandy. The strong backing that Cadillac had from both Quebec and Versailles at the outset was prompted in part by the expectation that the concentration of Indians and whites at Detroit would protect the former from the Iroquois and the Sioux, and at the same time enable the savages to learn the French language, intermingle, and intermarry with the French and thus create a mixed force that would be more than equal to the English and their allies.

To one who knew anything about the traditional policy of the Jesuits regarding the mixing of the races, it was not difficult to anticipate their reaction to all of this. From the beginning of their labors in New France they had opposed mingling the savages with the whites since they found that almost invariably it had a deleterious effect upon the Indians. But their opposition was not credited for what it really was; instead Cadillac and others of a like mind toward the Society of Jesus maintained that the priests fought the government's policy because they wished to control the Indian trade for their own enrichment. Although these charges were repeatedly advanced, there was never any substantial evidence produced to prove that the Jesuits were profiteering at the expense of their spiritual charges.

Moreover, on their side the Black Robes could show ample evidence of the disastrous effects that Cadillac's policies had on their missions as, for example, the reduction of the Indian population at Saint Ignace to only about twenty-five persons and for a time the complete abandonment of Saint Joseph Mission. In fact, by 1705 matters had reached such a pass that de Carheil, Marest, and Enjalran – much to the chagrin of the officials at both Quebec and Versailles – burned the mission buildings at Saint Ignace themselves lest they should be profaned and withdrew to Quebec. This action reduced the Jesuit stations to Saint Francis Xavier at Green Bay where Jean Charlon, S.J., had gone in 1701 to relieve the aged and enfeebled Nouvelle whose forty years of missionary labor were closed in death the following year.

Long before they had taken the drastic measure of setting fire to the mission and withdrawing, however, the Jesuits had given warning of what, in their judgment, had become the ruination of the cause they had tried to serve among the savages. In this regard Father de Carheil was especially outspoken, and in a letter of August, 1702, from Saint Ignace to the Governor of New France he laid bare the evils with which he and his confrères had had to contend from the French soldiers and traders. If, he said, the king wished to save the missions and to support religion, then the Jesuits would beg His Majesty to believe that there was no other means of doing so than to eradicate what he termed "two Infamous sorts of Commerce." They were the trade in brandy and, as he expressed it, "the Commerce of the savage women with the french," both of which were carried on in a public manner. The pernicious effects of the commandants and their garrisons on the Indians were so bad that, as de Carheil remarked, "we can truly say that they are the greatest scourge of our missions."[27]

According to Father de Carheil, these French soldiers and traders pretended to render service to the king; actually, their services consisted of the following: maintaining a public tavern for the sale of brandy; sending soldiers from one military post to another to carry thither the commandant's wares and brandy; converting the forts into places that the Jesuit was ashamed to call by their proper name, where, he stated, "the women have found out that their bodies would serve in lieu of beaverskins"; finally, gambling which was carried to such excess that when the traders assembled they and the soldiers spent not only all day but all night in this pursuit. They maintained that they needed the women for cooking, cutting wood, doing the laundry, and making shoes and leggings. In fact, they used them as prostitutes, and the most scandalous evil of all, said de Carheil, was that the traders had come to feel it so necessary to have the women at the trading posts "that they

[27] De Carheil to de Callières, Michilimackinac, August 30, 1702, *Jesuit Relations*, LXV, 195.

cannot do without them even on their journeys." As a result there was a steady traffic of prostitutes between Montreal and Michilimackinac. Summing up his views on the military, the Black Robe told the governor:

> I have therefore no hesitation in telling you that if trading Commandants and garrisons of trading soldiers be again stationed in our missions up here, we have no doubt that we shall be Compelled to abandon them, because we shall be unable to do anything for the salvation of souls.[28]

As cogent as may have been the Jesuit's arguments against the evils of brandy and women, and as clearly detrimental as both were to winning the Indians to the Catholic faith, the reasoning was lost on a man like Cadillac. With the Detroit commander economic gain was a prime consideration and the most that the missionaries could expect was that he would continue to favor Frontenac's policy of trying to regulate the liquor traffic under French civilian rule, a method that had been proven quite futile. Since the Jesuits continued to insist that the total ban demanded by the Bishop of Quebec be enforced, the result was a series of mutual recriminations that embittered relations between Cadillac and the Jesuits with little real remedy applied to the unquestioned harm that brandy wrought in the lives of the savages.

Meanwhile the nascent community of Detroit was struggling to get a start in life. On October 5, 1703, a fire destroyed the settlement and consumed the earliest ecclesiastical records. The church was rebuilt the following year, however, and the first entry in the new register for February, 1704, was a recording of the baptism of Cadillac's infant daughter. The most serious threat to the life of the community arose from the Indians of the region who resented the removal of the Christian tribesmen like the Hurons and the Ottawas to Detroit. Their slowly gathering wrath found a plausible reason for explosion in June, 1706, when the temporary commandant, Etienne Venyard, Sieur de Bourgmont, apprehended an Ottawa Indian in a trifling fault for which he beat him so severely that the man died. At that the braves of three of the surrounding villages swooped down on the town and in the course of the fighting Father Delhalle, trying to act as intermediator, was shot and killed. Detroit's first pastor was buried in the village church, and after an interval of two months his place was taken by a fellow Fran-

[28] *Ibid.*, LXV, 217.

ciscan, Dominique de la Marche. While the French were successful in beating off other attacks in 1707 from the Foxes and the Mascoutens, the former tribe, an especially arrogant and wily lot, continued to be a major peril by their unceasing intrigues to create turmoil among the other Indians and by their designs against Detroit itself. In fact, the Foxes were to the area now embraced by Michigan and Wisconsin in the mid-eighteenth century what the Iroquois and Sioux had been at an earlier date to the upper Great Lakes and the trans-Mississippi West. The danger was so real at Detroit that the commandant ordered the destruction of the second church which had been built outside the palisade, lest the Foxes and their allies use it to fire the other buildings.

During most of the eighteenth century the Franciscans served Detroit as its spiritual guides, the tenure of two of these priests covering a period of sixty years. One of these lengthy pastorates was that of Bonaventure Liénard who made his first entry in the register on June 22, 1722, and who continued on at Detroit until September, 1754. It was Liénard who first used the title of Saint Anne for the church, as it was he who first designated Detroit as a canonical parish, his predecessors having signed themselves simply as almoners of the military post. Not very much is known about the religious life of the village during Father Bonaventure's long term of office, but a definite increase of population had taken place, for by the time he withdrew the community counted about 500 souls. As the western base of operations for the French in the closing years of their rule in North America, Detroit's importance and prestige grew, and it was the increased numbers of the faithful that made it necessary to provide a more commodious church. It was Liénard's successor, Father Simplicius Bocquet, who supervised this undertaking, a friar whose pastorate extended to the summer of 1782 which was, therefore, almost as long as that of his predecessor. By the time that Henri Marie du Breuil de Pontbriand, sixth Bishop of Quebec, arrived in March, 1755, for his visit of several weeks to that distant part of his diocese the new church was ready to be dedicated. Pontbriand was the first incumbent of the See of Quebec to perform episcopal functions in what was later the United States on the occasion of his visits to Detroit and to the French fort where Ogdensburg, New York, stands today. He was also the last Bishop of Quebec to serve under the French regime, dying as he did at the Sulpician seminary of Montreal on June 8, 1760, just three months before the surrender of the colony to the British.

Before speaking of Detroit in the period of transition from French and British to American rule, something should be said of the final efforts of the Jesuits in the old Northwest. As we have seen, Fathers Enjalran, Marest, and de Carheil became so discouraged by Cadillac's policy of drawing off the Indians to Detroit, by his general opposition, and by the hostility of the Fox tribesmen that they set fire to the mission buildings at Saint Ignace in 1705 and departed for Quebec. But their action met with the prompt and firm opposition of both the colonial and home governments. Bowing to the royal command, therefore, in the summer of 1706 Marest returned to Michilimackinac and Aveneau resumed his residence at Saint Joseph for whose Miami Indians he gave in all eighteen years of his life. But at Sault Sainte Marie the possibilities of revival were too remote, and following the death there of Charles Albanel, S.J., in January, 1696, it was not until 1834 that the Sault again saw a Catholic priest in residence. At Michilimackinac the withdrawal southward of so many of the savages, and the deadly fear in which the remainder lived lest they fall afoul of the Foxes, deprived the mission of its former strength. After the fort had been transferred, therefore, to the tip of the lower peninsula about where Mackinac City is now located, the Jesuits followed with their mission headquarters in 1741. From that date until the mission was finally abandoned in 1766 there were stationed there four Jesuits in succession, the last being Marin-Louis Le Franc. But through much of that time the services of even a single missionary must have seemed superfluous, for with a largely depopulated area round about it the Jesuit residence was hardly more than a stopping off place for itinerant missionaries.

Upon their return to the West the Jesuits at Saint Joseph Mission became a special target for Cadillac's ill will because they did not hasten the removal of the Miamis and Potawatomies to Detroit with the speed that he desired. Claude Aveneau, S.J., was made to feel the displeasure of the Detroit commander, as were his assistants, Fathers Jean Mermet and Jean Baptiste Chardon. The latter came to Saint Joseph in 1705 and continued battling against great odds until 1712 when the attacks of the Foxes – instigated by the Iroquois and the English – finally made him despair of accomplishing any good and he returned to Michilimackinac. With Father Chardon's departure Saint Joseph was without a resident priest for the next seven or eight years. It was this same Jesuit who later felt the scourge of the Fox warfare against Saint Francis

Xavier Mission at De Pere, and it was Chardon who had the melancholy experience of being the last of his order to serve the Green Bay mission when it was finally abandoned in 1728 with the demolition of the neighboring fort.

Meanwhile, however, the Jesuits had not reconciled themselves to the permanent loss of Saint Joseph, and from about 1720 to the disastrous year of 1763 the baptismal register revealed that Black Robes were there at intervals, working among the relatively small group of Indians as well as the whites who manned the fort. Between June, 1738, and April, 1752, when Pierre du Jaunay, S.J., served intermittently at Saint Joseph, the number of whites was never large, there being about fifty soldiers stationed there through the 1740's. As for the Indian population, it had steadily declined and by 1763, the year of the formal cession of the colony to Britain and of Pontiac's uprising, there were only about 100 Potawatomie warriors, ten Miamis, and ten of the Illinois braves with their families. In May of that year Saint Joseph fell victim to an attack from Pontiac's followers and the garrison was either massacred or taken away as prisoners. During the American Revolution the old post figured in several frontier skirmishes between the British and the Americans and Spaniards. In the summer of 1780 a British raid on Saint Louis brought retaliation in the form of a raiding party from Cahokia that attacked Saint Joseph and made off with considerable plunder. More dramatic, perhaps, was the Spanish force that set out early in January of 1781 from Saint Louis and marched across country in the dead of winter to strike a blow at the British before they could mount another assault against the Mississippi settlements. On February 12 the Spaniards occupied the fort, reduced it for the most part to ruins, and were back in Saint Louis by the early days of March without having lost a single man.

Nearly twenty years before these events the last Jesuit, Pierre Potier, had signed the baptismal register at Saint Joseph Mission in June, 1761, and with that the final chapter of its spiritual history under the Black Robes was closed. Of those who had exercised their ministry at this mission one, Pierre du Jaunay, S.J., lingered on in Michigan for a few more years among a remnant of the Ottawa tribe at l'Arbre Croche. At this northern post near the present town of Harbor Springs Father du Jaunay functioned until his recall in 1765, having as an alternate for part of the time up to the spring of 1760 Father Jean Baptiste de la

Morinie, S.J. But the fate of all these missions had been sealed and by the end of the decade there would be left in the old Northwest only one member of the former French provinces of the Society of Jesus and he, as we shall see, had elected to serve as a secular priest.

Before the action of the French government brought the final eclipse of the missions in the western country another brief but unsuccessful attempt was made by the Jesuits to open a new missionary territory. The French were anxious to prevent the Sioux from attacking their line of communications between Lake Superior and the West, as well as to prevent them from allying with the Foxes. And to the combined motives of defense and commercial gain they added the hope that an expedition to the Sioux country might also establish a mission among these fierce people and in this way gradually tame them and bring them under some kind of control. As a consequence the government made appropriation for two priests to accompany the group. Thus in the company that left Montreal in June, 1727, under command of René Bouchard, Sieur de la Perrière, there were two Jesuits, Michel Guignas and Nicolas de Gonner. They arrived at Lake Pepin in September, and at a point about six miles from the present town of Lake City the French erected Fort Beauharnois. And in the small chapel, to which was given the name of Saint Michael the Archangel, there was offered that autumn the first Mass in the future State of Minnesota.

But the settlement on Lake Pepin did not prosper. An inundation the following spring wrought widespread damage and resulted in a number of the colonists losing heart and returning home, and the persistent hostility of the Sioux discouraged others as well as provided a cause for many of the shareholders to withdraw their support from the enterprise. Nor were the spiritual aspects of the undertaking in any happier state. While Father de Gonner remained only a brief time, his confrère stayed on only to be taken captive by the savages in October, 1728, and for about five months he was held a prisoner. But this grim experience did not daunt him, and upon being set free he went back to his Sioux apostolate where he remained until 1736, having in the end, however, nothing to show for the misery and sacrifice he had endured at their hands.

While Father Guignas was endeavoring to reach the souls of the Sioux two other Jesuits entered this far western region. In 1731 a government permission was issued to Pierre Gaulthier La Vérendrye to explore at his own expense for an opening to the western ocean with the promise of a monopoly of the fur trade in the territory he would traverse. When the La Vérendrye expedition reached Michilimackinac they were joined by Father Charles Mésaiger who accompanied them westward, although his stay was brief since a break in health made it necessary for him to return to Quebec before he had been able to determine finally what could be accomplished among the Indians. The La Vérendryes – father, three sons, and nephew – were a sturdy lot, and during the next three years they explored an immense area, staked out claims, and built a number of posts such as Fort Saint Pierre on Rainy Lake in 1731, Fort Saint Charles on the Lake of the Woods in the following year, and Fort Maurepas on Lake Winnipeg in 1734. These were notable gains, to be sure, for the French fur trading interests, to say nothing of the La Vérendrye party being the first white men to see the western plains of Minnesota, the Dakotas, and, perhaps, even eastern Montana. Moreover, even major reverses, such as the loss in 1736 of an entire group numbering one of his sons, did not deter the older man who continued his exploring and trading activities in these distant outposts until his death in December, 1749.

But however valuable La Vérendrye's achievements may have been for exploration and trade, they contributed nothing of permanent worth to the missions. Of the four Jesuits who saw service in this region between 1727 and 1736, de Gonner and Mésaiger remained only a brief time, Guignas was finally compelled to give up after nine years of futile effort, and the fourth forfeited his life on this soil. In 1734 the elder La Vérendrye was called back to New France on business, and upon his return the following year he was accompanied by Pierre Aulneau, S.J. Father Aulneau's hope of finding an opening among the Sioux, however, was no better rewarded than that of his predecessors. In June, 1736, therefore, he joined a convoy at Fort Saint Charles, headed by Jean Baptiste La Vérendrye, son of the explorer, which was bound for the East to secure needed supplies. The group had gone hardly more than twenty miles from the fort before they were fallen upon by a band of Sioux who murdered the Jesuit, young La Vérendrye, and nineteen others at what came to be called Massacre Island in the Lake of the Woods. Coming in the same year as Father Guignas' withdrawal, it was not surprising that this tragedy should have written a bloody end to the Jesuit attempts to gain the Sioux for the Christian faith.

As we have seen, the establishment of Detroit, together with the general unrest during and after the Fox upheaval, had put the northern missions into a state of permanent decline. As far as Detroit and its environs were concerned, as long as Cadillac remained in command there it was futile to think of making up for the losses in that area. But in 1711 he was assigned to Louisiana and with that a new prospect opened. Of all the western Indians to whom the Black Robes had ministered the Hurons were, perhaps, the most fruitful in the sense of lasting conversions and the missionaries were at pains, therefore, not to lose complete contact with the scattered units of this tribe. Thus they were aware that the Hurons who had been brought down by Cadillac from Michilimackinac to Detroit were not happy and that they wished to get away. Consequently when the opportunity presented itself a mission was opened for these Indians at Detroit in 1728 with Father Armand de la Richardie in charge. Although they had retained a dim recollection of certain Christian practices, de la Richardie found that in good measure he had to begin their instruction all over again. His first years were heartbreaking ones, but by 1735 his persistence was repaid when he counted approximately 600 neophytes who gave evidence of sincere conversion. By this time de la Richardie had become a beloved figure in their midst, and when the Hurons moved in 1742 far to the north to Bois Blanc Island he accompanied them. In all the Jesuit gave eighteen years of his life to this tribe before he left them in July, 1746, much to their sorrow and regret.

One of the besetting weaknesses of the Hurons, as of so many other Indians, was the curse of inter-tribal warfare which often exhausted their strength and disrupted their lives to a degree that normal missionary activity among them was rendered impossible. Not long after Father de la Richardie had gone trouble of this kind broke out, and his successor, Pierre Potier, S.J., whom the Indians did not especially like, was not equal to restoring peace. It was a compliment to the confidence that the redmen reposed in de la Richardie that a delegation of chiefs made the long journey to Montreal to beg him to return, and upon his arrival at Detroit in October, 1747, there was general rejoicing. Following a series of conferences with both the Indians and the government officials, de la Richardie succeeded in getting the latter to appropriate

5,000 livres for the reconstitution of the mission at a new site since the buildings at Bois Blonc Island had been destroyed by the enemy faction. The Jesuit chose a place called Pointe de Montreal a little below Detroit on the opposite side of the river where Sandwich, Ontario, is located. Precisely when the Hurons moved to Sandwich is not known, but they were settled there by October, 1749, with de la Richardie supervising their affairs until his return to New France in 1751 when Father Potier once more took over.

At that time, of course, no distinction was made by the government between the two sides of the Detroit River so that the two communities lived on in close proximity, each having its own priest, Bocquet, the Franciscan, at the town proper and Potier, the Jesuit, with the Indians across the river. After some years the progress and stability of the Indian mission warranted in Bocquet's judgment its being raised to the status of a parish, and as a result of his petition to the Bishop of Quebec permission for such was granted in August, 1767, with the Franciscan formally erecting the new parish and reporting his action to the bishop in October of that year. The change marked no real break in administrative affairs, however, since from the time that they had come to the Detroit area in 1728 the Jesuits had had little or nothing to do with the parish proper. Here, then, at the Huron village of Sandwich, Father Potier, like Father Meurin, the ex-Jesuit who died at Prairie du Rocher in 1777, continued his ministrations as a secular priest, and it was here that he, the last of his once numerous company in the Northwest, was found dead beside the fireplace of his residence on July 16, 1781.

During the course of the eighteenth century there gradually developed at Detroit most of the features of parish life as we have seen them in the French villages on the Mississippi. Following the British occupation in 1760, there was a general exodus of the French so that at one time there were only six Catholic families within the palisade. But unlike their counterparts in the Illinois Country, the *habitants* of Detroit did not move very far away. Rather they spread out to the rural areas in the vicinity so that at the time that the Americans took possession of the town in 1796 the bulk of Saint Anne's parishioners were farmers who lived on their lands up and down the river. Saint Anne's, too, had its *marguilliers* or church wardens, and the temporal business of the parish functioned through what was called the *fabrique* or parish corporation, generally centered in three *marguilliers* of whom one was elected each year.

The parish revenues were derived from various sources such as the collections taken at Mass on Sundays and holy days of obligation, the sale of cemetery lots, and the stipends for baptisms, weddings, and funerals. But the largest and most dependable source of income came from renting the pews in the church, while occasionally a benefactor would surprise the pastor and his flock with a sizable contribution. The pastor's salary came from the tithes which were usually paid by each farmer at Easter in the form of one twenty-sixth of the grain harvested the previous summer, from the so-called *quête de l'Infant Jesus*, a forerunner of the Christmas collection of more recent times, and finally from occasional gifts from members of the parish. As in most places in colonial times, there was an abnormal number of holy days of obligation when the faithful were expected to refrain from manual labor. In fact, the thirty-four holy days prescribed in 1694 was in time found to have such an adverse effect on the farmers' work schedule that in 1744 Bishop Pontbriand reduced them to fifteen. There was nothing approaching a parochial school as it is known today, of course, although the priest conducted regular catechetical instruction for the children to insure that they would know the essential doctrines and practices of their faith.

In the last half of the century Detroit witnessed a number of administrative changes that at times put a heavy strain on the frontier village and its Catholic inhabitants. With France's defeat the British moved to occupy the western forts, and late in November, 1760, they took possession of Detroit. For the first time the town now had a non-Catholic element in its population, although the situation was eased by the promise of freedom of worship that was contained in the terms of the colony's surrender, and the honoring of this pledge on the part of the British enabled the Catholics to surmount the problem of a mixed population without grave consequences. Far more disturbing than the presence of a few non-Catholics in their midst, was the Indian uprising which took its name from Pontiac, the Ottawa chief, who had inspired it. The objective of the savages was to chase the British out of the entire Northwest, and they succeeded to the extent of forcing the capitulation of all the forts except Pittsburgh, Niagara, and Detroit. Detroit's turn came in May, 1763, when the Indians laid siege to the town and for the next 123 days it was submitted to the most harrowing experience in its history.

The ordeal of the siege of Detroit was in the end successfully overcome, it is true, but it seemed for a time that there would be little chance for the community to settle down to a period of prolonged peace and constructive effort, for not long thereafter the first rumblings of the approaching revolution of the Americans against the mother country were heard even in this remote outpost. Yet it profited by its distance from the main scene of operations and Detroit never became the focal point of a major campaign. A further powerful factor in the French Catholic population retaining the peace and, too, their loyalty to Britain during the war, was the unflinching allegiance of the Bishop of Quebec to the British cause. Briand's example and his stern admonitions to his flock concerning the Americans, whatever might have been the personal feelings of the priests and people, helped to hold them in line and thus the British commander at Detroit had little to complain about regarding their conduct on that score.

Less than six months before the Americans and British signed the provisional peace of November, 1782, Father Bocquet's long pastorate came to an end, and with his departure that summer Detroit saw the last of its Franciscans pastors. Thereafter the parish and the surrounding settlements were cared for by a succession of secular priests who were sent from Quebec, including Jean François Hubert, a future Bishop of Quebec, who spent four years in and around Detroit, and Edmund Burke, the Irish-born priest whose distaste for Americans was only one of the reasons for his tactless and unhappy two years in the area. Burke, who was to die in 1820 as the first Vicar Apostolic of Nova Scotia, left in July, 1796, one week in advance of the formal American occupation of Detroit. But the village was not long without a priest, for Michel Levadoux, a French Sulpician who had been among the earliest refugees fleeing to this country from the revolution in his own land, arrived on August 14 of the same year. About a year after he had reached the United States in July, 1791, Levadoux had been assigned to Cahokia, and during most of his time there he had enjoyed the assistance of a young confrère, Gabriel Richard, also French-born. After Levadoux had had an opportunity to estimate the extent of priestly labors required in the Detroit area, he appealed to the Bishop of Baltimore for help, and John Carroll agreed to move the thirty-year-old Richard northward to assist him. With Father Richard's arrival in Detroit on June 3, 1798, the town, then approaching its first centennial as a white settlement, may be said to have entered upon a new chapter in its religious history.

CHAPTER TEN

LOUISIANA UNDER THE FRENCH

After the death of La Salle in 1687 over a decade elapsed before any serious attention was paid to the continuance of the grant that he had received to the territory to which he had given the name of Louisiana. During most of that time the French government was so preoccupied with the War of the League of Augsburg, or King William's War as it was known in America, that it could think of little else. It was not that Louisiana had been forgotten, for a number of proposals for its future were laid before Louis XIV. But only after the Treaty of Ryswick of September, 1697, had restored peace, and rumors had arisen that the English were preparing to occupy the mouth of the Mississippi, was action taken. To forestall the English, the Minister of Marine, Louis Phelypeaux, Comte de Pontchartrain, authorized in 1698 an expedition to the Gulf of Mexico, the leadership of which was placed in the hands of Pierre Le Moyne, Sieur d'Iberville, who had distinguished himself, along with his brothers, in fighting the English in the Hudson's Bay region. Iberville was Canadian-born, the son of Charles Le Moyne, one of the great seigniors of New France, and he had associated with him in the new venture his brothers, Jean Baptiste Le Moyne, Sieur de Bienville, and François Marie Le Moyne, Sieur de Sauvolle. The mouth of the Mississippi was one of the first instances where the interests of all three of the major colonial powers converged at a given time. As a consequence of that fact, as soon as news of what the French intended had reached Madrid, the Spaniards hurried to fortify Pensacola in November, 1698, lest they should land there and encroach on

Spanish claims. As it turned out, the precaution was no useless gesture since Iberville's ships appeared before the Pensacola harbor in January, 1699, and demanded admission. It was the refusal of the Spaniards that brought the newcomers to the site of old Biloxi where in the following month they laid the foundations for the first permanent French settlement in the lower Mississippi country.

As in practically all of France's undertakings of this sort, priests were identified with it from the outset. Since the Franciscans were the regular chaplains of the army and navy, it was no surprise to find one with Iberville when he sailed in October, 1698. Moreover, this friar was no stranger to America, for the chaplain in this instance was Anastase Douay who will be remembered as one of the survivors of La Salle's last tragic journey of 1687. Having identified the mouth of the Mississippi and built a fort, Iberville then returned to France in May, 1699, for reinforcements, leaving the original group under the direction of his brothers, Bienville and Sauvolle. Unlike many of his contemporaries in French public life, Iberville was friendly toward the Jesuits, a sentiment that was Franciscan reflected in the journal of his first voyage when he learned that the friar did not wish to remain in the colony. Iberville had then written: "I am quite distressed not to have a Jesuit missionary who would quickly learn the language of the savages of the region." [1] The omission was corrected on Iberville's second voyage when Paul du Ru, S.J., accompanied him to Louisiana as both chaplain and agent of his order to investigate at firsthand the prospects for establishing missions among the Indians.

The task that faced the colonists whom Iberville brought with him when he sailed again for the new world in September, 1699, was in no sense an easy one. They were expected to create a suitable habitation out of a wilderness that was subject to all the usual pitfalls, plus the hazard of sudden and violent storms that frequently brought in their wake severe inundation over large areas of land, as well as periodic epidemics of yellow fever, and other diseases. Yet they lost no time, and so earnestly did they go about their difficult task that Father du Ru felt he could not hold them to more than attendance at an early Mass on Sundays. For example, on February 7, 1700, he noted in his journal

[1] Iberville's Journal, April 19–21, 1699, Pierre Margry (Ed.), *Déscouvertes et établissements des Français dans l'ouest et dans le sud l'Amérique septentrionale (1614–1754). Mémories et documents originaux* (Paris, 1880), IV, 196.

the appropriateness of the gospel of that Septuagesima Sunday which contained the parable of the laborers in the vineyard. And he commented, "Certainly there is no one to be found at either nine o'clock or at noon to be set to work," and the labor, as he said, went on up to supper time. His inability to celebrate Sunday in the ordinary way with vespers and a sermon seemed to make the Jesuit slightly uneasy. "I shall be more careful to celebrate the festivals in the future," he said. "A little more devotion will not hinder the work."[2]

In the brief period of a little over four months that he was in Louisiana, Father du Ru's observant eyes and alert mind took in a number of features which were to characterize the colony in later days. He contacted several of the Indian tribes, and built a church and made what he called "a kind of catechism" for the Bayogoulas, one of the Muskhogean family that included the Creeks, Choctaws, and Chickasaws. On March 12 he arrived at Natchez only to learn that Father de Montigny, the seminary priest, had left just two days before, and in a letter which the missionary had confided to the Indian chief the Jesuit read that during de Montigny's time there he had baptized 124 children and some adult Indians who were ill. The following week at the village of the Taensas, du Ru met de Montigny, and in the light of the trouble that was soon to overcast the relationship between the two groups of priests, the Jesuit's comment is of special interest. He said: "He is a saintly man and I hope that we shall cooperate to promote religion and show by our actions that, though wearing different habits, we have the same purpose."[3]

Easter that year fell on April 11, and on this occasion Father du Ru was able to celebrate with the full festival requirements of a high Mass, vespers, and a sermon, at which the people attended with what he described as "such humility that I believe God will be pleased." In the early days of the colony these Louisiana pioneers encountered many misfortunes, some of which the Jesuit recorded; but they also had their consolations as, for example, when one of the men during the course of a trip up the river in April, 1700, shot a deer which provided food at a time that it was needed; and later when what du Ru called an even more substantial consolation came their way in a herd of buf-

[2] Ruth Lapham Butler (Trans. and Ed.), *Journal of Paul du Ru [February 1 to May 8, 1700]. Missionary Priest to Louisiana* (Chicago, 1934), p. 8.

[3] *Ibid.*, p. 41.

falo of which six or seven were shot down. It was no time for fastidious manners and delicate tastes since, as the Jesuit said, there was no vessel in which to cook the meat so they were reduced to eating the buffalo roasted before a fire. "On the average," he remarked, "fifteen or sixteen men eat two buffalo at one meal." Nor was anything wasted since all the meat was dried and put on a rack so that it could be picked up on their return.[4] One of the final observations made by Father du Ru before he sailed back to France with Iberville on May 28 foreshadowed a spectre that would frequently haunt the colony in the coming years, namely, a slave uprising. Having already boarded the *Renommée*, he made the following entry for the last date in his journal, May 8:

> We have heard in all the villages here that quite a large group of negroes and of mulattoes, men and women, have deserted and are established in a separate district where they persist in their revolt.[5]

The French regime in Louisiana lasted in all for seventy years from the founding of the original settlement in 1699 to the arrival of the first Spanish governor in August, 1769, and during that time there were four major changes in the government. These political changes, of course, affected the ecclesiastical life of the colony and, therefore, before proceeding to the story of the Church it may be helpful to summarize them briefly. The administration of the Le Moyne family, largely military in character, continued without much success from the beginning until 1712 when it was forced to give way with Louis XIV's grant of the colony to a company founded by Antoine Crozat. But Crozat was no more successful than his predecessors, and in 1717 his group yielded its charter to the crown which, in turn, granted it to the Company of the Indies headed by the Scotsman, John Law. Under these auspices Louisiana continued to be governed until 1731, more than a decade beyond Law's personal ruin and removal from the French scene. Then once again the crown took over and Louisiana remained its direct responsibility until the surrender to Spain in 1769. In the course of these changes the historian of the Church meets with a somewhat bewildering succession of officials with quite different attitudes toward ecclesiastical affairs. The one fairly constant figure was

[4] *Ibid.*, p. 65.
[5] *Ibid.*, p. 71.

Sieur de Bienville who occupied various offices amid all these changes, and who finally retired from Louisiana at his own request only in May, 1743.

With France deeply involved after 1701 in the War of the Spanish Succession – Queen Anne's War in America – and for years thereafter heavily in debt, it was to be expected that the infant colony would be left largely to its own resources. Furthermore, the armed conflict on both sides of the Atlantic prevented the Louisiana pioneers from devoting their efforts exclusively to building up the colony since they had to remain on the alert against the dangers of invasion from several quarters. Consequently, Iberville and his men were happy early in 1700 to welcome the trusted old lieutenant of La Salle, Henri Tonty, who found it to his advantage to shift his fur trade from the Illinois Country to Louisiana and to cast his lot in with the Le Moynes. In Tonty they had a man whose long and varied experience with the savages was almost unexcelled by any European of his time, and this experience was soon put to good use when he acted as the colony's intermediary with the Chickasaws which resulted in a conference in which the Chickasaw and Choctaw chiefs made an alliance of friendship and trade with the French. The agreement was of more than local significance because it removed for the time being the threat that these powerful tribes might combine with the English and their Indian allies from Virginia and the Carolinas in an attack on the French. Experience had likewise shown after several years that the original location at old Biloxi was not a suitable one, and in 1702 the settlement was moved to Mobile Bay where Fort Louis was built. This new location about fifty-four miles from the sea was more advantageous for checking the Spaniards at Pensacola and, too, less subject to the damaging storms and fever epidemics at old Biloxi.

It was here at Fort Louis, the forerunner of present day Mobile, Alabama, to whose present site the little colonial capital was moved in 1710, that there was centered one of the numerous feuds over jurisdiction with which the ecclesiastical life of Louisiana was torn in its early years. By reason of the favor that they enjoyed with Frontenac and La Salle it was the Franciscans who had been given the first chance in Louisiana, and they had won from the Congregation de Propaganda Fide in December, 1685, the erection of a prefecture apostolic with Hyacinth LeFebvre, one of their order, as prefect. But the friars had reckoned without Bishop Saint Vallier of Quebec, who strongly opposed the division of his diocese without his knowledge and who promptly lodged strong protests both at Rome and in Paris. As a consequence Louis XIV appointed a commission composed of François de Harlay-Chanvallon, Archbishop of Paris, François d'Aix de la Chaise, S.J., Louis' confessor, and the Marquis de Seignelay, to hear the dispute. After examining the matter the commission recommended the suppression of the Louisiana prefecture, and the king thereupon asked the Holy See that this be done. Soon thereafter La Salle was murdered, the Franciscans withdrew from the missions in the Mississippi Valley, and nothing further was heard of the matter for some years. But when it began to appear likely that Louisiana would become a reality, the Franciscan commissary general in May, 1699, again petitioned Propaganda for the prefecture. Nothing came of the petition, however, and Father Douay, the friar who had come out with Iberville's original group, let it be known that he did not wish to remain in Louisiana. The way would then seem to have been opened for the Jesuits.

There is no need to repeat what has been said about the conflict between the Jesuits and the priests of the Society of Foreign Missions of Paris in the Illinois Country, beyond the fact that after the decision of June, 1701, over the Tamarois mission had been rendered in favor of the seculars, the scene of their rivalry shifted to the area around Fort Louis. It is a long and complicated story, the details of which need not detain us here. Suffice it to say, there was more at stake among the interested parties than a question of ecclesiastical jurisdiction in a remote and little known colony. At the time the fires of the Jansenist and Gallican quarrels were still burning fiercely in France, and the controversy over the Chinese rites had only added fuel to the flames. Since the ultimate decisions over the Louisiana missions were taken in Paris by men strongly influenced by their partisanship in these larger issues, it was understandable that considerable bitterness should have entered into the case before it was settled. In all of this there was ardent feeling both for and against the Jesuits, it being recognized that they were the chief foes of both the Jansenists and the Gallicans, as well as the principal protagonists of the Church's acceptance of certain customs of the Chinese pertaining to their ancestors and to Confucius, which other missionaries stoutly opposed as tantamount to the admittance of idolatrous practices in order to gain converts. With this background it is easy to see how difficult it was for the principals to judge the question of Louisiana's missionary jurisdictions solely on its merits.

Briefly stated, the problem was as follows. Iberville wished to have priests, preferably Jesuits, who could act as missionaries to the Indians in his colony. The Jesuits were eager to secure the assignments, but only on condition that they be given a territory to themselves where they would be free of the authority of the vicars general of the Bishop of Quebec. The Tamarois case was still fresh in their minds and they did not want to have a repetition of it in Louisiana. On the opposite side was Bishop Saint Vallier of Quebec, a prelate of Gallican leanings, and the directors of the Society of Foreign Missions who were arrayed against the Jesuits in the Chinese rites case. The members of this Society, as we have seen, had been doing missionary labor in the Mississippi Valley since 1699, and Saint Vallier had given the faculties of vicar general to their superior.

The Bishop of Quebec was in France at the time that the case came before the authorities for settlement. During the course of the lengthy negotiations he remained adamant against the Jesuits' petitions for a separate jurisdiction and the appointment of one of their own number as vicar general. Nor was the bishop moved either by the intervention of Pontchartrain, Minister of Marine, or by the consideration that the Society of Foreign Missions did not have sufficient men to staff both the white parishes and Indian missions in Louisiana. In July, 1703, Saint Vallier made a decisive move which, in a sense, closed the case when he erected Mobile into a canonical parish and put the seculars in charge of it in perpetuity. Having failed entirely to persuade the bishop, the Jesuits meanwhile had appealed to the Holy See and in September, 1703, the Propaganda granted their petition for a separate jurisdiction. But it had come too late, for Saint Vallier's action in regard to the Mobile parish convinced the Jesuit superiors that an attempt on their part at this time to force the issue would lead to a major war with Quebec. The provincial sent orders, therefore, that his men were to quit the colony. By the time that the news reached Louisiana there were only two missionaries to whom it applied, Joseph de Limoges who had served among the Houma Indians, and Pierre Dongé, chaplain of the garrison at Mobile. Limoges was the first to leave and with his confrère's departure in September, 1704, the active role of the Society of Jesus in Louisiana was ended for over twenty years.

Quite apart from the jurisdictional dispute, the spiritual affairs of the colony in the early years did not prosper any more than did its temporal concerns. According to the terms of their grants from the crown, the Le Moynes, Crozat, and John Law were all in turn charged with the responsibility for making suitable provision for the Church. For example, the royal patent establishing Law's Company of the West contained a clause which stated that the glory of God was to be kept especially in mind by procuring, "the salvation of the inhabitants, Indians, savages and Negroes," who were to be instructed in the Catholic faith. Moreover, the company, it was said

shall be obliged to build at its expense churches at the places where it forms settlements; as also to maintain there the necessary number of approved ecclesiastics, whether it be parish priests or such others as shall be suitable, in order to preach the Holy Gospel there, perform Divine Service, and administer the sacraments; all under the authority of the Bishop of Quebec. . . .[6]

In the first years Iberville and his brother who governed the colony as lieutenant of the king after the former's departure, made repeated efforts to furnish priests for both the whites and the savages. But they were dealing with a particularly difficult situation. The feud between the Jesuits and the seminary priests, the conflicts between Bienville and the seculars after the latter took over, the absence of any support from the home government, and the Le Moynes' own limited resources made it impossible to effect a satisfactory arrangement. Moreover, there was lacking the promise of a healthy and prosperous future to attract the additional settlers who were needed to build up the colony. The lowlands were subject to repeated epidemics, such as that of the yellow fever brought in on a ship from Havana in 1704 which within the next two years took a good many lives, including Tonty, Father Dongé who died aboard ship returning to France, and Iberville who succumbed to the disease in Havana. These debilitating circumstances continued through most of the Le Moyne regime, and by 1708 out of nearly 2,000 colonists who had come to Louisiana less than 400 were left, of whom about 120 were soldiers, eighty Indian slaves, and around sixty roving Canadians.

For a brief time Father Antoine Davion was the chief spokesman for the Church. As a member of the Society of Foreign Missions he

[6] Le Page du Pratz, *Histoire de la Louisiane* (Paris, 1758), I, 77–78.

had been in this part of the world since 1699 where he had worked among several of the tribes in the Mississippi Valley, concentrating for a while on the Yazoos near what is today Fort Adams, Mississippi. But when his confrère, Nicolas Foucault, was murdered in July, 1702, by the Koroa Indians, Davion retired to Mobile Bay rather than to invite a similar fate. There he witnessed the last of the Jesuits take his leave in September, 1704, the same month that he welcomed the arrival of Henri Roulleaux de la Vente and Alexandre Huvé, pastor and curate respectively, of the Church of the Immaculate Conception which Davion, acting for Bishop Saint Vallier, formally erected on September 28 as a parish of the Diocese of Quebec.

Between 1704 and 1720 the priests of the Society of Foreign Missions held a virtual monopoly of the religious life of the colony, and during that time only two more of their group were sent to help supply the needs of the colonists and Indians, namely, Dominique Marie Varlet, who later became a schismatic bishop, and the Abbé F. Lemaire. During these years Davion exerted himself in behalf of the savages at the Tonica village and Father Saint Cosme was stationed among the Natchez; but nothing was done to advance the faith among other Indian tribes, although a number of them had requested Bienville to give them a missionary. It was obvious that the seminary priests were not equal to the task, and matters were not improved when their superior, de la Vente, who was also vicar general of Quebec, fell to fighting with Bienville and alienating others by his arbitrary ways.

The religious scene in Louisiana did not change substantially after Cadillac, who was Crozat's choice for governor, had taken over from Bienville in June, 1713. The latter had hoped to be named to the office, but his disappointment did not carry him as far as to preclude him working for the new regime. Eager to make the colony economically profitable, it was Cadillac's hope to exploit the lead mines and to open trade relations with the Viceroyalty of New Spain. While good in themselves, neither of these objectives, of course, was directly calculated to enhance the position of the Church. But the Church, too, was dependent for its welfare on the prosperity of the inhabitants, and in time it profited from the attempt to trade with the Spaniards in that it led to the founding of Natchitoches, the oldest white settlement in the present State of Louisiana which became second only to New Orleans as a religious center. In pursuance of their goal, therefore, the French despatched an expedition from Mobile in 1713 under the leadership of Louis Juchereau de Saint Denis which made its way along the Red River route to the present site of Natchitoches. Here Saint Denis gave orders for his men to erect a trading post and warehouse, and with that he proceeded westward into the Spanish domain.

It was the approach of the French to territory that they had grown accustomed to think of as their own that alerted the Spaniards to occupy eastern Texas, as we saw when we treated the Texan missions. Alarmed by the boldness of Saint Denis — who, incidentally, was arrested and taken to Mexico City where he made little headway with the officials, except to acquire the daughter of one of their number as a wife — plans were now pushed forward, and in 1716 the occupation began in earnest with the missionaries playing a leading part. Learning that the Spaniards were on the march eastward, and aware of the strained relations of France and Spain at the time, Bienville, in turn, hurried a company of soldiers to Natchitoches where they built Fort de Saint Jean Baptiste. Thus by the early days of 1717 the two powers confronted one another along the ill defined frontier in what is today northwestern Louisiana.

It was under circumstances such as these that Father Antonio Margil, O.F.M., as we have seen, founded his missions for the Indians of east Texas, and by the autumn of 1716, he had reached a point only about twenty miles west of the French post, and there he established the Mission of San Míguel de Linares. If the Spaniards and French continued to eye each other with mutual hostility, such was not the case with Fray Antonio. Hearing that Natchitoches was without a priest, he did not hesitate to make the trip to Fort de Saint Jean Baptiste to give the French the consolations of Mass and the sacraments. Since no provision had been made by the French for religious services, Bienville gave permission for the Spanish friars to continue their visits to the post. Soon thereafter, however, Spain and France were again at war, and Margil and his confrères were poorly repaid for their kindness when in the fall of 1719 the local French commandant, acting on orders from Bienville to take over their mission at Los Adayes, plundered San Míguel and drove off the friars and their Indian charges. But with the restoration of peace early in 1720 the Franciscans were back by September, 1721, and for a half century San Míguel struggled on and continued to provide a spiritual oasis where the French, who during their first decade at Natchitoches had not even built a church, found priests to minister to their needs.

A year before the renewal of war in the summer of 1718, the resources of Crozat had become exhausted and in August, 1717, he surrendered his Louisiana grant to the Duke of Orleans. The regent, desperate for a way out of France's financial woes, and like most of his countrymen taken in by John Law, now grasped at the Scotsman's dazzling prospects of how he intended to make the colony yield a fortune. Their charter, as we have seen, charged the new proprietors with the duty of providing for religion, and the directors of the Company of the West, as it was originally called, first undertook to carry out this obligation by inviting in the Discalced Carmelites of France. These friars accepted the offer, and they secured from the Congregation de Propaganda Fide a prefecture apostolic with Father Jacques de Saint Martin as prefect. In August, 1720, the prefect and two of his confrères arrived in Louisiana, and one of these, Father Jean Matthieu de Saint Anne, first signed the parish register for a baptism at Mobile on January 18, 1721. With this development the Louisiana assignment of the priests of the Society of Foreign Missions came to an end, Father Huvé making his last entry in the Mobile register a few days before the Carmelite's name appeared. The latter remained at Mobile for some time, and in 1722 he had the distinction of winning the first converts recorded for the area when he received two Calvinists into the Catholic fold.

But by this time Mobile had begun to take second place to the settlement that was rising about 150 miles to the southwest on the Mississippi River. For some time Bienville had been urging a location on the great river itself, realizing the superior advantages of proximity to the main artery of trade and the rich loam afforded by the lands along the river. He had been passed over again for the governorship in 1716 when Cadillac quit the colony, but the new company recognized his talents and in February, 1718, Bienville, now thirty-eight years of age, was nominated as governor and given the cross of the Order of St. Louis by the regent. The new governor lost no time in carrying out his idea, and after choosing a site about 110 miles from the mouth of the Mississippi the land was cleared and New Orleans, named for the regent, was underway by the end of 1718. For a long time it was hardly more than a small and unattractive settlement stretching along the river banks, although in 1722 the capital of the colony was moved to New Orleans from Mobile. While the plans for the new town had called for the construction of a church, for many years only a dilapidated warehouse was available for religious services. Such was the situation when Father Pierre F. X. de Charlevoix, S.J., came down the river early in 1722. In a letter to the Duchess de Lesdiguières he said:

> I have at last arrived in the famous city called *La nouvelle-Orleans*. . . . The eight hundred fine houses, and the five parishes, which the *Mercury* gave it some two years ago, are reduced at present to a hundred barracks, placed in no very great order, to a large storehouse built of wood, to two or three houses which would be no ornament to a village in France, and to the half of a miserable warehouse which they had, indeed, wished to lend to the Lord, and, of which he had hardly taken possession, when they despatched him to lodge under a tent. . . .[7]

It was a dismal enough picture, but that did not mean that Father de Charlevoix believed New Orleans was without a future. On the contrary, he predicted that one day, and that day, perhaps, not too far off, New Orleans would be an opulent city and the metropolis of a great and wealthy colony. The climate, the fertility of the soil, the industry of the inhabitants, the great river, and the colony's proximity to Mexico, Havana, and the English colonies – all, according to de Charlevoix, gave New Orleans advantages that even Rome and Paris did not have.

It would be a long time before New Orleans would approach de Charlevoix's predictions, but even then it was gaining ground, and a census of November, 1721, showed a total of 470 inhabitants, including 172 Negro slaves, twenty-one Indian slaves, and twenty-nine white servants. What gave the town hope for the future were the large accessions of colonists who were now pouring into Louisiana, immigrants who had come to occupy the great tracts of land granted by John Law to the *concessionaires*, as they were called, that is, to French noblemen, officials, and business men. With a view to providing a governmental structure, the company divided the colony into nine districts, one of which embraced the Illinois Country which was detached from Quebec

[7] De Charlevoix to de Lesdiguières, New Orleans, January 10, 1722, *Journal d'un Voyage fait par ordre du Roi dans l'Amérique septentrionale, addressé a Madame la Duchesse de Lesdiguières* (Paris, 1744), VI, 192–193. Hereafter this work will be referred to as: de Charlevoix, *Journal*.

and made a part of Louisiana. Thus from the Gulf of Mexico to the Illinois Country land was parceled out in immense tracts to the *concessionaires* whose settlers were recruited by the company's agents or by the proprietor himself. Many of these people proved to be excellent colonists, especially the families from the Rhineland who settled in large numbers some miles above New Orleans in a district along the Mississippi which came to be called the German Coast.

The concessions had a direct bearing on the Church in that a number of them had their own priests who had been engaged to accompany the emigrants. The system of concession chaplains, as it was called, grew out of the stipulation contained in the grant that each concession should have a chaplain with the *concessionaire* enjoying the right of patronage. As it turned out the system was largely a failure due to the lack of proper provision for the chaplains' support and the brief tenure of most of these men. Yet there was a time before 1722 when the southern end of the Mississippi Valley counted eight priests with the status of concession chaplains, although no one of them ever became a part of the permanent scene on the familiar colonial plantations to which the concessions gave rise. For the years that they were in Louisiana we have hardly more evidence than their names and locations with fragmentary records of their ministry.

One of the most memorable and enduring features of Bienville's time as governor was the introduction in September, 1724, of Louis XV's edict concerning the Negroes, a set of regulations that lasted down to the American occupation in 1803. The large number of slaves brought in by the Crozat and Law regimes made some kind of regulation imperative, for without it the civil and ecclesiastical authorities would have been even more powerless than they actually were to effect elementary justice for the slaves. The *Code Noir*, as it came to be called, was a detailed set of laws that fixed the legal status of the Negroes whether they were free, manumitted, or slave. Specific obligations and prohibitions were laid upon the slaves' master in such matters as provision for their religious instruction and marriage, as well as for their clothing, shelter, food, punishments for their misdeeds, and for their manumission under certain conditions. In regard to marriage, all priests were forbidden to marry one slave to another without the master's permission, marriages between whites and blacks were likewise proscribed and priests forbidden to officiate at such unions, and whites were forbidden as well to live in concubinage with blacks whether they be slaves, manumitted, or free-born.

Moreover, the code related to others besides the Negroes. Its first article, for example, decreed expulsion from the colony of Jews, another prohibited the exercise of any religion except the Catholic, and still another prescribed confiscation for Negro slaves placed under the supervision of a non-Catholic. Thus the *Code Noir* was a clear example of transference to France's colonies of the union of Church and State that obtained in the mother country. The regulations pertaining to the Negroes were on the whole helpful, but it was ironic to find Jews expelled and Protestants prevented from practicing their religion when the authority over the Catholic Church was at times vested in the hands of civil and military officials who, though nominally Catholic, were notoriously irreligious and immoral, such as the commandant at Natchez during the late 1720's whose brutal regime helped to provoke the Indian massacre of 1729.

In no part of the future United States was there more trouble during the colonial period on the score of ecclesiastical jurisdiction than in Louisiana. And one does not need to be an expert in canon law to appreciate how priests like the concession chaplains, appointed by lay landowners in France and beholden to them for their support, would only add to the confusion. The roots of the problem were manifold and need be given only in summary. Remoteness from the centers of ecclesiastical authority in Quebec, Paris, and Rome, ignorance of actual conditions in the colony, conflicting interests of missionary-minded religious orders, and the oddities that characterized diocesan administration in the last years of Bishop Saint Vallier—all these played their part in creating and sustaining the trouble. Thanks to the superb propaganda campaign of John Law, the name of Louisiana had become a familiar one in France, even though most of the people who used it had little or no true knowledge about it. Nor was the roseate picture immediately dispelled by Law's bankruptcy in 1720. It was natural, therefore, that the provincial of the Capuchins of Champagne should believe that there was sufficient missionary promise in Louisiana to warrant an appeal to Propaganda in April, 1722, for a prefecture apostolic. Since a Carmelite prefecture had been erected there only two years before it seemed questionable whether another should be granted, and in their uncertainty the officials of Propaganda turned to the apostolic nuncio in Paris for his opinion, and he vetoed the Capuchin proposal.

Administration of the Church in Louisiana was further complicated by the fact that Bishop Saint Vallier had given over ecclesiastical authority in the colony to his coadjutor, Louis François Duplessis de Mornay, a French-born Capuchin, who was consecrated in April, 1714, and who continued to exercise authority in Louisiana until his resignation of the See of Quebec in September, 1733, although he had never seen America. De Mornay was strongly Gallican in his sympathies, and when the Company of the Indies, as it had come to be called, sought to provide for the Capuchins in the colony, regardless of the Holy See's failure to grant the prefecture, they had little difficulty in persuading the coadjutor to approve their action. Thus by a decree of the company's commissioners of May 16, 1722, Louisiana was divided into three ecclesiastical jurisdictions as follows: all west of the Mississippi from the Gulf of Mexico to the confluence of the Ohio and the Mississippi was to go to the Capuchins whose superior was to be a vicar general of Quebec and reside in New Orleans; all above the Ohio was to be under the care of the Jesuits whose superior was likewise to hold the rank of vicar general and reside in Illinois; thirdly, all east of the Mississippi as far as the Ohio River was to be under the Carmelites whose superior, also to be a vicar general of Quebec, was to live at Mobile.

This arrangement, however, lasted only a little over six months. At the time that the Carmelites had secured their prefecture in 1720 from the Holy See without reference to the French government, de Mornay was in Spain. His Gallican sensibilities had been offended by this direct appeal to Rome, and on the grounds of having infringed upon the rights of the See of Quebec on December 19, 1722, the Carmelite district of the previous May was suppressed by the coadjutor and their district added to that of the Capuchins. Although they had been in the colony since 1720, the Carmelites chose not to dispute de Mornay's ruling and in the spring of 1723 all but one of their order returned to France. With the white friars out of the way the Capuchins were now in possession of everything on both sides of the Mississippi as far as the Ohio where the Jesuit territory began.

The first four Capuchins arrived in Louisiana in September, 1722, with Father Bruno de Langres as superior, although in the following spring he was replaced as superior and vicar general by Father Raphael de Luxemburg. Their arrival was badly timed, for on September 12 a hurricane had hit New Orleans and for more than twelve hours it continued to batter the area as far north as Natchez and east to Biloxi. In New Orleans the church, the hospital, and about thirty houses were destroyed, and according to de Charlevoix, "In the settlements above and below the city there was not a building standing." [8] Under these conditions it was not surprising that the Capuchin's first months in the colony should have been so unhappy. And the new superior did not fail after six months time to make their plight known and to charge the company with negligence in making proper provision for the church and the priests' residence. Father Raphael informed the Abbé Gilles Bernard Raguet, the Sulpician in Paris whom the company had engaged as ecclesiastical director of their Louisiana interests. He stated that the friars were compelled to live in three small rooms, one which they used for a combined chapel and kitchen, a second in which they all slept, and a third which held their provisions and supplies. Moreover, they had little or nothing to live on, and he urged Raguet, therefore, to see to it that the company fulfilled its obligations.

There could be little doubt about the justification for Father Raphael's complaints, although the inability of his own order to furnish the necessary number of missionaries weakened the Capuchins' case. In fact, fully aware as they were of the friars' failure to measure up to expectations in this regard, the company officials in December, 1723, made the unexpected move of decreeing that the Capuchin territory between Natchez and the Ohio River was to be given to the Jesuits since the former could not staff it. The Capuchins were indignant at this action, nor were they mollified at being told again that churches and residences for their missionaries would be built at company expense, and that the latter would likewise furnish the vestments and other equipment needed for divine services. Chagrined as he was, the Capuchin superior turned to Bishop Saint Vallier with whom he lodged a vigorous protest against the company's negligence and arbitrary ways. But the Bishop of Quebec replied in July, 1725, that he had not been consulted about these matters by the coadjutor and the company and,

[8] Pierre F. X. de Charlevoix, S.J., *History and General Description of New France*, translated by John Gilmary Shea (New York, 1872), VI, 69–70. Hereafter this work will be referred to as: de Charlevoix, *History*.

therefore, he would have to inquire into them. Saint Vallier advised Raphael that when the Jesuits arrived it would be well for the sake of peace and harmony to regard them simply as priests of another jurisdiction. Meanwhile with a view to softening the blow for the loss of so large a slice of their territory, the company assured the Capuchins on June 27, 1725, that the remaining portion of their mission district would continue intact, and that no other religious order would be permitted to enter it without their consent.

Father Raphael was by no means satisfied with the arrangement, but there was not much that he could do about it, and the conditions disclosed by his visitation of the Capuchin district in 1726 did little to lift his spirits. At that time the friars were in charge at six white settlements and were at least calling at intervals at four Indian missions if they were not in permanent residence. The colony was now in its twenty-seventh year and at only two of the six white settlements was there a church, and in neither case was it fully adequate. New Orleans and Natchez, the two largest towns, revealed a very poor record in Sunday Mass attendance with only about thirty persons at the former and twenty at the later fulfilling their obligation. In almost all cases except Mobile the priests' residences were shabbily furnished and too small for their needs, and in no one of these settlements was the annual stipend paid by the company, 600 livres, sufficient to keep the priest in a state of decency. As for the Indian missions, which stretched from that for the Apalache some miles from Mobile to Natchitoches on the Red River, conditions were even worse insofar as provision for the needs of the missionaries was concerned.

The situation uncovered by Father Raphael was reported by him to the colonial governor and intendant with the request that they, in turn, seek the proper remedy with the company officials in Paris. While not disputing the validity of the Capuchin's recommendations, the government was slow to move, and it was not until April, 1727, that New Orleans saw the dedication of its first real church, named for Saint Louis of France, although by this time the town was almost ten years old. The same was true elsewhere, as at Pointe Coupée on the west side of the Mississippi where the little chapel of Saint Francis of Assisi was dedicated in March, 1738, and on the German Coast above New Orleans where the sturdy German immigrants got their first church about 1740, the first of a series of edifices at this settlement to be called the 'red church' from the color of their paint. In spite of many handicaps the Capuchins, who between 1722 and 1769 numbered about thirty-eight priests and a few lay brothers in the colony, held on until the end of the French regime, and at one time or another they staffed ten parishes or mission stations for the whites of which four ultimately had to be abandoned. Of the remainder of these early Capuchin foundations four are still in existence, namely, Saint Louis Cathedral and Saint Charles Borromeo at Destrahan, both in the Archdiocese of New Orleans; Saint Martin's in Saint Martinville of the Diocese of Lafayette; and the Church of the Immaculate Conception at Natchitoches which is in the Diocese of Alexandria.

With the Company of the Indies so remiss about its obligations to support the Church, it is not surprising to learn that nothing was done for education. Father Raphael opened a school for boys at New Orleans in 1725, but the company declined to give anything for its maintenance and after six or seven years of financial and legal struggle the school disappeared.[9] It would doubtless have been a similar story for the girls had not eight Ursuline nuns from Rouen been induced to come to Louisiana in August, 1727, by Nicolas Ignace de Beaubois, S.J., former superior of the Jesuit missions in the Illinois Country. In November of that year the nuns opened a school, and by the following spring they had sixteen boarders and twenty-five day pupils among whom were seven Negro girls. These religious wrote one of the happiest and most constructive chapters in Louisiana's colonial history, for they not only maintained the school against heavy odds, but they likewise staffed the only hospital in the town, undertook the care of the orphans, gave catechetical instruction to both Indian and Negro children, and in May, 1730, established the first Sodality of the Blessed Virgin in New Orleans.

Yet in spite of the beneficent influence of the Ursulines on the community, they received little in return insofar as proper housing and material support were concerned. For seven years they lived in cramped quarters in a makeshift residence, and only in July, 1734, was a new and adequate convent ready for their occupancy. Thrown in large measure on their own resources, with the aid of Father de Beaubois the sisters acquired a plantation, a source from which they ultimately

[9] Samuel Wilson, Jr., *The Capuchin School in New Orleans, 1725. The First School in Louisiana* (New Orleans, 1961), pp. 20–21.

realized some profit. Meanwhile nothing was done for the educational needs of the boys, and when at last an agreement to build a boys' school seemed to offer hope, the agreement was cancelled by the government in January, 1744, and three-quarters of a century were to elapse before Louisiana had a Catholic school for boys.

Given the kind of environment provided by New Orleans in its early history, it was to be expected that the priests and sisters should be more than ordinarily anxious about inculcating moral as well as intellectual values in the young through the medium of schools. The town had more than its share of adventurers, prostitutes, and ex-convicts, and the influx of ne'er-do-wells that resulted from John Law's propaganda, both in Louisiana and the Illinois Country, brought a noticeable decline in the moral tone of society. A number of Frenchmen lived in open concubinage with either white or black women, attendance at religious services was slight, the payment of fees for the support of the Church was all but non-existent, and the interference of the civil officials in ecclesiastical affairs was more or less constant and frequently detrimental.

These conditions ultimately became known at Quebec, and in July, 1721, they drew a stern pastoral letter from Bishop Saint Vallier in which he predicted that "the maledictions of God" would descend upon the colonists if they did not mend their ways. He was determined to use all his power, he said, to withstand public vice, and instructions were given that the sacraments should be denied to all those "who in contempt of divine and human laws go so far as to commit scandalous impiety by their words, or by their actions, or by public concubinage. . . ."[10] The vicar general was ordered to impose public penance on persons who, having been warned, persisted in their sinful ways. It was an action worthy of a vigilant bishop intent upon restoring morality among his people, but like so many efforts of this kind, those who respected and obeyed the prelate's commands were not in any particular need of the admonitions, while those who did need them, for the most part simply flaunted Saint Vallier's orders and continued their way of life much as before.

The struggle of the Louisiana clergy against immorality was rendered all the more difficult by the lack of unity in their own ranks, a condition that was in part aggravated by the awkward and arbitrary

[10] Shea, *History*, I, 561, gives the text of the pastoral letter.

regulations issued by the company officials. This was especially true in the feuds that broke out after 1725 between the Capuchins and the Jesuits, a series of disputes that lasted with varying intensity to the latter's banishment from the colony in 1763. To understand this element of weakness in the Louisiana Church it is necessary to trace in a general way how it evolved. After the Illinois Country had come under the Louisiana government in 1718 it, too, felt the authority of the Company of the Indies in its ecclesiastical affairs. For example, directives were issued from Paris which changed the boundaries of the Jesuit missionary district to include the Yazoo Post, the missionaries' long-standing policy of segregation of the whites and Indians met with opposition from the company, and various other orders were given that pertained to the missionaries' salaries, location, number, etc. Having observed the events since his advent to the Illinois Country in 1720, the energetic new superior, Father de Beaubois, decided to seek rectification by a direct appeal to the highest authorities, and with that in mind he left in November, 1724, and proceeded first to New Orleans and then to France.

Twenty years had passed since the Jesuits had been formally withdrawn from Louisiana, although in the interval the colony had been visited by a half dozen or more of their number who stayed for a brief time but were in no sense a part of the company's official enterprise. In that interval it had become clear to everyone that the Capuchins were not capable of staffing both the Indian missions and the white settlements. Regardless, then, of what the directors of the company might think of the Jesuits – and some were not friendly – they were compelled to acknowledge that there was no other religious order better equipped to handle the savages, including the ability to hold them aloof from the blandishments of the English. Pressed by this need, therefore, the company entered into a discussion with the Jesuit superiors in Paris and in August, 1724, the Abbé Raguet, who had recently been engaged as the company's ecclesiastical director, and Louis D'Avaugour, S.J., procurator for the North American missions, signed a contract which provided for the reopening of the Jesuits' Louisiana mission. In return for the seven missionaries that were promised, the company agreed to pay each man an annual salary of 600 livres (about $110) with an additional 300 livres to outfit each new mission, to build the churches and priests' residences where it was judged suitable, and to furnish free passage for the missionaries on the company's ships. Neither Raguet nor D'Avaugour knew colonial conditions at firsthand, although the Jesuit procurator's arrangements were seconded by Father de Charlevoix who had returned some months before from his two-year tour of French America.

The Paris negotiators had proceeded, of course, without reference to the superior from the Illinois Country, but upon his arrival in September, 1725, de Beaubois soon made known his opposition to the contract. Obviously he knew more about these matters than almost anyone in Paris at the time, and the lengthy memorandum that he prepared helped to convince his superiors that the contract of August, 1724, was inadequate to cover the needs of the missions. After prolonged negotiations, in part of which de Beaubois shared, the old contract was set aside and a new one was signed on February 20, 1726, which received the royal assent the following summer. The Jesuits were herewith put in complete charge of the colony's Indian missions and the Capuchins were confined to the white settlements. The new document incorporated a number of de Beaubois' proposals, for example, permission for the Jesuit superior to reside in New Orleans, although not to perform ecclesiastical functions without the consent of the Capuchin superior, and the company's grant of a plantation near New Orleans to the Jesuits to help supplement their income. The annual salary for each of the ten missionaries promised by the Jesuits was again fixed at 600 livres, but each man was also to get a bonus of 200 livres per year for five years with an additional 450 livres for the purchase of necessary equipment for new missions. Once more the company promised to build the mission churches and priests' residences, to provide the sacred vessels and vestments for religious services, and to give the missionaries free passage on the company's ships. And on this occasion it was stated that in order to assist the evangelization of the Indians, "it shall be forbidden the French to establish themselves *pêle-mêle* with the Savages, and those French who shall be found among the savages shall be ordered to leave."[11]

With the conclusion of this contract and the naming of Father de

[11] Jean Delanglez, S.J., *The French Jesuits in Lower Louisiana, 1700–1763* (Washington, 1935), p. 113. Most of the text of the contract is printed here, pp. 112–114. Delanglez is in sharp disagreement on some points with another study in the same series, viz., Claude L. Vogel, O.F.M. Cap., *The Capuchins in French Louisiana, 1722–1766* (Washington, 1928).

Beaubois as superior of the Jesuits with the rank of vicar general for their Louisiana missions, the stage was set for trouble. In practically every major question that arose during the two years that followed de Beaubois' return to New Orleans in March, 1727, he and the Capuchin superior found themselves at odds. Nor were their differences confined to religious matters; they extended to politics as well. The colony's financial losses had made Bienville *persona non grata* in the eyes of the company directors, and in 1725 he was recalled, leaving the sentiments of the inhabitants divided between his followers and those of the *commissaires* who had been sent out to investigate his administration. Here de Beaubois ranged himself openly on the side of the fallen governor, with whom he had returned to France in 1725 and with whom he had formed a close friendship, while Father Raphael was just as closely allied with Bienville's archenemy, Sieur de la Chaise, who had been in Louisiana since 1723 with the rank of *commissaire ordonnateur.*

The Company of the Indies had, indeed, wanted the Jesuits as missionaries, but the directors who had come to know Father de Beaubois would have preferred another for superior. In pursuit of what he considered the interests of his order, the Jesuit's brusque and aggressive manner often alienated others, and judging from the sequel, it would have been better for all concerned had another been chosen. But de Beaubois was the man selected by the provincial, and in March, 1727, he landed at New Orleans from the same boat that brought Etienne Perier as successor to Bienville. With the advent of the full contingent of Jesuit missionaries in the course of the next year, there were by 1728 twenty-two priests in the colony, namely, three seculars in the Illinois Country headed by François Le Mercier at Cahokia, ten Jesuits of whom nine were scattered throughout eight Indian missions with de Beaubois, their superior, living in New Orleans, and eight Capuchins and a single Franciscan associated with them, at the eight white settlements with Raphael as their superior.

Mention has been made of the disputes—and they were many and varied—that now ensued between the superiors of the two orders, in all of which there could be traced as a root cause the contrary interpretations placed on de Beaubois' status as vicar general of the Bishop of Quebec. According to the contract of 1726, his faculties as vicar general were confined to the Indian missions of his own order. But de

Beaubois had sought a wider sphere of action by writing directly to Bishop Saint Vallier — unknown to the company directors and the Capuchins — and had asked for the powers of vicar general in New Orleans. In his reply of August 4, 1726, Saint Vallier stated that "as vicar-general you may exercise all the functions you wish in Louisiana and in New Orleans." Having set no limits upon de Beaubois' powers as vicar general, it became, according to the bishop, "more a question of what is becoming than of what you have the right to do, [and] I leave it to your prudence to decide what you will do." [12]

Insofar as the Bishop of Quebec was concerned, therefore, there were no doubts about de Beaubois' powers even in New Orleans. Unfortunately, the problem was not solved so simply, for twelve years before Saint Vallier had given over jurisdiction of Louisiana to his coadjutor, Bishop de Mornay, upon the latter's consecration, and the coadjutor was not only unalterably opposed to the Jesuit exercising ecclesiastical powers there but of his being in the colony at all. Since Saint Vallier sent his reply to de Beaubois in France where it missed him, the letter had to be forwarded to Louisiana and it was a full year before it reached the Jesuit superior. Less than six months later the bishop died on December 26, 1727, and de Mornay succeeded automatically to the See of Quebec.

Meanwhile the quarrel between the superiors in New Orleans had become public, and the laity, including the government officials, had taken sides with consequent grave scandal to the entire community. It showed up especially in regard to the Ursuline nuns whom de Beaubois had been responsible for bringing to the colony, and for that very reason de Mornay had been opposed to their going at all. Upon the nuns' declaration that they wished de Beaubois as their superior, the war between the two camps flared anew, and to such a degree of bitterness was it carried that the Capuchin superior became opposed even to the Ursulines' school. There were likewise criticisms of de Beaubois' exercise of his powers as vicar general for the Indian missions, and his ministering to the personnel of the Jesuit plantation was viewed as an encroachment on the Capuchin's authority as vicar general of the region. Mutual recriminations multiplied, and certain partisans of both groups went to such extremes that finally the crisis brought action from Paris. The company remonstrated with the Jesuit provincial about

[12] Saint Vallier to de Beaubois, Quebec, August 4, 1726, *ibid.*, pp. 169–170.

his subject's conduct in the colony, the former agreed to replace him, and in August, 1728, there reached de Beaubois the letter of the Abbé Raguet which informed him that he was recalled to France. By reason of the death of the missionary designated to take his place as superior, de Beaubois' departure was delayed until April of 1729 when Father Mathurin Le Petit, the priest at the Chocktaw mission, took over as his successor.

With Father de Beaubois' removal peace might have been restored to the distracted Church of Louisiana under his mild mannered successor had it not been for the aftermath of the Natchez disaster which occurred less than six months later. In Paris the Natchez affair put a new cast on everything relating to the colony. We have already seen how it led to Bienville's rehabilitation and return as governor; even more surprising, it was indirectly the reason for the reappearance of de Beaubois. Upon reaching France the energetic Jesuit lost no time in representing his views to all who would lend an ear, and for that purpose he drew up a lengthy apology about his time in Louisiana. What made a special appeal to the hard pressed officials of the company, burdened as they were with finding a remedy for the economic ills of the colony, was de Beaubois' assurance that if permitted to return he would find a way to clear up the debts owed by the Society of Jesus to the colonial regime, to render the missions self-supporting, and to convert the Jesuit land into a model plantation that would prove an incentive to other settlers. In spite of the prejudice that some of the company men had against de Beaubois, they could not help but acknowledge his business acumen, and these promising proposals won him another hearing.

Yet regardless of the Jesuit's enticing promises of what he could do, how was the Company of the Indies to get around the hostility of the colony's highest ecclesiastical authority, Bishop de Mornay? As it finally came about, it was the crown, not the company, that had to face the ultimate test with de Mornay since, as we have seen, the company's trade monopoly was surrendered and they retired from the scene. After July 1, 1731, therefore, the date on which the crown assumed control, in matters relating to de Beaubois there were no longer the unfriendly directors to deal with, but rather the Comte de Maurepas, Minister of Marine and the Colonies, who was sympathetic and whose basic approach to the problem was the practical one of putting the colony's finances in order. And in the execution of this policy Maurepas had the support of Louis XV's prime minister, André-Hercule Cardinal Fleury. But not even Cardinal Fleury and Comte de Maurepas could budge de Mornay who had not forgotten de Beaubois' appeal over his own head to Bishop Saint Vallier at Quebec. Far from being awed by de Beaubois' highly placed intercessors, the Capuchin prelate made it unmistakably clear to all concerned that if de Beaubois went back to Louisiana he would be placed under interdict.

When, therefore, the king decided, upon the advice of his counselors, to have Father de Beaubois return as superior of the Louisiana missions, although not as superior of the Ursulines or as vicar general of any part of the colony, Bishop de Mornay revealed that he had no intention of allowing himself to be circumvented even by His Majesty. He promptly issued instructions to Father Raphael as his sole vicar general, to put all the Jesuits in and around New Orleans under interdict should de Beaubois reappear there. As has been mentioned, the Jesuit superior reached New Orleans in March, 1732, but by reason of the slow pace of communication at the time it was another year before de Mornay's letter was brought in on the ship that carried Bienville back as governor. In the interval matters had at first gone peacefully enough between de Beaubois and Raphael, but when friction once more arose the Capuchin, once in possession of de Mornay's decree, had a powerful weapon in dealing with his adversary. Before issuing the interdict the vicar general consulted Governor Bienville and Edmé Gatien Salmon, the intendant, both of whom were sympathetic to the Jesuits. In spite of their sympathies, however, they were reluctant to be drawn into a purely ecclesiastical quarrel and declined to give a commitment, and Raphael then proceeded to make public the orders of Bishop de Mornay. Apparently, the vicar general was allowed certain discretionary powers in enforcing the interdict, however, for when the final illness and death of Mother Marie de Saint Augustin Tranchepain, superior of the Ursulines, occurred in November, 1733, he lifted the ban at the request of the sisters so that de Beaubois was able to attend her in her final hours. Since there were only three Capuchins then in the New Orleans area the interdict worked a real hardship because of the number and location of the Catholics who needed spiritual care. In the town proper there were 626 whites, including children, with 878 more whites within a radius of fifty miles, to say nothing of 3,695 slaves. Thus the total of over 5,000 widely scattered souls put a heavy burden on the three friars for which they could get no relief from the Jesuits while the latter were forbidden to exercise their ministry.

The author of the interdict, Bishop de Mornay, had had in general a rather unhappy career, and he was never a successful or popular churchman. His refusal to take up residence in New France gradually brought him into disfavor at court, and he was finally summoned and told that he must proceed without further delay to his new world diocese. Rather than leave France the seventy-year-old prelate resigned his see in September, 1733, and was succeeded by his coadjutor, Pierre-Herman Dosquet. As a former director of the Society of Foreign Missions, Dosquet had a long record of opposition to the Jesuits in the Chinese rites case, and it came as no surprise, then, when he made no substantial change in the policies of his predecessor. After it had become clear that Dosquet intended to follow in de Mornay's footsteps in regard to the Louisiana Jesuits, the Paris superiors concluded that there was nothing to be gained either for religion or their order by persisting in a course contrary to the wishes of the ordinary of the diocese. Thus the decision was made to recall Father de Beaubois, and he left Louisiana for the last time in the spring of 1735.

The lengthy digression on the Capuchin-Jesuit controversy was necessary if one is to understand the true nature of the Church's life in Louisiana in this period and the factors that impeded its progress. Another major setback was suffered as a result of the rising of the Natchez Indians late in 1729. In accordance with the contract of 1726 the Jesuit missionaries began arriving in the next year and proceeding to their respective stations in the Illinois Country, on the Wabash River, and at the other points on the Mississippi and its tributaries where tribes like the Arkansas, the Yazoos, and the Alibamons, whom they had been sent to convert made their headquarters. Three of these missionaries, Paul du Poisson, Jean Souel, and Jean Dumas, came out from France in the spring of 1727, and after a stop in New Orleans they began their trip up the river in late May. By mid-June they had reached Natchez which du Poisson described in some detail in a letter to a fellow missionary. He was impressed by the location of Fort Rosalie, situated high above the Mississippi, from which the river could be seen winding its way southward for miles with the lands of the *concessionaires* on either side. Du Poisson mentioned the Indian village about three miles distant from the French settlement, and in view of what was to happen here two and a half years later, it was especially pathetic to find him saying that these savages were about the only tribe among whom one could see a hope for orderly government and religion.[13]

Fort Rosalie, it is true, was a flourishing post at the time that the Jesuits passed up the river. The French community then numbered about 700, and the brisk trade in tobacco and other products of the rich soil made it the most successful settlement in the colony. The fort had been built in 1716 by Bienville to protect the trading post and its residents from the neighboring savages. But a major source of trouble at Natchez from the outset was the proximity of the two races, a juxtaposition which, as the Jesuits had always insisted, inevitably led to grief wherever it was tried. Some years before Gabriel Marest, S.J., an experienced missionary then stationed at Kaskaskia, elaborated on the results of French influence on the Indians for one of his confrères. If, he remarked, the French who thought of coming to live among the savages were like those whom he had formerly known at Kaskaskia, men "who edified our Neophytes by their piety and by the regularity of their morals," nothing could be more consoling to the missionaries or more helpful to the progress of the gospel. But if, as it was feared, some of them should come and openly practice debauchery and, perhaps, irreligion, all would be over with the mission, for as Marest said

> Their pernicious example would make more impression on the minds of the Savages than all that we could say to preserve them from the same dissolute conduct; they would not fail to reproach us—as they have already done, in some places with abusing their readiness to believe us, saying that the Laws of Christianity are not so severe as we teach.[14]

In brief, that was part of what happened at Natchez where at first the Indians were friendly toward the French. But gradually a combination of bad example and arbitrary and despotic actions on the part of several of the French commanders dissipated the good will and goaded the savages into an attack. In 1723 Bienville had fought a campaign against them in which they had been beaten, but in spite of appearances the Natchez had not been subdued. Plans were stealthily

[13] Du Poisson to unnamed missionary, Arkansas Post, October 3, 1727, Louis Aimé-Martin (Ed.), *Lettres édifiantes et curieuses. . . .* (Paris, 1838), I, 754.

[14] Marest to Barthélemi Germon, S.J., Kaskaskia, November 9, 1712, *Jesuit Relations,* LXVI, 293–295.

laid for ridding themselves of their hated neighbors, and the Yazoos, a tribe over 100 miles to the north, joined in the conspiracy. On November 28, 1729, they struck suddenly and within an hour or so over 200 French men, women, and children perished, and about eighty women and 150 children—with almost as many Negro slaves—were taken into captivity, According to the account of de Charlevoix, "Of all the French who were at this post, the most populous of all, only about twenty escaped, and five or six negroes, most of them wounded."[15] Father du Poisson had arrived at Natchez only two days before from his Arkansas mission, and he had just finished his Mass when the massacre began and he was among the victims. Less than three weeks later the Yazoos, having returned to their village from the uprising, fell upon the French garrison at the Yazoo Post and on this occasion Father Souel was also murdered. And before the area had quieted down another missionary, Etienne Doutreleau, S.J., had a very narrow escape from a like fate early in the new year at a point not far from where Souel had met his death.

The Natchez rebellion was in every sense a major disaster for the colony. Not only had the missions lost two valuable men, but the Indians for hundreds of miles were put in a state of unrest and sullen acquiescence which told on the Jesuit neophytes as far away as the Illinois Country. Fort Rosalie was, it is true, rebuilt and continued in French hands until 1764 when the British took it over under the name of Fort Panmure; but the post never recovered the position it had known before the massacre. Heavy losses were also sustained elsewhere in the colony, since many of the residents of the plantations fled from their unprotected lands to New Orleans in terror of the roving bands of Natchez who were still on the loose. More than six months after the event the unsettled state of affairs that still obtained was reflected in a letter of Father Le Petit to the Jesuit procurator in Paris. The New Orleans superior acknowledged that the rebellion had retarded progress, but they consoled themselves, he said, in the belief that the misfortune would be productive of good results in deciding the French government to send troops for the pacification of the colony. Revealing the atmosphere current at that time, he continued:

Although they have nothing to fear at *New Orleans*, either from the smaller neighboring Tribes, whom our Negroes alone could finish in a single morning,

[15] De Charlevoix, *History*, VI, 82–83.

or even from the *Tchactas* [Chickasaws], who would not dare to expose themselves on the Lake in any great numbers, yet a panic terror has spread itself over almost every spirit, particularly with the women.

All of this, however, would pass with the arrival of the soldiers whom they were expecting daily. As for the missionaries themselves, they had remained altogether tranquil. "The perils to which they see themselves exposed," said Le Petit, "seem to increase their joy and animate their zeal."[16]

For a long time Louisiana had been in a languishing condition economically, and the disruption of normal life that followed the uprising, plus the necessity of punitive expeditions against the rebellious tribesmen, only accentuated the trend. But the troops that Father Le Petit and his confrères had eagerly expected never arrived, for with the news of the Natchez disaster the Company of the Indies took a step in an entirely different direction. The frantic appeals of Governor Perier for men and arms to push the campaign of extermination against the offending red men proved, in a sense, to be the *coup de grâce* for the company's enterprise in Louisiana. The directors decided that the risk of incurring further financial losses was not worth running, and in 1731 they thereupon cancelled their trade monopoly and receded the colony to the crown.

Meanwhile the Governor of Louisiana had been doing his best, with the aid of the Chocktaw allies, to bring the Natchez to heel, and he could show considerable success with about 450 savages taken captive and sold into slavery in the West Indies. But the Natchez were not his only worry. In the same year that the company surrendered its trade monopoly there occurred one of those disquieting episodes in which the Negro slaves made a break for liberty. According to de Charlevoix, the plot originated among the Chickasaw Indians who were in the pay of the English. The savages sent a trusty Negro to New Orleans to tell his people that it was up to themselves if they wished to gain their freedom and to live in comfort among the English. The plan, as revealed to Perier by a Negress who knew what was intended, called for the slaves to rise during the parochial high Mass, to set fire to the houses of those who were at church, and then to escape. Having been tipped off in time, the authorities arrested a colored woman who

[16] Le Petit to D'Avaugour, New Orleans, July 12, 1730, *Jesuit Relations*, LXVIII, 223.

was the mainspring of the conspiracy along with four of the male ringleaders. They were promptly convicted, and as de Charlevoix described it, "the woman was hung and the men broken alive, and these examples, which showed the rest that their secret had taken wind, was [*sic*] enough to keep the rest in their duty." [17]

With the company's men passing off the scene in 1731 there was need for a strong and confident hand to grasp the reins of government, and no one could think of a man better fitted for the difficult assignment than Bienville. For six years he had been living quietly in retirement in France, smarting under the injustice that he felt had been done him by his enemies. But his hour of vindication came when Louis XV summoned him to resume the governorship. Conditions having reached so low an ebb in Louisiana, the appointment brought widespread satisfaction among all but Bienville's enemies, and there was general rejoicing when the familiar figure landed again at New Orleans in March, 1733.

It would be pleasant to record that the recall of Father de Beaubois ended all trouble between the Jesuits and the Capuchins, and that religious peace was restored to the colony. Such, however, was not the case, and it was really not until the banishment of the Jesuits in 1763 that all friction was finally eliminated between the two orders. Yet that did not mean that there were not intervals of peace as, for example, when Father Raphael a few days before his death in February, 1734, lifted the interdict from the Jesuits on condition that de Beaubois would be recalled. As we know, that came about in the spring of 1735, and the next period of disturbance was due, not to a renewal of the old quarrel between the two groups of religious, but to the harsh and authoritarian regime of Raphael's second successor as Capuchin superior and vicar general, Father Mathias de Sedan. In fact, it was Mathias' own brethren who raised the loudest and most effective objections to him, and after an investigation of his rule by the authorities of the order in France he was deposed in June, 1739, and his place taken by Father Philippe de Luxembourg, a tactful and moderate friar, with whom the Jesuits worked without serious difficulty.

A further contributing factor to the unhappy state of the Church in Louisiana was the series of rapid changes through which the See of Quebec passed in these years. Saint Vallier, it will be remembered,

[17] De Charlevoix, *History*, VI, 119.

died in December, 1727, and de Mornay's regime lasted less than six years when his resignation was practically forced in September, 1733, because of his refusal to reside in the diocese. The fourth bishop of the see, Dosquet, then took over, but after a little over five years he became so dissatisfied with conditions which he despaired of being able to change that he resigned in January, 1739. The fifth ordinary of the see, François-Louis Pourroy de l'Auberivière, was thereupon appointed, consecrated, and took up residence in Quebec only to die a few weeks later in August, 1740. Almost a year went by before the consecration of the sixth bishop, Henri-Marie de Pontbriand, in April, 1741, but with this prelate there ensued an uninterrupted administration of almost twenty years. In considering the Louisiana Church and its difficulties, therefore, it should be kept in mind that the diocese of which it formed a part had within fifteen years five bishops, of whom one never saw the diocese, another served only a few weeks, two resigned after relatively brief periods, and not any one of the five prelates ever visited Louisiana.

In the absence of the ordinary, the government of the colony's religious affairs was vested in the vicars general who were both resident and non-resident. It was in the capacity of a non-resident vicar that Saint Vallier had used de Mornay, and when the latter took over as ordinary he engaged a French priest, Pierre de la Rue – better known as the Abbé de l'Isle Dieu – who from the time of his appointment in 1734 until his retirement in 1776 at the age of eighty-eight, conscientiously performed the duties of the office. In addition to these vicars general in Paris there was always at least one official of that rank in the the colony, and sometimes two or three priests held the rank simultaneously. In a situation of this kind it was of paramount importance, then, that those chosen should be men of agreeable disposition who were endowed with tact and understanding.

Throughout the eighteenth century the Louisiana Church experienced both the fortunate and the unfortunate in the choices made for vicar general. For example, after his appointment as bishop, de Pontbriand sought to acquaint himself with the background of his responsibility in Louisiana by reading a good deal of the correspondence for the previous decade. Evidently the regime of Father Mathias as Capuchin superior and vicar general made a quite unfavorable impression on him, for just before he sailed for New France in May,

1741, there arrived the latest batch of mail from the colony bearing news of further bickering among the Capuchins, and the new bishop determined then and there upon a drastic remedy. He summarily suppressed the Capuchin vicar generalship and put the friars' entire Louisiana mission under a Jesuit vicar general. Fortunately, the Capuchin provincial chose a benign old friar, Charles de Rambervillier, to send out to Louisiana as the new superior, and during the remainder of Father Charles' lifetime he and the Jesuit vicar general, Pierre Vitry, got along very well and an unwonted quiet settled over the colony's religious life.

Not long after the deaths of Fathers Vitry and Charles which occurred in 1749, the reverse side of the coin began to show. The successor of Vitry as Jesuit superior and vicar general was Michel Baudouin, while Father Dagobert de Longuory, a reasonable and moderate friar, succeeded to Charles' place as head of the Capuchins. As long as Dagobert was in office no serious trouble arose, although he, too, questioned Baudouin's authority in some particulars. But it was otherwise with Father George de Fauquemont who arrived in February, 1753, to replace Dagobert. The new superior was a strong minded man who was intent upon regaining the freedom of action that his order had lost twelve years before. Soon friction was again the pattern with the chief centers the Ursuline convent where the friars were determined to be spiritual directors of the nuns, at the military hospital where the chaplaincy was the bone of contention, and in the parishes where such rites as the celebration of marriages, and the administration of the sacraments generally, provided a source of trouble. If Father George overlooked any item that might enhance Capuchin prestige at the expense of the Jesuit vicar general, it was more than made up by his confrère, Father Hilaire de Geneveaux, who showed himself even less scrupulous than his superior in defying the vicar general.

Fundamentally, the quarrel reduced itself to a contest between the representatives of normal ecclesiastical government, namely, the bishop of the diocese and his vicar general, and the Capuchins who in good Gallican fashion attempted to by-pass the bishop and his vicar when they would not agree with them and to place their reliance on the civil authorities. When, therefore, the friars found that they were making no headway in Louisiana they decided upon carrying their case to France. Father Hilaire was the spokesman, and upon his arrival in 1755 he laid the Capuchin grievances before the Parlement of Paris. The significance of this move might easily be missed were one to overlook the fact that at the moment the parlement was waging a fierce campaign against the anti-Jansenist clergy, among whom, of course, the Jesuits were the most conspicuous and forceful group. Speaking of the parlement's recent conduct, one historian has remarked, "By the beginning of 1755 . . . priest-baiting had become general, and the harshest measures were approved."[18] Circumstances, then, favored the Capuchins, and in conformity with their Gallican ideas the parlement proceeded to call in question Bishop de Pontbriand's act in having eliminated the Capuchin vicar general, alleging that the *placet* of the crown had not been received, and insinuating that the prelate's action was the result of his having been hoodwinked by the Jesuits. Much was likewise made of the latter's alleged violation of the agreement of 1726 between the two orders for separate missionary districts in Louisiana under their respective superiors.

In all of this, to be sure, the Capuchins had ignored the Bishop of Quebec. But de Pontbriand had no intention of allowing his authority in his own diocese to be flaunted. He prepared a five-point statement in 1755 which reasserted the Jesuit vicar general's authority and the Capuchin's obligation to recognize it, and he sent the document to Father Baudouin with instructions that he should secure the friars' adherence to its terms in writing. Nor did he give up, as we shall see, when the Capuchins refused to sign the statement upon its presentation in July, 1756. Meanwhile their attempt to annul the Jesuit vicar's authority by invoking the rule of his own order, proved no more successful. The friars challenged Baudouin on the score that the Jesuit rule forbade its members to accept ecclesiastical offices of any kind. On this point, however, de Pontbriand's vicar general in Paris, the Abbé de l'Isle Dieu, sought a confirmation from the Holy See, and in December, 1755, Pope Benedict XIV issued a brief dispensing Baudouin in this particular, an action which the pope made known to the General of the Jesuits.

When news reached him of Father Hilaire's trip to France and his petition to the parlement, Bishop de Pontbriand was greatly annoyed. Once again he confirmed Baudouin's authority and this time he issued a decree placing Fathers Hilaire and Dagobert under interdict unless

[18] Pastor, *History of the Popes*, XXXV, 257.

they immediately obeyed. The interdict was certified to the two friars in January, 1758, but on this occasion Hilaire's defiance became so flagrant that sympathy was alienated from him in every quarter. The whole matter reached a climax when he went as far as to forbid, on his own authority, a visiting Spanish Franciscan to say Mass in a private home even though the visitor had obtained permission from Father Baudouin. The owner of the house now sued the Capuchins, and the case came before the Superior Council, the highest governing body in the colony. They rendered a decision that Hilaire's religious superior should send him back to France immediately, and if he should threaten to disobey, then the government would expel him by force. By this time the Capuchins' opposition was broken and on October 27, 1758, Father Dagobert and his two confrères then in New Orleans signed de Pontbriand's five-point ultimatum of three years before that had enjoined their recognition of his vicar general. With that the controversy that had disrupted the religious life of the colony intermittently for over thirty years was finally ended.

Few things in the history of the Louisiana Church exposed more clearly its fundamental weaknesses than the Jesuit-Capuchin conflict. First, and most important, was the absence of a resident bishop who could use his authority to nip these inter-clerical disputes before they got out of hand. The ideal, of course, would have been a separate diocese for the colony; but even a coadjutor or an auxiliary bishop in residence, were he an able and prudent administrator, would have mitigated the evil effects of the quarrels among the religious. Actually, Louisiana was only fourteen years short of a century old before a bishop came to reside there, and all that while the Catholics had been deprived of the Sacrament of Confirmation. Moreover, without a bishop no effort was made to establish a seminary and to recruit candidates among the boys of the Catholic families for the diocesan priesthood. Thus no hope was held out that within the foreseeable future normal ecclesiastical government might be established. During this same period a school for boys or a seminary would have been well nigh impossible among the English-speaking Catholics along the Atlantic Coast because of the penal legislation and the general prejudice against Catholics. But in Louisiana, where the Catholic religion was the only one allowed by law, there was no such excuse for the absence of a training center for future priests.

A further weakness in the early years was the dependence of the priests who came to the colony, whether they were the concession chaplains, the members of the Society of Foreign Missions, or members of one of the religious orders, on the trading companies. The directors of the companies held virtually absolute power since it was the companies that paid the priests' salaries and provided their living quarters, as well as the churches with their equipment for divine services. But when the representatives of the companies did bestir themselves to fulfill their obligations to the Church they generally showed little ability in handling ecclesiastical business, and more often displayed little conscience about the needs of religion if they happened to conflict with their material interests. Nor was there much improvement after 1731 when the crown took over and sought through the Ministry of Marine and the Colonies to provide for the Church. Thus the Louisiana Catholic community limped along until almost the end of the century before an Auxiliary Bishop of Santiago in Cuba – under which Louisiana had meanwhile passed – came in 1786 to reside in the colony, and with this step the way was gradually opened for the erection of a separate diocese seven years later.

Preoccupation with the religious controversies should not blind the historian to the more constructive side of the work done by the missionaries during these same years. A word should be said, therefore, about the Jesuits' missions among the savages before they were closed out by the decree that banished the Black Robes from Louisiana. But here one cannot find the wealth of detail that was true of an earlier day, the reason for which must be sought in Europe. Among the many losses sustained in consequence of the feuds over the Chinese rites and the French government's struggle to impose the so-called Gallican liberties, was the *Jesuit Relations*. The pamphlet war that arose over the rites in the Orient became so furious that the Holy See in 1673 ordered a stop put to all publications bearing on the Church's missions unless they bore the written permission of the cardinals of the Congregation de Propaganda Fide. But Clement X's brief headed directly into the rising storm over Gallicanism, and when the famous articles of the Gallican Church appeared in 1682 among them was a prohibition of any recognition in France of the authority of the Roman congregations. Since the *Jesuit Relations* were published under the auspices of the Paris provincial, the celebrated reports, which have provided historians with so rich a mine of information on colonial North America, were brought to a close, and as a consequence we know far less about eighteenth-century conditions than we do those of the preceding century.

During the thirty-six years that followed their return to Louisiana in 1727, Jesuits served for varying lengths of time at the three white settlements of Mobile, Natchitoches, and New Orleans. At the first named the parish registers showed five of their number substituting at intervals between 1725 and 1740 for the Capuchin pastors when the latter were absent; while at Natchitoches, Pierre Vitry, S.J., served as pastor of the mixed congregation from early in 1734 to April, 1738. It was under Vitry's supervision that Natchitoches got its first church in 1737, the year that a census of the parishioners showed 112 whites, 107 Negro slaves, and fourteen Indian slaves. In New Orleans the Jesuits were found as chaplains at the military hospital and the Ursuline convent, as well as occasionally lending assistance to the Capuchins in the parishes of the colonial capital and its neighboring villages. Sodalities were established for both men and women under Jesuit direction, and the spiritual welfare of the slaves on their own plantation occupied a considerable amount of their time and effort since by 1763 the latter numbered thirty-six families.

But these assignments were incidental to the Jesuits' main business in the colony which was the conversion of its Indian tribes. And here they had their own peculiar problems, and in the final analysis very little success. For the first twenty years of Louisiana's history there was no traffic in brandy which was a merciful boon for the cause that was uppermost in the missionaries' minds. But as the rivalry between the French and English for the mastery of the tribes east of the Mississippi intensified, the Louisiana officials felt less and less inclined to make efforts to enforce the regulations of the king and of the Bishop of Quebec banning the trade. The principal reason was the success which the English had in drawing off the savages with liquor, a policy that by 1737 had yielded such telling results that in that year the French introduced the trade. The usual evil effects on the Indians followed in due course with their accompanying heartaches for the missionaries.

A second problem pertained to the sex relations between the French and the Indians. The missionaries' policy of strict segregation of the two races was well known, but here in Louisiana it suffered an especially acute strain. In the Illinois Country the scandal of open concubinage of white men and red women had been in part mitigated by the importation of white girls from New France. But in Louisiana white girls were scarce, and Frenchmen simply took the easiest way to acquire a mate. During the reign of Louis XIV marriages between couples of this kind were regarded as legal, providing the woman became a Catholic. But as the eighteenth century wore on French officialdom grew increasingly hostile to such unions. In some cases the opposition would seem to have stemmed from hardly more than personal repugnance; in others from an official's conviction that neither of the partners desired to contract a permanent union, and from the fear that if the man should die the Indian woman would return to her tribe and the colony might thus lose the value of her husband's goods.

For the priests, of course, the question was one of morals. There was record as early as 1699 of marriages of this kind having been performed in the Illinois Country, and early in the next century the missionaries in Louisiana sought to regularize the unions of French men and unconverted Indian women on a broader basis. The Jesuits petitioned their Roman superiors for a general dispensation from the Holy See for the impediment of disparity of cult in order to rectify as far as possible what they could not prevent. In other words, if white men and Indian pagan women insisted upon living together, then in order to avoid scandal and preserve some semblance of community morals, the pagan mate should be given an elementary instruction and then be married to her white partner in a Christian ceremony. To do less, was for the priest an intolerable burden on his conscience as a guardian of morals; yet to do as much, was often to bring down the frown and active hostility of the civil authorities. Whether or not the dispensation came through from Rome, is not clear. The parish registers of Post Vincennes showed that as late as 1750 marriages of this kind were being performed there, while in Louisiana the prohibition against an Indian widow inheriting her white husband's estate remained to the end of the French regime. As in so many other matters, the problem was never satisfactorily solved, and as long as the French continued in the colony it remained a subject of fairly constant embarrassment and vexation for the missionaries.

Strained relations between the men of Church and State were not, as we know, in anyway unique to Louisiana; the student of the

Church's history in colonial America meets with them wherever he turns. In Louisiana as elsewhere the policies of civil and military officers were usually directed toward what they conceived as their material interests, and insofar as cognizance was taken of religion at all, it was to have the latter subserve political ends. That was true of the brandy trade as it was in most other questions, such as the government's decision to abandon a number of the military posts because they were thought too expensive. In making the decision little or no consideration was given to the fact that these forts were the only protection which the missionary might have at times when the savages became threatening. A further instance was the monetary assistance which the government was pledged to give the missionaries. Not infrequently, it was handed over with reluctance and only after long delays, and even then as a calculated investment for the State, not as a benefit to the Church. The civil and military authorities knew full well, of course, that the priests were the best instrument available for taming the savages and holding them in the line of French obedience against the allurements of the English; and for that reason their needs could never be entirely ignored. Yet unless a missionary could prove to the officials' satisfaction that a policy of State would be advanced by building and sustaining a mission in a given locality, he might be left without a roof over his head, or without a decent spot in which to say Mass, as happened to the last Jesuit who served at the Arkansas Post.

When one turns to survey what was actually accomplished in the Indian missions maintained by the Jesuits in Louisiana in this period it is largely a story of successive failures. Their efforts were concentrated on four main tribes: the Arkansas, Yazoos, Chocktaws, and Alibamons. The first tribe lived west of the Mississippi and had been visited by the seminary priests shortly before the Jesuits appeared in 1727. It was Father du Poisson who opened the mission among the Arkansas, but his time was short, for as we have seen, he was murdered by the Natchez two years later. Yet in spite of the meager hope held out by the Arkansas as prospective converts, the Jesuits continued for the next thirty years to come to the Arkansas River Valley. But ultimately the superstition and deeply rooted pagan practices of these savages, plus the utter indifference to religion of the French garrison at the fort, made it useless to continue. The French did not even provide a fitting place to conduct divine services, and they saw nothing incongruous about the missionary having to say Mass in the commandant's eating quarters where the chickens roamed freely about the room. The situation finally became too much for Father Louis Carette, and in August, 1758, he left, and his departure marked the end of the mission. The Yazoos had also had some instructions in the Christian faith from the seminary priests before Father Souel reached them. But the measure of their appreciation for the gospel message was shown two years later when they murdered the Jesuit in December, 1729, and once more a mission was closed forever.

The two main tribes with whom the Jesuits endeavored to make some headway on the east side of the Mississippi were the Chocktaws and the Alibamons. In the vast area over which the former roamed there was no military post to afford protection for Father Le Petit and his successors, among whom was the first Canadian-born Jesuit, Michel Baudouin. They continued their labors, nevertheless, and although the long and exhausting journeys which they had to make between the widely separated Chocktaw villages were a severe trial, it was mild in comparison to the hardship and frustration that they experienced by reason of the almost constant warfare. The English were intent upon making peace between the Chocktaws and the Chickasaws which, if it were successful, would spell the doom of the French in Louisiana; and for that reason the latter were equally active in keeping the two tribes in arms against each other. Ultimately the white men's jockeying for the Chocktaws' allegiance led to a split in the tribe and created a situation akin to civil war. Through twenty of the thirty years that the Jesuits spent in the Chocktaw country, therefore, there was active fighting with, it need hardly be said, practically no success in bringing the Indians to accept Christianity.

Nor were conditions any more prosperous among the Alibamons whose homeland was in the valley of the Coosa and Talapoosa Rivers. Here there was at least a French military post in Fort Toulouse which had been built in 1714 and which kept the savages in a little more awe of the white man than would otherwise have been the case. But in this instance the eagerness of the French to prevent the Alibamons from going over to the English led them to introduce the brandy trade, and once the natives got the taste of the fire water it became so consuming a passion that the Alibamons proved to be one of the worst of all examples of Indian addiction to drunkenness. These were formidable handicaps, and yet from the time that Father Alexis de Guyenne arrived among these Indians late in 1727 through the futile term of Guillaume Morand, S.J., who came in 1736, and on to Father Maximilien Le Roy who was with the tribe from 1751 until the expulsion of his order from the colony twelve years later, the Black Robes persisted. In the case of none of these missionaries, however, was any real progress made in bringing the Alibamons or any other tribes of northeastern Louisiana into the Catholic fold.

Before recounting the sad story of the Jesuits' banishment from the colony something should be said about their plantation, which was the source of a good deal of worry to them, as it was of annoyance to the Capuchins and of opposition on the part of certain civil officials. From the outset of the Louisiana enterprise all the missionary groups found it next to impossible to exist in decency on the meager annual salary of 600 livres per man which was paid by the trading companies, and after them by the crown. The result was that not only the Jesuits, but also the Capuchins and Ursulines, were compelled to look for other sources of income. The sisters supplemented their funds by their school and by working in the hospital as well as by a plantation worked by slaves, while the friars had some income from parochial fees, and also got revenue from a plantation about three miles below New Orleans which was worked by slaves.

During the time that Father de Beaubois had spent in New France he had observed how the missions there benefited from the large Jesuit farm near Quebec, and it was the hope of obtaining something of the same kind for his order in Louisiana that prompted in part his trip to France in 1725. His first attempts met with rebuffs, but in April, 1726, Bienville agreed to sell his plantation to the missionaries, a large tract at New Orleans of about twenty acres or more along the east bank of the Mississippi which carried with it three Negro slaves, the livestock, and the buildings for the price of 12,000 livres. On his way back to Louisiana in 1727 de Beaubois purchased sixteen additional slaves in Santo Domingo for the plantation, and the outlay of so much capital put the Jesuits heavily into debt, although by June, 1730, they made the final payment on the plantation. Once they got the latter underway it proved to be a profitable enterprise, and in time it was enlarged by the purchase of more land. The Jesuits concentrated on the cultivation of cotton, for which they had their mill, and on indigo, the manufacture of which de Beaubois revived in the colony. And it was due to them that sugar cane finally became a permanent staple in Louisiana. In addition a flourishing fruit orchard was developed, additions were made to the livestock, and the chickens, doves, and other fowl were also made to yield a return.

For all of this variegated agriculture the labor was performed by the Negro slaves who quickly became a familiar feature of life throughout Louisiana after their introduction about 1717. Although the Church had condemned the slave trade more than once — most recently by Benedict XIV's letter of 1741 to the faithful in Brazil — human slavery *in se* had not been condemned as contrary to the natural law, even though various popes had deplored the institution and had insisted upon the moral obligations of masters to treat their slaves with kindness and consideration. Both the Jesuits and the Capuchins had slaves on their reductions in South America in this same period, and it was not surprising, therefore, to find them on the Louisiana plantations of these religious. Care was taken to see that the slaves received religious instruction, and there were probably no more conscientious masters in the colony than they were in carrying out the detailed prescriptions of Bienville's *Code Noir* of 1724.[19] In fact, the insistence of the Jesuits upon baptizing and marrying their own slaves at their plantation chapel was one of the sources of grievance on the part of the Capuchins who contended that it was a violation of their parochial rights. In spite of the criticism of the friars, and of certain politicians who grew envious of the success of an enterprise for which they could claim no credit or from which they could derive no benefit, the Jesuit plantation continued its successful course to the end of the owners' time in the colony. And when it was confiscated and sold at auction in July, 1763, with all its movable property, it was found that the 136 slaves, divided between thirty-six families living in the forty-five slave huts, 180 head of cattle along with other livestock, two houses, barns, and other out buildings brought a total of 955,752 livres (about $180,000), of which 287,350 livres were paid for the plantation and the buildings.

[19] For the text of the *Code Noir* cf. the appendix in Charles Gayarré, *History of Louisiana*, 4th ed. (New Orleans, 1903), I, 531–540. Regarding the articles relating to the Jews and the Catholic religion, Gayarré said: "By what concatenation of causes or of ideas these provisions concerning the supremacy of the Roman Catholic religion and the expulsion of the Jews came to be inserted into the Black Code, it is difficult to imagine." (I, 362–363).

But some years before the liquidation of the Society of Jesus and its properties in Louisiana, there had begun the series of events that would lead not only to the Jesuits' expulsion but as well to the end of the colony's French regime and its replacement by that of Spain. Let us speak of the political change first. Repeated reference has been made to the rivalry between France and Britain in North America, and it had been gradually building up to a point where finally fighting broke out at the Forks of the Ohio in April, 1754, and with that was launched the French and Indian War. For over two years hostilities were confined to the new world, but early in 1756 the English made an alliance with Prussia which was followed in a few months by that of France with Austria.

The stage was now set for the Seven Years' War, as it was called in Europe, and Great Britain led off with a declaration of war on France on May 15, 1756. The sequel is too well known to need retelling here; suffice it to say, for the first four years the French were for the most part the victors. But in June, 1757, William Pitt took the helm as British prime minister, and with his skillful and effective planning the British forces in both the old and new worlds soon began to take on new life. The year 1759 proved disastrous for the French, and by September, 1760, Pierre François de Rigaud, Marquis de Vaudreil, who had become Governor of New France after his ten years (1743–1753) in the same office in Louisiana, was compelled to surrender the entire province. At the time that Spain had begun to throw its weight to the side of France the British had declared war on the sister Bourbon monarchy in January, 1762, so that in the Treaty of Paris of February, 1763, that ended the fighting, major changes were made in the possessions of all three of the principal colonial powers. Canada passed to Great Britain, as well as all French territory east of the Mississippi, including the port of Mobile, the Ile d'Orleans alone excepted. In the Anglo-Spanish aspects of the peace settlement Cuba was restored to Spain and East and West Florida became British possessions; and Louisiana – ceded by France to Spain in the secret Treaty of San Ildefonso of November, 1762 – now passed to the Spaniards. The actual turnover, however, in a number of cases was delayed, and in Louisiana almost seven years were to elapse before the first Spanish governor made his appearance at New Orleans in August, 1769.

To return now to the Jesuits' last days in colonial Louisiana. Enough has already been said about the opposition that developed in France around the middle of the eighteenth century to the Society of Jesus. The objective of their enemies was long in taking shape, but by the end of the 1750's it was clear for all to see. Arrayed against the order were not only Louis XV's powerful mistress, the Marquise de Pompadour, but the Gallicans, the *philosophes*, and the Society's old foes, the Jansenists. And at the opportune moment a member of the beleaguered order, Antoine Lavalette, S.J., put a weapon into their hands which furnished the pretext for the final attack. Father Lavalette had for many years been indulging in financial manipulations and trading operations in the West Indies in connection with the Jesuits' missions there. He had been ordered by his superiors to cease, but he had willfully persisted until bankruptcy overtook him with about 4,500,000 livres owed to creditors which he could not pay. One of the firms with which he had done business brought suit before the consular court in Paris in November, 1759, and with this the campaign against the entire Jesuit Order took on new life. From this time to the promulgation of the decree of the Parlement of Paris of August, 1762, that condemned the Jesuits and ordered their suppression, events moved at a more rapid pace, and by the end of that summer the 3,049 members of the five French provinces, including 142 men on the foreign missions, faced a practically hopeless prospect with little or no chance of saving anything from the storm that had gathered around them.

The spirit that had characterized the campaign in the mother country was not long in being transmitted to the colonies, and on July 9, 1763, the Superior Council at New Orleans — acting on orders from Paris — declared the suppression of the Society in Louisiana and the Illinois Country. It need hardly be said that the members of the Superior Council were in no sense competent to judge the constitutions of the Society of Jesus, for it was on the strength of the alleged inherent evils in their rule that the order was struck down. They were charged as well with having violated the agreement on which they had been admitted to the colony, and particularly as it related to the vicar generalship of the Capuchins. It was stated that everywhere the Jesuits went, they had been more concerned for the advancement of their order than they had for the conversion of the native peoples, and insofar as Louisiana was concerned, it was added that "they have made very few conversions in the posts of this colony, where their ambition has often been the cause of dissensions."[20]

We have already seen the disposition that was made of the Jesuits' New Orleans plantation and its goods. The contents of the plantation chapel, along with that of the other chapels at the various missions, were ordered to be turned over to the Capuchins, and in several cases the chapels were razed to the ground and even the graves in the adjacent cemeteries were desecrated. What followed in the lives of the thirteen Jesuits – twelve priests and one lay brother – during the next six months was described a year later by François Philibert Watrin, the superior of the Illinois Country missions at the time. What especially grieved Watrin was the charge that the Jesuits "had not taken any care of their missions; that they had thought only of making their estates valuable; and that they were usurpers of the vicariate-general of New Orleans."[21] So keenly did he feel this injustice that Father Watrin devoted a major portion of his lengthy document to its refutation. He stated that upon their return to France many had expressed to them their astonishment and horror at what had taken place in Louisiana, and that it had been remarked that this sort of thing, "was only to be expected from open enemies of the Catholic religion." The ex-religious at that time being in so delicate a position, it is understandable to find Father Watrin adding, "the Jesuits could only answer these sayings by silence."[22]

The procedure that had been carried out at New Orleans in July was repeated in the Illinois Country in the autumn. The missionaries were ordered to assemble at Fort Chartres on the Mississippi, and even Father Julien de Vernay at Post Vincennes, who had been ill for six months, was not excepted but rather compelled to make the difficult overland journey through the wilderness. Here, too, an inventory was taken of their property which was then sold at public auction. Mentioning how stripped and forlorn they found their former home when they returned to it after the sale, Watrin then spoke of the chapel. He said:

[20] Delanglez, *op. cit.*, p. 511. The text of the decree is printed here, pp. 509–513.

[21] François Philibert Watrin, "Banishment of the Jesuits from Louisiana," Paris, September 3, 1764, *Jesuit Relations*, LXX, 221.

[22] *Ibid.*, LXX, 265.

They found their chapel in a still more melancholy condition: after the sacred vessels and the pictures had been taken away, the shelves of the altar had been thrown down; the linings of the ornaments had been given to negresses decried for their evil lives; and a large crucifix, which had stood above the altar, and the chandeliers, were found placed above a cupboard in a house whose reputation was not good. To see the marks of spoliation in the chapel, one might have thought that it was the enemies of the Catholic religion who had caused it.[23]

The twenty-seven day voyage down the Mississippi began on November 24, and all that the ex-religious were allowed to take with them were their mattresses and blankets, a small quantity of clothes, and some food which, incidentally, they shared with the forty-eight Negroes who had been their former slaves and who were now being taken to New Orleans. In the crisis that had come upon the Illinois missionaries it is pleasant to recall that with their arrival at New Orleans the civil officials exerted themselves to make life as comfortable as possible for them, and that the Capuchins now came forth to show their fallen rivals every kindness and consideration. Alluding to the treatment that the refugees received from the friars, Watrin stated, "during the six weeks which elapsed before they embarked, there were no marks of friendship which they did not receive from these Reverend Fathers.[24] By the summer of 1764 most of the ex-Jesuits had departed for Europe except Fathers Baudouin, Meurin, and Potier, who remained to serve as secular priests under the Bishop of Quebec, Baudouin in and about New Orleans, Meurin in the Illinois Country, and Potier at Detroit.

[23] *Ibid.*, LXX, 281.
[24] *Ibid.*, LXX, 289.

CHAPTER ELEVEN

LOUISIANA UNDER THREE FLAGS

The year 1763 marked a sharp break in the history of both Church and State in North America. With France expelled from the continent, a new era opened for the Catholic Church as well as for the international relations of the new world. The vast territories that had been ruled from Quebec and New Orleans were now subject to new masters, and the future of Catholicism was in part to depend on the Church's relations with the English Protestant rulers of Canada and the Floridas and with the Spaniards who came to replace the French in Louisiana Following the peace settlements of 1763, there was an interval of twenty years during which the heartland of the continent, traversed for over a century by the missionaries, soldiers, and *coureurs de bois* of France, witnessed the sporadic raids of Englishmen upon Spaniards and vice versa. Simultaneously a new factor was coming to the fore, the independent American, with whom, as it gradually became clear, the future lay. Meanwhile many of the French inhabitants of the posts around the Great Lakes and in the Mississippi Valley had departed after the defeat of the armies of Louis XV. But many, too, remained to leave a certain stamp upon future American settlements all the way from Maine to Minnesota, and southward through the old Illinois Country to New Orleans. We shall speak later in another connection of some of these pioneer white communities on the American frontier. Here it is necessary to give an evaluation of the colonial missionary efforts of the French before returning to Louisiana to trace the life of the Church through the forty years between the advent of Spanish rule and the sale of the colony to the United States in 1803.

Were one to judge the French missions solely on the basis of the number of permanent conversions to Catholicism made among the American redmen, they would undoubtedly be reckoned a failure. For if one considers the thousands of Indians in the dozens of different tribes to whom the gospel was preached between 1613 when Fathers Biard, Massé, and Quentin came to Maine's Mount Desert Island to the government's expulsion in 1763 of Father Jean Jacques Le Prédour, missionary to the Alibamons, the Chocktaws' priest, Nicolas Lefevre, S.J., and the others, there were exceedingly few who had accepted Christianity and who had shown its civilizing influences in their lives. True, the Abenaki in Maine produced a good number of solid Catholics, and so did the Hurons in whose ranks there were a few converts of remarkable sanctity. But the number, in comparison to the over-all Indian population reached by these French priests, remained negligible.

Yet in spite of the lack of response on the part of a majority of the savages to the gospel message, among those who brought that message the one who showed a disposition to abandon them was the exception. On the contrary, priests of the Society of Foreign Missions, Franciscans, Capuchins, and over 300 of the finest specimens of French manhood enrolled in the Society of Jesus, gladly gave all or a major portion of their adult lives to this disappointing apostolate. The training of all these men had, of course, been intended to prepare them for suffering and reverses, and having been taught to judge everything from a supernatural point of view, obstacles and frustrations at times only enhanced their courage and determination. The missionary reports of the period are replete with examples of this spirit, such as that of Father Marest who in 1709 detailed for a confrère the formidable difficulties he had encountered among the Illinois tribes. Yet he concluded, "If our Missions are not so flourishing as others on account of a great number of conversions, at least they are precious and beneficial to us, on account of the labors and hardships which are inseparable from them."[1]

Even a visitor on tour in the new world like Pierre de Charlevoix, S.J., manifested the same sentiment when quite by accident he came upon

[1] Gabriel Marest to Barthélemi Germon, S.J., Kaskaskia, November 9, 1712, *Jesuit Relations*, LXVI, 255. According to the estimate of Arthur E. Jones, S.J., the total number of Jesuits who worked in New France and Louisiana between 1611 and 1773, including the lay brothers, was 320. (*Ibid.*, LXXI, 120–181).

a dying Indian child and was able to baptize it. Should the fatigues and dangers of his journey be useless in every other respect, he said, the baptism of this single child would have made it all worthwhile since, as he remarked, "according to all appearances, if I had not come to Pimiteony this child would never have entered Heaven where I do not doubt she will soon be."[2] And amid his uphill struggle at the Arkansas Post, Father du Poisson's reactions to the fickle and stubborn tribesmen there were much the same. He told the editor of the *Lettres édifiantes* that what he would beg most of him would be prayers that he might give all his strength to their conversion. And both his sense of realism and the secret of du Poisson's inner consolation were reflected when he added, "to judge humanly, no great good can be done among them, at least at the beginning. I hope everything from the grace of God."[3] Nor was this steadfast dedication to a cause that yielded such meagre results, true of the Jesuits alone. Father de Montigny of the seminary clergy, for example, told a friend not long after he reached the Illinois Country that all the hardships that he and his associates had to endure would not be counted as lost if "we only baptize a great number of children who otherwise would die without baptism."[4] Testimony of this kind to the supernatural ideal that sustained the missionaries could be multiplied from their correspondence, for it was the strongest single factor in fighting the corroding discouragement and sense of futility that attended their oftentimes unprofitable labors.

If the achievements of the French missionaries are measured against those of their Spanish brethren, the latter's record is the more impressive one. A leading authority on the Spanish missionary era has stated that before their expulsion in 1767 the Jesuits of New Spain alone had probably baptized not less than two million Indians.[5] A figure such as this dwarfs the number of savages who received the sacrament at the hands of the French priests. And apart from numbers, the Spaniards excelled their French contemporaries in the success they had in bringing the Indians to a sedentary way of life and to the acceptance

[2] De Charlevoix to de Lesdiguières, Pimiteony, October 5, 1721, *Journal d'un Voyage*, III, 389.

[3] Du Poisson to Louis Patouillet, S.J., Arkansas Post, 1726 [the year is incorrect here; it was 1727], *Jesuit Relations*, LXVII, 263.

[4] De Montigny to Delisle [n.p., n.d.], Delanglez, *op. cit.*, pp. 380–381.

[5] Bolton, *Rim of Christendom*, p. 12.

of at least the elements of civilization. Nowhere in French colonial America was there to be found anything in number and size to match the missions and pueblos of the Southwest and California. The French had some success in this regard at the Indian villages on the Saint Lawrence where they not only supervised the religious life of the natives, but introduced them to farming, weaving, and other features of civilized living; but it was on no such scale as obtained among the Spaniards.

Needless to say, comparisons of this kind are not intended to depreciate the labors of the French missionaries, but only to impress upon the mind of the reader a clearer notion of the extent and nature of the success or failure of the general Catholic missionary enterprise in this period. And if the French suffer by comparison with the Spaniards, the reasons are not difficult to discover, for major differences of policy between the two colonizing powers account in good measure for the fate of the missions in their respective possessions. For example, the Spaniards were both more generous and more consistent in their supply of material assistance to the missionaries and their neophytes than was true of the French. To be sure, this was largely dictated by the hope of making the savages a peaceful and productive element of the colonial population, capable of ultimately perpetuating Spain's religion, language, and social customs among their own kind. The French were also interested in keeping the Indians at peace and of making them productive, especially of furs, but never to the degree of expending upon them the money, time, and care that characterized the colonial regime of Spain. In that sense the latter's policy was much more calculated to last than the often shortsighted emphasis of the French on earning a fortune in furs.

The difference in attitude toward the native peoples showed up particularly in such questions as that of language and of intersocial marriage. The Spanish officials insisted upon the missionaries teaching the savages the Spanish language, while their French counterparts, on the contrary, were intent that the priests should learn the Indian dialects and deal with them in their own tongue. As for marriages between whites and Indians, Spain generally took a benign view of them and put no legal barrier in the way of such unions. As a result in time they became so numerous that their offspring constituted an entirely new class, the *mestizos,* who played an important role in the later years of Spanish rule in America. Among the French, marriages of this kind were, indeed, permitted in the early period, but as time went on there developed a strong prejudice against them, and it was not uncommon for a priest who wished to officiate at such a union to encounter keen opposition from the local civil authority. Both the language and interracial marriage questions reflected, of course, the contrasting views taken by the two colonizing powers of the native peoples. Spain wished to make the Indians, insofar as that was possible, like the Spaniards in a way that would never have suggested itself to the French. While the former found the Indian worthy to share, at least to a minor extent, in creating a new society and in shaping its destiny through the *mestizos*, the French never encouraged the natives to aspire to association of this kind with the white overlords, and the halfbreed was never accorded the same position in the social stratification of the French colonies that his opposite number had among the Spaniards.

In both colonial empires, as we have seen, the missionaries acted as agents in various capacities for their respective governments, and at times the secular authorities leaned heavily on them, especially when it was a matter of taming the savages and keeping them aloof from alienating influences like the English. In both cases, too, the missionaries were paid their salaries by the government, and were also dependent on its soldiers for protection and on its good will for the material suppliers needed for their chapels and dwellings. In both domains, as we know, the civil authorities often failed to live up to their obligations to the missions, but in the final reckoning the Spaniards had a better record than the French. This is not to suggest that the Spaniards always lived up to their promises, for we know that they did not. But the point is, at the outset they pledged more than the French, and in the sequel they actually gave more to sustain the Church's operations among the redmen. As a consequence, the Spaniards' stake in the missions was always much greater than the French as the ultimate results were more far flung and lasting.

One can get some idea of the comparative commitment in the two empires from the fact that when Charles III's decree of 1767 expelling the Jesuits from his dominions was executed in the new world it struck 678 members of the order in the Viceroyalty of New Spain alone – not even half of whom were in the missions, but rather were teachers in the colleges and schools or were serving as parish priests. In contrast there were something over 300 Jesuits who served through the whole of the colonial period in the North American colonies of France, and that was no mean number. But when set alongside the more than doubled figure of their Spanish confrères laboring in a single viceroyalty, it was small. And in terms of enduring influence on the native population, the picture is pretty much the same. Long after the memory of the French Black Robes and friars had faded among the tribes of the Mississippi Valley, large numbers of the converts of their Spanish brothers still held to the Catholic faith that they had been taught. And while they remained within the pale of the white man's influence the same could be said for the farming methods, the domestic animals, the tools of labor, and the building techniques—all of which they owed to the missionaries.

But if after a century and a half of French missionary effort the results were so slight, it was due largely to the circumstances beyond the missionaries' control. Ranking high among the causes was the extreme difficulty of trying to master numerous Indian dialects in such a way that the abstract concepts and beliefs of Catholicism might be successfully conveyed in languages which were rich in concrete terms but poor in words connoting abstract principles. A further major obstacle that never lost its force was the struggle to get the Indian mentality to accept the Christian doctrine of self-sacrifice. As one might expect, the idea of self-denial, such as that of fasting during Lent, was nonsense to the savages, and it was grist for the mill of the tribal medicine men who were constantly on the alert to undermine the missionaries' teaching, and whose propaganda often proved a fertile cause for their failure. Likewise the priests' frequent clashes with the civil and military personnel retarded progress, as did the failure of the latter to perform their obligations to the missions.

Still another cause arose from the marked change that came over religious life in France. Whereas in the early stages of the missionary movement the great Catholic revival, of which it was a belated expression, had provided numerous recruits and generous financial assistance, as the seventeenth century wore on the effects of the Catholic Reformation faded amid the splendor of the Sun King's reign where men's minds were directed to other goals; and the missions were made to feel the difference. For example, in 1683 only one newcomer arrived in the colonies for a missionary assignment. By this time the religious orders were experiencing a decline in vocations to what they had known a half century before, and there were now fewer men to volunteer for the missions than had been true in the days of a Jogues or a de Brébeuf.

Moreover, as it became evident that it was futile to anticipate any real progress among many of the Indian tribes, there was a growing tendency for the missionaries to transfer their zeal to their own countrymen. And for that reason by the end of the French regime there were probably more white men in New France, the Illinois Country, and Louisiana under the spiritual care of the priests than there were Indians. While this change of priestly service from the savages to the whites was, in a sense, an added reason for the diminished vigor of the missionary apostolate, it constituted a sufficient contribution to the religious life of colonial America to warrant mention in its own right. And here, it should be said, was one place where the French clergy made every bit as deep and favorable an impression on the lives of the white settlers as their Spanish brothers did in their own white settlements.

Throughout the French colonies the old military and trading posts in time gave rise to a number of American towns and cities. At Detroit, Mobile, and Vincennes – to name only a few – this was true, and in the social life of these frontier communities the Catholic Church played a leading role. Amid their rough surroundings the spark of religion often burned very low; yet it was never totally extinguished, thanks to a succession of French priests. Thus when the onrush of events occasioned by the American Revolution reached beyond the mountains and engulfed the West, the militiamen of the new-born states and the other fighting men found that among the most influential men in these towns was the priest. Father Gibault at Cahokia is the case most frequently cited, but there were others like the two ex-Jesuits, Sébastien Meurin at Kaskaskia and Pierre Potier at Sandwich near Detroit.

Nor was there any essential change during the period of transition experienced by the western country before it came under full American sovereignty. And here the persecution of the Church by the French revolutionary government after 1790 played a decisive part, for it brought to the new United States a large number of French refugee priests whose first assignments were to these French-speaking communities in the West. The Sulpicians, Michel Levadoux and Benedict Flaget, were cases in point, the first appointed to Cahokia and the second to Vincennes, just as a little later there came Gabriel Richard who was to make himself felt at Detroit, the Trappist, Marie Joseph Dunand, in Perry County, Missouri, and the itinerant missionary, Etienne Badin, who became a familiar figure throughout three or four states of the new West. In the American wilderness these cultivated refugee priests kindled anew the fire of religious faith that their fellow countrymen and fellow priests had originally lighted during the missionary era. And by the same token they enriched the lives of the inhabitants of these settlements – Catholics and non-Catholics alike – by their cultured minds and manners.

In that connection one of the most perceptive foreign observers of contemporary American life and its historic roots has stated that the old towns of the Middle West are more American and more touching to the historical imagination than the large cities. Among these he mentions Vincennes and Bardstown, Kentucky which were once, as he says, "centres of civilization, of learning, of religion, of commerce."[6] And it was the Catholic faith, held over from the French colonial regime in the case of the former and imported from Maryland in the case of the latter, that accounted in good measure for their character. Early in the nineteenth century both Vincennes and Bardstown – and the same could be said for Saint Louis, Mobile, and Detroit – had each its cathedral and college for boys staffed in the main by bishops and priests from France who had helped to establish in their midst a relatively high civilization before the frontier, as Americans understand that term, had entirely passed beyond their limits. In fact, it was the French who gave to many of the communities of the region the names they still bear, for example, Saint Louis so called for Louis IX, Louisville named after Louis XVI, Marietta, Ohio, for Marie Antoinette, as well as Dubuque, Duluth, Marquette, and Vincennes which perpetuate the memory of a trader, an explorer, a missionary, and a military commander of French birth or extraction.

In assessing the contribution of the French missionaries, therefore, the part they played in helping to shape the early development of the oldest towns of the Middle West should not be forgotten. In their person was found a stabilizing factor, for it was the priests who made the ancient and rich traditions of Catholicism come alive which, in turn, provided a softening and refining effect on the rough and raw elements

[6] D. W. Brogan, *The American Character* (New York, 1944), p. 12.

of the frontier. What has been said of the missionaries' influence has, of course, pertained largely to the external and material aspects of life. But there was another realm, hidden from the historian's gaze, in the inner recesses of men's souls where that influence was known only to God and to the individual inhabitant who sought out the priest for counsel and guidance. Many of the French settlers were, indeed, heedless of the priest and their religious duties; yet at the end of life, if given an opportunity, most of them gladly availed themselves of the priest's comforting ministrations to make their peace with God. Finally, the story of the sufferings of the missionaries likewise made a deep impression on future generations. Nearly three-quarters of a century after the Jesuits had been expelled from the American missions, one observer recorded the effect that their sacrificial lives had upon the missionaries of his own time. And it was not mere sentiment or fancy that prompted his tribute when he wrote:

> That which they did in America was prodigious. They conquered more people by the word than the armies by the sword and by fire. Their victories cost no tears; the blood that they shed, was their own. Their glorious example still guides today the missionaries of Europe, and impels them to penetrate, often even at the peril of their lives, into the still unknown parts of America in order to bear the light of Christianity.[7]

We have now reached the span of years that lay between the end of the French regime and Louisiana's purchase by the United States in 1803. Its treatment is somewhat awkward in that while these forty years are rightly regarded as part of the colonial era, the European power that is normally identified with Louisiana's early history was no longer present. Yet if the story of Catholicism is to be brought abreast of the time when the area passed under American sovereignty—as has been done in the case of the colonies already discussed—it is necessary at this point to trace the development of the Louisiana Church as it occurred under the brief period of Spanish rule.

The news of the transfer to Spanish sovereignty was received with anything but pleasure by the French inhabitants. The tardiness of the Madrid government in assuming control gave time for the opposition to crystallize, and Antonio de Ulloa, who took over as temporary governor in March, 1766, had to face a rebellion which threw the colony into turmoil and uncertainty that lasted for the next three years. But

[7] Aimé-Martin, *op. cit.*, I, 817–818.

with the arrival in August, 1769, of Lieutenant General Alejandro O'Reilly, an able Irish-born, Spanish-trained officer, with a force of 3,000 troops, the rebellion was quickly crushed and five of the ringleaders were arrested and shot, including Nicolas Chauvin de la Lafrénière who as attorney general had been one of the chief agents in the Jesuits' undoing six years before. Thereafter the political disturbances gradually quieted down under O'Reilly and his successor as governor, Don Luís de Unzaga.

The transition from French to Spanish rule was at first not much more agreeable to the ecclesiastical authorities than it was for the more politically active laymen. Nonetheless, O'Reilly was formally received by the Capuchins at Saint Louis Church with a *Te Deum* and as much display of ceremony as their limited resources would allow. The change brought a transfer of the colony from the jurisdiction of the See of Quebec to that of Santiago de Cuba whose bishop, José de Echevarría y Elguezúa, was now made responsible for its spiritual well being. It was no easy task, for with the change of governments the already small number of priests was further reduced when some of the French Capuchins departed. And while Father Dagobert of Longory, the superior, and five or six other friars remained on, they were in no sense equal to the demands made upon them. The shortage of priests was emphasized in February, 1770, when Dagobert reported that there was need of eighteen religious if all the vacant posts were to be filled. Now that the Spaniards were in control, it was no longer necessary for them to maintain the military post and mission on the border between eastern Texas and western Louisiana, and in June, 1773, the government ordered San Míguel to be abandoned and there thus passed away the only Spanish mission in Louisiana. But its abandonment offered no substantial relief to the Capuchins, and when Governor Unzaga issued his report in July, 1772, he had high praise for the zeal of the friars, but once again he made it clear how inadequate their numbers were to carry on their obligations to a growing population living in widely scattered communities.

Reports of this kind had been reaching Cuba, headquarters of the Spanish government in Louisiana, from O'Reilly, Unzaga, and Father Dagobert for some time, and finally the Bishop of Santiago felt constrained to do something about it. His solution for the problem took the form of an appeal to the Spanish Capuchins to come to the assistance of their French confrères. The bishop's action brought grave misgivings to many, lest dissension should arise between the two groups of friars, and it was not long before it became evident that the fears had not been unfounded. In July, 1772, Father Cirillo de Barcelona reached New Orleans at the head of a band of four Spanish Capuchins, and before the Spanish superior had been very long on the scene the nationalist tensions were reflected in the long scolding letters that Cirillo was sending back to Cuba about his French brethren and their defects.

While there would seem to be little doubt about the zeal and tireless industry of the Spanish superior, he was a man of violent temper, given to sudden impulses, and possessed of a strong ambition to have his own way. They were characteristics that were to prove costly to the harmony of the Catholic community in Louisiana, as well as to the friendly relations with his own superior, Bishop Echevarría. The inter-Capuchin feuds gradually faded out, however, with the withdrawal of the French friars, and Father Dagobert's death in May, 1776, removed one of the last major links with the previous ecclesiastical regime. With Dagobert's passing Father Cirillo was not only superior of the friars, but likewise vicar general for Echevarría, and, too, pastor of Saint Louis Church. His position was a strong one, therefore, and it must be said to his credit that he made a serious attempt to enforce the canon law and to bring order out of the chaotic conditions that prevailed in some congregations. He endeavored, furthermore, to make provision for the expanding population by opening new parishes wherever it was found feasible. Among the newcomers were a group of immigrants from the Canary Islands who had come under the auspices of the government. Some of the islanders settled at the Post of Opelousas where the first church was built in 1776 and others at Galveztown at a later date where they became members of the parish of Saint Bernard. The German congregations were meanwhile growing also and were in need of more adequate facilities for religious worship.

But the principal worry of Father Cirillo on this score was probably making provision for the largest single group of immigrants to reach Louisiana in the second half of the century, namely, the Acadians. Their tragic story will be told in more detail elsewhere. We are concerned here only with those exiles of the deportation of 1755–1756 who found their way to Louisiana through the course of the next thirty years. The first arrivals reached the colony indirectly, that is, either by ship from the Atlantic ports or the West Indies to New Orleans, or by the overland route from Maryland, Pennsylvania, and Virginia whence they treked through the forests and descended streams like the Tennessee, Ohio, and Mississippi Rivers on flatboats. The first group arrived in the autumn of 1756 and from that time to 1784, when the nearly 1,600 who had found a temporary shelter in France were finally freed by the government to return to the new world, they continued to seek refuge in Louisiana. Most of them, of course, were farmers who took readily to the lands assigned to them in the southern and western parts of the colony.

It was at the Attakapas Post that the Acadians became the chief founders of the future Saint Martinville which came to be recognized as their principal center. Here along the Bayou Teche was the colorful region of Evangeline Labiche, the original of Longfellow's heroine. Yet here, too, as elsewhere, they maintained their identity, "as sharply distinguished from the Louisiana French Creoles as from the French-speaking Canadians,"[8] among whom others of their fellow exiles settled. The number who finally made their home in Louisiana has been the subject of considerable difference of opinion. That they were fairly numerous can be seen from the fact that in the early months of 1765 alone there were 656 Acadians to whom lands were allotted. In 1787, thirty-two years after the deportation, Governor Estevan Miró ordered a census to be taken, and at that time there were 1,587 Acadians in the colony. In all likelihood the total number did not exceed 2,500 and it may, indeed, have been closer to 2,000. In any case, it was a sizable population increase, and since they were practically all Catholics it was the Church's duty to provide for their spiritual care.

In 1776 Governor Unzaga was promoted to Caracas and in January, 1777, Bernardo de Gálvez, only twenty-nine years of age at the time, took possession as the new governor, and during the eight and a half years of his term of office he continued for the most part Unzaga's support of the Capuchins and their work for the Church. The new governor enhanced his popularity with the inhabitants by his liberal commercial policies and, too, by taking a native Louisiana woman for a wife. Thus when Spain declared war on Great Britain in June, 1779, and the colony

[8] Lawrence Henry Gibson, *The Great War for the Empire. The Years of Defeat, 1754–1757* (New York, 1946), p. 343.

became embroiled with the English in Florida, de Gálvez found better support for his campaigns than would otherwise have been true. Baton Rouge was taken from the British in September, 1779, Mobile fell the following March, and the prime objective then became Pensacola. Three attempts were made by de Gálvez to capture the port, but finally he succeeded with a force of over 7,000 men, including 725 Frenchmen and a Hibernian regiment of 580 Irish officers and soldiers. And with the fall of Pensacola in May, 1781, the British hold on West Florida was broken.

Spain had entered the conflict on France's pledge that if they were victorious against the English the Floridas would be restored to Spanish sovereignty. Insofar as the Catholic Church was concerned, the victory of the Bourbon powers was a boon since once the English occupied the province after 1763 Catholic activity had come practically to a standstill, except for the feeble congregation at Mobile. Large numbers of the former Spanish residents left Florida for Cuba and Mexico, and the only gain of strength, and that was not much, had come from the approximately 1,200 immigrants from Minorca. At Saint Augustine the bishop's residence was given over to the Church of England and the Franciscans' convent was made into a barracks for troops. Such was the measure of the Catholics' loss in the former Spanish colony. But with de Gálvez' conquest there was renewed hope for Catholicism in Florida.

Spain's acquisition of East and West Florida in the peace settlement of September, 1783, accentuated, however, a problem that had already given cause for concern, namely, the shortage of priests. In an effort to meet the need King Charles III had issued a decree in October, 1779, providing for six more Capuchins, and these friars had arrived early in 1781. Among them was Antonio de Sedella whose first entry in the register of Saint Louis Church for a baptism on February 3 heralded the opening of a career that would last for almost a half century and that would provide the Louisiana Church with some of the stormiest episodes in its history. For the present, however, the newcomers helped to relieve the shortage. But there was left much to be desired by way of the administration of ecclesiastical affairs, for example, the conferring of the Sacrament of Confirmation. The sacrament had never been conferred in the colony, and although Charles III had secured in 1779 from the Holy See a grant of faculties to the Bishop of Santiago for twenty years that enabled that prelate to sub-delegate the superior of the Louisiana missions for this purpose, there is no evidence that it was ever used.

The widespread irregularities in ecclesiastical administration, and the great distance from the seat of the diocese in Santiago de Cuba, thus made the naming of a bishop for Louisiana all the more imperative as the colony grew in population. Finally Charles III proposed to Pope Pius VI that an auxiliary bishop should be appointed for Santiago with the understanding that he would reside in Louisiana. On September 14, 1781, the king nominated Father Cirillo with the consent of Bishop Echevarría who agreed to set aside an annual sum of 3,000 pesos for his support. Cirillo was notified of his appointment as early as July, 1782, but the customary delays ensued and it was not until March, 1785, that he was consecrated in Cuba and only in August of that year did he return to New Orleans. But at last Louisiana had a resident bishop 103 years after La Salle had first explored the area and conceived his plan for a colony.

By the time that the bishop-elect departed for Cuba to be consecrated he had completed twelve and a half years of residence in Louisiana and was thus well acquainted with its problems. Generally speaking, they had been reasonably good years in the relations of Church and State, even if Cirillo had met with trouble from a civil official who apparently believed he had the authority to issue decrees of separation for quarreling husbands and wives. The Capuchin was quick to declare the lay official incompetent to judge in this matter, but in 1783 he encountered another kind of problem as pastor of Saint Louis Church when a murderer sought refuge within the church and invoked the right of sanctuary. Cirillo was somewhat doubtful about the law's applicability in this instance, but the civil and military authorities were not disposed to recognize any such right. As a consequence the case dragged on for some years and was the subject of a good deal of correspondence without it ever reaching a clear cut decision. Shortly before his departure Cirillo took the somewhat fatal step of announcing that he had named Sedella as temporary pastor during his absence, and that Fray Antonio was also now superior of the Capuchins and assistant vicar general of the Bishop of Santiago.

The return of Cirillo de Barcelona to New Orleans as a bishop in August, 1785, marked a number of changes in the Church's life. West Florida had been added to his jurisdiction for which he was to receive an increase of 4,000 pesos for his annual allowance. With his consecration the Spanish government also abandoned the policy of restricting the Louisiana mission stations solely to the Capuchins, with the result that before long secular priests and members of other religious orders began to make their appearance. In September, 1787, the new Diocese of Havana had been erected by the Holy See, and with that Louisiana and the two Floridas were transferred to the new see from Santiago. Since the Church was governed everywhere throughout the Spanish Empire by the *real patronato*, it was to be expected that it would be introduced into Louisiana. That is the explanation for the leading role taken by Charles III in the ecclesiastical changes just mentioned, and the system was continued and after 1785 all applications of priests for assignment in the colony passed through Sedella's hands as vicar general to the government officials for final approval. The majority of the inhabitants were still French, of course, and their resentment of the Spanish priests was one of the most unpleasant things that Bishop Cirillo and his fellow friars had to face. Moreover, Estevan Miró, who succeeded de Gálvez as governor in July, 1785, had a very high concept of his role as overseer of the Church, and when he found certain pastors whom he believed to be remiss in their duties he did not hesitate to issue peremptory orders to Cirillo for their removal.

In addition to the problems created by the government officials and various residents of the colony, there were also the accidents of nature that added to the woes of the churchmen. In 1779 a severe storm struck New Orleans and the Charity Hospital of Saint John was virtually ruined. But the disaster had the happy sequel of bringing forward Don Andres Almonester y Roxas, a wealthy layman, who provided the funds to rebuild the hospital, marking the first of many generous gifts of this devout layman to the cause of religion. On Good Friday, March 21, 1788, a devastating conflagration destroyed over 850 houses in the town along with Saint Louis Church and the bishop's residence. It was a sad blow from which New Orleans was some time in recovering. But most serious of all, perhaps, was the prevalence of a high degree of immorality among the nominally Catholic populace, many of whom ignored the Church completely and by their ridicule and open contempt of religion proved a sore trial to Cirillo and his priests in their attempts to restore the moral tone of the community.

No one could fairly charge Bishop Cirillo with a lack of the sense of his duty, even if at times the manner in which he chose to execute it would have profited from a greater concession to tact. Thus in the late summer and autumn of 1785 he conducted a visitation tour of New Orleans and the neighboring communities during which he made serious efforts to bring about a more orderly religious life, and in so doing aroused a good deal of criticism much of which was probably inevitable. When news reached him late in the autumn that Bishop Echevarría was ill, the Capuchin prelate suddenly terminated his activities and quite inadvisedly set out for Cuba on the pretext that his superior would need his help. Not only did the trip retard his work in Louisiana and Florida, but Echevarría was not in the least thankful for his coming without being summoned. The result was that the relations between the two bishops became seriously strained, and Cirillo's obstinacy about returning to Louisiana after repeated requests from the civil officials finally ended in his receiving strict orders to be gone. Nearly three years had passed since he had left the mainland, but in early July, 1788, he crossed to Florida where he was engaged in a visitation tour until the following summer. From the departure of Cirillo in the late autumn of 1785 until his return to New Orleans in August, 1789, Sedella had been acting head of the Church in Louisiana, a fact that was to tell against the auxiliary bishop's attempt to resume his position as the ranking churchman in the colony.

There was no doubt that the Capuchin bishop would have been better off had he remained on the scene, but even his incomplete visitation had taught him a great deal. There are few things that open the eyes of a bishop more effectively to the state of religion among those in his charge than a conscientious visitation of the parishes and missions of his jurisdiction, and in this respect Cirillo's experience was no exception. Among the things that had shocked and saddened him was the state in which he found the Negro population living. In many cases the masters had neglected entirely to see that the slaves had any religious instruction, and they had paid little heed to the regulations of the *Code Noir* concerning the blacks' labor on Sundays and holy days of obligation and those that pertained to the married state among them. Cirillo reported on these infractions to the Bishop of Havana who, in turn, informed the government at Madrid. As a consequence King Charles IV issued an edict in May, 1789, which demanded that spiritual ministrations be furnished regularly for the slaves, that the men and women be segregated, and that manual labor not be exacted of them on Sundays and holy days. The royal edict likewise emphasized the evils of concubinage and illegitimacy among the slaves and ordered the masters to rectify the abuses.

Needless to say, many of the planters were annoyed at the royal edict, and even more so at Bishop Cirillo for having reported the situation. They sought in every way possible to escape the regulations of the *Code Noir* by pleading such excuses as the lack of availability of priests to afford the slaves religious services. And though there was some increase thereafter in the number of Negro marriages, concubinage and illegitimacy among them remained almost the norm. Cirillo's reform efforts were not, to be sure, confined to the blacks, and his regulations against the Jansenist practice of keeping children from holy communion until they were fourteen years of age, and of the adults absenting themselves from the sacraments for years at a time, were not calculated to increase his popularity amid the atmosphere that then prevailed. While the bishop did his best to improve conditions, morals in Louisiana remained in a very low state in his time there, but for that matter, the same was true for years after he had left the colony.

One of the things that Bishop Cirillo's Florida visitation was not long in uncovering was that the growing English-speaking population called for English-speaking priests. Here again he had been anticipated by the King of Spain who as early as December, 1778, had commissioned two Irish-born priests to assist with the Minorcans in East Florida. These two recent students of the Irish College at Salamanca, Thomas Hassett and Michael O'Reilly, had volunteered for the missions and were assigned to help the hard pressed Minorcan priest, Father Camps, with his fellow countrymen on Florida's east coast. But Spain's declaration of war on Great Britain had intervened, and the result was that Hassett and O'Reilly were assigned to other work and had to wait until 1784 before they finally took up their labors in Florida. But their appointment helped to set a precedent for future action, and they became the first of twenty Irish priests who in as many years were to serve in Louisiana and Florida. Meanwhile Cirillo's appeal for priests who understood English did not go unanswered, and in 1787 Fathers William Savage, Gregory White, Constantine McKenna, and Michael Lamport came out and were assigned, the first three to the Natchez district and Lamport to Mobile. Before Louisiana's purchase by the United States fourteen more Irish priests followed, among whom were both seculars and regulars, the most noteworthy of the former being Patrick Walsh. The regulars numbered two Carmelites, a Dominican, and a Franciscan, and it was Fathers Constantine McCaffrey and John Brady who resumed where their Carmelite brethren had left off in Louisiana over seventy years before.

While Bishop Cirillo was absorbed with matters pertaining to his episcopal office, Fray Antonio – or Père Antoine as the French called him – was gaining stature at New Orleans. Sedella was thirty-two years of age at the time of his arrival in 1781, having been born at Sedella in Granada and as a young man having joined the Castile province of the Capuchin Order. He was a person of unquestioned ability who possessed considerable social grace and a suavity of manner that helped to win him a wide circle of friends and admirers. But this accommodating way often worked to the detriment of religion in that Sedella could apparently bring himself only with the greatest reluctance to become aroused over moral lapses among the local populace, and for that indulging spirit those who placed little premium on good morals were naturally grateful. We have already seen how he came to occupy important offices in the first years of Cirillo's episcopacy. In his early years he had likewise become *persona grata* to Governor Miró, and it was the latter who had nominated him for the post of pastor of Saint Louis Church to which he was appointed by Bishop Echevarría in July, 1787. Since June, 1782, he had also been director of the Charity Hospital, but he resigned that office in September, 1786, because of the press of so many other obligations, his withdrawal from the hospital being one of the few public posts that the friar ever voluntarily relinquished. He was already superior of the Capuchins, assistant vicar general, and assistant ecclesiastical judge when his position was further enhanced on July 21, 1787, by his appointment as Commissary of the Holy Inquisition, an appointment of which Miró was appraised from Cuba shortly after it had been made. It was a formidable concentration of power in the hands of a man of Sedella's ambition and aggressive nature, and in the sequel it proved to be a test to which his humility and balance were not equal.

It was scarcely surprising, then, that Bishop Cirillo should have gradually come to realize that ecclesiastical business was being conducted more and more at Sedella's bidding rather than at his own.

And the early favor that the friar had enjoyed with Governor Miró was dissipated once the latter discovered that he was siding with Miró's chief rival, the royal auditor, who happened to be from the same province in Spain as Sedella. Early in 1790 the bishop believed that he had found a way out of the difficulty, namely, to have Sedella appointed a chaplain at Pensacola. Miró was in agreement, but then a question arose about their right to remove a pastor from his parish and reduce him to the rank of a chaplain, whereupon the governor made the blunder of consulting the auditor. The latter lost no time in tipping off his friend at what was in store for him, and Sedella became fighting mad at this attempt to get him out of the way. And by this time he had a large enough following in New Orleans to cause Cirillo to think better of forcing the issue, so the bishop decided to recall the appointment lest, as he confessed to Miró, there should be an uproar in the city.

The next move in the game to get rid of Fray Antonio was to persuade him to return to Spain, a plan with which at first he seemed to agree, only to undergo a complete change of mind when the time came to depart and to remind the bishop and the governor that as Commissionary of the Holy Inquisition he possessed power and jurisdiction quite independent of either of them. And he further let it be known that if they did not desist he would open a war on the colony's non-Catholics on the score of their heretical beliefs. It was a shrewd move, for Miró was aware of Madrid's desire to attract Americans and other outsiders for economic reasons, and if Sedella were now to launch a heresy-hunt the prospect for success in that direction would be dim, indeed. But the arbitrary conduct of his highhanded confrère finally exhausted Cirillo's patience and he appealed to Governor Miró for assistance in removing him by force. The governor and the bishop agreed on a plan, and on the night of April 29, 1790, a sergeant and eight soldiers were sent to arrest the friar and take him to a waiting boat in the river whence he was deported to Spain. While his enemies in both Church and State rejoiced at his removal, Louisiana had by no means seen the last of Sedella, and a little over five years later he returned, this time in the company of the first ordinary of the new diocese of Louisiana! We shall have occasion, therefore, to meet Père Antoine again.

While the removal of Sedella brought temporary improvement to domestic affairs at New Orleans, the colonial regime was too badly ridden by factions for anything like real peace. The party of Governor Miró had the support of Bishop Cirillo, but on the other side was the royal controller or intendant, Don José Orne, who had with him Father Joaquín de Portillo, the new Spanish Capuchin pastor of Saint Louis Church. Joaquín was not lacking in energy, and his vigilance in behalf of the laws of the Church brought on feuds with the civil authorities over such matters as the unlawful burial of a Negro slave girl in a private garden in June, 1791, and in the following month a quarrel with Miró over Negro slaves who were found working on a holy day of obligation. A further source of trouble was the replacement of Saint Louis Church that had been destroyed in the fire of March, 1788. At that time there were only two chapels in New Orleans, namely, those at the Ursuline convent and Charity Hospital, but they were too small to accommodate the parishioners and there was a pressing need, therefore, for a new church. Once more Almonester proved his worth when he advanced the money to get the construction underway in the early spring of 1789. But between that time and the completion of the edifice in December, 1794, building operations were interrupted a number of times because of feuds between the *cabildo* or governing council and Almonester which, in turn, more often than not involved the clergy and the members of the *fabrique* as the board of *marguilliers* or church wardens came to be called in the time of the Spaniards.

The task of regularizing religious life was furthered, however, by the appointment of Father Teodoro Tirso Henrique Henríquez as an auxiliary vicar general and ecclesiastical judge for Louisiana by Filipe José Trespalacios y Verdeja, Bishop of Havana. This appointment of February, 1792, proved helpful in that Henríquez, with Cirillo's guidance, issued a set of rules for the clergy which established a more uniform code of clerical conduct before Henríquez quitted the colony in the summer of 1793. But it was more difficult to make any progress in the realm of education. As early as 1772 a government school had been opened by Governor Unzaga, but the French inhabitants were not sympathetic to having their sons educated under Spanish auspices, and consequently the school had not prospered, having no more than thirty students at any time and once dropping to only six. Even the arrival in 1787 of six Franciscans, several of whom were prepared and willing to teach, did not alter the situation since the French persisted in hiring tutors or sending their sons to private schools conducted by laymen. The Ursuline nuns, however, had meanwhile continued their faithful service to elementary education for the girls, and in 1748 the first American-born girl, Marie Turpin, entered the community as a lay sister. She was the daughter of a Canadian father and an Illinois Indian mother and had been raised under Catholic auspices in the Illinois Country. A second native, Martha Delatre, followed in 1756, and in 1778 for the first time the predominantly French character of the community was broken with the admission of two Spanish women. Here, too, Almonester was extremely generous in the sums of money he gave to the nuns for the repair of their convent and the building of a new chapel and additional classrooms.

As much as the Spaniards might have wished to follow their cherished policy of isolation from foreign influences, it proved impossible in Louisiana. In fact, that policy was in conflict with the government's ambition to further the colony's economic life. If trade and commerce were to flourish, obviously concessions would have to be made in the strict code of religious and ideological objectives that generally motivated the representatives of the crown. In this respect the influx of Americans proved to be the chief source of embarrassment, for most of them were either Protestants or persons of no particular religious affiliation. Since the Spaniards had taken over and made their own the French regulations concerning religion, the Madrid government sought a way out of the dilemma by decreeing that new settlers were not to be molested on the score of their religious faith, but their worship would have to be conducted in private. Inevitably, this led to a severe cleavage between the Catholic and non-Catholic elements of the population, a gap that widened as the number of the in-coming Americans increased. The problem was especially acute in regard to marriages of couples that involved either one or both Protestants since by an order of November 30, 1792, from King Charles IV such unions would have to be contracted before a priest, although the latter was not to use the customary formula nor was he to give the nuptial blessing. It requires no strain on the imagination to picture how regulations of this kind would produce friction and a worsening of relations between the varying religious groups.

As the eighteenth century drew to a close there were other outside influences that played as much or more havoc with the regulations governing the colony's religious activities than the non-Catholic Americans. One of these was the growth of Freemasonry. In 1793 a lodge was established in the vicinity of New Orleans of which a considerable number of Spanish officers, many Frenchmen, and influential creoles became members, and shortly thereafter a second lodge was set up. The philosophy of the Freemasons, of course, contributed to the damage that had already been done to the Catholic faith by the old Jansenist and Gallican schools of thought, and the growth of the spirit of the Enlightenment with its rationalist philosophy, of which the Freemasons were one manifestation, also took its toll. With these influences at work in Louisiana society for a score or more of years the ground was prepared for the revolutionary ideas that began to be exported from France in the last decade of the century. Thus by the time that Baron Francisco Luís Carondelet took over as governor in December, 1791, the colony was flooded with revolutionary tracts and pamphlets, the works of Voltaire and Rousseau were enjoying a revived popularity, and the general results on the traditional Catholic faith of the people were such as to reduce the number of those who faithfully practiced their religion to an almost insignificant minority.

In an atmosphere of this kind it was small wonder that Bishop Cirillo should have found cause for grave complaints. In September, 1789, he reported to Charles IV that he received so little support that he could not live and function in New Orleans as a bishop should, being unable to have even a pontifical Mass according to the rubrics prescribed by the Roman *Rituale*. This sort of thing had long since ceased to be news to Madrid, for successive governors had urged that something be done about the Church's sorry plight. The consequence was that in June, 1791, the King of Spain requested Pope Pius VI for a division of the See of Havana in the hope that if Louisiana were established as a separate diocese it might have a wholesome effect on the Church. Time had to be allowed for the intricate negotiations between Church and State called for by a case of this kind, and it was not until April 25, 1793, that the pope erected the Diocese of Louisiana and the Floridas with two canons to serve as the nucleus for a cathedral chapter. Thus three and a half years after the establishment of the See of Baltimore as the first American diocese, Rome erected the second diocese in territory that was soon to become part of the United States. But in the case of Louisiana, unlike Baltimore, the model followed was that for episcopal sees in Europe and throughout the Spanish dominions, that is, with a cathedral chapter attached.

With the establishment of the new diocese Bishop Cirillo was recalled and given an annual pension. The agnostics and scoffers, needless to say, were glad to see him go, for though he had failed to stem the tide of unbelief he had made an earnest attempt to withstand its corroding effects. Cirillo had set up several new parishes such as that at Baton Rouge in 1792 where Father Charles Burke was made pastor, and in the following spring Valenzuela (Plattenville) got a parish with the Spanish Capuchin, Bernardo de Deva, in charge. Unfortunately, the Capuchin prelate had lessened his own effectiveness by a bad temper and peremptory manner which got him into trouble not only with civil officials but also brought unnecessary grief upon his head from many of the laity. In fairness to him, however, it must be said that the religious situation during the eight years that he had served as a bishop in Louisiana was enough to try the patience of men of far more even disposition than he was. That the fault could not be laid mainly on Cirillo's untactful ways was proven by the time he died in October, 1799, when the situation was not markedly improved after four years of the conscientious rule of the able churchman who followed him.

The new Diocese of Louisiana and the Floridas was bounded on the north and east by the Diocese of Baltimore and on the south and west by the Dioceses of Durango and Linares. In fact, the area was so immense that no one was quite sure where certain of its boundaries left off. For the new post the Holy See approved the nominee of the Spanish crown, Luís Ignacio Maria de Peñalver y Cárdenas, Vicar General of the Diocese of Havana, a Cuban-born churchman who was forty-four years of age at the time. Pending his arrival in New Orleans, ecclesiastical affairs were in the hands of Father Patrick Walsh, one of the six Irish priests who had come out from Spain in 1792. Walsh had no easy task, but he managed the diocesan business with efficiency, tact, and sound judgment, and he had the good fortune to have the support of Governor Carondelet. Among Walsh's problems was that of maintaining clerical discipline, staffing the missions, and caring for the refugees from the French Revolution who had begun to reach Louisiana in considerable numbers, among them being three Poor Clare nuns who had come down the river from New Madrid, Missouri, in November, 1794. Another disastrous fire on December 8 of that year destroyed within a few hours over 200 houses in New Orleans, but two weeks later the city had the satisfaction of witnessing Father Walsh officiate at the formal dedication on December 23 of Saint Louis Cathedral whose generous donor, Don Almonester, was rewarded by the King of Spain with the right to sit in the sanctuary, to receive the liturgical kiss of peace at Mass and to exercise the right of patronage over the parish.

More than two years elapsed between the erection of the diocese and the arrival of its bishop, but on July 17, 1795, Peñalver finally reached New Orleans, and on the same boat Antonio de Sedella returned to the scene of his former activities. Following his deportation five years before, Sedella had appealed his case to the King of Spain, and although initially there had been a period in which the final outcome was in doubt, the fact that he had manouvered Miró and Cirillo into sending him back to Spain as a practical prisoner, rather than as a missionary who had voluntarily withdrawn from his post, told in his favor. The friar's New Orleans friends wrote numerous testimonials in his behalf and they showed their regard in a practical way by engaging a lawyer to plead his case. In the end he won a complete vindication, Miró and Cirillo were charged in his removal with having usurped powers that did not belong to them, and on October 22, 1794, King Charles IV issued a royal decree ordering Bishop Peñalver to reinstate the friar as pastor of the cathedral, news of which the bishop communicated to Governor Carondelet shortly after his arrival. The Capuchin was thereupon installed at his old post, but this was the only office that he held during Peñalver's administration of the see.

Bishop Peñalver did not lose much time in getting down to the duties of his new office, and in August he opened a diocesan visitation in the see city. He had brought with him Father Hassett, who with eleven years of service at Saint Augustine behind him, now joined the clergy of New Orleans. When it is recalled that Governor Carondelet had reported in January, 1794, that there were nearly 45,000 people living in the provinces of Louisiana and West Florida for whom there was need of a minimum of thirty-five priests and that only twenty-two were then available, it will be better understood how much the presence of the Irish priests meant to the new diocese with its twenty-two parishes separated in some cases by hundreds of miles. Yet of the twenty Irish who came in the period before the American purchase, all but four were engaged in Florida so that Louisiana did not profit proportionately from their services.

After having spent over three months surveying conditions in the diocese Bishop Peñalver completed a report for the Minister of Justice at Madrid which he signed on November 1. At the outset he made it clear that he had no illusions about the failure of his diocese to measure up to the reform canons of the Council of Trent. To Peñalver the toleration of Protestants in the colony encouraged the bad Catholics in feeling authorized to go on living without any religion at all. Many adults, he said, died without ever receiving the sacraments, and of the 11,000 souls in the cathedral parish, it was his belief that hardly more than 300 to 400 complied with the precept concerning the annual reception of the sacraments. This was especially noticeable, he thought, among the regiment of soldiers stationed in New Orleans of whom not more than thirty had discharged this duty in the previous three years. Moreover, not more than a fourth of the city's population attended Mass on Sundays, to say nothing of holy days of obligation. Most of the men, both married and unmarried, lived in concubinage, and the marriage contract was almost never entered into by the slaves. Observance of Lent and other days of fast and abstinence throughout the year was practically unknown, and it was the prelate's impression that in general there was little sense of religion in those who had been baptized.

When the bishop turned to the causes for this deplorable state of affairs, he ascribed it in part to the spirit of rebellion that pervaded so large a part of the populace. "Rebellion is in their hearts," he said, "and their minds are imbued with the maxims of democracy."[9] Were it not for the wisdom and vigilance of Governor Carondelet, he was of the opinion that there would long since have been an explosion, and unless a man of that caliber were to succeed Carondelet it was likely to happen in the future. The homes of the people, he reported, were filled with books against both religion and civil authority which they were permitted to read without let or hindrance, and at their dining tables they were wont to entertain themselves and their guests with shameful and sacrilegious songs.

What, then, were the bishop's recommendations? First, as to the schools, the Spanish school maintained by the government was properly

[9] Peñalver's report on religious conditions, November 1, 1795, Charles Gayarré, *History of Louisiana* (New York, 1854), III, 377.

enough conducted. But as for the French schools, only one had received a license from the government, and since Peñalver was ignorant of the religious faith professed by the teachers in these schools, he had prescribed for them the Spanish regulations in regard to education. While he had words of praise for the Ursulines' school, his disapproval of its French atmosphere was evident when he wrote:

their inclinations are so decidedly French, that they have even refused to admit among them Spanish women who wished to become Nuns, so long as these applicants should remain ignorant of the French idiom, and they have shed tears on account of their being obliged to read in Spanish books their spiritual exercises, and to comply with the other duties of their community in the manner prescribed to them.[10]

So much for the education of the girls, which on the whole he considered worthy of commendation, even if it was the faint praise that the Ursulines' education of the future mothers of the colony at least assured the fact that their convent training would make them "less vicious than the other sex." The elementary training of the boys in the Spanish school was satisfactory, but since there was no college to which they could be sent thereafter, these boys usually returned to their homes which were mostly situated in the country where, he said, "they hear neither the name of God nor of King, but daily witness the corrupt morals of their parents. . . ."[11] It was a dismal picture, surely, and the officials in Havana and Madrid under whose eyes Peñalver's report may have fallen must have wondered, indeed, what, if anything, could be done to restore religion to its rightful place.

Allowing for the bishop's training and background as exclusively Spanish, it is a bit difficult to feel much sympathy for him in ascribing the moral waywardness of his flock to the extraneous influences of the non-Catholics and their democratic ways. The point is that Louisiana morals were not appreciably better in the days before a non-Catholic American was ever known in the colony. Moreover, the lack of understanding of the French sympathies of the Ursuline nuns revealed something of the bishop's own narrow nationalist outlook, for it was scarcely to be expected that a group of French religious who had been on the scene nearly seventy years before Peñalver's coming, for over forty years of which the convent existed in an entirely French colony,

[10] *Ibid.*, III, 378.
[11] *Ibid.*, III, 379.

were likely to be very quick to change over to an acceptance of the Spanish language and Spanish customs.

The nationalist spirit of the Bishop of Louisiana and the Floridas showed in another way that militated against his success. Like all his predecessors who had exercised episcopal power in Louisiana from the time of Bishop Laval to his own day, Peñalver had no seminary for the training of native boys as future diocesan priests. He was thus left dependent on volunteer missionaries of any and all nationalities, both secular and regular. Fortunately, most of these men were zealous and conscientious priests, even if a few proved to be a source of grief to the bishop and to the faithful. But the fact that they were mostly non-Spanish was not at all to the prelate's liking. Of the twenty-two parishes in existence when he arrived, eight were in the hands of Irish priests, six were governed by Frenchmen, and the remaining eight parishes were held by Spanish Capuchins of whom five had already completed ten years of service and were, therefore, eligible to request their recall. It was not, indeed, an ideal situation, and the fact that they were separated in some instances by hundreds of miles from the see city was one of the principal obstacles which Peñalver encountered when he thought to convoke a diocesan synod of his clergy. In the end he had to give the idea up and instead he substituted a lengthy letter of instructions in which he outlined in detail the priests' duties to the whites and to the Negroes, as well as recalled to their minds the Church's regulations governing the administration of the sacraments, the keeping of careful parochial records, and certain admonitions pertaining to their own spiritual lives.

But where the bishop showed a lack of understanding of the situation in which he was placed, not to mention the lack of any perception of the political realities of the time, was in his attitude toward the non-Spanish clergy. Their failure to make any substantial headway in converting the non-Catholic Americans in their parishes, prompted Peñalver to remark that for the Spanish government to continue to furnish financial aid to foreign priests who did not know Spanish would "only serve to foment [in these people, that is, the Americans] the erroneous opinions they have received from their parents."[12] Peñalver's low opinion of the Americans now migrating in increasing numbers into

[12] Peñalver to Llaguno, November 1, 1785, Michael J. Curley, C.SS.R., *Church and State in the Spanish Floridas, 1783–1822* (Washington, 1940), p. 259. Curley prints parts of the Peñalver report not contained in Gayarré.

his diocese, as well as his judgment concerning the failure of the Irish and French priests to bring these people into the Church, represented an unhappy state of mind for a bishop situated as he was. True, he was in the colony only six years, but even had he been given a longer span of time in Louisiana it is doubtful if he would have found it possible to enter more sympathetically and realistically into the problems of his heterogeneous clerical body and the mixed population among whom they moved. It was evident that the habits and training of a lifetime were too strong to alter sufficiently the pronounced Spanish views of Bishop Peñalver to enable him to feel at home in the kind of social patterns that were then evolving in Louisiana and Florida.

In 1796 the bishop, accompanied by his secretary, Father Ysidro Quintero, and Father Antonio de Sedella, extended his visitation tour to the parishes along the Mississippi, to the most distant interior posts such as Natchitoches, and later to Florida. Besides Louisiana and East and West Florida, Peñalver was also responsible for the Catholics in the Illinois Country and in the area now occupied by the States of Arkansas and Missouri. It was small wonder, then, that this immense jurisdiction absorbed so much of his time in routine matters, and that during his administration he found it possible to establish only three new parishes. At no time did he ever have a sufficient number of priests. New Orleans required for Saint Louis Cathedral, the only parish in the city, a pastor and several assistants, and priests had likewise to be found for the chaplaincies of the Ursuline convent, the hospital, and the military barracks. There would seem to have been no dearth of priests who visited the see city for brief periods, but many of these were mere birds of passage and were soon on their way again. In fact, in the years between 1795 and 1802 there was record of no less than twenty-two priests who were there at one time or another, including seculars, Capuchins, Carmelites, Franciscans, and one Mercederian. But not many of these were men on whom Peñalver could count for any prolonged or sustained assistance. And besides the cathedral parish there were other congregations that were now becoming fairly large in size, for example, Saint Bernard at Nueva Galvez — for many years the only parish below New Orleans — Saint Charles Borromeo at the German Coast, Ascension Church at present-day Donaldsonville, and Saint Gabriel Parish at Iberville. Moreover, until Spain's cession of Louisiana to France in October, 1800, Baton Rouge and Feliciana were in

Peñalver's charge, although thereafter they passed to the Bishop of Havana as part of West Florida which Spain had retained.

One of the most remarkable pastors whom the bishop met on his visitation tour was Michel Bernard Barrière who served at Saint Martin's at the Attakapas Post from 1795 to 1804. Barrière became noted for the trips he made in and around the Bayou Teche in search of strayed Catholics, and the mixed character of his flock was revealed when Peñalver visited his parish in October, 1796, and ordered him to keep separate registers for the whites, blacks, and those of mixed blood. Father Barrière was to become the center of a somewhat celebrated case in Church-State relations within a few years which we shall mention later. After his visit to Saint Martin's the bishop proceeded to other stations and finally brought his visitation tour to a close in November at Natchitoches where he remained almost a week. This remote spot had had a checkered history, and for long periods the parish had been without a resident pastor. During these vacancies the Catholics had to carry on as best they could, and in 1794 a bizarre character, David Cantor, undertook to hold religious services until he was finally apprehended by the authorities. In spite of the fact that the local clergy were augmented in these years by a number of priests fleeing from the French Revolution, the rate of deaths, retirements, and incapacitations for one reason or another generally exceeded the rate of replacements. And conscious as he was of the risks involved in entrusting to strange priests the care of distant missions, Peñalver always tried first to give the newcomers a period of trial at close quarters so that he might test their priestly fitness for parochial assignments.

On August 1, 1797, a new governor was named for Louisiana in the person of Manuel Gayoso de Lemos. The internal peace was not improved by Gayoso's laws concerning the non-Catholic residents. Shortly after taking office he issued the customary new legal regulations which included the following: liberty of conscience was not to be allowed hereafter beyond the first generation; children of non-Catholic parents were to be baptized as Catholics and refusal to comply was to be punished by banishment; and no non-Catholic ministers were to be allowed in the colony. In all of this the governor and the bishop worked in harmony, these regulations representing to their minds a necessary procedure for protecting the faith of the majority.

It was about this time, too, that Peñalver first began to detect in some parishes a recalcitrant spirit on the part of certain *marguilliers* who were intent on asserting their right to a voice in the naming of pastors when a parish became vacant through the death or retirement of the incumbent. The bishop little realized, of course, that here was the foreshadowing of one of the most severe crises that episcopal authority would have to face in Louisiana in the years to come. Meanwhile Peñalver's reports to the officials of the crown continued to be written in a highly pessimistic vein, and in 1799 he complained bitterly about such things as the tolerance of prostitutes around the military barracks, the influence of the Masonic lodges, the scandalous conduct of certain magistrates who were living in open sin, and the mounting threat to religion from the loose living people who were entering the diocese from the western parts of the United States.

On the subject of the Americans, the Bishop of Louisiana and the Floridas had ample cause for concern. As we have said, Peñalver showed little comprehension of the complicated character of the population, but in fairness to him it should be stated that one could scarcely imagine a more lawless, immoral, and dangerous lot of Americans anywhere at that time than those who began descending on the Southwest shortly after the American Revolution. That is not to say that all those who then turned their eyes in the direction of Louisiana, or of Florida, were of that kind; but the predominance of this type made it understandable that the conservative Cuban-born bishop should see in them one of the major perils to the Catholic faith of his people. This is not the place to trace the tangled story of Spanish-American relations after the Revolution. Suffice it to say, the differences between the two nations were highlighted when Spain suddenly closed the Mississippi River to navigation by Americans in June, 1784. At first an effort was made to reach a solution of the difficulties through diplomacy. But the prolonged negotiations of John Jay, then Secretary for Foreign Affairs, and Don Diego de Gardoqui, first Spanish Minister to the United States, resulted in a draft of a treaty which the American Congress found unacceptable in August, 1786, by reason of its provision for closing the Mississippi to Americans for the next twenty-five years. And with that the two governments made no further move for some years to reach an agreement.

This failure of diplomacy by no means ended the matter. Too many people were economically dependent on the Mississippi as a lifeline of trade, or were anticipating it as the channel to a fortune, to permit the situation to remain static. The result was almost a decade of free-lance efforts by traders, land speculators, spies, backwoodsmen, Indian chiefs, and shady characters like James Wilkinson of Pennsylvania and the half-breed, Alexander McGillivray, to settle the fate of the Southwest on their own terms. The fantastic situation created by these people continued to run its course until October, 1795, when Thomas Pinckney succeeded in getting Spain to agree finally to recognize the boundary claims of the United States as the Mississippi on the west and the thirty-first parallel on the south. Moreover, the Treaty of San Lorenzo also contained the important provision that Americans were to be accorded the right of navigation of the Mississippi and of depositing their goods at New Orleans with the right of reshipment from there for a period of three years. The muddled character of this episode was due to the fact that Spain, long since in decline, was unable to defend the far flung frontiers it claimed, and the new government of the United States was still so bedeviled by pressing problems on the Atlantic seaboard that it was either ignorant of or unable to control the rough elements of its western population. But in the meantime the feuds and intrigues that filled the more conservative residents of the Southwest with foreboding, and the irrepressible onward march of Americans carrying their lawless ways and loose morals into the Spanish colony, gave justification for the grievances of Bishop Peñalver.

By this late date, however, complaints lodged at Madrid were often ignored by the enfeebled government of Charles IV, or when action was taken it proved ineffective to remedy the evil. An example of the latter was the king's orders for the destruction of the Masonic lodges in Louisiana which inflicted no more injury on them than the uneasiness of a temporary scare. And the local government, too, was weak, among other reasons because of excessive changes in personnel. Twice within a year the governor was changed, and in June, 1801, Juan Manuel de Salcedo arrived as the ninth and final Spaniard to rule over Louisiana. A man of good morals in his private life, Salcedo was now too old to keep a firm grip on the reins, with the result that the confusion in public affairs only increased. One of the worst calamities of Salcedo's administration was the smallpox epidemic in which the medical authorities prescribed inoculation, or the inducing of a mild form of the disease to render persons immune. Unfortunately, what was then intended as a purely scientific remedy became embroiled in a theological dispute when Peñalver and his clergy—seconded by the governor—forbade inoculation as an unwarrantable experiment that endangered the patient's life. Public opinion became aroused and there was severe criticism of the clergy, especially after more than 600 Negro slave children died of the disease.

Before the diocese had reached the ninth anniversary of its establishment it lost its first bishop. On July 20, 1801, Luís Peñalver was promoted to the archiepiscopal See of Guatemala, and he departed in early November. While Peñalver's episcopacy had been able to show little progress in Louisiana and Florida, his going was a loss in the sense that he had at least maintained the idea of a high moral standard before the public mind, and he had been the source of strength and comfort to the religiously inclined part of the population. The Spanish crown lost no time in nominating a successor in the Spanish Franciscan, Francisco Porro y Peinado, who happened to be living in Rome at the time and who was consecrated there less than two weeks after his predecessor had left New Orleans. The sixty-two-year-old prelate delayed his voyage to America because of the winter, but he set out via Genoa in the late spring and by early June, 1802, he had reached Málaga. By this time, however, the terms of the secret Treaty of San Ildefonso of October, 1800, in which Louisiana had been ceded back to France, had become known, and the second Bishop of Louisiana and the Floridas was now confronted by an entirely new situation. Rather than embark for a diocese that was now part of the dominions of the formidable Napoleon Bonaparte, Bishop Porro postponed his departure and in the end he was appointed Bishop of Tarazona in Spain and never saw his American see.

The awkward provisions made by the Archbishop-elect of Guatemala for governing the diocese after his departure contributed at this point to a period of canonical uncertainty that was to plague the Church well beyond the date when Louisiana was purchased by the United States. Briefly the case was as follows. Peñalver had left Louisiana before he had received the bulls elevating him to Guatemala; therefore, in the strict canonical sense, he was still ordinary of the diocese. Wishing to insure the fact that the Church in Louisiana and Florida would be in responsible hands, the bishop had appointed Thomas Has-set, one of the two cathedral canons, as administrator about three weeks before he left, and on the day he departed he named Patrick Walsh as assistant to Hassett. This arrangement ignored the other canon, Francisco Pérez Guerrero, who in his chagrin protested Walsh's appointment to the governor, and continued to challenge it until his death early in 1803. Once Peñalver was entirely quit, canonically speaking, of Louisiana, Hassett had doubts concerning his own canonical status. In the absence of a metropolitan, he turned, therefore, to Juan José Diaz de Espada y Landa, Bishop of Havana, as the nearest suffragan bishop for advice. But the latter felt incompetent to render a judgment, and in the end Hassett carried on until his own death in April, 1804. At that point Walsh assumed full control and went unchallenged for an entire year until his authority was called in question from two sources, namely, by Sedella in Louisiana and by Bishop Espada insofar as Walsh's exercise of power in the Floridas was concerned.

But before matters had reached that phase the rapidly changing political picture had added far greater complications. In Bonaparte's plans to revive the French empire in the new world, Louisiana had come to occupy a prominent place. It was relatively easy for him to coerce Spain, and in the secret Treaty of San Ildefonso of October, 1800, he forced the transfer of the colony back to France, although Spain continued to govern Florida. As word of this treaty gradually leaked out it brought profound anxiety to President Thomas Jefferson who foresaw grave consequences for the Americans with France at the mouth of the Mississippi. The president, therefore, instructed Robert Livingston, American Minister to France, to initiate a move to purchase a tract of land that the United States might later make into a port for themselves. Fortunately, fresh dissensions had meanwhile arisen between Bonaparte and Britain in Malta and Hanover, and the likelihood of a renewal of war in Europe caused the first consul to make a sudden shift in his plans for an overseas empire and to propose the sale of the entire colony. Agreement was reached in late April, 1803, and Louisiana thus passed to still another master, and that less than two months after Clement de Laussat, the French commissioner sent to take over from the Spaniards, had made his belated appearance at New Orleans.

If the prospect of a French government at the mouth of the Mississippi had made Jefferson feel uneasy, it had been no less disturbing to those residents of Louisiana who cherished their Catholic faith. Since 1790 the Church in France had suffered a severe persecution, the details of which were familiar to the Louisiana Catholics from the refugees who had sought a home among them. The thought of passing under a regime that was the heir of the Jacobins naturally filled them with misgivings. Thus when the Spanish officials had notified Father Hassett to inform the priests of the impending change to France, the majority of the clergy had declared they would leave. They had been receiving a small monthly salary from the King of Spain which they could not conceive the French as continuing; moreover, those who were Spaniards felt a deep distaste at the thought of living under a French government. As it turned out, less than half of the twenty-six priests actually left Louisiana, but the Church suffered a real blow when sixteen of the twenty-seven Ursuline nuns departed for Cuba in May, 1803, after having received permission from Charles IV of Spain to retire to Havana. The depletion in the ranks of the priests and religious was one of the most grievous burdens that Father Hassett had to bear in the final months before his death in April, 1804.

In the few months that he had spent in the colony the conduct of the French commissioner had not been such as to offer much assurance to the Catholics. For a reason that is not clear, he summarily removed Father Michel Barrière, pastor of Saint Martin's Church at Les Attakapas, and appointed in his place an ex-Jesuit by the name of Etienne Viel. Laussat took this action without any reference to the ecclesiastical authorities who protested vigorously, contending that Barrière was the rightful pastor. Both Barrière and Viel had come out directly from France some years before as refugees from the revolution, and their differences now caused factions to form about each with a scandalous climax on one particular Sunday when the two priests and their respective supporters tried to prevail at the church. The case dragged on and was still not settled when the Americans took over. Governor William C. C. Claiborne sought the advice of Father Walsh who stoutly defended Barrière's right to the parish, and finally the latter was reinstated at Saint Martin's and his rival withdrew to France where he died some time later. Among the many perplexing problems of his new office that Claiborne reported to James Madison, Secretary of State, this uproar over parochial rights was one, but the report of May, 1804, would not be the last time that Madison would be confronted by vexing questions relating to Catholicism in Louisiana.

With the colony's formal cession to the United States in November, 1803, Father Hassett felt bound to inform the Bishop of Baltimore of the state of the Church there, for, as he told Carroll, he had no doubt that it would soon fall to the bishop's lot to provide for its future. There were then twenty-one parishes of which some were vacant for lack of priests. Hassett rehearsed what had happened when he had interrogated the priests at the time that the colony was ceded to France, only four having then indicated that they would continue. And then reflecting the almost equal uneasiness felt by many of Louisiana's Catholics about the Americans, he added, "whether many more than the same number will remain under that of the U.S. God only knows."[13] He was glad to say that the cathedral was in good condition and that its appointments were decent and adequate for divine services. As for himself, he felt that he would have to leave Louisiana on account of his failing health, but his assistant, Father Walsh, for whom he had high praise, had decided not to abandon his post.

It was hardly a message that would bring cheer to the heart of one who was already overburdened with the responsibilities of an immense diocese. Yet one aspect of affairs in Louisiana was to receive a fairly prompt and satisfactory solution before Bishop Carroll had been formally invested with jurisdiction over the vacant see. Naturally concerned about the future of her community, Mother Thérèse de Saint Xavier Farjon, superior of the Ursulines, had written to Carroll in early November, 1803, to inquire how they were to fare under the United States. The bishop referred the letter to the Secretary of State at Washington with a recommendation of the sisters, and in March, 1804, the superior wrote directly to President Jefferson. The Ursulines' misgivings were entirely set at rest when the president told the nuns that he knew of the good work that had been done by their institution, and they breathed more easily when he added, "Be assured it will meet with all the protection my office can give it."[14]

[13] Hassett to Carroll, New Orleans, December 23, 1803, Edward I. Devitt, S.J. (Ed.), "Letters from the Archiepiscopal Archives at Baltimore," *Records of the American Catholic Historical Society of Philadelphia*, XX (1909), 273.

[14] Jefferson to Farjon, Washington, May 15, 1804, Henry C. Semple, S.J., *The Ursulines in New Orleans* (New York, 1925), pp. 61–62.

Would that all the problems of the Church in Louisiana might have been settled as readily as that of the Ursuline convent. But such was not to be, for by spring of 1805 Father Antonio de Sedella had broken into open war against Father Walsh's authority, and had carried along with him not only the *marguilliers* of the cathedral but Governor Claiborne as well, and the Church was threatened with a real schism. Both Carroll and Walsh had previously informed the Congregation de Propaganda Fide of the change of sovereignties in Louisiana and had requested the Holy See to direct them how to proceed. Replies were despatched to both men in late September, 1805, to the effect that Walsh's authority was now at an end, and Carroll was to assume the post of administrator until a bishop should be appointed. If it was unwelcome news to the Bishop of Baltimore who already had more than he could properly attend to, it probably came as a relief to Father Walsh who, in any case, was not to be affected for very long since his faithful years of service were terminated by death on August 22, 1806.

PART THREE

THE ENGLISH MISSIONS

CHAPTER TWELVE

MARYLAND

When one turns from the story of the North American colonies of Spain and France to that of the Catholics in the English settlements that stretched from Massachusetts to Florida, he encounters a far different world. In the case of both the Spaniards and the French – with the exception of the latter's few Huguenot settlements – the religious character of their North American undertakings was entirely Catholic, even if the spread of that faith, as we have seen, was frequently not their principal motive. In the matter of time, too, there was an important difference. The first permanent English settlement of 1607 at Jamestown in Virginia lacked only fourteen years of being a century after Ponce de Léon had attempted to settle Florida in 1521. In fact, Spain was almost as far in advance of the French as it was of the English, for Ribault's colony at Port Royal Sound in 1562 and Laudonnière's effort of two years later on the Saint John's River – both Huguenot in origin and both destined to end in quick failures – left it to Quebec in 1608 to provide France's first permanent settlement on this continent.

Throughout most of the sixteenth century the preeminence of Spanish leadership in western Europe was an established fact by reason of its superior land armies, its fleets, and the tremendous wealth drawn from its overseas dominions. But as the century drew to a close this preeminence began to fade, and although the debeat of the Armada in July, 1588, did not at once usher England into a commanding position on the seas, it did herald a downward course for Spain that continued almost uninterruptedly through the seventeenth and into the eighteenth century. And the more that Spain declined the more marked was the emergence of the English and the Dutch as the new masters of the seas and the lords of trade and commerce.

During the course of the religious revolution that swept over much of western Europe in the early sixteenth century Spain had become so closely identified with Catholicism that the fading fortunes of its European position and of its overseas empire were associated in many men's minds with a falling off of Catholic strength. In fact, a unifying theme in the English propaganda for colonies was that every advance made against the Spaniards was a blow against the papacy, and if there was one subject that was sure to win an enthusiastic hearing among Englishmen of wealth and rank it was anything that seemed calculated to lessen the power and prestige of the Catholic Church. Running simultaneously, then, with rivalry over the command of the seas and the trade that passed across them, was the eagerness with which the exploits of John Hawkins, Martin Frobisher, Humphrey Gilbert, Walter Raleigh, Francis Drake, and the other Elizabethan freebooters were credited as services to the Protestant cause. It was a favorite subject with English ministers of religion who were among the most outspoken and consistent promoters of a colonial empire. As one writer has said:

> One particular political issue the clergy kept alive. That was the danger to England from Catholic Spain. The Protestant clergy unanimously agreed that Spain must be thwarted in her colonial empire. From the reign of Elizabeth to the end of James's life, and later, the preachers waged an incessant and bitter war against Spain. . . . With the increase of Puritanism, the attack on Spain intensified, and English Puritans on two continents continued an ideological war against Spain. . . . The preservation of the Protestant faith and the English realm depended upon clipping the wings of the Spanish eagle. This argument cannot have failed to carry conviction to many a zealous English Protestant who may have been deaf to other pleas.[1]

Thus there was joined to avarice for material wealth, anxiety to grasp unclaimed lands, and jealousy for the mastery of the seas, as leading motives for English efforts in the new world, a determination to crush Catholicism. If today statesmen and men of business should have a religious motive for their actions they are usually careful to

[1] Wright, *Religion and Empire*, pp. 155–156.

conceal it beneath a mask of liberal toleration. But their sixteenth-century predecessors, reflecting the intensely religious interest of the age in which they lived, had no such scruples. Their religious outlook deeply colored their political and commercial undertakings and they were at no pains to conceal the fact. The triumph of materialism was still far in the future, and while the undisguised motive of many of these sixteenth-century men was greed for gold and silver, religion did not cease to be a prime factor in their political and commercial calculations.

By the time that England had entered seriously into the competition for an empire in North America the religious scene in western Europe had radically changed from what it had been in the days when a Vasco da Gama, a Columbus, and a Cabot were staking out the first claims of the European powers to possessions overseas. In the intervening century the German world had witnessed the outbreak of the Protestant Revolt, and after a generation or more of maneuvering, sparring, and outright war the Peace of Augsburg of September, 1555, foreshadowed the permanent division of the German-speaking lands between the Catholic and Protestant camps. Nor was there a clear cut victory for either side in France. Although the Catholics still predominated at the opening of the seventeenth century in the posts of power, the Edict of Nantes in April, 1598, had represented a compromise in the sense that it gave a temporary check to the devastating civil war that had wracked the country ever since 1562. In Spain an increasingly strong central government had guarded against the incursion of Protestantism, and the sincerely devout Catholic masses were in this way saved from the divisive conflicts that weakened the Germans and the French.

In England the religious revolution of the sixteenth century was in many ways unique. What Hilaire Belloc called the 'English accident,' in characterizing the separation of the nation by Henry VIII from the spiritual allegiance it had paid to the Holy See for over a thousand years, afforded an example of religious change imposed from above. Yet it would be quite misleading to picture the severance of the ties that had bound England to Rome as solely the doing of the king. Had there not taken place in the hearts of many Englishmen a deep defection from the old faith it would scarcely have been possible for Henry VIII and his minions to accomplish the fundamental changes brought about before the death of the king in 1547. Even if one is not prepared to accept fully the dictum of George Macaulay Trevelyan that it was anti-clericalism "equally felt among the learned and the vulgar,"[2] that made possible the break with Rome and the dissolution of the religious houses, it was true that the state of the English clergy – and the attitude of the laity toward them – was not a wholesome one. When confronted by the royal demand that they repudiate the pope and swear allegiance to Henry VIII as the supreme head of the Church in England, virtually the entire hierarchy, along with a majority of their priests and religious, gave way. Their action made real the remark of Saint John Fisher, Bishop of Rochester, the sole member of the hierarchy to withstand the king, when he told a delegation of bishops sent by Henry VIII to the Tower to try to persuade him to take the oath of supremacy, "The fort is betraid even of them that shoulde have defended yt. And therfore, seeing the matter is thus begunne and so faintly resisted on our parts, I feare we be not the men that shall see the ends of the miserie."[3] This is not the place to recount the complicated history that lay behind the churchmen's defection, although their state was neatly summarized by England's fallen chancellor, Saint Thomas More, when he described them to his daughter, Margaret Roper, as "a weake Cleargie lackinge grace to stand to their learninge."[4]

In any case, by the time that the English established their first permanent colony in Virginia in 1607 nearly a half century had passed since the enactment in 1559 of the Elizabethan Acts of Supremacy and Uniformity with their accompanying oaths, measures that put the kingdom once more – and this time permanently – in the Protestant camp after the brief reign of the Catholic Queen Mary Tudor. It was a half century that was used to excellent advantage by the promoters of the Protestant cause, and if Anglican and Puritan, Presbyterian and Quaker, disagreed seriously about doctrine and thus nullified the Act of Uniformity much to Elizabeth's chagrin, they had no trouble in agreeing on the exclusion of Roman Catholics from every aspect of public life. These were the years when Catholic activity was gradually forced

[2] G. M. Trevelyan, *English Social History. A Survey of Six Centuries. Chaucer to Queen Victoria* (London, 1942), p. 101.

[3] François Van Ostroy, S.J. (Ed.), "Vie du bienheureux Martyr Jean Fisher, Cardinal, Évêque de Rochester (1535)," *Annalecta Bollandiana*, XII (1893), 159.

[4] Elsie Vaughan Hitchcock (Ed.), *The Life of Sir Thomas Moore, Knighte, written by William Roper, Esquire* (London, 1935), p. 78.

underground and the long night of the penal age, destined to endure until the early nineteenth century, descended upon the Catholic community. Under these circumstances it was to be expected that the spirit in which England's North American settlements were born should be hostile to Catholicism, and given the vigor and persistence with which that spirit was cultivated throughout the entire colonial period, it should occasion no surprise that enmity toward the Catholic Church emerged as the English colonists' most viable and deeply cherished prejudice.

It was in June, 1578, that Queen Elizabeth I issued her patent to Sir Humphrey Gilbert for his ill fated colony and thus formally inaugurated English colonization in the new world. Encouraged by Walter Raleigh, the Anglican chaplain to the English ambassador to Paris, Richard Hakluyt, not long thereafter prepared an elaborate treatise on the advantages of American colonization for the queen which he presented in person in 1584. Hakluyt's *Discourse of Western Planting*, to give it the abbreviated title, laid great stress on the need to combat the Spaniards in order to counteract the spread of their superstitious worship in America, and, too, to put an end to their cruel enslavement of the Indians, evidence for which he drew from the works of Bartolomé de las Casas, O.P. The young minister was likewise at pains to give a detailed refutation of Alexander VI's right to divide the new world between Portugal and Spain, as he was to convince Her Majesty of how much colonies in North America would mean to the prestige and economic welfare of her kingdom. It was a highly persuasive document in which the author used every argument that he could think of to win over the queen, and concerning the motives that prompted him one student has remarked, "none was stronger than his zeal for the Protestant faith, with its corollary hostility to Catholic Spain." [5]

While there is no doubt that Hakluyt's work exercised a strong influence in favor of England's colonizing ambitions and that his various arguments were used over and over again, his exhortations for the conversion of the native peoples to the Protestant faith so that they might be saved from the superstitious beliefs of the Spaniards and Portuguese, remained largely a dead letter. True, there were exceptions like John Eliot and John Mayhew; but in the main the English settlers gave little heed to the spiritual welfare of the redmen with the result

[5] Wright, *op. cit.*, p. 48.

that the colonial period came to a close with very few Indians having been evangelized by the Protestants. Yet the propaganda value of this approach, insofar as it might be directed against the Spanish papists, did not lose its force, for the man who could mount any kind of argument against the pope and those who acknowledged his authority was as likely to win a sympathetic hearing in 1760 as was true two centuries before. A leading Protestant historian summarized the point when he stated:

> Thus from the beginning of the agitation for English colonization of America to the very outbreak of the War for Independence the Protestant crusade against Roman Catholicism was a major motive in projecting, in planting, and in extending the English colonies in America.[6]

Amid the stir that accompanied the early stages of the colonizing movement it was natural that English Catholic families of means should have become interested in the possibility of finding in the new world the freedom of worship that was denied to them at home. Unfortunately, the extant evidence on these projected undertakings is slight and one cannot, therefore, speak of them in any detail. But that several Catholic lords, among them Sir George Peckham and Sir Thomas Gerard, were associated with Gilbert's attempt to found a colony in Newfoundland in 1583, is certain. While the Catholics would seem to have been free to practice their faith there, Gilbert's death at sea while returning to England, and the colony's abandonment soon thereafter, deprived the project of any chance to set a lasting precedent in this regard. Nor did a similar effort in 1605 involving Thomas Arundel, another Catholic lord, fare any better. And when the idea of founding a refuge in the new world was presented to Father Robert Parsons, who with Blessed Edmund Campion had opened the Jesuit mission in England in 1580, he vetoed it as too risky an investment for the Catholic lords' money. Parsons feared that an enterprise of this kind would further deplete the dwindling Catholic ranks in England, and he felt that the chance of converting the Indians was too uncertain to warrant the venture on that score. In consequence participation in the colonizing of North America on the part of more than an occasional Catholic here and there was postponed for about a generation.

Meanwhile Protestant Englishmen were deterred by no such doubts.

[6] William Warren Sweet, *Religion in Colonial America* (New York, 1942), p. 12.

The doubts earned by earlier commercial corporations like the Muscovy and Levant Companies prompted others to seek their fortune through organizations of this type, and soon the East India Company and the London Company came upon the scene. It was the latter, operating under the special patronage of the crown, that succeeded in planting the first enduring English colony at Jamestown in 1607. During the next 125 years twelve more permanent colonies were either founded or taken over by the English in the coastal regions between the vague frontier of New France on the north and that of Spanish Florida to the south. In all but three of the thirteen Catholics figured in only a negative way as the subject of penal measures of one kind or another, and that whether there were any subjects of the pope present or not. For example, when Sir George Calvert, whom we shall meet later as the founder and first proprietor of Maryland, went to Virginia as a member of the London Company in 1629 to seek a home for his coreligionists, it was soon made known to him that in this predominantly Anglican colony there was no place for Catholics. In Massachusetts Bay no Catholic was known to have appeared during the first twenty years or more of the colony's life; yet that did not prevent the Puritan government from enacting an anti-priest law in May, 1647.

In this way there gradually evolved a fixed pattern of treatment for Catholics in English America, and when the final one of the thirteen colonies was brought into being in 1732 by a charter granted to James Oglethorpe and his associates by King George II, full religious freedom was promised to all future settlers of Georgia "except papists." The century and a quarter during which the colonies were forming was in consequence a dismal time for Catholics, and there would seem to be little gain in rehearsing here the numerous and repeated anti-Catholic steps taken by these early American governments. We shall, therefore, confine ourselves in the main to three colonies, namely, Maryland, New York, and Pennsylvania, where for at least a brief span of years, Catholicism knew something approximating an organized existence, with mention of certain key events which from time to time related to the Church and its faithful in the neighboring parts of English-speaking America.

Before treating the half century within which the three colonies in question became further extensions of the English crown in the new world, something should be said about the general state of the Catholics in England in the early seventeenth century. By the year of Maryland's establishment in 1634 a century had already passed since Henry VIII's Act of Supremacy had been placed on the statute books in June, 1534. In the intervening time Catholics had known alternate periods of persecution, uncertainty, and hope as the politico-religious pendulum swung back and forth. But once the Elizabethan measures of 1559, which we mentioned above, had been enacted and put into execution the expectations that the dominant Protestant trend would be reversed faded from the minds of all except the most optimistic Catholics. True, the proscribing of the old faith was the occasion for the migration of numerous Englishmen to the continent where they established ecclesiastical colleges and convents that they could not have at home. And it was from one of these, the English College at Douai in the Low Countries, that the first four priests arrived back in England in 1574 to begin their hazardous assignment in their native land. Six years later Robert Persons and Edmund Campion landed from the continent to open the Jesuits' English mission, and between these two groups of priests not only were many held in their Catholic allegiance, but others who had lapsed were won back and even a few converts were brought over from Protestantism.

But the pull away from Catholicism was far stronger than its attraction for Englishmen in the last forty years of the sixteenth century. The vehemently Protestant spirit of the government was, of course, a prime factor, but external events also contributed to the decline of the traditional faith. The excommunication of the queen by Pope Pius V in 1570, no matter how well intentioned, proved a disaster of the first order for the harassed English Catholics, and the defeat of the Armada eighteen years later removed any serious hope they might have entertained of assistance from Spain. Still another major blow was dealt them near the close of Elizabeth's reign in the trial and execution in 1601 of Robert Devereux, the Earl of Essex, since a number of prominent Catholics had been associated with the ventures of the erstwhile royal favorite, and his fall was accompanied by the departure of the last of the Catholics who had lingered on in the circles of the court. From the outset of the religious change in England there had been a far stronger and more persistent profession of Catholicism in the north than there was in the region of London, the Midlands, or in the South and West. Yet the fact that twenty Catholics – eight secular priests, one Jesuit, and eleven laymen—were executed in the city of York alone between 1588 and 1603, to say nothing of those who suffered a like fate at Durham, Newcastle, and other northern towns, was unmistakable evidence of how intensely the current was running against the old faith even in that part of the kingdom that had defended it most stubbornly. In other words, no section of the country was any longer safe for those who adhered to their spiritual allegiance to the pope.

With the death of Elizabeth in 1603 and the coming of James, the first of the Stuarts, it was natural that the Catholics should once again have permitted themselves to speculate if the change of dynasties might not bring with it an improvement in their religious affairs. Both an affirmative and a negative response to such hopes could be read in certain happenings in the years that followed. The fact that the new king restored the earldom of Arundel to Thomas, the young son of Philip Howard who had given his life for the Catholic faith in 1595, was a favorable sign, and one might interpret the more benign atmosphere that accompanied the prolonged negotiations for the marriage of the Prince of Wales to a Spanish princess in the same category. Although these diplomatic exchanges ended in failure, it was not until 1623, two years before James I's death, that they were finally abandoned, and in the interim they had occasioned a restraining influence on the conduct of the royal officials in carrying out the government's policies toward the Catholics.

Far more significant than these favorable omens, however, was the deep detestation of the Church of Rome which the son of Mary Queen of Scots had imbibed in his native Scotland and which he brought with him to England and maintained to the end of his life, regardless of what appearances may at times have otherwise suggested. Thus James' rigid Protestantism was not altered by his personal attachment to those among his favorites who were either Catholics themselves or who had Catholic families. This was true in the case of George Villiers, Duke of Buckingham, who enjoyed extraordinary favor with the king in the latter's last years, a status that he retained in the reign of James' son and successor. While the duke was not himself a Catholic, his mother and two brothers became converts to the Church and were able, especially Lady Buckingham, to win various favors and exemptions for their Catholic friends and relatives. But the true mind of James I was not revealed here but rather in the fact that when the young favorite married Lady Catherine Manners, a Catholic, he was made to fall in with the king's insistence that she become an Anglican. In the end nothing of a lasting character was owed to these highly placed persons, for as one writer has said, "away from the febrile atmosphere of the Court the great mass of the Catholics plodded on quietly bearing their burdens."[7]

No era of relief dawned for the English Catholics, therefore, with the advent of the Stuarts. And had James I felt disposed to change his customary attitude in that regard he would have found justification for remaining in his present mind in the supreme folly of Guy Fawkes and his associates. The Gunpowder Plot, by which these misguided men sought to advance the Catholic cause by blowing up the king, lords, and commons on November 5, 1605, not only failed of its objective, but it left an indelible imprint on the English mind. Long after James I and his contemporaries had passed from the scene the priceless propaganda value of this episode continued to be exploited by the enemies of the Catholic Church to the constant embarrassment of Catholics in every part of the English-speaking world.

Such in brief was the religious temper of the England into which there was born about 1580 of an old and substantial Yorkshire family George Calvert, who was destined to open for the beleaguered Catholics the first really promising prospect of a friendly haven beyond the seas for their religious faith.

Into his relatively short life of fifty-two years the first Baron of Baltimore managed to crowd a great many varied activities both successful and otherwise. From his appointment in 1606 as private secretary to the powerful Sir Robert Cecil, chief minister of James I, young Calvert's rise was swift and his favor with the king increasingly strong. His official career continued until 1624 when he surrendered all hope of further advancement by announcing his conversion to the Roman Catholic Church. Following the dictates of his conscience, he thereupon resigned his post as one of James I's principal secretaries of state, an office that he had held for six years, as well as his seat in Parliament. But to the king's credit his secretary's conversion did not deprive the latter of the royal good will, for in accepting Calvert's resignation in

[7] David Mathew, *Catholicism in England, 1535–1935* (London, 1936), p. 72.

January, 1625, James retained him as a member of the privy council and raised him to the peerage as Baron of Baltimore.

While still a young man George Calvert had shown an interest in colonization, having become in 1609 a member of the Virginia Company (formerly the London Company) and some years later he also associated himself with the New England Company. Having acquired a grant of land in Newfoundland in 1620, he made several attempts during that decade to plant a permanent colony in Avalon as it was then called. But the weather conditions were so adverse that colonists could not be induced to remain, and in 1629 Calvert asked King Charles I for a grant in a milder climate far to the south. Before he received the king's reply he set off from Avalon for Virginia where Lady Baltimore had preceded him the previous autumn. But as has been said, he was soon made to realize that Virginia was no place for a Catholic, and when the oaths of supremacy and allegiance were presented to him Calvert departed for England. Stiff opposition from former members of the Virginia Company was now encountered when he tried to secure a grant of land south of Virginia, and in the end Charles I settled his problem by issuing the patent for lands lying between the fortieth degree of north latitude and the Potomac River and extending westward from the ocean to the longitude of the river's first source, the whole to be called Maryland in honor of Queen Henrietta Maria, wife of Charles I. But by this time the earthly course of the first Baron of Baltimore had been run and with his death on April 15, 1632, the grant that passed the great seal two months later devolved on his son and heir Cecilius.

While George Calvert was not a great man in the commonly accepted meaning of that term, he was a person who merited well of posterity for his sterling character and splendid integrity, qualities often lacking in those who frequent the circles in which he moved. The single fact of his public conversion to Catholicism in 1624 when every earthly inducement would prompt him to remain an Anglican, proves as nothing else could the depth of the man's sincerity and moral rectitude. In general historians have not been conspicuous in their praise and credit to Calvert for setting on foot what was for that time an altogether unprecedented experiment in religious freedom. And in this regard it is disappointing to find one of the best historians of colonial Maryland acknowledging Calvert's trustworthiness, honor, and keen sense of justice, and then adding that Baltimore was in no way ahead of his time "except perhaps in religious matters." The words of the same writer to the effect that "In this respect he was tolerant and sympathetic, benevolent rather than liberal . . ."[8] doubtless read more convincingly a quarter century ago than they do today. In any case, the judgment was less than generous, to say the least, and less than one might expect from so learned an authority in the history of colonial America as Charles M. Andrews.

The charter that Cecilius Calvert inherited at the age of twenty-seven was substantially the same as that issued to his father for the latter's colony of Avalon. As for its provisions touching religion, three points were especially noteworthy. 1) the proprietor was given express and absolute liberty to erect and found all churches and chapels; 2) the right of control was vested in him as patron for all churches of whatever kind; 3) he was expressly exempted from all laws of mortmain which otherwise would have made it impossible for him to convey properties to religious bodies. This charter, granted to a Catholic who intended to use it to establish a refuge for his coreligionists, deliberately employed loose language such, for example, as stating the need for adopting the laws to their new surroundings. In this way, by emphasizing England's liberties rather than its penalties, the colony was able to escape from the penal code. And since it was stated that all men were free to come and to acquire all just liberties, it has been remarked, "penal laws and restrictions were free to stay away."[9] It was by design that a good number of questions remained unanswered, for it would have been unwise to be too specific about the freedoms allowed to Catholics in an English colony at this time.

In the case of the Avalon colony George Calvert had tried the experiment of taking out both Protestant and Catholic ministers of religion, but it had not succeeded. His son, therefore, decided to leave that matter to the colonists themselves, although he availed himself

[8] Charles M. Andrews, *The Colonial Period of American History* (New Haven, 1936), II, 280.

[9] Thomas Hughes, S.J., *History of the Society of Jesus in North America. Text.* (Cleveland, 1907), I, 242. The curious situation created for a Catholic by Baltimore's charter was accentuated with the proprietor being made patron of all the churches in the colony. It is interesting to speculate on the question of *communicatio in sacris* in his disposal of benefices of the Church of England. Hereafter this work will be referred to as: Hughes, *Text.*

of his father's appeal to the Society of Jesus to interest itself in his colony. As a result in June, 1633, the General of the Jesuits, Mutius Vitelleschi, gave a hesitant consent to Richard Blount, the English provincial, to proceed to appoint men if he thought it wise to do so. From the outset, however, it was made clear that the Jesuits would have to undertake the mission as gentlemen adventurers like the others since there could be no support of their activities from the colonial government. In the end Blount appointed Andrew White and John Altham, two priests, and Thomas Gervase, a lay brother, to accompany the expedition. In the months before sailing the Jesuits were closely associated with Cecilius Calvert's efforts to interest prospective settlers, for the proprietor was intent upon establishing a colony that would be economically sound and thus attractive to future colonists. But the spiritual motive remained uppermost in the enterprise, and in both Father White's *Declaratio Coloniae* which he prepared in February, 1633, and in the proprietor's instructions of the following November the spiritual welfare of the colonists and the conversion of the pagan Indians received prime consideration.

Much time was lost during 1633 by the proprietor's struggle to offset efforts to deprive him of certain rights vested in him by the charter, by the technical demands of the Lords of Admiralty about the two ships scheduled to carry the colonists, and by having to overcome the false reports to Star Chamber that the ships had been permitted to sail without their papers being in order. In fact, after they had sailed the *Ark* and the *Dove* were called back to London, but they finally managed to get cleared on November 22, 1633. The Catholic passengers contrived to escape taking the oath which would have forced them to deny papal authority either, as one writer has said "by concealment or by boarding the vessels secretly farther down the Channel."[10] The majority of the 200 to 300 persons on board the two ships were Protestants, as was borne out by Father White's comment concerning an epidemic of fever during the voyage from which "about twelve died, among whom were two Catholics."[11]

Baron Baltimore's anxiety for the peaceful establishment of his colony was reflected in the instructions which he wrote out in advance of sailing for his brother Leonard, the governor, and his commissioners to

[10] Andrews, *op. cit.*, II, 286.

[11] "Narrative of a Voyage to Maryland," by Andrew White, S.J., Ellis, *Documents*, p. 106.

the effect that while crossing the ocean they should see to it that no offense was given to the Protestants, that Catholic services be performed "as private as may be," and that on all occasions when there was "discourse concerning matters of religion,"[12] the Catholics should be told to be silent. These instructions were proof, if any were needed, of Calvert's sincerity in desiring to establish a colony that would be free from religious quarrels. And though differences on this score ultimately disrupted the peace of Maryland, as Andrews has said:

> the significant fact remains that in no other colony of the period was the experiment even tried of Roman Catholics and Protestants actually living side by side on terms of equality, amity, and forbearance. In that respect the settlement of Maryland holds a unique place in the history of English colonization.[13]

Counting the stops in Barbados and Virginia, Maryland's pioneer colonists were approximately four months in reaching their goal, landing, as they did, on March 25, 1634, at what was called Saint Clement's Island. Andrew White described how Mass was first celebrated and he then continued:

> After we had completed the sacrifice, we took upon our shoulders a great cross, which we had hewn out of a tree, and advancing in order to the appointed place, with the assistance of the Governor and his associates and the other Catholics, we erected a trophy to Christ the Saviour, humbly reciting, on our bended knees, the Litanies of the Sacred Cross with great emotion.[14]

With the Protestants holding their own service, the colony was thus formally launched with these religious ceremonies, whereupon Governor Calvert proceeded to contact the neighboring Indians. Endeavoring to convince the natives of the white man's sense of justice Calvert purchased a strip of thirty miles of territory from them and took possession of the Indian village to which he gave the name of Saint Mary's, and at this spot there soon began the construction of a chapel and a fort.

Once the difficulties and uncertainties about the boundaries of the colony had been for the most part resolved, virtually absolute power over the ten- to twelve-million acre domain was vested by the charter in

[12] "Baron Baltimore's Instructions to His Colonists, November 13, 1633," *ibid.*, p. 101.

[13] Andrews, *op. cit.*, II, 291.

[14] White, *op. cit.*, p. 107.

Cecilius Calvert. And from the original settlement until the proprietary family lost the charter Maryland's political and social development reflected this aristocratic character. At the head of the social hierarchy stood the members of the proprietary family, relatives, and friends who held manors of the proprietor of about 6,000 acres each. Next in rank were some sixty families who held manors of from 1,000 to 3,000 acres each, and from these – along with the proprietor's relatives and friends – were drawn the members of the governor's council which in time came to constitute the upper house of the assembly. Far more numerous than the lords of the manor were the freeholders who held tenements of the proprietor ranging in size from less than 100 to over 1,000 acres, and it was their representatives whom the deputy governor summoned to discuss colonial business and who after 1650 sat apart from the lords of the manor as the lower house of the assembly. After tobacco had been introduced from Virginia it soon established itself as practically the exclusive staple of Maryland as well as its currency. And along with tobacco there came the Negro slaves who performed the labor on the expanding plantations. Unlike the indentured servants who hired out their labor for a period of time, the slaves, of course, could not look forward to ultimate freedom and a responsible status in colonial society.

During the colony's early years there was probably no single group that was made more aware of the proprietor's strict interpretation of his powers than the Jesuits. Their original motive in coming to the new world had been the evangelization of the Indians as well as the ministration to the Catholic settlers. But since anything like close co-operation between Church and State as then obtained in the colonies of Spain and France was out of the question in Maryland, it was agreed that in order to insure their support the Jesuits should take up lands as gentlemen adventurers the same as laymen. Thus beginning with a small parcel of ground near the chapel in Saint Mary's City they gradually added other tracts like the 2,000 acres which included Saint Inigoes Plantation and Saint George's Island with its 1,000 acres which were washed by the Potomac River. These were acquired under authority of Baltimore's so-called Conditions of Plantation issued in August, 1636, which allowed each adventurer 2,000 acres for every five men brought to the colony. On the ground, therefore, that Fathers White and Altham had been responsible for thirty men coming out in 1633, and that he and Father John Knolles had brought nineteen more in 1637, Father Thomas

Copley (alias Philip Fisher), the successor of White as superior, felt warranted in applying for more land. In this way the Society of Jesus came by 1727 to have a total of 9,133 acres on which slave labor was used the same as on the manorial estates of the laity.[15]

But to return to the relations between the Baron of Baltimore and the Jesuit missionaries which hampered the progress of the Catholic faith in early Maryland, the prolonged dispute arose chiefly over jurisdiction and property rights. Baltimore resented the Jesuits' acceptance of lands from the Indians without reference to him, as he was likewise critical of their attempts to evangelize the natives without his permission. And in an effort to offset the Jesuits he made provision for English secular priests to take over some of the missionaries' responsibilities in his colony. On their side the Jesuits regarded Calvert's conduct as unwarranted interference in the business that had brought them to Maryland, and as the feud continued both parties appealed to the Holy See.

As in most cases of this kind neither side was entirely free from blame. Baltimore's attempt to displace the Jesuits by secular priests in an area to which the former had been assigned, only threatened to make matters more complicated. Yet even had the proprietor's action in this instance been entirely proper it would not have accomplished his objective since the two secular priests, Gilmett and Territt, who left England late in 1642 were not long in the colony before they went over to the side of the Jesuits. In addition, Calvert's exaggerated suspicions and fears of the latter's motives and actions made a peaceful settlement of their differences exceedingly difficult. As for the missionaries, they did not seem to appreciate the fact that the Catholic proprietor – ultimately accountable to a government strongly biased against Catholics – was in no position either to grant them the kind of favors that would have been routine procedure in the days when England was Catholic, nor was he able to permit them complete liberty of action in Maryland had he been so disposed. The principal grievances of the Jesuits against Baltimore were summarized by one historian of Maryland as follows:

> they objected to the introduction of the Secular clergy into Maryland; to the payment of quit-rents in corn; to the obligation of military service on the part

[15] Thomas Hughes, S.J., *History of the Society of Jesus in North America. Documents* (Cleveland, 1908), I, Part I, 233. Hereafter this work will be referred to as: Hughes, *Documents.*

of their servants, and to being assessed for the building of a fort; to the rule that their adherents should be considered amenable to the civil laws in temporal affairs in common with the rest of the settlers of the colony; and finally, they protested against the determination of the Proprietary that they should not receive lands from the Indians except according to the terms of his charter.[16]

To make matters worse Copley, the Jesuit superior in Maryland, and his chief adversary, John Lewger, a convert to Catholicism to whom the proprietor had given numerous offices and a great deal of power in the colony, were both men of iron will and singular tenacity and as a result in their hands the dispute only seemed to harden.

The unhappy affair dragged on for a number of years with attempts made at mediation by various persons, including the proprietor's sister, Anne, Mrs. William Peasely. But it was the conciliatory policy of Father Vitelleschi, General of the Jesuits, to whom the dispute had been appealed by the English provincial, that prepared the way for a settlement that in the end met practically all of Baltimore's terms. Vitelleschi counseled Father Edward Knott that for the sake of peace he should forbid his men in Maryland to accept any landed property without Baltimore's consent. Thus the Jesuits were compelled to resign all claims to the land ceded to them by the Indians and to agree to take no more; to accept the English statutes against pious uses, and to agree neither to take any more lands without the express permission of the proprietor nor to claim any privilege or right that they did not have in England. Moreover, no missionary was to be sent to Maryland without the proprietor's permission, and any missionary already there, or to be sent later, was to be recalled within a year if Baltimore demanded it: finally, no missionary was to be allowed in the colony without taking an oath of allegiance to the proprietor. Naturally, the Maryland priests were not pleased in having to curtail their activities in this fashion, but they bowed to their superiors' judgment that the future of the mission was worth the sacrifice. For as the general remarked when giving the order to comply to the provincial in England, "I should be sorry indeed to see the first fruits which are so beautifully developing in the Lord, nipped in their growth by the frost of cupidity."[17]

[16] William T. Russell, *Maryland: The Land of Sanctuary* (Baltimore, 1907), p. 149.

[17] Vitelleschi to Knott, Rome, December 5, 1643, Hughes, *Documents*, I, Part I, 31.

All the while the Jesuits had continued their work among the Indians with in some instances remarkable success, and with good prospects of being able in time to broaden their field of operation. Encouraged by the Patuxents' initial friendliness, Andrew White went to reside among them in June, 1639. But after King Maquacomen's good will toward the English began to cool the governor urged White to withdraw lest he should be killed or seized as a hostage. The missionary then passed over to the other side of the peninsula to the Piscataways where his efforts were rewarded by the tayac or emperor receiving instruction and being baptized in July, 1640. Governor Calvert, Secretary Lewger, and other officials were in attendance at the ceremony at the tribal center on the Potomac River about fifteen miles south of the present city of Washington, D.C. About the same time John Brock, S.J., the superior, was evangelizing the redmen at Mattapany, John Altham was at Kent Island, and Father Copley was in charge of the chapel at Saint Mary's City. In all the nine priests and two lay brothers who had come to Maryland between 1634 and 1641 were profitably employed not only among the native Indians and Catholic white settlers, but they even made some converts among the Protestants as the missionaries' annual letter of 1638 made known:

> among the Protestants, nearly all who have come from England, in this year. . . . , and many others, have been converted to the faith, together with four servants, whom we purchased in Virginia. . . . for necessary services, and five mechanics, whom we hired for a month, and have in the meantime won to God.[18]

[18] "The State of Catholicism in Maryland, 1638, Ellis, *Documents*, p. 111. This account also speaks of a Jesuit who went outside the colony and met two Frenchmen who had not practiced their faith for years. One was near death and the missionary prepared him by administering the last sacraments, and the other man likewise received the sacraments and was reconciled to the Church (*ibid.*, p. 112). In this same year 1638 there arrived in Maryland from England, Fulk and Giles Brent with their sisters, Margaret and Mary. The Brents had trouble with the proprietor, however, and c. 1650 they moved to Virginia where, in spite of the anti-Catholic laws, they occupied important military and civil offices up to the time of George Brent's death in 1699. A recent writer has summarized their position in the predominantly Anglican colony as follows:

> That the Catholic Brents of Stafford County, in the century and a quarter preceding the Revolution, experienced a practical toleration despite anti-Catholic laws is a conclusion which the scanty records of their activities certainly support. Secured initially by their isolation in the wilderness, their service as guardians of the frontier, and their inconspicuous religious practice, it was safeguarded by friendships and associations with fellow gentry. Amorphous

But this bright prospect was soon overcast. In addition to the quarrel with Baltimore and his representatives in America, the Jesuits suffered severe losses in the yellow fever epidemic which struck the colony in 1641 and which took the lives of Fathers Knolles, Altham, and Brock, as well as that of Brother Gervase who had migrated with the original band in 1634. And a still more serious detriment to their progress was the unremitting warfare waged against Maryland by its avowed enemy, William Claiborne, who had begun his opposition to the Calverts as early as 1630 and who continued it until his death nearly a half century later. For a proper understanding of the case, which had its focal point at Kent Island in Chesapeake Bay to which both Claiborne and Calvert laid claim, and which drew its bitterness in part from the former's deep seated hatred of Catholicism, a word should be said about the spirit in which Calvert's Catholic representatives had administered the Maryland government during the first few years.

The position of the proprietary regime was, to be sure, a delicate one with a majority of the colonists belonging to the Protestant faith from the outset and that majority growing all the time, while the principal governmental posts were in the hands of Catholics like Leonard Calvert, John Lewger, the secretary, and Thomas Cornwaleys and Jerome Hawley, the commissioners. Yet these Catholic officials went to extraordinary lengths to avoid giving any pretext for complaint on the score of religious discrimination. For example, when William Lewis, Father Copley's overseer at Saint Inigoes, came upon two of his Protestant servants reading a book that was abusive of the pope and the Jesuits, he reprimanded them severely. The servants reported Lewis and in July, 1638, he was brought to trial after an investigation by Cornwaleys and was convicted of having offended against the procla-

this toleration was, and more extensive on the seventeenth-century frontier than in the established society of the eighteenth century. But it was real: it conferred tangible benefits. Although it was, on several occasions, severely tested, it survived, because at each crisis the central authorities of the colony so willed. To conclude from this single, and perhaps signal, example of the Brents that humbler Virginia Catholics were suffered to live out their lives in peace and quiet would be dangerous. But surely their chronicle does amply illustrate the statement that a mere enumeration of anti-Catholic Acts passed by the Assembly will provide no very accurate picture of Catholics and Catholicism in colonial Virginia.

Bruce E. Steiner, "The Catholic Brents of Colonial Virginia. An Instance of Practical Toleration," *Virginia Magazine of History and Biography*, LXX (October, 1962), 409.

mation banning disputes about religion and a heavy fine was imposed. In this instance not only the defendant but all the principals involved—except the two servants—were Catholics, yet all approved the sentence, including Lewis' Jesuit employer. Three years later Thomas Gerard, a Catholic, was arraigned for having taken away the books and the key from the Protestant chapel, and in March, 1641, he was made not only to restore these articles but to pay a fine of 500 pounds of tobacco toward the support of the first Protestant minister that should become available to conduct services in the chapel.

What was even more remarkable, perhaps, and certainly in the end more harmful to Catholic interests, was the benevolent attitude of the proprietor and his deputies toward those who were harassed because of their religious beliefs in other colonies. Thus in 1643 Samuel Gorton and his followers who had suffered much at the hands of the Puritan majority in Massachusetts were offered a haven in Maryland, and a similar invitation was extended to a group of Puritans in Virginia who had come from New England some years before. The latter had run afoul of the Anglicans when they brought three Puritan ministers into the colony and thus occasioned an act of the Virginia assembly in March, 1643, against any minister who did not conform to the doctrines of the Church of England. Calvert did not abandon his friendly attitude toward the Puritans, and in 1649 about 300 of them migrated from Virginia and settled along the Severn River near present day Annapolis. There could be no question, therefore, about the fundamentally just—and generous—policies pursued by the Maryland government toward those of other religious faiths.

To return to Claiborne and his feud with Calvert, the determination of which was to be decided on a broader basis than their differences over Kent Island. Back in England the Puritan element in the Long Parliament had gained the ascendancy over King Charles I, and when he saw that he could not prevail he had left the capital and in August, 1642, he raised his standard at Nottingham for what was the formal launching of the civil war. Needless to say, the mood of the Puritans was decidedly hostile to the Catholics, and it was as a result of their pressure in Parliament that during the years 1641 and 1642 eleven priests were executed for their faith. The future of Maryland was directly involved, therefore, in the outcome of the civil war in the mother country. We need not be detained here with details of the military operations that were set in motion once the news from England reached the colonies. Suffice it to say, an open bid was made by Claiborne, Richard Ingle, and their followers to overthrow the proprietor's regime, and the more the Puritan party prevailed in England the bolder did the enemies of Calvert become. Claiborne was not himself a Puritan in religion, but that did not prevent his using the Puritans of Maryland as convenient and willing allies in furthering rebellion against the government that had befriended them.

By 1643, then, Maryland was in a state of grave disruption and during the course of the fighting Governor Calvert was forced to flee to Virginia, the manorial estates of the Catholic leaders became a prime object of attack, and from the autumn of 1644 to December, 1646, Claiborne and his group were in full control. In 1645 Fathers White and Copley were seized, put in chains, and sent to England where they were tried for having broken the penal law against priests coming into the country. Pleading that they had not come of their own accord, they were acquitted and banished to the Low Countries. While he was unable to fulfill his wish to return to Maryland, White managed to get back to England where he died in December, 1656, while Copley succeeded in 1648 in returning to Maryland where death overtook him four years later. Meanwhile their confrères, Roger Rigbie and John Cooper, had eluded the Puritans and escaped to Virginia with the aid of their Indian neophytes, and there they both died in 1646. With the death of Father Bernard Hartwell, the superior, the same year it meant that in twelve years the Jesuits had lost eight men by death and two by banishment as prisoners, and for a brief time there was not a single priest in Maryland. One of the few consoling features of that dark time was the friendliness of the Indians whom the missionaries had instructed on both shores of the Potomac to the Piscataway and up the Patuxent to Mattapany, and among whom a considerable number had been admitted to baptism. Both at this time and later matters were not improved by the numerous rumors and false stories that circulated throughout the colony, a phenomenon which prompted one historian to say:

Few colonies suffered more from innuendo and whispering manoeuvres than did Maryland, not only during the lean years when the proprietor was fighting to save his province but even to a greater extent afterward when he and his successor were employing every agency possible to save their prerogatives.[19]

Leonard Calvert refused, however, to be counted out and after his initial defeat he gathered a small army in Virginia and fought his way back to power. But Maryland's first governor did not long survive his return, for he died on June 9, 1647, and in the following year, in an effort to meet Protestant criticism, Baron Baltimore appointed William Stone, a Protestant, as governor and named five councillors of whom three were Protestants. The return of the proprietary regime opened the way for the Jesuits and in March, 1648, Copley informed the General of the Society that he and Father Lawrence Starkey had resumed their missionary labors in the colony. But conditions were still so dangerous that the Catholics had to practice their religion almost by stealth in the face of the steadily increasing number and power of the Puritans who were ever on the alert to pick a quarrel with the papists.

With the civil war going against King Charles I, to whom practically all the English Catholics had rallied, the future was no brighter for Catholics in the mother country than it was in the colonies. And with the seizure of the king, his trial, and execution in January, 1649, the way was opened to the Puritan Commonwealth which heralded even a darker time ahead for the adherents of the Church of Rome. It was in circumstances such as these that Baltimore prepared the text of a law intended to guarantee religious toleration in Maryland and thus save his colony from the threat of a war over religion. Governor Stone introduced the act to an assembly composed of both Catholics and Protestants with the former in a slight majority and on April 21, 1649, it was passed. The 'Act Concerning Religion,' as it was called, deserves an honored place among the documents embodying American liberties since it was entirely unprecedented in the English-speaking world of that time. Yet it introduced nothing new into the colony, for the previous fifteen years Maryland had witnessed a policy of toleration in matters of religion. But a formal enactment of this kind to prevent future religious dissension among Christians of different denominations – and that by the joint action of Protestants and Catholics – was, indeed, new.

The toleration act did not, it is true, extend to all men since those

[19] Andrews, *op. cit.*, II, 309.

who did not believe in the Trinity or the divinity of Christ were not admitted to its benefits. Moreover, the punishments prescribed for legal infractions on the score of blasphemy, profaning the sabbath, and calling opprobrious religious names entered into Maryland legislation a harshness of tone that had not hitherto been heard there. But this was a reflection of the Puritan atmosphere that had called the act forth, as well as evidence of a Catholic proprietor trying to meet half way the demands of this powerful element in his colony. Regardless of the act's defects, therefore, the fact that Calvert took the pains to draw it up and to send it to America, and the further fact that the mixed assembly passed it, offers proof of the sincerity of the proprietor and his colonial legislators. As it turned out their sincerity proved no match for the Puritans' narrowness and ingratitude, but the toleration act was not rendered less significant for that.

The admittance of the Virginia Puritans had proved a costly act of hospitality for Maryland. Once settled at Providence (later Annapolis) they entrenched themselves and made ready to seize power at the first opportunity. And when in September, 1651, the old enemy, William Claiborne, and Richard Bennet, one of the Puritans who had sought refuge in Maryland, were named among Cromwell's commissioners to reduce to obedience the English settlements along Chesapeake Bay, it was inevitable that trouble would follow. In March, 1655, a petty civil war broke out and the Puritans' quick victory enabled them to install themselves as complete masters of the colony for the next three years. The familiar pattern followed with the harassment of the Jesuits and the Catholics generally, and in the missionaries' annual letter for 1656 the author described the attack on the Jesuits' residence. He then remarked:

> With almost the entire loss of their property, private and domestic, together with great peril of life, they were secretly carried into Virginia; and in the greatest want of necessaries, scarcely and with difficulty, do they sustain life.[20]

But the death of Oliver Cromwell in September, 1658, brought another turn of the political wheel, and since Richard, his son, had neither the will nor the ability to grasp the reins firmly and to throw back the mounting tide of discontent which the dour Commonwealth regime had inspired, the royalists, with support from most of the coun-

[20] "Persecution of the Maryland Catholics, 1656," Ellis, *Documents*, p. 119.

try, brought about the restoration of the Stuarts without any great difficulty. In May, 1660, Charles II entered London, and in July of that year he restored Baltimore's proprietary rights in Maryland, whereupon the latter appointed his son, Charles, as governor and instructed him to reinstate the toleration act of 1649.

It is not necessary here to recount in detail the varying political fortunes that Maryland experienced during the next quarter century. Suffice it to say, that although the Calverts emerged from the turmoil that began with the civil war in a strong position in relation to the London government, the autocratic character of their regime became the object of increasing pressure and criticism in the colony itself. But neither old Cecilius Calvert nor his son, Charles, who became Governor of Maryland in September, 1661, and who retained this office along with becoming proprietor upon his father's death in 1675, was disposed to yield any of their rights. There could be little question about the general benevolence of their rule, but there was likewise little doubt that by the late 1670's the proprietary family and its close associates had become unpopular with many. The spirit that had motivated Nathaniel Bacon in April, 1676, to rise in rebellion in Virginia made its way across the bay, and in November of that year the deputy governor, Thomas Notley, had two malcontents hanged in Maryland. Criticism centered in good measure on the proprietor's insistence that he retain complete review and an absolute veto over the legislation passed by the assembly. While he was fundamentally a good man, Charles Calvert was not gifted with the kind of political astuteness that might have enabled him to ride out the storms that gathered around him. For example, when the lower house of the assembly resisted his demands he did not hesitate in December, 1670, to limit the suffrage by cutting off all freemen of the colony who had less than fifty acres of land or a personal estate valued at less than forty pounds sterling. Six years later he went further and where previously the sheriffs had been authorized to issue writs for four deputies to the assembly from each county, Calvert cut the representation of each county to two deputies. Added to these unpopular measures was the widespread belief that the colonists were being taxed for the benefit of the Calverts and their close friends. The fact that these favored few were almost all Roman Catholics, and that by 1675 the Catholics were estimated to be only one-twelfth of Maryland's approximately 20,000 people, needless to say, only added fuel to the fires of discontent.[21]

Nor were there lacking those who stood ready to light the fires at the first favorable opportunity. Josias Fendall, the disgraced former governor and traitor, was still on the scene, and by 1681 he had found an ally in a former Anglican minister by the name of John Coode who had been elected to the lower house of the assembly in 1676, and who from that time until his death over thirty years later gave more than his share of trouble to everyone with whom he dealt. Fendall, Coode, and their following did not scruple to hatch intrigues against the Catholics and to circulate stories to the effect that it was the latter who were guilty of murders attributed to the Indians. To add to the mischief the Reverend John Yeo, an Anglican minister, in May, 1676, wrote a lengthy letter to the Archbishop of Canterbury which gave a highly damaging picture of the condition of Anglicanism in Maryland. While Jesuits and Quakers, he said, went about promoting their false doctrines, "noe care is take or Provision made for the building up Christians in the Protestant Religion. . . ." Thus the papists and the Quakers were making converts among the people, and the colony was deteriorating into what Yeo called "a Sodom of uncleanness & a Pest house of iniquity."[22]

The Yeo letter alarmed conservative Anglicans and was influential in arousing opinion against Baron Baltimore on both sides of the Atlantic. Nor was the bad impression that it created cancelled out by such support as the proclamation of a group of prominent Maryland Protestants in May, 1682, which repudiated the misrepresentations and false stories circulating about the proprietary regime. Challenged in certain of his charter rights, and faced with a serious boundary dispute

[21] Maryland's estimated 20,000 people in 1676 had grown to 25,000 by 1688, three years before the colony passed from proprietary to royal status. Cf. Evarts B. Greene and Virginia D. Harrington, *American Population before the Federal Census of 1790* (New York, 1932), p. 124. Of the 20,000 colonists of 1676 it was estimated that about one-sixth belonged to the Church of England, three-fourths were members of other Protestant sects, mostly Puritans, and not more than one-twelfth or approximately 1,670 were Catholics. For these percentages cf. Sanford H. Cobb, *The Rise of Religious Liberty in America* (New York, 1902), p. 380.

[22] Yeo to Archbishop of Canterbury [Gilbert Sheldon], Pesuxant [*sic*] River, Maryland, May 25, 1676, William Hand Browne (Ed.), *Archives of Maryland. Proceedings of the Council of Maryland, 1667–1687/8* (Baltimore, 1887), V, 131.

with Pennsylvania, Baltimore felt that the solution for these problems was to be found only in England. The proprietor departed for the mother country, therefore, in 1684, and the transaction of this business, attended by the customary delays in official circles, dragged on so long that he was still in England late in 1688 when the so-called Glorious Revolution broke out with King James II's flight to France. Events moved swiftly and on February 13, 1689, Parliament proclaimed James' Protestant son-in-law and daughter, William and Mary, the rightful sovereigns of England.

News of the change reached the American colonies in April of that year, the same month that witnessed the formation of a group in Maryland calling themselves – to give the abbreviated title – the Association in Arms for the Defense of the Protestant Religion. Friendly voices lifted in behalf of the lord proprietor were now too late to offset the popular clamor, and thus the declaration issued in late March by sixteen respected Protestants to the effect that they had investigated the circumstances surrounding the government's renewal of an annual treaty of peace with the Indians, and that they had found no evidence to suggest the plot attributed to the Catholics who were allegedly leaguing with the redmen against the Protestants, carried little weight. Mention has already been made of the damage done by false rumors in Maryland, and these mischievous stories were rarely at a higher premium than during 1688 and 1689. The renewed scare concerning a popish plot being hatched with the French and their Indian allies, therefore, created the right atmosphere for Coode and his force of about 250 crudely armed followers when they seized Saint Mary's City in July, 1689, and put the proprietor's deputies to rout. The latter at first sought refuge at Mattapany but by August 1 they surrendered to the superior force of the rebels.

Although the final outcome was never in serious doubt, during the next year and a half the opposing parties fought strenuously by means of petition and pressure on the London government for the possession of Maryland. In the end, however, Baltimore lost and on January 15, 1691, King William gave orders that Sir Lionel Copley should be named as first royal governor thus annulling Calvert's charter and opening the way for Maryland as a royal province. Copley arrived in America in April, 1692, and the first act of the assembly summoned by him was to give formal recognition to William and Mary as King and Queen of

England. The assembly's second action was no less significant when it passed a bill establishing the Church of England as the official religion with a tax of forty pounds of tobacco to be levied on each citizen for the support of the ministers of that faith.

During the generation between the Stuart restoration and the change to a royal province the Catholic faith made some progress in Maryland. Between 1667 and 1674 a total of 260 conversions from Protestantism, or reconciliations to the old faith by lapsed Catholics, were brought about by the missionaries.[23] There might well have been more had there been a larger number of priests, a subject about which Baron Baltimore complained when he received a visit late in 1669 from Don Claudio Agretti, secretary of the Internuncio to Flanders, who was on a special mission to England for the Holy See. The baron told Agretti that over the previous quarter century Propaganda had failed to respond to his pleas for priests for the missions of his colony. Actually, between 1660 and 1674 nine or ten Jesuits had gone out, although most of them had remained but a brief while, and at the time that Agretti was in England only Fathers William Pelham and Michael Forster were in Maryland. An individual missionary could, however, do much as was true of Peter Manners (alias Pelcome), a convert, who in the two years that he spent in the colony before meeting an accidental death in a swollen stream in the spring of 1669, had not only restored a number of Catholics to the practice of their faith but had also made nearly 100 conversions.

In due time Don Agretti reported his English visit to Rome, and in a session of the Congregation de Propaganda Fide in September, 1670, a communication was drawn up which requested Baron Baltimore to furnish the Congregation with the names of priests of approved merit to whom Propaganda might issue faculties for his colonial missions. As a consequence of this action an approach was made to the English Franciscans, and in a meeting at London in October, 1672, the superiors of that order decided to send Father Thomas Massey and a companion to open a mission. The lack of documents prevents one from saying much about this Franciscan effort which continued for nearly a half century. But we do know that the friars were welcomed at the outset by the Jesuits, for in the latter's annual letter for 1673 the newcomers' arrival was noted, to which was added, "between whom and ours there

[23] Hughes, *Text*, II, 80.

is a mutual fraternal charity and an exchange of necessities to the general good of Catholic affairs."[24] Other than the names of some of these Franciscans, like Polycarp Wicksted and Basil Hobart who were appointed in May, 1674, we know little about their work. They were never more than six in number—for most of the time only three or four—and with the death of Father James Haddock in 1720 the mission came to an end.

In 1674 a French Jesuit, Jean Pierron, took the occasion of some leisure time on a winter assignment in Acadia to make a tour of the English-speaking colonies from Massachusetts to Virginia. Although he aroused suspicion in Boston and was cited before the general court, he managed to escape and to proceed on his way southward. He was shocked by the large number of unbaptized persons whom he encountered and by the seeming indifference of the English settlers to the question of baptism for themselves and their children. In a description of Pierron's trip which was sent to the Jesuit provincial in France it was said:

> In Maryland, he found two of our Fathers and a Brother, who are English, the Fathers being dressed like gentlemen, and the Brother like a farmer; in fact, he has charge of a farm, which serves to support the two missionaries. They labor successfully for the reduction of the heretics of the country where there are, in truth, many catholics, among others the governor.[25]

Since Maryland Jesuits were obviously not able to take care of the entire colony, and since Pierron knew the dialect of the local Indians, he volunteered his services to his own superior for work in Maryland. But the superior was not persuaded of the wisdom of the suggestion, for as he told the French provincial, Pierron's offer should have originated with the English Jesuits, the Englishmen and their French confrère belonged to two different assistancies of the Society, and finally a considerable amount of money would be needed to carry out such a project. For all these reasons he declined to let Pierron go to Maryland.

An added factor in the bleak picture of Catholicism in these years in Maryland and the other English colonies was the absence of any regular form of ecclesiastical government either in America or, for that matter, in England. With the advent of James II, a Catholic, to

[24] Extract from the annual letter for 1673, Hughes, *Documents*, I, Part I, 134–135.

[25] Claude Dablon to Jean Pinette, Quebec, October 24, 1674, *Jesuit Relations*, LIX, 73–75.

the throne in 1685 provision was made for a Catholic bishop and in September of that year John Leyburn was consecrated by Pope Innocent XI and came to London where he was the first bishop of the Church of Rome to be in the country in sixty years and the first to function openly for nearly 130 years. Leyburn had nominal authority over the Catholics in the colonies, but it would be quite unreal to think of him or any of his successors as having exercised more than a remote and vague jurisdiction. And, needless to say, Leyburn's public ministrations were cut short when James II lost his throne in 1688 and there began the sternly Protestant regime of William and Mary. Yet Bishop Leyburn continued on until his death in 1702 and from time to time under his four successors who filled the office of Vicar Apostolic of the London District the American Catholics would receive a directive, and their priests would sometimes seek faculties for the performance of their religious duties from the bishop resident in London. But with American independence this authority, slight as it had been, came to an end, and in 1783 a request for faculties by two American-born priests who were returning to the United States was declined by Bishop James Talbot on the grounds that he no longer had any jurisdiction over their homeland.

But if Catholicism made no very notable gains in seventeenth-century Maryland, Anglicanism made less. In spite of the fact that from the beginning the latter had enjoyed complete freedom to establish its own religious institutions, it was not until around 1650 that the first minister of that denomination appeared in the colony. In this instance, and in others during this period, the Church of England's prestige suffered more, perhaps, from the unworthy character of its ministers than it did from the absence of ministerial services. By 1676 the number of ministers had risen to three, and it was one of these, John Yeo, who, as we have seen, in that year wrote to Archbishop Sheldon of Canterbury to express his dismay at the sorry state of Anglicanism and the advances that were being made by the Quakers and Catholics.[26]

Regardless of the character of the Anglican ministers, however, the

[26] This condition of the Church of England in Maryland was general throughout the colonies. One historian has said, "The influence of the Anglican Church continued to decline until during the American Revolution it reached its lowest ebb. Its history throughout the entire colonial period is one long recital of disappointment, of wasted opportunities, and gradually diminishing strength." Thomas J. Wertenbaker, *The First Americans, 1607–1690* (New York, 1927), p. 138.

Maryland assembly's act of 1692 buttressed their position by calling for the division of the colony into parishes of the Church of England which were to be governed by vestrymen, with every taxable inhabitant forced to pay forty pounds of tobacco annually to a fund for the building of Anglican edifices and for the livings of their ministers. And this was a mere foreshadowing of what was in store for the Catholics in the colony that their coreligionists had been responsible for founding. The 'no popery' cry that Coode had raised in 1689 when he overthrew the Calvert government and that proved so successful in rousing the populace, continued to epitomize the spirit of governmental officials in their enactments even though, as has been said, "There is not a single recorded instance of Romanist violence against Protestants in the history of the province."[27] During the administration of Governor Francis Nicholson who arrived in 1694 the mounting hostility to Catholicism was reflected in measures such as the assembly's law of 1696 which pointed toward compulsory attendance at Anglican services – though this was annulled three years later by the royal council – the law transferring the capital of the province from Saint Mary's City in the heavily Catholic county of the same name to Annapolis with its solid Protestant environment, and the memorial sent to the governor in 1698 by the upper house of the assembly expressing alarm over the fact that during an epidemic then current some Anglicans without a minister of their own were summoning Catholic priests in their illness and succumbing to the latter's wiles by becoming converts to the Church of Rome. Moreover, in 1699 a test oath was administered to office holders which was highly effective in keeping Catholics out of office by its insulting references to transsubstantiation, the Virgin Mary, and the Mass. In 1700 the assembly took a further step and demanded that the *Book of Common Prayer* be used in all churches of the colony, but in this instance the protest of the Presbyterians and Quakers was strong enough to kill the measure.

The next twenty years witnessed the enactment in Maryland of a penal code against Catholics that was a faithful reflection of what was then transpiring in the mother country. Beginning with an act of the London government in 1688 that forbade those who would not take the oaths of supremacy and allegiance to keep arms, ammunition, or a horse worth more than five pounds or to vote in elections, the laws

[27] Cobb, *op. cit.*, p. 384.

steadily increased. In 1696 a bill barred Catholics from being counsellors-at-law, barristers, attorneys, or solicitors, and four years later another measure struck at their principal stronghold, ownership of land, by making them incapable of inheriting or purchasing land. Priests were made subject to imprisonment for life, and an informer who would report a priest saying Mass and win a conviction was awarded £100. Thus the dreary process went on, and even though these laws were often not strictly enforced, they were on the statute books and could be, and were, invoked whenever it pleased the authorities to do so.

It was in these same years that Maryland inaugurated its penal age for the Catholics. With the coming of Governor John Seymour in February, 1703, a period of special energy ensued due to his deep hatred of everything Catholic. For example, in 1704 two Jesuit missionaries, William Hunter and Robert Brooke, were hailed before Seymour, the former for having consecrated a chapel, the latter for having said Mass in the old chapel at Saint Mary's City. They had as their lawyer Charles Carroll who had come to Maryland in 1688 as Calvert's attorney general, a colorful fellow who had succeeded in making good in a business way even if his tenure of office had been too brief to permit him to accomplish anything worthwhile. Carroll was a man of admirable courage, and when the case of the two Jesuits came before the governor and his council in September, 1704, he presented himself in their defense but was denied admittance. In the end the priests were let off because it was their first offence, being given a long harangue by Seymour about what would happen to them were they to resume their illegal activities.

The remarkable man who had sought to defend the Jesuits' legal rights was the grandfather of the Catholic signer of the Declaration of Independence. During these dark years the Catholics had no more able champion of their lost liberties than Carroll, the attorney general, as he was known, who retained his fire and vigor up to his death in 1720. The spirit of the man was well conveyed by a biographer of his grandson who said of him:

> . . . . in spite of the tremendous odds against him he usually managed to make fools, single-handed, of the entire House or the entire Governor's Council.
>
> He was a magnificent fighter because he never knew when he was beaten.

He was incorrigibly optimistic. Circumstances could not defeat him. He always kept hoping for a turn of the wheel.[28]

With such a man to speak for them the beleaguered Catholics at least had someone to voice their grievances in a striking way even when he could not bring relief from their burdens.

It would take the 'incorrigible optimism' of old Charles Carroll to withstand the pressure on the Catholics during the closing years of his lifetime when so much of the legislation against them evinced, as has been said, "a peculiar malignity of spirit. . . ."[29] In 1704 a Catholic bishop or priest was forbidden to exercise his functions in any public religious service in Maryland under penalty of a £50 fine or six months in prison, and if caught and judged guilty a second time, he was to be banished to England. The only service permitted Catholics was that held within the limits of what was termed a "private family of the Romish communion." Fearing that the Catholics' numbers might grow through immigration, the same law imposed a fine of twenty shillings for every Irish servant imported into the colony, a law that was renewed in 1714. In 1715 a bill permitted the children of a Protestant father and a Catholic mother to be taken from the latter if the father died, and in case the son of a Catholic family became a Protestant, the father lost control of him but was, nonetheless, compelled to support him. In 1716 there was added an oath of abjuration for all elected to office, and two years later the ballot was denied to Catholics unless they abjured their faith. The ultimate in this type of legislation was reached, perhaps, in an effort to secure for Protestantism the heirs of Catholics by promising them that they alone would inherit the property if they abjured. And, too, parents were to be fined £100 for sending their children abroad to be educated as Catholics.

Many of their Protestant neighbors felt a deep sympathy for the harassed Catholics and in December, 1704, the assembly actually suspended the law against saying Mass for a period of eighteen months as long as it was said privately in a Catholic home. There was also a slight mitigation from the mother country when Queen Anne in January, 1705, intervened to assure Catholics of this right of private worship, and in the spring of 1707 to order that the assembly pass the

[28] Ellen Hart Smith, *Charles Carroll of Carrollton* (Cambridge, 1942), p. 16. Hereafter this work will be referred to as: Smith, *Charles Carroll.*

[29] Cobb, *op. cit.*, p. 397.

required measure assuring them of this right. From this time on, then, there was nothing but private Catholic worship in Maryland, and the year that Fathers Hunter and Brooke stood trial the old chapel at Saint Mary's City was ordered to be demolished lest it again become the center of Catholic devotion.

Circumstances such as these set the pattern for private religious services in the homes of the Catholic families or in the chapels of the Jesuits' residences up to the American Revolution. For the most part no support was given by the laity for the support of the clergy, the latter living on the income from their plantations. Fortunately, the Jesuits' estates yielded a good return and they were able from time to time, therefore, to make additional purchases such as the 458 acres bought by Father Thomas Mansell in July, 1706, at Bohemia in Cecil County near the friendly Pennsylvania border. Certainly the Catholics' numbers at this time should not have frightened their Protestant fellow colonists, for the census ordered to be made throughout the counties by the Maryland sheriffs in 1708 turned up a total of about 34,000 – including 4,657 slaves – of whom only 2,974 were Catholics, and nearly half of these were in Saint Mary's County.

Following the purchase of the Bohemia property in Cecil County, the Jesuits acquired other tracts of land in the region to a total of about 1,700 acres, and after a time the chapel of their manorhouse, known as Saint Francis Xavier Mission, became a center of worship for the Catholic families who had settled in the neighborhood, as it was the headquarters from which the priests made periodic visits to scattered Catholics over the Pennsylvania border and to places like Mount Cuba in what is today the State of Delaware. As has been said, the amount of progress they could show was controlled by the number of missionaries available, a figure which continued to fluctuate throughout the century with new recruits arriving at intervals such as the four who came in 1711 and the six new men in 1724. Many of these, however, remained only a short time, yet the general impression of their activity was strong enough to alarm men like Governor John Hart who on more than one occasion tried to rouse the Anglican ministers to action by citing the increasing number of converts to Catholicism that were being credited to the Jesuits. Up to his death in 1715 the former proprietor, Charles Calvert, who had not lost his territorial rights when the charter was annulled, was not unmindful of the missionaries and in September, 1712, he renewed his benefactions by ordering Charles Carroll to act as his agent in paying 1,000 pounds of tobacco each to the Jesuit superior, Robert Brooke, "and the rest of his brethren, being in all eight persons," as it was said, with a further 1,000 pounds to be paid to James Haddock, superior of the Franciscan mission.[30]

The benefactions of the old baron were soon offset for the Catholics by a fresh blow when in January, 1713, Benedict Leonard Calvert, his son and heir, apostatized from the Church in the hope of recovering the family's proprietary rights in the colony. It proved to be a quite futile move, however, for Benedict died in the spring of 1715 only a few weeks after his father. But his sixteen-year-old son, Charles, who was represented to King George I as a Protestant, was invested with the rights of the original charter as fifth Baron of Baltimore, and from that time until the end of the colonial period there was the added disadvantage for Catholics of living under a Protestant proprietor.

Normally the Catholics went about their business in a quiet manner and little was heard from them. True, they had been deprived of all civil rights such as voting and holding office, but they were not seriously disturbed in their economic affairs. Thus a number of these families emerged into the revolutionary generation with considerable fortunes, and in the lives of none of them does one hear of grave economic hardship. For those Catholics who had to earn their living by working on the plantations of Protestant masters, the nearly thirty annual holy days of obligation of the eighteenth century proved a real difficulty. In an effort to bring them relief, in 1722 the Jesuits petitioned their provincial in England, Father Robert Beeston, who, in turn, sought help from Bonaventure Giffard, Vicar Apostolic of the London District.[31] Bishop Giffard understood the problem and on December 21

[30] Hughes, *Text*, II, 469.

[31] A striking picture of the trials of the English Catholics at the time is contained in a letter of Bishop Giffard in which he said: "Since the 4th of May, (1714) I have had no quiet, have been forced to change lodgings fourteen times, and but once have lain in my own lodging." One of his greatest crosses arose from the activities of spies among whom were two apostate priests who had turned priest-catchers and informed on his whereabouts. He said, ". . . I may say with the Apostle, *in carceribus abanduntius.* In one I lay on the floor a considerable time; in Newgate almost two years; afterwards in Hertford gaol; and now daily expect a fourth prison to end my life in." Giffard to unnamed correspondent, October 7, 1714, quoted from the *Catholic Miscellany* of 1827 by W. Maziere Brady, *Annals of the Catholic Hierarchy in England and Scotland, A.D. 1585–1876* (Rome, 1877), pp. 151–153.

of that year he approved a regulation drawn up by the Jesuits which permitted farm hands to do servile labor between May and October except on the feasts of the Ascension, Whitmonday, Corpus Christi, and the Assumption. These regulations were apparently in force until Pope Pius VI reduced the number of holy days of obligation for the English Catholics generally in March, 1777.

As for the intellectual life of the Maryland Catholics, there was, indeed, very little. For a few years during the mid-seventeenth century the Jesuits attempted a small school which was attached to their manor-house at Newtown and which was conducted in part by Ralph Crouch, a lay master. But aside from this the only other school was that opened about 1745 at Bohemia Manor where boys like Charles Carroll, the signer, and his cousin, John, the future archbishop, as well as young Neales, Brents, and sons of other well known Catholic families received their elementary training. Needless to say, it was illegal for the Catholics to conduct a school of their own, and thus those just mentioned had to exist by stealth and were subject, therefore, to quite irregular sessions. Moreover, the Catholics were forbidden by law to send their children abroad to be educated as Catholics. So apart from occasional tutoring from a few itinerant Irish schoolmasters – who were thought dangerous enough, however, for a group of Anglican clergy to protest their presence in October, 1753,[32] – or from their parents, the Maryland Catholic children got very little. Parents of means, however, paid as little heed as they dared to the law about sending their children outside the country with the result that a considerable number of youth – both boys and girls – enjoyed as good, if not better, educational advantages than their American contemporaries at the schools maintained by both the male and female English religious communities on the continent. It was to such a school, Saint Omer in French Flanders, for example, that both Charles and John Carroll were sent after their days at the little academy at Bohemia Manor.

Apart from formal schooling, intellectual advantages for all colonials of whatever religious persuasion were exceedingly limited. There were no large libraries at their disposal, and even that of Harvard College,

[32] On the subject of education among the Maryland Catholics cf. Richard J. Purcell, "Education and Irish Teachers in Colonial Maryland," *Catholic Educational Review*, XXXII (January, 1934), 143–153; and Thomas Hughes, S.J., "Educational Convoys to Europe in the Olden Time," *American Ecclesiastical Review*, XXIX (July, 1903), 24–39, which treats particularly of the 1760's.

the largest in the colonies, had only about 3,200 titles in 1723. Maryland's only library of any size, aside from those of certain individual families, was the one which had been connected with the state house at Annapolis since 1697 and which was merged in 1704 with the library of King William's School after the state house fire. Wealthy men, of course, often had fairly good collections of books, and that of Charles Carroll of Annapolis was the principal source from which his son, Charles of Carrollton, drew much of his early knowledge. Yet as late as 1784 there was still a scarcity of books among these Marylanders, for in that year Father Joseph Mosley of the Eastern Shore told his sister in England:

The book of *The History of the Church*, which you sent me, some years ago, has contributed much to our numbers; it is forever agoing from family to family of different persuasions. Be so good, if you know of any books of equal force, that have appeared of late years, to contribute your mite towards our successes, by sending them to me. New books of that kind are not with us.[33]

In economic matters, as has been said, the Catholics fared much better. Some families were able to accumulate considerable fortunes, and Charles Carroll became one of the richest men in the colonies with thousands of acres of land on most of which he raised tobacco, with a town house in Annapolis having its private chapel—a residence which he turned over to his son, the future signer, when the latter married—and the handsome estate of Doughoregan Manor in Howard County where the old gentleman retired and spent much of the time before his death in 1782. About the mid-century Carroll had purchased 12,000 acres between the Potomac and Monacacy Rivers and let it out in small farms with the result that many tenants in Saint Mary's County moved north bringing into the area names like Darnall, Boone, Abell, Brooks, Payne, and Jameson.

With the passage of time the Jesuits likewise increased their land holdings either by purchase or gift. Thus in 1729 James Carroll devised the estate of Whitemarsh in Prince Georges County to the Society of Jesus, a tract of 2,000 acres that was located fourteen miles from Annapolis and about a half mile from the Patuxent River. This property

[33] Joseph Mosley to Mrs. Dunn, Jr., Saint Joseph's, Talbot County, Maryland, October 4, 1784, Edward I. McDevitt, S.J. (Ed.), "Letters of Father Joseph Mosley, S.J., and Some Extracts from His Diary, 1757–1786," *Records of the American Catholic Historical Society of Philadelphia*, XVII (1906), 306.

came to have great importance for the Jesuits and by 1764 there were twenty-nine working slaves attached to it as well as thirty-six supernumeraries, that is, aged, infirm Negroes, and children. But the income was no more than enough from the plantations to meet the Jesuits' obligations since they had to depend entirely on it to cover their personal expenses as well as to meet the demand of their provincial in England for £200 a year for the general missionary fund. Moreover, the Maryland religious had to meet the expenses of passage for new recruits coming out from England as also the passage for those who were returning to the mother country, and there was a considerable amount of travelling back and forth by these men.

Had there been no plantations none of the Jesuits' activities would have been possible. That is why the agitation for the seizure of their landed properties, which became part of the general 'no propery' campaign in 1754, posed such a grave threat to the Jesuits' future. Fortunately, the threat passed and their estates remained intact. Their ownership of slaves to work these lands also raised problems that were not always easily solved, and Father George Hunter while on retreat at Port Tobacco in December, 1749, reflected the uneasiness of some of his brethren when he confessed that he was disturbed by the talk he heard from some of his confrères concerning the Negroes' labor rather than an emphasis on their souls. One of the most vexing problems involved the Sacrament of Matrimony. If a slave of one master wished to marry the slave of another, it devolved upon the conscience of the priest who performed the ceremony to see that they would not be separated. Father Mosley encountered cases of this kind as, for example, in November, 1770, when he noted in his diary that the Jesuits had bought Jenny, the slave of a certain Charles Blake, after she had been married to Jerry, a Negro belonging to the Society. More than a half century later it was still a problem for Father Francis Neale at Saint Thomas Manor who fretted over the fact that his best Negro had married a woman with three little girls who belonged to another master. Since the latter asked $500 for the woman which was more than the Jesuits felt they could pay, Neale remarked, "I shall be obliged to sell our man, not to separate man and wife." [34]

Generally the slaves were given small patches of ground to till for

[34] Francis Neale to Francis Dzierozynski, Saint Thomas Manor, January 10, 1826, Hughes, *Documents*, I, Part I, 383.

themselves on which they grew vegetables, raised chickens, etc. At times they illegally gathered oysters on Sundays and holidays and sold them for a slight profit. Along with their food and lodging the masters provided working clothes, a physician's care when they were ill, and other necessities, as well as paid a county tax on each slave between the ages of eighteen and forty-five, all of which cut down on the profit from their labor. In fact, the expenses were often so high as to wipe out the profit, and Brother Joseph Mobberly, S.J., one of the most experienced of the Jesuit plantation managers, envied his Pennsylvania confrères whose farms were not handicapped by having slaves as was the case on Maryland's tobacco plantations. That in some years there was, indeed, little left over we know, for even at a time when the Society of Jesus owned over 12,000 acres in Maryland and 620 acres in Pennsylvania, their American superior found it hard to meet the £200 demanded by the English provincial. In other words, a relatively light tax of eight to ten cents per acre to meet the provincial's assessment proved on occasion to be a real burden.

As for the moral life of the slaves, Father Mosley is again one of the most satisfactory contemporary witnesses. Replying to his sister's inquiry on this point in 1774, he stated that the Negroes belonging to the Catholic masters were all Christians and were carefully instructed in their religious faith. He then continued:

> some are good, some very bad, some docile, some very dull. They are naturally inclined to thieving, lying and much lechery. I believe want makes them worse thieves and liars, and the innate heat of the climate of Africa and their natural temper of constitution gives them a great bent to lechery. The Negroes of all other Persuasions are much neglected, as you imagine, and few ever christened.[35]

At a later date Father John Carroll testified concerning the slaves, relations to their masters and he remarked how much freedom the latter allowed them. ". . . . a *priest's negro*," he said, "is almost proverbial for one, who is allowed to act without control." Referring to the British attacks on the plantations along Chesapeake Bay during the Revolution when the invaders gave the slaves a chance to get away, Carroll related that while the Negroes belonging to other manors crowded aboard the

[35] Mosley to Mrs. Dunn [Tuckahoe, Talbot County, Maryland], October 3, 1774, McDevitt, *op. cit.*, p. 299.

British ships, those who belonged to the priests declined to go. And of the two who were seduced into sailing off with the British, one returned at the first opportunity. "The rest," he concluded, "either absolutely refused, or ran into the woods to prevent being carried off." [36] One could scarcely ask for stronger evidence of good treatment than this.

Through most of the colonial period there was a close parallel between the Catholics' situation in England and that in the American colonies. Hope of recovery of their lost status died hard in English Catholic hearts, and it took the pathetic failures of the Stuart attempts to stage a return in 1715 and again in 1745 to make certain that the path to favor and power had definitely been closed to them. Gradually it became clear that the new dynasty of the Hanoverian kings — brought in by Parliament's special act of succession of June, 1701, because of their Protestantism — was not to be dislodged. And as this certainty dawned more and more of the Catholic families defected from the old faith during what one of their historians has characterized as an age of "dispirited discouragement." It was the period when during the 1720's and 1730's Robert Walpole was forging so strong a government that it gained the distinction of having produced England's first prime minister, a regime described as "Whig and profoundly Protestant in its policy," which made itself felt in every aspect of the nation's life. As for the Catholics and how they fared in this setting, it has been said:

> If Walpole ever did maintain that 'every man had his price' one point was obvious, he did not even trouble to buy the Catholics. At the same time strong as was the antipathy towards the old religion its weakness secured it from persecution, save of that passive kind which exclusion from all employments must imply. The Court was now the centre of the sincerest anti-Catholic feeling, the tone being set by George II's consort, Caroline of Anspach.[37]

Such in brief was the plight to which the English Catholics had been reduced for most of the eighteenth century, a condition that was mirrored in the lives of their American coreligionists. Nearly thirty years ago there appeared a book which detailed with crushing force the

[36] "The Present State of the Catholic Missions Conducted by the Jesuits in North America. By Rev. Patrick Smyth" [unpublished reply by Rev. John Carroll], *American Catholic Historical Researches* [New Series], I (July, 1905), 202–203.

[37] Mathew, *op. cit.*, p. 129.

dismal image of Catholicism as seen through the eyes of eighteenth-century Americans.[38] Every type of printed material — almanacs, tracts, pamphlets, novels, and ballads — carried references of an unfriendly nature toward the Catholic Church, and as the author of this impressive work said in regard to the newspapers, "To cite the colonial newspapers which printed anti-Catholic items would be to call the roll of the colonial press." [39]

Given this thorough cultivation of the mother country's traditional attitude toward Catholicism, it was to be expected that events bearing only a remote relationship to the Church would often be interpreted in terms of the hostile designs of the American followers of the pope. Thus when the Young Pretender, Charles Edward Stuart, raised his standard in Scotland in 1745 colonial Catholics were branded as Jacobites no matter what they may have thought about the Stuart cause. The Jesuits were constantly watched and not infrequently arrested, and in July, 1746, Governor Thomas Bladen issued a proclamation warning Marylanders of the activities of the priests and charging them with alienating the affections of some from the British crown in connection with the Stuart uprising. Not infrequently it was a matter of more than empty warnings. In 1745, for example, Father Richard Molyneux suffered arrest on the flimsy charge of his having been in Lancaster at the time of the negotiation of a treaty between the English and the Indians. It proved a sore trial to the priest even if he was discharged without a sentence after Charles Carroll had interceded for him.

In an intellectual climate of this kind the slightest provocation was seized upon for fresh abuse. When the two executors of the estate of James Carroll, namely, Charles Carroll of Annapolis and Dr. Charles Carroll, an Annapolis surgeon who had left the Catholic Church, fell out in 1750 over the handling of the estate with the former wishing to close it and the latter refusing to co-operate, it provided the occasion for a new Protestant-Catholic clash. Repercussions from this feud mounted until the deputies in the lower house of the assembly in a sort of frenzy passed a law calling for perpetual imprisonment of every priest found exercising his functions in the colony and demanding that all persons educated in or professing Catholicism who did not six months after reaching eighteen years of age take an oath of supremacy were to be

[38] Sister Mary Augustina Ray, B.V.M., *American Opinion of Roman Catholicism in the Eighteenth Century* (New York, 1936).

[39] *Ibid.*, p. 182.

disabled from inheriting property. Fortunately, this extreme measure failed of passage in the upper house which brought the Catholics to address a formal letter of thanks to that chamber for saving them from what would have been an unmitigated calamity.

But the harassed Catholics of Maryland no sooner managed to escape from one threat to their security and peace than they were confronted with another. And by the mid-century these threats were coming so fast, and carrying with them so much force, that Charles Carroll began to lose heart. In 1752 he made a trip to France to seek a grant of land along the Mississippi from the government of King Louis XV with the intention of removing himself from the increasing menace in his native colony. He had already disposed of land worth around £2,000 and had administered a thorough shock to his son at this determination to quit Maryland. Nothing came of Carroll's action, however, although it was not because of an improvement in conditions in Maryland. In a review of the situation for his son in 1760 Carroll dwelt upon the baseness of the government's action of four years before when both houses of the assembly inflicted double taxation on the Catholics, and the proprietor who, as Carroll remarked, "knew us innocent of the calumnies raised against us," signed the measure. Revealing both the gravity with which he viewed these events and the love he had for his son, he said:

> From what I have said I leave you to judge whether Maryland be a tolerable residence for a Roman Catholic. Were I younger I would certainly quit it; at my age (as I wrote you) a change of climate would certainly shorten my days, but I embrace every opportunity of getting rid of my real property, that if you please you may the sooner and with more ease and less loss leave it. However, my most valuable lands and slaves shall be kept to the last that you may chuse for yourself, and make yourself as happy as possible. It is my greatest study and concern to make you so.[40]

The tensions of wartime, needless to say, only enhanced the feeling against the Catholics. For years the English and French had been fighting to gain the mastery in North America, and when their final

[40] Carroll to his son, n.p., July 14, 1760, Kate Mason Rowland, *The Life of Charles Carroll of Carrollton, 1737–1832. With His Correspondence and Public Papers* (New York, 1898), I, 43. In 1767 an English physician, Sir Henry Jerningham, who had settled in Maryland led a move for another Catholic exodus to Louisiana; although he corresponded with the Spanish governor, Antonio de Ulloa, who encouraged the idea and gave a pass to a certain James Walker to act as prospector for the Maryland Catholics, the scheme failed when Ulloa left the colony in November, 1768. (Hughes, *Text*, II, 546–548).

contest was ushered in in the spring of 1754 by armed encounters in the region of the present city of Pittsburgh, it was the signal for new assaults from the enemies of the pope. The *Maryland Gazette* on May 16 renewed the suggestion of seizing the Jesuit properties and of punishing those whose children went abroad to school. Once again a feverish excitement overtook the assembly about the dangers from a popish plot, and with a view to checking the too numerous influx of Irish servants, and of German and French papists coming in via Pennsylvania or through Newcastle on the Delaware, they projected still another law. But like a good number of bills in this period the most recent measure failed to win sufficient support to pass both houses. Periodic arrests of priests continued, however, as Father James Beadnell found out in September, 1756, when he was taken up for having come from Bohemia to say Mass in several houses and also for, allegedly, trying to win a Quakeress away from her religion. The case dragged on for some months, but in April, 1757, Beadnell was acquitted. Benedict Neale, S.J., of Deer Creek had a similar experience, being arrested for what was termed treason with the French in an indictment drawn up at Frederick in October, 1756; but he, too, was freed at the Annapolis assizes the following February on the ground that the charges had been unfounded.

As though there were not enough internal hazards to overcome, the Catholics' lot was rendered more complicated by the arrival of a group of coreligionists from outside the province in the persons of the unfortunate Acadian exiles. That unhappy chapter in the history of Anglo-French rivalry began in the fall of 1755 when the British resorted to forced removal of about 7,000 of these simple farmers and fishermen from their homeland and shipped them southward to the inhospitable ports of the American coast. Maryland public opinion had not yet been calmed over the assembly's attempt in the previous spring to raise money for the defense of the frontier against the French and their Indian allies. During the course of the debates on this issue all kinds of false charges were hurled at the Catholics, and it was on the score of their political unreliability – in the face of the Catholic nation with which England was then at war – that the double taxation bill mentioned above was enacted. Both Catholics and their opponents plied Governor Horatio Sharpe with petitions about the bill, but in the end he gave way before the pressure of the Protestant element, declined to veto the measure, and it became law. Sharpe's action was all the more blameworthy in that he later confessed in a report to the proprietor:

upon the Whole, my Ld I must say that if I was asked whether the Conduct of the Protestants or Papists in this Province hath been most unexceptionable since I have had the honour to serve your Ldp, I should not hesitate to give an Answer in favour of the Latter.[41]

Into a colony already plagued by wartime fears and rumors of this kind there came in November, 1755, the five ships bearing to Maryland its allotment of 913 Acadians. Catholics were forbidden to house their French-speaking coreligionists, and Charles Carroll told his son, "I offered the government to take and support two families, consisting of fourteen souls, but was not permitted to do it."[42] The Acadians were divided between Baltimore, Annapolis, and the river settlements along the Patuxent and other streams, but those who were assigned to Baltimore fared better than the others since most of them found employment and were afforded a fairly reasonable prospect for the future. They were likewise able to get spiritual consolation from Father John Ashton, chaplain to the Carrolls at Doughoregan Manor, who said Mass for them in a house that became Baltimore's first congregational center of Catholic worship. Resentment against the Acadians was sharp in some parts of Maryland as in Talbot County where an address to the assembly was drawn up in February, 1757, urging that they be removed from the province as a menace. As was true throughout most of colonial America, the Acadians who were deported to Maryland made no lasting impression on the life of the community. This was not their fault since for the most part they continued in a depressed state, were unfamiliar with the language and customs of their new surroundings, and only a minority of them ever really settled down and relinquished the hope of returning to their home. Consequently, the Maryland Catholics drew relatively little strength from their presence, and a generation later John Carroll spoke of the inroads that had been made on their religious faith by certain French immigrant freethinkers whose propaganda and bad example had deprived a number of Acadians of their ancestral attachment to the Catholic Church.

[41] Sharpe to Baltimore, Annapolis, December 16, 1758, William Hand Browne (Ed.), *Archives of Maryland. Correspondence of Governor Horatio Sharpe* (Baltimore, 1890), II, 318.

[42] Carroll to his son, n.p., July 26, 1756, Rowland, *op. cit.*, I, 27.

The Treaty of Paris of February, 1763, not only ended the French and Indian War, but it marked the opening of the decade preparatory to the American Revolution. With France expelled from the North American continent, and with Britain's gradual alienation of its erstwhile loyal subjects by its economic policies, a new phase of life opened for the colonists. It was a change that the Catholic minority also felt, but before we discuss what the years after 1763 held for them generally it may be well to conclude this particular treatment of Maryland with a brief summary of their position at this time. Almost from the founding in 1634 there had been occasional mixtures of national background among the Catholics in Maryland, but the majority had always remained English with the Irish – mostly servants – constituting the second largest number. In the month that the first Continental Congress adjourned Father Mosley gave his sister a detailed description of his coreligionists and their way of life. After speaking about the Negro slaves, which we have already seen, he went on to say:

> Our Congregations are a mere medley of English, Irish, Scotch, French, Dutch and Country-born. If you mean by 'people of the country,' *Indians*, we've ne'er one in any of our Congregations; the law forbids us to meddle with them. I think the families of the English stock are the glory of our flocks, edifying, virtuous, good Christians, and well instructed in the Faith. . . .[43]

Mosley's remark explained why the Jesuits had been able to show no progress with the Indians, and as for the superior status of the English Catholics, that was to be expected since they were by far the most numerous. The largest supplementary group, as has been said, were of Irish birth or descent with most of them belonging to the servant class, although the Catholic Carrolls who traced their origins to King's County, Ireland, were a striking exception in this regard.

The Maryland Catholics' numbers remained to the end of the colonial period relatively small with various estimates given by different writers. But the 7,692 reported for the late 1750's as against 92,308 Protestants was probably not far off the mark. The Catholics' economic status could in part be gauged by the fact that in 1759 they were found to hold 316,150 acres of land in contrast to the 3,636,321 acres owned by the Protestants. Their spiritual life, as has been said, was cared for by itinerant missionaries whose activities were well described in the

[43] Mosley to Mrs. Dunn [Tuckahoe, Talbot County], October 3, 1774, McDevitt, *op. cit.*, p. 299.

letters of Joseph Mosely, S.J., to his sister. For example, he spoke of riding horseback at times up to almost 300 miles in a single week, and hardly ever riding less than 150 miles in a week. In 1766 he detailed the location of the six missions he was then serving in a way that made it clear how he could run up so high a weekly total of mileage. He said that the chief congregation was ten miles away from his residence, the second largest was twenty miles; the third, twenty-four; the fourth, twenty-two; the fifth largest was the station where he resided; and the sixth congregation was twenty-two miles distant. He visited these six stations at least once every two months, and in addition there were two others — thirty-nine and ninety miles distant respectively — which he visited twice a year. "This, you'll say, is still hard," he concluded. "It's easy, Dear Sister, to what it was." [44]

The life of a missionary in colonial Maryland was, to be sure, a strenuous one; but it was not without its consolations. Less than a year before his death Mosley gave evidence of that fact in stating that when he began Saint Joseph's Mission in Talbot County in 1765, in an area where a priest had never before lived, he found only a few Catholics. Twenty-one years later, however, he was able to count between 500 and 600 communicants which made him feel that his labors had not been in vain.[45] One might add that if the missions on Maryland's Eastern Shore — served by only one other priest beside Mosley who lived fifty miles distant from him — were able to show this modest progress, the Catholic congregations elsewhere in the province did even better, for it was Saint Mary's and its neighboring counties that represented the centers of whatever strength the Maryland Catholics had.

[44] Same to same, Tuckahoe, Talbot County, October 14, 1766, *ibid.*, p. 201.
[45] Same to same, Tuckahoe, Talbot County, July 20, 1786, *ibid.*, p. 309.

CHAPTER THIRTEEN

NEW YORK AND PENNSYLVANIA

NEW YORK

A decade before the founding of Maryland there was begun the active settlement of the only one of the thirteen original colonies that owed its origins to the United Netherlands. It was an English sea captain, Henry Hudson, in the hire of the Dutch East India Company, who, in searching for a northeast passage to India in 1609, had come upon the mouth of the river that today bears his name and had claimed the area for the Dutch. Hudson's employers did not at once sense the value of this rich fur bearing region to the south of the Saint Lawrence River, and another decade was to pass before the area took on greater value in Dutch eyes. With the 1620's, however, they began in earnest and in 1624 a fur trading post was built at Fort Orange (Albany) and two years later Fort Amsterdam was erected at the tip of Manhattan Island. From the beginning the Dutch Reformed Church was the favored religion, and in the 1640 edition of the original Charter of Freedoms and Exemptions it was stated that no public worship would be permitted except to the members of that church. Insofar as Catholics were concerned, for a long time the situation remained very much as Father Isaac Jogues found it in the fall of 1643 when he was rescued from the Mohawks and brought to New Amsterdam by the Dutch. He discovered only two Catholics in the town at that time and, in fact, not until the 1680's was there enough Catholic activity to warrant the attention of the historian of Catholicism.

As a result of the Anglo-Dutch trade rivalry of the early seventeenth century the clashes between the two powers grew and finally led to armed conflict in 1652 in the first of three brief trade wars which continued at intervals until the final English victory which was marked by the Treaty of Westminister of February, 1674. On the eve of the second war in March, 1664, King Charles ceded to his brother, James, Duke of York, an immense area of the continent between the Connecticut and Delaware Rivers, and in August of that year, in an effort to dislodge the Dutch, a small English fleet seized New Amsterdam without firing a shot. With the exception of a year and a half in 1673–1674, during which the Dutch managed to regain temporary occupation of their former colony, the future of New York, as it was known after 1664, was in English hands.

From the outset the colony's Dutch founders had shown the anti-Catholic bias of their Calvinist motherland, a prejudice that was only a trifle less vigorous than that of New England and Virginia. Needless to say, this sentiment was in no way mitigated by most of the English who now began to make their homes in New York. Thus neither the Dutch — who for some years remained a majority of the population — nor the English found it to their liking when the proprietor, the Duke of York, was converted to the Roman Catholic faith in 1672. Moreover, the normal hostility toward all things Catholic was rendered sharper by the feverish agitation and hatred associated with the Titus Oates Plot, the first news of which broke in August, 1678, and which continued for several years both in England and in the colonies with thirteen priests being executed for alleged treason in the mother country in the single year 1679.

From the English seizure of the colony in 1664 to the opening of the reign of King James II in February, 1685, New York was ruled as a proprietary colony by a series of appointed governors whose task was not made easier by the necessity of trying to reconcile the proprietor's possession of absolute authority and his expectation of revenues from the colony with the inhabitants' demands for a voice in leveling taxes and making laws. If one is to understand, therefore, the background to the brief moment of power and freedom for the Catholics of New York that came near the end of this period, the nature of the regime that the Duke of York introduced should be kept in mind. Matters were simplified at the outset when the proprietor transferred the southern portion of his huge grant to Lork Berkeley and Sir George Carteret, that is, the lands lying between the lower Hudson and Delaware Rivers, for what was to become the colony of New Jersey. In the remainder of the province, centering around the Hudson River Valley and Long Island, the approximately 10,000 Dutch who stayed on after the conquest resented, needless to say, certain features of the new regime, but they accepted the change without too much difficulty once they had been reassured concerning their property and religious rights.

It was rather the increasing number of English settlers who were the source of the most serious trouble. The Duke's Laws, introduced by Governor Richard Nicolls in March, 1665, made no provision for the colonists to elect their own representatives to act with the governor and his council in the making of laws. True, they were given the right to elect their local officials from among the freeholders, but this was slender consolation for the lack of any voice in the colonial government. Thus a fundamental grievance was established at the beginning of English rule which continued for almost twenty years to aggravate relations between the proprietor, governor, and council on the one hand and the majority of the population on the other. To this political complaint was added an economic grievance when the proprietor sought to make his rich province yield more revenue through increased taxes.

On the vital question of religious freedom, however, the New York colonists had no just grounds for complaint. At the time that the colony was retaken from the Dutch in 1674 the Duke of York appointed Major Edmund Andros as governor, and he instructed him to the effect that, providing that there was no disturbance of the public peace, he was to permit

> all persons of what Religion soever, quietly to inhabit within ye precincts of yor jurisdiccon, wthout giveing ym any disturbance or disquiet whatsoever, for or by reason of their differing opinions in matter of Religion.[1]

Yet this broadminded policy was no more successful in appeasing Protestant prejudice and suspicion in New York than it had been in Maryland a generation before. When the proprietor from time to time appointed Catholics to official posts, therefore, regardless of whether or not they functioned with ability, the fact of their religious faith told heavily against them. Among them were Anthony Brockholls who was Governor Andros' first councilor and later acting governor, Major

[1] Instructions of the Duke of York to Andros, July 1, 1674, *Documents Relative to the Colonial History of the State of New-York* (Albany, 1853), III, 218.

Jarvis Baxter, also a member of the governor's council and commander of the troops at Albany, Bartholomew Russell stationed at the fort in New York City, and Matthew Plowman who was customs collector for the port of New York.

Such in brief was the situation in New York when in September, 1682, the proprietor appointed the most prominent Catholic in the history of colonial New York to the post of governor as successor to Andros. Colonel Thomas Dongan was Irish-born, a close friend of the Duke of York's, and a man who had served the British crown as Lieutenant Governor of Tangier for three years. By reason of York's desire to settle first certain matters that he had in hand with the proprietors of New Jersey who were then in England, Dongan's departure was delayed and he did not arrive in New York until August, 1683. That the proprietor had been influenced by the agitation for representative government in his American colony was evident from the instructions that he issued to the new governor who was told to summon a legislative assembly as soon as it was thought practical and to permit the freeholders to elect deputies to represent them in this body. In consequence of this directive an election was held in September and on October 17 there met the first legislative assembly since New York was founded sixty years before. It consisted of Governor Dongan and the five members of his council and the seventeen deputies who had been elected by the freeholders. During their first session they passed in all fourteen laws as well as the Charter of Liberties and Privileges, a bill of rights which was enacted on October 30 and which contained the following important declaration concerning religion:

> Bee It enacted by the Governor Councill, and Representatives now in general assembly, mett and assembled, and by the authority of same. . . .
> THAT Noe person or persons, which profess faith in God by Jesus Christ, shall at any time, be any ways molested, punished, disquieted, or called in question for any difference in opinion or matter of religious concernment, who do not actually disturb the civill peace of the Province, butt thatt all and every such person or persons may, from time, and at all times freely have and fully enjoy his or their judgements or consciences in matters of religion throughout all the Province, they behaving themselves peaceably and quietly, and nott using this liberty to licentiousness, nor to the civill injury or outward disturbance of others.[2]

[2] *Ecclesiastical Records. State of New York* (Albany, 1901), II, 864. When King James II nullified this charter in 1686 he allowed the clause concerning religious freedom to stand.

Thus New York joined—if only for a brief time—the company of Maryland, Rhode Island, and Pennsylvania in the grant of a broad religious freedom. That it proved a reality for the balance of the time that Dongan held the governorship, we know from evidence such as the letters that the Dutch ministers wrote during the ensuing years to the classis in Amsterdam testifying to the peace and growth of their Dutch Reformed congregations, and from the welcome that Dongan extended to the Huguenots fleeing France after the revocation of the Edict of Nantes in 1685, a group who were soon to lay the foundations of the settlement at New Rochelle.[3]

Thomas Dongan was a remarkable administrator. In fact, a leading authority of this period of American history said of him, "He proved to be one of the very best of all the colonial governors."[4] And for no single policy did he win more praise in after years, perhaps, than for the foresight he displayed and the energy he put forth in furthering England's interests in relation to the Iroquois Indians and to the rival French on the northern reaches of his colony. Dongan was aware before he came to America of the significant part played by the French Jesuits in the extention of French influence among the redmen in the Saint Lawrence Valley and the region of the Great Lakes, and it was his original idea to introduce English Jesuits into New York who might counteract the influence of their French confrères with the natives. With that in mind negotiations were begun with Father John Warner, the English provincial, and when Dongan sailed for America in the summer of 1683 he had with him Father Thomas Harvey, S.J. The Jesuits' plans were summarized for the General of the Society when Warner told him:

Father Thomas Hervey, the missioner, passes to New York by consent of the Governor of the Colony. In that Colony. . . . is a respectable city, fit for the foundation of a College, if faculties are given, to which College those

[3] When the Jews in New York petitioned Dongan in September, 1685, for the right to trade and to practice their religion, he recommended the petition to the Mayor of New York. The municipal government refused the request, but before Dongan left office he obtained the right for the Jews to engage in wholesale trade, and the fact that two Jews, Isaac Henriquez and Simon Bonan, appeared on the rolls of the freemen for 1687–1688, and that a synagogue was opened in New York before Dongan's term had expired, would indicate their favorable position in the days of the Catholic governor. Cf. John H. Kennedy, O.M.I., *Thomas Dongan. Governor of New York, 1682–1688* (Washington, 1930), pp. 86–87.

[4] Herbert L. Osgood, *The American Colonies in the Seventeenth Century* (New York, 1904), II, 131.

who are now scattered throughout Maryland may betake themselves, and make excursions from thence into Maryland. The Duke of York, the lord of that Colony, greatly encourages the undertaking of a new mission. He did not consent to Father Thomas Hervey's sailing until he had advised with the Provincial, the Consultors and other grave Fathers. . . .[5]

Actually, the prospect was not nearly as promising as the provincial thought it was, for there were very few Catholics in New York, the prejudice against the Church was deep and widespread, and—as it turned out—Dongan was not in power long enough to effect any lasting arrangements for the Catholics. Nonetheless, the Jesuits went ahead with their plans and between 1684 and 1686 four more of their number, Fathers Henry Harrison and Charles Gage and two lay brothers, joined Harvey in New York. They opened a little chapel in Fort James for the few Catholic families, and they also staffed a small school which, according to unfriendly observers like Jacob Leisler, was frequented by the sons of some of the leading non-Catholic citizens like Judges John West and John Palmer, Captain John Tuder, and James Graham.

Meanwhile Governor Dongan had not relinquished his objective in regard to New York's French and Indian neighbors. In late July, 1684, he met a group of Iroquois chiefs at Albany where the English peace covenant with them was renewed. And while thus maintaining good relations with the Iroquois, the principal Indian foe of the French, at the same time he encouraged them to continue their harassment of the tribes of the Five Nations who were allied to the French. Moreover, Dongan issued a series of strenuous protests to the government at Quebec against French encroachments on territory that England regarded as its own, and the French were put on notice that there would be no yielding by the English in their claim to act as overlords of the Iroquois and protectors of the latter's territories as far north as Lake Ontario. As for the English Jesuits' part in all this, as it turned out Dongan never had enough of these men to implement his original plan to send them among New York's Indian tribes, nor did he really have to face the necessity of doing so. In the end, therefore, Dongan could take satisfaction in the success of his policy in laying the ground so well that an ultimate recognition by the French of the English claims came in the Treaty of Utrecht in 1713. But it had been due to Dongan's perceptive planning,

[5] Warner to Charles de Noyelle, February 26, 1683, Henry Foley, S.J., *Records of the English Province of the Society of Jesus* (London, 1878), VII, 343.

his show of force at the right time, and his resolution in pushing his sovereign's interests rather than to any missionary work among the Indians by the English Jesuits.

Thomas Dongan had repeatedly advised the London government of the advantage to be derived from a strong union of the American colonies to counterbalance the French threat and to insure protection against the latter's Indian allies. The idea was slow in making its way through Whitehall, but in June, 1686, it was finally determined to proceed with a union of all the New England colonies which were joined under the authority of Sir Edmund Andros as Governor of the Dominion of New England. Two years later the plan was extended to embrace all the colonies north of Pennsylvania and on this occasion James II issued a new commission to Andros with provision for deputy governors in the respective provinces. As a consequence of these changes Dongan was recalled. But he decided to remain in the new world, and after his successor took over in August, 1688, Dongan retired to manage his large estate on Staten Island and his farm at Hempstead. Summing up his administration, Charles M. Andrews said of him:

> he showed himself efficient, just, and conciliatory, though at times perhaps over-inclined to leniency, loyally devoted to his superiors in England and equally faithful to the people he governed.[6]

But the former governor's merits were to receive short shrift from the people who were soon to come to power in New York. Opposition to King James II had been steadily mounting in England during the previous three years on the score of his frequent arbitrary conduct in relation to Parliament and the consequent alienation of both rival political groups soon to be known as Whigs and Tories, but even more so, perhaps, because of the king's Catholic faith and the favoritism shown to his coreligionists. When, therefore, on June 10, 1688, there was born to James' Catholic wife, Mary of Modena, a boy child the nation was faced with the prospect of a Catholic dynasty. It was the signal for launching a series of secret manouvers in behalf of James' Protestant son-in-law and daughter, William of Orange and the Princess Mary. Once the so-called Glorious Revolution got underway most of the support that James II had managed to retain now fell away so that he was in no position to counter the moves against his throne. When he realized,

[6] Andrews, *op. cit.*, III, 121.

therefore, that his enemies were about to close in on him he fled to France in December, 1688, where King Louis XIV offered a friendly refuge to James and his family.

By the time that news of these stirring events reached America in April of 1689 the English Parliament had almost two months before proclaimed William and Mary as rightful sovereigns. The stage was now set for raising the standard of revolt against certain colonial governments where discontent had accumulated. We have already seen the violent change that at this time brought an abrupt end to Calvert's proprietorship in Maryland. New York had its counterpart to Maryland's John Coode in the person of a German-born soldier, Jacob Leisler, who had come to the colony in 1660 in the hire of the Dutch West India Company. Leisler had an especially virulent hatred of Catholicism so that after his assault on the government of Lieutenant Governor Francis Nicholson on June 1, 1689, and his expulsion of that official, a rabidly anti-Catholic policy was inaugurated in New York. Leisler assumed the title of commander-in-chief and by the end of the year he took over that of lieutenant governor as well, and he and his associates did all they could to give widespread circulation to the rumors and false stories of an impending French and Indian attack in which the Catholics were said to be aligned with their French coreligionists.

Orders were now issued for the arrest of all reputed papists, the franchise was abolished for Catholics, and those of that faith who were then holding office were suspended, a measure that touched only a very few among whom were Major Jarvis Baxter, commander of the garrison at Albany, and Ensign Bartholomew Russell who was stationed at the fort in New York City. A warrant was issued for the arrest of former Governor Dongan who during the next year or more was hunted like a criminal. It was only by virtue of his dexterity in avoiding Leisler's dragnet that he was ultimately able to get back to England in 1691 where in the years that followed he repeatedly but vainly sought to gain some compensation for his confiscated American properties. In 1698 Dongan inherited the title of Earl of Limerick, but his distinguished services to the crown earned no consideration in the days of his misfortune and he died in London in relative obscurity and poverty in 1715 at the age of eighty-one, loyal to the last to the cause of the exiled Stuart whose father had been his friend and patron in better times.

When the storm struck New York the Jesuits narrowly escaped the wrath of Leisler and his fellow rebels by hasty flight. Father Harrison returned to Ireland and Father Harvey took refuge for a time in Maryland whence he stealthily made his way back to New York to minister to the scattered and proscribed Catholics until his health failed and he returned once more to Maryland where he died in 1696. Needless to say, the little chapel in Fort James was closed and the Catholic school quickly liquidated. During the period from Leisler's seizure of the government in December, 1689, to the arrival in March, 1691, of Henry Sloughter, the man appointed by William III as governor, the policies of Leisler created the deepest differences among the populace. Since the latter's expulsion of Nicholson two years before was viewed as a usurpation, his refusal to surrender to Sloughter now led to his arrest, his trial for treason, and – along with his son-in-law who was an accomplice – to his execution on May 16, 1691.

The few Catholics who may still have been lingering on somewhere in the colony probably breathed more easily at news of the death of Leisler, although they were to find no comfort from the government that succeeded him. Like Maryland, New York was at this time declared a royal colony and Benjamin Fletcher, successor of Sloughter, as governor, succeeded after a hard struggle with a reluctant assembly in getting through a measure in September, 1693, that resulted in the gradual establishment of the Church of England in four of New York's most important counties. Any Catholic living in those counties would have to contribute, therefore, to the support of the Anglican ministers. But the government after 1688 was so hostile to Catholics that it is doubtful if any remained in New York. That very fact made all the more incongruous the severity of the measures taken against them during the administration of Richard Coote, Earl of Bellomont, who in 1697 became Governor of New York, Massachusetts, and New Hampshire. He was a son of the notorious Richard Coote who in the days of the Cromwellian invasion of Ireland had committed so many outrages against the Catholic population, and thus Catholics living within the son's jurisdiction had little reason to anticipate any mercy.

The fear and suspicion of the French that dominated the thinking of so many English colonists at this time were not dissipated in September, 1697, by the Treaty of Ryswick that closed King William's War. During the interval between that temporary truce and the renewal of Anglo-French warfare in May, 1702, the clashes along the vague boundaries of their respective possessions in North America took an increasing toll in lives and property. It was this atmosphere that served as justification for the draconian law against Jesuits and 'popish missionaries' which was enacted on August 9, 1700, and which provided that all priests residing within the colony were to depart before the following November 1. If they failed to obey and were caught, they would be subject to perpetual imprisonment, and if they escaped from prison and were apprehended they were to be punished by death. Moreover, anyone who knowingly harbored "any Jesuit preist [*sic*] missionary or other Ecclesiastical person of the Romish Clergy.[7] . . ." was to be fined £200, one half of which was to go to the government and one half to the informer who had reported the name of the priest's host, and the latter was to be further punished by being set in the pillory for three days.

Nor was there any relief from these penal measures through the remainder of the eighteenth century. But even their harshness was no security against irrational outbursts of fear and hatred of Catholics such as occurred in 1741 when the misconduct of some Negro prisoners and the partial burning of the chapel in the municipal fort gave rise to a wild tale that the Negroes were plotting to massacre the whites in New York City. In the midst of the excitement there arrived a letter from General James Oglethorpe of Georgia to the Governor of New York which warned the northern colonists of the danger from Spanish spies who were said to be mostly priests intent on burning the principal English towns. At this juncture a frenzied spirit seized the New Yorkers who in looking about for spies fell upon an innocent non-juring Anglican minister by the name of John Ury. He was brought to trial on the charge of being the chief conspirator with the Negroes and of being a Catholic priest living in the colony in violation of the law of 1700. Ury and the Negroes were denied counsel and in the so-called trial that followed they were quickly condemned to death, the minister being hanged on August 15 while the Negroes were either hanged or burned to death.

Little wonder that a few years later an Anglican minister writing from the village of Chester above New York City could say, "There is not in New York the least face of popery."[8] Even after American inde-

[7] *Ecclesiastical Records, State of New York* (Albany, 1901), II, 1369.

[8] Letter from a certain Reverend Backhouse, Chester, New York, June 26, 1748, Shea, *History*, I, 396.

pendence had been declared the anti-Catholic prejudice persisted and when a constitution was framed for the state in 1777 all religious denominations – including the Catholics – were given freedom of worship, but the latter were denied full citizenship. They were deprived of their civil rights by a clause that demanded an oath of abjuration of all foreign allegiance "ecclesiastical as well as civil."[9] The intent was clear and a revision of the constitution in 1801 brought no change. Five years later, however, when Francis Cooper, a Catholic, was elected to the state legislature and refused the oath, he became the subject of a memorial to the legislature which was signed by 1,300 Catholics in New York City asking that the restriction be removed. The assemblymen now repealed the offending clause and on February 7, 1806, Cooper took his seat at Albany as the first Catholic in the history of New York State to hold an office of public trust above the municipal level.

PENNSYLVANIA

In many ways the story of the Catholics in Pennsylvania is the most pleasant and positive of any of the original thirteen colonies. The fact is due largely to the spirit of broad tolerance that informed the Quaker settlements from the outset, and to the persistence with which they maintained their principles, often in the face of severe pressure from London to conform to the normal pattern of restrictions on religious liberty. By the time that King Charles II in March, 1681, issued the grant to William Penn, son of Sir William Penn of naval fame, in order to clear a debt which the crown owed to the late admiral, the younger man was thirty-seven years of age and had already lived through some highly eventful years by reason of his religious opinions. Having joined the Society of Friends, Penn became an ardent convert whose zeal in spreading his Quaker beliefs through preaching and writing earned him several prison sentences. Thus his personal conviction concerning the desirability of religious tolerance, his association with the Quakers, and his personal friendship with the Duke of York with whom he shared his view on religious tolerance – although not his opinion of Catholicism, to say nothing of his terms in prison – gave him a rich and varied preparation for the religious aspects of his colonizing endeavors.

Once the grant of the lands west of the Delaware River had been

[9] "The Dawn of Religious Freedom for American Catholics, 1776–1791," Ellis, *Documents*, p. 143.

made over Penn set to work in earnest to interest others in his project. Before drawing up his plans for the government of the colony he wrote several pamphlets describing Pennsylvania which he spread widely through England, Wales, and Ireland, as well as distributed them on the continent in Dutch and German translations. This early propaganda met with considerable success, and since there were already living within the borders of Penn's colony a number of Dutch Reformed and Swedish Lutherans, the advent of the English, Irish, German, and Dutch newcomers, taken all together, constituted the most polyglot American community so far established under English auspices. That being the case, it was all the more important that the proprietor should have held the views that he did on religious toleration. If any prospective settlers should have entertained misgivings on the score of religious freedom, their minds would have been set at rest by the thirty-fifth clause of Penn's Frame of Government which he drew up in 1682 while still in England and which read as follows:

> That all persons living in this province, who confess the Almighty and eternal God, to be the Creator, Upholder and Ruler of the world; and that hold themselves obliged in conscience to live peaceably and justly in civil society, shall, in no ways be molested or prejudiced for their religious persuasion or practice, in matters of faith and worship, nor shall they be compelled at any time, to frequent or maintain any religious worship, place or ministry whatever.[10]

The Quaker proprietor lost no more time than was necessary in getting his 'holy experiment' underway. In 1681 he sent out his cousin, William Markham, as deputy governor and in October, 1682, he came himself to America. Penn's liberal attitude in religious matters had long ago aroused the suspicions of the more orthodox, and it was probably no great surprise to him to learn that a rumor had been spread that he was dead and had died a Jesuit, both of which items he was happy to deny in a letter of August, 1683. While there is no reason to believe that Catholics would not have been treated decently had they appeared in some numbers, in the first days of Pennsylvania's history, actually it was several decades before there were enough of them to attract much attention. Doubtless priests passing back and forth between Maryland and New York had traversed parts of the colony, although there

[10] Francis Newton Thorpe (Ed.), *The Federal and State Constitutions, Colonial Charters, and Other Organic Laws* (Washington, 1909), V, 3063.

are no extant records of such visits, and the development of Pennsylvania's colonial Catholicism is, therefore, almost entirely an eighteenth-century story.

The Quakers and the Catholics shared one thing in common, namely, they were both religious minorities and they both had numerous enemies. Pennsylvania's founder thoroughly understood that fact, and thus it was to be expected that Penn – like Calvert before him – would have to walk circumspectly lest he call down the wrath of powerfully entrenched groups like the Puritans and the Anglicans. At the first session of Pennsylvania's assembly held in Chester in December, 1682, however, he and his associates went quite far for that time in enacting a law which stated that office holding would be open to all who professed a belief in Jesus Christ as the Saviour of the world. Although this principle excluded Jews, Unitarians, and unbelievers, its admittance of Catholics proved much too generous for the government of William III with the result that during the next twenty years the political tug of war between the proprietor and his deputies on the one hand and the popular element in the colonial assembly on the other, was at times made to take second place to the contest between London and Philadelphia over Penn's interpretation of religious toleration.

In 1693 the crown in effect annulled Penn's generous policy by demanding that all office holders subscribe to the oath then in use in England. The colonial government fought off this demand for a time, but London was not to be denied and in 1701 the request was repeated and two years later the government of Queen Anne returned to it once more. Obviously the colonists had offered stout resistance to the pressure from the mother country or these repeated demands would not have been made. But the Quakers were not in a position of sufficient strength to flaunt indefinitely the demands of the crown, and in 1705 the assembly gave way – much to Penn's chagrin – and exacted an oath of office holders. This oath not only continued the exclusion of Jews, Unitarians, and unbelievers, but it expressly demanded an abjuration of the Catholic doctrines of transsubstantiation, veneration of the Mother of God and the saints, and the sacrifice of the Mass, and it was not until 1776 that this requirement was eliminated in the broad liberties embodied in Pennsylvania's declaration of rights of September of that year.

In spite of the fact that they were barred from holding office after 1705, the mild regime of William Penn attracted Catholics to Pennsylvania, especially after the penal age had begun in neighboring Maryland. As they increased in number their presence, needless to say, did not go unnoticed, and among the earliest evidence of them in the Quaker colony was the description of religious conditions in America given by the Reverend John Talbot, an Anglican minister in Burlington, New Jersey, who reported uneasily to the Society for the Promotion of the Gospel, the missionary arm of the Church of England, that an Independency had been set up in Elizabethtown, Anabaptism had appeared in Burlington, and what was probably to his mind the worst symptom of all, there was a rumor of "the Popish Mass at Philadelphia." [11] A few weeks later the same minister told one of his colleagues:

> I saw Mr. Bradford at New-York, he tells me mass is set up and read publicly at Philadelphia, and several people are turned to it amongst which Lionel Brittain [*sic*], the Church-warden is one and his son another. I thought that Popery wou'd come in amongst Friends the Quakers, as soon as any way.[12]

What substance was there to this rumor about the Roman Mass being offered in the Quaker capital? In all likelihood it was true, for as we have already seen, the Maryland Jesuits bought property at Bohemia Manor in Cecil County close to the Pennsylvania border in 1706, and from time to time these priests made excursions into Pennsylvania and Delaware in search of scattered Catholic families. Although there was no record of the priest's name nor of the place, Mass was said to have been offered at Christmas, 1707, when Brittin and several others were received into the Church as converts. This ominous development concerning the Mass was soon known on the other side of the Atlantic where Penn, charged with it, felt compelled to relay the matter to his deputy, James Logan, to whom he wrote: "Here is a complaint against

[11] John Talbot to the Society for the Propagation of the Gospel, January 10, 1707–8, Martin I. J. Griffin, "The First Mass in Philadelphia," *American Catholic Historical Researches*, XII (January, 1895), 39. Speaking of Catholicism, Talbot continued: "I thought the Quakers would be the first to let it in, particularly Mr. Penn, for if he has any religion 'tis that. But thus to tolerate all without control is to have none at all." Actually, Penn was at the time in prison in England for debt on account of his colony of Pennsylvania.

[12] Talbot to George Keith, Westchester [New York], February 14, 1707–8, *American Catholic Historical Researches*, XXII (April, 1905), 122.

your Government, that you suffer publick Mass in a scandalous manner. Pray send the matter of fact, for ill use is made of it against us here."[13]

In spite of annoyance of this kind, however, to the great credit of William Penn and his associates nothing was done to impede the Catholics, and even a law of 1730 for the protection of church property that restricted its benefits to Protestant churches, raised no difficulties or unpleasantness for them. As the early shadowy character of their Pennsylvania beginnings gradually passed there emerged by 1720 the figure of their spiritual leader, Father Joseph Greaton, S.J. During the 1720's Greaton led the life of an itinerant missionary through northern Maryland, southeastern Pennsylvania, and in and around Philadelphia. But in 1729 he took up residence in the city which by this time had become the metropolis of the English colonies with a population variously estimated from 10,000 to 12,000 people. With the immigrants into Pennsylvania drawn largely from Protestants of the German Palatinate and northern Ireland, the tiny Catholic group got no appreciable increase through that source.

Nonetheless, there was a sufficient number of the faithful to warrant taking steps for a church and in May, 1733, a layman by the name of John Dixon conveyed the deed for a lot on Walnut Street to Father Greaton. Here a tiny chapel and priest's residence were erected, and thus for the first time since the chapel at Saint Mary's City, Maryland, had been closed Catholic colonists again had a place where they could gather for public worship. That this freedom was genuine we know, for in the spring of 1741 Father Henry Neale, a young English Jesuit who had arrived in Philadelphia a month before, told his provincial: "We have at present all liberty imaginable in the exercise of our business, and are not only esteemed, but reverenced, as I may say, by the better sort of people."[14]

Not all of Pennsylvania's immigrants from the Palatinate were Protestants in these years, and as the number of German Catholics grew

[13] Penn to Logan, London, July 29, 1708, Deborah Logan and Edward Armstrong (Eds.), *Correspondence between William Penn and James Logan* (Philadelphia, 1872), II, 294.

[14] Neale to Charles Shireburn, Philadelphia, April 25, 1741, Hughes, *Documents*, I, Part I, 342.

both in the city and in the rural areas west of Philadelphia, it became necessary to make special arrangements for their spiritual care. For some time the English provincial and his advisers had been considering ways of strengthening the Pennsylvania mission, but since their confrères could not speak German an approach was made to Father Franz Retz, General of the Society, for German-speaking members of the order. The appeal met with favor and in 1741 two Germans, Theodore Schneider and William Wappeler, arrived in Pennsylvania as the first of a succession of Jesuit priests from the German states that would continue to the eve of the Revolution. In the year of his arrival Schneider established a station at Goshenhoppen near the present village of Bally, and in February, 1743, he built there a humble dwelling from which he went forth on his periodic visits to the surrounding settlements and even as far distant as New Jersey where the union of East and West Jersey in 1702 had brought among other new laws one that restricted religious freedom to Protestants. In addition to these assignments, Father Schneider also took care of the German Catholics in Philadelphia. Father Wappeler centered his operations at Conewago in Adams County where he began Sacred Heart Mission, and in 1742 he erected a small stone chapel at Lancaster. It was at Conewago, too, that Wappeler purchased the first portion of the Jesuit farm which in time became one of the main sources of support for the Society's undertakings in the Quaker colony.

A further factor contributing to the success of the Jesuit missions in Pennsylvania was that in May, 1740, Sir John James, a wealthy English Catholic, made his will and set aside the sum of £4,000 the income from which was to be used by the Jesuits for their Pennsylvania missions. The James Fund was a real help to these missions and a quarter century later the superior of that day, Father George Hunter, reported to the provincial that the income for 1765 had amounted to £80 which he had divided equally among Saint Mary's in Philadelphia, Saint John Nepomucene in Lancaster, Saint Francis Borgia at Conewago, and Saint Paul Mission in Goshenhoppen.

But in spite of the freedom that they enjoyed the Catholic colonists in Pennsylvania remained few in number. Fortunately, a census taken in 1757 by Robert Harding, S.J., successor to Father Greaton, enables the historian to speak with some certainty. The total number of Catholics was then 1,365 about equally divided between the 692 men and the 673 women. Philadelphia accounted for 378 of whom 150 were said to be Irish or English and were under the care of Father Harding, while the 228 Germans were the responsibility of Father Schneider. The next largest concentration was in Lancaster County where Father Ferdinand Farmer had 202 in his congregation all of whom were Germans. The latter were by far the largest national group as was evident from the fact that they numbered 949 of the total while 416 were designated as Irish or English Catholics.

In a colony that at the time was estimated to have between 200,000 and 300,000 inhabitants the fright that periodically seized many Pennsylvanians on the score of the few Catholics living among them, was a testimony to the viability of an historic bias if nothing else. How so many could be so frightened of so few can hardly be explained on any other grounds than the traditional prejudice that so readily lent itself to exploitation, as well as to the astonishing success enjoyed in colonial America by rumors. With France joining Spain, its Bourbon partner, in March, 1744, in war on England rumors again flourished, and with them heightened suspicion of the Catholics. For example, the Jesuit superior, Father Richard Molyneaux, happened to be in Lancaster on business for his order at the time that the commissioners of Maryland, Pennsylvania, and Virginia met there for a conference with the representatives of the Six Nations who ceded to England on this occasion their lands in the Ohio Valley north of the river. Molyneaux's presence was given a sinister interpretation to the effect that he was an agent of the French to prevent the Indians from ceding their lands. And out of this there came the story of the Jesuit's indictment for treason with the whole tale gathering further embellishment as it traveled from place to place. How far these exaggerated accounts colored the judgment even of men in a position to know better, was well illustrated in the year that King George's War broke out when Lewis Morris, Governor of New Jersey, warned George Clinton, his fellow governor in New York, of the threat to their colonies posed by the French and Indians and the danger of the Catholics being leagued with them. He said:

> Pennsylvania is in much like condition and I fear our enemies know it too well. They have there a popish chapel and numbers of Irish and Germans that are Papists and I am told that should the French appear and 1500 to 2000 men, they would in that Province soon get ten or twelve thousands together, which would in that case, be not a little dangerous to these and neighboring colonies.[15]

If Morris was representative of opinion in official circles about the numbers and strength of the Catholics and their affinity for the French, it is not difficult to see how the ordinary colonist could become thoroughly terrified at the prospect in their midst of the spiritual subjects of the pope.

Needless to say, this atmosphere was not improved in November, 1755, when three ships docked at Philadelphia bearing 454 Acadians, the Quaker colony's allotment of these unfortunate exiles. They arrived at a time when stories of massacre and pillage by the French and Indians were still coming in from the western settlements where the defeat of Sir Edward Braddock's army that summer had deprived the frontier inhabitants of their defense. And adding to the colonists' anxiety was the knowledge that priests frequently accompanied the French in the West from the time when Father Jacques de la Bretonnière, S.J., and two other priests were members of the Longueuil expedition of 1739 to the more recent presence of two Franciscan friars who were chaplains to the troops in the western forts, namely, Fathers Gabriel Anheuser at Presqu'Ile (later Erie) and Denis Baron at Fort Duquesne. Under the circumstances it was natural that the Pennsylvanians should view the French-speaking Catholic Acadians with suspicion as sympathizers with their principal foe. All things considered, however, the Quakers treated the exiles fairly well, and through the efforts of men like Anthony Benezet, the kindly and generous Quaker of Huguenot descent, they fared better in Pennsylvania than they did in most other colonies.

One of the most severe trials for the Pennsylvania Catholics was probably the so-called popish plot of 1756 which was concocted on the basis of allegedly treasonable correspondence discovered during

[15] Quoted in Joseph L. J. Kirlin, *Catholicity in Philadelphia* (Philadelphia, 1909), p. 55.

the war which purported to sell out England's interests to the French. A flurry of excitement ran through the colony, officials became more than ordinarily vigilant, and here and there a Catholic was subjected to unpleasant scrutiny. News of the plot travelled far and wide, and that summer the Governor of New York, Sir George Hardy, revealed the general pattern of thought about the cause of the trouble when he told Governor Morris:

I am rather Inclined to think, the Treasonable Correspondence must have been carried on by some Roman Catholics; I have heard you have an ingenious Jesuit in Philadelphia.[16]

Father Harding was not, indeed, lacking in ingenuity, as his successful ministry of more than twenty years in the city bore witness, but it was not directed to the sort of thing implied by Hardy. In fact, nothing of an incriminating nature was uncovered against any of the Catholics during these feverish days. An indication that the most recent false alarm had done no permanent injury to the Catholics in the eyes of the public authorities was shown the following year when the latter raised no question about the Catholics enlarging Saint Joseph's, their original Philadelphia chapel, to accommodate the growing congregation. And in May, 1759, they bought a further plot of ground on Fourth Street on which there was built in 1763 Saint Mary's Church, their second house of worship in the Quaker capital. Moreover, their coreligionists in the countryside west and north of Philadelphia continued to prosper. A good index of that prosperity were the Jesuit farms which were located at Saint Paul's Mission in Goshenhoppen (500 acres) and Saint Francis Regis Mission at Conewago (120 acres), and which contributed substantially to the support of the missionary undertakings of the priests.

During the course of the developments that have been traced in Maryland, New York, and Pennsylvania there was practically no indication of Catholicism in the other ten colonies. In most cases the Catholic Church had been proscribed at an early date, as in Virginia where the act against Catholics and their priests of March, 1642, set the tone

[16] Hardy to Robert H. Morris, Fort George, New York, July 9, 1756, *Pennsylvania Archives*, Series I (Philadelphia, 1853), II, 694.

for the remainder of the colonial period, and in Massachusetts Bay where the stern provisions of the anti-priest law of May, 1647, represented in a general way the Puritan mind well into the nineteenth century. There had, indeed, been progress in religious toleration during the century and a quarter that lay between Virginia's founding in 1607 and the establishment of Georgia, the final colony, in 1732. In the interval the intolerance of Protestant for Protestant that had characterized the early seventeenth century had lost a good deal of its sharpness. But the feeling toward Catholicism had not essentially changed. Thus the charter that James Oglethorpe and his associates received from King George II in 1732 embodied a broad grant of liberty of conscience, and the free exercise of their religion, to all inhabitants of the province "except papists." [17] Instead of Catholics, therefore, it is groups like the forty-two Protestant families from Salzburg, Austria, that one meets in Georgia's colonial history, a band that migrated in 1734 to Georgia to escape the intolerant policy of the local archbishop.

That some Catholics were resident at one time or another in all the colonial settlements was doubtless true. But most of these people were but shadowy figures who left no impression on the history of the colonies where they resided. Rather the story of the scattered Catholics in all the colonies outside Maryland, New York, and Pennsylvania resembled those found in South Carolina in the early eighteenth century by Dr. Francis Le Jou, an Anglican missionary working under the auspices of the Society for the Propagation of the Gospel. Through Le Jou's correspondence one can trace the loss to the old faith of a considerable number of Catholics. For example, early in 1709 he told the Society's secretary:

> . . . . two Strangers that were Papists come of their own accord to our Church and another who is reputed also a Papist and has been long settled here is very desirous to do better than he has done. I am in a few days to baptise four of his Children. . . .[18]

Two years later the same minister reported that there were no professed papists in his parish, to which he added, "and few I thank God

[17] Thorpe, *op. cit.*, II, 773.

[18] Le Jou to Secretary of the Society, Goose Creek, South Carolina, February 18, 1709, Frank J. Klingberg (Ed.), *The Carolina Chronicle of Dr. Francis Le Jou, 1706–1717.* (Berkeley, 1956), p. 52.

that I hear of in the Province. . . ." Some of the local families were suspected of being Catholics, but Le Jou did not bother them since they came to church, behaved well, and did not present themselves for communion. If, he said, they should attempt to receive communion, "I would do my duty and speak to them of what the world does suspect. . . ."[19] It is evidence of this kind that tells what happened to many who had been born and raised in the Catholic Church and who, either through lack of facilities for worship or for some more culpable reason, were among those lost to the Catholic faith whose true number was known only to the recording angel.

[19] *Ibid.*, Same to same, Goose Creek, South Carolina, September 18, 1711, p. 102.

CHAPTER FOURTEEN

THE REVOLUTIONARY GENERATION

On February 10, 1763, there was signed in Paris the treaties that brought to an end the Seven Years' War, or what was called in the new world, the French and Indian War. Not only had Great Britain triumphed over France, but likewise over Spain, the sister Bourbon monarchy, against which the British had declared war in January, 1762. By the provisions of the peace settlement France was compelled to cede Nouvelle France or Canada and all the central part of the continent east of the Mississippi River, while Britain also got the Floridas from Spain and was thus put in possession of the entire Atlantic Coast and all the territory inland as far as the Mississippi. And in the final major territorial change in North America, France ceded the immense area of Louisiana west of the river to Spain. With these changes the position of the Catholics in the thirteen colonies was somewhat eased for a time since there was no longer any immediate fear of their collaborating with the French and Spanish coreligionists. A comparative quiet settled over the inter-denominational scene, therefore, until the furor raised by the Quebec Act a decade later.

Meanwhile an internal problem arose among the Catholics on the score of their ecclesiastical government. Changes such as those brought about by the treaties of 1763 were bound to affect the Catholic Church, for if the number of the faithful in the original English colonies was very small, practically the whole population of Canada, as well as most of the scattered white population of the Great Lakes and Mississippi Valley, were at least nominally Catholic. From time to time the question of providing a bishop for the Catholics in the English coastal and island settlements had arisen, but nothing had come of it. And one of the principal causes for putting off the matter was the difficulties encountered by the Anglicans when they made efforts to bring a bishop to the colonies from England. By the late 1750's when the Anglicans made their final major attempt before the American Revolution to introduce episcopacy, the politicians in London had become too wary of arousing further American opposition by yielding to the suggestions on this score of the Archbishop of Canterbury, the Bishop of London, and other Anglican leaders. They sensed that a move of this kind would only add to the resistance that many Americans were already beginning to offer to the crown's economic and political policies. And they were right, for few things were calculated to alert the New England Congregationalists more quickly than the prospect of the British government sponsoring the introduction of episcopal rule in their midst.[1] And if the Anglicans found it impossible to have bishops in America, *a fortiori* there was less chance that the Catholics might succeed in doing so.

The origin of Catholic ecclesiastical rule in Britain's American colonies is lost in obscurity. There is no evidence of any express action taken by the Holy See for these regions until the second half of the eighteenth century, and as far as one can see faculties were either given by bishops from whose diocesan ports the missionaries sailed for the new world as, for example, for Nouvelle France by the Archbishop of Rouen, or by the major superiors of the respective missionaries who would seem to have had the power of conferring faculties from the Congregation de Propaganda Fide. In October, 1696, however, Pope Innocent XII sought to regularize the practice by a brief which demanded that missionaries in general apply for faculties to the vicars apostolic in whose jurisdiction they lived, and this brief was confirmed by Benedict XV in 1745.

Insofar as the American colonies were concerned, the question was

[1] For a recent discussion of this question cf. Jack M. Sosin, "The Proposal in the Pre-Revolutionary Decade for Establishing Anglican Bishops in the Colonies," *Journal of Ecclesiastical History*, XIII (April, 1962), 76–84. Cf. also Carl Bridenbaugh, *Mitre and Sceptre. Transatlantic Faiths, Ideas, Personalities, and Politics, 1689–1775* (New York, 1962), especially pp. 260–313. Bridenbaugh says, "Closely related to the issue of episcopacy in the colonial mind was the hereditary fear of Rome, which the colonists shared with the English, especially the Nonconformists" (p. 333).

raised in 1756 by Richard Challoner, coadjutor to Benjamin Petre, Vicar Apostolic of the London District, when either at the instance of Propaganda or of Bishop Petre, Challoner prepared a report on what he knew about the American situation. He confessed that he was ignorant of any positive action by Rome in regard to these missions, but he supposed that the latter came under the jurisdiction of the London vicar apostolic since that was the capital of the British Empire and it was from London that one had the best opportunity for communication with the American settlements. Vague and uncertain as it was, Challoner's report at least had the good effect of being the occasion for the Holy See's first official cognizance of the North American colonies of Great Britain when the Prefect of Propaganda, Giuseppe Cardinal Spinelli, in March, 1759, informed Challoner that since the time of James II the Vicar Apostolic of the London District had authority over these new world missions, a jurisdiction that had been confirmed by a decree of Pope Benedict XIV in January, 1757, giving Bishop Petre faculties for six years "over all the colonies and islands in America subject to the British Empire." After Petre's death in December, 1758, these faculties were confirmed for six years to Challoner as his successor, and it was the latter's anxiety over his greatly increased American responsibilities that prompted him in May, 1763, to solicit a clarification of his position through his Roman agent, Monsignor Christopher Stonor.

The Holy See replied that the problem was much too vast to be decided without due deliberation and a request was, therefore, made of Challoner for more information. At this point the London vicar apostolic's communications encountered a series of mishaps which delayed matters, for both his reports of August, 1763, and of March, 1764, failed to reach their destination, which made Challoner suspicious that the government agents had tampered with his mail. In any case, a further letter to Stonor on August 28, 1764, got through in which the bishop begged Rome to inform him just how far he might go in granting faculties to missionaries in the new world. On Christmas Eve of 1764 Propaganda replied with faculties for Challoner for the newly acquired British possessions, saying that the question of a resident bishop there would be taken up later.

In the meantime rumors of this exchange of views between London and Rome reached the Catholics in America, and alarm was at once felt by both clergy and laity because of their awkward political situation resulting from the penal legislation. A further cause of uneasiness for the Jesuit missionaries in the colonies was the Holy See's recognition of the exiled Charles Edward Stuart as rightful King of England, and the fact that the pretender's brother, Henry Cardinal York, was influential in the appointment of bishops in the British dominions and he was known to be strongly anti-Jesuit. Consequently, the priests in Maryland and Pennsylvania were on the alert against a York appointment, while the laymen were fearful that a Jacobite incident of some kind might be laid at their door by their suspicious Protestant neighbors. It was for these reasons that a petition bearing the date of July 16, 1765, was signed by 256 colonial Catholics and forwarded to Father John Dennett, English Jesuit provincial, protesting against sending a bishop to America. The petition, signed by leading men like Charles Carroll of Annapolis, Henry Darnall, and Ignatius Digges, embodied their objections under the following headings: the appearance of a bishop would afford an excuse for renewed persecution; his functions would have to be public; they would not be within the legal limitations of family services as then obtained in Maryland; finally, such action was unprecedented by anything that the Anglican Church had been able to do in that regard.

Beyond this joint effort Charles Carroll wrote personally to Bishop Challoner, mentioning the same arguments as the petition and remarking:

> Should an Apostolical Vicar, or priest of any other denomination be sent amongst us, I am fearful the peace and harmony, which has so long subsisted, will be very soon banished.

He was at pains to let Challoner know that the Jesuits had not prompted the action since, as he said, "uninfluenced by 'em I write this." If in spite of their protests a bishop should be appointed, Challoner should if possible stop him from proceeding to America. For, said Carroll,

> such a step, I am afraid, will create great troubles here, and give a handle to our enemies to endeavor at the total suppression of the exercise of our religion, and otherways most grievously to molest us.[2]

[2] Carroll to Challoner, July 16, 1765, Hughes, *Text*, II, 591.

The vicar apostolic was not convinced, however, that the Jesuits had not inspired the laymen's action, for over a year later he told Stonor:

> I believe I never told you how much those gentlemen [the Jesuits] were alarmed upon hearing the first rumour of a Bishop being designed for North America: and what opposition and subscriptions they procured from the laity there, which they would have had me to have sent to Hilton [an alias used for Rome] but I desired to be excused. By which I plainly see it will be no easy matter to place a Bishop there, although there be so many thousands there that live and die without confirmation.[3]

In any case, Bishop Challoner had not been won to the American position, and he continued to work for a bishop for Britain's new world possessions. For example, when he had to renew his application for faculties for these colonies in 1771 he again urged upon Christopher Stonor their need for a resident bishop, remarking once more how many Catholics were dying without having received the Sacrament of Confirmation. Actually, the vicar apostolic was not well informed about American conditions as he revealed in September, 1756, when he referred in a letter to Stonor to the government in the colonies having been "a little hard upon them of late years," which was a far milder interpretation of the pressures that followed the alleged popish plot than the colonists themselves would have given. Again in August, 1763, he made reference to Pennsylvania and Maryland where, he maintained, "the exercise of religion is free," a statement with which his spiritual charges in the latter colony would not have agreed.

A further suggestion made by Challoner to Stonor that showed the bishop's lack of acquaintance with the American scene was that the Bishop of Quebec, "who is not at so great a distance," might administer confirmation to the Catholic colonists.[4] He little realized the complications involved, for the death of Henri-Marie Pontbriand, Bishop of Quebec, in 1760 had prompted the British authorities to reject the clergy's first choice for a successor and it was not until 1766 that Joseph Olivier Briand was finally approved and consecrated in Paris, although his title of Bishop of Quebec was not recognized by the government. It is not altogether clear how the same idea arose at Rome, but in early

[3] Challoner to Stonor, September 12, 1766, Edwin H. Burton, *The Life and Times of Bishop Challoner, 1691–1781* (New York, 1909), II, 138.

[4] Same to same, June 4, 1771, Burton, *op. cit.*, II, 144.

September, 1771, Giuseppe Cardinal Castelli, Prefect of Propaganda, asked Briand to undertake a confirmation tour to the Atlantic Coast colonies, or if he could not do so personally to suggest someone who could discharge this duty. Some months before another request to Challoner from Propaganda for further data on the American missions had brought a lengthy communication embodying a description of the Church on the mainland and in the West Indies as he knew it. He took occasion at this time to renew his suggestion about the Bishop of Quebec making the journey southward, and in closing he brought the Jesuits into the picture again when he said:

> Those Fathers display an unspeakable reluctance to receive within their midst a Bishop, under the pretext that there might be a persecution by the Secular Government, to the ruin of the mission.[5]

By the opening of the 1770's, however, relations between the colonies and the mother country had begun to deteriorate and to affect seriously any plans for a change in ecclesiastical government in the former. When, therefore, Bishop Briand was requested by Propaganda to go south to confirm he stated that he would first consult the missionaries in that region. He asked Father Bernard Well, S.J., a missionary then in Canada, to inquire of his confrères at Philadelphia to get their reaction to the proposal. Father Ferdinand Farmer replied in late April, 1773, with the familiar arguments against the idea, namely, that the bishop's presence would cause a commotion, that the Anglicans were not permitted to have a bishop, etc. The reply from Philadelphia undoubtedly brought relief to Quebec, for Briand did not lose much time in informing the Holy See of Farmer's opinion and stating that under the circumstances it would be inadvisable for him to undertake the journey. And when one recalls the uproar that ensued a few months thereafter over the passage of the Quebec Act one is prompted to admit that Briand had acted wisely.

Thus ended the final attempt before the American Revolution to provide regular episcopal government for the American Catholics, and another decade passed before the question rose again. For nearly a century and a half after the settlement of Maryland, then, the Catholics of these colonies had continued with no personal acquaintance with the normal rule to which their coreligionists elsewhere were accus-

[5] *Ibid.*

tomed. It is a fact worth remembering when one reaches the post-revolutionary years and finds so much resistance being offered to the authority of the first bishop of the United States. Meanwhile the Revolution came on in 1775 and within a short time all vestiges of British authority disappeared in the thirteen mainland colonies save that exercised over the Catholics from afar by the Vicar Apostolic of the London District. Of that fact his biographer stated:

> It is indeed a strange and curious fact to remember, but it is none the less true, that, during the rest of Bishop Challoner's life, his jurisdiction over his American priests and people remained the only remnant of authority in the hands of an Englishman that was still recognised in America. King and Parliament and Ministry had lost their power, but this feeble old man, living his retired life in an obscure London street, still continued to issue his faculties and dispensations for the benefit of his Catholic children in Maryland and Pennsylvania.[6]

During the course of the decade after 1763 life did not radically change for the Catholics. As has been said, there was even a certain measure of improvement in their situation in that they were for the most part let alone. Yet the irritation felt against recent parliamentary enactments did not distract the Protestant colonists from their traditional temper and attitude toward the Catholic Church. Most of the inhabitants, for example, would probably have agreed with Samuel Adams in 1768 when he stated, "I did verily believe, as I do still, that much more is to be dreaded from the growth of popery in America, than from the Stamp Act or any other acts destructive of civil rights. . . ."[7] In spite of this fact, however, Father George Hunter, S.J., superior of the missions, and the fourteen Jesuits in Maryland and four in Pennsylvania who were serving under him, went about their work relatively unhampered by any major obstructions. New churches, or the repair or enlargement of old ones, at Frederick, Port Tobacco, Newton, and on the Eastern Shore of Maryland, were an outward indication of progress made during this quiet time. Likewise at Lancaster, Pennsylvania, a church was so well constructed that it continued in use for divine services until the mid-nineteenth century, and it was these same years that witnessed the construction of Saint Joseph's in Philadelphia.

[6] *Ibid.*, II, 148.

[7] Boston *Gazette*, April 11, 1768, Charles H. Metzger, S.J., *Catholics and the American Revolution. A Study in Religious Climate* (Chicago, 1962), pp. 13–14.

The problem of clerical replacement became more acute as time went on, for the Society of Jesus was itself under severe strain and in 1773 it succumbed after a long and painful struggle to the pressure brought to bear on the Holy See by Portugal, Spain, and France. Thus when Father Theodore Schneider died in May, 1764, after nearly a quarter century of fruitful labor among the German Catholic colonists his assignments were taken over by Ferdinand Farmer who had simultaneously to fulfill his own duties without much assistance until a Belgian-born missionary, John B. de Ritter, S.J., arrived in May, 1765. The dwindling ranks of the priests sustained further losses with the death of the young Joseph Hathersty in May, 1771, who was followed to the grave a year and a half later by the veteran Robert Harding. At no time had there been an adequate number of priests for the tasks they were expected to perform throughout the widely scattered Catholic settlements, a condition that became especially noticeable in the years before and during the Revolution when fewer recruits came to America from England.

The suppression of the Society of Jesus by Pope Clement XIV on August 16, 1773, was a sad event for Catholicism in America as well as in Europe. From the time that the three Jesuits landed in 1634 with the original Maryland colonists until the year of the suppression approximately 144 members of the Society, including lay brothers, had served for varying lengths of time in the colonies. In the year of the suppression there were 274 men in the English province of whom 135 were laboring in the British possessions. The bull of suppression had directed the bishops throughout the world to assume control of the Jesuit properties in the name of the Holy See and to see to their personal transfer to the status of secular priests. Thus on October 6, 1773, Bishop Challoner informed Father John Lewis, the American superior, of the Holy See's action and he told him that he was under instruction to secure the priests' acceptance of the formula of submission which he was then to forward to Rome.[8] The London vicar had neither the

[8] Two weeks after writing to Lewis, Challoner summarized his actions in regard to the ex-Jesuits for William Walton, Vicar Apostolic of the Northern District, in a letter of October 21, 1773. He stated that Thomas More, provincial of the former Jesuits, had promised him that whatever remained of the Society's temporal possessions after its obligations had been met, he would leave "to the mission." Challoner then remarked: "For the securing of this, & the management of our affairs in North America, I have made him my Vicar over his quondam

wish nor the ability to replace the ex-Jesuits in the colonies, so Father Lewis carried on as Challoner's vicar general until the latter's death in 1781.

That there was no exodus of the clergy from America in consequence of the suppression of the Society, or of the war with the mother country that followed so soon thereafter, was the best testimony of their loyalty to the people whom they had been serving. In that connection Father Ferdinand Farmer remarked to a German friend early in 1778:

> After the Suppression all our missionaries remained in their own places and offices (I speak of Pennsylvania and Maryland); yes, and they continued their manner of life, with the single change of the office of Provincial [Mission Superior?] into that of Vicar General.[9]

The Jesuits' French and Spanish confrères, as we have seen, had some years before suffered a worse fate in the central and western parts of what would become the United States. For there was the important difference that the English missionaries were not hunted out as had been true of their French and Spanish brothers. The results, therefore, to the English Catholic colonists were slight since the former religious remained on to care for their spiritual needs. It was into a situation of this kind that there came in the late spring of 1774 Father John Carroll, himself an ex-Jesuit, after an absence of twenty-seven years from his native land. Carroll, who was thirty-nine years of age at his return, became the first priest after the Declaration of Independence to refuse obedience to Lewis acting as Challoner's vicar general. He continued to reside quietly at his mother's home at Rock Creek near the present city of Washington where he employed the faculties that he had brought with him from abroad in ministering to the Catholic families of the neighbhood.

brethren in my district, as I take him to be a very worthy man, and believe this will be the best means to cement us together." Manuscript Collections, St. Cuthbert's College, Ushaw, Durham, England.

[9] Farmer to Christian Mayer, January 29, 1778, Hughes, *Documents*, I, Part II, 953–954, n. 6. William P. Treacy, *Old Catholic Maryland and Its Early Jesuit Missionaries* (Swedesboro, New Jersey, n.d.), stated under date of 1775, "Anthony Carroll left for England on the 7th or 8th of May" (p. 180). But Carroll would not be an exception to the rule since, as Hughes explained, this Irish-born priest arrived on June 26, 1774, and left the next year; to which he added, "He came merely on private business" (*History*, II, 699). The writer is indebted to his friend, Charles H. Metzger, S.J., for the reference to Treacy's work.

Meanwhile the conditions that led to the break with England were gradually accumulating, and in no link in that chain of events, as it turned out, did the Catholics as such have more at stake than in the Maryland controversy over a revenue grant to the ministers of the Church of England. Upon the expiration of the grant the lower house of the assembly refused to renew it, and from a question relating solely to the fees paid to the ministers the quarrel broadened into one involving the taxing power of the crown for the salaries of colonial officials in general. Governor Robert Eden, upholder of the royal interests, resented the legislators' interference, and when a deadlock between the two houses occurred he seized the opportunity to prorogue the assembly and to issue a proclamation on November 26, 1770, that arbitrarily fixed the salaries at the old high rate. Widespread discussion ensued among the colonists, and in January, 1773, the Maryland *Gazette* began the publication of a series of letters between two adversaries who signed themselves 'First Citizen' and 'Second Citizen,' whose identity in time became known, the former as Charles Carroll of Carrollton the latter as Daniel Dulany, one of the leading lawyers of Maryland. For the crown's power to tax to be boldly assailed was in itself still something of a surprise, but for the attack to come from a Roman Catholic seemed almost unbelievable to men like Dulany and his sympathizers. Yet Carroll's was the popular side, and he proved extraordinarily skillful in pleading it in the face of Dulany's arguments. As one of Carroll's recent biographers has said, not too long before practically everyone would have thought it an impertinence for a Catholic to have spoken out on a public issue, but "Now amazingly, they were applauding what the Roman Catholic said." [10]

As the debate progressed and Dulany continued to lose ground he did not hesitate to invoke religious prejudice in an effort to discredit his opponent. Thus he caustically inquired:

> Who is he? He has no share in the legislature, as a member of any branch; he is incapable of being a member; he is disabled from giving a vote in the choice of representatives, by the laws and constitution of the country, *on account of* his principles, which are *distrusted* by those laws. He is disabled, by an express resolve, from interfering in the election of members, on the *same account*. He is not a protestant.

To this attack Carroll calmly replied in the *Gazette* of May 6:

[10] Smith, *Charles Carroll*, p. 108.

> To what purpose was the threat thrown out of enforcing the penal statutes [against Catholics] by proclamation? Why am I told that my conduct is very inconsistent with the situation of one who owes even the *toleration* he enjoyed to the favor of government? If by instilling prejudices into the Governor, and by every mean and wicked artifice, you can rouse the popular resentment against certain religionists, and thus bring on a persecution of them, it will then be known whether the toleration I enjoy be due to the favor of government or not. . . .[11]

But the appeal to religious prejudice failed, for it was plain that Carroll had the better of it, and in the end the letters of First Citizen proved the leading factor in determining the landslide for the popular party in the Maryland election of May, 1773. For the Catholics, the significance of the episode lay in the fact that one of their proscribed minority had for the first time since the advent of the penal laws been accepted by the general populace as the champion and spokesman of a popular political cause. It was a new role for an American adherent of the Church of Rome, and its implications were not lost on Carroll's coreligionists.

But before the Catholics could realize any advantage from the increased prestige won by Charles Carroll of Carrollton they were destined to undergo another wave of criticism and abuse. For almost a decade after the peace treaties of 1763 the French inhabitants of the Great Lakes and Mississippi Valley were ruled in good measure by the British military. It was a highly unpopular regime, and in 1772 the French in the Illinois Country petitioned for a civilian government, a request that led the British to a full scale review of Canada's future. News of Parliament's consideration of a permanent government for their neighbors reached the Americans in August, 1773, and at once occasioned uneasiness lest there should be any recognition accorded to the Canadians' religious creed. When, therefore, the text of the enactment that had passed Parliament in June, 1774, reached America the following September, it confirmed their worst fears. Not only had the Quebec Act recognized the right of the French to the free exercise of their religious faith and their native law, but Parliament had gone further and cut off the Atlantic Coast colonies from the lands that they claimed in the West by giving over these territories to the government at Quebec. Now they would be surrounded by French-speaking Catho-

[11] *Ibid.*, p. 111.

lics on both the north and the west. The effect of this intelligence was immediate, and for the next few months the colonies rang with the familiar denunciations of the Church of Rome, as well as of everybody and everything that they fancied had any connection with the new legislation. In fact, historians of the Revolution are agreed that the Quebec Act constituted one of the major causes for the armed rebellion against British rule.

It is impossible to treat here the course of agitation in any detail, but it is essential that something be said of the equivocal stand taken by the Americans in regard to Canada once they sensed the importance of not alienating its inhabitants if their own military plans were to be successful. And in that connection no aspect of the affair was more revealing than the official letters drawn up by the representatives of the united colonies in the autumn of 1774.

From the adoption by the Continental Congress on September 17 of the resolutions against Great Britain passed the previous week by a convention in Suffolk County, Massachusetts, to the letter addressed to the Canadians on October 26, the name – and the fancied iniquities – of the Roman Catholic Church were frequently heard in official circles at Philadelphia. Not only did Congress make the anti-Catholic language of the Suffolk Resolves its own, but it adopted similar language in its letter of October 21 to the British people. The latter were told that Americans could not suppress their astonishment that the British should consent to establish in America a religion which, they said, "has deluged your island in blood, and dispersed impiety, bigotry, persecution, murder and rebellion through every part of the world."[12] And in the summary of grievances which were drawn up for the king five days later there was mention of the establishment of the Catholic religion in the territories that bordered on the western and northern boundaries of what was called "the free protestant English settlements. . . ."[13]

Yet on the same day that they petitioned George III in these terms the Congress addressed a letter to the inhabitants of Quebec in which they enumerated the rights in defence of which they had taken up arms and asked the Canadians to join in the fight. They then stated:

[12] "Reactions of the Continental Congress to the Quebec Act, September 17–October 26, 1774. Ellis, *Documents*, p. 134.

[13] *Ibid.*, p. 136.

We are too well acquainted with the liberality of sentiment distinguishing your nation, to imagine, that difference of religion will prejudice you against a hearty amity with us. You know, that the transcendent nature of freedom elevates those, who unite in her cause, above all such low-minded infirmities.[14]

Having already secured their basic freedoms in the Quebec Act, the Canadians remained quite unmoved by the appeal of the Continental Congress, knowing, as they did, the true sentiments of the majority of that body toward their religion. Had there been any hesitation at Quebec, in all likelihood Bishop Briand's vigilant and determined opposition to the Americans would probably have stiffened the wavering, although, actually, no sizeable number of Canadians showed any disposition to be beguiled by the American effort to make them allies in the war against the English.

With the outbreak of fighting the inhabitants of the thirteen colonies – the Catholics not excepted – were confronted with the necessity of a decision for or against the mother country. In the circumstances in which they found themselves the Catholics could hardly have remained neutral. From the standpoint of religion there was little for them to choose between the British government and that of practically all the colonies except Pennsylvania. Parliament's recent generosity toward their coreligionists in Quebec might, indeed, have afforded a reason for retaining their loyalty to the crown, especially when the same measure had occasioned such a bitter outcry from their fellow colonists against the Catholic Church. Nor was the excitement stirred up by this episode confined merely to talk. For example, in the Mohawk Valley of New York life was made so unpleasant for a group of Catholic Scotch Highlanders by their neighbors that they withdrew to Canada with their priest, Father John McKenna, who was commissioned chaplain in the British army by Governor Guy Carleton not long after his arrival in Montreal in the autumn of 1776. In similar fashion a school teacher by the name of John Heffernan had his school broken up in Baltimore and he felt compelled to depart, as was also true of a certain John Maguire and his wife who were hunted out of Delaware.

To be sure, acts of this kind were bound to have a sobering effect on the Catholics when they thought of the popular cause. Yet their memory was not so short as to permit them the illusion that the Quebec

[14] *Ibid.*, p. 135.

Act represented a permanent change in the crown's policies toward the Church. Even if it were, there were considerations besides religion which entered into their thinking. They, too, had felt the burden of increased taxes imposed by the mother country, just as they also had been attracted by the arguments for representative government even though they did not then enjoy either the right to vote or to hold office. In other words, economic and political factors were mingled with religious considerations when the majority of the Catholics made their ultimate decision in favor of the Revolution.

Before it had become clear what position most of the American Catholics would take an attempt to involve the Canadians in the war by direct invasion brought some interesting developments among the Catholics of that country. The American military plans involved a two-pronged advance northward with Benedict Arnold going through Maine toward Quebec while General Richard Montgomery, who assumed command of a force of about 1,000 men after General Philip Schuyler's health forced him to give up, proceeded toward Montreal which was captured in November, 1775. In spite of the general loyalty to Britain that obtained among the Canadians, enough sympathizers with the American cause were found among them to make up two regiments. To one of these, commanded by Colonel James Livingston, there was appointed through the agency of Arnold, a Catholic chaplain in the person of Father Louis Eustace Lotbinière. When the Americans' early victories turned into defeat and they had to retreat in the early summer of 1776 this first Catholic chaplain enrolled in the armies of the United States accompanied the troops southward and spent most of his remaining time in the service in and around Philadelphia.

The short lived character and ultimate failure of the Canadian venture was not unrelated to the address to the British people, written by John Jay, Richard Henry Lee, and William Livingston for the Continental Congress a year before, a document which naturally put the Canadians on their guard against men who would speak in such insulting terms of their religion. As has been said, the Bishop of Quebec felt strongly about the Americans, and he did not hesitate to excommunicate anyone who joined them, and even those who defied Briand's order and later returned to Canada were denied the sacraments on their death bed if they would not openly recognize their guilt. For the most part, however, the Canadians needed no persuading to keep them free of involvement, although there continued to be some exceptions such as Father Pierre Huet de la Valinière, S.S., who was so vociferous a friend of the revolutionary cause that in 1779 he was sent out of the country by the British and came to the United States where for a decade or more he served on the American missions.

While the Americans were still hopeful of engaging the Canadians on their side this expectant mood accounted for putting an end to an annual celebration against the pope that for many years had been widely held throughout the colonies. In most of the principal towns November 5 was an occasion for burning the pope in effigy to commemorate Guy Fawkes Day, the anniversary of the attempt in 1605 of that Catholic zealot and his associates to blow up the parliament building in London when King James I, the royal family, and the members of Parliament were scheduled to be assembled there. Having assumed command of the army in the summer of 1775 at Cambridge, Massachusetts, George Washington, who was quite free of religious bias at any time, entertained high hopes that the military expeditions into Canada would enlist the aid of that country. Obviously the antics of Guy Fawkes Day were not calculated to serve that end, and when the commander-in-chief heard, therefore, that plans were afoot among his troops to hold the customary celebration he acted at once. He issued a general order on November 5, 1775, which expressed his surprise that there would be officers and soldiers "so void of common sense" as not to see the impropriety of "that ridiculous and childish custom of burning the Effigy of the pope," at a time when Americans were soliciting Canada's help. At such a time and in such circumstances to insult their religion, said Washington, was "so monstrous as not to be suffered or excused."[15] And with that strongly worded order no more was heard of the practice among the revolutionary armies. Thus the exigencies of the new situation in which the Americans found themselves were gradually wearing away some of the more notable and time honored traces of their hostility toward the Church of Rome.

A recent scholar who has investigated the status of the Catholics of this period has concluded that they could hardly have numbered more than about 20,000 in 1776 out of a total population of around 2,500,000.[16]

[15] "George Washington Bans Guy Fawkes Day in the Army, November 5, 1775," *ibid.*, p. 135.

[16] Metzger, *op. cit.*, p. 96.

Most of these people, as we know, were concentrated in Maryland and Pennsylvania, and it will be worthwhile, therefore, to say something about Catholic reaction to the war in these two provinces. The majority of the estimated 20,000 Catholics lived in Maryland where there was a long and grim history of penal legislation which was bound to figure in the Catholics' reckoning as they watched the first uncertain steps of their new state government for signs of its religious policy. Another factor that entered into their thinking was the precedent already set for them on the burning questions of the day by their most distinguished member, Charles Carroll of Carrollton. From the time when Carroll's First Citizen letters of 1773 had put him in the forefront of the rebel cause he had kept that position in the eyes of Protestants and Catholics alike by his approval of the burning of the *Peggy Stewart* in Annapolis harbor in October, 1774, with its cargo of English tea, and his outspoken views in favor of independence before others who were members of Maryland's convention or the First Continental Congress had said much about it.

Moreover, as we shall see, Carroll confirmed his early stand by later accepting a congressional commission to go to Canada in the spring of 1776 and by his signature affixed to the Declaration of Independence later that same summer. Nor was he in any way frightened off from the goal he had set for his country by the tumult raised against his Church by the Quebec Act. He held to his 'popery' just as firmly as he adhered to his views on independence, and this in spite of the fact that at the very time other Americans were finding the widespread fear of Carroll's Church a motive for recruiting men for the army. As the Reverend Daniel Barber, a Congregationalist minister who later became a convert to Catholicism, was to write, "The real fears of Popery, in New England, had its influence; it stimulated many timorous pious people to send their sons to join the military ranks in the field, and jeopardize their lives in the bloody contest. The common word then was, 'No King, No Popery.'"[17]

The Maryland Catholics, among whom those eligible for military service would probably not have exceeded 3,000 if they numbered that many, did their duty during the war in various capacities whether as regulars in the Continental Army, in the militia, in the burgeoning navy, or in the more prosaic task of working their plantations and farms

[17] Daniel Barber, *The History of My Own Times* (Washington, 1827), p. 17.

to provide the food and other essential items for the fighting men. The bulk of these people lived in Saint Mary's and Charles Counties, and the names listed among the militia for those counties, for example, Fenwick, Neale, Spalding, Abell, Mattingly, Mudd, and Brooke told unmistakably of Catholic families some of whom had been in Maryland for well over a century. Furthermore, the repeated recurrence of the Christian name of Ignatius told the same story, reflecting the devotion inculcated in these Marylanders by their Jesuit missionaries for the order's founder, Saint Ignatius Loyola. By the same token the periodic British raids into these counties showed the importance attached to their agricultural products by the enemy, eager as he was either to capture and carry them off or to destroy them before they reached the hands of Washington's soldiers.

And what has been said of the laity may likewise be said of their clergy who remained at their posts even though many of them were English by birth and had strong ties with the mother country. For example, the family of Father Joseph Mosley of Maryland's Eastern Shore urged him to come home to England. Acknowledging to his sister that there were, indeed, reasons which might prompt him to do so, yet his services were necessary where he was and his fellow priests would not hear of his departure. "I am really between hawk and buzzard," he said, "I know not what step I best take." In the end a sense of priestly duty was the overriding consideration, and Mosley was probably expressing the mind of most of the priests toward the war when he told his sister, "A Clergyman's call has little to do with civil broils and troubled waters. . . ."[18] The fact that the clergy's estates along Chesapeake Bay seemed to have been a favorite target for British men-of-war would indicate how their erstwhile fellow countrymen felt about them. True, no Catholic chaplain accompanied the troops, but since the normal procedure was to select a chaplain from the same religious faith as a majority of the men to be served, and since no priest joined the Pennsylvania loyalist regiment and no Maryland regiment was either exclusively or predominantly Catholic, no priests were found in service of this kind. All things considered, then, Father Mosley was reflecting the general situation among his coreligionists when he said that of all

[18] Mosley to Mrs. Dunn, Tuckahoe, Talbot County, Maryland, August 16, 1775, Edward I. Devitt, S.J. (Ed.), "Letters of Father Joseph Mosley, S.J., and Some Extracts from His Diary, 1757–1786," *Records of the American Catholic Historical Society of Philadelphia*, XVII (1906), 301.

those whom he knew "every Catholic . . . , not one excepted,"[19] had pledged their allegiance to the new United States.

In the case of Pennsylvania an entirely different religious background accounted for the fact that by 1776 its inhabitants showed such a wide variety of national origins and religious affiliations. Whereas the Catholics of Maryland were largely of English and Irish birth or descent, those of the neighboring province—far fewer in number than their Maryland brothers—were in the main Germans with the Irish and English making up the remainder. A census of the Pennsylvania Catholics in 1757 had revealed a total of only 1,365, and thus the next two decades would probably not have increased their numbers much beyond two or three times. Allowing for the aged, children, Negroes, and the disabled, the men eligible for armed service would, therefore, be very limited. Since there was evidence of around 300 Irish Catholics enrolled in one of the most famous of the province's fighting units, the Pennsylvania Line, and since the Irish were outnumbered among the Pennsylvania Catholics by both the Germans and the English, it would not seem unreasonable to conclude that 500 or more Catholics of this province saw service in the armed forces, a record that has prompted one historian to describe as "patriotism written in capital letters."[20]

Moreover, it was in Pennsylvania that most of the Catholic names prominently associated with the fighting in the American Revolution arose. For example, the Irish-born Stephen Moylan, brother of the Bishop of Cork, began his military career by leading a band of volunteers to join Washington's army at Cambridge. He later filled a succession of offices such as muster-master general of the Continental Army, aide-de-camp to Washington, a member of the latter's staff, quartermaster general, colonel of the Fourth Continental Dragoons, and finally for his conspicuous service in November, 1783, Congress conferred on Moylan the highest military honor won by a Catholic during the war, the rank of brigadier general. In fact, the Moylan family deserved well of the new republic for three brothers of the general gave substantial assistance to the cause in one way or another.

Besides the Moylans there were other Pennsylvanians like Captain John Barry who distinguished himself in his command of a number of ships whereon his exploits gave a much needed prestige to the infant

[19] *Ibid.*

[20] Metzger, *op. cit.* p. 235.

American navy. Another was Joseph Cauffman, a Catholic physician, who volunteered in the spring of 1777 while still in Vienna. Cauffman was assigned to the frigate *Randolph* as ship's surgeon, but a promising career was cut off when he was lost at sea in March, 1778, in an accident which occurred during a battle with a British cruiser off Barbados. Still other Catholic Philadelphians of prominence in the war were Thomas FitzSimmons and his brother-in-law, George Meade, who raised a volunteer fighting unit in 1775. Their principal service, however, was through the privateering activities of their shipping firm and its trade with the West Indies which helped to secure provisions for the French naval vessels after they entered American waters. FitzSimmons fought in the Princeton campaign, but more important was his appointment in the spring of 1777 to the State Navy Board of Pennsylvania where he rendered effective aid in the construction of ships and the stocking of military stores. Meanwhile Meade's most notable benefits to the Revolution came in the form of a generous contribution to the fund for the support of Washington's army which was then in such a dangerously weakened condition at Valley Forge, an act that at the time amounted to a gift in view of the slight prospect of repayment of the money. The patriotic conduct of FitzSimmons and Meade help to right the balance for the transactions of another Philadelphia Catholic shipping merchant, James Mease, whose generous subscription of £5,000 sterling for Washington's army was, unfortunately, offset by his shady dealings with Benedict Arnold for the disposal of surplus military goods for their personal gain.

Just as there was a James Mease to demonstrate that all Catholics of the revolutionary generation were not immune to the temptation to make a quick fortune at the price of honor, so other Philadelphians of Mease's religious faith were far from sharing the enthusiasm for the Revolution shown by men like the Moylans, Barry, and FitzSimmons. The attitude of some of these people probably sprang from their natural conservatism which dictated that it was better to take one's chances with the imposition of British duties which could, indeed, often be eluded than to lend encouragement to overturning the government and ushering in a chain of evils that might terminate in the destruction of public order, business, and property alike. And for these Catholics of the Tory persuasion there was the added consideration of the discrimination that had been practiced by most of the colonial regimes against their Church, a policy that had been brought up to date, so to speak, by the blatant hostility toward Catholicism of many of the revolutionary leaders. A combination of these incentives might well make them feel that they had nothing to gain by putting in with the rebels.

In any case, a number of Catholics were of this mind, and when military reverses caused the British commander in Philadelphia, Admiral Richard Howe, to conceal his hitherto open contempt of Irish Catholics as soldiers, a Catholic by the name of Alfred Clifton, who attended services at Saint Joseph's Church, emerged to put himself at the head of an enlistment campaign for a regiment to fight with the British under the name of the Roman Catholic Volunteers, an action to which Howe gave his approval in the fall of 1777. The top strength of this group was reached in August, 1778, with 331 men of English, Irish, and German background as well as of various social strata from Lieutenant Colonel Clifton, who was described as an English 'gentleman,' to a shopkeeper by the name of Dennis Dougherty who sold rum, sugar, and snuff. The Roman Catholic Volunteers' peak strength soon fell away, however, and by the time that Howe was replaced as commander by General Henry Clinton they had been reduced to 180 men, and since they continued to dwindle both in numbers and discipline in October, 1778, Clinton finally had the eighty remaining effectives absorbed into a regiment called the Volunteers of Ireland which had been raised the previous spring at the instance of the British commander and Lord Francis Rawdon. Although this unit remained intact until the spring of 1782, its later inglorious history in South Carolina and elsewhere need not detain us since it had little or no relation to the Catholics as such.

Insofar, then, as the Catholics' conduct during the war was concerned, the facts demonstrate that neither of two extreme interpretations given by historians of the last century can stand. First, George Bancroft's indictment of the Catholics in 1874 as having been guilty of widespread disaffection toward the revolutionary cause and of numerous desertions from the American army, was not true. Neither was the equally extreme statements made in rebuttal two years later by John Gilmary Shea to the effect that there were no Catholic Tories and that they were all staunch patriots. The truth was that the great majority of the Catholics of Maryland and Pennsylvania accepted the break with England in much the same spirit as their neighbors of other faiths and proceeded to do their duty in conformity with that fact. Yet this was not the case with all their coreligionists since the action of the Philadelphia group described above made it clear that the Tories found some sympathizers among the adherents of the Church of Rome.[21]

The changed conditions of society during wartime often render it impossible – or at least highly inexpedient – for men to indulge their customary prejudices. In this respect the Revolution was no exception. From the equivocal conduct of the Continental Congress in October, 1774, in addressing the inhabitants of Canada and King George III on the same day in contradictory terms regarding the Catholic religion, it became increasingly clear that the traditional manner of referring to that subject would have to be muted if it were not to militate against the goal that was then uppermost in the minds of most Americans. Nowhere was that more strikingly illustrated than in the latter's persistent belief that the Canadians might be induced to join them in the conflict against Britain. Thus on February 15, 1776, the Continental Congress passed a resolution to send a committee of three to Canada for this purpose, and the three selected were Benjamin Franklin, Samuel Chase, and Charles Carroll. That the last named was chosen was not too remarkable in view of his early and notable contributions to the revolutionary cause. But what was surprising was that Congress should have the same day added the request that Carroll's distant cousin, Father John Carroll, should be associated with the mission. Upon learning from John Hancock about two weeks later that the commission would soon be ready to set out, General Charles Lee replied:

> I should think that if some Jesuit or Religieuse of any other Order (but he must be a man of liberal sentiments, enlarged mind and a manifest friend to Civil Liberty) could be found out and sent to Canada, he would be worth battalions to us.

Lee had discussed his idea with others and found that they concurred, and he then told Hancock, "Mr. Carroll has a relative who exactly answers the description."[22] Actually, as we have seen, Congress had anticipated Lee, and in informing his friend, James Warner, of the appointment of the committee, John Adams added, "But we have done

[21] For a detailed account of this and other matters relating to the Catholics in the Revolution the writer is indebted to the scholarly volume of Father Metzger.

[22] Lee to Hancock, New York, February 27, 1776, *American Catholic Historical Researches*, XXIV (July, 1907), 225.

more. We have empowered the Committee to take with them, another gentleman of Maryland, Mr. John Carroll, a Roman Catholic priest, and a Jesuit, a Gentleman of learning and Abilities."[23] Just how Adams managed to reconcile this high estimate of Carroll with his well known horror of all Catholic priests, and especially of Jesuits, is not clear.

In any case, Congress had acted and it was now up to Charles Carroll to carry out its instructions. His cousin was in no sense elated by the news. While not at all insensible of the honor, John Carroll was his customary honest self in stating that he felt bound to make known to Congress how little they might hope to derive from his services on such a mission. His clerical training had precluded his knowing anything about diplomatic negotiations, and what was more, he was seriously concerned lest the sacred character of his priestly office should be jeopardized by this undertaking. He remarked:

> I have observed that when ministers of religion leave the duties of their profession to take a busy part in political matters, they generally fall into contempt, and sometimes even bring discredit to the cause in whose service they are engaged.[24]

It was an eminently wise attitude for a priest to take, one of the earliest evidences, incidentally, of the uncommon balance and good judgment of this man which within the next decade would so strongly recommend him as the proper person to lead the infant American Church.

In spite of the fact that the commissioners were furnished with in-

[23] Adams to Warner, Philadelphia, February 18, 1776, Edmund C. Burnett (Ed.) *Letters of Members of the Continental Congress* (Washington, 1921), I, 354. For a man with Adams' anti-Catholic prejudice he paid an extraordinary tribute to Charles Carroll. After informing Warren of the plan to send the commissioners to Canada he stated that he had met Carroll a year and a half before in Philadelphia and "was much pleased with his Conversation." He heard that the Marylander had a fortune of £200,000; he found him a well educated man and, of course, in the present circumstances his Catholic faith was an asset. Adams then stated: "In the Cause of American Liberty his Zeal Fortitude and Perseverance have been so conspicuous that he is said to be marked out for peculiar Vengeance by the Friends of Administration. But he continues to hazard his all, his immense Fortune, the largest in America, and his Life. This Gentleman's Character, if I foresee aright, will hereafter make a greater Figure in America" (I, 354).

[24] Undated memorandum, Peter Guilday, *The Life and Times of John Carroll, First Archbishop of Baltimore, 1735–1815* (New York, 1922), I, 96–97. Hereafter this work will be referred to as Guilday, *Carroll.* Carroll did not know that John Adams thought of his role as being at hand "to administer Baptism to the Canadian children and bestow Absolution upon such as have been refused it by the Toryfied Priests in Canada." Burnett, *op. cit.* I, 352.

structions by Congress which were intended to reassure the Canadians that their religion would be fully respected – such as Washington had furnished to Arnold on the latter's invasion the previous September – they encountered strong opposition to their mission. Enough has already been said to make clear why this was so, such as the Canadians' contentment with the Quebec Act, the warnings of Bishop Briand, the presence among them of people like Father John McKenna and others who were refugees from American anti-Catholic feeling, as well as the remnants of the armies of Montgomery and Arnold still lingering around Quebec. From the Continental Congress' standpoint, therefore, the mission was a total failure. Meanwhile Father Carroll was the occasion for a few exciting moments on his own in ecclesiastical circles. When the delegation arrived in Montreal in late April he had presented a letter of introduction from Father Ferdinand Farmer to Father Pierre Floquet, also an ex-Jesuit, and the last of that group who was friendly to the American cause. Floquet had already incurred the wrath of the Bishop of Quebec for his disapproval of the Quebec Act, and his cordial reception of Carroll and his permission for the latter to say Mass in his house gave added offense. The fact that Floquet had received back through Colonel Moses Hazen the Jesuits' old house in Montreal which had been taken as a prison by Governor James Murray, was bad enough, but the knowledge that he was hearing the confessions and giving communion to the men of the two companies raised by Hazen was too much for Briand and in June the priest was suspended.

There being nothing that they could do to alter the climate of opinion in Montreal, the American commissioners prepared to depart. Father Carroll joined Dr. Franklin at Saint John's on May 12 in order to accompany the latter who had become quite ill, while Chase and Charles Carroll traveled together and arrived in Philadelphia some weeks behind them. By late May Franklin and his companion had reached New York where the old doctor stated in a letter to their colleagues, Chase and Charles Carroll, "I find I grow daily more feeble, and I think I could hardly have got along so far, but for Mr Carroll's friendly Assistance and tender Care of me." [25] The association proved to be a meaningful one seven years later when the Holy See initiated an exchange of views on how to set up an ecclesiastical government in the United States with the American Minister to France, a post then

[25] Franklin to Chase and Charles Carroll, New York, May 27, 1776. Albert Henry Smyth (Ed.), *The Writings of Benjamin Franklin* (New York, 1906), VI, 449.

held by Franklin who had not forgotten his experience on the trip home from Montreal. The final word on the ecclesiastical aspects of the ill fated mission was meanwhile spoken by Bishop Briand in a pastoral letter of December 31, 1776, in which the doughty prelate viewed the American failure in Canada, on both the military and diplomatic fronts, as a sign of divine vindication of his position.

By the time that the American commissioners returned from their futile mission the issue of independence had been practically determined, and the governments that ruled the thirteen erstwhile colonies were beginning to consider the constitutional adjustments which the new situation demanded. We are interested solely in the changes that related to the subject of religion, and here it is to the individual states that one must turn. For the Continental Congress took no cognizance of religion from October, 1774, when it despatched its letter to the Canadians until, as we shall see, nearly a decade later when an inquiry from the Holy See to Franklin as American minister in Paris concerning the Church's future government in the new Republic, caused Franklin to ask the opinion of Congress. Father Carroll made the distinction between the national and state governments when his old friend, Father Charles Plowden, expressed his curiosity to know about the prospect of religious freedom for the American Catholics. Carroll replied that it was to the states that this problem pertained, and he was happy to inform Plowden – in a more optimistic vein, as it turned out, than the situation then warranted – "that the fullest and largest system of toleration is adopted in almost all the American states." He rejoiced that there were beginning to be indications that England and Ireland were moving in the same direction, which prompted him to add, "I cannot help thinking you are indebted to America for this piece of service." [26]

There was a wide variety in the way that the individual states undertook to handle the question of religion. The first notable break with the past occurred in Virginia where a renewed outbreak of Anglican bigotry against the Baptist preachers pushed the problem to the fore. As a result of this agitation when the state convention assembled in 1776 many petitions were sent in asking for the disestablishment of the Anglican Church. A bill of rights, framed in the main by George Mason, but containing a section on religion of which Patrick Henry and James

[26] Carroll to Plowden, February 28, 1779, Annabelle M. Melville, *John Carroll of Baltimore. Founder of the American Catholic Hierarchy* (New York, 1955), p. 55.

Madison were the authors, was adopted on June 12, 1776. The new legislation not only established the principle of freedom of religion for all men according to the dictates of their conscience, but it likewise brought about the separation of Church and State by declaring an end to a privileged status for any church. It was a good beginning, although the Old Dominion's final enactment on this subject came only nine years later with the passage of a special act establishing religious freedom in October, 1785, a document which was drawn up by Thomas Jefferson and seconded by Madison after a long and bitter fight with the vested Anglican interests in a series of debates that Jefferson characterized as "the severest contests in which I have ever been engaged." [27]

In contrast to Virginia's liberal settlement a number of the other states maintained their colonial restrictions on religious freedom with discrimination against certain groups. For example, New Hampshire held four conventions between 1776 and 1784, but the favored status of the Protestant religion stood throughout, as did a colonial law making the church a town institution to be supported by public taxes.[28] Connecticut followed much the same course, for although it did not adopt a new constitution the bill enacted in 1784 for securing the rights of conscience left no room for Catholics and Jews. New York's convention of 1777 excluded ministers from public office and destroyed the last remnants of its moribund Anglican establishment with the repeal seven years later of all laws granting privileges to that church. But more to the point were John Jay's fierce attacks on the Catholic Church in the New York convention of 1777 which carried the day against the counsels of moderation sounded by men like Robert Livingston and Gouverneur Morris. True, freedom of conscience and worship were established, but all naturalized citizens were compelled to take an oath of allegiance to New York State, "and abjure and renounce all allegiance and subjection to all and every foreign king, prince, potentate, and State in all matters, ecclesiastical as well as civil." [29] It was a provision that, as we shall see, kept Catholics out of office in the state until 1806.

New York's next door neighbor, New Jersey, drew up a new constitution in 1776 that granted complete freedom of worship, although

[27] Philip S. Foner (Ed.), *Basic Writings of Thomas Jefferson* (New York, 1944), p. 432.

[28] Thorpe, *op. cit.*, VI, 2451–2457.

[29] Thorpe, *op. cit.*, 2638.

only Protestants were guaranteed the enjoyment of civil rights and a religious test was imposed which confined public offices to "persons professing a belief in the faith of any Protestant sect. . . ." [30] In the same year Delaware's convention gave a broad grant of religious freedom in worship, but restricted office holding to those who believed in the Trinity and the divine inspiration of the Scriptures.[31] North Carolina's qualification for holding office was much narrower in that no one who denied the existence of God and "the truth of the Protestant religion," [32] was capable of holding office, a restriction which was removed in part in 1835 by the plea of the state's most distinguished Catholic layman, Judge William Gaston, who won the substitution of 'Christian' for 'Protestant,' after failing to get office holding free of all restriction. South Carolina took no action on religion in its convention of 1776, but it more than made up for the omission two years later. At that time ministers were excluded from the governorship, lieutenant governorship, and the legislature until two years after they would have quit the ministry, and a union of Church and State was assured with the declaration that, "The Christian Protestant religion shall be deemed, and is hereby constituted and declared to be, the established religion of this State." [33] Yet the customary pattern of Church-State union was not followed in that a provision was made that no one was to be coerced into paying for the support of a religious worship that he did not wish to uphold.

The southernmost state, Georgia, granted freedom of conscience in its constitution of 1777, but all members of the legislature were required to be of the Protestant religion.[34] At Massachusetts' first convention which took place in 1780 a constitution was drawn up that granted freedom of conscience and worship, but the privileged status of the Congregational Church was continued with provision being made for support and maintenance of "public Protestant teachers of piety, religion, and morality," [35] a feature of the Church-State union that lasted down to 1833. As for Rhode Island, no new state constitution was framed at the time of independence, and since its colonial charter had long contained a general grant of liberty of conscience and worship,

[30] *Ibid.*, V, 2597.
[31] *Ibid.*, I, 566.
[32] *Ibid.*, V, 2793.
[33] *Ibid.*, VI, 3255.
[34] *Ibid.*, II, 779.
[35] *Ibid.*, III, 1889.

no changes in this regard were needed to bring the state's instrument of government abreast of recent developments.[36]

Let us now see what was done in two states where the Catholics were most numerous. The first substantial break in the penal code that had fettered the Maryland Catholics for the better part of a century came in 1775 when all free men having an estate valued at forty pounds or over were admitted to the franchise "without religious distinction," a right that was restricted in the Declaration of Rights adopted on November 11, 1776, to those who were Christians. Maryland like New York excluded ministers from public office, but the Church of England was given ownership of its properties forever and thus there was avoided the quarrel that plagued Virginia for so long a time. To the Catholics it must have been a source of joy and relief to learn that their state now espoused the principle

> That, as it is the duty of every man to worship God in such manner as he thinks most acceptable to him; all persons, professing the Christian religion, are equally entitled to protection in their religious liberty. . . . nor ought any person to be compelled to frequent or maintain, or contribute, unless on contract, to maintain any particular place of worship, or any particular ministry. . . .[37]

It heralded such a welcome new day for Catholic Marylanders that they were in no way disturbed by the oath of allegiance which was imposed and by the fact that theirs was the only state to appoint a form of public prayer for the government. The last item irked the Anglican ministers and the majority of them refused to conform, whereupon they were confronted with the alternative of paying a treble tax for their disobedience or leaving the state. Most of them departed with the result that the Anglican churches either fell into desuetude or were taken over by other denominations.

As for Pennsylvania, its action was embodied in a Declaration of Rights adopted on September 28, 1776, that contained the following article:

> That all men have a natural and unalienable right to worship Almighty God according to the dictates of their own consciences and understanding: And that no man ought or of right can be compelled to attend any religious worship, or erect or support any place of worship, or maintain any ministry,

[36] *Ibid.*, VI, 3212–3213.
[37] *Ibid.*, III, 1689–1690.

contrary to, or against, his own free will and consent: Nor can any man, who acknowledges the being of a God, be justly deprived or abridged of any civil rights as a citizen, on account of his religious sentiments or peculiar mode of religious worship: And that no authority can or ought to be vested in, or assumed by any power whatever, that shall in any case interfere with, or in any manner controul, the right of conscience in the free exercise of religious worship.[38]

It was an enactment with which Pennsylvania Catholics could have no quarrel, even if some of the more advanced spirits among them might have shared Franklin's disappointment in the restriction of office holding to those who believed in God and in the divine inspiration of the Scriptures. With Maryland and Pennsylvania having thus liberated their Catholic subjects from all legal restrictions four months after independence was declared, the latter were able to lend their efforts to the war after the fashion of men who had a personal stake in its outcome.

Civil liberties having been attained as a consequence of the new conditions created by the war, the Catholics experienced a further boon to their religion from a series of events that occurred outside the country. Even before independence had been declared the Continental Congress had sought outside help, although little encouragement had been forthcoming from tentative approaches such as those of Silas Deane in Paris. True, there was little love for England to be found in Paris, Madrid, The Hague, and other European capitals, but there was also little confidence that the Americans were equal to their undertaking until the defeat of Burgoyne at Saratoga in October, 1777. That made a difference. The French foreign minister, Count de Vergennes, now became convinced that the rebels represented a good risk, although for some months his attempt to implement that conviction was thwarted by the terms of the Family Compact of 1761 with Spain, where fear of the British fleet rather than regard for the British themselves slowed down the consent to France's action. Finally, however, the obstacles were overcome and on February 6, 1778, France entered a treaty of alliance with the United States for the prosecution of the war with Deane, Franklin, and Arthur Lee signing for the Americans.

With the strength and prestige of His Most Christian Majesty's government enrolled on the side of the Americans their cause took on a

[38] *Ibid.*, V, 3082.

more promising aspect on both sides of the Atlantic. In August of 1778 there arrived in Philadelphia Conrad Alexandre Gerard as France's first Minister to the United States and the first diplomat accredited to the American government. The fact that the new minister was a Catholic was not lost upon the Tories whose newspapers, as has been said, made much of the coming of the ally's ships ladened with "tons of holy water, crucifixes, hair shirts, and other 'trappings of popery.'"[39] And the distressed Tories were in for more of the same thing, for though Spain was not brought in as an ally of the United States, the Spaniards were prevailed on in June, 1779, to declare war against Britain, and before long another Catholic dignitary, Don Juan de Miralles, appeared in Philadelphia as agent of the Spanish government. Thus the nucleus of the new nation's first diplomatic corps was Catholic. Moreover, in fulfillment of the terms of the treaty of alliance French fleets entered American ports and a French army arrived to take the field against the common foe. Chaplains accompanied all these forces so that between 1778 and the end of the Revolution over 100 priests had served the French on American soil. Only three of the priests in the French service, however, remained in the country after the war, namely, Paul de Saint Pierre, O.Carm., an Irish-born Capuchin by the name of Charles Whelan, and John Rosseter who later joined the Augustinians and exercised his ministry in and about Philadelphia.

Many an American must, indeed, have entertained grave misgivings as he observed the freedom with which these priests moved about, to say nothing of the official courtesies which his government now felt compelled to pay to Catholic religious services held under French or Spanish auspices. For example, on July 4, 1779, a *Te Deum* in Saint Mary's Church in Philadelphia drew the president and members of the Continental Congress at the invitation of Gerard, the French minister, when the sermon was delivered by Father Seraphim Bandol, a Franciscan friar, who was chaplain on *Le Languedoc*, a unit of the fleet. Again on May 8, 1780, members of the Congress attended a solemn requiem for the Spanish agent, de Miralles, at Saint Joseph's Church, as a number of the same body did again – in company with a delegation of the Pennsylvania assembly – when Saint Mary's was the scene of a thanksgiving service on November 4, 1781, for the victory at York-

[39] Thomas A. Bailey, *A Diplomatic History of the American People* 5th ed. (New York, 1955), p. 20.

town. To be sure, these were merely acts of courtesy, yet they undoubtedly gave a feeling of uneasiness to those who from childhood had been taught to abhor everything connected with the Church of Rome.

Needless to say, those who had opposed the Revolution from the outset did not fail to make the most of these disturbing events. The historic prejudice was thus made to do double duty in papers like the *Royal Gazette* and the New York *Gazette* by arousing the populace on the score of the Catholic menace, and at the same time using this point to deflate the rebels' diplomatic victory in securing the French alliance. And when the hour arrived for Benedict Arnold's treason in the fall of 1780, he issued a proclamation to the military in which he ridiculed the attendance of members of Congress at the requiem Mass for de Miralles where, he said, they were participating in the rites of a Church "against whose anti-Christian corruptions, your pious ancestors would have witnessed with their blood."[40]

But whatever were the private thoughts to which the fulminations of Arnold and the Tories may have given rise, they did nothing to dim the enthusiasm with which the majority of Americans greeted the French alliance. In fact, if the Tories were to have judged matters by the Pennsylvania legislature's establishment in 1779 of the University of Pennsylvania from the old College of Philadelphia by a charter that called for the board of trustees to number the senior ministers of all the city's religious denominations, including Father Ferdinand Farmer of Saint Joseph's Church, they might have concluded that the country had already succumbed to the baneful influence of this increase of Catholics in their midst. In this way, incidentally, did Farmer become the state's first Catholic to hold civil office. In the same manner people of the loyalist persuasion would have been disturbed by the address to the Canadians which Charles H. T. Count d'Estaing, commander of the French fleet, issued at Boston in the name of King Louis XVI on October 28, 1778. D'Estaing made a special appeal to the Catholic clergy whose labors, he said, merited their being constituted "a body in the State" and given part in the government. The flambouyant rhetoric of the French admiral stirred some Canadian hopes that they might gain their liberty from the British, and even the

[40] Proclamation of General Benedict Arnold to the Officers and Soldiers of the Continental Army, New York, October 20, 1780 [John Almon], *The Remembrancer* (London, 1780), Part I, 21.

Catholic Indians in Maine got wind of the changed state of affairs and sought to use it to get a priest. D'Estaing's proclamation was sent to them and in November, 1778, the tribesmen in the region of Saint John's River were told that both the King of France and the latter's minister at Philadelphia had been approached in their behalf.

The allegiance of these Indians whose lands lay astride the area between the Americans and the British colony to the north, was a matter of importance to both the military and civil authorities. In a circuitous way the coming of the French was responsible for reactivating for a time the Catholic mission among these Indians. During an Anglo-French naval battle one of the latter's ships was captured and brought into New York, and among the prisoners was the chaplain, Father Hyacinthe de la Motte, O.S.A. He was one of a group who were exchanged for English prisoners and who were transferred late in 1778 to Boston where the Massachusetts government, searching for a priest through whom they hoped to hold the Indians, engaged de la Motte. He arrived in Maine in the spring of 1779 and as an emissary of the King of France and a friend of the United States he summoned the tribesmen to meet him at Passamaquoddy. Unfortunately de la Motte was not suited by temperament for the work and after a few months his lack of tact compelled Colonel John Allan, Massachusetts superintendent of the eastern redmen, to request his recall. The Indians had, nonetheless, made their point in having a priest return to their villages with the consent of the Massachusetts government.

Meanwhile the war was also having its effect on the inhabitants of the distant settlements around the Great Lakes and through the Mississippi Valley most of whom were French-speaking Catholics. Mindful of his responsibility to these people who lived in this remote part of his diocese, Bishop Briand sent Father Jean François Hubert to Cahokia in the Illinois Country in 1778 where he remained until the next year ministering to the inhabitants there and in the surrounding villages. At Detroit an old Franciscan friar, Simplicius Bocquet, was still carrying on when Hubert came there in October, 1782. Father Simplicius, whose ministry at Detroit dated from 1754, was recalled to Quebec at this time and the spiritual needs of the people were taken care of by Hubert and Father Louis Payet, the new pastor of the town. For the next fourteen years Detroit remained under British control until the treaty between the United States and Britain finally terminated their occupation, and in January, 1796, the Bishop of Quebec informed Bishop Carroll that the area was now part of the Diocese of Baltimore.

More directly related to the war and the Catholic Church in the western country, however, was Kaskaskia located along the Mississippi River in what is today southwestern Illinois. Since 1768 Father Pierre Gibault had been stationed there and he was still there at the time that George Rogers Clark succeeded in getting the Virginia government to attempt the seizure of this western territory from the British. Clark was commissioned a lieutenant colonel and he set out in May, 1778, at the head of his 175 militiamen for the long trek to the West, arriving at Kaskaskia on July 4 where they experienced no difficulty in entering this French village. When it became known to Father Gibault that their goal was Post Vincennes about 240 miles to the east, the Americans' friendly treatment of his parishioners, plus his sympathy with their cause, prompted him, as we have seen, to volunteer his assistance. Since he realized how strongly his superior, Bishop Briand, would deprecate anything of this kind, he kept in the background when the expedition departed on July 14 and the village doctor, Jean Baptiste Laffont, was ostensibly the Americans' chief guide.

But it was Father Gibault with his approach to the people of Vincennes by way of what he described for Clark as "hints in the Spiritual way that would be conducive to the business," [41] that made him the effective intermediary for the quick surrender of the post. So notable a part had he played, in fact, that Gibault became an object of execration at British headquarters in Quebec, and especially to Colonel Henry Hamilton and his troops at Detroit who, a recent writer has said, "could hardly wait to get their hands on him, though fortunately they never did." [42] In Clark's report he made known what Gibault had done, and in 1780 Governor Patrick Henry issued an official expression of commendation and gratitude to the priest and the Virginia legislature likewise passed a resolution of thanks.

While Father Gibault's American sympathies were doubtless sincere, it was apparently his fear of Briand that at times caused him to speak and write of his own share in these events in a quite ambiguous way. Yet even his misgivings on this score did not prevent him two

[41] John Bakeless, *Background to Glory. The Life of George Rogers Clark* (Philadelphia, 1957), p. 88.
[42] *Ibid.*, p. 107.

years later from describing for George Rogers Clark the sad condition to which the Kaskaskia had by that time been reduced and begging his assistance. Yet in spite of their misfortunes, Gibault assured him, "we are of good courage and are so good Americans that we are ready to defend ourselves to the death against any who attack us. I pray you to accept my respects," he said, "and to employ me in any way in my power for your service."[43]

To Father Pierre Gibault, then, one of the last of the seminary priests of Quebec whose missions had been inaugurated in the Illinois Country almost a century before, there was owed a major share of the credit for delivering that area into American hands. Patrick Henry, Governor of Virginia, expressed that thought in the instructions he sent to George Rogers Clark late in 1778 urging him to try to bring the inhabitants of Detroit under American rule as he had those in the Illinois Country and along the Wabash. Recommending that Clark consult with others, Henry said, "Perhaps Mr. Gibault, the Priest (to whom this country owes many thanks for his zeal and services) may promote this affair."[44] Gibault may, indeed, well have felt ill repaid for his efforts when after Virginia's annexation in 1778 of what it styled the 'County of Illinois,' there was imposed a military regime the harshness of which created a general dissatisfaction that endured until the Ordinance of 1787 finally cleared the doubts about the area's sovereignty and provided a friendlier rule for its inhabitants.

In one other region of what would one day be the United States the Catholic Church underwent certain changes as a consequence of the war, and that was in Florida. One of the conditions on which Spain had entered the fighting against Britain was that France would help to deliver Gibraltar and Florida into its hands. With that as an objective, Don Bernardo Galvez, Governor of Louisiana, opened a whirlwind campaign in September, 1779, that struck the British in the region of the Gulf of Mexico and compelled them to surrender in turn Baton Rouge, Fort Panmure at Natchez, Mobile, and finally Pensacola. With these victories came a change of ecclesiastical personnel as, for example, at Mobile where Immaculate Conception Church at first got a Spanish Mercedarian, Salvadore de la Esperanza, for pastor, although not for long since parochial changes were numerous there during the succeed-

[43] Gibault to Clark, Kaskaskia, May 10, 1780, Clarence Walworth Alvord (Ed.), *Kaskaskia Records, 1778–1790* (Springfield, 1909), pp. 518–519.

[44] Henry to Clark, December 15, 1778, *ibid.*, p. 62.

ing decade. A group of Spanish Capuchins from Louisiana had followed Galvez' army into Florida and when Pensacola fell on May 8, 1781, they took charge of that church. Further east the little colony of Minorcans at New Smyrna had found no mitigation of their hardships from the British after the latter acquired Florida in 1763, and in 1777 the approximately 600 survivors left with their priest, Father Pedro Camps, and moved up the coast to Saint Augustine. Here Lieutenant Governor John Moultrie was more considerate of their needs, although facilities for their religious life were sadly lacking with the parish church of the little provincial capital practically in ruins and the old Franciscan convent in use as a military barracks. In any case, the Minorcans' time under British rule had not long to run, for in the peace settlements of 1783 Florida was ceded back to Spain.

It was not surprising, of course, that there should have been little general progress among the Catholics during the decade and a half after 1775. The disturbed conditions would allow for no real advance, although most of the congregations in Maryland and Pennsylvania held their own reasonably well due to the fidelity of their priests. As has been said, these men remained at their posts in spite of such inducements as the urging of their families that they should return to England, as was true in the case of Father Joseph Mosley. The deaths of two able missionaries like Fathers Matthias Manners (Sittensperger) in June, 1775, and George Hunter in June, 1779, increased the load of work since no new recruits came out to America in these years. Father John de Ritter continued his round of regular visits to the rural German settlements like Goshenhoppen and its neighbors, and he included as well Reading, Easton, and Allentown in his tours with the first baptisms performed in the last named place in March, 1774. Father Robert Molyneaux remained in Philadelphia most of the time where at intervals he had the company of Ferdinand Farmer who made the city his headquarters. Farmer was often absent on far-ranging trips in search of scattered Catholics that probably made him the most active itinerant missionary of the war years. He covered an increasingly large area to the north with trips into Somerset County, New Jersey, to the new mining districts in Passaic County where he ministered in the homes of German settlers attracted by the iron mines and furnaces, and even as far as Fishkill, New York, where in October, 1781, he baptized fourteen persons. Farmer's register showed 139 baptisms for northern New Jersey in 1775 with 170 for the year 1781 and 129 for the following year. On one of the last of his northern tours he left Fishkill on November 4, 1783, and may even have visited New York City after its evacuation by the British three weeks later. It is little wonder that he died on August 17, 1786, at the age of sixty-six a worn out man.

In the meantime the priests in Maryland carried on under what were, perhaps, more trying conditions than those with which their Pennsylvania brothers had to contend. The reopening of the church in Baltimore in 1775 for at least a monthly Mass added to the obligations of Bernard Diderick to whom this duty was assigned. In the countryside, as previously mentioned, British men-of-war sailing up Chesapeake Bay took a toll on the properties of the clergy by shelling buildings and stealing slaves and provisions. Saint George's Island which belonged to the clergy was occupied for a while by Virginia's royal governor, John Murray, Earl of Dunmore, and at Newtown the priests' house was turned into a hospital for American soldiers. The war likewise interfered with the conduct of religious services due to lack of supplies as, for example, the holy oils needed in anointings. Since they could not be had through the customary channel, the vicars apostolic in England, priests in both Canada and the United States profited by the action of Juan de Miralles, Spanish agent in Philadelphia, who in May, 1779, helped to make good the deficiency by securing the oils from the Bishop of Santiago de Cuba.

All things considered, then, the fortunes of the American Catholics took a turn for the better as a consequence of the Revolution and the changes that it brought in its wake. The Catholic minority was still exceedingly small, obscure, and for the most part of very modest means, but the historic decade that closed in 1785 with the final peace treaties had brought one basic difference: the Catholics were now free to worship God openly according to their traditional faith; moreover, two states where they lived in greatest numbers had made them for the first time free to enjoy their rights as citizens.

CHAPTER FIFTEEN

IN SEARCH OF A BISHOP

The ultimate outcome of the war was decided when the combined American-French forces accomplished the defeat of Lord Cornwallis at Yorktown and he sued for terms of surrender on October 17, 1781. True, desultory fighting continued elsewhere, but the final issue was no longer in doubt. By the spring of 1782 John Adams had won the recognition of the United States by The Netherlands, and in the following October he secured a substantial loan and a treaty of amity and commerce. Faced with certain defeat, Britain was not adverse to driving a wedge between its enemies, so when a rift appeared in Franco-American relations over France's wish to delay the peace for Spain, the British accepted the Americans' terms in a preliminary treaty on November 30, 1782, while the definitive treaties by which they concluded the war with the United States, France, and Spain were signed on September 3, 1783.

It was a time when the Catholics would obviously be preoccupied with the problems relating to the newly won freedom in both their religious and civil rights. Yet before their leaders could give their undivided attention to these matters the Catholic community was to experience the shock of the first formal apostasy among its priests. Charles Wharton, born in Maryland in 1748, educated at Saint Omer, Bruges, and Liége after he became a Jesuit, remained in Europe until June, 1783, when he returned to Maryland and took up residence on his estate. A visit to Father John Carroll prompted the latter to tell his English priest friend, Charles Plowden, in September of that year that

Wharton showed real talent and, he thought, too much intelligence to be guilty of the doctrinal errors bruited about him during his time as chaplain to the Catholics in Worcester, England.

But Carroll was mistaken, for since July, 1782, evidence had been slowly accumulating that Wharton was no longer a sincere Catholic, and in May, 1784, he went to Philadelphia where he gave his *Letter to the Roman Catholics of the City of Worcester* to the printer. Written in a polished and cultivated style, this personal apologia for leaving the Church professed a love for the Catholic clergy and a regret that he had felt compelled in conscience to act as he did. The *Letter* was well timed in that its principal argument centered on the author's desire for intellectual freedom which, he said, he could not find in the Church. Feeling was then running high for freedom of every kind, and the liberty of religious opinion was no exception, with the result that Wharton's polite accusations seemed to reveal the Church as the foe of freedom at precisely a time when such a charge would create the maximum offense in the minds of most Americans.

In other words, the attack of the ex-Jesuit was a serious one and the Catholics realized that it would have to be answered to offset the damage that Wharton had done. In this situation practically all the Catholic leaders – clerical and lay alike – turned to John Carroll as the man best equipped to perform this unpleasant duty. Father Molyneaux invited him to come to Philadelphia to prepare the reply, acknowledging, however, that his efforts to find the necessary books at the Logan Library, the best in the city, had not been very successful. Carroll had meanwhile learned that the library at Annapolis was a good one, and it was there that he wrote most of his *Address to the Roman Catholics of the United States of America.* As mentioned before, Wharton's repudiation of traditional Catholic doctrines like transsubstantiation, the infallibility of the Church, and the impossibility of salvation outside of the Church, were expressed in so measured and dignified a way that it made them all the more effective, and by the same token, all the more difficult to answer. But Carroll replied in kind with a matching dignity that admitted no bitterness of tone or invective in a detailed answer that ran to 116 printed pages or about twice the size of Whaton's *Letter.* In the course of his reply he was able to show that Wharton's scholarship was not beyond criticism since he had used some of his patristic and theological sources inaccurately.

Carroll's *Address* was effective enough to bring a second communication from Wharton as well as two other replies in England in 1785, one by a Franciscan, William Pilling who warned the Worcester Catholics against their former chaplain, and the other by Father Joseph Berington which was addressed to John Hawkins, a Benedictine friend of Wharton's who had also left the Church. In September, 1786, Plowden stated that their mutual friend, Father John Thorpe, had reported that the *Address* had been well received at the Roman Curia, an exception being the criticism of a certain Abate Cucagna of the Irish College who did not fancy the American's interpretation of the doctrine *extra ecclesiam nulla salus.* As for Wharton himself, he soon joined the Protestant Episcopal Church, married twice, and served as Rector of Saint Mary's Church in Burlington, New Jersey, from 1798 to his death in 1833. He was again heard from by way of published criticism of Catholic doctrine in 1833 when he challenged the explanation of Anthony Kohlmann, S.J., on the Sacrament of Penance. Thus was there launched in the United States what was to become an abundant literary output in the field of Protestant-Catholic polemics.

The Wharton controversy was the occasion for an exchange of views between John Carroll and Joseph Berington which is worthy of mention by reason both of the subject and of Carroll's later prominence. The latter had used Berington's book, *State and Behaviour of English Catholics from the Reformation to the Year 1780*, to advantage in answering Wharton, but a number of the author's fellow churchmen were highly critical of what they regarded as its doctrinal errors. Among these was John Douglass, Vicar Apostolic of the London District and Berington's own superior, who went so far as to suspend his faculties. Part of the trouble arose from his support of the Catholic Committee, a group composed mostly of laymen intent on the political emancipation of the English Catholics and not much inclined to heed the conservative clergy. The fact that the priest was a cousin of Bishop Charles Berington, Vicar Apostolic of the Midland District, who was himself a member of the Catholic Committee and generally sympathetic to its work, did not save him from being twice suspended by Douglass. But in 1801 Berington made a public recantation of his errors, was reinstated, and from that time until his death in 1827 at the age of eighty-five he kept clear of such censures.

During his early years, however, Joseph Berington's advanced views on various questions such as the relations of Church and State more than once drew the fire of contemporaries, including Carroll's friend, Father Plowden, for what were thought his minimizing tendencies of the Church's rights *vis-à-vis* the State. Yet Plowden's disapproval did not cause the American to back away from Berington, nor did it prevent Carroll from expressing admiration for his writings and from urging him to tackle two problems in a future book, namely, to ascertain what he called "the boundaries of the spiritual jurisdiction of the Holy See," and also "the use of the Latin tongue in the publick Liturgy." Revealing the liberal turn of mind of the man who was soon to be named the first American bishop, Carroll said:

I consider these two points as the greatest obstacles to Christians of other denominations to a thorough union with us, or at least to a much more general diffusion of our religion, particularly in N. America. . . . With respect to the latter point, I cannot help thinking that the alteration of the Church discipline ought not only be solicited, but insisted upon as essential to the service of God and benefit of mankind. Can there be anything more preposterous than an unknown tongue; and in this country either for want of books or inability to read, the great part of our congregations must be utterly ignorant of the meaning and sense of the publick office of the Church.[1]

Opinions of this kind arouse opposition today, to say nothing of the late eighteenth century, so it was not surprising that when Berington used Carroll's letter in his feud with Bishop Douglass that alarm should have been expressed in conservative quarters. John T. Troy, O.P., Archbishop of Dublin, for example, informed Carroll that the question of the vernacular had become a debated issue in Ireland and that he had written a sixty-page pastoral letter against it. An Irish Franciscan, Arthur O'Leary, also wrote in a critical vein, and in 1786 this friar published a review of the vernacular controversy to which he appended a defense of the Franciscan Pope Clement XIV in suppressing the Jesuits, an appendix that brought a sharp rejoinder from Carroll.

Berington was in complete agreement with Carroll's stand on the vernacular as he told him in March, 1788, and according to him, the only part of the latter's *Address* that had drawn criticism in England was the appended note on the suppression of the Society of Jesus. He had heard rumors that Carroll might be made a bishop and he hoped that they might prove true. He was outspoken in his criticism of what

[1] Carroll to Berington, n.p. [1787], Guilday, *Carroll,* I, 130.

he considered the abuses of the Roman Curia, and he hoped that the American Church would get off to a good start without the burden of what he termed "those obstacles which the Court of Rome ever has, and ever will throw in the way of a Church miserably constituted as is that of the English Catholics." Foreseeing great possibilities for the Church in the United States to fix a new pattern in the Church-State relations, Berington concluded:

Certainly were I circumstanced as you in America seem to be, I would shut my eyes on the 14 last centuries, and only consider what was the prerogative of the See of Rome during the Apostolic ages and the years immediately succeeding to them. All that is *essential* then existed; the rest is abuse and usurpation.[2]

It would be interesting to know Carroll's reactions, but if he replied no copy would seem to have survived.

At the time the situation in the United States was still uncertain for the Catholics both as to the form that their ecclesiastical government would take and the relations that the Church would have to the State. On the first point they had theoretically remained under the jurisdiction of Bishop Challoner until his death in January, 1781, and then continued under that of his successor, James Talbot. Practically, however, the connection had been pretty much severed at the Revolution with Father John Lewis continuing on as Challoner's vicar general. Knowledge of the old bishop's death reached America only about the time of the victory at Yorktown, and that Bishop Talbot made no pretense to jurisdiction over this country became clear in 1783 when two American priests, John Boone and Henry Pile, applied to him for faculties on their way home and he declined to grant them.

Meanwhile the problems of internal organization of the Catholic community had not gone without consideration. Among the priests, who then numbered between twenty and twenty-five, John Carroll, perhaps, had the matter most at heart, and in 1782 he wrote out a so-called Plan of Organization which sought to put the clergy's affairs on a systematic basis. Ever since his return from Europe in 1774 he had acted apart from his fellow priests in that he felt they were deluding themselves about the prospects of a restoration of the Society of Jesus, and that their lack of energy made it impossible to deal realistically with the problems then confronting the Catholic minority. With that

[2] Berington to Carroll, Oscott, March 27, 1788, *ibid.*, I, 132.

in mind Carroll was at pains to outline in his Plan of Organization a way to settle the properties of the suppressed Society by common consent. He would have them placed in the hands of an administrator who would supervise them for the benefit of the spiritual good of the people and the sustenance of the clergy generally, not as a trust, so to speak, against the day when the Society of Jesus would be restored. In other words, Carroll's breadth of view embraced the needs of the Church in general and not merely those of any single group. In all of which there was no lack of affection for the stricken Society; on the contrary, Carroll's sense of outrage at the wrong done the Jesuits was clear from the note he appended in 1784 to his reply to Wharton. Moreover, he was just as alert and as critical of the hostile attitude of the Congregation de Propaganda Fide toward the ex-Jesuits as any of his confrères, and in commenting in September, 1783, on the rumors then circulating concerning Propaganda's designs on the Jesuit properties in Europe, he remarked to Plowden that if any emissaries of the Congregation were to come to the United States they would "certainly return empty-handed." [3]

The Plan of Organization stirred the priests to action, and on June 27, 1783, John Lewis presided at a meeting of six of their number at the Whitemarsh plantation midway between Georgetown and Annapolis when their missions were divided into three districts, in each of which the clergy were to appoint two delegates to a general meeting. Meanwhile they exchanged views on the proposed form of government and finally by October, 1784, they were ready for formal adoption of a constitution which contained nineteen articles on the form of government for the priests, six on rules for individual members, and eight for their properties. A formula of promise was added which each member of the Select Body of the Clergy, as they were henceforth called, was asked to sign. It was this document that served as the clergy's rule of life until 1806 when the Jesuits were restored in the United States. That the situation called for regularization beyond this, however, was obvious if for no other reason than to provide for the thinning ranks of the clergy. As Father Mosley said regarding the priests in the autumn of 1784, "We are all growing old, we are very weak handed, few come from England to help us." [4] Four priests had died between June, 1775, and Novem-

[3] Carroll to Plowden, n.p., September 26, 1783, *ibid.*, I, 167, n. 3.

[4] Mosley to Mrs. Dunn, Saint Joseph's, Talbot County, October 4, 1784, Devitt, *op. cit.*, p. 306.

ber, 1782, while no new recruits had arrived between the return of Carroll (1774) and that of Leonard Neale in April, 1783.

One of the principal actions taken by the priests at their meeting in November, 1783, was the appointment of a committee to draw up a petition to the Holy See requesting that Father Lewis, their superior, be given certain episcopal faculties such as administering the Sacrament of Confirmation, blessing altar stones and chalices, and granting faculties to newly arrived priests. The American government, they maintained, would not permit a bishop, and the case of the Anglicans was adduced as an example of the difficulties that would be encountered on this score. The customary lengthy interval ensued, and then on August 20, 1784, Carroll received a letter from Father John Thorpe at Rome informing him that on June 9 Pope Pius VI had named him superior of the American missions and that as soon as additional data about the American situation were received he would be named a bishop. News of the appointment also came from Plowden, but this time it was accompanied by a rather ominous note to the effect that the Apostolic Nuncio to France, Archbishop Giuseppe Doria Pamphili, had inaugurated negotiations with Benjamin Franklin, American Minister to Paris, concerning the future government of the American Church. Annoyed at this ignoring of the American priests, Carroll told Plowden:

> Nothing can place in a stronger light the aversion to the remains of the Society than the observation made by you of a negotiation being carried on relative to the affairs of religion with Dr. Franklin, without ever deigning to appy for information to the Catholic clergy of this country.[5]

Carroll said that he would protest directly to Franklin were it not that it would put him in too conspicuous a position. For he was equally distressed by the knowledge that Rome was considering him for the miter, and if his fellow priests agreed that he could decline the appointment without serious injury to religion, he would certainly do so.

Meanwhile the committee of three appointed to frame a memorial against a bishop had finished its work and Father Bernard Diderick, spearhead of the anti-episcopal group, sent it for Carroll's perusal. Diderick was determined not to have a bishop, although he made it clear that should such prove to be necessary the committee would have no objection to Carroll. The memorial stated that six of the twenty-two

[5] Carroll to Plowden, n.p., September 18, 1784, Guilday, *Carroll*, I, 175.

priests had been named to confer on matters relating to the Church's future, and they now desired to inform the pope of the reasons why they did not wish to have a bishop. There were strong Protestant prejudices against bishops in the United States, there was no means of support for such an office, and there was likewise no means to bring a greater number of missionaries to this country.

Although at the time John Carroll was in substantial agreement with the committee's views, he told Thorpe that he had been compelled to withdraw from the meeting where the memorial had been framed because of illness, and he had later learned that the committee's action had displeased some of the priests who were not present. He regarded Diderick's appointment to the committee as a mistake since in his judgment he lacked both prudence and a knowledge of the world. In the interval a third notice of his appointment as superior reached Carroll through the French minister, François Barbé de Marbois, and finally on November 26 the official documents arrived from Leonardo Cardinal Antonelli, Prefect of Propaganda. Obviously the memorial in favor of Lewis' episcopal faculties had not reached Rome in time to prevent Carroll being named superior, but it probably slowed down the pace of his appointment as a bishop.

That Rome should have been perplexed on how to proceed in organizing the American Catholics on a permanent basis, was altogether understandable. For the first time in its long history the Holy See was confronted by the necessity of providing an ecclesiastical rule for a small group of its adherents living in the midst of an overwhelming Protestant population in a country that had adopted a republican form of government and that was located over 3,000 miles away. The Roman Curia had, indeed, for several centuries dealt with matters relating to North America, but transactions pertaining to the possessions of Spain and France offered no precedent for the present situation. Nor could any guiding principle be found in Rome's previous dealings with the English in that part of the world, for it was now out of the question to think in terms of the vicar apostolic in London who had maintained at least nominal jurisdiction over the American missions for nearly a century. Moreover, the organization to which practically all the priests in the new republic had belonged was no longer in existence to offer any help, the Society of Jesus having been suppressed a decade before the close of the American Revolution. Given these circumstances, it was not extraordinary that the Cardinal Prefect of Propaganda should have turned for enlightenment to France as the recent ally of the Americans. At the court of Versailles the long established papal nunciature afforded a ready channel through which the Holy See could initiate an inquiry as to the best course for it to pursue in the United States and, perhaps, there also could be found the financial assistance that would be needed to place that infant Church on a firm foundation.

Such in brief was the background that lay behind Cardinal Antonelli's instructions of January, 1783, to Archbishop Doria Pamphili. He suggested that the nuncio approach the government of Louis XVI for guidance in the matter, as well as with a view to having inserted in the peace treaties that still remained to be concluded what Antonelli called "an article concerning the free exercise and the maintenance of the Catholic religion," in the new republic.[6] But the moment was ill timed, for the French were then in a bad humor with their wartime allies over the latter's failure to respond to France's wishes concerning the peace settlement and the repayment of its loans. For that reason the foreign minister, Charles Gravier, Count de Vergennes, declined to make any attempt to influence the government at Philadelphia, and in the summer of 1783, therefore, Doria Pamphili brought Antonelli's proposals to the attention of the American minister. Franklin became quite enthusiastic and, in fact, he went beyond the nuncio's request that he sound Congress about Rome's appointment of a man to head the American Church. Not only did he state that Congress "would not fail to give its tacit approval" to anyone selected by the Holy See in concert with himself, but he spoke in terms of choosing "a French ecclesiastic" who would reside in France and administer his office through a representative in the United States.[7] Thus it was Franklin who was responsible for introducing the notion of a French churchman ruling the American Catholics from outside the country, an idea that gave rise to deep resentment when it was learned on the other side of the Atlantic.

The turn taken by the negotiations at this point was important, for it both disclosed the American official policy and helped to set a prece-

[6] Antonelli to Doria Pamphili, Rome, January 15, 1783, Edward I. Devitt, S.J., "Propaganda Documents. Appointment of the First Bishop of Baltimore," *Records of the American Catholic Historical Society of Philadelphia*, XXI (December, 1910), 188.

[7] Franklin's observations on the note of Doria Pamphili, undated, *ibid.*, XXI, 196.

dent for the future. In his letter to Elias Boudinot, President of the Continental Congress, Franklin stated among other things:

I send also a copy of a note I received from the Pope's Nuncio. He is very civil on all occasions, and has mentioned the possibility of an advantageous trade America might have with the Ecclesiastical State, which he says has two good ports. . . .[8]

Doria Pamphili's note had summarized the manner in which the Catholics had been governed in America up to that time, and he stated that since it might happen that there would be no priest in the United States judged worthy of the episcopal office, he was anxious to learn the reaction to a situation where, as he expressed it, "it would be necessary that Congress should consent" to choose a person from "among the subjects of a For. Nation" that was friendly to the United States.[9] Months elapsed before the matter came before Congress, but in the spring of 1784 it was included along with other business arising from the correspondence of the American representatives abroad, and it was settled by the passage of the following resolution:

Resolved, That Doctor Franklin be desired to notify to the Apostolical Nuncio at Versailles, that Congress will always be pleased to testify their respect to his sovereign and state; but that the subject of his application to Doctor Franklin, being purely spiritual, it is without the jurisdiction and powers of Congress, who have no authority to permit or refuse it, these powers being reserved to the general states individually.[10]

A reply of this kind probably produced a slightly baffled reaction among the Roman prelates, accustomed as they were to the active interest – and interference – of most governments in the choice of bishops. That any government should volunteer that it had no competence in the matter signalized to the Roman Curia as few things could better do that a new phenomenon had risen in the world of statecraft.

That there was a variety of interests at work in this case was clear from the correspondence of diplomats in both Paris and Philadelphia for whom political considerations were usually uppermost. For example,

[8] Franklin to Boudinot, Passy, September 13, 1783, *The Diplomatic Correspondence of the United States of America* (Washington, 1837), I, 369.

[9] National Archives, Record Group II, "Papers of the Continental Congress," No. 82, II, 429.

[10] Resolution of May 11, 1784, Gaillard Hunt (Ed.), *Journals of the Continental Congress, 1774–1789* (Washington, 1928), XXVII, 368.

Franklin was still under the impression that the American Catholics were ruled by a spiritual superior in London, and it was this thought, as he confessed to Vergennes, that made him uneasy and prompted him to wish that the appointment should go to a churchman who, as he said, "is of this Nation [France] and who may reside here among our Friends."[11] The same reasoning lay behind his suggestion that Louis XVI's government confiscate some of the English monastic houses in France and use the revenues to finance the Church in the United States, a suggestion that was immediately vetoed by Cardinal Antonelli when he heard of it. In Philadelphia, Franklin's counterpart, Anne Cesar la Luzerne, French Minister to the United States, was closer to the realities of the situation when a few weeks later he informed Vergennes:

> The Catholics would not be pleased with a foreign Bishop, but they could very well choose the worthiest of their priests and present him to His Holiness for consecration, if he judges him qualified for the episcopal functions.[12]

All the while the American priests themselves were not approached for their views. Smarting under this neglect, and still nursing resentment over Propaganda's hostility toward their suppressed Society, these ex-Jesuits were anything but pleased with recent developments. Carroll illustrated their mind when he assured Father Plowden that there was no question about the Americans' desire to preserve their spiritual allegiance to Pope Pius VI. But of one thing Plowden could be certain and that was

> that no authority derived from the Propada. will ever be admitted here; that the Catholick Clergy and Laity here know that the only connexion they ought to have with Rome is to acknowledge the Pope as Spirl. head of the Church; that no Congregations existing in his States shall be allowed to exercise any share of his Spirl. authority here; that no Bishop Vicar Apostolical shall be admitted, and, if we are to have a Bishop, he shall not be in partibus (a refined political Roman contrivance), but an ordinary national Bishop, in whose appointment Rome shall have no share; so that we are very easy about their machinations.[13]

[11] Franklin to Vergennes, Passy, December 15, 1783, Jules A. Baisnée, *France and the Establishment of the American Catholic Hierarchy. The Myth of French Interference, 1783–1784* (Baltimore, 1934), p. 57.

[12] La Luzerne to Vergennes, Annapolis, January 31, 1784, *ibid.*, p. 79.

[13] Carroll to Plowden, Maryland, April 10, 1784, Hughes, *Documents*, I, Part II, 619–620.

It was an instance where the normally balanced judgment of John Carroll was unsettled by his deep suspicion and antipathy for Propaganda, for a few months later when this same Congregation appointed him mission superior, the sobering effect of his new responsibility left little disposition to attempt any implementation of the challenging assertions made to his English friend.

Father Carroll's talents had brought him to the attention of practically all the principal participants in these transactions, among whom was Archbishop Doria Pamphili who turned to la Luzerne in May, 1784, for a confidential opinion of the American priest as a candidate for the episcopacy.[14] With the departure of la Luzerne the following month the French representatives for the remainder of the decade, Barbé-Marbois and Louis-Guillaume Otto, took a conservative attitude toward French involvement in American ecclesiastical affairs and cautioned their government against it. They were conscious of the widespread anti-Catholic feeling and of the belief of so many Americans that the Catholic Church was an enemy of political freedom. As Otto told Vergennes early in 1786, if a foreign power should be found assisting the Catholics it would only increase native American hostility; besides, he maintained, it was to France's interest to see that the American Church should not be too closely linked to the French, "since it would be one motive the more to excite the subjects of his Majesty to emigrate."[15]

The prolonged negotiations with their attendant uncertainty over the form the ecclesiastical government should take, and the man to be named to rule the Catholics, were suddenly terminated on June 9, 1784, when Cardinal Antonelli appointed Father Carroll as superior of the American missions. What caused the Prefect of Propaganda to move so quickly at this point, we do not know. But that he considered Father Lewis too old for the appointment, and that Carroll's aloofness impressed him as an indication of the latter's lack of personal ambition, were certain. Moreover, as he stated to Carroll:

you have given conspicuous proofs of piety and zeal, and it is known that your appointment will please and gratify many members of that republic,

[14] Doria Pamphili to la Luzerne, Paris, May 12, 1784, Devitt, *op. cit.*, XXI, 206–207.

[15] Otto to Vergennes, New York, January 2, 1786, Baisnée, *op. cit.*, p. 94.

and especially Mr. Franklin, the eminent individual who represents the same republic at the court of the Most Christian King. . . .[16]

At the same time Antonelli asked for a full report on the state of the Catholic religion in the United States, and he suggested that if Carroll would select two American boys whom he felt had a vocation to the priesthood and send them to Rome, they would be received at the Urban College of the Propaganda and educated gratis.

It was no easy task for the Propaganda officials to conduct this business to a successful conclusion in view of their own ignorance of many of the circumstances involved, and, too, of the prejudice of the American clergy against the Congregation. And in the latter respect the English correspondents of a number of these American priests did not help matters. In fact, at one point Plowden allowed his prejudices to carry him to such extremes that Carroll rebuked him for adopting the language of what he called "some of the prints on your side of the water," that represented Americans as "under imperious leaders and the trammels of France."[17] Yet the experience had likewise been trying for Carroll upon whom the others relied to keep a watchful eye out lest American interests be jeopardized, while at the same time he had to guard against creating the impression that he was projecting himself into a post of leadership. Sensitive though he was on this score, he held firmly to his belief that the Holy See should not erect a missionary jurisdiction in the United States. "To govern the spiritual concerns of this country as a mission is absurd," he told Plowden, "seeing there is a regular clergy belonging to it."[18] And if the Americans might have had any hesitation about the matter their English friends more than made up the deficiency as, for example, Father Thomas Talbot who rejoiced when he thought the American Church had escaped from the rule of Propaganda. "Your reasons are special," he said, "and Rome must come in at last to grant a jurisdiction ordinary."[19]

Unaware of Rome's official action of June, 1784, in naming Carroll, the American priests held a meeting the following October during which they approved their constitution, declared against having a bishop, and said that he would have no support from their lands.

[16] Antonelli to Carroll, Rome, June 9, 1784, Guilday, *Carroll*, I, 203.

[17] Baisnée, *op. cit.*, p. 132, quoting an undated letter.

[18] Carroll to Plowden, n.p., September 15, 1784, Baisnée, *op. cit.*, p. 146.

[19] Talbot to Carroll, London, September 21, 1784, Hughes, *Documents*, I, Part II, 624.

Throughout the entire affair it was Propaganda that worried these men and not anxiety over coming under the rule of a French bishop. That Carroll shared the view of his fellow priests was clear when he remarked early in 1785 to Father Thorpe that the American clergy were no longer missionaries and were not, therefore, under the Congregation's jurisdiction. The same idea is found at this time in his correspondence with the papal nuncio in Paris and with the Prefect of Propaganda, whom he begged to understand the delicacy of the position of the American Catholics and asked that every possible concession be granted in order to avoid stirring up the hostility of their non-Catholic fellow citizens. In this Carroll had the support of others such as Barbé-Marbois who spoke in a similar vein to Vergennes, and of John Thorpe who in December, 1786, went as far as to think it possible to guarantee the future against the efforts that he fancied Propaganda would make to fasten its grip on the Church in the United States by having France promote an ordinary bishop for the Americans.

Once the official documents had reached John Carroll he was faced with the necessity of a decision concerning his acceptance or rejection of the post of superior of the American missions. While he was reluctant to assume the heavy burden – especially in view of the very limited faculties granted to him by Propaganda – his keen sense of responsibility compelled him to recognize that it might, indeed, be a duty for him to do so. As he told the clergy in a circular that solicited their opinions:

> Nothing but the present extreme necessity of some spiritual powers here, could induce me to act under a commission, which may produce, if long continued, and it should become public, the most dangerous jealousy.[20]

In general the priests agreed that Carroll should accept Propaganada's appointment, even though some still had misgivings about what would evolve from this arrangement. While he continued to sound his fellow priests and to turn over the matter in his own mind, Carroll acted to the extent of sending out instructions to the clergy which outlined the conditions for gaining the indulgences attached to the jubilee of 1775 which the Holy See had extended to the United States. The ensuing weeks did not increase Carroll's confidence in his ability to fulfill the assignment that Rome had asked of him, for he found his faculties so priests. But the letter of appointment had stated that these arrangements

[20] Circular letter of Carroll announcing his appointment as superior, n.p., n.d., Shea, *History of the Catholic Church in the United States,* II, 251, n. 2.

limited that he could not even, in turn, grant faculties to newly arrived were meant to be only temporary, so conscious as he was of the handicaps and doubts that surrounded the undertaking, in the end Carroll's sense of duty overcame his reluctance and on February 27, 1785, almost four months after he had received the official notice, he informed Cardinal Antonelli of his acceptance.

In his letter of acceptance Father Carroll spoke cautiously of the enduring character of the new religious freedom in the United States, and noted the fact that complete civil liberties were still denied to Catholics in some states. He alluded to the difficulties experienced by the erstwhile Anglicans, now called Episcopalians, in establishing a bishopric and mentioned that in doing so they had erected a national church with no dependence on a foreign superior. Catholics were free to invoke the same principle of religious freedom as the Episcopalians, but Cardinal Antonelli need have no fear that they would follow the latter's example in setting up a national church since both clergy and laity were too devoted to the Holy See to renounce its authority. At present there was no need for a bishop, but when that time came Carroll hoped that the utmost concessions would be granted by Rome in order to allay Protestant suspicions. Moreover, he expressed the desire that the future bishop would be an ordinary rather than a vicar apostolic, and that if the Holy See would not allow the priests to propose his name, that a method would be devised that would avoid as much as possible arousing bad feeling among the people of this country, both Catholic and non-Catholic.

In the letter of appointment the Prefect of Propaganda had requested Carroll to furnish the Roman officials with a complete report on the state of Catholicism in the United States. With that in mind the latter used the interval between late November, 1784, and the time when he replied to Antonelli's letter to gather data on conditions in various parts of the country, with the result that by March, 1785, the first detailed report on American Catholicism was submitted to the Congregation de Propaganda Fide. It was divided into three sections: the number of Catholics, their general living conditions, and the number and quality of the priests. Carroll estimated that there were then about 15,800 Catholics in Maryland of whom around 9,000 were freemen, adults, or children over twelve years of age while about 3,000 were white children with around the same number of African slaves of all ages. In Pennsylvania he thought there were about 7,000 Catholics among whom were a few Negroes. Virginia, in his opinion, had no more than 200 Catholics who saw a priest only four or five times a year, and he heard of other Catholics elsewhere, for example, of around 1,500 in New York, but he had no exact information concerning them. As for the vast area that stretched between the Appalachian Mountains and the Mississippi River, he had been told that there were many Catholics there – most of them French-speaking – but he knew of only one priest working among them, a German Carmelite who had come to this country by way of France.

Under the second heading the Maryland Catholics were described as chiefly planters of whom a few were well to do, while in Pennsylvania their coreligionists were mostly farmers with some merchants and mechanics in Philadelphia. On the whole the Catholic people seemed to be religious, but many were deprived of regular services because of the lack of priests, and Carroll expressed a certain uneasiness about the great numbers of immigrants whose religious practice was poor in contrast to that of the native Americans. True, moral abuses existed because of contacts with non-Catholics, but abuses also arose from national traits like the fondness for dances, for reading novels, and the free relations between the sexes. Added to all this there was the basic weakness of a lack of religious instruction for the children, a situation that was especially acute among the Negroes.

As for the priests, there were at the time nineteen in Maryland and five in Pennsylvania, but of these five were either seventy years of age or near it, others were in bad health, and one was suspect of immoral conduct. Carroll had given the latter another chance, but he intended to watch him and if need be to deprive him of his faculties even if some Catholics had to go without religious services. He made clear his attitude on this point when he said:

> I am convinced that the Catholic faith will suffer less harm, if for a short time there is no priest at a place, than if living as we do among fellow-citizens of another religion, we admit to the discharge of the sacred ministry, I do not say bad priests, but incautious and imprudent priests.[21]

In general, however, he had words of praise for the zealous labors of the priests who, he stated, were supported "chiefly from the proceeds

[21] Report of Carroll to Antonelli, March 1, 1785, *ibid.*, II, 260.

of the estates; elsewhere by the liberality of the Catholics." There was no ecclesiastical property properly so called since the lands from which the priests gained their living were held "in the names of individuals and transferred by will to devisees." Although there were no Catholic schools, educational facilities for prospective candidates for the priesthood were not entirely lacking in that there was a college in Philadelphia to which Catholic students were admitted, and it was proposed to establish two more colleges of the same kind in Maryland. Moreover, the Catholics were thinking of establishing a seminary in which young men could be trained for a life suitable to the ecclesiastical state.[22]

Assuming responsibility for the spiritual welfare of 25,000 or more Catholics scattered throughout the new republic would have been an awesome undertaking in any period, but it was especially so just at this time. Through the 1780's an air of deep uncertainty continued to pervade men's minds about the future of the new nation as the centrifugal political forces retained their ascendancy over the efforts of those who sought to implement a strong national government with authority to speak for all the people. The individual states clung tenaciously to their rights and privileges, and they eyed each other with so much jealousy that, as has been said, they were put "in some ways more self-consciously at odds than when they had all been British colonies." The new Constitution that was born out of the anxious sessions of the convention that sat in Philadelphia through the summer and early autumn of 1787 only increased the suspicions of many Americans of that day; and no attempt on the part of those who came to be called Federalists to define and delineate the nature of the union that was intended to hold the states together, escaped serious challenge. Furthermore, these attitudes persisted up to and beyond the inauguration in April, 1789, of the national government under George Washington, and in circumstances of this kind, therefore, it was no wonder, as a recent writer has said, "that the President's hands shook as he held his inaugural address and read out its blameless sentiments." [23]

The weakness of the State contributed, needless to say, to the further weakening of an already enfeebled Church since the latter could not exist in a vacuum, and a situation such as the government's exhausted financial credit that brought Robert Morris, Superintendent of Finances,

[22] An English translation of the report is given in Shea, *History*, II, 257–261.

[23] Marcus Cunliffe, *The Nation Takes Shape, 1789–1837* (Chicago, 1959), p. 14.

to resign his office in despair in January, 1783, made itself felt in ecclesiastical as well as business circles. In fact, in both Church and State the basic defect was similar, namely, a lack of authority at the top, for as the months passed and the numbers of the Catholic laity increased by natural growth and by immigration, and as more priests from abroad were attracted to this country, Carroll realized all too keenly how inadequate his ecclesiastical powers were. This crippling factor was given a partial remedy, it is true, in July, 1785, when Cardinal Antonelli enlarged Carroll's faculties to permit him, in turn, to grant faculties to newly arrived priests so that they might perform the functions of the ministry. But knowledge of Antonelli's action did not reach the superior until March, 1786, and by that time it was not easy to overcome the effects of the initial handicap.

From the outset of his term as superior of the missions Father Carroll's most acute problems centered around the clergy, that is, their insufficient number to supply the demands of Catholic groups in widely separated sections of the country, their moral fitness for the ministry, the suitability of certain of the newcomers for the American apostolate, and, finally, the problem of furnishing proper training for young men who showed a leaning toward the priesthood so that a source of supply might be secured for the future. Carroll mentioned to Father Plowden in the summer of 1785 that requests for priests were reaching him from all quarters, but he was unable to supply them. He begged Plowden to urge missionary minded priests whom he might meet to consider the United States, and he hoped that he would soon have on deposit in London enough money to pay the passage of six men.[24] He had not forgotten Propaganda's offer to educate two boys at the Urban College, nor the offer of the French government to pay the expenses of eight ecclesiastical students in the seminary at Bordeaux. Unfortunately, however, there were no candidates to avail themselves of these burses.

Even though John Carroll did not possess the powers of a bishop, one of the principal duties of the episcopal office devolved on him with his appointment as mission superior and that was to visit the stations of which he had been placed in charge. It was impossible for him to cover all the far flung settlements, but he undertook in the mid-summer of 1785 to visit those in Maryland where he administered the Sacrament of Confirmation to the faithful prepared by the nineteen priests then

[24] Carroll to Plowden, June 29, 1785, Guilday, *Carroll*, I, 237.

resident in the state. While on this trip Carroll crossed the Potomac River and visited the northern counties of Virginia, but in August he returned to his mother's home at Rock Creek to await cooler weather. On the whole the Maryland missions were in good condition, although they were just then beginning to lose a number of their members with the migration of the first Catholic Marylanders beyond the mountains to Kentucky.

In September, 1785, Father Carroll set out for the north where his principal responsibilities centered in Pennsylvania and New York, for another three years would pass before New England got its first permanent Catholic community, if one excepts the Catholic Indians in what was later to become Maine. Pennsylvania was in many ways the most promising of the areas visited, for here Carroll found a number of relatively flourishing congregations in the rural districts west of Philadelphia which had been settled almost a half century before by Catholics of German birth. For example, Father James Pellentz reported around 1,000 souls in his congregation at Conewago, while Father John B. de Ritter had about 500 at Goshenhoppen with Father Luke Geissler numbering about 700 in and around Lancaster. In Philadelphia the two pioneer congregations, Saint Mary's and Saint Joseph's, were in the care of Fathers Robert Molyneaux and Ferdinand Farmer, and besides these two ex-Jesuits there were at this time three other priests in the city, namely, William O'Brien, O.P., and Thomas Hassett, a secular priest, both Irish-born, and Pierre Huet de la Valinière who had been deported from Canada some years before because of his American sympathies.

Insofar as New York was concerned, the Catholics had no organized life since, as we have seen, after 1688 the official attitude had been so hostile that few if any Catholics had settled there. True, the law of 1700 against popish priests was repealed in 1784 by the legislature so that a priest could thereafter freely enter the state and exercise his ministry. The first priest of whom Carroll had word in New York was an Irish-born Capuchin by the name of Charles Maurice Whelan who had seen service with the French navy. In November, 1784, Father Farmer informed Carroll that as his vicar general he had warned Whelan he must first have faculties before he administered the sacraments. But the friar had proceeded without any permission which was an ominous sign of the trouble that he would cause in the years ahead.

Not only was Father Whelan's action a sample of the kind of disobedience that Carroll had to contend with from a number of immigrant priests in these early years, but it likewise furnished a painful illustration of the superior's inability at the moment either to furnish these men with faculties or to curb their disciplinary infractions. In the circumstances Farmer advised Whelan to apply for faculties from Propaganda through the nuncio in Paris which he did in January, 1785, enclosing a recommendation that he had received from Michel Guillaume de Crèvecoeur, French consul in New York. The friar described the poverty of the New York Catholics for Archbishop Doria Pamphili and remarked how they would not even have a place where Mass could be offered were it not for a Portuguese gentleman who loaned them a part of his house for that purpose. Whelan claimed that since his arrival he had made converts of "a great many of every denomination," and he added that a priest working in New York would need to know Irish, French, and Dutch.[25] Farmer was still uneasy over the Capuchin administering the sacraments without faculties, but after a visit to New York he told Carroll that the friar's conduct was not giving scandal, although he was not a very prudent person nor did he possess the ability for good public speaking and the gift of ingratiating himself with others. Obviously there were reasons, therefore, why a superior might withhold full confidence from Whelan, but in the circumstances Carroll felt warranted in taking the risk of granting him temporary faculties until Rome could be heard from, and this he did on April 16, 1785.

The trouble with Father Whelan was only a foreshadowing of the grief that John Carroll was to experience from the New York Catholic community before it had been placed on a stable basis. In June, 1785, a group of laymen had themselves incorporated as the 'Trustees of the Roman Catholic Church in the City of New York' and purchased ground on Barclay Street for a church. And an already confused situation was made more complicated when another Irish-born Capuchin, Father Andrew Nugent, appeared on the scene and was given temporary faculties by Carroll to act as Whelan's assistant. The friars soon fell out, and with that the peace of the congregation was shattered with the laity dividing into quarreling factions behind the two Capuchins. The trustees who had gone over to Nugent now insisted that Whelan

[25] Whelan to Doria Pamphili, New York, January 28, 1785, *ibid.*, I, 250–251.

withdraw entirely which he refused to do. Matters thus went from bad to worse, and in an effort to assert the Church's rightful authority Carroll made a vigorous protest in which he told the trustees:

> The great source of misconception in this matter is that an idea appears to be taken both by you and Mr. Whelan that the officiating clergyman at New York is a parish priest, whereas there is yet no such office in the United States.[26]

He stated that there was no warrant for withdrawing Whelan's faculties, and if the latter should depart the congregation would find itself without a priest who had the power to care for its spiritual needs.

Father Carroll's efforts to clarify the issues and to establish the canonical principles involved were, however, largely wasted, for after a brief lull the congregation of Saint Peter's Church became embroiled in the late summer of 1787 in a series of even worse disturbances. In the hope of restoring peace Carroll went to New York in October only to find himself on two successive Sunday mornings routed from the church by the violence of the followers of Nugent. So riotous was their conduct that on both occasions Carroll failed in his attempt to offer Mass in the church and had to withdraw to the house of Don Diego de Tardoqui, the Spanish minister, in order to do so. With New York then the national capital and the whole ugly affair bruited throughout the city, Carroll's embarrassment over the scandal given by the Catholics and his own personal humiliation were enhanced by the chagrin he felt in learning about this time that Nugent's previous record in Ireland had been a very bad one and that his misbehavior had caused the Archbishop of Dublin to suspend him from his priestly functions. As he later told Charles Plowden, he suspected that Nugent had forged the credentials he had presented when he came to the United States since, as Carroll remarked, he had been detected to be "a most infamous fellow, and there is no excess of which he does not seem capable."[27]

Infamous the Irish friar certainly was, so much so that his extreme conduct gradually cost him his following and proved an assistance to Father William O'Brien, O.P., whom Carroll had appointed to take charge of Saint Peter's at the time of a visit to New York in October, 1787. Needless to say, O'Brien did not immediately prevail, but this strong

[26] Carroll to the Trustees of Saint Peter's Church, Rock Creek, Maryland, January 25, 1786, *ibid.*, I, 265.

[27] Carroll to Plowden, March 1, 1788, *ibid.*, I, 282, n. 22.

minded Irishman found that time told in his favor. As reluctant as Father Carroll may have been to have the New York Catholics resort to the civil courts against a priest, in the end it proved the most effective way to rid themselves of Andrew Nugent. Fortunately, in the act of the New York legislature of April, 1784, that removed the inequalities and disabilities of religious groups other than the Anglicans, there was a clause to the effect that no changes made by the present act were to be construed as having altered the constitutions or governments of any of the churches, "so far as respects, or in any wise concerns the Doctrine, Discipline or Worship thereof."[28] It was not difficult for the trustees to prove from Nugent's assertion that he was subject to no authority save that of Christ and the New York magistrates, not even to that of the pope, that if Saint Peter's were left in his control it would be used for the practice of a faith quite at variance with that for which the church had originally been established. By this method, then, Nugent was ousted, and even though he hired a house and continued to say Mass, it was for a steadily dwindling congregation. Apparently convinced after a time that his cause had been defeated, he decided to return to France, and in order to further that idea the trustees of Saint Peter's took up a subscription to pay for his passage on *Le Telemaque* which sailed from New York on January 4, 1790. With that the distracted congregation which had suffered so much at his hands saw the last of the troublesome friar.

The New York situation has been described at some length for two reasons: first, it was these disorders of Saint Peter's more than any other single factor that convinced the priests generally of the need for a bishop with full authority to deal with disruptive elements within the American Church; secondly, New York's Catholic community in the late 1780's afforded one of the earliest examples of a phenomenon that was to become widespread in the succeeding decades under the name of lay trusteeism.

Space will not permit us to relate in detail the beginnings of organized Catholicism in the other large cities along the Atlantic Coast and in the rural areas that lay to the west and beyond the mountains. But before the origins of the lay trustee movement are described, something should be said about the Catholic communities in general, especially

[28] Samuel Jones and Richard Varick (Eds.), *Laws of the State of New-York* (New York, 1789), I, 109.

in Boston and Philadelphia, since nothing could better illustrate how desperately an effective ecclesiastical authority was needed to govern the unruly elements that had now begun to make their appearance. In Boston, however, it was not the abuse of lay trustees that lay behind the Catholic community's stormy beginnings. It was rather a series of incidents of equal folly and embarrassment caused by two French-born secular priests, Claude Florent Bouchard de La Poterie and Louis de Rousselet. From the former's arrival in the fall of 1788 until the departure of the latter in 1791 Boston's small group of Catholics were victims of the ambitious schemes and restless manouvers of these two men. Both had been granted faculties by Carroll after having presented what seemed proper credentials, but in both cases defiance of all authority finally compelled Carroll to suspend La Poterie and Rousselet. Fortunately, in August, 1792, there came to Boston another French priest, François Matignon who with his friend, Father Jean Cheverus who arrived four years later, were able in time by their eminent good sense and their piety to repair the damage done by their predecessors.

In Philadelphia during the Revolution the Catholics had prospered under the spiritual direction of Fathers Robert Molyneaux and Ferdinand Farmer. The death of the latter in August, 1786, was a severe loss not only to Philadelphia but to the Church generally, and Father Francis Beeston who came first as assistant to Molyneaux and then was named his successor, found the rising discontent of the Germans in the English-speaking congregation his most difficult problem. The nationalist sentiment which played as much havoc with the peace and harmony of the Catholics here as in any place in the United States in the early years of the republic, was furthered by two German Capuchin brothers, John and Peter Heilbron, who arrived in the city unannounced in October, 1787, the same month as Father Laurence Graessl who had been asked to come to this country by Farmer before he died. Carroll's appointment of Graessl to take charge of the German Catholics was the signal for trouble, for the Heilbrons had won over a part of the congregation, and resenting Graessl's advantage, they had no scruples about ministering to their fellow countrymen without faculties.

Matters in Philadelphia were not made easier for John Carroll when a committee of German laymen, headed by Adam Premir, bought a lot for a church in February, 1788, and wrote to the superior for permission to build. While Carroll granted his approval, he expressed uneasiness lest the proposed church should not have enough financial support to maintain it and, too, over the possibility of it becoming a divisive factor among the Philadelphia Catholics. He likewise took occasion to make it clear that Father Graessl had been put in charge of the congregation. The superior went as far as he could to meet the Germans' wishes, even at the cost of incurring Father Beeston's displeasure over the division of his flock.

The next move came with the legal incorporation of both groups, that is, the English-speaking congregation of Saint Mary's which was incorporated on September 13 and the 'Trustees of the German Religious Society of Roman Catholics' three weeks later on October 4, 1788. This establishment at Holy Trinity Church, which opened in November, 1789, of the country's first Catholic congregation formed on a nationalist basis, and the ensuing dispute between Graessl and the two Capuchins when the trustees sided with the friars, heralded more than a generation of strife for the Church in Philadelphia. Not only did the German congregation go into schism for a time, but later Saint Mary's Church became engulfed in even graver dissensions as a result of three refractory Irish-born priests who abetted the lay trustees in their war against ecclesiastical authority. The rebels refused to obey Carroll in the years up to the erection of the new Diocese of Philadelphia in 1808, and after Michael Egan, O.F.M., first Bishop of Philadelphia, came to live among them in November, 1810, he was defied in the same manner.

Generally speaking, outside the cities and large towns the Catholics in the rural areas pursued their religious life in an uneventful way. At the time that he accepted the office of mission superior in February, 1785, Carroll told Cardinal Antonelli that he heard there were many Catholics beyond the mountains who were mainly French-speaking and for the most part destitute of priests, but he confessed that he knew little for certain about them. Later that same year Carroll's own native state was to furnish the first sizeable addition of Catholics to this western country when around twenty-five families migrated from Saint Mary's County to the neighborhood of Pottinger's Creek a few miles from the village of Bardstown, Kentucky. The next few years witnessed other Marylanders moving to Kentucky so that by the end of the decade Nelson and Scott Counties had a considerable Catholic population.

The great distance and the lack of means of communication between these frontier settlements and the Atlantic Coast made the task of supplying them with priests doubly difficult. In fact, until Stephen Theodore Badin, the first priest ordained in the United States, arrived in Kentucky in November, 1793, to begin his long and useful life in the Middle West, these pioneer families had to remain content with brief periods of ministration such as that given by Charles Whelan, the Capuchin whom we have already met in New York, and William de Rohan, a wandering priest whose career in Kentucky and elsewhere was overshadowed by personal weaknesses that detracted from the good that he accomplished. Yet it was to de Rohan that there was owed in 1792 Kentucky's first Catholic house of worship in Holy Cross Church at Pottinger's Creek.

A further obstacle to Carroll's effective administration in the West was the jurisdictional uncertainty, since for over a century the whole region had been regarded as part of the Diocese of Quebec, and Father Gibault, a priest of that diocese, was still functioning at Vincennes. In the hope of clarifying matters Carroll appointed Father de la Valinière as his vicar general for the West. But the latter's tactless and aggressive manner helped to bring on differences with Gibault who considered himself vicar general of Quebec, and in the end only fresh complications were the result. Carroll finally determined in May, 1788, to appeal directly to Bishop Jean-François Hubert. By an exchange of correspondence the two men agreed that since Detroit was still held by the British, for the time being they would consider Michigan as under Quebec, but for the rest of the western country all official acts of Carroll or his vicar general would be confirmed by the Bishop of Quebec. Hubert explained that he could not recall Gibault due to the lingering resentment of the British against his conduct during the Revolution, and he cautioned the American superior to be watchful of de la Valinière because of his "turbulent spirit," while at the same time paying tribute to the former Canadian's general good character and morals.[29]

We have already mentioned the stable condition of the predominantly German rural settlements west of Philadelphia where established congregations like those at Conewago, Goshenhoppen, and Lancaster had their resident priests who at intervals visited the growing number of Catholics in towns like York, Reading, Easton, and Carlisle. Moreover, by this time Catholics had begun to appear in western Pennsylvania, as Father Farmer learned when he received a petition in July, 1785,

[29] Hubert to Carroll, Quebec, October 6, 1788, Guilday, *Carroll*, I, 297–298.

signed by seventy-three of their number who asked that a priest be sent to them at least once a year. Two years passed before one was available and then a wandering and uncertain German Franciscan by the name of John B. Causse ministered to the families around Greensburg long enough, it was said, to encourage them to purchase property for a church in March, 1789. At the end of that year Theodore Brouwers, O.F.M., came to the neighborhood, and intending to settle down permanently, he bought a farm called Sportsman's Hall in April, 1790, near the present Latrobe where Saint Vincent Archabbey stands today. These western Catholics, however, were fated to suffer ill fortune with their early priests, for Brouwers died in less than a year and left a faulty will that gave still another German Franciscan, Francis Fromm, an opportunity to practice his nefarious ways by involving the property in a lengthy litigation and defying Carroll's authority to the point of creating a schism before he departed for Philadelphia in 1798 where he died in the yellow fever epidemic unreconciled to the Church.

In Maryland the mission stations of colonial days were still in use in the southern counties, either in the chapels attached to the residences of the ex-Jesuits or in those maintained by the wealthier Catholic planters in connection with their manor houses. In the northern counties the 1780's witnessed the beginnings of a number of future parishes as itinerant missionaries visited southeastern Pennsylvania, northwestern Maryland, and some of the settlements in the nearby counties of Virginia. For example, at Hagerstown which got its first resident priest in Father Denis Cahill, property was acquired in 1794 on which Cahill erected a chapel and a priest's house. He made trips to Martinsburg, Shepherdstown, and Winchester in Virginia with occasional calls also at Fort Cumberland in Maryland and Chambersburg, Pennsylvania, while the priest who resided at Conewago did a similar service for communities like Hanover in Pennsylvania, and Taneytown, Maryland. Thus the widely separated Catholic families were given a chance to maintain contact with the Church, and as their numbers increased the missionaries were able to lay the foundations of future parishes throughout an area that was still generally looked upon as part of the West into the early nineteenth century.

In Baltimore, to which John Carroll moved from his mother's home at Rock Creek early in 1787 to take residence at the priest's house adjacent to Saint Peter's, the moral laxity among recent immigrants from France was a source of anxiety to the superior. In a letter to Plowden he said of them:

They are everywhere a scandal to religion, with very few exceptions. Not only that, but they disseminate, as much as they can, all the principles of irreligion, of contempt for the church and disregard for the duties which both command.[30]

According to Carroll, these transplanted products of French rationalism were also guilty of corrupting the Acadians and their descendants who had been in Baltimore for a generation following their expulsion from Nova Scotia. The city that was soon to be the seat of the new bishopric, and which in 1790 had 13,500 inhabitants, had had its own peculiar problems, therefore, for Carroll. His obligations there were rendered more difficult by the repeated and lengthy journeys that he was compelled to make to other parts of the country while still remaining in charge of Baltimore's pioneer congregation at Saint Peter's. About the few and widely separated Catholics on Maryland's Eastern Shore his mind could rest easily as long as the veteran Father Mosley lived, but when that splendid missionary died in June, 1787, another care was added to the superior's lot.

South of Maryland, aside from the several hundred Catholics scattered through Virginia's northern counties who were attended at intervals by priests from Maryland, there were few of Carroll's charges in the Old Dominion. In North Carolina the Church had at this time at least one devoted adherent in a remarkable widow, Mrs. Margaret Sharpe Gaston, who raised her children in the Catholic faith and who offered her home in New Bern as a place where Father Patrick Cleary, a canon of Funchal, Madeira, could say Mass when he came there around 1784 to look after some property to which he was heir. In South Carolina there had been a handful of Catholics in Charleston from a fairly early date, and in 1788 Carroll sent them Father Matthew Ryan who during his stay of about two years bought an abandoned Protestant church which was fitted up for services, the congregation numbering about 200 souls when Father Christopher Keating succeeded Ryan in 1790. Having heard that the New York Catholics had been given financial assistance by the King of Spain in building Saint Peter's Church, the Charleston trustees made an appeal to Charles IV through the

[30] Carroll to Plowden, October 23, 1789, Shea, *History*, II, 286.

Spanish consul. Aware of the claims of ecclesiastical patronage made by the Spanish crown, Carroll was uneasy at their action lest the request should afford further excuse for charging the Church with foreign connections, and above all of inviting the *real patronato* to American soil. For as he told the Charleston trustees, "neither you gentlemen nor the ecclesiastical superior in these States can effectually interfere in the appointment of clergymen protected and supported by foreign princes. . . ."[31] As it turned out nothing came of the petition to Madrid so there was no further worry on that score.

Father Keating had in the meantime grown discouraged by the difficulties and disappointments encountered in Charleston and in March, 1791, he departed. Not until the spring of 1793 was Carroll able to find a priest to replace him when he appointed Simon Felix Gallagher who had recently arrived from Ireland with seemingly authentic credentials. Gallagher's advent to Charleston opened a long and painful chapter in the city's Catholic history, for his contempt of ecclesiastical authority and the scandal of his personal life, combined with the rebellious spirit which he fostered in the lay trustees of Saint Mary's Church, brought on one of the most disgraceful and damaging conflicts that the American Church was to experience. Finally, in Georgia, the last of the southern states, the years before Carroll's consecration as a bishop gave indication of the presence of hardly more than an occasional Catholic within its borders.[32]

Such in general were the conditions that obtained among the American Catholics during John Carroll's time as mission superior. Before tracing the course of events that led to his choice as the first Catholic bishop of the United States, it may be helpful to summarize the causes of the lay trustee movement since this, more than any other internal problem, was to plague the Church throughout the whole of Carroll's episcopacy and for many years thereafter. With the hatred and suspicion of Catholicism so deep and widespread among Americans, and with

[31] Carroll to Trustees of Saint Mary's Church, Charleston, Baltimore, June, 1790, copy, Guilday, *Carroll*, II, 736.

[32] For a recent account of Catholicism in the Carolinas with reference to Georgia and Florida as well, cf. Richard C. Madden, "Catholics in Colonial South Carolina," *Records of the American Catholic Historical Society of Philadelphia*, LXXIII (March-June, 1962), 10–44. Monsignor Madden mentions one Catholic, Richard Hawley, former Governor of Georgia, who came to St. Augustine, Florida, in December, 1784, to receive the sacraments (p. 40).

the country's civil laws so strongly favoring lay control of church temporalities, it is little wonder that many non-Catholics should have looked on with ill disguised glee at the internecine struggles within the Church of Rome. Those of nativist mentality saw in the efforts of men like Carroll and his successors to establish ecclesiastical discipline and the precepts of canon law, a splendid opportunity, as one writer has said:

to preach the undemocratic nature of a religion which refused to allow the people control of their own churches and to decry the manner in which Popery sought to evade American laws.[33]

The causes that lay behind the abuses to which the lay trustee movement led in the years after 1785 are not difficult to determine. First, was the absence of a strong ecclesiastical authority with adequate power to cope with the dangerously libertarian trends that characterized both religious and secular circles in the early years of national independence. Secondly, the fact that during the colonial period the Catholic community had never known what it was to be governed by bishops meant that at times even the best behaved priests were ignorant of the principles of normal ecclesiastical rule, to say nothing of the native born laity and of numerous recent arrivals from foreign lands. Thirdly, the entire spirit that then enveloped the new republic was against the kind of ecclesiastical control to which Catholics were accustomed in other countries, for not only did the administrative policy of the Protestant churches give wide discretionary powers to their laymen, but the laws of the various states pertaining to such matters as legal incorporation of trustees and the latter's control of church temporalities favored the laymen. Seeing their Protestant neighbors proceed to organize their respective congregations with the encouragement of the law, it was natural that the Catholic laity should decide to do likewise. And once they had tasted power, like the trustees of Saint Peter's Church in New York and of Holy Trinity Church in Philadelphia, they were loath to relinquish it to a distant churchman who claimed the right first to give them permission for their own actions.

In addition to these causes there was the further circumstance that as the eighteenth century drew to a close the make-up of the Catholic community — until then largely of English stock in Maryland with many of German birth or descent in Pennsylvania — became more com-

[33] Ray Allen Billington, *The Protestant Crusade, 1800–1860* (New York, 1938), p. 300.

plex with newcomers of Irish, French, Spanish, and other national origins arriving in ever greater numbers. That few things divide men more sharply and more enduringly than differences in language and nationality, is a commonplace. Among some of the new arrivals were people who had known either in Europe, or in new world possessions of the European powers like Louisiana, the institution of the so-called *jus patronatus* or right of patronage whereby laymen enjoyed the right of providing the priests for vacant ecclesiastical offices as well as the right to dismiss them at will. The attempt to introduce among the Catholics of the United States this right of patronage was accompanied by the assertion that such a right obtained in this country, a claim that John Carroll and his successors vigorously denied.

Many non-Catholic Americans, as has been mentioned, delighted in the struggles that they witnessed within the Church of Rome, and far from doing anything to quiet them, the trustees and rebel priests were at times abetted by outsiders who urged them to vindicate their rights as citizens of a free country. Thus from the 1780's on, as one historian of trusteeism has said, "to the latter decades of the last century there was probably not a single year during which the disease of trusteemania was not epidemic, or better endemic, in some diocese in the country. . . ."[34] Not until there dawned a consciousness and acceptance by both clergy and laity of the Church's norm of government by bishops, and until the number and caliber of the bishops were strengthened in the United States, was a lasting remedy found for these disrupting tactics. In conclusion one should mention that the opening in 1791 of Saint Mary's Seminary at Baltimore provided for the first time in this country regular training for the priestly state, and consequently through the instruction of the Sulpicians future diocesan priests learned how its temporalities should be managed from their study of canon law and the history of the Church, a training which the scholasticates of the religious orders would in due time impart to their own future priests.

Central to the defeat of the trustee excesses was the supply of future priests of a dedicated and reliable character. At the outset of Carroll's term as superior there were about twenty-five priests in the United States, practically all of whom were members of the suppressed Society of Jesus. But a new day was now at hand, for as we have seen, during

[34] Robert F. McNamara, "Trusteeism in the Atlantic States, 1785–1863," *Catholic Historical Review*, XXX (July, 1944), 139.

the 1780's there began arriving clergymen of quite another background and spirit. Conscious as Carroll and his former confrères were of how the need to provide a living for these outside priests might threaten the property interests of the suppressed Society, and conscious, too, of the deep prejudice that obtained at the Congregation de Propaganda Fide against the ex-Jesuits, Carroll had urged at the clergy's meetings in 1782 and the following years the necessity of securing legal incorporation so that their lands might be held without fear. Since most of them were dependent for a livelihood on the income from their estates, one can appreciate their concern, especially in view of the rumors that reached them from time to time about Propaganda's confiscation of the properties of the former Jesuits in Europe. They were highly sensitive to criticism, therefore, as one can understand, while allowing that on occasion the sensitiveness of some of their members carried them too far.

In the light of these facts we can better appreciate the discomfort of the ex-Jesuits when a slashing attack was made on them by an Irish-born secular priest who had come to this country and had served for some months in one of the mission stations. Father Patrick Smyth, pastor of Dunboyne in the Diocese of Cork reached the United States late in 1787 and was appointed successor to Father James Frambach at Frederick, Maryland. Smyth remained there until March, 1788, when he informed Carroll that he was coming to Baltimore to give over his faculties and return to Ireland. He expressed gratitude for the superior's generosity and kindness, while at the same time complaining that the families of English blood and background had been cool toward him. As it turned out Smyth spent a month as Carroll's guest before sailing for home.

Following Father Smyth's departure a letter written by him to a Mr. Robert Welsh of Fells Point was handed to Carroll who found therein a harsh indictment of the former Jesuits on the score of their having pre-empted the best ecclesiastical livings in the country for themselves. Smyth stated that he knew six or seven Irish diocesan priests who would gladly come to the United States were it not for the prejudice that obtained in favor of what he termed "a certain description of ecclesiastics." Stung by the charges, Carroll at first thought of answering Smyth, and he even wrote out the rough draft of a reply. But upon the advice of

Archbishop Troy of Dublin and others he finally decided not to proceed with it.

Anxious, however, that the correct version of American conditions should be made a matter of record for the Irish clergy, Carroll sent a lengthy defense of the ex-Jesuits to William O'Brien, O.P., the most prominent Irish-born priest in the country at the time, and O'Brien, in turn, passed on the information to the Archbishop of Dublin. Several months later in writing the latter Carroll referred to the Smyth affair. To be sure, said the American superior, there was a great need for priests in the United States, but he wished to make it clear that this need, pressing though it was, did not mean they were prepared to take in every wandering priest who turned up on these shores. Revealing how well he understood the special requirements of the American milieu, as well as how guarded his recent experiences with some immigrant priests had made him, he remarked regarding Irish priests who might have the American missions in mind:

> But one thing must be fully impressed on their minds, that no pecuniary prospects or worldly comforts must enter into the motive for their crossing the Atlantic to this country. They will find themselves much disappointed. Labour, hardships of every kind, coarse living, and particularly great scarcity of wine (especially out of the towns) must be borne with. Sobriety in drink is expected from clergymen to a great degree. That which in many parts of Europe would be esteemed no more than a cheerful and allowable enjoyment of a friendly company, would be regarded here in our clergy as an unbecoming excess. Your Lordship will excuse this detail, and know how to ascribe it to its proper motive, that gentlemen applying to come to this country may know what to expect.[35]

But Carroll had not yet heard the last of Smyth. Not only did the latter circulate false charges against the American clergy in private letters, but he did far greater damage by a lengthy diatribe which he printed in Dublin late in 1788 under the title *The Present State of the Catholic Missions conducted by the Ex-Jesuits in North America.* A copy of this pamphlet reached Carroll in January, 1789, and he composed a detailed rebuttal which he proposed to publish until the strong urging of his friends dissuaded him. In his reply Carroll corrected Smyth's false version of the early Jesuits' relations with the first Baron

[35] Carroll to Troy, Baltimore, August 11, 1788, Guilday, *Carroll,* I, 312.

of Baltimore, along with the author's statement that Catholicism had been the established religion in colonial Maryland. The superior also described the present poverty of the former Jesuits and defended them against the accusation of neglect of duty in not expanding their missionary districts. Unfortunately, however, the Smyth pamphlet was widely read and when it reached Rome the Prefect of Propaganda, Cardinal Antonelli, made close inquiries about the United States missions from the two American boys who were then enrolled at the Urban College. Nor was Smyth's the only attack of that kind that Carroll and his fellow priests had to endure, for the year after Smyth's pamphlet appeared the notorius Abbè La Poterie in Boston put one into print which he called *Resurrection of Laurent Ricci; or a true and exact History of the Jesuits.*

If the haunting concern of Carroll and his associates about a certain supply of worthy priests was ever to be solved it was beginning to appear that it would only be through the opening of a seminary. But since the resources at their disposal were so very limited the most that they could hope for at the time was a school wherein boys might be prepared for entrance into a seminary. The subject was discussed at the second clergy meeting in November, 1786, and it was resolved to begin a subscription for funds at once in the United States, the West Indies, and Europe. The clergy agreed to set aside £100 from their common funds for the purpose of a school to be located at Georgetown, then in the State of Maryland, and a committee of five priests, headed by Carroll, was appointed as directors of the future institution. Needless to say, progress was slow, for even in its embryonic stage the future Georgetown College experienced a number of setbacks before the little academy opened its first classes in November, 1791, more than a year after Carroll's episcopal consecration.

Meanwhile Father Carroll had not forgotten Antonelli's offer to educate two American boys free of charge at the Urban College of Propaganda. American lads with a vocation to the priesthood were not easily found at that time, and even if they were available, obstacles like the oath demanded of the Propaganda students slowed progress since Carroll declined to proceed until he had Antonelli's promise to waive the requirement of the oath for the Americans. News of this concession reached the superior in late March, 1786; yet not until July, 1787, had the two prospective seminarians, Ralph Smith of Maryland, age fourteen, and Felix Dougherty of Pennsylvania, age thirteen, been found and made ready to depart. They sailed that month and after spending some time in France finally reached Rome in January, 1788, where Carroll's old friend, Father John Thorpe, promised to keep an eye on them. The boys remained for almost a decade during which they completed their humanities and a good part of the philosophy course. They made satisfactory progress in their studies, and on Pentecost Sunday of 1796 Dougherty preached in Latin before Pope Pius VI in the Sistine Chapel. But in the next year both men dropped out, Smith because he found he had no vocation and Dougherty because of ill health. Although the latter entered Saint Mary's Seminary at Baltimore in 1798 he soon withdrew, and thus the first two American seminarians sent to Rome did not reach their goal, and it was over thirty years before any other students from the United States appeared as candidates for the priesthood in the Eternal City.

When the clergy's representatives gathered at Whitemarsh in November, 1786, for their second meeting there were other problems that they had to face besides that of providing the means of clerical training, for example, the need for legal incorporation in order to protect their properties. But as it turned out the most important item of business was a petition to the Holy See for a bishop, convinced as most of them had become by the disorders in New York that nothing short of one with full episcopal powers could handle the dangerous situation then developing in the United States. Father Charles Sewall was authorized to send out a circular letter soliciting the opinions of all the priests in the country, and although there was still opposition to both a school and a bishopric from a few like Father Bernard Diderick the circular in good measure helped to silence this opposition. The three men selected to compose the petition to the Holy See were John Carroll, Robert Molyneaux, and John Ashton, a task for which Carroll felt a real distaste lest, as he told William O'Brien, O.P., some should think that he was anxious to have a mitre placed on his head.

From the earliest days of the negotiations over his post as mission superior Carroll had insisted with the Holy See that he felt the erection of a missionary vicariate in the United States would be a mistake. And what he witnessed on his visitation tours after 1785 convinced him of the correctness of his original view. In spite, therefore, of his awareness of the risk he ran of being misunderstood in advocating a bishopric, he emphasized that point of view strongly in the petition which he and his two associates sent off to Rome under date of March 12, 1788. The petitioners asked the Holy Father to appoint a bishop as soon as possible and to make the diocese immediately subject to the Holy See. Moreover, at least for the first time, Pius VI was also asked to permit the priests to elect the bishop. Carroll followed up this document with a lengthy report to the Cardinal Prefect of Propaganda that gave further details of the New York scandals, and he told Antonelli that Don Diego de Gardoqui, the Spanish diplomatic representative in New York, agreed with him about the need for a diocese with a bishop in charge.

Once the petition of the three American priests reached Rome matters moved forward. The assent of Pope Pius VI was given to their requests and Antonelli so informed them on July 12, 1789. In his letter the cardinal gave a surprisingly free rein to the Americans when he told them:

> By you, therefore, it is first to be examined in what city this espiscopal see ought to be erected, and whether the title of the bishopric is to be taken from the place of the see, or whether a titular bishop only should be established. This having been done, his Holiness as a special favour and for this first time, permits the priests who at the present time duly exercise the ministry of the Catholic religion and have care of souls to elect as bishop a person eminent in piety, prudence, and zeal for the faith, from the said clergy, and present him to the Apostolic See to obtain confirmation.[36]

Upon receipt of this directive the memorialists announced to their fellow priests on March 25, 1789, that they were setting the date for the election which would be held at Whitemarsh on the following May 18. On that occasion Baltimore was unanimously chosen as the site for the episcopal see, and John Carroll was elected by a vote of twenty-four to two to occupy it.

The names of Baltimore and Carroll were forwarded to Rome and after Pius VI's confirmation of the clergy's choice was given the formal bull, *Ex hac apostolicae*, erecting the new diocese was issued on November 6. Cardinal Antonelli accompanied the official documents with a letter in which he suggested that the bishop-elect should apply for additional faculties if he felt they were needed, urged him to make visitations, to watch for abuses, and to forbid anyone to undertake

[36] Antonelli to Carroll *et al.*, Rome, July 12, 1788, *ibid.*, I, 352.

the care of souls or administration of the sacraments without his permission. He then stated:

If you be short-handed for Priests see to it, as to what country it is best to invite recruits from, but take care lest quarrels and dissensions may arise from the diversity of character and disposition which generally exists amongst the natives of different countries. For which reason, principally, we do not permit Italian priests to go thither; and besides, they very rarely speak English. *Impose not lightly hands on any man*: but enlist amongst the Clergy only such as have given proof of piety and learning in the Seminary.[37]

It was counsel that Carroll knew how to value, although at times the circumstances in which he found himself did not permit him to carry it out as literally as he might have wished. In the bull *Ex hac apostolicae* it was stated clearly twice that the election of the bishop by the priests on this occasion was by reason of a special grant and for this time only, which was an indication that the request that the priests had made at their Whitemarsh meeting of the previous May, namely, that future choice of bishops be left to the clergy, would not be granted.

The move to strengthen the government of the American Church came only a few months after the inauguration of a strong central authority for the United States itself. During the uncertain time when Father Carroll was struggling to keep order with little real power to do so, the government of the Articles of Confederation was continuing to expose its weaknesses and to make it apparent to most men that the national government must be given more authority to rule. The ultimate result of this situation was the convening of a constitutional convention in the early summer of 1787 in which there sat two Catholics, Thomas FitzSimons of Pennsylvania and Daniel Carroll of Maryland, brother of the mission superior. Both men were Federalists and both lent their influence to adoption of the Constitution while the issues was being debated by the individual states. At length the requisite number of states needed to ratify the instrument was secured, and on April 30, 1789, George Washington took the oath as first President of the United States at New York.

The Constitution itself had said nothing about religion except to state that no religious test should ever be required as a qualification for any office or public trust held under the United States, a liberal

[37] Antonelli to Carroll, Rome, November 14, 1789, *ibid.*, I, 357.

provision that raised opposition to Catholic office holders here and there. In the same vein the *Gazette of the United States* on May 9, 1789, carried an article signed 'E.C.' and entitled "The Importance of the Protestant Religion Politically Considered," which proposed that Protestantism be made the established religion of the new republic. John Carroll did not let it pass unnoticed, and on June 10 the *Gazette* printed his reply in which he remarked that the blood of Catholics had flowed as freely (in proportion to their numbers) to cement the fabric of independence as that of any of their fellow-citizens. They had concurred with perhaps greater unanimity than any other body of men, in recommending and promoting that government, from whose influence America now anticipated all the blessings of justice, peace, plenty, good order and civil and religious liberty. He pleaded that the principle of religious freedom be kept inviolate, referred to the unfairness of certain state constitutions in this regard, and then speaking of the new nation he asked:

> Ought she not rather to treat with contempt these idle and generally speaking interested speculations, refuted by reason, history and daily experience, and rest the preservation of her liberties and her government on the attachment of mankind to their political happiness, to the security of their persons and their property, which is independent of religious doctrines, and not restrained by any?[38]

Actually there was no real peril to religious freedom on the national scale, for the religious complexity of the population and the conviction of the foremost national leaders helped to guarantee the preservation of the principle which had been enshrined in the Constitution and its amendments. As we have said, Catholics had every reason to rejoice at this turn of events, and following the action taken by delegations representing several of the prominent Protestant churches, a committee of Catholics, consisting of Father Carroll and four laymen, Thomas FitzSimons, Daniel Carroll, Charles Carroll of Carrollton, and Dominic Lynch of New York, addressed a letter of felicitation to the president. They expressed their profound admiration for his past achievement both in war and in peace and their confidence in his administration of national affairs in his new post. They mentioned their recently won rights as citizens, a boon which they deeply cherished, alluded to the fact that some state constitutions still restricted men of their religious

[38] *Gazette of the United States*, June 10, 1789.

faith, and stated that when they prayed for the preservation of these rights and for the national welfare they would not omit to pray for the president since, as they said, they could conceive no human means more likely to promote the welfare of the United States than "the prolongation of your health and life, in which are included the energy of your example, the wisdom of your counsels, and the persuasive eloquence of your virtues."[39] Washington replied on March 12, 1790, and after thanking the Catholics for their prayers and good wishes he called attention to the contribution that their coreligionists had made to the revolutionary cause in the following way:

> I presume that your fellow-citizens will not forget the patriotic part you took in the accomplishments of their Revolution, and the establishment of their government; or the important assistance which they received from a nation in which the Roman Catholic religion is professed.[40]

Preoccupied as he thus was with the affairs of both Church and State, Carroll found himself more than ordinarily busy in the winter of 1790 due to the necessity of making plans for his consecration. The Holy See had left him free to choose both the location and the bishop who would consecrate him and this became one of the first decisions he had to make. After giving thought to Quebec, and to Dublin by reason of Archbishop Troy's invitation, he finally decided to accept the invitation of his friend, Thomas Weld, to be consecrated in the latter's private chapel in Lulworth Castle in Dorsetshire by Charles Walmesley, O.S.B., Vicar Apostolic of the Western District.[41] That Carroll should have favored Lulworth Castle was understandable, for there he would meet a number of old friends whom he had not seen since 1774, and to no reunion did he look forward with more anticipation than that with the Weld's family chaplain, Father Charles Plowden. He sailed in early

[39] "The Catholics' Congratulations to President Washington, 1789, and His Reply, March 12, 1790," Ellis, *Documents*, p. 171.

[40] *Ibid.*, p. 172.

[41] A good idea of the kind of family the Welds were was contained in a letter of James Talbot, Vicar Apostolic of the London District, to his brother, Thomas, Vicar Apostolic of the Midland District, written from Gosport on September 8, 1788, during a visitation tour that had taken him to Marnhull where he stopped with a certain Mr. Wright. He then said: "From thence I went to Lulworth Castle where I staid five days, and was never in my life more edified by y saintly conduct of Mr. and Mrs. Weld, and y good behaviour of all y family, especially y children, who are very numerous and brought up in a truely Xtian manner." Manuscript Collections, St. Cuthbert's College, Ushaw, Durham, England.

June and both going and returning he had the company of James Madison who was likewise going to England for his consecration as the first Virginia bishop of the Protestant Episcopal Church.

The consecration took place on August 15 with Bishop Walmesley assisted by three priests, and young Thomas Weld, the future cardinal, then seventeen years of age, holding the missal over the bishop-elect's shoulders. In his sermon for the occasion Plowden contrasted the freedom enjoyed by Catholics in the United States with the limitations still binding their coreligionists in England, remarking how revolution within the British Empire had wrought such a favorable change for the Church in the new world. After the consecration the new bishop remained for a few weeks with his Lulworth friends and then went up to London where a considerable amount of correspondence awaited his attention, a task to which he addressed himself at intervals between that time and his sailing for home on October 8.

Bishop Carroll's stay in London proved to be memorable in more ways than one. Through the summer Father Thorpe kept him informed of developments at the Roman Curia touching American affairs, and in early July he reported that the Holy See had been requested by a group of Frenchmen interested in a colonizing project in the American West to appoint a bishop for the region. The colony in question was called Gallipolis and was located in Ohio, a part of the land speculations of the Scioto Company that was to come to grief after a few years. The first group of colonists had left France in May, 1790, and others followed until ultimately several thousand Frenchmen were committed in one way or another to this unhappy venture. Among them was Pierre Joseph Didier, a Benedictine of the Congregation of Saint Maur, whose brother was one of the land purchasers. Anxious to further their business in every possible way, the promoters thought that having a bishop in Ohio would serve this end, and Dom Didier was of the same mind. Fortunately, the request, made through the nuncio in Paris, found the Prefect of Propaganda unwilling to act without reference to the Bishop of Baltimore. Although Antonelli granted Didier faculties as vicar general *in spiritualibus* for seven years, he did so only on condition that it would not conflict with Carroll's jurisdiction. Thorpe's letter was the first intimation that the new bishop had of the matter, and before sailing he explained to Antonelli by letter the dubious character of the undertaking, and thereafter nothing more was heard about a bishop for Gallipolis.

Another scheme with similar ecclesiastical aspects grew out of the plan of certain French settlers in northern New York to convert the Oneida Indians. In April, 1789, a petition had been sent to Pope Pius VI for Father Jean Louis Victor Le Tonnelir de Coulonges, a priest of their choice, to be made a bishop. The agent was Jean de la Mahotière who presented the request in person to the nuncio in Paris, Archbishop Antonio Dugnani, and who wrote a letter to Pius VI assuring the pope that provision had been made for a chapel, vestments, and other necessary equipment, and that six Capuchins were ready to return with him to the new world to begin work among the Indians. Dugnani took his time about the matter, but in August, 1790, he forwarded the case to Cardinal Antonelli. While the latter lauded the idea of converting the savages, he once again showed an awareness of the American situation by stating that before he would make any further move he would wish to know whether these Indians were living within the Diocese of Baltimore or that of Quebec; if they were not in either diocese, then he would submit Mahotière's request to the pope. With that another ill advised ecclesiastical dream was thwarted and Carroll was freed from the threat of a rival jurisdiction within his diocese.

But the London visit brought more positive results than heading off madcap schemes for planting bishops in the midst of the American wilderness. Conscious as he was of his lone position, Carroll asked Thorpe even before he had been consecrated to make inquiry if Propaganda would not be willing to give him a coadjutor bishop so that if he should die suddenly there would be no awkward period of suspended authority in the See of Baltimore; but to this Thorpe recommended that he let the matter await his return home. Carroll's friend likewise told him of a conversation he had with Cardinal Antonelli in which the latter had emphasized that now that Carroll possessed full episcopal powers he should not hesitate to use them against unruly priests. Moreover, the cardinal was willing to consider any reasonable changes that Carroll might suggest in the wording of the consecration oath of bishops to suit American conditions.

A week before the consecration ceremony Mother Ann Hill, an American-born Carmelite of the Hoogstraet convent in the Low Countries, and a cousin of Bishop Carroll's, had written him to say that Mother Bernardine Matthews, also American-born, and three other nuns had sailed for the new world in the spring to open a convent in the United States. These first American contemplatives arrived during the bishop's absence and were settled at Port Tobacco in Charles County under the guidance of Father Charles Neale, one of five members of that well known Maryland family who had joined the Society of Jesus before its suppression. In this way one of the communities of religious women in the Low Countries to whom American Catholic girls had been sent to be educated during the penal days and with whom a number had remained as members, had now made a return to the new world at a time when the tables were threatening to be reversed with the Church of the old world endangered by the rising tide of revolution in France.

It was, indeed, an eventful time for Catholics on both sides of the channel, for in the single month of July, 1790, the National Assembly in Paris not only abolished the kingdom's historic provinces, the parlements, and the hereditary nobility with its titles and coats-of-arms, but it also enacted the Civil Constitution of the Clergy which struck a fateful note for the Church and its time-honored place in the French State. Simultaneously in England the Catholic community was distracted by a heated controversy over the question of giving the crown the right of veto in the selection of bishops. It was thus in an atmosphere of uncertainty between the defeat of Charles James Fox's motion in March, 1790, for relief of all religious dissenters and the introduction into the House of Commons of a new Catholic relief bill in February, 1791, that Carroll's visit to England was spent. It was little wonder that he should have found himself caught up in the differences among his English friends, but he shrewdly managed to escape involvement, for as he told Archbishop Troy:

> Since my arrival I have carefully avoided taking any part in the present controversy amongst the Catholics, though I have been urged on all sides.

He would go only as far as to say that in his judgment the oath of loyalty which the British government was then seeking to exact of the Catholics was inadmissible.[42]

On September 27 Bishop Carroll summarized for the Prefect of

[42] Carroll to Troy, London, October 3, 1790, Guilday, *Carroll*, I, 381.

Propaganda the principal happenings in both the United States and Britain of which he lately had knowledge. Another contingent of colonists had left for Gallipolis in Ohio in spite of his wishes, and in what was quite another aspect of his affairs, the hope was expressed that he could get classes underway at the school in Georgetown soon after his return home. He lamented the calumnies of Smyth and La Poterie, but as for Antonelli's suggestion about employing clergymen who had never been Jesuits, he stated that during the more than five years that he held the post of mission superior, of the thirty priests to whom he had given permission to exercise the ministry only seven had been ex-Jesuits. But the most hopeful note of all was the news of the visit paid Carroll in London by Father François Nagot, superior of the Seminary of Saint Sulpice in Paris, who had been sent by Jacques-André Emery, the Sulpician superior general, to interview the bishop about founding a seminary in his diocese.

True, the Civil Constitution of the Clergy had only passed the National Assembly on the previous July 12 and as yet it was not clear how far its stringent clauses would be enforced. But perceptive churchmen like Emery read the implications of the act and correctly anticipated the storm long in advance of Pius VI's condemnation of the act in April, 1791. Gravely preoccupied by the fear that his beloved Society now faced extinction unless a refuge could be found outside France, Emery first invited Bishop Carroll to be the Sulpicians' guest in Paris, and when he declined on account of the disturbed political conditions there, the superior general then determined to send Nagot to London. But he had also enlisted the papal nuncio on his side, and in forwarding an outline of Emery's proposals Archbishop Dugnani told Carroll:

> The first condition of their crossing would be that it would cost neither you nor the residents of the United States anything; they themselves will find the means from their own resources to defray the expense of the undertaking.[43]

It was an astonishing offer, to be sure, and Carroll's surprise must have increased as he learned further details, for example, that the Sulpicians were prepared to provide not only a staff of veteran professors

[43] Dugnani to Carroll, Paris, August 24, 1790, Joseph W. Ruane, *The Beginnings of the Society of St. Sulpice in the United States, 1791–1829* (Washington, 1935), p. 22.

and spiritual directors, but even several young men as the nucleus of a student body, to say nothing of their own passage money and the expenses connected with acquiring property and a building to house the seminary. Little wonder that he should have told Lord Arundell of Wardour a few days before sailing of the gratitude he felt to divine Providence for this extraordinary turn of events, although, as he said, "I feel great sorrow in the reflection, that we owe such a benefit to the distressed state of Religion in France."[44]

It was during Nagot's time in London in September, 1790, therefore, that the main lines of the transaction were worked out for what became easily the most enduring benefaction to the American Church deriving from Carroll's visit to England. The bishop had no Sulpician connections in his personal background, but after having seen their work at close range for a brief time and being well enough informed in general ecclesiastical matters, he appreciated fully the truth of what Bishop Hubert of Quebec later told him about the coming of the Sulpicians, even if he probably demurred at having the outcome interpreted as a sign of his own providential role in the undertaking. At a time when Nagot, his three Sulpician confrères, and their five seminarians had already been in Baltimore about five months, Hubert wrote:

> You could not, my Lord, build a more solid foundation for the preservation and growth of the true faith in this country. The individual merit of this director [Nagot], the reputation of the house to which he belongs, are so many arguments which prove that God, in calling you to the episcopate, has given you the wisdom and administrative ability necessary to fulfil its requirements.[45]

His business in England concluded, the Bishop of Baltimore prepared to depart for home, sailing on the *Sampson* from Gravesend on October 8 for what proved to be a rather stormy crossing of two months duration. He arrived in Baltimore on Tuesday, December 7, and immediately took up residence in the modest little rectory adjacent to Saint Peter's Church that was to be his home for the next quarter century. On the following Sunday he took official possession of the procathedral, as Saint Peter's came to be called, with five priests and the trustees meeting him at the door and escorting him to the little sanctuary. He had been set to rule over a diocese that was coterminus

[44] Carroll to Arundell, October 4, 1790, *ibid.*, p. 32.
[45] Hubert to Carroll, Quebec, December 5, 1791, Guilday, *Carroll*, I, 389.

with the United States in which about thirty-five priests were then serving some thirty churches and many more mission stations for a Catholic population that numbered, perhaps, around 35,000. The search for a bishop had been a long and trying experience, but at last the American Church, infant as it was, had an organized character and a man at the helm who was equal to the burden that he had been asked to bear. That Carroll had a high concept of his office was clear to anyone who knew him, and that he felt this keenly was evident in the sermon he preached on the day of his installation when he said:

It is no longer enough for me to be inoffensive in my conduct and regular in my manners. God now imposes a severe duty upon me. I shall incur the guilt of violating my pastoral office, if all my endeavours be not directed to bring your lives and all your actions to a conformity with the laws of God. . . .

After particularizing what he meant the new bishop confessed that his heart sank as he contemplated what lay ahead for him. Yet he found his consolation in the assurance of God's help, and his conscience was clear, for God knew how much he had dreaded to be made a bishop. "He will not abandon me," he said, "unless I first draw upon His malediction by my unfaithfulness to my charge."[46] It is pleasant to record that more than 170 years have passed since that December day of 1790; it has been the unanimous verdict of all who have studied the history of the Church's first quarter century of organized life in this country that there was never anything in the conduct of John Carroll to suggest any infidelity on his part that had ever earned the abandonment of Him Whose cause he had served with dedication and distinction.

[46] "Bishop Carroll's Sermon on Taking Possession of His See, St. Peter's Pro-Cathedral, Baltimore, December 12, 1790, Ellis, *Documents*, p. 173.

INDEX

INDEX

INDEX

INDEX